"This is another well done, honest and heartfelt piece of writing from Kirk Alex. It's short, easy to read, and well worth the reader's time."

—Paul Lappen, Dead Trees Review


Praise for: **ZOOK**

"Strange twisted story. But great read."

—NetGalley


Praise for:
**Working the Hard Side of the Street —
Selected Stories / Poems / Screams**

". . . this is a nicely put together piece of work."

—*BookLore*


"This book is excellent. It's full of honest, heartfelt writing that certainly shows a very different view of Hollywood."

— *Paul Lappen, DEAD TREES REVIEW*


"**WORKING THE HARD SIDE OF THE STREET— Selected Stories / Poems / Screams** is an anthology of powerful, caustic, original tales and poems by Kirk Alex about the ups, downs, and hard knocks of Hollywood's seamy underbelly. The perspective of a "fly- on-the-wall" cab driver provides a piercing realism and insight into the vicious clashes and personal struggles that lie hidden underneath the entertainment capital's glossy, photo-touched exterior. **WORKING THE HARD SIDE OF THE STREET** is recommended as a gut-wrenching read for both its candor and bravado."

— *THE MIDWEST BOOK REVIEW*

# BY KIRK ALEX

# LUSTMORD:

## Anatomy of a Serial Butcher

### Book One (of Two)

Presented as a Novel

## KIRK ALEX

TUCUMCARI PRESS

Tucson — 2017

**Lustmord: Anatomy of a Serial Butcher – Book One** is dedicated to Tom Biederman, and to the memory of Ziggy, Darcy and Neil for providing the author with shelter (when shelter was desperately needed). I can't thank you enough.

Last, never least, to the memory of the amazingly gifted writer/artist and #1 fan of horror, who reminded more than a few of us that horror should be/deserves to be treated with the same respect as any other genre, the late, great Chas. Balun.

# A WORD OF CAUTION

## (updated & revised, with a rant or two tossed in)

> "And if you gaze for long into an abyss, the abyss gazes also into you."
>
> –Friedrich Nietzsche

Translation: this one is not for the faint of heart, nor the weak of belly. Foretold is forewarned.

I started **LUSTMORD: Anatomy of a Serial Butcher** back in 1987—and it is January 2017 as I write this. How many years is that? Twenty-nine? Thirty? Give or take. I say give or take because somewhere in there, during the mid 1990s, I had to lay off the thing for about five years. Why? Nightmares. Cold sweats. Unable to sleep. Why? Subject matter. Some of it was too damned horrific and the images wouldn't go away at the end of the day. Five years. Not to mention another three years when I could only face the book for about four or five months at a time. The shit was sick and depraved. Fucking brutal. I needed a break.

And so the first eBook version was released sometime in 2013 and the reception was far better than I could have hoped. Always makes a writer feel pretty good that the sweat and toil had not been for naught. Great. Walk away from it, start something new. As I had intended and did.

Only it wasn't that easy to cut ties completely. From 2013 up until the end of 2016 things kept nagging at me. Having to do with backstory.

Cecil's childhood, to be specific. Had crucial facts been merely touched on, others even left out altogether? I did what I could to ignore it. I'd spent enough years on the book and that was that. Novel was done and I was not about to go back and re-visit what had been a trying enough experience the first time around. One is ready and willing to give up a lot for a book, but not one's sanity. Hey, my sanity was tenuous at best and always had been. But that's for another time and place.

I liked being positive and happy; appreciate the good people in my life. Better believe it. We learn: Good peeps are like precious gems and treasured as such. Value the cool folks in your life & never miss an opportunity to let them know how much they matter.

Anyway, it had taken a while to recover from the effects of the debilitating tome and I felt I was doing just fine, had been working on other things, as stated, away from horror, a bit more on the lighter side. I preferred infusing a degree of humor in just about everything I write, no matter the genre. My humor is never in your face slapstick (the kind that has no place & falls ass-flat in horror or a thriller, just go ask Tobe Hooper and how all that Three Stooges idiocy effing ruined what might have otherwise been a decent Texas Chainsaw Massacre sequel.) Am talking about the one with the late, great Dennis Hopper. And to this day, Tobe doesn't get why people like me hate that fucking flick. Hey, Tobe, horror is supposed to scare the shit out of peeps, brother, not make them want to giggle. If I want comedy I'll turn to the great comedies of yesteryear—with Rodney Dangerfield, Laurel and Hardy, W.C. Fields, Jonathan Winters, all of whom I love, by the way, including the original Three Stooges. I'll pop in *It's a Mad Mad Mad Mad World* if I want to laugh, not Texas Chainsaw Massacre #2, but I digress.

Back to the thriller opus at hand: I was good with the version released, and so were my readers. So there it was: my attitude. It was settled. No more. No way. Onward and upward, or something like it.

Well, we know different, don't we? Certain books have a way of getting under our skin. The detail that had been lacking in the initial version of the novel was fading in in bits and pieces of its own accord, no matter how hard I fought against it. Here and there, through my subconscious that refused to be ignored, images kept surfacing, knocking at my noggin. And so, I did the only thing there was *to do*: I started writing some of this stuff down, and pretty soon the words and sentences took over and the notebook started filling up. I wrote things down and kept writing things down, from 2015 up until about/just prior to 2017, when I could no longer keep putting off incorporating this new material into the novel and making it available for the upcoming 6x9 paperback version.

There was fan mail, to be sure, requests for not only more background on the Biggs character, but readers wanting to know if he was coming back. Whether Bishop Cecil O. Biggs and his alter ego, the clown called Trusty, would ever make another appearance I had no way of knowing, but what I did have was more on the origins of his own quirks and what basically left that irreparable crack in his psyche and turned him into the remorseless killing machine years later, with nothing but loathing and contempt for his brethren and sistren.

And so on Dec. 31, 2016 I sat at my desk, flipped open my laptop, opened the notebook crammed with all types of jottings and scribbles containing snatches of dialogue, fresh character insights and background detail, and went to work.

Eventually it became evident that there was more to that single stretch of kindness, brief as it was, that he'd experienced in his life as a child and the older couple with the pet hog who had befriended him and that Cecil had grown quite fond of and wished he could have been adopted by. Fact was, they were his only source of light in that otherwise perpetual combo of fear and despair that his childhood was. And who knows, he may have even gone a different route entirely later on as an adult, had his friends Flora and Truly Turnbull and their pet pig not only been extracted from his needy grasp, but so abruptly and with such viciousness that the resulting gap had been too much of a shock for his young mind to comprehend, let alone bear.

And so the details were all there, now all that remained was to read *from the beginning*, as I had countless times in the past over the years, the nearly half million word horror novel and weave this new information in. Daunting? More so than was usual for me and what I was used to. You better believe it. And there didn't seem to be any recourse but to tackle it head-on. My attitude always has been: No point in taking on a project unless you're willing to give it your all, (no matter that it damned near *put me* in the loony ward initially.) And if you think this is a stretch and/or far-fetched, look up a U.K. crime writer named Derek Raymond (who wrote the mind-twisting crime noire novel entitled *I Was Dora Suarez*) and see the emotional state it left him in, and there's others; they're easy to look up on the Net. Point being: *Fuck with evil*—and guess what? Evil has a tendency to *fuck you back*. That's what the Nietzschean quote at the top of this forward is about. There is no such thing as a free lunch.

Logging in 14 to 16 hour days or more and getting by on next-to-no-sleep, I got through it, survived it. Eighteen days later, the revised and updated Lustmord: Anatomy of a Serial Butcher contained thousands of additional words.

This is that new version, dear reader. From my end, I felt it was worth the time and effort. You tell me if it works for you at yours.

If I could have just one thing taken away from this novel, and I don't write message thrillers, folks; I don't believe in getting up on a soap box and preaching to the reader or even dispensing advice, this is what it would be: *be kind to your offspring*. To anyone who thinks this isn't much, or who thinks it's overstated, I've got news for you: it's the most important thing there is.

This entire enterprise begs the question then, doesn't it? If it was such a task to write and clearly it was, and had taken not only a heavy toll on its author, but three long decades of hard work to pull off, why go anywhere near the subject matter, then? Because had I an inkling it was going to be anywhere near this tough or that it would take thirty years to complete, there is no way in hell I would have so much as attempted it. I was in my mid 30s when I started it, sixty-six is mere months away. No-way-in-fucking-hell.

Still does not answer why the *topic* was chosen. Why fool with something this cynical and psychologically draining? Because as a writer I have to bounce around, move from genre to genre, or else I lose interest—and because if I'm going to do a book about a sociopath, you better believe one thing: I am going to treat the material with absolute honesty. There is no other way. I did not want to whitewash (or sugarcoat) any of it, the way certain writers like to do, or the way some, rather, most Hollywood flicks treat the material: by having the unpleasant stuff happen off screen, or else it's done with gimmicks and cheesy effects. I wanted it raw, and I wanted it to be disturbing—not only physically, but more importantly, on a psychological level—because when it happens, the way it happens in real life, that's what it is: appalling, venal, sickening and twisted and scars/marks anyone within its vicinity for life afterwards, including the guilty cretin who leaves this kind of unspeakable trauma and dread in his or her wake.

So I repeat, read at your own risk. The author/publisher is not responsible for any nervous breakdowns, facial tics, insomnia, depression, loss of appetite, loss of hair, sexual dysfunction, bouts of insanity, marriages and/or relationships disintegrating, time spent in therapy, stays in the bughouse, shakes, quakes, headaches, heart problems, prostate issues, vomiting, nausea, episodes of anxiety, suicidal tendencies or a sudden, inexplicable urge to do bodily harm to your fellow humans, and any other ailments, be they large or small, that you may experience as a result of having read **LUSTMORD: Anatomy of a Serial Butcher.** You have been thoroughly advised. Proceed at your own peril.

K.A.
January 17, 2017

"I've been called everything but a human being."
—Cecil O. Biggs

# CHAPTER 1

**They were into it.** Heard more than he wanted to.

"J.J., don't!"

"Shut your mouth, whore!"

"I'll be good! I promise, J.J.!"

"I told you to shut your hole!"

"Don't hit me, J.J. You better not hit me no more!"

"I'll beat you to death! Filthy heifer cunt!" Slaps and screams followed. "Why, you ain't even a good whore! Where's my whiskey money, bitch? Spent on shoes and ice cream for that worthless little shit? Why come? Since when are the little bastard's wants more important than mine?"

More slaps followed, screaming. The next sound was the male's, a deep grunt, as though on the receiving end himself. Furniture was thrown, dishes. The woman shrieked.

"We're out of ass-wipe, over-the-hill heifer, and you got nerve to waste money on ice cream and shoes for the little pissy!" Dogs barked; a real ruckus was in progress up there. The boy pretty much ignored it all. Went about in a calm way burning his spiders, tearing wings off flies.

The view from where he stood at the grimy rear window on this tenement landing between the third and fourth floors gave one about as much hope and peace of mind as the hell going on up on the fourth floor: a back parking lot with cracks in the pavement, pot holes and loose cement chunks and gravel that had, over time, become the unofficial dumping site for neighborhood wrecks. Autos of all makes and sizes, pickup trucks, vans, gutted. Some without doors and windshields or wheels, had been abandoned to rust on wood or cinder blocks, bricks, piled rocks.

Knee-high weeds grew from fissures in the pavement. There were scattered stacks and piles of threadbare tires and strips of black rubber throughout; rusted out mufflers, gas tanks, radiators and grills; engines that had long ago been stripped of anything useful.

Down, toward the right-hand part of the parking lot-cum-junkyard, where the dumpster was located and over-flowing to capacity with refuse, dead foliage, and an assortment of fractured and discarded bargain-basement, low-rent coffee tables and nightstands, sofas and chairs, toasters, crock pots, washers and dryers, refrigerators and other appliances, large and small, with additional mounds of plastic trash bags bloated and splitting at the seams, that surrounded it at the base, were a couple of stray dogs engaged in the act, something the boy had been exposed to enough times in the past, so that in and of itself held no real interest; only these two were caught up/entangled in such a way that he had never witnessed until now. Stuck, they were, ass-to-ass, literally; on all fours, heads at opposite ends. Evidently attempting to separate, to untangle, and not able to do so.

One would pull one way for a while, dragging the other with him, then the other mutt would pull, or try to, in his direction, forcing the other dog to back up, neither getting anywhere.

Mexican standoff? He couldn't say. All he knew was it was the Latino part of town. East LA. What was going on?

It was only moments earlier that they had been in front of the building. Fucking, to be sure, but doing it the way they were supposed to: the male, forepaws atop the other's hind end, while he pumped away from behind. The boy's mother, with whom the boy had walked up, having been thoroughly disgusted by the sight, had flung one of her pumps at them. The dogs hadn't bothered to separate—maybe even then had not been able to—instead had hopped the short distance to the left of the tenement to where the driveway and entrance to the lot in back was. And here they were, still at it, only coupled in this baffling manner.

What was it J.J., his dogcatcher step-daddy had said to him about it that time? Couldn't recall the exact words. "Ever see 'em stuck, boy, it's 'cause the bitch has got her snapper locked on the male's prick and he ain't gettin' out until he shoots his load in her. Then the head of his prick, fat like a light bulb, goes down; only then can the male take his dick back.

Now, them young males don't get it; and it's fun to watch 'em panic, an' struggle to pull out. Ain't happening, no way. What a man who knows dogs does then is to calm the asshole down. Only thing that works. Calm the motherfucker down."

Cecil wondered if that's what was going on, if only in a casual way. Because the mongrels, the junkyard, and the heaps hardly mattered beyond what went on in them at night, as well as during the day: local prostitutes, some who lived in the building, sneaking about with their johns, junkies in a crazy frenzy to slam a needle somewhere, bums seeking out vehicles with missing seats to take a dump in.

He'd taken more than one girl to one of the forgotten sedans himself, gotten them to pull their panties down and show him what they had.

None of that rated this mid-morning. No. What mattered and preoccupied his thoughts were the spiders and fat flies he enjoyed burning to a crisp on his side of the window, the flies who threw themselves mindlessly against the pane, and the spiders lying in wait in various corners of the window frame and the traps they had spun for the purpose of snagging a meal.

The boy stood at the window, book of matches in hand, doing the thing that sent the familiar sensation through him: setting things on fire, living or not; fire did it for him. Even though it was beyond his comprehension how or why the mere sight of fire and destroying things in this fashion had the effect that it did on him, it did not stop him from yearning for more of the same.

Drawing his attention above his head, in a web in the upper right corner of the frame, a newly trapped fly struggled to untangle itself, to no avail. Spiders knew what they were doing. The web was sinewy, tough, and this spider's latest victim was not going anywhere.

As expected, the spider emerged soon enough from within its lair. Moved toward the prey. With bated breath, the kid waited until the predator was practically upon the doomed insect before striking the match, reaching up, and roasting them both.

There were other flies he pounced on, clutched in his fist, and dealt with. Large, glistening green flies, who made the loud buzzing, grating noise that added to the thrill, he caught and relieved them of their wings. They were incredibly easy to grab: dumb flies who kept throwing themselves against the grime-streaked glass as if they expected to be able to drill through somehow and escape out there to join up with thousands of their ilk at the dumpster below and anywhere else throughout the lot.

The boy snatched them up, yanked the wings off, and watched with something like inner satisfaction as they kicked out with their spindly legs on their backs, on the sill, kicking out frantically, that enhanced the experience for him. There was no denying it, no explaining it: the combo, fire and subsequent death, not only heightened the senses all around, but clearly left him in a state of arousal, just as there was no denying he felt responsible for what was taking place up there on the fourth floor.

Coco Garcia, the gap-toothed, obese Mexican woman who lived across the way from them in the other apartment and everyone knew to be a prostitute, who had, in fact, turned his mother on to some of her johns, poked her head out through her partially opened door.

"They're at it again, huh, kid? I wouldn't take that off no man. I hope she beats the shit out of his fag ass this time."

The boy said nothing. Looked up at her, then turned away to mind his spiders and flies. He was down to his remaining match and that bothered him. The big woman shook her head at the ongoing racket. She withdrew back into her place and closed her door.

"Lemme get this straight, bitch: You stayed out all night and a good part of the morning, and all you got to show for it is a handful of change? Why, you ain't even good at whorin'! To call you a whore would be an insult to all the hard-working whores out there! Hear what I'm saying, bitch? You ain't even good at whorin'! You don't rate!"

"It's the boy's birthday, Joe. I wanted to do something for the boy this once."

"You ain't even got enough coins left here for a bottle of *rotgut*—"

"He needed shoes, Joe. It's his birthday."

"How many times I gotta hear about the bastard's birthday, *goddamn you!* I ain't got enough here for a taste, and you got nerve to spend on shoes and birthday cakes and ice cream!"

"Can't you do without this one time? We'll get some money later—"

"Why should I have to do without, bitch? Why should I have to suffer? Didn't I tell you to abort the bastard? Didn't I?"

"There was no money for it, asshole! You drank everything I brought in—like you're doing now!"

"You're blaming me? *It's my fault?*"

There was a loud slap. The woman screamed. There was tumbling. Someone being thrown against a wall. More screaming and yelling. Mad dogs barked inside the apartment.

Eight-year-old Cecil Omar Biggs stood at the landing between the floors, struck the last match and burned a plump spider with it. Through with that, he was back on the green flies: easy to catch, while they kept at the filthy windowpane, buzzing away. He'd sever their wings and lower them on the window sill on their backs. Liked to watch them kick wildly this way.

He had an unusually large one now. Was desperate to burn it. Went through his pockets in search of matches. Dug up a book. No matches left in it. Kept searching, found another. A single match left. Struck it. Lowered the flame toward the frantic fly: the fat fucker. He wanted to kill them all. Nothing gave him more pleasure than killing these fuckers. And then he got him but good. The last match. That was it. Gone. All of them. What would he do? Keep catching them and tear their wings off. He'd have to find some more matches somewhere soon. While happening to look up toward the top of the windowpane at a couple of flies banging their heads against the glass, his eyes wandered up toward the ceiling, up there in both corners, large cobwebs, too, but he couldn't reach those. He wished that he could. There were also plenty of dead moths along the window sill that he felt like frying . . . but he needed matches for that.

The landing was littered: beer cans and soda bottles, cigarette butts and empty cartons, bologna packaging and candy bar wrappers, used condoms and Tampons. He shoved his worn sneaker around in there, in search of a possible match, a lighter . . . and found nothing. He cursed. Needed fire. The yelling and fighting in their apartment kept on: more things being broken; his father's dogs barked. Then he heard John Joseph release a deep howl. The apartment door opened like a cannon shot, and his mother, heavily made-up as usual, both eyes swollen, mouth bleeding, with all that wild dark hair flying and not a stitch of clothing on her, scrambled down the flight of stairs toward him.

There was panic and terror in her peepers; even, incredibly enough, to some degree, a kind of glee. He noticed, too, a couple of her front teeth were missing this time.

She descended the stairs in her clumsy, harried way, with John Joseph, drunk and slobbering, nose and jaw bloody, in his soiled OD green army boxers and worn, mis-matched white socks, staggering in the doorway, the birthday cake haphazardly balanced on the palm of his left hand, while he held onto the doorjamb with the other to steady his aim. He cursed and hurled the cake at her, the birthday cake that she'd only bought moments earlier. J.J. sent the cake flying through the air as she neared the landing where the boy stood. The youngster turned his back in time. The cake grazed the top of her head, and a good deal of it deflected and spattered the back of the boy's neck.

"Half a whore!"

"Up yours, faggot!"

The boy's mother continued on down the next flight to make her way toward the lobby below.

"I'll kill you, bitch! Kill the both of you!"

John Joseph ducked back inside, to reappear seconds later with the box the boy's new footwear was in and pitched the shoes, one at a time, at the eight-year-old.

One shoe bounced off the top of the boy's head and went sailing through the windowpane, causing him to pivot enough for the second shoe to nail him between the eyes. The blow sent the kid spinning into the corner, his face buried in his hands. He wasn't crying, merely doing his best to deal with the throbbing pain.

# CHAPTER 2

John Joseph Biggs staggered back into the apartment, slammed the door shut, and could still be heard cursing and carrying on at the top of his lungs.

"That's right: kill you both, so help me! Cake and ice cream, when I ain't even got enough to wet my beak! Good-for-nothing, two-bit half-a-whore! Cake and ice cream! No ass-wipe in the crapper, but there she is throwing good money away on nothin'! Out of dog food, out of ass-wipe, nothin' left to drink—and the bitch throws money away with both hands! What I get for marryin' a madwoman! My own goddamned fault, right there. Could've married up—no, not me; I had to marry down! Insane over-the-hill heifer! Probably got Mad Cow. Wouldn't be surprised."

The boy was squatting in the corner of the landing and wiping his bloody nose with the back of his sleeve. There was no stifling the tears by now.

He heard the door to their apartment open again. Looked up to see Juicer Joe leaning against the door jamb and pointing a shaky finger at him.

"What was you doin'? Playin' with matches, boy? How many times I gotta tell you not to play with fire? Wasn't enough you burned our home down—forced us to have to move to a place like this what we can't even afford."

"I wasn't playing with matches."

"Like hell you wasn't. What you sittin' there for like an asshole? Get that old twat in here before she goes out and kills herself!" his stepfather yelled at him, barely able to hold onto the jamb, vomit and blood dribbling down his chin. He had one of his barking large mutts with him on a leather belt, the belt buckle end of which he had a difficult time holding on to.

"You heard what I said, Pissy? Go get your mother! What are you waiting for?"

"What can *I* do? She never listens to me. . . ."

The father swiped at his chin with his hand, staggered back inside, to reappear a short while later with a beer bottle. Noticed that a good swallow of brew remained. He drained it, and the bottle was hurled at the cowering boy, caught him across the lower back and knocked him off his feet.

The kid was doubled up on the floor, wincing in pain.

"*You heard what I said, Pissy?* Quit your fakin' and bring that confused tramp in here before she throws herself under a bus. Wouldn't break my heart none if she did. Trouble is ain't got no insurance on the bitch. Can't never scrape enough together to take out a policy on the wretched heifer! Understand what I'm sayin', boy?"

Cecil looked up. Could not move from the pain and remained lying on the littered floor of the landing. "And don't you dare so much as think about runnin' off to that molester's place, neither, boy! I catch you again at Turdbull's I'll not only waste his sorry ass, but I will slaughter that pet hog of his and be happy to do it! I will! You can count on it, boy! Chop him up into pork chops to sell to the Mex butcher down the street! Ya hear? Ya hear what I'm sayin', Pissy? I catch you at that pedophile's again, you little motherfucker, you won't hardly like what I do!"

The boy, bothered to his very being, by the ugly and untrue things that were being said about the only kind friend he'd had in the world, didn't dare respond; didn't dare utter a word. But then it happened. Couldn't stop himself. "I would if I could . . . only he's dead. And you killed him."

"What was that?"

"You killed him, and set his house on fire."

"You're a damned liar, Pissy!"

"Killed his pet pig. Fed pork chops to your friends. Even made me eat a pork chop before I knew it was Parfrey, then laughed afterwords when you let me know. You admitted as much it was Mr. Turnbull's pet Parfrey. Only you don't recall on account you was drunk at the time. You can ask around; ask your redneck friends you get drunk with; ask ma. Go ahead."

"Best shut your lyin' trap, boy. Ain't nothin' but a worthless bag of pig waste! Hear what I'm sayin'? Before I give ya another dent in that lop-sided skull of yours to match the one you already own! How's that, boy? Want a second dent? Cave your temple in to go with what you got when you was still inside your mamma's belly?"

"He was an old man and he was my friend; him and Parfrey was my only friends. You stole his money and beat an old man who could hardly walk, J.J. You did! And you burned him down so no one would know it was you done it; you and them redneck billies you drink with. *It was you!*"

"Now I know for sure you burned our home down! Was merely guessin' at it before! Testin' you out. Ain't guessin' no more! *Am I?* To get back at me! You scurvy little prick! I'll cripple you and that homely tramp now for sure! Guarantee it! Got my word, Pissy! Free myself! *Cripple you both!* Be worth goin' to jail over! Sure would! Give myself the best gift of all: *Freedom!* Good for nothin; the both of you!"

The door directly across the way from their unit opened, and the same tired, wasted street whore who lived there stuck her head out.

"The fuck you want, skank?"

The woman's eyes were about half open, not that it mattered, because the appallingly bad bleach job that was her hair hung over them. She had on a black bra that was several sizes smaller than it should have been and revealed a far greater amount of the flab that made up the enormous bosom than was flattering. The large, moth-eaten black underpants she wore managed to detract even further from the overall bloated and disagreeable appearance. This was a big woman who easily weighed in excess of two hundred pounds.

"Can you spare a drink, J.J?"

"Get your *nasty, hog bitch ass* back in that *smelly sty* you crawled out of. This is family business."

"*Besame culo, pendejo.*" She flipped him the middle finger.

"Who you calling '*pendejo*,' you tub of shit?"

John Joseph yelled at the dog to go after her. The woman withdrew quickly enough back into her place, slamming the door shut in time.

J.J.'s attention was back on the boy. Yanked on the makeshift leash, pulling the dog back, who would not stop barking and tugging on the belt. This was one manic animal. Out for blood. Anyone's blood.

"Get up, you little turd! I end up goin' to jail I'll know it was you ratted me out! Suspected you'd be no good; felt for sure you'd turn out like this before you was even born! While still inside that dirty street whore's belly! Sure did! In the womb. Was right, too, wasn't I? *Are you gettin' up? Best get up.* I'll turn this beast on you, so help me!"

The canine tugged too hard, causing the drunk to trip on his feet and stagger against the door jamb, driving his face into it, exacerbating the bleeding nose. He cursed. Wiped the blood with the back of his hand. The man gave the dog a few whacks on the head with the buckle end of the belt, then pointed at the youngster.

"Get him, Mojo! Get the little snivel snot down there! *Get him!*"

The dog charged, pulling the drunk to the stairs. Caused him to miss a step, and down he went, falling on his backside and tumbling down the rest of the way to the landing, cursing both: child and dog.

The boy managed to scramble out of the way in time, crying for help, pleading.

"Daddy, don't! Please, Daddy! Please, Daddy, no! I'll get her! Daddy! Daddy!" Clearly wetting his pants by now.

John Joseph rose to his knees, hissing, in a rage. "Who you callin' *'Daddy,'* Pissy? After what you just said to me? After you done disrespected me with your lies? Daddy? After them foul insults you dared insult me with? If I told you once I musta told you a hunnerd times: I ain't your *Daddy*, boy! Just 'cause I married that whore mama of yourn that don't make me your Daddy! I ain't nobody's Daddy! Whore needed management, is all; somebody with know-how to guide her along, show her what's what, find her tricks, dicks to suck—and I happened to be available at the time. About it! Nothing more to it! So don't you dare insult my intelligence by implying I was the one impregnated that dumb bitch! You hear? Hear me, you worthless motherfucker!"

He probed for something to pick up out of the pile of litter to throw at the kid. Settled for a nondescript bottle. Flung it. Found an empty whiskey fifth. Threw that down the flight of stairs at the fleeing boy. Missed. The bottle hit the wall. John Joseph could be heard shouting over the breaking glass.

"Don't you *never, never, ever* call me *'Daddy,'* boy! I didn't ask to be your Daddy! Only married the nasty heifer on account I musta been outta my mind at the time!"

He felt like chasing after the kid. Was in no condition. Only the dog didn't get that. Kept tugging, and forced the man down to his knees once more.

John Joseph rose, kicked the animal, then began whacking away at it with the belt buckle, drawing blood. Yanked hard on the makeshift leash, and made it back up the stairs to the apartment door. Went in. Slammed it shut.

# CHAPTER 3

Cecil Biggs held onto the handrail as he descended the stairs with measured steps and could clearly make out all the commotion his mother was the cause of in front of the tenement: traffic jams and

**near-wrecks, and the slobbering dog catcher who had married his mother before he was born and given him his name had yelled at him to bring her back; cursed him, thrown the shoes at him, to go out there and fetch her; thrown those bottles at him, threatened to turn one of his dogs loose on him if he didn't.**

Only how was he supposed to do it? How was he supposed to get her to stop carrying on and come back inside? This was never easy, never even made sense. The only way anyone was ever able to control her when she got this bad was to surprise her from behind and force her into a straitjacket. And since he did not have a straitjacket, nor was old enough or strong enough to get her into one (even if he'd had one in his hands), what was the purpose? Why bother with it?

But he did as told, tears streaming down his dirty face, tears brought on by fear of what she might do to herself this time, tears brought on by fear of what John Joseph would do to him later if he failed.

His back hurt. Made walking a task.

He proceeded down the last flight of stairs to the lobby. What's the use? It won't work. Never did. He was stuck. Nowhere else to go. No one to turn to. If he ran away, where would he go? End up where? Rollers would catch him and bring him back and make it worse for him, like before. The straitjacket seemed to be the *only* answer, not that he wished the assholes in their white coats would appear and do that to his mother again as they had in the past. Ma had never liked being taken away this way, not that anyone could blame her. She always screamed and kicked and did her best to resist and fight back. And if it was painful for the boy's mother, it was painful for the boy as well to see it happen.

He paused there, leaning against the mailboxes covered in graffiti, the pain in his head and back forcing him to take a breather. He didn't have to bother with what they'd written about him and his family, he knew it from memory. You see something enough times it sticks with you. He wished he could have blocked it out, only there it all was:

WHAT'S FRUITY ALL OVER & got NUTS In-side? J J Biggs
with A MOUTHFUL OF <u>TESTICCLES</u> pissy-the-sissy drips
urine in his PANTIES J.J. pimps his WIFE COCO GARCIA IS
A HORE & Got <u>Penis Breath</u> PISSY IS A <u>PUSSY</u> CHARLETT
BIGG IS A DIRTY STANKY HOAR J.J. IS HER PIMP JOHN
JOSEF BIGG is a Di-generate wife beat<u>(HER)</u> BLOw JOBS <u>R</u>
<u>US</u>/see CHARLOTTe BuGGS, <u>plus</u> JJ BIGS IS A turd & Dirty
Dog Napper - QUEER 4 SURE

There was something about Cecil's misshapen head; there always would
be. Kids never stopped teasing him about it. Their favorite label for him,
other than "Pissy" was "Football Head."

Sissy the Pissy FeLL OUT of bed and PUT a DENT in his
HEAD / I'd rather be DEAD than be like <u>"FOOTBALL</u>
<u>HEAD"</u>!!

Never mind that it had nothing to do with any kind of accidental fall
from a bed that caused it, but J.J. battering his pregnant mother before she
gave birth to him, and then picked up where he'd left off once he'd been
born to spite her for not having listened to him and aborted him. The oval-
shaped indentation above the right brow, very near, but not quite as high
as the hairline was the result of those assaults.

There was more graffiti. The words ran together after a while, blurred. The
way he preferred it. Had trained himself over time for it to happen this way.
He wiped his eyes, but the pain would not let up. He winced, gritted his
teeth. Looked up. Moved to the center of the lobby. Continued looking up
between the banisters to see John Joseph glaring down at him from above with
a gun held loosely in his hand and clumsily being aimed down at him.
"Should bury you both . . . is what I should do."
The boy heard him retch, and stepped back in time to avoid being
rained on by the bile.

He made it across to the entrance. "What am I supposed to do? He'll shoot me if I don't do what he says." He might. He's threatened to lots of times before, pointed a gun in his face and pulled the trigger . . . only the gun never had bullets in it.

This time could be different. Could be he means it this time.

How do I talk her into coming back inside? How do I bring her back to the apartment before the men in the white coats show up? She wouldn't pay any attention to me.

His mother always liked to laugh hysterically when she got like this; was either laughing or cursing out everybody, sometimes both: laughing *and* cursing at the same time, and it embarrassed him, always.

He knew his pants were wet and that was something else he couldn't do anything about.

# CHAPTER 4

The boy walked outside, stepping into the blinding East LA sun, and could see his mother a short distance away, on his right, standing on the sidewalk of this busy street, bending over for everyone to see whatever it was they wanted to see: she seemed to be saying that all those people in passing cars could kiss her big naked butt as far as she was concerned—and then she rose and shook her large breasts at them, thrust her chest out that way and shook it all very well for them, and Cecil's face remained flushed as he shook his head, wanting to talk to her, wishing to communicate with his mother, wishing to tell her to stop, to please stop and come back inside.

On the verge of tears all over again, he stood and watched and found it unbearable.

"Ma. Please, Ma. Ma . . ."

Charlotte Yvonne Biggs paused long enough in place to look down as a heavy stream of urine poured out of her. Once finished, the expression on her face was clearly one of great satisfaction and she resumed with the shouting and laughing, cursing and weaving, and she was off the sidewalk now and running down the middle of the busy thoroughfare causing more near-wrecks and congestion.

*"MA!"*

The woman was in a world of her own. People in cars did their best to avoid slamming into her without slamming into other cars or utility poles and streetlights.

Ma, don't, he felt like yelling out again. When he opened his mouth to call out to her, warn her that she could get run over, traffic noise drowned him out: bus and truck horns and even a jackhammer going strong not far from there with plenty of dust everywhere and it made it difficult to see what was going on at the end of the block with the DWP street crew where his mother was headed. A yellow panel truck appeared from the left, made every effort to go around her, to swerve and prevent the inevitable. There was no way this time.

The boy screamed with all that he had in him, yelled to his mother to look out for the truck, to get out of the way, not to do what she was about to. And he knew that it would not do any good, that this would be it, the one time finally that she would succeed.

It had been her wish for so long. He'd witnessed her suicide attempts before (only somehow each and every time she had failed; come close— but failed.) This time she would do it for sure.

The panel truck slammed into her, hard, and his mother's body went flying into the air like a human rag doll, and as she dropped back down was struck by a black sedan coming from the opposite direction, was propelled back up, and finally came down, bounced and rolled on the ground near the street crew, knocking some signs and barricades over and was swallowed up by dust and the incredible noise created by the jackhammer.

This is what she had wanted. A way out. To die.

# CHAPTER 5

**In his recurring nightmares thirty some years later, everything was not always crystal clear as the jackhammer operator had remained obscured by a good deal of dust and diesel exhaust, but Cecil Omar Biggs remembered the intermittent glimpses of the jackhammer operator's goggles, the hard hat, the sleeveless khaki shirt, the mud-caked Levi's and construction boots, and his mother's blood spattering, covering the workman as the bit continued to bore into her and tear apart her skull and chest.** And in these flashbacks, Cecil Omar Biggs saw himself as a young boy standing there and screaming his lungs out, trying to stop it, screaming so hard that his guts ached, his own skull throbbing to such a point that he felt it would surely explode, screaming and shedding rock-hard teardrops and running toward the slaughter that did no good at all, as the bit continued its dirty work down across his mother's upper body, tearing it open and drawing that bloody mess out, that whole sickening, tangled mess.

Not that he understood it or even had a clue why it was happening, but he could've sworn he saw the man curse/shout over the din, words like: *"Bust up my marriage, will you? Ruin my life, will you?"*

Cecil had no real idea what it meant, what the jackhammer operator was exactly in a rage about, all he wanted was for him to stop doing what he was doing to his mama, just stop it, not that Cecil's tears and wailing phased the ditch digger any; on the contrary, he appeared to be getting his kicks: determined as well as demented, his jaw and face, and then rest of his head seemed to undergo a type of surreal/fluid-like transformation to that of an eyeless/skinless human skull from which blood poured from both eye sockets, nose cavity and jaw, while he continued to drill with maniacal fervor.

*"DON'T DO IT! PLEASE DON'T! YOU'RE HURTING MY MOM!"*

"Your mother?" the psycho with the death skull said through clenched teeth and a mouth without lips, while looking up momentarily. "This whore? She's a whore. GET IT? *WHORE.*" He was back focusing on the very mayhem he was the cause of. *"Why'd you have to tell my wife? Why?"* The ditch digger resumed boring through the body at his feet, all the while his fly swelling and his rigid groin bursting forth, literally tearing through the zipper. The thing had a head on it the size of a doorknob from which blood spurted, then flowed as if from a garden hose, rained down on the spattered, mutilated body of Cecil's mother, finishing her off. It was then the crimson that flowed from the man's penis turned to sparks, fire; fire shot from his member and engulfed what used to be Charlotte Yvonne Biggs.

Cecil's screaming had gone on for quite some time afterwards, the son unwilling to give his mother up, unwilling to accept what he saw happen to her with his own eyes.

He stood there sobbing, until absolutely spent, and collapsed in the mound of dirt at the overturned MEN WORKING sign and barricades.

Initially unaware that the spattered workman, his member back inside his pants and no longer visible or a threat, had dropped the J-hammer and picked up a sledge. Advanced with it toward him. Cecil realized what was about to happen to him quickly enough. Rose. Taking several, awkward, backward steps away from the mound, backed into John Joseph, his stepfather, standing there in his worn army jacket that had no stripes because he'd been given the boot years before for doing things with and to recruits—in the middle of the night while they slept soundly in their bunks. Heard his mother bring it up enough times during their fights.

J.J. had the jacket on, but no trousers, instead was still in those green army boxers with the urine and blood stains, mismatched socks. Had his large hands clamped down on his shoulders. Held him in place. Prevented him from going anywhere. Wouldn't let him go, no matter how desperately Cecil struggled to free himself. That's when the workman, no longer bearing the death's head skull, instead had returned to normal, whatever "normal" was—and began swinging the sledge.

It was here that Cecil O. Biggs, adult version, became aware that he was trapped in a not unfamiliar nasty flashback and that it was spiraling out of control, taking him places that he did not wish to be taken. *Enough was enough.*

He did his best to scream out, beg for help, freaking at all of it, at what had been done to his mother, screaming to be saved himself, given a hand, rescued from the ugliness of everything; had his mouth wide open, head shaking violently—only not a sound seemed to be emerging.

He'd fought with this for ages, going on for the past thirty-seven years: nightmares and flashbacks, that refused to go away and would not stop reminding him at the way his mother, the unhappy broad, had cashed-in her chips.

The only possible respite he could hope to look forward to, from the onslaught that the dream had deteriorated into, was to yank himself out of it through sheer will and determination and snap awake. Always far easier said than done, no matter how often in the past he'd managed it.

The nightmare was clinging and would not let him be.

You have to fight it. Resist. With everything you have in you. Refuse to go any further. The battle was on. As a result of the effort, he was in and out of it presently, the struggle yielding dividends, yet he was unable to free himself entirely (in one clean break, which was always the desired objective) even though, way off in the distance, there was what vaguely/faintly sounded like the ringing of a telephone.

Fuck this shit. I've had enough. I want out. *I NEED OUT. I WANT OUT. NOW.* Do it. Pull yourself away from it.

Eventually, gradually, the ringing sound could not be mistaken for anything other than a phone, *his phone.* In his bedroom. Telephone bleating. That's when the adult version of Cecil Omar Biggs broke through at last, jerking himself—if not wide-awake—at least awake.

# CHAPTER 6

**He sat up.** Was in a cold sweat. Back stiff due to the Kevlar vest he rarely slept without.

Didn't have to squeeze his groin to know he was hard down there. Squeezed just the same. Like iron. These flashbacks/nightmares, as bothersome as they were, as heavy as their toll was on his psyche, seldom failed to leave him in a state of arousal. Still, it was some price to pay.

Biggs was forty-five years old these days and just as disorientated as ever. The indentation above the right brow was far more pronounced and resembled a misshapen oval that overlapped into and was part of his hairline. The dark eyes, his mother's eyes, pain-wracked and tear-filled.

He dabbed at his face with a corner of the bed sheet that reeked of something he not only was used to, but found a type of undeniable comfort in: BO. His own. Body odor was acceptable, so long as it was not someone else's.

He wiped his neck and armpits. Something like a cockroach, dropping out of nowhere, landed on his chin and ran up toward a corner of his mouth. He slapped at it on instinct, killing it, whatever it was, and just as instinctively spat it out.

Cockroaches wouldn't let you be—like the phone, that phone, that wouldn't stop ringing. Seemed it would go on forever if he didn't pick up.

Did what he was able to collect himself. Turned the volume down on the police scanner that he preferred to leave on around the clock, just as he liked to leave the all-talk and/or all-news AM radio station on while he slept.

He turned down the radio. Hit the record button on the answering machine next to the phone, and lifted the receiver.

"Church."

"You're a bitch."

It was the redneck next door: one Martin Thurman Roscoe, known to one and all as Marty, speaking in a deeper tone than was normal for him (in a feeble attempt to disguise his voice). He was also drunk.

"What was that?"

"You heard. You and that fruit Marvin. Couple of fags. *Tutti and Fruity*. Coupla bitches."

"You're wrong, crevice wipe."

"I know what I'm talking about. Nigger-lovin' faggot is what you are."

"Your mama must have been gang-banged by a pack of rabid mongrels to have engendered a white trash imbecile like you."

Biggs had been able to get it out without losing his composure for a change. He hung up the phone. The bullshit never ended. Redneck asshole.

Faggot? He was no faggot, not by nature. Didn't suck dick, didn't fuck men in the ass, and vice-versa. He was about bitches. Tits and cunt. Where did the redneck get the idea he was homo? Because he ran with Marvin? Marvin wasn't queer. So what gives?

# CHAPTER 7

**It bothered him a little more than it should have.** He needed to keep calm, the nerves steady. He shut the recording device off. Turned the volume up on the news station.

According to the digital clock radio it was only 10:30 in the a.m. Way too early for him to be up. Might as well stay up now. Besides, you got that 2:00 p.m. appointment at the Westwood VA. Can't miss that. Shouldn't. Took you long enough to make up your mind to set it up.

Stay awake. Check the mail.

Even though his primary mailing address was a P.O. Box that he rented on a yearly basis at the North Hollywood post office, and where he received correspondence that mattered, the rest of his mail, usually advertisements and junk of that ilk (that he never sent for) was being sent to this address here.

Check it all the same. Take a look at the cars. Check to see that they're still there and haven't been vandalized overnight.


Where was the *Elavil*? He reached for the *Elavil* container on the night stand on his left (knowing full well that it was empty), had been empty for nearly two weeks now, or was it three?

Lack of medication had to be the cause behind his most recent depression attack. The blues were much worse than was usual for him.

Then he noticed the pile of empty *Preparation H* boxes in the waste basket by the dresser; the last tube he'd squeezed all the balm out of on top of it all. The sight was a needless reminder, as all he'd had to do to be aware of the pain in his burning rectum was move an inch, or not move at all; the ache was always there. Goddamned hemorrhoids. Against his better judgement, he released a fart, and it felt like being jabbed with steel bristles down there. Asshole was on fire. What it felt like.

A second fart wanted out and he suppressed it, held it back. He wiped his face some more with the sweat-stained bed sheet having forgotten that he had the clown makeup on. Ruined the sheet now for sure. Not that it hadn't needed washing to begin with. Some Man of the Cloth you turned out to be.

He thought he might like to die right now, maybe go out like his mother. Why not? What was the point in getting out of bed? You've got to make that interview today—if you're interested in getting the prescription refilled and updated.

How do you get away from yourself? How do you escape your existence? How do you ditch hell? How do you do it? You're wasting your time, he finally concluded, asking questions like that. You're stuck with it, stuck with who you are.

He looked at his surroundings: bulletproof blanket, the cluttered bedroom; stuck with it all. Chained to the nightmare.

The bed was a mess and so was the room. Stacks of the *Wall Street Journal* about on the floor, pictures of hardcore starlets he'd cut out from underground smut rags and slick porn publications adorned the walls. Cunts being drilled by massive cocks. If they weren't being fucked, their faces were in the process of being drenched in cum.

There were also autographed glossies, eight-by-tens, of various strippers and hardcore cunts who worked various LA, Nevada and Arizona clubs. The local peelers he'd gotten to know well enough: Pearleen Bell went by *Peaches LaBelle*; Lana "Da Bottom" Sepulveda's stage name was *Lady Likkerish*; Stella Martel took her clothes off as *Stunning Stella Storm*; and there were others.

This is what kept him going. That need for pussy; that deep, inexplicable craving for cunt. He hated being a slave to it as much as he despised the bitches themselves for it. Still, it made him want to hang around. Kept him from blowing his brains out. Couldn't tell if that was good or bad.

But the bitches came and they went. At least these three, and a couple of others, lived in the Valley and were house dancers, regulars at the *Casbah Hideaway – Cabaret & Nightclub*—and they'd gotten acquainted.

He'd spent enough bucks for the privilege. Hated to. Only there was no other way. *Money talked, bullshit walked.* It was the oldest cliche around, but true. Money was honey—and it drew gold diggers like flies to dog crap. On the other hand, they weren't all dancers and porn starlets.

He had a series of color photos taped to his dresser mirror and on the wall surrounding it that he had taken with a telephoto lens of a gorgeous high school cheerleader, photos taken from a distance, without the subject's awareness, an undeniably attractive Latina named Olivia Candida Duarte who lived with her family in a part of the neighborhood that was not as rundown and seedy as the block his own place was on.

He also had stills from some of his favorite slasher flicks up there on his walls and door: freaked out sluts drenched in their own blood on the run from some mask-wearing, machete- or ax-wielding psycho determined to take them out.

He had a poster on the ceiling of a fat retard fuck about to carve up a helpless cunt in pain hanging on a meat hook, another of some dorky male having his melon bashed in by the same psycho with a sledge.

There were slick bondage mags on his floor as well as publications on flicks with ultra violent content, at least what the so-called mainstream considered "ultra violent."

Quite a few of these VHS horror movies that these magazines featured were about in stacks on the worn carpet. There was plenty of hardcore porn in there as well, with titles like *Cuckoo for Culo, Beach Blanket Bunghole, Cunt Blanche, Assholes Anonymous, Cornhole Confidential, Double-D Nymphos Triple-Teamed,* et al.

Some of these strippers that he favored, namely Lana Sepulveda, Stella Martel, others, had appeared in a hardcore porn video or two. On the other hand, Peaches LaBelle, quite possibly the hottest of the exotic dancers, didn't do triple-X on film—that he knew of. Then again there was no way to be sure; these sluts had more aliases and stage names than you could keep track of, although the soft-X type titles she had appeared in (that he *was aware of*) he had copies of.

LaBelle pumped dumbbells in the buff, hosed down a Porsche in the skimpiest pair of cutoff jeans and tiniest of Ts.

In one of the videos shot at some seaside resort somewhere south of the border, they had her showering in her birthday suit, spreading soap suds all over those impressive hangers and running a washcloth between her ass cheeks; got the twat, too. There was the post-shower masturbation finale on the bed with a vibrator in hand being inserted into the moist and glistening cooter, the licking off of said moistness by her very own ruby-red lips and tongue, and the subsequent further sliding in-and-out of her cunt with that vibrator until the bogus climax. In fact, all of it was bogus. *One major con.*

It was: Give us your hard-won cash, and we'll give you sleight of hand. He knew it. And it pained him to spend good money on this crap, but when you were obsessed with cunt, you paid. It was clearly an addiction. There was no denying it. Porn and splatter.

Had additional stacks of these videos on either side of the eyeless, decades old teddy bear perched atop the combo tee-vee/VCR on the dresser, as well as additional videos on makeshift shelves to the right of the banged up dresser. Sucking and fucking. Butchering and mayhem. It was there. True crime paperbacks. Books on pop psychology and scholarly texts. Man couldn't exist on smut and bloodshed alone. Well, he might try—and get along well enough—but for him something would be missing.

His eyes shifted back to the teddy bear. Tired. No eyes. A childhood memento. There was nothing remotely sentimental attached. He'd held on to it as a perpetual reminder of what he'd lived through as a youngster, stainless-steel-proof what useless/worthless cretins humans were. Bottom line. People were shit. All he'd had to do was take a look at the teddy bear—whose eyes had been gouged by John Joseph, and real eyes from a live pup inserted in their stead—to be sobered up about society. Biggs didn't need to keep staring at it to remember what had been done to him, what he'd survived.

# CHAPTER 8

**You need to get out of bed.** Get out of bed. Act required motivation that wasn't there.

What he did next he did so with hesitation, as always; great trepidation. Paused to stare at a couple of faded photos, taped to the top of the mirror, of the only love he'd experienced as a youngster; the only friends he'd ever known, the only ones who'd shown him genuine kindness and affection: Mr. Turnbull, Truly Turnbull and his pet hog Parfrey. Long gone. Taken out by John Joseph and his druggie street freaks. It pained him. Even now. Lo these many years later. Hurt went deep.

He stared at the photo: Mr. Turnbull in his sinister clown makeup as Trusty Lusty; then to the right of his friends: Cecil, in his pre-teen years, smiling with his arm lovingly around the hog's neck. Parfrey, black and ugly and repulsive, not unlike a wild boar—and yet, this had been the appeal; why he had been drawn to the pig. It was easy to relate; there were unspoken things in common. Biggs had felt ugly and unappealing enough himself. Inside and out. Unworthy, unwanted—unloved. The dented forehead and scars and welts were equal to Parfrey's horribly frightening slobbering jaw and fangs; bulky skull and huge, ragged ears. But to Cecil, this was what had made him so appealing and handsome. Lovable, even. They were drawn to one another. It had been love at first embrace. And this is what had made him so unique and special to the hog's tender-hearted owners, Mr. and Mrs. Turnbull. Friends. Caring. Genuine. Long gone presently. Flora Turnbull's heart had given out. And Truly? Deep-sixed by the alkie bigot. Beaten senseless and robbed of his precious coin and stamp collection and anything else of value that he had and his house summarily torched. His pet hog had been butchered by J.J. and his psycho crew and afterwards eaten.

Made him sick to his belly to think about it. So why do it? Because it belongs to me. It's mine. They live on inside of me—until the very end. This was his way of honoring them: by thinking of them, reminding himself of the kindness he had been shown. If they hadn't mattered to anyone else, they mattered to him. If he, as a child, hadn't mattered to the abusive creeps who had raised him, by keeping his friends' memories alive he was reminding himself that there had been a time when someone had actually given a damn; someone had provided him with sanctuary and a caring word; had fed him when he was hungry, and most often he was; had provided him with not only clean clothing and footwear, but clothing meant for a boy, as opposed to the dress and other girly attire his mother and her homo boyfriend had forced on him that they had filched from the lowliest thrift stores.

This was exactly why he made the effort on a daily basis to address/pay his respects/give a nod to the images that represented the two people and their pet hog who had been there for him in his times of great need. The other reason, of course—prior to leaving the domicile on his way to the haunted house (the times he did the makeup here as opposed to at the Bordello of Fear)—was to see if his version of Trusty Lusty's makeup compared to what Mr. Turnbull wore in the picture. Some days he was closer than he was on other days. This current incarnation that covered his face was not bad at all, if you considered he'd slept with it on, and then had to whack at the roach that had resulted in further smearing near chin and mouth. He reminded himself that he'd also unintentionally wiped quite a bit of it off with the bed sheet a moment ago. Got to expect it to be off and smudgy.

He did one last thing in their honor: Stared and studied the two Parfrey masks that he had hanging from the coat rack in the corner, full head masks that he'd fashioned himself with needle and thread a while back. Actual skin masks he'd peeled off of pig heads he purchased on a regular basis from a meat market in Pacoima. It troubled him that they appeared worn, shabby. Steady use at the haunted house had been the cause. He'd have to stop by the same butcher shop pretty soon to pick up a few more heads and sew enough masks for future use. His haunted house business was about to be shut down indefinitely by the DA's office because Greta

Otto—one of the crazier and more unpredictable members of his church board—had lost her cool and gone after a customer, as well as a couple of his own Mex employees, with an axe handle. The customer he'd been able to pay off, now the former employees, janitors, in the country illegally, were threatening to sue. After money. Trying to shake him down for a substantial amount of cash. They wanted to take away what took a lifetime to build up. It was envy. Those who were able were always envied by those who were never capable of anything. The Roscoes next door were a perfect example. So were chronic trouble-makers Glassy and his low IQ, mentally-challenged punk buddy Felix. Out to grab what was his, instead of going out and working for it.

His eyes were on a yellowed-by-age newspaper clipping on the mirror above the stuffed animal, having to do with someone he'd been involved with once, a certain Puerto Rican porn whore who'd gone by *Mistress Payne*, aka Mona Pleeze, aka Mona Payne, the professional disciplinarian he'd got his hands on back in 1978 and held captive in a homemade coffin for ten days—not ten months or ten years, but ten days—and for that they'd made him do five years in Atascadero, forensic institution for the criminally insane. Misguided fuckers.

He'd spent good money on the bitch, plied her with expensive drugs, bought her clothes and trinkets. He'd only been trying to get his money's worth. Besides, how else was he supposed to keep her from running off? He'd only kept her in the oblong box because he hadn't been able to trust her. Trust took time. She'd finally been able to con him into believing she was on his side. Took her with him to the Glendale Galleria to buy ice cream cones, and the whore had slipped away and fingered him. Told a bunch of lies about him. Half-truths. Shit she made up because he'd turned the tables on the dominatrix. *She was the one* who was supposed to be meting out the pain; the emasculating cunt made her living this way, and when he turned all that around she didn't like it—and fingered him to the enemy.

Let it go. Fact is, you got caught. She flapped her jaw. Ratted you out. Dead bondage queens tell no tales. Your mistake was you didn't shut her up when you had the chance.

There were some other clipped out articles on missing women (and a few men) throughout Southern California the police suspected the same perp (or perps) were behind, but were not certain. Didn't have enough "to go on." As soon as they had more "to go on" they were sure to release it to the media. It was all in Biggs's collection of old newspaper clippings from the *Herald Examiner* to the *LA Weekly*, the *LA Times*, the *Daily News*, the *Orange County Register*; even a Spanish language paper or two.

It didn't concern him; this was nothing more than a way to pass the time, keep up with what was going on in this hopeless life and world he was stuck in.

There were boxes of stale doughnuts on both end tables, additional paperbacks that specialized in bondage and torture scenarios; some dealt with bestiality: bitches being fucked by Great Danes; bitches caressing horse penises. What a society. Whores were the gutter.

There were *Twinkie* and *Ding Dong* wrappers strewn about the room; candy bar wrappers: *Three Musketeers* and *Butterfinger.*

In the closet, on the other side of the room, to the right of the mini fridge that sat to the right of the dresser, with the sliding door open, and in full view on the floor were *U-Haul* cardboard boxes full of handcuffs, leg irons, bottles of chloroform, dildos and rubber vaginas, vibrators, a gas mask or two, ankle holsters, shoulder rigs. Up on the shelf, shotgun mics and headsets, boxes of cartridges for a variety of handguns in his collection, among which was a *.357 Magnum Colt "Python"* that he liked to keep under the pillow while he slept, insomnia notwithstanding. That reminded him. Checked under the pillow to make certain it was there, that he hadn't misplaced it.

*Mag* was there. Where else would it be? Held it, while being drawn to and unable to ignore the framed wedding photo next to the lamp on the end table on his side of the bed, a wedding that had not taken place that long ago after all, no more than two years ago, in the Philippines, to a twenty-four-year-old Filipino nurse named Tillie Marie who had wanted out of the marriage out of the blue. Had hired a Beverly Hills Jew lawyer to file a civil suit against him for mental anguish, of all things. Mental anguish. *Irreconcilable differences.* After all he'd done for her. Had wanted and gotten her divorce, had wanted and gotten her alimony. All the money he'd spent on her during the courting phase, not only on her, but her entire family; not only prior to the wedding, but close to two years that they'd spent corresponding, all that money spent on *Candygrams* and postage, endless stream of *Hallmark* cards for every known occasion invented by man, not to mention the thousands spent on plane fare: round-trip for him, one-way for her. The wedding itself, that had taken place in the Philippines and cost so much it pained him to even think about it. It was due to his innate generosity that she was able to move to the States, where she had always wanted to live.

Ungrateful whore. User. Turd-World deceptive cunt. Not only was the alimony killing him psychologically (and otherwise), and the child support, among other things, but she'd had his young son by now and refused to let him see him, pretty much. Had custody. Controlled the situation. The rare visits he was allowed, at locations of her own choosing, she made it nearly impossible to spend quality time with him. He and the kid were never left alone to enjoy their moments together. Although she was never there with the kid, her many Filipino friends were, more like bodyguards, as far as he was concerned—so that it made it virtually impossible to bond with his own offspring, if indeed he was his. She claimed the kid was his, so did her lawyer, so did the court. Judge said he was the father. And you're going to pay alimony, Mr. Biggs, as well as child support—and we're going to give her, although she does not deserve it and has no right to lay claim, some of your hard-earned assets. Try to do something about it. Go ahead.

California courts always ruled in the bitch's favor. Don't like it? Move to Saudi Arabia.

Wouldn't even tell him what she'd named him for the longest time, and he never would have found out anything if he hadn't hired a private detective. "Send the money to her lawyer's office," he was told, "and she'll get it. We're not disclosing her whereabouts. Do not attempt to contact her."

The restraining order saw to that. He got the message.

She had named the kid *Honesto*, of all things. *Honesto Cipriano*. Goddamn her. He could have taught the kid a thing or two about the "fair sex." Not only were they all whores, but gold diggers on top. Scheming, conniving, manipulating opportunists.

What right did she have to backstab him? All he'd done was slap her around a couple of times because she'd refused to participate in a ménage with hookers he'd brought home and paid good money for. There was no way any one cunt could ever satisfy his sexual needs, and the bitch needed to get used to it. All would have been fine, except she pulled a double cross, like Mona Payne, and ran off, got her divorce, and was now attempting to have the alimony "adjusted." Inflation, they claimed. Mental anguish. Where? The only anguish he witnessed was the anguish she and her ambulance chaser lawyer put him through. This was what they were trying so hard to nail him to the cross on. He was Christ on the cross: modern-day version, not that he ever believed Christ had ever existed, but he certainly was the one being crucified monetarily and otherwise, by the slant-eyed shrew.

And after all of it, the hell of it, he still missed her. Hadn't expected to miss her, but did. More than that, though, he missed all the cash she had cost him and continued to cost him, and he never would get the chance to teach his young son about bitches, how to handle them, keep them under your thumb, beat them down, keep them way down. Always. Cunt had him. Honesto Cipriano is the name she gave him. It was the "Honesto" part that bothered him. Honesto. Named by a conniving slut who did not know the meaning of the word.

Some of what they were going on about on the radio filtered through in the background, penetrated his thoughts and the malice he felt for Tillie

Marie and what she'd put him through and continued to put him through.

He picked up on a name. Pamela Alice Phelps. Had been forced to stop on a shoulder of the 101 north of Malibu late one night a month ago due to a flat tire, and not seen since.

They broke for a commercial for *Prep H*. That reminded him: would have to pick up some.

News was back on.

*"The search continues for eighteen-year-old Helen Irene Sanchez who was last seen five months ago in a Culver City shopping mall talking to two men in a tan panel truck."*

There was something about a Woodland Hills school teacher named Connie Higgins. Missing since Friday night. Police were hoping someone would come forward with information that would help in the investigation. There was a bit about a dead jogger found in Griffith Park that morning. Male. Mid thirties.

*"The body of a female in her twenties was also discovered nearby."*

LAPD were receptive to clues and tips; any information that would help. Good luck, thought Biggs. Turned the radio off. Lowered the framed wedding photo that he was in with "Agenda" Marie. What her name should have been. User! She was a user, and he'd clearly been used.

Well, he'd fucked the shit out of her cunt and asshole and mouth for a year and a half anyway. It had cost him plenty to be sure, but he did get some, got his share—and now *she* was out to *get more*. Was asking for more money. She was an RN. Pulled in a substantial salary. Enough to provide for the kid—but there she was, changed lawyers and suing to increase the child support and alimony, making a nuisance of herself, not unlike the cockroaches and rug beetles he was being invaded by.

# CHAPTER 9

**He crawled out of bed.** Left side/Safe side. Where the arsenal was kept. A number of roaches hurried past his feet, scurrying away. Some seeking shelter behind the four-and-a-half-foot-high black file cabinet, or else behind the heavy-duty safe next to it. Safe was as high as the file cabinet and about as wide as a large kitchen refrigerator. This was where he kept his rifles, shotguns, additional handguns and ammo, and was damned near unmovable. The only way to get at the pests was to spray between the two, or directly behind. Some ran across the floor to hide behind the dresser.

Where was the *Black Flag?* Looked about. Nowhere to be seen. Thought to check under the bed. Good place for it. Crouched to reach it. His back was at it again. *The Pain.* Like being jabbed with steel bristles across the tailbone region and above it. It froze him up every time. He'd sought medical attention for it, had taken *Percodan* and others. Nothing ever helped much. Doctors couldn't tell him what brought it on, could not even begin to pinpoint the source of the pain, and had no idea what the solution was.

One did suggest spine surgery, that Cecil was absolutely, adamantly against. He saw, with his own eyes, over the years, what this type of tricky operation did to people: left them hunched over, unable to walk straight, upright—ever. It was not for him.

No, thank you.

Some of the quacks had gone so far as to imply that it was (possibly) psychological. Psychological? Bullshit to that. As far as he was concerned, there was no mystery as to the initial cause: John Joseph hurling whiskey and beer bottles at him years ago, when he wasn't busy flailing away at him with broom sticks (and/or just about anything he could get his hands on).

What added to the confusion was that the pain dissipated on its own eventually. Always. It came and it went. Never knew when it would strike—or leave him. There were times when lifting anything (be it light or heavy, or simply sitting in a chair, if slouching) did it, or bending down to pick up something under his bed, triggered it; although, for the most part, there was no real rhyme or reason for it.

He had his hand on the *Black Flag* canister, but did not dare move; the pain wouldn't allow it. He straightened himself in slow gradations. Stood still. Waited. Winced. Clenched his teeth. Christ. It was gone by about eighty percent, and so were most of the pests.

He sprayed behind the file cabinet, the safe. Behind the nightstands, and back of the dresser. Nothing he did, no matter how much he sprayed, kept them away forever. Even Boric acid allowed for nothing more than temporary respite. And to bring an exterminator in was out of the question.

Canister was empty. He went at them with his bare feet, needing to crush as many as he was able. Gave him a feeling of superiority. It was not unlike killing flies and burning spiders as a kid; something like eliminating humans.

Then it happened, as he knew it would: *stubbed* his big toe on the right foot. Cursed and cursed plenty. A large roach hurried up the wall. Biggs shook the canister, hoping there was enough pesticide left in it. No dice. Nothing but air, and it took a lot more to stop roaches.

Pissed, he flung it, hard, at the wall. Canister promptly bounced back, as he suspected it might. Boomeranged against his mouth. Hurt bad enough. Day was starting out perfect. Omens everywhere. Of bad shit to come.

"I love my life."

Biggs tasted blood inside his mouth. He looked in the dresser mirror. Clown in the fucked up makeup stared back. Lower lip was bleeding, or was it upper? Both? Goddamned *Black Flag*. He stared at the image that didn't look away.

"Wouldn't you want to be me? Yes—you. Wouldn't you like to be me?"

Needed something to dab at the blood with. Grabbed a corner of the bed sheet. Dabbed away. Wiped more sweat from his forehead and neck with the sheet. He got his feet into the scuffed black leather shit-kickers, grabbed the carabiner with the key rings and countless keys, and walked to his door in his sweat-stained boxers. Reached for the shoulder holster hanging from a chair there. Strapped it on.

Holstered the *.357*, and got into a plaid shirt over that. There was enough of a bulge where the gun was, but the shirt concealed it well enough. He dropped the pepper spray in the left shirt pocket. Looked around for his glasses.

There was a stack of books on the night stand that he'd browsed through the night before in hopes that it would help induce sleep. Even after putting in a long and exhausting night at the Bordello of Fear, he still had not been able to fall asleep right away. Worried. The pending lawsuit. Fear of being shut down. Mr. Turnbull, who had willed him the business, might be turning in his grave right now at the clumsy way he had handled the situation with Greta and the Mexican illegals he'd had working for him and who were now doing everything they could to shake him down for a frighteningly substantial chunk of change. This was how they repaid him for showing compassion by hiring them in the first place. Never mind that they'd had papers, forged documents, no doubt, all of it: bogus social security cards, counterfeit license and IDs. Fuck it. I'll deal with them later. It's an issue I'll have to resolve in my own time and manner. But not now. Not now. It was Halloween. The biggest night of the year for the haunted house business—if he was still in business. Temple City honchos had been threatening to shut him down unless he resolved the complaints against the Bordello. Never mind that the so-called complaints were blatant attempts to squeeze him for cash. What did it matter to them? It didn't.

He'd drive out there tonight and find out if the Bordello, his golden goose, was still there for him. Maybe stop by where the peelers lived and do his Peeping Tom bit with Marvin, then maybe check in on Liv Duarte, prick-teaser extraordinaire, before moving on to the Casbah for the special Halloween show the Cabaret owner had been promising his loyal customers for more than a month now. *Fear and Pussy,* had a nice sound to it.

His eyes were on the stack of books, the one on top in particular. *The Devil's Dictionary* had given him a mild chuckle or two. The others hadn't done much for him: a couple by economists Milton Friedman and Henry Hazlitt, a tome on the Nazi bag of excreta named *Hitler* by John Toland.

The thing that he resented about "Uncle Adolf" and his kind was that he'd never be in their league. You'd have to have a real military to make slaughter on that mass scale possible, because without it you were nothing more than an amateur, Boy Scout. The thing that he found puzzling and disagreed with the little man was this single-minded determination to go after primarily the Jews.

He didn't get it. Why not go after all of them: Chinese, Japanese, blacks, Hispanics, whites, Ruskies, Filipinos, Slavs, Mohammedans, Agnostics, Atheists, strippers, whores (same thing), virgins, shopkeepers, politicians, actors, moviemakers, factory workers, janitors, teachers, lawyers, preachers, butchers and bus drivers, models and call girls (same thing), joggers and tennis players, rollerbladers and cyclists, soccer players and junkies; the rich, the poor, the bright and the low-brow?

Why not go after everyone?

Why discriminate? Why make the Semite your principle target? The Semites only made up a small portion of the picture anyway. How relevant is that?

But the old boy, *Schicklgruber*, had made his bed and was lying in it. Illiterate cocksucker had dug his own grave and was dozing in it and so were most of his pissant followers. Once they were "relieved" of their "armor," the pathetic punk pussies were left standing there shitting in their *SS* and *Wehrmacht* and *Luftwaffe* panties like a certain junkie he knew of who liked to hover around his property and case his domicile, a junkie they called "Ace," other times called "Glassy" for that blue marble of an eye in his socket where a real one used to be, and his equally worthless buddy Felix Monk. The only reason he thought of them at all was because his cars were on his mind. You couldn't think of one without the other. They went hand-in-hand like sex and violence, like bitches and pain, like Romeo and Juliet.

His glasses lay on top of the Bierce book. Held them up against the desk lamp. Glasses were dirty. Lenses dust-covered with prints and smudges.

He wiped the lenses with a shirttail. Put the glasses on. The tinted bifocals were nothing more than reading glasses. Upper sixty percent of the lenses was plain glass and were lightly tinted, the lower were prescription. Although he wore them at all times, he didn't have to, and did so because they were stylish and enhanced his appearance—to the extent it was possible with that damned dented forehead. He wore them— even when he didn't have to. If he didn't, they got misplaced. By leaving the glasses on his face he knew where they were and wouldn't have to look for them the times he needed them. The bigger plus yet: it was far easier to tell people that you had to deal with whatever you felt like telling them, whatever far-fetched, fabricated tale you felt like weaving when they couldn't quite read your eyes. Sometimes they could, but for that they'd have to be close in, too close, as well as indoors—because the tint lifted considerably when the glasses were worn indoors.

Leave them on. Check the mail and the cars. See how your "faithful staff" is doing, what they're up to.

He was back at the dresser. Stood in front of the large mirror. Held a pocket mirror against the back of his head, over the area where he suspected his hair to be thinning. Hair *was* thinning and he didn't care for it. You wanted to hold on to your hair no matter how old you happened to be, no matter that Father Time dictated, usually, otherwise.

Years before he had gone in for a tat in the crown region and had promised to himself that if it ever became so visible that you could actually make out what it was that he would go back to shaving his head; he would cut all his hair off and shave his skull.

Shaving your scalp had its drawbacks, it revealed the crater that made up part of your forehead, but it also made it possible to conceal one's true age. Twats couldn't tell how old you were if there weren't any tell-tale gray hairs to give your true age away.

There was a white ball cap, stained with sweat and a degree of general grime, with black script across the front that stated:

## GOD'S #1

He put it on. Picked up the foot-long, heavy aircraft aluminum black Maglite. Unlocked the door. Stuck his head out. Hallway was quiet enough.

No doubt about it, he felt put upon by these "self-imposed" precautionary measures, because the house was owned by him, a house that he had turned into the United Christian Church of Re-Newed Hope a few years back; he also knew well enough, with the sort of erratic board members and staff he had on his hands, it made sense to be cautious.

# CHAPTER 10

**Biggs listened.** Shone his Maglite up and down the dark hallway. Did not see anyone lurking about, which was good, since they were all supposed to be in the basement safely tucked away for the time being—only the stench of excreta was stronger than usual.

Biggs directed the Maglite at the floor a yard to his left, and saw the pile, a puddle of urine, and it did not make him feel good. Hadn't these screwballs learned anything by now? How many times had he said to them that they ought to be using the john in the basement or the honey buckets that he provided them with? That they were ruining his property by crapping all over his hardwood floors this way?

He'd been patient with them, but things were just getting out of hand lately. Didn't matter that he'd been protective of the whole lot, had wanted them to have a place where they could shower, have a bed to sleep in and buckets to crap in the times he was out or unavailable; given them the roof over their heads; was able to relate to them in ways that others, out there, could not and did not wish to relate.

Was this his reward now? Having to pick up their waste after them? Did it not matter to them that they were an integral component of the picture and that a certain responsibility came with it? Responsibility to the church as well as to the Bishop of said church? Someone who provided shelter as well as made survival possible?

The stench was too much. Far worse than the norm.

*"I got you out of the institutions, goddamn it! Got you off bus benches and sidewalks! Gave you a place to live, fed you! The least you can do is shit in the honey buckets and not on my floor!"*

The more he thought about it, the angrier he became. What was it going to take to get them to abide? *"The next one shits on this floor is going to have his asshole sealed tight with a fucking blowtorch! You think I'm kidding? Try me. Just try me."*

Biggs reached back inside his dresser drawer for a couple of chain leashes with carabiners. Changed his mind. He would go with what he had downstairs instead. Should be able to dig up one or two in the cabinet in the Fun Room.

Rummaged around through old locks, keys, candles, flashlight batteries, extension cords, in search of the tape measure. Found it. Grabbed a pencil, small notepad. Jammed them in his shirt pocket.

# CHAPTER 11

**He locked his bedroom behind him and walked toward the front.** Flipped the switch for the overhead light. Checked his entrance. Door seemed in good shape. The other door in the foyer there, on his right, that led to the second floor and the Prayer Hall, hadn't been tampered with, either. He was relieved. Door was a bit loose maybe, but the lock held. Tested the living room door across from it. Solid. Hadn't been tampered with.

He walked back down the hallway, watching where he stepped. Paused at a door past his own, same side of the hallway. Pounded on it. In a moment the door opened, and a sleepy-eyed light-skinned African-American appeared, holding a larger-than-average black rat against his chest. The rat, one of four that Marvin cared for, had been "tagged" MC Snagglepuss by him and was gnawing on a dog biscuit.

"Clean it up, Free Ride."

Biggs entered the john across the way. Marvin R. Muck remained in the doorway. Took a quick whiff of the stale, odiferous air, and knew what the problem was and it did not make him happy, neither was he thrilled at the way Cecil had taken a cool street name like "Free Base" and turned it into something as lame-ass as "Free Ride." But he put up wiff it. Tolerated it. For the time being. There was other things about the "gig" he wasn't crazy about either, but the pluses, there was enough pluses that made up for it, fringe benefit', that made him want to keep hangin' around a while longer.

Beat livin' in condemn' buildins in Hollyweird, beat diggin' around in dumpster' in back of *Fatburger* and *Wendy'* and Von' supermarket; beat muggin' old bitches and blind beggas in wheelchair for chump change.

Yo. Had to beat the street', the wet mothafuckin' street' when it be rainin' in LA like a mothafuckah, an' be cold in the winter time, too. Yeah. Most of the time. This don't be one of them time, though. When you had to pick up after the geek'. Prob'ly it was Mr. Pimple took him that major dump on Brotha Trusty's floor.

Marvin was another one who had a bughouse or two in his past, another one who had done his share of time in bullpens and jail cells, orphanages and foster homes.

Although merely in his twenties, the teeth were already tobacco stained.

The naturally curly hair was light brown, with the exception of the layer across the very top that was as close to platinum as he was able to make it with a do-it-yourself hair-bleaching kit. A couple of old scars, knife wounds, more-than-likely, crisscrossed below the lower lip. The left earlobe had been gnawed off by rodents in Seattle, Oregon, and Hollywood motel rooms many years before while left unattended night after night by his crack-addicted, street-walker mother. Part of his upper lip, the area surrounding the nostrils, contained visible discoloration, reminders of the botched cosmetic surgery and the attempted reconstruction to repair that part of the nose and section of upper lip. Primarily explained Marvin's strong love and respect for the creatures. This had been the only way he could think of of overcoming his tremendous fear of them. *Love 'em. Make 'em yo friend. Can't beat 'em? Make 'em yo pet.*

The scars not only left him self-conscious, but made it that much tougher to pull in the hot hoz, the kind of *Grande culo* bitches that made his meat hard. Not impossible, just tougher, in that he had to run a better game on 'em to get that booty.

As bothersome as the facial flaws were, they did not draw half as much negative attention as the eyes, if one got a good, close look at the eyes, if that were at all possible, because Marvin R. Muck, aka Free Base, very often wore tinted sunglasses to conceal his eyeballs for this very reason. Wearing the rose-tinted shades, day or night, was the only way he had of concealing from the world the weird and off-putting thoughts and ideas that were usually spinning around in his head, thoughts and fantasies that he had no control over and did not understand, thoughts and notions that, very often, confused and unsettled even him.

But the bishop had made him "deacon" fourteen months ago and Marvin and his pet rat had a roof over their heads these days and that's what mattered, that's all that mattered—for the time being.

Sure, the mofo had promised to buy him some ferret'. Marvin had wanted a couple of ferrets. No problem. Move in. What Bigg' said. Help me out around the church. I'll get you what you want. All the coke you can huff. All the pussy you can bang. Free rent and grub. You get to ride around in a pimp mobile and pick up cunt.

Sounded good, thought Marvin. Only the mothafuckah bought him three rat' instead of the ferret' he wanted. Said ferret' cost money. What Bigg' said. Ferret' eat meat. Said too many peep' in the church was meat-eater'. Had him enough meat-eater' as it was.

And the "grub"? Grub be Mulligan stew, most of the time. Fuckin' cook didn't know how to cook. Jambalaya, they calls it. An' tap water to wash it down wiff. Most of the time. Sometime' Bigg' give him a candy bar for dessert. Sometime. Or else it was *Twinkie'*. Had him cases of *Twinkie'* down there in the cooler. *Twinkie'* and *Ding Dong*. Was tight wiff it, too.

This is what went through Marvin Muck's mind presently as he stood there, rubbing sleep from his eyes. What the dream had mostly been about: ferret'. Fuck the ferret', thought Marvin. Do what the dude tell' you, he reminded himself, or you and Snagglepuss and the rest of your pet homie end up right back in that shootin' gallery on Yucca, maybe a return visit to the bughouse, maybe for good next time. I hope not.

His nose dripped and he was desperate for a snort of blow. Cecil coulda let him have some, instead there was a yellow bucket on wheels with a mop in it that he kicked out of the crapper and into the hallway.

Tossed Marvin a pair of generic, powder-free/latex-free synthetic white gloves.

"How about if you put the fucking beast down and get with it?"

Marvin returned Snagglepuss to his cage and stepped back out. Dragged the mop and bucket toward the stench.

Biggs handed him a dust pan and a broom. Marvin swept up what he was able. Dumped it in the john. Flushed it away.

"Buncha *boo-shit*."

Biggs was back in the closet. Reached down for a one-half-gallon jug of *Skaggs Alpha Beta Lemon Ammonia*.

"Here." Tossed it to him. "Pour enough in the water. Get it good, Marvin. This is supposed to be a House of Worship."

Years ago, in reform school, where he'd had his share of chores and working the mop, Marvin had tattooed the epithet **FUCK U** across his right palm, and now he was giving Biggs a perfunctory salute with this hand behind his back. He did not like cleaning up after staff and members of the board any better than he did years before in juvie; did not like cleaning up after them "fuckin' tard'," but there he was, doing it, mopping someone else's floor again.

Remember the street'. You be doin' the deacon' job, Brotha Marvin. If you want to keep livin' here wiff Brotha Bigg' you gonna havta keep cleanin' up and bein' the flunky an' gofer.

# CHAPTER 12

**Biggs withdrew his *Magnum* and went in search of the guilty board member who had dared take not only a dump, but a major one, in his hallway.**

Biggs figured it was Norbert Fimple, the big, greasy slob who could never get enough to eat and was always breaking into the walk-in cooler in the basement or else it was the kitchen and busting the locks off cupboards and eating up provisions.

Cecil took several steps down toward the rear where the kitchen was located to discover that the kitchen door, on his right, had been left ajar. The lock and part of the jamb damaged. He walked in.

Mr. Fimple was nowhere to be found. On the other hand, what he discovered in the fat fool's stead, was at least one of the chickens he'd left behind. Probably hadn't been able to get his hands on it. The hen was on the kitchen counter, picking at remnants of ground up meat in and around the grinder and the hopper itself.

There were chicken feathers on the dining table and the floor. The cage was still up there, hanging from a hook in the ceiling. The way Biggs had it rigged, there was a rope strung along the ceiling via steel hooks, to the wall of pennies at the far side, where the long end was tied to an eyebolt in the wall, above the kitchen counter, but below the cupboard.

Instead of untying the rope, and simply lowering the cage in order to get at the hens inside, there had been two, he hadn't had the sense to do that, Fimple had climbed up on the table and pulled off the crime in his habitually clumsy and confounding manner. Hadn't even bothered to turn the light off, either.

# CHAPTER 13

**It bothered Biggs.** Bothered him considerably. One whole chicken snatched. Probably destroyed. Wasted. At least both refrigerators looked to be in good shape, the locks intact, as were the locks on the cupboards. He stepped beyond the barber's chair. Tested the lid on the white, five-foot-long freezer on the floor that sat against the wall of pennies. Locked. Lid hadn't been tampered with.

Where would he look now? Had Mr. Fimple been able to break in upstairs through the door across the way from the kitchen? Into the Prayer Hall? He hoped not. Doubted Mr. Fimple would have been interested in going upstairs. Wasn't any food left up there. No *Kool-Aid* or crackers. Made allowances during open house only. He doubted Norbert would have been interested in going upstairs. Behemoth had been after grub. Could never get enough. Would have really made Cecil's blood boil if that had happened. This was supposed to be a church, was it not? The Prayer Hall with its tremendous cross and altar and neat rows of chairs and benches that made up the makeshift pews were supposed to be relatively clean and tidy, after all.

Biggs checked the back door. It was locked. Checked the door opposite the kitchen that led to the flight of stairs to the second floor, that he allowed no one but himself access to, was also in sound condition. Locked. However, the basement door, back at the halfway point in the hallway, had been pushed open with such force (and left hanging haphazardly) that the lock had been punched out of the jamb, the bottom and middle hasps left dangling. This meant more work, more repairs. Mr. Fimple would have to be punished once again.

Biggs lifted the door. Propped it against the wall on his left. He aimed his Maglite down at the darkness and stench that was the basement. Shifted the light around. Heard muted, rustling sounds, pecking sounds, like tiny feet running off. He aimed the light at the source. Spotted two, large, dripping wet rats scurry across the cement past the door in the floor to flee the intrusion that his Maglite represented.

He did not like venturing into the abyss without proper lighting. The insomniacs had unpredictable ways about them. He had left the black-and-white tv set on for them in the Bunk Room, but the screen being of moderate size hardly gave off enough illumination.

He stepped back. Flipped the light switch on the wall. Why he did this he had no idea, because the geeks had decimated the bare, forty-watt bulb that had hung from the ceiling above the stairs weeks ago. Probably Norbert. Once again. Ate pulverized glass. Drywall, too. Not to mention chicken. Raw. Norbert Fimple. Mr. Norbert Fimple.

He flipped the switch again. Same results. What did you expect? Could have replaced it. Only he wasn't about to keep wasting money that the fuckers, or rather, Norbert would only break again and probably consume.

If that red night-light down there in the game area hadn't been made of hard plastic he would have eaten that, too. Wouldn't put it past him.

Ate most anything. Living or dead. Had pounds of silverware in his belly, nuts and bolts. You could easily hear metal clanging when he walked. And now he was down there somewhere feasting on a live chicken, sucking its blood.

Cecil's only hope was that Mr. Fimple showed enough sense not to eat the feathers. He doubted it. If he ate the feathers, he might choke. More trouble. Something he had enough of.

Lack of light was always a bitch. Well, he had the Maglite. The Maglite would have to do. He shone it at his feet to make sure he did not step on anything that would send him tumbling down the staircase.

# CHAPTER 14

**He descended with caution, all the while reminding himself if Norbert Fimple were to leap out at him he would simply have to blow his big ass away.** Put him down. Drill a couple of rounds into his slobbering fat face and that would be the end of it. As much as he needed staff and board members for the sake of the church and its tax exemption status, Norbert was beginning to annoy the hell out of him. Just not worth the trouble, that's all. If he had to shoot him, and he was indeed prepared and willing, he could always replace him, not that Norbert Fimple had been all that impossible to handle, because he remained docile for the most part, never spoke or caused real trouble. About the only time he got out of line actually was when he craved food—which was more often than Biggs liked—and then he'd break out of the Geek Cell and go searching for grub, be it down there in the walk-in or upstairs in the kitchen refrigerators.

Biggs reached the bottom. Paused there. Looked around. Basement had a way of being eerie, feeling eerie. He probed at nooks and crannies with the Maglite's beam. He was 6'3", lean, tough enough, and able to take care of himself. Was not afraid of much in this world. Nothing surprised him; not much fazed him anymore. Yet, he had to admit: coming down here, in his own basement, gave him chills at times, made him apprehensive. He didn't like the feeling, didn't like having to go below—not like this, not for reasons of this nature.

He should have gone and replaced that lightbulb above the landing, higher light bill or not. No; he was right not to. What's the point in replacing bulbs if the loons kept destroying them? Or else left the goddamned light on forever. It always came down to one thing, one thing only: he had to pay for it out of his own pocket.

Besides, they had the tv, they had the night-light—and Betty Lou had the flashlight. He'd given her a smaller version of the black Maglite he held in his hand. For reading her *Bible*. Had given her rechargeable batteries and a recharger to go with it. Small price to pay for keeping them happy.

What the hell did they need anything else for anyway? They did nothing down here. Slept most of the time, mumbled or wailed, said silent prayers, or giggled at each other or giggled at nothing. Farted, belched, shrieked, played checkers, or masturbated; other times they sang hymns to themselves. Very often it was to some imagined deity. What would they need light for? The mental defectives were generally better off with the way things were, better off if outside light, sunshine, did not confuse them; if sunlight, or any kind of seriously noticeable brightness did not shine through to add to their existing confusion.

How would you explain the guilt then? Did he not allow them to dine in the kitchen from time to time? Were they not allowed to spend time in the Prayer Hall on the second floor on occasion? Should be enough. If not, too bad.

Biggs took another step. Listened for chicken sounds, listened for clanging of metal, shifting of silverware. What he heard instead was munching, crunching, squishing.

Maybe the rats. Couldn't tell.

"Norbert?"

If Norbert were the source of the munching and burping he didn't respond, not that he ever would. Norbert Fimple never spoke to anyone, never uttered a word.

Chicken was probably gone. Cecil's gut feeling was that the leghorn was history. He still had two left up there: the one in the kitchen, and there was that one in the cage in the living room closet. He would have to remind himself later to grab the one running around loose in the kitchen and put it back in its cage.

Biggs aimed the Maglite to his left, against the wall. Shone it down fast enough to see a fat rat nibbling on a chunk of meat so fresh that blood dripped from it. There was a chicken feather stuck to the meat in the rat's jaw. That didn't seem to bother it. Slimy cretins were not unlike Norbert, ate whatever was at hand, whatever they could sink their choppers into.

Biggs braved a third step, and the rat disappeared with the meat, cutting in front of him, and headed directly toward the pit. Pit was oblong and about six feet deep, five feet of which was water. There was a door that lay flat over the pit with a heavy lock that kept it in place. The door had a series of holes in it about the size of a silver dollar. One hole in particular was at about the mid-point, the center.

The rat wasted no time scurrying under the door, hitting water. Biggs could hear the creature swimming, kicking around in the blood and crud.

A female voice, coming from beneath the door, made a desperate sound for help at this time, sobbing, pleading momentarily, and then it got quiet.

Biggs walked past the pit. Shone the light directly ahead of him, into the john in the corner. *The Diaper Man* was in there. Olin Goodfellow. His large ass on the toilet. Shitting and farting. Shone the light to the right, the Geek Room, the one with the bunks and the small black-and-white tv. Door had been torn from its hinges. What else? What did you expect? Expected as much. He would take a closer look in a minute.

Moved on. The door to the Furnace Room was next. Tested the door. It was locked. Door was intact. Fimple wouldn't go in there. Nothing to chew on in there, nothing to ingest. Did an about-face. Aimed his light at the door to the Mattress Room behind the stairwell. Seemed in good shape. Then across the way, on his left. Shined his light at the entrance to the Fun Room. Didn't look as though anything had been disturbed there. Walked over to make double-sure.

Continued moving to his left. Past the Fun Room and the play area with the patio furniture, taking steps toward the walk-in cooler. Munching grew in volume, munching, burping. Smacking of lips and sucking of fingers. Fimple had no class whatsoever.

Biggs reached the cooler door. Thick. Heavy. Saw the "handle" that had been yanked out of the wall—to the right of the door, at about the same level as the actual handle—the chain and lock that hung from the handle on the door itself.

Held the *.357* out in front, and with great caution, stepped inside.

# CHAPTER 15

This was a large, walk-in cooler with plenty of room to move around in: twelve feet deep, fifteen feet long; eight feet from floor to ceiling, a cooler that Biggs had helped design and install after buying the two-story house six years ago upon his release from the hospital.

The hand-printed legend across the top of the metal door, having been written in a combination of blood and crayon, read:

## <u>His</u> ABATTOIR

Biggs waited there, listened to the slobbering, munching sounds. He knew it had to be the behemoth mouth-breather, Norbert Fimple. Biggs aimed the light high, to his left. The dog carcasses he had left hanging on meat hooks were still there, so was the jackrabbit.

He shifted the light to his right, away from the roadkill. Aimed it at the metal floor in front of him and the puddle of blood that had collected there and was congealing. A waste.

He moved the light around. Held it on the bare female feet dangling. Moved the light up. Scanned it up to include the blood-covered legs, pubic area, bare hips and belly. Up further . . . over the larger-than-average breasts, long hair that was matted, over the blood-covered young woman's pained face, more sticky stuck-together hair, up along her long arms and strapped-together wrists that hung from a chain in the ceiling.

The woman's eyes opened weakly when the harsh light hit her face, then shut closed. Unable to deal with it. She made no effort to say anything or make a sound of any sort. She knew well enough not to cause problems.

"Shit, Connie. Your makeup is smeared."

Well, at least the animal carcasses had been spared, and so had the victims.


Cecil aimed the light on the other woman: Sandra Harcourt, hanging on a hook from a rod across the ceiling, even in worse shape. If not from the sharp meat hook imbedded a fraction to the left of her spine, than from the thirty-six-degree temperature and dropping. Cecil could almost see his breath now as he moved deeper into the cooler. He walked right up to the woman with the pleading, pained look on her blood-stained features that said: *either please take me down, help me, or please put me out of my misery.* Cecil couldn't tell which. Certainly one or the other had to be on her mind. Wouldn't you want to be finished off and put out of *your* misery if you were hanging on a hook this way? No doubt.

He ran his hand up between her thighs. Inserted the middle finger inside the vagina. It was moist in there. Was it blood?

He moved away. There would be time for that later.


To the left, near the corner, were two large, suitcase-shaped metal chests with rope handles, that Biggs himself had built, with a little assistance from

Big T, a board member. One of the chests had been turned over, the contents spilled out.

Fortunately, the female heads, up high on the green wire shelf against the wall in back of the hanging vics, remained intact. The bishop had gone to great pains to do the makeup just right and the dark wigs coiffed to his liking.

The damp air had a tendency to pull the hairdos down over time, but that was something he could always tend to later. The important thing was that they were safe and beyond Mr. Fimple's reach. At least the heads that mattered appeared untouched. Could have been worse, he said to himself, although it was bad enough, in that plenty of detritus littered the metal floor. Quite a mess: fingers, partial torso, rectums, livers, intestines and general viscera.

It was one untidy scene, and there was no real reason for it. Nothing justified it. It was Fimple. There was no way to satiate his appetite; as he, even now, jammed a *Twinkie* in his mouth and chased it with a cherry soda. He was licking his grubby fingers, oblivious to anything else.

Bits of skin and flesh juice covered his mouth and chin. Feathers were in evidence. There was blood on his black shirt and green Chino pants—and more feathers, that once upon a time were part of a chicken that lay dead on the metal floor by his bare feet, its head having been twisted off. Looked like the hen had been drained of blood. Sucked dry, no doubt. The goods in the industrial freezer hadn't been tampered with. However, the limbs inside one of the chests had been molested. Obviously plenty of it having been devoured and were inside Fimple's belly by now.

Norbert had filled himself with raw flesh and blood, and was presently in the process of topping it off with dessert: *Twinkies* and cherry sodas. Looked like he'd put away a dozen or more *Twinkies*, a few cans of soda. Cecil's own private stash. It irked him. Not only was it about the dent it put in his wallet, chickens and *Twinkies* cost money, but the mess would have to be cleaned up, or else the risk of slipping on blood, and whatnot, was far greater than he dared think about.

If that weren't bad enough: Norbert was barefoot. Not that it in and of itself was anything unique. Had Biggs wondering how he was able to take the cold metal floor of the walk-in. He'd given him shoes in the past. Fool refuses to wear them. Part of it, Cecil supposed, had to do with corns and bunions. About the only type of footwear Fimple was amenable to were sandals and flip-flops—and neither lasted very long at that.

The real reason behind the concern for him was the threat of illness or injury whenever the fools ran around like this. In either case, threat of illness or any kind of physical wound that had to be tended to usually resulted in having to use costly medical supplies or dip into the budget.

"You know what I told you about breaking into the kitchen, Mr. Fimple; what I would do to you if you went in there and left a mess. There's chicken feathers all over the fucking linoleum, and that's the least of it. There's chicken shit all over the floor and counter up there."

# CHAPTER 16

**Biggs unlocked the lock on the chain that hung from the walk-in cooler door.** Unfastened the chain itself. He wrapped one end around his fist, stepped back inside and proceeded to whip Norbert Fimple across the face with it. He didn't give a damn if the retard's bifocals got destroyed in the process this time. He'd had enough.

"I warned you about this, Norbert. I told you to stay away from the cluck-clucks, keep out of the kitchen, the cooler. If you're hungry, all you have to do is wait to be fed like everyone else. Very simple. Easiest thing in the world for anyone to remember—anyone but you, that is."

It had to happen. Just as Biggs knew it would. Missed Fimple and whacked himself across both shins. He tossed the chain to the side. Hopped about for a bit. Rubbed his legs. It was the rhino's fault, all of it. What Norbert reminded him of: *a wild rhino son of a bitch.*

It took a moment for the pain to go away, although it wouldn't entirely.

Biggs straightened himself. Went on the attack anew. Using the Maglite this time. He was past fretting if it got damaged making contact with the back of the rhino's hardened skull.

Due to Mr. Fimple's indiscriminate penchant and unexplained need to consume and swallow anything he could get his beefy hands on, whenever his enormous belly shifted, or he managed to take a step or two, only to get knocked back down again, the resulting sounds reminded one of a toolbox being lifted at an awkward angle and the nuts and bolts, screws and nails inside sliding from one end to the other.

This is what was taking place presently with Mr. Fimple rolling about, kicking out, jerking his body from side to side; the silverware in his belly and all the metal objects that had found their way inside his stomach made quite a racket that only added to the grunts and groans and general chaos of what was taking place.

Cecil smacked away, hitting the barefoot behemoth across the back of his neck and upper shoulders with such ferocity that the assault dislodged the man's dentures and sent them skidding across the littered floor.

Bishop paused to catch his breath. Glanced about to see where Norbert's false teeth may have landed. Couldn't spot them. Too much crud on the floor. Crud and feathers.

"Get up, Norbert. It's Pit Therapy this time."

Norbert shook his head adamantly at the mention of the pit and refused to budge. It didn't seem to matter how hard he was beaten, his fear of the pit far outweighed anything else that might be done to him.

"I need a hand over here!"

Biggs could have continued to clobber away at Mr. Fimple with the Maglite and decided against it. Maglite seemed intact. Why risk damaging it, after all? Solidly crafted Maglites such as this did not come cheap.

He lifted the chain off the floor and did some more whipping with it and watched tears and snot run down the big man's bruised and swollen face.

Another break was in order.

"I need support, Marvin! Where are you?"

Muck appeared at last.

"About time."

Biggs tossed him the key to the padlock on the door over the pit. "Get the heifer out of the hole. Mouth-breather's got discipline coming. He'll never learn otherwise."

Marvin did as told. Unlocked the door. He lifted the door open and helped the disorientated woman climb out. Although willing to comply, and clearly on her feet, Theresa Denise Klopp could not help faltering. Muck did what he could to assist.

Made no kinda sense to let good bush go to waste. Tall ho still had her some good booty left, no lie. Them pretty blue eye' an' hair coulda been workin' the track for 'em, makin' coin. Wished he ran the show. Damn right. Wasn't no more than a month ago they snatched this trim in a *Lumber City* parking lot in Valencia. Looked fine, too; she did. Only tight-ass Cecil be wantin' to give the ho that nasty jambalaya that the ho don't want. Don't blame her, neither. Lots of that fine figure she had damn near be gone now. Mothafuckah don't want to give nobody some good food— and the hoe' get weak, get sick, die—an' if they don't die natural, the fool see to it that they be ice'. If I had it my way, I be doin' it different. Clean the bitches up, get 'em some good wardrobe and kicks at the *Goodwill*— and take 'em to eat at some class joint like *Mickey D* or *Jack in the Crack*— and then let 'em work the track. What I would do, me.

Fuck it. Be nothin' but a waste of time thinkin' like that.

He walked her to the bottom of the stairwell. Helped her to sit down, so that her back rested against the wall.

"You be all right, sugar-bush. *Mack Daddy Muck* got hisself a *plan*. Gonna make you my *bottom ho*."

A perturbed Biggs had been watching, standing there by the cooler door and taking it in. Marvin's sissified behavior did nothing but fuel his rising anger.

"The hell you waiting for? Second Coming of Malcolm X? I need assistance over here. *Assistance.*"

"Yo. Assistance. Everybody be needin' assistance."

Muck hurried back to the cooler. Biggs handed him the chain, and the two of them proceeded to take turns beating on Norbert Fimple until the big man had no choice but to scramble out of the cooler in an effort to escape the onslaught. His assailants pursued him with great fervor and intensity, clubbing him over the head with chain and Maglite and even fists and boots, until Norbert, seeking refuge, staggered into the water in the pit on his own.

"Success. Hard won/hard fought."

"Sho-nuff. Mothafuckah sound' like he got hisself a hardware store in his belly, or a *Home Depot.*"

"Gimme the key."

Marvin handed it over. Biggs re-attached the padlock key to the ring of keys. Closed the door over the pit.

"Stand on it. Make sure he stays put."

Muck did that. Cecil walked to a cell toward the front, Roscoe side. Unlocked the door to the workshop he usually referred to as the Fun Room and did so for a reason: on his right was a butcher's block, saw bench. There was an old style copper tub in the center. On his left, hanging from the wall, was a rectangular board he had fashioned himself from a solid oak door and screwed a series of iron eyebolts into: two at either corner at the top, halfway down there were two more, and a couple at the bottom. Nylon rope restraints dangled from these eyebolts. There were also ankle shackles at near the bottom. One of the bottom eyebolts had a long chain attached that ran along the cement floor and was secured to one of the bathtub's claw feet.

At the far side of the torture board was a floor-to-ceiling steel cabinet, bolted heavily into the cement, as everything else was here.

The single window, high up, he had boarded up with solid planks: inside, outside, in addition to the meshed bars that protected the basement from external as well as internal elements. Should hard-up dopefiends allow their curiosity to get the best of them, and they managed to pry the planks and bars off, break the window and attempt to crawl inside—a surprise awaited them: a nice little trap of his own design just waiting, above the window, up near the ceiling, to be triggered.

Every little precaution that he was able to create and implement made him feel that much safer and fortified against all of them out there, the miscreants, vermin, who were green with envy because of what he had/owned—and they didn't.

He unlocked the steel cabinet. Selected a couple of chain leashes with carabiners and placed them on the butcher's block. Went back inside the cabinet for a first-aid kit that came in a case. Placed it next to the leashes. On the bottom shelf of the cabinet was the fifty-foot industrial electrical cord with the bare wires exposed at one end that he would need.

He was careful as he crouched, for fear his back would act up again; carried it outside the door and dropped it there. He returned to the cabinet for the long hose they would also need, picked it up and carried it out and left it beside the electrical cord.

Biggs closed and locked the cabinet back up. Grabbed the chain leashes, the first-aid case, and stepped out. Locked the room. Lowered the first-aid kit, picked up the cord, and returned to the pit.

"Open it."

Marvin lifted the door up, and Cecil attached the leashes to the loops on either side of the iron collar on Mr. Fimple's neck. The chains were then threaded through separate holes in the door and the door was closed back over it. Marvin was instructed to take the electrical cord and plug it into the socket in the wall by the stairwell.

# CHAPTER 17

**Norbert may have been hurt and bleeding, but not to the extent that he didn't gradually become aware of what was about to take place.** He was able to pick up movement, glimpses, of the electrical cord, through holes in the door above his head. At first he nudged it open an inch or two, then followed that by an all-out effort. With folded forearms, shoved hard up against his side of the door, throwing Cecil clear off the door itself as it slammed open against the cement floor.

Norbert attempted to climb out of the pit. Was too heavy and clumsy and in way too much pain to pull it off. He was whacked across the head and neck a few times with the cycle chain by the bishop that rendered Norbert's efforts not only ineffective, but left him dazed and helpless. He succumbed.

The door was shut over the pit once again. Padlock locked in place. Marvin Muck held the prong end of the orange electrical cord in search of the socket in the wall that was supposed to be somewhere in front of the bottom step of the stairwell and about twenty feet from the rectangular-shaped hole in the floor. Illumination was lousy. The red-haloed light way back at the other side, in back of Biggs, the Roscoe side of the basement where the wall of books was, hardly helped. It was way too weak.

Muck searched for it, while Cecil held his end: a wire in each hand, making sure that they were fairly apart and stayed that way.

"Got it plugged in?"

"Prob'ly."

"There's no *probably* about it. It's either plugged in, or it's not."

"Got it plugged in. Yo."

## CHAPTER 18

**Biggs was lying on his belly over the door that covered the pit, poking the wire in his left hand in one of the holes in the door, while running the other wire through a separate hole in his right, all the while pressing his right eye up against a hole in the center of the door somewhere, doing his best to guide the wire down.**

The left wire touched water, and was kept there, while he strained in vain to connect the right wire to the metal collar on Fimple's neck. Nothing doing. Fimple, not as utterly brainless as perceived, kept himself down in the water up to about his chin, and there was no way for Cecil to make out where the goddamn collar was. Furthermore, he didn't dare risk touching the water with the hot wire in his right hand from fear that it would short-circuit the entire system.

Well, dumb-ass Norbert was being clever, although hardly clever enough. That was the purpose of the chain leashes. Live and learn. One had to be smarter than the geeks. Cecil called Marvin over. Had him grab the chains. Told him to step back to the north of his head by a good yard.

"When I order you to yank, I want you to yank. He needs to be pulled up. Understand?"

"Yo. Ain't got to tell me *twiced.*"

"I didn't say it '*twiced.*'"

"I know that."

Cecil shook his head. Let it go.

"Do it."

Marvin went to work. Thin and wiry as he was. Pulled back, hard. Stepped back some even. Had to. Yanking on the chains.

"Pimple be one heavy mothafuckah."

"Wrap them around your wrists."

Cecil had his eye over the hole about the size of a large coin. He liked what he was seeing down there. The former used car salesman was being uprooted by the neck, so that the stainless steel collar was visible at this point. Biggs played around with the wire in his right hand, maneuvering this way and that. It took effort and concentration. Everything required concentration.

Finally, at last, the wire connected, if briefly, and Fimple got buzzed. Not enough, not for him, but some. Sparks materialized. The bishop felt a sense of accomplishment. He renewed his determination, even though Norbert kept doing his best to dip below the surface.

"He's submerging again. Don't let him go underwater. I want him up, out of the water. Pull back, hard. Do it, Marvin. Get him up against the door."

Muck was working up a good sweat. Went for it. Gritting his teeth, seemed to be making progress.


Biggs searched out the collar down there. Connected. More sparks. And Fimple jerking about so hard that he caused Marvin to slip and fall. Marvin cursed. Biggs looked up. Did not have to say a word. Muck was back on his feet, and yanking on the leashes again. Biggs refocused on Norbert down in the pit. Had the wire against the collar for a decent amount of time this time, shocking Fimple a good deal. He did not keep the wire there, as he did not wish to kill him, merely teach him a lesson. *Pit Therapy*, that's what the bishop liked to call it. Not much different from what they did to him over the years at the VA, Camarillo, and Atascadero.


He stuck the wire back down there, touching the collar, and watched current go through Norbert; well, his reaction each and every time. Made him jump around like a *spaz*. Frankly, if he had known Norbert was going to be this much trouble he would have left him on that bus bench in front of LA City Hall to begin with.

"You gonna kill him, man. Yo."

"Nah. Not my intention. Norbert can take a lot more than the average sinner, a lot more."

# CHAPTER 19

**Biggs realized that Norbert had had enough at last.** Told Marvin to pull the cord from the wall. He unlocked, then lifted the door open all the way. When he looked down what he saw was a dazed geek. Hardly moving or coherent.

"How are we doing, Norbert?"

Norbert Fimple remained too out of it to respond.

"You bring it on yourself every time, Norbert, and that's the truth. I don't enjoy punishing members of the inner circle in this manner—but punish you I will when you break the rules. We have rules around here and they will be abided by. I won't have you destroy my property. That door up there will have to be repaired, maybe even replaced. You better hope I have one in the garage that will fit. Then there's the kitchen door, Bunk Room door—that will need work."

Biggs turned his head in the direction of the walk-in. His attention was back on the big man in the pit.

"As if that weren't bad enough, you did some damage to the cooler door handle. It's uncalled for. There's no excuse for it. I won't stand for it, Norbert."

It took a while, but Norbert was blinking, showing life.

"Surprised he ain't chill."

"Told you: Norbert can take way more than the average heathen. Isn't that right, Mr. Fimple?"

Norbert was hacking, spitting up water.

"Get up, Norbert. You get put in a cell all by yourself this time. Solitary confinement."

"Siberia?"

"Siberia."

Norbert attempted to climb out of the pit on his own, and in his disoriented state was having a difficult time of it.

"Help him out, Marvin. Can't seem to make it. Seems he can use a hand."

"Sure. Dude can use a hand."

Marvin stood at the edge of the pit. Reached down. Norbert grabbed his hand with one of his, and rolled up and out of the water, onto the cement floor. Rested on his side to catch his breath. He was bleeding from his nose and mouth; one of the ears. There seemed to be traces of vomit.

"Life can be tough enough, only certain individuals always have to make things just a little tougher. Don't know why that is—only know that's the way it is."

"Norbert don't be gettin' nothin'. Got to be told two time'."

"Yeah? Like somebody you know?"

"I don't be knowin' nobody like that."

Biggs's attention was back on Norbert. "What am I supposed to do with you, Mr. Fimple? Do you want me to shoot you? Is that what you want?"

Norbert said nothing. Did not so much as shake his head in response.

"I don't think you want that. I know I don't. I don't want to shoot you. I worry about you—but you have to stop causing me all this trouble. Doors cost money, lightbulbs cost money. I didn't get where I'm at today by squandering funds. I've been destitute in my time, and let me tell you: it's no fun. The world will shit on you when you're broke and can't fend for yourself. I know, believe me; I know what that's like. It's taken years to get where I'm at and I'm not about to let someone like you bring me down."

Biggs thought if he went the distance, made him disappear, if he got rid of him right now, he'd only have to go to some nut house and recruit another psycho and break him in. Bus benches and sidewalks were no different: nutcases too defective to be taught anything, too out of it usually to be controlled to his liking—and that was too much work, too much of a hassle.

He'd been through it too often, been through it with all the other members of staff and board, and yet he needed them for the illusion a staff and board of directors created, if he intended to continue to benefit from the 501 tax exemption status as a church, if he intended on keeping and holding on to this two-story house with basement and attic and garage in back and a '72 Rolls and new *Fleetwood Cadillac* and his half a mil-plus stock portfolio—which he damn well did. He valued it all, every bit of it; he wasn't that "touched" just yet.

Furthermore, if he needed to be reminded of the hell that awaited him by bringing in someone new, all he had to do was take a look at the twisted, off-kilter geek from South Dakota, or was it North Dakota? Namely, Olin Goodfellow. All you had to do was take a look at that sack of pig slop named Goodfellow to be reminded how tough it was to bring in someone from the outside and teach them how to comport themselves.

Norbert Fimple rose to his knees, and with additional help from Biggs and Marvin, made it all the way to his feet. It soon became evident that the big man had soiled himself; the buzzing session had caused him to piss and crap his trousers. It had happened before. Nothing new there. The odor was unmistakable, on top of all the other odors in a dungeon that reeked of all types of noxious fumes.

At least the man was standing on his own two feet. Hardly at that. Some caution was warranted here, lest he fell and split his head open.

# CHAPTER 20

**They walked him to the street side of the basement and a cell that was located between a storage closet and a holding pen Biggs liked to call the Mattress Room.** The cell they escorted Norbert to had been commonly known as Solitary Confinement—until Ionesco, the Pinko Punisher, started referring to it as "Siberia." The name stuck. Cecil had a fair knowledge of Stalin and the Bolsheviks from having read up on the Commies over the years and thought the tag fit.

Although Ionesco had never set foot in the Soviet Union, let alone

Siberia, he had spent a week in this cell himself a while back and upon his release had made a promise to Cecil, his "true American *comrade*," that he would never again do anything to piss him off enough to be "sent back to *Siberia*."

"Got me this sick feelin' Norbert could be carryin' a load in his drawer'. I know he done took a dump upstairs. A dude like him got enough doo-doo in him for five ghetto pimp'."

Biggs gave Muck the silent stare, then went about unlocking the door to "Siberia." Marvin hadn't been able to hold the big man up by himself. Mr. Fimple's legs gave way and he dropped to the floor outside the door to the cell.

"Could be we went too far this time."

"He brought it on himself. Think I enjoy seeing him like this?"

"Should give the fool some dry skin' to wear. Brogan', too. Gonna come down wiff somethin'."

"Like what?"

"Like ammonia. Or his death of cold."

"You mean *pneumonia*."

"Yo. Could be."

"That would leave me demoralized."

"Not you. Maybe the rest of them. Want the geek' to be depress'?"

"They were born *'depress.'*"

Biggs unlocked the storage room next to the cell. Gave Muck the spigot key and told him to go get the hose where he had left it by the Fun Room door and connect it to the tap out by the pit. He also had to remind him to leave the nozzle end.

Marvin managed to accomplish the chore without a single mishap, and was back. He was instructed to help Mr. Fimple out of his soiled pants and boxers, wet shirt. Marvin proceeded without bitching. May have even felt a bit of compassion about all of it. Norbert was a messed up dude. His ho run off on him. Took the kid. Shit like that could make a homie lose his mind—and never want to sell another used ride. What he done before he got like this. What he was told by Cecil.

Biggs dragged the nozzle over and hosed the behemoth down thoroughly. Found a couple of towels in the storage closet and tossed one of them at the flunky. Wiped what remained of the Trusty makeup on his face with the other. Marvin walked Mr. Fimple into the cell. Helped him dry his head and shoulders, upper body in general, and let him do what he could as far as drying his legs and privates on his own.

"Don't try to play with the man's dick. I'm watching."

"Man, fuck you. Yo. I don't be playin' wiff his dick. *Pit Therapy* fucked him up. Too much shock treatment. Can hardly dry his private part' without help."

Biggs was back in the storage room. Re-emerged with a stack of folded clothing: dark green chino pants, green shirt, army boxers. Handed them over to Marvin, who in turn assisted Mr. Fimple into them.

"You happy, rapo?"

"I could be mo' happy if I had a ho workin' the track an' makin' bank."

"Prostitutes get busted. It wouldn't be long before the rollers came looking for us. You can't seem to get that through your head. Why should I risk losing everything because you have this wild notion to be the next Iceberg?"

Marvin was about to do some more running of the mouth. Biggs waved his hand, shutting him up and letting him know to get with the next step: Mr. Fimple would need something to defecate in for the duration of his isolation.

"Grab a honey bucket, roll of ass-wipe. Jug of water. Drop his dirty clothes, including the towel, in the washer by the john before you do that. Pour in two cups of concentrated detergent. Using hot water. Then wash your hands. Got all that?"

"Yo."

"Oh yeah: I think his dentures fell out in the cooler somewhere. Don't concern yourself if you can't find them. We'll pick him up another set next time we visit a boneyard."

"*Boneyard?*"

"Where do you think those came from?"

"Ain't thought about it."

"You know they came from a stiff. You don't think I would spend good *'coin'* on fake teeth for him? Problem is they don't always fit right. Only thing to do is to keep trying until you find a set that works. It's a crap shoot."

Marvin was clearly disgusted. Kept it to himself. Even so, pictures popped in his mind's eye that turned his stomach.

"That reminds me: could use footwear, too. Check his feet for glass before you do the other stuff."

Marvin bent down. Pulled a shard from the big man's big left toe. Found another piece in the heel. Tossed them in the corner.

"Don't do that. He's liable to swallow them."

Marvin retrieved the shards. Cecil had him drop them in a jar in the storage closet. Muck gathered up the dirty clothes and left to do what else he had to.

# CHAPTER 21

**Biggs picked up the first aid kit, and returned to the cell.** Mr. Fimple was lying on the floor on his side, his back against the wall on the left. Biggs knelt beside him. Poured peroxide over the cuts, applied *Band-Aids*.

"I give you shoes but you refuse to wear them. Flip-flops never last you long. What am I going to do with you? Step on a rusty nail and could lose a foot. That's begging for it. Now, taking a foot off is no skin off my nose, Norbert, if it has to be done—only what good would you be around here?" Biggs shook his head. "What's the use? Cause me enough grief to have a meltdown. Look, these break-ins and constant penchant for grub . . . You've got to behave yourself, Norbert. Show some patience. We'll have Greta heat up some of that jambalaya for you later, maybe. You have to be patient, develop a better sense of patience, otherwise I'll starve your ass down to nothing. You'll be a big bag of bones, Norbert, if you don't stop destroying my property."

Biggs felt an obligation to remind him again of the damage done. "I have to replace that door upstairs now, repair the jamb, replace the lightbulb; replace two other doors. The handle that was in the wall to the right of the walk-in cooler door will have to be bolted into the wall again—because without it there is no way to keep the cooler door locked. You know all this—and yet you continue to fuck up, continue to cause me grief. Repairs take time and cost money—and I'm getting tired of it. You think I have a money tree growing in the backyard? There's no money tree back there. The only money I see is the money I generate. I can't go to the government for a handout; I can't go anywhere for a handout. They don't give a shit about me, or any of us. If that weren't bad enough, they're threatening to shut down the Bordello of Fear. You have no idea how crucial that revenue stream is. Glorified pencil pushers don't care if we live or perish." Biggs took pause, looking at the as yet stunned big man. "Know what they pay out there? They pay shit out there. Peanuts. Crumbs. Average salary. Try to get a job and see what they pay in the real world. It's hell. I have to watch how I spend my money. I know all too well what it's like to be broke and at the assholes' mercy. I don't ever want to be broke again—ever. I'd rather be burned alive than be destitute and begging for a handout."

Fimple struggled to adjust himself to a sitting position. Leaned his back against the wall and got his fat face caught in a cobweb. Brushed and rubbed against the wall to shake it all, to get rid of the spider racing down his face, over his Adam's apple and chest.

"Take it easy, Norbert. It's just a spider. That's all it is. Spider. I love spiders. . . ."

Biggs stepped in and gave Norbert's chest a hard backhand that flattened the spider out of existence. He wiped the spider's guts against his own boxers. Biggs found himself cursing under his breath right after he did this.

Marvin was back with a ten gallon paint can and a gallon jug of tap water, roll of TP. Placed them on the floor. He reached in his shirt pocket for Norbert's eyeglasses. One of the lenses was cracked, the frame bent.

"Put them on his face. Won't last him long anyway."

Marvin did that. Adjusted the specs. Norbert remained in a zombified state pretty much. He may have reacted a bit to the episode with the spider a moment ago, but for all intents and purposes, he was clearly out of it.

Marvin produced a couple of dog biscuit treats. Dropped them on his lap.

"The toilet paper is to wipe your fat ass with after you've taken a dump in the bucket, and not to jerk into. Try to remember that. Ass-wipe is not free; otherwise I might be inclined to let you wipe with old issues of the *LA Times*, for the useless Lefty rag that it is."

Biggs looked at Marvin. Asked if he had any luck locating the man's dentures. With thumb and index finger, Marvin gingerly reached inside a trouser pocket, extracted the false teeth, and just as gingerly placed them on Fimple's lap.

"Look' like some of them chopper' be broke."

"Don't sweat the small stuff. Never sweat the small stuff."

They unhooked the chains from the loops on the metal collar on Norbert's neck and walked out. Biggs closed the cell door and locked the heavy padlock, leaving Mr. Norbert Fimple to ponder his latest predicament in utter darkness.

# CHAPTER 22

**The deacon was instructed to take Terri Denise Klopp and return her to the pit.** Marvin went about to do as told, only the woman was no longer at the stairs where he'd left her.

"Where the ho go?"

Biggs looked at him. Shook his head.

"This is what I'm talking about: Cunts can't be trusted. You can't trust a cunt."

He raised his eyes to the ceiling, not that there were answers to be found there.

"What are you waiting for? Go get her."

Marvin scrambled up the flight of stairs to the first floor. Cleared the landing, and stopped. Took a breath in the alcove. Using great care and caution, he stuck his face out past one corner, then the other—looking up and down the hallway.

"Ain't no use, ho. All you be doin' is gettin' the bishop all pissed off. Heard what I said? Show your ass, ho."


The door to the john was closed. He walked to it. Reached for the doorknob. Turned it slowly. Opened the door. No one in there. Approached the utility closet next to it. Door, like the other, was closed. Wondered if she was in there. Hiding out. Had to be in there. Prob'ly hiding under them pile of kicks, or else found the sliding door to the livin' room closet. Where else was she gonna go? Open the damn door, then, he said to himself. Got his hand on the knob and took his time pushing the door in—to find his upper body drenched in ammonia.


Marvin whirled out of there and into the hallway, screaming and rubbing his burning eyes.

The woman proceeded to whack away at his face and neck with a mop handle and Marvin was on the floor yelling for assistance of his own. Biggs came up from behind and whacked her hard across the nape and side of the face with the flashlight. She was down, not out, but on the floor. He had his *Magnum* aimed at her. Hammer cocked.

"It's back in the pit for you, *missy*. With a little bonus added on top."

He looked at Marvin. Kicked at his feet. "Get up. You're useless to me. Get your ass up, I said."

Marvin rose. The ammonia continued to sting.

"Go wash your eyes out."

While Marvin did that in the bathroom, Biggs resumed whacking away at the woman on the floor before him simply because she'd had the audacity to do what she just did.

"What's taking so long? I need a hand over here."

There was no response from Muck.

When Biggs stepped in the john to check up on him—didn't want to risk the fool going blind—Marvin was bent over the sink, delicately splashing water into his eyes with both hands like some kind of sissy. Biggs shook his head. Idiot had a way of trying his patience. He turned the shower on. Grabbed Muck by the nape and stuck his face under the shower head so that the water sprayed his eyes.

"Keep your peepers open."

"Be hurtin' like a mofo."

"You have to keep them open."

# CHAPTER 23

**Biggs returned to Theresa Denise Klopp, who had managed to crawl to the rear door and was clawing against it, twisting the doorknob (knowing it was futile).** Biggs gave her several whacks with the Maglite just because it made him feel good inside, and for no other reason this time. Yelled out to his right-hand man.

"What's taking so long? Marvin?"

"Eyes ain't right. Seein' triple an' shit."

"What you get for being careless."

Marvin staggered out of the john at last, cursing. Insisted he was blindsided.

"I don't want to hear it. We're taking her back down." Biggs's stare was on the female. "I envision shock therapy in your immediate future this time, bitch."

Marvin attempted to grab the victim by the wrists. She resisted. His counter was to deliver a punch to her belly. Watched her double over. The deacon shoved her in the direction of the entrance to the basement. Biggs shoved Marvin out of the way, and kicked the woman in the ass and watched her tumble down the flight of stairs.

It was a nice move, Biggs thought. Only there he was with a tinge of regret, fearing that it may have resulted in a broken neck, or worse—therefore, making pointless the Pit Therapy session that he had planned for her.


The bishop and the deacon climbed down the stairs. The whore was nearly out, but not quite. No broken neck, that he could detect. No broken back or legs or arms. Resilient cunt. All the better.

"I hate it when subjects try to pull a double cross; when unrepentant sinners try to out-con the sharpest con artist of them all—because, you see, it can never happen."

They attached the chains to the loops on the iron collar on her neck. "Have a heart, please. Have a heart."

"You don't want to be sayin' somethin' like *that* to somebody like Cecil, ho."

Biggs had Marvin re-plug the extension cord into the wall.

"Ho ain't gonna be able to take it like *Pimple.* That damn Norbert be like one of them grizzly bear. Can take a lot. This here ho don't look like she can take it."

"She'll take it. Or she'll die taking it."

Biggs had the cord untangled. Held the raw ends in his left hand. Re-holstered the *Magnum.*

"Drag her ass over to the pit."

Marvin did his best, tugging on the chains. The woman fought him, resisting. He had no choice but to literally drag her over and dump her in.

Biggs ordered him to run the free ends of the chains through holes in the door. Once this was accomplished, the door was closed over the pit. Biggs was on hands and knees, as before. Held a wire in each hand.

It was a matter of selecting the right holes to slip the wires through. It was a good thing he'd made the holes the size of a large coin and easy enough to see where the wires were going as he peeked through yet a third hole. With his left hand, he drove the wire through and down into the water, with his right he was at the other end of the door, slipping the wire in in order to have it connect to the collar on her neck.

And all this he watched while peering through a hole somewhere in the center. Well, this took a degree of skill. The wire in the water was no big feat; it was the other that usually proved a challenge, because the victims, the bright ones, got the idea to duck under, and trying to connect the wire to the collar was not easy. He kept his eye glued to the hole in the door to see exactly where he was. If she attempted to submerge, he would have Marvin yank on the chains to pull her out, for if the wire in his right hand touched the water itself it could mean short-circuiting the entire electrical system. Wouldn't want that. Had the same concerns when Norbert was buzzed. Sure, Big Tex might be able to repair the damage, but why go to the hassle if one were able to prevent it? He'd had it happen to him once or twice in the past. What a bitch. Live and learn. Caution was the way to go. He kept his eye down against the hole, while poking around with the wire that he held in his right hand, guiding it. Touched the collar just enough to witness the resulting sparks. The sparks, although never great, were usually enough to cause a tingle in his nuts. It was akin to burning flies and spiders as a young firebug. Gave him wood. Something like when Juicer Joe sledged his pet Rottie to death, or even when the truck plowed into his Mama. No denying it. You could try, but it would be a less-than-honest way to go through life.

Sparks were all right. Sparks, and a trapped heifer with no place to hide.

The cunt jerked around some, then ducked under. Just as he knew she would. Nothing original there. Biggs cursed, not that he was pissed, simply amused by the lame action.

"She's under water. Stupid cunt is under water, hiding out."

Marvin asked if he ought to yank up on the chains again to pull her back up, to force her to surface.

"No need. She'll have to come up for air eventually."

And this she did. When it happened, Biggs was there with the exposed wire that he held in his right hand. Played with it, shifted it around, until he connected with the metal collar on her neck. Sparks ensued. The victim flapped around. Biggs lifted the wire to give her a chance to recoup for a bit, then resumed the procedure. Continued with it, never leaving it down there long enough to do serious damage.

"Don't want you to expire just yet, only teach you a lesson. Cause me grief and aggravation and this is the way I work it, the way I deal with it."

Finally, the last zap seemed to take a heavier toll on the victim than he intended, and Biggs decided it was enough. A slight slip-up on his part.

"Ho be gone?"

"Don't worry about it. She's not gone."

Biggs yanked the cord out of the socket in the wall. Lifted the door open. Checked her eyeballs. The pupils were not dilated. That was a goofball error the ever over-rated Hitchcock made with the Janet Leigh character, post shower assault: her pupils *were not* dilated. And they should have been. They should have been. Fuck Hitchcock. At least this bitch here still had life left in her.

The chains were detached, the door closed over the pit, and the padlock locked. He had Muck go back up and finish up.

# CHAPTER 24

**Now that that was over and done with, he felt a need to reassess the damage and check the other rooms thoroughly.**

The grunting and general flatulence that came from the john in the corner continued unabated. Biggs shone his Maglite in there. The bald-headed, cross-eyed, diaper-wearing putz from South Dakota (or was it North Dakota?) was still on the throne doing his business.

Olin Goodfellow, the portly forty-year-old, horse-molesting farmhand had his stuffed Porky Pig doll with him that he was clutching to his bosom.

The newcomer was a tough one to teach new tricks. At least he wasn't taking a dump in the tub as he did all during that first week he was here. But a taste of the pit had educated him enough to the point he was using the bathroom the way it should be used. Well, most of the time. At least the rest of the time he went in his diaper. Gave Marvin less to complain about that way. Crap in the tub tended to clog up the drain. Dirty diapers weren't a problem for the washing machine. Not yet, anyway.

To the right of the john was the Bunk-cum-Geek Room. Biggs looked the door over. Dislodged bottom hinge. Busted lock and part of the jamb. Would require work.

Goddamned Fimple. All of these doors, with the exception of the bathroom door, had a ten-inch-by-ten-inch meshed glass Judas window with a small curtain over it. In a couple of the cases, the Mattress Room, as well as the Fun Room, had a curtain on both sides of the window.

Bunk Room's door curtain was on the outside (that Biggs liked to keep drawn usually when administering Pit Therapy—in order to keep the geeks from witnessing the process—unless he wanted them to see it).

Fimple had not only managed to tear the small curtain to shreds, but yanked the curtain rod right off. It was relatively minor, yes, compared to the serious damage done to the doors, still . . . It rankled. Compounded the situation.

Basement door ruined, kitchen door fractured—and now this one. Made it three doors that either needed repair or replacement. Then you had the walk-in door "handle" that he didn't even want to think about. How often could you bolt the thing into the steel wall without running out of places to drill new holes into?

# CHAPTER 25

**Biggs stepped in.** The room contained a dozen bunks: a row of three double-bunks on the left side of the room, the same number of bunks on the right. A plastic jug of water hung on a rope from every one of those bunks. He was always on Marvin's case to make sure that those jugs had plenty of tap water in them. And on special occasions, he, Biggs, saw to it that there was *Kool-Aid* in the jugs in place of plain water.

Say it was someone's birthday. Well, that individual received not only *Kool-Aid*, but an extra *Pop-Tart* or two. Not to mention all the times the lot of them were invited to dine upstairs in the kitchen and treated to dog biscuits and the extra helping of Greta's jambalaya. Meaning he did what he could for them; went out of his way even, quite often, and this was the thanks he got. Indifference to Fimple's reckless behavior. Wait. There was more. In addition to his aforementioned kindness, there was the idiot box. "Glass teat." High up, on the far wall, perched on a shelf was a thirteen-inch black-and-white television set. Did it matter? Did it make any difference to them? Apparently not. His kindnesses went unappreciated.

He looked about to make certain that all the other church board members and staff were accounted for. To his right, in this bunk-free area, weathered, ninety-two-year-old Miss Betty Lou Rutterschmidt in her wheelchair with that huge *Bible* open and resting across her skinny lap and all those stained, old, Raggedy Ann-type dolls attached to the back rest.

Having had a strong desire her entire life to have kids, lots of kids, and never having been able to make the dream happen, she had, instead, developed a habit of collecting all sorts of dolls of this nature, as well as, many years before, while up at the institution in Central California, she had "adopted" the sixty-seven-year-old woman who lay on the foam mattress at her feet, alternately snoring and farting.

The farts seemed to compete in volume and audio with the snores. Biggs could not tell whether the snores or the other had the winning edge. Although what was not easy to ignore were the gaseous fumes that competed with the otherwise existing odor of the basement.

Mildred Elizabeth continued to snooze. She had dragged her mattress out and was curled up on it down there. Didn't have enough sense to do her sleeping in her assigned bunk.

Let them. They had beds to sleep in, pillows, blankets and sheets—and yet some preferred to crash on the cement in this fashion. Logic? Don't look for logic and/or common sense here, thought the bishop.

He was ready to move on, check out the hole in the wall that Fimple must have caused when he yanked his chain out of it. Only the cockroach caused him to linger a bit longer here.

A large enough roach having difficulty moving through Miss Betty's wiry, white hair at above the brow. Scrounging around for something to eat? Or looking for a place to take a roach-dump?

If he slapped at it to get it out of there, or did anything of the sort, he only risked waking the tired old woman who required more rest than the others. At her age, she spent a good deal of her time dozing, in dreamland; and when she wasn't doing that she had her nose buried in her beloved *Bible*.

Let her. Saw the chain hanging from her neck. Would let her hang on to it for the same reason. No point rousing the gravel-voiced old heifer. Chain was Norbert's. A yard or so in length. Behemoth had managed not only to pull the one end out of the wall above his bunk, but break off the end on his wrist.

He'd let her keep it for the time being, as he had allowed her to retain one or two other "items" to defend herself with against anyone who was brazen enough to attempt to take the flashlight away from her. Besides, it wasn't her fault that Fimple was loose. There is no way that she, or the daughter, could have done anything to prevent it.

It was the others. The lot of them. Bloody Sam had his *Wild Bunch*, I've got my *Crazy Bunch*. Their fault. Blame was theirs. They could have done something to prevent it. Then again, *why would they?* No skin off their noses that his property was being vandalized on a daily basis.

His eyes cased the others. In a bottom bunk, on the same side of the room, was reed-thin, silver-haired six-foot-five "Big Tex" Leo Nix in that jockstrap with the colorful rhinestones that he always wore. Big T. was stretched out on his mattress, scratching his scrotum and muttering to himself.

"I left Texas for this?"

He looked up. Winced at the bright Maglite that Biggs held in his hand. *"Listen to me, Bishop. You gotta tell that puke-suckin' Commie scum up there to keep his pie-hole shut."*

Big Tex was whining about Julian Ionesco, the Rumanian in the bunk above him, whom he very often deliberately referred to as the "Red Menace," or the "Pinko Punisher," whenever the two engaged in one of their verbal exchanges that they were known for.

Ionesco, who had emigrated to the US twelve years before with his wife Anastasia, and had for a time earned his living as a New York City cabbie, then subsequently drove a taxi in LA, and was, for a period, "Butler to the Stars," spoke in a pronounced, far-from-easy to decipher Eastern European accent, and would not/could not clam up about Europe, Rumania in particular, constantly ran his mouth about it (when he was not lamenting the passing of his beloved spouse, who had succumbed to cancer a while back.)

It was not so much the constant bemoaning of his deceased wife that irked the man from Texas, since this type of loss was not difficult to relate to or be understanding about, but the never-ending praise of Paris and

Berlin, Vienna and Brussels, Rumania and the city of his birth, Bucharest, the Balkans, and the ever-present besmirching of the US and the way it did not live up to his dreams and vision of what he thought it would be, from what he had heard and seen in Hollywood movies; the constant reminder of what a letdown and disappointment it was, is what riled the cowboy.

"Don't like it?" Big T. had spat out more than once. Did so presently. "Who twisted your *chorizzo* to come here, *amigo?* Ain't nobody gripped you by the nutsack and forced your depraved *Commie ass* to fly eight thousand miles to these here United States so you can bellyache about how you're disappointed because Doc Holiday is long gone and Wyatt Earp ain't runnin' Dodge these days and Injuns is doin' all their scalpin' at the gaming tables. That's right: own casinos. Gettin' fat on greenbacks an' drunk on gold. About time, too, I say. You bet. Now, cowboys, on the other hand, I can help you out with. Ain't got to go far—on account you're lookin' at a genuine, Stetson-wearin', rootin-tootin' bronc-buster from the Lone Star State. *Texas. The Real McCoy.* Still got somethin' to bellyache about? Don't like my country? Eat a *cowpie and die,* is my final piece of advice to you, *Pinko bag of steer manure.*"

The balding, squat Rumanian was not disagreeing. "*Ja ja.* We are *comrades.* We are all *comrades* here."

"There goes the sumbitch again with that *comraide shit.*"

"Pipe down. I don't want to hear about it. I have a bunch of doors that are ruined—and all because you people allowed Mr. Fimple to get loose. All you had to do was keep him subdued long enough to give me a chance to catch up on some desperately needed sleep. You couldn't even do that."

"Please turn the heat up, Bishop Biggs," a black woman in her thirties said. This was Patience McDaniel. Wrapped in a dark brown monk's robe that Biggs had given her a while back. He, in fact, kept enough of these robes on hand for all of the members of his staff and board of directors for when snoopers from various government agencies came sniffing around to make certain and to satisfy themselves that "all was well" with the United Christian Church of Re-Newed Hope.

Patience, curled up in her favorite, the fetal position, was in a bottom bunk, at the far end, left side of the room, and she was shivering. She was always shivering. Seemed to be her natural state. Eyes shut. Wasn't interested in tv, food, water, drugs or booze, not even sex. Was after but one thing always—be it summer, winter, spring or fall, not that Southern California was known for its seasonal changes—to keep warm.

"Please turn the heat up."

Biggs ignored her, as most everyone always did. In the bunk above her, lay the tall lady named Greta Otto, who at times was either called *"The Leaper"* or *"The Jumper,"* for good reason.

A Cupid mask covered the Amazon's face. With the exception of Biggs, none of them had any idea what she looked like underneath that facade, and the one time Biggs got his glimpse some time back had been more than enough to keep away from her.

Greta's features had been disfigured over the years by a series of suicide attempts: first by fire, and then by acid—by her own hand—as well as a number of leaps from a rooftop or two, all prior to becoming a member of the group.

The rest of Greta's attire consisted of a far-from-clean negligee, worn black sweater over that, black leather *Wehrmacht* jackboots with hobnails and heel irons. She used her robe the way one would a blanket, to cover herself with.

He let her be.

The television was on, but no one had interest in what the idiot box had to offer. Somehow they seemed to sense it was all a bunch of horse dung, no matter how you added it up. Not that it mattered any to Biggs; he left the set on as a means of providing them with some light, so that they wouldn't break a leg or arm while climbing out of their bunks to use a honey bucket or make it to the basement john.

Then, too, there was that door in the floor that covered the pit that he thought anyone might easily trip on if he didn't at least allow for some illumination. The crimson-tinted night-light in that area outside the walk-in cooler where the patio table and chairs were was quite weak and hardly adequate.

His attention was drawn to the bunk on his left presently, lower berth, and the character lying on his belly. Lawrence Sassounian was his name, and he was a forty-year-old former psychotherapist and carpet cleaning technician out of Azuza, who was usually either banging his forehead against the hard-edged steel part of the frame above his pillow, or else banging the right side of his face and head against the wall in back of him.

There must have been something like the head of a nail sticking out or else the constant back-and-forth rubbing and banging against the frame that caused it, because there was blood on his face as well as on the grimy white bra and cheerleader skirt with the red, white and blue cleats that he had on.

Lawrence Sassounian, who was partial to "Laura" or "Sassy," was an individual of few words and preferred to "express" himself through self-mutilation and/or self-cannibalism. It was because of this that Biggs had gone to the trouble of individually taping his fingers and thumbs with gauze and medical tape. Cecil had gone to the trouble of taking the time to do likewise with the man's toes on both feet.

Even though it was rather obvious, with the clogs he wore, that gauze and medical tape had been torn off several of them and toenails and tips of toes were missing. Had been severed. How Sassy may have been able to accomplish this without access to a cutting implement was a mystery.

This was not the only disfigurement the man had inflicted upon himself. Sassounian's lower lip, having been at some point chewed off by the man and was a series of cracked scabs and tiny blisters bloated with puss and blood, didn't help matters. There hadn't been anything that Cecil could have done to prevent it, either.

The stained skirt and white bra had seen better days, as had the female scalp with the long, dark brown strands that sat atop his practically bald dome.

Biggs gradually realized Sassounian had something in his mouth that he was chewing on. Looked like an ear. Perhaps merely part of one.

The bishop held Sassy's head still long enough to brush back the hair over the other ear. Still bleeding. About a third of it gone somehow, the former therapist having found a way to cut it off—and it was in his mouth. His own ear—and he was banging his head against that nail in the wall.

Biggs understood perfectly why: he'd refused to let him have the panties and other undergarments he'd lifted from the same source he'd lifted the skirt. Tough. There were other issues, no doubt. The gender reassignment he was intent on wasn't happening fast enough as far as he was concerned. It didn't matter to him that this type of surgery was not only exorbitant, but clearly out of the question for other reasons that Biggs didn't feel like going into.

"Do you have any idea how difficult it was to 'acquire' that shit in the first place?" said the bishop to him in a guarded tone, not wanting the others to hear. "The risk involved? Better yet: Do you even give a damn? From the looks of things I don't suppose you do."

Biggs resumed in his normal voice: "I don't much care what you do to yourself, Sassounian. Can't control that; can't watch you night and day. What I do give a damn about is my property. You're damaging my property. The mortgage isn't even paid off and you're trying to bring me down; you're causing me problems. I have a tough enough time sleeping as it is."

Sassounian kept at it: banged his forehead against that steel bar by his pillow, then would lift his head, sitting up, and rub the right side of his face and temple against the wall behind him and the nail head sticking out, while he chewed the ear in his mouth. Made no difference to him what anyone said or thought. Had his own agenda. This was Sassy's way of coping.

"Knock it off, Mr. Sassounian, before you knock my wall down. Some of these walls are made of nothing more than wood and Sheetrock, planks and two-by-fours. Constructed with my own two hands—for the most part."

Lawrence Sassounian wouldn't stop. Biggs gave his left leg a kick. Then again. Not that it did any good. Whacked him over the head with an open palm that knocked the female scalp right off, exposing open sores across the top of his noggin.

"All you're doin' is makin' him feel good," said Big Tex. "Pole smoker loves to be whupped."

"You have a point."

Biggs left the Bunk Room for a few minutes. When he returned he held a pair of pink panties, matching shade of red lip gloss, hand mirror and a violet barrette in his left hand; in the other he held a fresh *Band-Aid* and a tube of *ChapStick*.

"You get the goodies, so long as you apply the lip balm to your lower lip, then the *Band-Aid*. Deal?"

Sassounian stopped carrying on of his own accord. Placed the scalp back on his head. He accepted the lip balm and applied it to the appropriate lip; then did the *Band-Aid*. He winced, but went ahead. *Band-Aid* was a bit askew. It was better than nothing, thought Cecil. Let him have the other items—save for the hand mirror—as a peace offering.

Sassy's acceptance of what was being given allowed for a kind of truce between them.

"You happy? I get it: accessories make the outfit."

Sassy was eager to try out the barrette. Applied the lip gloss. Cecil held the mirror up for him to help out.

"No, not the lower lip, Sassy." But it was already too late, the determined one-time therapist had already drawn a coat of lip gloss across the *Band-Aid*.

# CHAPTER 26

**Taking the mirror with him, Biggs stepped out of the Bunk Room.** He paused at the damaged door. Knew the size by heart. Measured it all the same and jotted the figures down. Waited there until the cross-eyed fellow from South Dakota returned with his stuffed Porky Pig doll.

Swine Vomit walked to a bunk in the middle, right-hand side, bottom tier. Slipped, lost his balance, and dropped to the cement with a thud.

No one bothered to notice or gave a damn, no one that is, with the exception of Patience McDaniel. The mishap had jarred her out of her usual dazed-and-confused state. She helped Goodfellow up and onto his mattress, and returned to the security of her own bunk. Wound the robe about her, the blanket, resuming the fetal position, eyes closed, shivering.

Biggs had taken it in. Patience had a way of being helpful. It was this kind of support—should he have been able to get from the rest of them—that would have made his existence easier, at least to some degree. The burden would not be resting entirely on his shoulders if some of the others gave a damn about his situation and what a struggle it was to keep the church going and the overhead manageable.

"Use the paint buckets to go in for the time being. There is enough drinking water in the water jugs to tide you over for a while. I have to run an errand. You can behave yourselves for a few hours."

He found a way to secure the door with a longer chain. Locked it. Biggs continued to the right: Furnace Room door. Seemed intact. Nothing in there he would want. To the right of this door was a bookcase, from floor to ceiling. Then you had the walk-in cooler. Looking at it again only managed to aggravate the foul state he was in. Nothing he could do about the "handle" right now. The cooler itself ran the length from here to the wall on the right, that faced the Roscoes' prefab domicile. Another bookcase here, much larger, stretched from floor-to-ceiling and was over the window.

This bookcase was about twenty or so feet wide. This entire section here, about twenty feet by twenty feet, was like a game area where the geeks could play checkers and cards, or, if they so wished, draw with crayons, fill in coloring books.

There was the green, round patio table, steel, bolted into the cement floor, with green iron patio chairs all around. Bolted down as well. This way, if in a fit of rage, for whatever reason, they would not be able to split open each other's skulls by picking up a chair.

There was a yoyo on the table, dominoes, a beach ball on the floor at the base of the larger bookcase, ping pong table to the right of this, up against the wall that was part of the Fun Room.

There was the small night-light in the shape of an elf that gave off a weak red light and had been plugged into a socket somewhere. Biggs assured himself once more: This night-light was made of hard plastic and there was no fear that Mr. Fimple would attempt to chew and devour it.

The Fun Room-cum-Workshop was thirty-five feet by thirty-five feet. The door seemed fine here. He took a peek through the ten-inch-by-ten-inch meshed glass window. All seemed intact inside, as it should, since he'd just been in there earlier.

# CHAPTER 27

**Biggs climbed the stairs to the landing.** He stood at the seriously impaired door, shaking his head. There would be no way to repair it. The lock and the doorknob he was certain could be salvaged; the door itself would have to be discarded. *Son of a bitch.* Retards were costing him more than they were worth. It seemed that way at times. What else could he do? He was stuck with them. He'd have to measure the door and hope he had one in the garage that fit; anything to keep from having to spend money. This was the third door Norbert had managed to destroy in as many months. Number didn't include all the other ruined doors before that.

Then you had the kitchen door on top. He'd have to see if Big Tex could do something with it, save it. Possibly. Do a repair job on the door to the Geek Room. Three doors. *Three of them.* There was no end to it.


Marvin was through cleaning the floor and was now spraying the air with *Lysol.*

"Stuff is expensive. Don't use it all up. Save some for later."

"Yo. You know *Pimple* gonna drop another big load on the floor sometime, break more door'."

"You mean *Fimple.*"

"What I said: Fimple."

"No, you did not. You said *'Pimple.'*"

"Yo. I know what I be sayin'."


Biggs measured off the door. He'd replaced some of these doors so often he knew the particular sizes by heart. Measured all the same, to be on the safe side. Width and length. Jotted it down in the notepad. Measured off the kitchen door as well, in case they wouldn't be able to salvage it.


Marvin was still spraying the air, wasting disinfectant.

"What did I just tell you?"

"I'm doin' what you tol' me to do. Said to clean up. I be doin' it."

"I told you to stop spraying."

Marvin returned the *Lysol* to the utility room. Came out. Indicated the barking sounds that came from somewhere in the vicinity of the back door.

"Omar, hear it?"

"Don't call me that."

"Bet it be them Roscoe mutt' again."

Biggs paused to listen. Sounded like it may have stopped raining out there. It had been raining off and on practically the entire week and evidently had subsided, because what he heard definitely sounded like something else. Dogs growling and barking. Marvin was right. Biggs cursed. Walked down the end of the hallway to his back door. Unlocked it.

Bright midday sun blinded him momentarily. He looked down from the stoop. The dogs had a habit of usually digging and clawing at that basement window to the right of it. Not this time. Could hear them barking and scratching away around the corner of the house.

# CHAPTER 28

**Biggs withdrew the *.357 Colt "Python,"* discreetly held it against his side, not wishing to draw undue attention from any of the neighbors, and stepped down.** Marvin followed him to a basement window located on the redneck's side of the property.

Familiar-looking mutts were digging away frantically at the base of the window. Didn't matter to them that Cecil and Marvin were standing there taking it in.

The shaggy white dog (in dire need of shampoo and trim, especially over the eyes) was an overweight Lhasa apso bitch named Ziggy. The other, much smaller dog, another bitch, was a Boston terrier called Darcy.

The animals were clearly aware of the bishop's presence, and continued to dig away just the same. It was the smell that they were undoubtedly drawn to down there, the strong smell of burning flesh that emanated from the basement—even though Biggs and Marvin had not dumped any body parts in the furnace in over two months. Couldn't help noting again that they had chosen a different window this time. For whatever reason.

Beasts were nosy, and a nuisance. Like their owners. He stood there watching them, cringing and watching. They had managed to crawl through the fence again; that flimsy six-foot-high wooden fence that separated his property from his neighbors on the right. It didn't do any good to complain to Marty Roscoe and his wife Petunia about their dogs constantly getting into his backyard and sticking their snouts into his private affairs.

When would he break down and spend the money to have a proper fence put up, Cecil asked himself. Chain-link fence is what this called for, like what he had in the front. Fences cost money he wasn't willing to spend on something he shouldn't have to spend it on. It was Roscoe's fault, pretty much. Kept removing pickets, or his wife did—or both—from time to time, to snoop on him. Billy garbage. White trash busybodies interfering in his business. Humans respected nothing these days. Nothing was sacred. Well, they did respect one thing, even in the 80s; one thing still worked: force, *brute force*, the kind of brute force a powerful handgun made possible.

Remaining discreet, he moved the barrel up enough so that it was pointed in the dogs' direction. Probably should go back inside for a 9 milli with a silencer. *Magnum* is going to draw too much attention. It would take two shots. Was it worth it? In broad daylight? The noise, the attention. Didn't have his earplugs with, either.

"You gonna off them K-9, Cecil?"

"What of it?"

Biggs kept the gun aimed at them. The dogs were persistent in their effort to increase the depression they had created at the base of the boarded up window.

"Blood don't bother me, long as it don't be mine."

"I'd like to pummel them out of existence. Once and for all."

Biggs found himself lowering the business end of the *Magnum* when he realized Brenda, who lived across the street with her half-brother and grandparents, was standing on the sidewalk looking in his and Marvin's direction. Some of her teen girlfriends were with her. Unlike Brenda, they were preoccupied jumping rope. Brenda was the one wringing her hands and watching intently.

What was going on? Did the thirteen-year-old want to be initiated? They spread their legs at a young age these days. Wouldn't have mattered much to him. Dishwater blond hair, that he disliked, and all. Could always throw a dark wig over her head and go to work on her. Educate her in ways she didn't know existed.

It was the sight of the thirteen-year-old Brenda that made him take a closer look at the window. Should have thought of it right away. There was something furry and white, smaller than either dog, trapped between the hard wire mesh and the boarded up window. It had a collar on and a leash that trailed out below the window in the grass and weeds. Brenda's pet rabbit. Should have known. What was his name? Benson? Becker?

Marvin noticed the girl himself, then took a second look at the dogs. Cursed.

"*Bentley*. What them dirty mutt' be after."

Brenda was wiping her eyes. Cecil re-holstered the *Magnum*.

"Take the mangy mutts back. Lift them over to their side of the fence and drop them. Drop them hard enough and maybe they'll break a leg or two this time. Hopefully break a neck."

"Why me? You ain't helpin'? What if the big one mistake my black ass for a buffet, like he done before, and try to take a bite?"

"I'd do it myself, except I get sick to my stomach whenever I see that slobbering redneck moron and that chunky psycho cunt he's married to up close. Furthermore, you've got gloves on, I don't. Their dogs smell. I don't want that smell on my clothes."

Marvin stared at him. Was tempted to say: *Is you for real?* The way the basement be? And the *Abattoir*? And them *honey bucket*? Them dog' ain't got no smell to 'em. Ziggy like' to bite, is what it be.

"*What?*"

"Nothin'."

Using care and caution, the deacon got his arms under the Lhasa apso. Lifted him. Dog was unhappy and continued to make noise. Cecil didn't want to be around when Roscoe and his wife showed—should they show—because of the racket the dogs were creating. Felt like taking a walk to the front, check his mail maybe, check up on his cars, only there was no way he was about to trundle through the tall weeds and trash, not to mention dog piles left there by Ziggy and Darcy.

He walked toward the back. Would take a stroll down his driveway on the Crust side of his place.

"Be nice now, mothafuckah."

"You relay this message to Marty Roscoe: *Tell him to keep his dogs off my property.* If that repulsive heifer of his pokes her head out, if she happens to be home—I don't know that she is—but if she is, and gets abusive, or he starts showing off with that six-shooter, don't panic. Call me over. Don't mouth off, just call me over."

"What chu gonna do about *Bugs Bunny?*"

"I'd like to shove him in the microwave, or just let Mr. Fimple feast on him. Raw."

"Rabbit stew be a whole lot better than that jambalaya Greta be cookin' all the time."

"Keep your eyes peeled. The Flinger kid could be on the premises."

"*Wilmer?* Finger Lickin'? Figured as much."

"Take a good look in the back, both sides of the garage, after you drop the dogs off. I'm taking a walk down the driveway. I wasn't kidding about throwing them over the fence, either."

"I ain't doin' it. I ain't throwin' no dog over no fence."

"Get them out of my sight."

# CHAPTER 29

**Although as inquisitive and nosy as the Roscoes, the people on the other side of his driveway were far easier to tolerate.** Harold and Fay Crust were the middle-aged African-American couple who lived in the one-bedroom frame house on his left. There was a close-to-identical type of wooden fence that separated the two properties, only it was a shade of brown, old, weathered.

Best of all, though, the Crusts didn't own dogs. And that cat they had, that he didn't care for, at least didn't go around digging up holes outside his basement windows.

Biggs spotted the obese tom they called Delonzo crouched in the weeds at the foot of the fence up ahead. Seemed focused on a small rodent in front of him in the wet grass.

Delonzo forgot about the rodent the minute he sighted Cecil walking up, leapt up the fence with that large body of his; not only scaling it, but cleared it, and was gone in a flash.

Just as well, thought Cecil. He may have been tempted to pitch a rock at the copper-eyed, nasty-looking tom. Truth was, and he had to remind himself from time to time, he didn't mind the cat half as much as he minded Roscoe and Petunia's mutant mutts. Delonzo mistrusted and disliked people as much as Biggs did, and took off the second he sensed a human, any human he wasn't familiar with and was close enough to do him bodily harm. The dogs, on the other hand, lingered and barked at you on your own turf, as if it belonged to them. They'd stand their ground and go nuts, snarling and threatening. What balls.

Biggs walked along the driveway pocked with potholes full of water from the rains. Somewhere above, on a power line possibly, a large crow mocked him with as much relish as any henpecker he'd ever had the displeasure of crossing paths with.

He ignored the crow. Had to. Went about checking the wrought iron bars and mesh on his basement windows. Gripped and shook the bars for looseness. Bars and mesh looked to be in good shape. Solid, as were the boards on the windows themselves. This was wrought iron mesh, and not that cheap, run-of-the-mill window mesh used by homeowners to keep flies out. So the only explanation he could come up with for that gap in the mesh that the rabbit had been able to crawl inside of must have been caused by a potential home invader, a snoop, crook; lowlife criminal types who prowled the neighborhood looking for an easy score to buy their dope with. Must have been cut with tin snips.

Vigilance was the only recourse when you lived in a bordering-on-seedy

North Hollywood neighborhood such as this. Vigilance. You kept on your toes, or they took you under, pulled you down to their level of poverty and desperation. He'd been there before. Both: broke and desperate. Had had his share of it, and hadn't cared for it.

He stood in the littered, weed-infested driveway, taking in the brick and wood affair. Shabby? Maybe. It was his. He could have lived in a better neighborhood, upscale home, and that was the plan eventually, to move out. Mortgage was manageable and money was hard to come by; it was always hard to come by. Why squander when you didn't have to? Thrift was key. Save, don't spend—had mantra potential.

He looked up. The sun in his eyes. Squinted. He'd never liked the sun much. He kept looking, squinting hard. That's right, get burned. Real smart.

Windows on the first and second floors he'd outfitted with shutters, inside and out, in addition to bars—on all of them, with the exception of the four attic windows: dormer in front, one in back, and the standard-type single windows on either side.

Felt those windows up there didn't require outside shutters or bars; the inside shutters with the iron crossbar was adequate, although it wasn't unthinkable that certain home invaders were brazen enough to scale that high in order to hit a place. What he had up there would have to do. He felt comfortable enough with it.

He walked down the gravel driveway in his boxers toward the front, past tall weeds that grew in clusters here and there and glistened with moisture. Flattened milk and juice cartons littered the grounds. Crushed and punched out beer and soda cans that resembled misshapen miniature gondolas held enough water to draw small birds to them. Buzzing mosquitoes hovered over puddles acting like they wanted their share, although Biggs knew better; they were out for blood. Possibly his, if they could score without a hitch.

He supposed he should have collected the cans and turned them in for cash. Give Muck something to do. The freeloader hardly pulled his weight.

Cans and cartons weren't the only eyesore. There was rubbish; enough of it had accumulated to make it annoying even to someone as indifferent when it came to general appearance as he was. He'd never been all that fastidious about it, only this was supposed to be a church, was it not?

Should put Muck to work. Make him earn his keep. Have him cut the grass, pick up some of the trash; at least trim some of the weeds with the edger.

Wouldn't it make more sense to have the grounds looking a bit more on the "presentable" side? It was a matter of being better organized, not always that easy to pull off, especially when you had so many other things on your mind.

The noticeably less-impressive, one-bedroom dwellings on either side of Biggs house were nothing more, as far as he was concerned, than glorified Southern California bungalows. He called them as he saw them. What irked was the fact they were cleaner looking and their lawns kept up, at least to some considerable extent, the one that belonged to the black couple to the left of his place. Even the other one, to the right of the church, belonging to the redneck and his abhorrent wife, had a better looking, decent lawn.

Their front porch was cluttered, as Roscoe was a known pack rat, but the grass part of their sidewalk was periodically trimmed, as was their own lawn, surrounding the front porch and backyard. Roscoe wouldn't do the work himself, instead paid the Mexican Perez brothers or neighborhood punks like Flinger in vinyl records or worthless trinkets and figurines, to do it. Not that Cecil had never given it much thought, or that it genuinely bothered him any—until now. The way he had it figured: the waist-high weeds served their purpose. The majority of the juveniles in the area were reluctant to climb over his fence at night (or even during daylight hours) and break into his cars from fear that he might be lying in wait in the weeds with a ball bat or piece.

The same loud crow, or a different one, pulled him away from his train of thought. Through the nasty black bird's squawking he could hear the girls jumping rope in front of Lloyd and Fontana's place. Brenda and her prick-teaser friends.

He got close enough to be able to see them: the former mail carrier's granddaughter Brenda and her cunt girlies.

Brenda still standing there, wiping her eyes, looking unhappy over her missing rabbit. Well, they weren't going to cook it, he came close to assuring her, and that Marvin would bring him over as soon as he unloaded the dogs.

He couldn't go over there the way he was dressed—or call her over; even if he had wanted to go and see her, there was no way that he would. A man his age talking to a slit that young? Besides, he disliked that dishwater hair. Always had, always would. Two of her friends, whose blond locks were light enough to pass for platinum, he disliked no less.

Some went for the tow-headed type. He never understood why. Dusky beaver was always more enticing to him. Forget the fair-haired twats. The others with them were ethnic girlies. One black, the other Hispanic. Latinas reminded him of Tillie. Any high yellow reminded him of Tillie. Couldn't decide if that was good or bad. But they did.

Truth was, the fact that light hair held little or no interest for him made no difference, was immaterial, because the dark-haired and brown-haired jailbait fascinated him enough to want to stand there and take in all that virgin pussy. Dwell on the possibilities.

Ballbusters in the making. Every one of them. Would grow up one day to henpeck more than one feckless dork into a state of mental anguish to land them in the psych ward. But right now, they exuded joy, jumping rope. "Double Dutch" is what they called it, what they, to a one, were into at the moment—with the exception of Brenda, who stayed forlorn. Looked in his direction presently. Or was she? Interested in him? Why would she be? Unless she craved a "Daddy" to loosen up that unmolested, untouched young pee-hole?

Couldn't be it. Had to be the rabbit. Her pet had gone AWOL and she was worried. That's all. He didn't know. Then again: Who did? Who ever would?

He remained in place, standing and watching them jump rope, watching the summer breeze and the activity they were into lift their dresses and skirts high enough to reveal more thigh and a variety of panty as they bounced around, revealing enough skin to make him lust after it. Cunt was like money and kicks—you could never get enough. It's off limits, he reminded himself. Too close to home. Have to be careful about these things. He'd taken his share of chances before, but to even think about going after one of these cute little numbers would not have made much sense. There was no way he could have gotten away with it.

It wasn't until Biggs had walked close enough to his front yard to check on his shell gray 1971 *Rolls-Royce Silver Shadow* that he paid seventeen grand cash for sitting there, and the new deep-red, four-door *Cadillac Brougham* with the black vinyl top parked next to it that he noticed one-eyed "Meth Mouth" and his punk buddy Felix Monk sitting in their multi-colored, banged-up Toyota a couple of houses to the right of where the teeny boppers were hopping around.

Meth Mouth was Jesus Ortiz, better known as "Ace," also known as "Glassy." Nothing more than an ex-con junkie out on parole looking for a way to fuck up again in order to be sent back to the pen. Well, not really—but Biggs knew better. A born-loser like that wouldn't be able to stay out of the slam for very long. He'd known more than a few like him.

And that other pissant with him with the do-rag? Just another low-grade *mook*. Between the two they didn't have the brains of one of Roscoe's idiot canines. Wouldn't be surprised to discover they were responsible for damaging the mesh on his window.

The junkie and the a-hole had dark shades on and they were sucking down beers in brown paper sacks. Slumped low in their seats. Ace in front, the other in the back. No doubt casing his place, trying to nail his routine down; no doubt scheming how to get to his rides, maybe his gun collection, dope stash, and other things of value that he owned.

The cars were fine. None of the neighborhood punks had attempted anything overnight. All the windows were intact, the wheels still there.

Both cars were heavily insured, and were rigged with state-of-the-art alarms. That didn't always make him rest easy, not with desperate types like Ace and Felix hovering around his nest like those mosquitoes over the puddles of rain water.

He was well aware that it would have made better sense to at least leave one of the cars parked in the garage in the back. Well, garage space was taken up with all sorts of things: doors, freezers and furniture, tires and car parts, tools, stereos and speakers, tv sets and boxes and boxes of porn— and a few other items. Besides, he enjoyed leaving his fine "hoopties" sitting this way in the front yard for the simple reason it gave him great satisfaction to flaunt his wealth, even with shifty low-life imbeciles like Ace Ortiz and Felix Monk always sniffing around, aching to get their sticky fingers on them.

It's all right. Let them try it. Not only was he insured, but had the arsenal and means to stop them cold in their tracks should they ever attempt anything.

Keep the bait out there where it can be seen. That's what luxury automobiles like this were when it came to bitches: bait. Cunt magnets. Let the neighborhood wannabes dry up with envy, let all the moronic welfare cases in this near-barrio see that *you've got, and that they haven't.* Let the young cunts know who owns the brand new *Cadillac* and a mint condition '71 Rolls.

One of the blonds, not Brenda, noticed that he was in his underwear, and quickly enough the rest of them did, too. Giggles and snide remarks soon followed, as they always did. To Brenda's credit, though, she was not participating, and did what she could to get the others to stop it. She was not like Lloyd and her half-brother, after all.

Her pals were not about to relent. They pinched their noses, while pointing at him and chanting: "Stinky! Stinky! Stinky!"

Their mommies and daddies had taught them well. All came from dysfunctional homes. Had druggies and boozers and molesters and thieves and malcontents for parents.

It was Dicker, ultimately. His fault. Curmudgeon was always making waves behind his back. What did you expect from someone who carried mail all his life? Certified nobody. He was the one responsible for spreading rumors about "stench" emanating from his church. It was nothing more than gross exaggeration, as far as Cecil was concerned. The so-called stench wasn't nearly as bad as they claimed. He was certain of it. Wouldn't he have been aware of it if it were? Wouldn't he be as bothered by it as they, supposedly, were? Or was he so used to it at this point that it no longer fazed him?

He wasn't sure. What he was sure of, however, was how much satisfaction it would give him to hang the young heifers on hooks in his walk-in, the bitches, all of them: Lloyd Dicker, his grandson Wilburn Claude, one-eyed Jesus Ortiz and his greasy buddy, and a few others in the area.

The chanting was not letting up in spite of Brenda's concerted effort to put an end to it, and it was starting to get to him in a bad way. He could tell the pepper bellies in the sorry bucket were snickering. Fuckers. All fuckers. The way it always was for him: the world on his ass. *Society* causing him grief. *People.*

Just as he contemplated, toyed with the idea merely, of drawing his *.357* and taking care of business, commotion of some kind coming from the backyard, the left side of his Garage, to be more precise, by the hedges, pulled him away from the badgering teens, drew his attention, and he walked back there.

# CHAPTER 30

**Just as he had suspected upon first spotting the trapped rabbit behind his window mesh, Lloyd's other grandkid, Brenda's older half-brother "Twelve-Fingers" Flinger, was tussling with Marvin against the side of his garage.**

Bent teeth and the "Mohawk" that was a foot high and went straight up and kept this way with lots of gel, extra-strength. Kid wore leather wrist bands with inch-long chrome spikes. Had a mama who was an aging rock-n-roll groupie and was doing time, or had done time for hanging paper and soliciting a vice cop in a Beverly Hills hotel.

Marvin had the teen on the ground and he was pummeling him with both fists. By the time Cecil got there, Flinger had begun to hyperventilate. His eyes rolled back and he lost consciousness. Biggs shoved Marvin off of him. Knelt beside Finger Lickin'. Turned him on his side and slid the US Mail satchel, that he was rarely without, under his head.

"Ain't done shit to the young punk, me. Punk be actin'."

"He's epileptic."

Biggs dug around inside Flinger's satchel. Found a bottle of *phenobarbital,* a thermos. Shoved an anticonvulsant in his mouth. Uncapped the thermos, and poured soda in him to chase it.

"Couldn't you tell he was having a seizure? Hell's the matter with you?"

"Didn't know, me. Don't nobody say shit about it."

"You didn't know he was epileptic? You must be the only one, then."

"Fuck him. Young dude ain't got no invite to trespass."

"People are known to die from asphyxiation after a grand mal seizure like this."

"Dude was *snoopin'. Yo.*"

Flinger was regaining consciousness. He was coming back to. Stabilizing. Biggs helped him up.

"What was that?"

"You heard: caught him *peepin'* in the garage window."

"That right?" Biggs was looking at the teen now. "What did you expect to see in there?"

Wilburn Flinger remained on the woozy side and it took him a moment to respond.

"How could I see anything? Windows are dirty, and you got them boarded up; just like everything is boarded up around here."

"What was it you expected to see?"

"Beeves."

"*Beeves?* You're crazy. This is a church, not a slaughter house."

"That's what I hear."

"Who sent you?"

"Who sent me? Nobody sent me. It's my sister Brenda's rabbit: Bentley. Got caught in your basement window. I come over to free him. That's when I got the idea to find a stick or something to poke at it, make him come out the other side of the mesh."

"I'll ask you again: *Who sent you?*"

"I told you: Nobody did."

"How did your rabbit get caught in my window?"

"He ain't mine. Bentley belongs to my half-sis."

"How'd he manage to get stuck—on my property, of all places?"

"Petunia Roscoe's dogs went after him. He run inside the mesh to keep from getting mauled to death."

Marvin picked up a pair of binoculars off the ground. "He was carrying these."

"Belong to my grandpa. Lets me use them."

Binoculars had night vision capability. Biggs was familiar with the type. He looked at him without saying anything for a while.

Although the kid was eighteen, at a mere five foot two he was practically a dwarf, a wide one. Had a unibrow and a large head, with all that dark hair formed in a ridiculous do. An earring in the shape of a swastika hung from the left earlobe. There was a stud in one of the nostrils, a safety pin above his right eye. Black leather jacket had zippers along both sleeves, and other places; lots of zippers. Black cut-off jeans went down to below his knees, although up at the waist were way too low, lower than the elastic underwear band. Wore knee-length argyle socks. Boots were shit-kickers: black and scuffed, with five-inch heels, to compensate for lack of stature.

It wasn't until the teen wiped grass and general crud from his chin and mouth that Biggs was reminded that he had an extra pinkie on each hand. Flinger had a total of twelve fingers. Where the average Joe and Josephine had ten, flop-eared Flinger had a dozen. Possibly explained why he was so quick to flip people off at the slightest provocation: secretly hoped that the extra finger on each hand might one day be severed by an unhappy recipient, then he'd be down to ten—like everyone else.

"Yo. Ain't you gonna *aks* him what he be doin' way back here, when the *bunny* be *over there?*"

Flinger took the opportunity to give Marvin Muck the bird. Marvin was about to step in and knock him down again.

Biggs put a stop to it.

"Peeps want to know what's causing the smell. Thought I'd *investeegate* while I was back here looking around for a twig, something to poke at the rabbit with."

"But nobody sent you?"

"They didn't send me. Nobody sent me. Lloyd, my grandpa, keeps talking about the smell; he's bothered by it. But he didn't send me. Nobody sent me."

"Rutherford, my German shepherd. Got run over. Keeping him in the garage for the time being. Went out and bought formaldehyde and trying to learn taxidermy in order to preserve him. It's not easy to let go when a pet dies. It's like losing a member of your family. He *was* family. That's that. And you're trespassing."

"I know."

"You planted that rabbit in my window deliberately in order to have an excuse to snoop."

"Like hell that's what I done. Rabbit don't even belong to me." He pointed to his thirteen-year-old half-sister Brenda standing on the other side of the street, currently wiping her eyes with a tissue, or doing something like it; looking nervous and concerned.

"Believe me now? Bentley belongs to her. He don't belong to me, like I said. If he was mine I'd just throw him against the wall, head first. Rabbits are like cats: smell like a sewage plant. Something like the stench coming from your garage."

"We went over that."

"Keep telling Brenda if she don't keep that rabbit in his cage, he's gonna get run over one day."

"Exactly. That's what happened to Rutherford. Hit-and-run."

"Nobody run over Rutherford," said Marvin.

"The driver who ran him over," Biggs continued unfazed, "didn't even have the decency to stop and offer condolences."

"Maybe he got nervous," said Wilburn.

"Or just didn't give a damn," said Biggs.

Wilburn lifted the lid on his Tupperware container that he kept in his *US Mail* satchel to see if any of the eggs in there had survived the tumble. Three of the four raw eggs were cracked, and he turned the container upside down and let the yolk pour out and down his throat.

He swallowed the lot, shell and all, although some of the yolk and egg white missed his mouth and dripped onto his hands. Finger Lickin' dealt with it by licking his fingers and sucking his thumbs.

He retrieved the final, untouched egg, poked a hole in the shell with the fingernail on one of his two extra pinkies, and sucked the yolk out. Marvin Muck made a face like maybe he was about to get sick.

"You right, Cecil. Yo. Mothafuckah be *crazy*."

When Wilburn was done with that, he dug around inside the plastic container and produced a purple *Popsicle*, mostly covered in raw egg. He licked the egg off, and stuck the *Popsicle* in his mouth.

It was disgusting the way he went about it.

"Like a crack ho suckin' weenie head."

"Nothing like dessert. After you had a fine meal like that."

"Dessert? You call that dessert? You call suckin' raw egg' a meal? Even *jambalaya* be better than that."

Wilburn sucked his *Popsicle*.

Biggs handed him the binoculars. "You'll need these, the better to peek under the girls' dresses with."

Wilburn accepted the binoculars with a repeat of the earlier claim, as he walked along the Roscoe side of the church grounds to where the window was. Biggs and Marvin followed.

"They ain't exactly mine. Field glasses belong to Lloyd."

"So you come from a long line of Peeping Toms, that it?"

"There." Wilburn Flinger pointed at the frightened, trapped rabbit, caught between the wire meshed wrought iron bars and the planks over the pane itself. There was a gap; better yet, what looked like a man-made opening, that the animal had been able to crawl into, and was presently unable to budge.

"You cut that opening in my mesh?"

"No way." Wilburn picked up a twig off the ground. "I didn't want to cause more damage to it than was already there."

"What do you plan on doing with that?"

"Poke at it. Until it comes out the other side."

"Can't you see it's stuck? Animal is not going anywhere; it isn't able to."

"I can't think of nothing else." A flustered Wilburn Flinger turned his head, and could see his sister standing back there across the street, on the verge of tears. "Brenda's about to start crying again—and I just can't stand to see her cry. I ain't a rabbit lover; I don't get rabbits. Just as soon throw it at a moving truck and watch it go splat. Like I said: it's Brenda's. I have to do something. Maybe one of her girlfriend's will blow me if I can show them what a good guy I am."

Cecil selected a key on one of the many key rings on his carabiner. Inserted it into the lock in the wrought iron frame. Turned the key. He opened the frame and let the teen scoop the bunny up. Flinger seemed to lack the sense to say thank you, and walked off toward the chain-link part of the fence that fronted Biggs church and property.

Cecil swung the wrought iron bars in place and locked the frame. Saw that Flinger was about to try scaling his gate and couldn't believe it. If the kid broke a leg he'd have another lawsuit on his hands. He walked down to put a stop to it.

"You're not climbing over with Bentley in tow?"

"Got a better idea?"

Biggs unlocked the gate. Gestured he try walking instead. Flinger took him up on it. Brenda rushed in to take her pet in her arms. Kid had tears streaming down. She was the one who thanked Biggs for the effort.

"Don't mention it." If he were not genuinely touched by the girl's show of gratitude and emotion, he came close. It was rare for him. "Had a couple of pets myself as a youngster. They were killed and eaten by my own family. Something like that you never forget. Glad I could help."

# CHAPTER 31

**Biggs checked his mailbox.** Found the usual junk mail, advertisements, and porn solicitations. Someone had evidently put his name on a few smut lists. It didn't figure: he was the bishop of a church. Why send him gay porn and outcall service offers and hot oil rubdown enticements at discounted rates from that massage parlor but a few doors down from Slim Jessup's diner? Jessup owned the place, too, or at the least was one of the co-owners. That was the rumor. And the gay porn? It wasn't all gay porn, but a lot of it was. Who would do that to him? You get one guess: Petunia and Marty Roscoe. Unless it was Roscoe on his own. Just to fuck with him.

When he looked up he noticed that Brenda had walked back to her side of the street to join up with her friends and was reprimanding them for the chanting and jeering. They did stop upon her insistence. She realized what her brother was up to just then and shook her head in disgust. Called her grandfather Lloyd's name. Wilburn didn't seem fazed in the least. He was lying on his belly in the middle of the driveway and he had the binoculars glued to his eyes, which in itself would have been perfectly harmless, except that he had them aimed at the girls' behinds as they jumped rope.

Old man dicker soon enough limped up from his backyard with the aid of that metal cane. Paused at Wilburn's feet and swung that cane like it was a golf club, whacking him across the soles of his boots.

Biggs stood where he was, pretending to be immersed in his mail, while straining to hear what was taking place on the other side of the street between grandfather and grandson. Enough of it was discernible.

"What did you find out? I sent you over there to see what's causing the smell. Find out anything?"

"Yeah, I did. Dude's got bad breath like you, Gramps."

"Keep pushing, Wilburn, and you'll push yourself right out of the garage and onto a bus bench. I'm charging you rent from now on—"

"Rent?"

"And utilities. If you can send money to Manson and them other serial killer vermin, what you don't spend on drugs and hookers, you can damned well pay rent. Me and Fontana are damned tired of carrying your ass. About time your mother quit running around with that rock-n-roll trash out there in London and started taking care of her own kids."

"Fuck Bernice. She ain't shit."

"Don't talk about your mother that way." The old man more than understood the kid's bitterness. Had every right. Sure did. Took notice of his grandson's face for the first time.

"They do that to you? What happened over there?"

"Got the living crap beat out of me, is what happened. Thanks to you."

"Was it Biggs?" Lloyd was about to turn on his heels to go inside and get on the phone. "Calling Valley PD about this right now."

"Wouldn't do no good."

"Why wouldn't it? It's their job to protect the citizenry."

"I was trespassing, you old fool. Besides, it wasn't him. He helped me. Was having a seizure, too. It wasn't Cecil; it was the other one: the nigger."

"You need to stop using that word."

"What word?"

"Nigger. That's what word."

"Why?"

"Because it's the ugliest word there is. That's why."

"No, it ain't. There's one other that's worse."

"Name it, you little jerk. What is it?"

"Rent. And utilities."

"You're asking for it, ain't you, boy?"

"You sent me over there to get my ass kicked, and all you want to do is squeeze me for every dollar I got. Ain't got that much to begin with. Get nearly put in the hospital and all you want to do is stick me in some crappy shed and take my money."

"You ain't got any to speak of, as of yet—so hush up about it."

"You brung it up, Gramps."

"You didn't answer my question."

"Man, I'm sick of old people always giving me a hard time."

"What's behind the odor?"

"Rutherford. His dead dog. Got him hanging in the garage. Biggs is trying to learn taxidermy. So he can keep him around."

"Not likely. That dog of his hit the road, just like Tillie; like his wife. Had to get away from him. Can't say as I blame either one. Took his abuse long enough. His kind is always like that: abuse their women, beat on the dog—and wonder why they moved on."

"Yeah? You'll be asking yourself the same thing when I'm gone if you don't get off my back."

"The day you move out will be the happiest day of my life."

"You say that now, only you'll be crying your eyes out, you and Grandma both, when I pack up and hit the bricks. Tired of this shit."

"Go in the house. Let Mother take care of you, clean your face. You look a mess."

"Leave me alone."

Lloyd held his hand out. Asked for the binoculars. Looked like Wilburn was refusing to turn them over. "I didn't let you borrow them so you can sneak peeks under young girls' dresses. Hand them over."

"When I'm good and ready."

Old man Dicker raised his cane. Was about to smite the teen with it. Held it there. Poised.

"I will. I'll strike you down, Wilburn. Exactly why that nigger over there give you a beating. Got no respect."

Didn't seem like Wilburn was willing to go that far. The old man looked like he meant business. Flinger rose to his feet, lifted the leather strap over his head and relinquished the binoculars.

Biggs thought he heard him say that he was sorry. Yes. Apologized to his grandfather, and asked if he really meant what he said about charging him rent. Lloyd Dicker limped back down his driveway to his backyard without responding. Wilburn spit on the ground. Kicked his skateboard over, hopped on it, and skated out toward the sidewalk.


Ace and his buddy Felix Monk could be heard chuckling out loud in their beater; they were sucking on beers in those paper sacks and chuckling. One of them even made cat sounds, implying that Wilburn was nothing but a "pussy."

Wilburn "Finger Lickin'" Flinger did not waste any time, didn't think twice about it. Flipped them the bird. Skated up to the car on the sidewalk side, held that middle bone where it could be seen. Taking great pleasure in it.

Before he knew what was happening and could duck in time, beer was thrown in his face, then the beer cans. First the one, then the other, practically knocking him off his skateboard. Ace and Felix laughed out loud this time, then drove off in their multi-shaded bucket.

# CHAPTER 32

**Biggs turned to walk back.** Noticed his sign. Stood there shaking his head. As if he didn't have enough to deal with.

To the right of the stoop, roughly in front of the basement window, the height of an average human, the message the thirty-six-by-thirty-six-inch cathedral sign proclaimed was not the one he had instructed Marvin to put on there. Instead of posting a simple enough adage like LIFE IS SHORT, PRAY HARD, Marvin had made it:

## LIFE IS SHORT,
## PLAY HARD

Idiot couldn't be counted on to do anything right. Biggs unlocked the metal frame and opened the Lexan window. He unlocked the metal tray in back where the letters were kept, and while replacing the L with an R, correcting the blunder, he fought a strong urge to make it SOCIETY IS A WHORE, KILL MORE.

He swung the window back in place. Locked the frame, the tray in back. That's when it caught his attention. Thought it was just a mite peculiar: a *Kibbles 'n Bits* dog food bag. Sitting upright in front of his door. This was the type of dog food used by Roscoe and his bitch hog to feed their mutts. What was it doing there? Dog food sample? He doubted it. Leaned over to pick it up, instead froze in place upon seeing what was in it: a massive turd. Too large to have been made by any neighborhood dog he was familiar with—and large enough to have been excreted by a human—and the human who immediately came to mind was the same one who'd made the offensive phone call to him earlier: Marty Roscoe, the neighbor on his right, the one married to the loud and lumpy and repulsive beast named Petunia.

They badgered him with obscene phone calls, were responsible for the gay smut the postal service continued to deliver to his residence by having put his name on some smut list—and were now leaving excrement on his doorstep.

What did you expect? Lowlife was jealous; they all were. That was the point. Made Biggs feel good inside about that, gave him a certain satisfaction to rub it in and watch them turn green with envy. He had the means and ways, they had what was left: bitching and belching about how things were unfair and stacked against them—and retaliated the only way they knew how: by leaving "surprises" like this for him to discover and be disgusted by.

Let them do their worst. You're tough enough. Took years to rebuild your sense of self-worth. Years. Decades. And the battle wasn't over yet.

It was an ongoing, evolving aspect of his existence. Still, look where he had come from, the bottom, lower than the bottom, and look how far he had come.

Any time life's *Sturm und Drang* reared its ugly head, kicked him in the balls, did its best to tear him down, thoughts of the IRS and other clandestine government agencies, to disrupt his peace of mind, all he had to do was remind himself of all he had accomplished. Yes, there was still a lot more to do in order to get where he needed to be—but that was no reason to downplay, or even discount, the achievements.


With thumb and index finger, he pinched the bag by one of the creases (somewhere at about the middle, at least away from both the top and bottom—to be on the safe side) and carried it this way, well out in front of him, to the backyard.

Marvin Muck, the Fuck, not yet having picked up the trash that Flinger had knocked over, walked up, wondering what was up.

Without responding, Biggs raised the bag above the pickets, turned it, ever-cautiously, upside down, so that what had been inside rolled out and landed on Roscoe's side, the enemy's turf. He then dropped the bag after it. Noticed Petunia Roscoe peeking at them through her screen door, and then turn away without saying a word, for a change.

"How you know Finger Lickin' ain't the one?"

"Why would he? Gave him a whole bag of Hershey's Kisses last Halloween, not to mention a stack of paper money from the Civil War that absolutely has zero value. He doesn't know that. He figures all he has to do is sit on it for a few years and he's rich. No, it's the same 'intellectual' who likes to make obscene phone calls."

"That be *twiced* this year, and the year don't even be over. Redneck dude ain't right to be doin' that."

Biggs told him to let the trash go for the time being and follow him inside the garage and help him pick out the doors.

There were many different types of doors to choose from in there. Some older than others, some stacked on the floor, still others propped against either wall.

Cecil consulted his pocket notebook. Selected three that seemed like reasonable candidates. Measured them off to be certain, and had Marvin carry them inside the house.

When he stepped back out, he had him refill the hole outside the basement window Roscoe's dogs had been responsible for.

"Roscoe ain't right to be doin' all that. Dude be as bad as Wilber. Wouldn't be no surprise if it turn out he the one be Finger Lickin' true daddy."

"How do you figure?"

"Yellow eye'. Both a them got 'em. Gotta be Marty, and not that other one: Fred Flinger of the Flyin' Flinger Trapeze act that Wilmer always be talkin' about."

"It's *Wilburn.*"

"What I said, ain't it?"

Biggs did not want to hear about the Flying Flingers, nor did he give a shit who Wilburn's real daddy was. Instead reminded Marvin of a *faux-pas* of his own, for what good any of it did.

"You misspelled 'pray.'"

"Say what?"

"The sign. You fucked up my sign. Misspelled 'pray.'"

"Yo. I ain't misspell' nothin'. It look' better that way."

"How about if I dock your allowance for deliberately misrepresenting my message?"

"Allowance? I don't get no allowance."

"Go clean yourself up. We're taking a drive in the *Caddy*."

# CHAPTER 33

**Biggs drove south on Lankershim Boulevard past auto repair shops, low-rent motels, out of work illegals from South of the Border in worn, slept-in clothing kicking back in the shade pulling on beers in brown paper sacks, past upholstery shops, weather-beaten taco stands, doughnut huts, a Mexican movie house marquee with the title of Jorge Rivero's latest celluloid canker sore; muffler shops, a retirement home here and there, other greasy spoons.**

The streets were littered, terminal, the sun-bleached stucco bungalows having seen better days.

"See all those bottom-feeders over there?"

"Beaner'? I seen 'em. Wetback mofo."

"Makes me sick to look at them. They'll ruin this country one day—completely. There won't be much left of the American Dream at the rate these scavengers are nibbling away at it."

"They don't be different from the ones tryin' to squeeze my number one main homie for all the coin they can get."

"The ones I had working at the haunted house had papers; were above board. Had no idea they were wetbacks. Had to have someone to clean the latrines and mop my floors free of vomit and urine at some of the more effective exhibits."

"Fac' is, ain't never liked no mothafuckin' beaner, me, 'cept bangin' them beaner ho in they tight ass."

"Anyway, that would have been you, just like that: living like a cockroach among cockroaches—if I hadn't decided to help you out."

"I ain't never argued wiff it."

"Just don't ever forget it, either."

"I don't forget nothin'. Plan be to get a tricked-out hog of my own one of these day', me."

Biggs looked at him. "How will you do that? By mugging old women like Betty Lou and her daughter Elizabeth?"

"Was nothin' but chump change I got that time."

"Exactly my point."

"Still gonna get me a pimp ride of my own, one of these day'."

"Try getting a driver's license first."

"License? I can get it, me—if that be what I got to do."

"Why do I even bother?"

Biggs turned right on Vanowen. When they reached Hazeltine Avenue he drove south to Ventura Boulevard, away from Beverly Glen.

Marvin looked at the other man and could not figure out what was going on. They needed to go up Beverly Glen in order to get to the LA side.

"I thought we was going to the VA?"

"We are."

"I don't be gettin' it. You goin' the long way through Hollywood?"

Just then Biggs pulled into the nearest gas station on the north side of the street, cutting off traffic, and doubled back up Ventura Boulevard to Beverly Glen.

"Just making sure we got the FBI tail ditched."

"FBI?"

"That's what I said. FBI."

"They been followin' us? How you figure?"

Biggs said nothing. Not only did he suspect the FBI and IRS to be on his ass, but Meth Mouth and his pissant buddy Felix might be interested in nailing down his routine in order to make a move on his property. Why help them? It paid to be cautious.

He made a left on Beverly Glen Boulevard and took the *Cadillac* over the hill to the Los Angeles side. When they reached Wilshire, he turned right, taking it past Westwood Village. Got on the VA turn-off just beyond the San Diego Freeway. Stayed with it as it curved to the right.

It would have spared him a lot of driving time if he were to allow himself to get transferred to the Valley VA, only he did not wish to go through the hassle of having to get "re-acquainted" with a new "shrink," nor did he want to risk running into Roscoe and other veterans who lived in his neighborhood who might get wind that he was still on meds these days. The less they knew and suspected, the better off he was.

# CHAPTER 34

**It was another sunny, smoggy day in West Los Angeles and the manicured VA Hospital grounds had the appearance of a lush country club initially, but then all that seemed to change drastically as they got closer and closer to the buildings that much too much resembled barren army barracks: gray, lifeless; it all became clinical and foreboding, not unlike the grounds of a mental institution, which in fact, a good deal of it was.**

Passing the barracks-type building, they neared larger three- and four-story edifices, all gray and depressing.

As far as Biggs was concerned, he wanted no part of it. And yet, he had gone this far. . . . He needed the medication.

He pulled the *Cadillac* into the parking lot and sat there, watched doctors and nurses, "attendants" all in white coats, walking about—from one hospital wing to another, from their parked cars in the lot to one of three hospital wings.

He hated the smell of the place (recalled all too well what it represented to him), not that this particular hospital smelled any different from all the others. It made him feel edgy to be around so many cripples and crazies. Being around nurses and doctors (shams, every single one of them), he hated it as much as he hated the rest of it. Made him wonder how he ever ended up as a practical nurse—not that he should have been wondering about any of it.

Not many options had been available to begin with. Had originally been interested in being an MP—and they had turned him down. Military Police? Sorry, they'd said. Not for you. Made him a medic instead. He had gone along with it because he felt it was something he'd be able to do on the outside, once he got out. And the Bordello of Fear? Yes, it had been there for him all along, waiting for him to re-open and make it work. Only he had no real idea that he'd be able to turn it into a successful money-making venture again—as the original owners had. Now that it was, for years had been, certain nefarious forces were out to undermine and destroy all the hard work that had gone into it.

Your take on the hospital and grounds has zippo value these days. You're here, and you need to get out of the car. Only he sat, staring at the main entrance.

"What be the matter, home'?"

"Nothing."

Biggs withdrew the *.357 Magnum* from the shoulder holster to make sure that it was loaded. He stuck the *Magnum* in his right jacket pocket. Biggs liked having it there whenever he visited the VA. It allowed for more immediate access in time of need. One had no way of knowing when an emergency might come knocking. All he had to do was keep his hand in his pocket, fingers wrapped around the *Magnum* butt. That was it. He felt safer this way.

*I won't fuck with them, so long as they don't fuck with me.*

A long-haired 'Nam vet wearing a faded fatigue jacket hobbled out of the main entrance with a cane. Swung at some people with it. Shouted obscenities. He made it to the cab parked at the curb and the cabbie who had hopped out and was opening the passenger side door for him. Instead of getting in, the pissed off vet raised that cane and began to beat the cab driver with it, missing half the time. The vet hit the door and the roof of the taxi once too often, breaking his cane in half as a result. But that didn't stop him. The cabbie was on the ground with his hands defensively over his head and did what he could to roll out of harm's way. Pretty soon three orderlies were running out and were all over the long-haired guy in the fatigue jacket. They had him down on the sidewalk and kept him there.

A fourth orderly, carrying a straitjacket, quickly joined them. They worked on the kicking, raging vet. Got his army jacket off and eventually slipped the restraining canvas garment on him. Strapped him in, nice and snug, and literally carried him back inside the hospital.

Biggs sat there watching. Recalled the way they had done the same to him years before. But he'd had it coming, had fucked up. Hadn't always been smart enough back then to keep his mouth shut, to control his behavior in front of these assholes and others up at Atascadero like them. Initially, that is, and they had thrown him in with the lunatics, the screamers, the lost causes, the hopeless mental defectives so often and for such uncalled-for and painfully long stretches that he didn't want to even think about it.

Christ, he didn't want any part of what had just gone down. Keep your cool when you walk in there, he said to himself. Control is the key. *Control.* Don't attack anyone if you can help it. Don't shoot up the place unless absolutely necessary. Even if they start in on the innuendoes, the slick, sly accusations. Let it slide right off your back, Cecil. Like water off a duck's ass.

That's the ticket.

And then he thought about getting out of there, driving off and forgetting about getting the meds that he needed.

"Yo, Bishop. How about leavin' the sounds on for me while I be sittin' here waitin', Brother?"

"Drains the battery."

Biggs got out, taking the car keys with him.

"No, it don't."

"What's the matter with using your transistor radio?"

"Battery get' run down."

"They're rechargeable."

"Why come everything got to go your way all the time, man? Why you always got to be the one in control?"

"My money pays for everything."

"Why I got to get me some of my own, then. Shit."

Marvin reached down for the *Radio Shack* portable under the seat. Tuned it to something by a rap group. Reception was tinny. It would have to do.

Biggs pocketed the Caddy keys and took that long, slow walk to the hospital entrance, while keeping his right hand inside the fatigue jacket, fingers tightly wound around the gun butt.

# CHAPTER 35

**He'd only been made to wait twenty minutes this time and was shown to a small room by a young guy in a white frock.**

Another Freud idolizer, Biggs concluded, a student of psychology.

They kept giving him these young punks who knew nothing about humans, the human psyche and what made it tick. They gave him these snot-nosed, wet-behind-the-ears know-nothing twerps (male as well as female) who always put him through it by asking the same dumb questions every time and nodded their heads to his pat answers—as if any of it was supposed to amount to anything.

This future Sig Freud had a thick, light brown mustache, dark hair cut short and parted on the side, baby blue eyes that had never known much pain or probably never even been laid or had any inkling how to masturbate for max effect or done anything of any significance.

And they put him through it every time; and he put up with it because he needed the *Elavil.* Biggs recognized the guy's voice now as he spoke. He'd had him before.

"I'll be right with you, Mr. Biggs. Have a seat."

The psychology student left the room. Biggs loosened the grip on his gun. That's okay, he thought. It felt better being alone. Then he wondered where the buzzing was coming from. Inside his head, or somewhere else?

Turned.

Looked at the huge window on his right. Big fly was against the glass, buzzing around. Ascended to the top of the pane, and dove back down again.

Biggs focused in on it. See, proves you can't escape your destiny, your fate. Right there. You dream about them, you think about them; you hear that buzzing all the time and take it with you no matter where you go. Right there. The goddamn flies and jackhammer noise. Why don't these geniuses have something for that? For these flies? Why don't they come up with something that would help me shake the flies?

He got up from the couch and his back seemed to cramp on him. Easy does it, Cecil. Easy does it. He waited. Moved slowly. Rose to his feet and the pain seemed to leave him.

He walked over to the window looking up at the goddamn fly and he wanted to get his hands on it and pull its fucking wings off, catch that ugly, filthy fly and tear its wings off and put it on its back and watch it go crazy, watch it kick desperately with its legs, fight its fate, a fly's fate.

But he couldn't reach it. He was on his toes. Six feet three inches tall, and it was not enough to reach the goddamned fly. Just as he looked around the room for something to pick up and swat the insect with, young Sigmund Freud returned.

Biggs sat back down, the only thing left for him to do—that would not have resulted in dire consequences. He knew it. Knew it well.

*Freudy* was trying to be pleasant and he was smiling. Everything was just fine with Sigmund. No problems, no worries. The world was a swell place. Perhaps not perfect, but that was all right, because Sig Freud was part of the new breed and he and others like him would cure all that ailed.

He held a piece of paper in his hands. The *Elavil* subscription, no doubt.

"You look much better today, Mr. Biggs."

Bullshit, Biggs thought.

"The other day I was hoping the ceiling would come crashing down on me. I was lying in bed, wishing the ceiling would just crash on top of me." He didn't really know why he even bothered to tell any of this to the college kid. Just take the prescription, get the *Elavil,* and hit the road, Cecil.

"Why is that?"

"You're asking *me*?"

"I'm asking *you*, Mr. Biggs."

"You're the 'experts.' You tell me. . . . You tell me why I can't sleep most nights . . . and on the rare occasion that I manage to fall asleep, why is it I hope I don't wake up the next day?"

"It's depression. . . ."

"No shit."

Biggs's hand was back in his pocket, and he had his index finger inside the trigger guard. Although the college guy was not aware of the gun and had no idea what was going on, he was beginning to grow just a bit nervous around Mr. Cecil O. Biggs.

"It will pass. Like it usually does. It's a phase you're going through."

"You don't get it: I'm tired. . . . See no point to any of it. . . . Not only do I loathe this existence, but I loathe the filthy pee-hole I was squeezed out of. . . . This is why none of us could ever be clean or one hundred percent sane and mentally healthy. . . . Look how we're brought into this world: through some whore's dirty twat, some two-bit streetwalker's diseased and gamey snapper. As a species we never stood a chance."

"That's being rather cynical, isn't it?"

"You might call it that. I call it being realistic."

"Like I said: it's temporary."

Biggs's eyes were back on the fly. The buzzing seemed to dominate his attention.

"Sure. I can't expect anything, can I?"

"We can put you back on *Trilafon*. You can be put on both, like before."

Biggs let the fly go for the time being. *Trilafon* was the anti-psychotic drug with rather nasty side effects, more so than *Elavil*. Doctors all over the nation were way too eager to prescribe the deadly meds. The pharmaceutical corporations who manufactured the mind-altering toxins had their hooks into the medical profession, and deep. Everyone was corrupt. There was no one left to trust. They'd damaged him enough as far as he was concerned.

"No, thanks."

The bishop considered committing himself. If he did that, not only would they have him back on *Trilafon*, but possibly shock therapy. As he had learned many times over, shock therapy was far more enjoyable when he was the one doing the administering—*on others*.

"Your *Elavil* subscription has been updated. It should help you get back on track."

It was just as well he'd kept his mouth shut about having psychotic thoughts and/or wanting to commit himself, because just then some zonked out Korean War vet pressed his scarred, demented face up against the glass door, slobbering on it, licking the glass and shouting at the top of his lungs: *"FUCK-YOU! YEAH, YOU BUDDY! POSITIVELY YOU! MOTHERFUCKER!"* The old guy looked at the college kid. *"AND YOU! FUCK EVERY ONE OF YOU! HEAR ME? FUCK YOU ALL! AND FUCK YOUR SISTER, TOO, BUDDY!"*

Two orderlies in white coats moved up from behind to restrain and drag the yeller away, who could still be heard, shouting and making threats. "Fuck you and you and you, too. Your mother sucks mule dick, you hear? Your mama sucks mule pipe, and your daddy takes dog dick in the ass."

The college kid was silent. Waited for Biggs, whose attention was back on the fly up in the corner, to stop watching it and look at him. The guy cleared his throat. Biggs turned away from the fly. Thought how much pleasure it would give him to put two rounds into that nothing, West LA soap opera face. Bang bang. What a sight that would make; what a pretty sight to see all that rosy brain matter spatter all over the white walls and tile floor. Yeah; he would have liked that. One bullet right between the eyes—and watch the back of the twerp's skull explode something like a ripe watermelon or one of Wilburn Flinger's pomegranates. And then a second bullet for good measure. *Coup de grace.*

"Your sex drive. What's the status there?"

Biggs preferred looking at anything but the guy's face. This time he looked right at him. Said nothing.

"If you'd rather not respond . . ."

"The status of my sex drive is that it drives me crazy."

"How's that?"

"*How's that?* Most of the time I can't get enough no matter how much I get, the rest of the time I can't get it up." Scribble that in your file, he thought. Mustache wrote something down. Looked back up.

"Do you have a girlfriend?"

"I have many girlfriends."

"Would you like to talk to a sex therapist?"

"What for?"

The guy nodded. Didn't seem to give a damn one way or the other. Just doing his job. Logging in time. Until the day he would shuck the VA and land a lucrative gig in Beverly Hills, dealing with neurotic showbiz types, or maybe even their rude poodles. Movie people had shrinks that they took their poodles to.

The wannabe head quack wrote something else in his open file. Made Cecil curious, but not curious enough to inquire what exactly the guy was jotting down about him. The pros/the cons. Negative comments he was slamming down against his name and character. Like the time up at Atascadero because he hadn't felt like talking to anyone, he had written on a piece of paper that the devil had stuck a cookie in his throat and he couldn't speak. He had been called a Satan worshipper because of it. Negative comments/observations noted against him. A pile of it. Mountains of it. They kept writing things down and writing things down in that file that was as thick as Betty Lou Rutterschmidt's oversized *Bible.*

"Are you experiencing psychotic thoughts, possibly psychotic episodes?"

Just this: I'm a stalker by nature, Biggs came close to confessing. Predatory, if you will. It's in my blood. In this world you're either *predator* or you're *prey.* I've been both, you see. Predators tend to have a healthier life span, in my humble estimation, and more fun. Then thought better of it. Why reveal things that they would only be obligated to use against you eventually? What sense did that make? If he admitted to any of it they'd be dragging him away the same way they did the loose cannon a moment ago. After all, he was supposed to be cured. More or less.

"I get notions. Not exactly psychotic . . . but out there. . . . Possibly borderline."

"For instance?"

"Like I explained earlier: feelings of inadequacy. There's a hollowness; lethargy. . . ."

"You're depressed."

Some revelation, thought Biggs.

"Define: One in the hand is worth two in the bush."

Not if the two in the bush were dead, thought Biggs. No, the one in the hand wouldn't be worth two in the bush.

"Value what you have over what you don't."

It was too easy. These low IQ buffoons were beyond dumb. Marvin's fancy rats were brighter than this. Had to be. Roscoe's two dogs were sharper than this. And that rabbit: Brenda's pet rabbit, whose name presently escaped him: Belden, Bennett; no, Bentley, was more aware. Well, this was the VA. They had him working here. Wouldn't want to actually hire anyone genuinely brilliant, or even someone who came close. No.

The mind healer was writing something in his file. Looked up, without acknowledging whether he liked his response or not. He had more of the same, however.

"Define: An ounce of prevention is worth a pound of cure." This form of low-grade quizzing was not only an insult to his intelligence, not only pointless and idiotic, but so entirely ridiculous it was laughable. The irony of it was: they were the ones who were supposed to be sane and normal. This here lame performance by the wannabe shrink backed up everything he had believed about them all along: that they were certifiable, and in serious denial.

"Better to be safe than sorry."

The next one, though, damned near caused him to slip up.

"Define: If you bury the hatchet, don't mark the grave."

Cecil bit his tongue. Wanted to say: When you dump a body, make certain that you don't leave traceable evidence. He took his time. Forced himself to. A wrong answer could, possibly, have you back in a straitjacket. One never knew. Freud Jr. waited.


Biggs sighed. Cleared his throat.

"It simply means this: Let bygones be bygones. What's done is done. No point dwelling on the past."

The sissy in white seemed satisfied. Wrote things down. Like I said, thought Biggs: easy to please. So long as you played their game. Although it hadn't taken much to out-think the simple-minded fucker at all. World was full of them. Not much different from Charlotte Yvonne or J.J.

"You'll be fine. Just have to take it easy. . . ."

"Take it easy?" Sure, thought Biggs. I'm thinking of splattering your brains all over your starched white frock right now, and you're telling me to take it easy?

"Easy enough for you to say. . . ."

"Ride it out. It's a phase you're going through, a mild one. You've been there before, according to your file, but you're doing much better these days. What you're experiencing presently is a mild relapse—because you've been off the medication for a while. Once the medication kicks in you should be fine—"

"How long?"

The guy shrugged. "Anywhere from a few days to a couple of weeks."

Biggs didn't like to hear it and his expression showed it.

"Why did you wait to get your prescription refilled?"

"I don't like coming here. Place creeps me out."

"I understand. However, any time you stop taking your meds cold turkey, the way you did—it is going to result in your feeling this way. You are having a bout, experiencing a phase."

How many times did he have to be reminded of it? Skip it. The punk was wet-behind-the-ears. In diapers, practically. Baby powder residue on his ass. Like Olin Goodfellow. Now there was a head case.

"What if I went out and did something that could be construed as psychotic? What would you say, then?"

"For example?"

"Who knows? Just a hypothetical question."

"I understand. How would that get rid of your depression?"

"It might not. Then again: it might alleviate it. Might help me feel better. . . ."

"To do something 'that could be construed as psychotic'?"

"Could be a way to decompress. Pressure builds up, anyone would tell you that much. Life can be a bitch. There's the stress factor: living in a congested hellhole like Southern California." Biggs paused. "It's possible I'm 'out there' for having this perspective on things. . . ."

The psych major's nervousness became more obvious to Cecil, especially now that the guy could not even bring himself to look him in the eye longer than a few brief seconds at a time. The intensity of his black marble eyes bore right through them and they couldn't take it. Too weak, Cecil thought. No balls. Spineless lemmings lacking any sort of intestinal fortitude and/or genuine intelligence. And this guy was going to be another Siggy Freud? Of course.

"Look, you're not 'out there.' However, what you're getting at is starting to sound 'out there.'"

"I don't know. I get this ringing in my ears. . . . Sounds a lot like that fly buzzing around up there. Hear the fly? See it up there in the corner? The buzzing comes and goes. Sometimes it sneaks up in my sleep. . . ."

"Pick up your *Elavil.*" The guy couldn't wait to get rid of him, it seemed. "The depression will lift eventually. Don't do anything foolish. If your condition doesn't improve, come back and see us. That's what we're here for."

He handed him the piece of paper. Left the room. That was it. Cecil remained seated. He stared at the hallway through the open door, at the cripples (mental and otherwise) who walked past.

"I should have put one between your eyes, 'Freud.' Would that have lifted my depression any? It certainly wouldn't have hurt it any."

He was looking at the fly again, and thought: Maybe I could put a bullet between *my* eyes? Why don't I do that instead? Hell, only an asshole takes his own life. Only a dumb fucking jerk/total crazy-ass bastard is going to commit suicide. He wasn't about to start thinking along those lines again. Too much was at stake. He stood to lose all he'd worked for.

Biggs got up. Stepped into the hallway. Picked up his meds at the pharmacy in the other wing, can of soda, and was back out in the sunlight. Walked toward the *Cadillac.*

# CHAPTER 36

**Marvin still had that hip-hop crap playing on his portable radio.**

"Was they cool in there?"

Biggs leaned in through the passenger window and snatched the radio from the other man's grasp. Dropped it. Stomped the life out of it.

"Why, dude?"

"Because I loathe rap."

"Yeah? Ain't no worse than that fuckin' disco you be playin' all the time up at the cribby."

"Only to drown out the bitches' screaming and carrying on."

Biggs got in on the driver's side. Popped a single *Elavil* in his mouth and chased it with a pull from his soda.

"You owe me a boom box, Hoss. I don't be *boo-shittin'*, neither."

Biggs handed what remained of the soda to Marvin to finish off. It was always preferable to hearing him whine about not getting any. Muck drank it down, not at all happy at having had his radio crushed.

Biggs started the engine, not giving a damn one way or the other. Looked at Muck long and hard.

"Who sent you?"

"Who sent me?"

"I asked you a simple question: *Who sent you?*"

"Yo mama did."

"She's dead."

"I know ho be dead."

"Don't ever cross me, Marvin. . . . You ever cross me, it'll be the last time you cross anyone."

On that, Cecil O. drove the big car out of the parking lot. Got on the 405, north. Took it to the 134, and headed east.

# CHAPTER 37

**Rumor had been floating around for weeks now: certain Temple City bureaucrats with a hard-on for him were intent on putting him out of business for good, or at the least eager to shut him down until issues of violence related to the haunted house he owned were resolved to**

**their satisfaction.** Didn't make a bit of difference to the self-serving functionaries that the claims were counterfeit and made by individuals who were in the country illegally.

City left a notice on his front gate: **No Trespassing**. By the order of the office of . . . bla bla bla. In other words: Fuck you, Mr. Small Businessman. Frankly, we don't give a shit that Halloween is, by far, the most lucrative day of the year for the type of business that you're in. Illegals are human beings and they have rights. This is America. Yes, but what about my rights? As an American and a tax payer? You don't rate because your vote is rarely for our side.

He and Marvin had driven up to the Bordello of Fear in the Caddy. The old and quite impressive two story airplane hangar type of structure had been an actual slaughter house at one time. Cecil's long gone benefactor had purchased it just as it had been shut down and was about to be razed and turned into a Texas roadhouse type of joint. A ten foot tall wall surrounded his property. Black: all of it. Hangar and wall and gate. High end security system in evidence: one perched up at the top of the left side of the gate, its brother across the way on its right. Cecil even had cameras way up on the roof, near the large neon likeness of Trusty Lusty grinning his sinister grin, with blood flowing from his fangs and tongue. There it was, bigger than life: Large black neon letters, stating for one and all easy to pick up from a goodly distance: *Trusty Lusty's Bordello of Fear.*

Paid through the nose for the juice. His light bill high enough every month. Was worth it to him. Good for publicity to leave it on. Only what good did it do him when there was a large padlock dangling from the gate? Put there by his detractors. And his detractors were legion. Too many to count.

"You knowed they was gonna shut you down?"

"Suspected as much. Hoped that they had enough sense to let me get through the holiday. Hurts like a bitch to have to give up this kind of revenue."

"Pepper belly done it," said Marvin. "Tryin' real hard to shake my brother down." Biggs got out of the Caddy and walked up to the handful of people waiting there: concerned and bewildered. His employees. He apologized.

"No one had given me a heads-up, either. Been threatening to shut us down for weeks now. Didn't think they could be so mercenary as to actually put working people out of work like this."

"When do we open, Mr. Biggs?" One of the Hispanic-American males asked.

"As soon as I get word, Mr. Tampico, I'll let all of you know. I realize how much you depend on what you earn here. Paying off bills and putting food on the table only gets tougher in this what used to be a great nation. You can thank all the Marxist/socialist slime for being behind it. Liberals."

Contessa Arroyo and her significant other Prospero, felt a need to let him know how much they were going to miss that evening's tips and all the other weekends they wouldn't be open and making money. They had two young mouths to feed.

"This is still America," said Biggs. "No one is going to starve, not a single one of you will have to worry about going hungry, not if I can help it." He promised to have a bucket of the best jambalaya his chef Greta can make delivered first thing the next day to anyone interested. "How's that sound? And I don't mean only tomorrow, either, folks, or the next day. You have a difficult time scraping enough funds to buy groceries, you let me know. From now on until we re-open—and I guarantee you, we will re-open. I don't quit. Cecil Biggs never quits—on anything he starts. Bordello of Fear means everything to me."

"Me and my missus just might take you up on your offer, kind sir," said Yaphet Pound, an African-American, who was a jack-of-many trades at the haunted house for Cecil before this disappointing last act. "Sho is kind of you, Mr. Biggs," said Cheyenne Pound, the man's lady.

Marvin Muck felt it was his duty to chime in: "That jambalaya gonna make yo kids grow up to be big and strong; no shit, Contessa."

"Thank you again, Mr. Biggs. We are grateful for everything you have done for us and our family."

His employees walked off to their cars.

"Fuck it," said Biggs. "Might as well go and check in on the peelers."

"You sayin' you be bothered what jus' went down wiff the peeps, homes?"

"Yes. Why wouldn't I be? They're hard working Americans; and not out there with a sign that says; give me your hard-earned cash so I can go out and buy my crack and rotgut"

"Like them illegal trying to shake my boy Trusty down."

"Took the words out of my mouth."

"Did, didn't I?"

# CHAPTER 38

**Autographed eight-by-ten glossies were nice to have of potential victims you wanted to have your fun with, but hardly equalled looking at the genuine article up close.**

It was another lower-middle income North Hollywood neighborhood no more than a couple of miles from Cecil's own place that he and Marvin cruised later that night.

Biggs made a slow turn into a poorly lighted alley, killed his headlights, and had the *Cadillac* crawling past overfilled trash cans and dumpsters, gutted sofas and easy chairs, rusted bicycle frames without wheels, unusable car doors, charred box springs, and mattresses. Biggs was in his sinister clown guise, while Muck wore—far from willingly—one of those repulsive pig masks that smelled as nasty as it looked.

Fighting frustration as well as a need for a shot of nicotine, Marvin stuck an unlit cigarette in one of the pig nostrils.

"You trying to be funny?"

"I ain't tryin' to be nothin', me. You the one be playin' Trusty the Clown."

A single glare from Cecil O. was all it took for Muck to withdraw the cigarette from the pig nose and put it away.

The *Fleetwood Brougham* crept along until Biggs recognized the graffiti on a garage door and stopped the car. He killed the engine and both got out. They walked past another garage. Went through a flimsy wooden gate that Marvin absentmindedly allowed to bang shut, not that the resulting sound had been all that loud (considering the Mexican music that could be heard playing on various radios and stereo systems: *Los Lobos* came from one source, as did Freddy Fender from somewhere else in the distance); it still did not sit right with the bishop, who froze up and gave the other man a look that warned him to be more careful.

# CHAPTER 39

**They walked down the gangway.** Past scattered Frisbees, plastic, dairy product lids and containers, soda bottles and beer cans, toy trucks. Reached a three-story, salmon-tinted stucco residential building. The lights were on in most of the apartments on all three floors. The only floor Biggs and his flunky were interested in was the ground floor.

They crept up to the window near the back. Ducked their heads. Moved up against the cracked stucco under the window sill and inched their noses up high enough to be able to peek in on Amazonian Pearleen Bell, whose autographed B&W eight-by-ten glossy likeness or two adorned rarified wall space in the bishop's bedroom, as did many other pics he had cut out of various smut mags he had of her doing things with a vibrator or dildo: inserting one or the other in her luscious cunt, while inserting something into her even more luscious and sacred asshole. He had a video of her spreading soap suds across a *Corvette* windshield in a tight wet T that was nothing more than a strip of fabric across the front barely wide enough to conceal the thick, ripe nipples and jean cutoffs so brief they readily revealed snatches of moist cunt and glistening cunt hair and even allowed a treasured peek at that sweet spot known as "brown-eye." Butt-hole. Ass and butt-hole to die for.

She did these vids as *Afrodesia DeLyte.* Forty-four-inch tits packed into a 38 EE bra. Killer. Flat waist. Twenty-nine or thirty inches.

Then you had the ass: thirty-eight inches, maybe forty. Depended. Didn't matter. Woman weighed 154 pounds (give or take). To his liking. No skeletal skank here. Tits were full and round. Thick. No flab. Tits that sagged and were flabby repulsed him. She had double *Es. Thirty-eight, double Es.* Afrodesia DeLyte. Was better known to fans of her sizzling hot strip act as *Peaches LaBelle. LaBelle of da Ball.* Bitch had it. Shy one quarter of an inch, maybe two quarters of an inch, tops, of six feet. One-hundred-fifty-plus-pound *fuck machine.* Whore extraordinaire. Close enough to touch. Only no touching allowed.

The pink T-shirt she had on could not in any way conceal the abundance of tit flesh, nor the flat waist that accentuated it.

Some had it; some had way too much. He thought about plunging an ice pick into her neck so that blood sprayed him while he drilled her with his cock. Then, for the encore, spinning her around and spraying heavy scrotum nectar down her throat . . . and smashing her face and brains in with brass knucks for the *coup de grace.*

What dreams were made of. About the extent of it. Stop wishing. Make it happen, instead.

Rest of her was in black silk panties, black garter-belt, black fishnets and spike heels, as she sat at her sewing machine adding a finishing touch or two to a gold lamé cape that she planned on wearing at some point in her act.

Gold lamé, thought Biggs, for a teasing high yellow cunt with golden skin. That glowed. She moved (or breathed) ever-so-slightly/lightly, and the awesome tits moved with her—every time. How was it possible? It happened. They were heavy evidently enough, but she seemed to be able to handle the poundage. Big and fuckable. He ached to bury his tongue and nose deep in her butt crack.

He looked up at the wrought iron bars over the window. How tough would it be to get them off? Yank them off? Pry them off?—and how fast would they be able to do it—and jump in there before the bitch had a chance to start wailing and raising all kinds of hell and screaming rape?

Forget it. Drop the crazy notion before they drop a straitjacket over your dented head and give you a one-way ride back to the House of Psychos.

# CHAPTER 40

**Biggs and Marvin did the only thing they could do: watched as the stripper paused to go over to the dresser where she had a turntable sitting on top.** Flipped the record over. *Al Green. So tired of being alone. . .* She cranked up the volume. Reached inside her purse for a cocaine vial. Snorted. One nostril, then the other. Proceeded to return the vial to her purse and a small caliber pistol dropped out.

Probably *.25 auto*, thought Cecil. Six round mag. One in the chamber. It was good to know. He filed it away. You expected a tough cunt like her to be packing. Keeping one in the chamber was not always the smartest thing to do. Give her the benefit of the doubt. Assume she had one in the chamber—to make it seven caps.

Both men stared in awe as she bent over to pick the gun up off the carpet. Couldn't quite reach it; her hangers nearly flopped right out of the top of her T and a good portion of her well-shaped behind hung out all over those bikini briefs.

Marvin was transfixed. Only problem was: fuckin' Parfrey pig mask got in the way wiff what he was tryin' to get a better look at. Grabbed it from the bottom, and yanked back on it so that it sat up there on his forehead. Didn't give a damn if Cecil liked it or not. Bitch had her some fine pussy a dude be willin' to die for just to get him a taste.

He ogled. Could not believe his eyes. As often as they had seen this crack ho—on stage and right here showin' off half-naked in this cribby like she be doin'—an' the time' her and her crack-addict friend' been to Bigg' church, he found it hard to accept any hot ho could have a backyard like that.

Ho like' to pose, too. Bendin' over like she do at that ugly nigga Fritz McCoy' Casbah Hideaway. Yeah, thought Marvin, we seen Peach bend over and do a whole lot more. Reason they was actin' like they never seen it before was because the ho be able to do that to peeps.

Peach ain't got no rep for puttin' out, got no rep for gettin' down wiff them customer' at her work. She know' how to get they meat up when she be on stage, though; know' how to take over and make every swingin' dick in the place cry for pussy.

Some of them bitches, too, be hot for that high yellow booty.

Biggs rubbed himself. Wanted her. Felt like rushing in there with his *Magnum* and smacking her in the face with it to make her docile and then taking her right there on the carpet and having some fun. Maybe slitting her throat afterwards, instead of plunging an ice pick in her. Better yet, slitting her throat while he fucked her and seeing the blood spurt. But he would have to wait. Bide his time. And it would happen.

You don't want to end up back in the loony bin with all those loonies in there, because then you will never get anywhere at all, because then it will simply be beyond your reach. This way there's hope at least, but you have to work things out first. And it will pay off for you. Then, too, he risked losing the haunted house for good if he got taken away again. Had a management company run it last time he was gone. Assholes charged high rates and skimmed off the top, every time. Burned him good. Took advantage. Not much he could do about it. Did he want to go through that again? No, he did not want to go through that again.

# CHAPTER 41

**He nudged Marvin in the ribs to pull the mask back down, and they moved over to the next window and Pearleen Bell's roommate Lana "Da Bottom" Sepulveda, another stripper who worked the same club.** Lana Da Bottom was the same age, a long-haired Mexican-American dusky diva. She was five foot eight, and although her bosom was not as impressive as Pearleen's, she had plenty that men were always lusting after; and she had all the rest: flat stomach and curvy hips, a firm, well-shaped *culo*. Lana was known as *"Da Bottom"* for a reason, and she had great legs, muscular, dancer's legs.

It had been months since the girls (along with Stella, whose room was to the right of this one) had performed their private little dance routine at his house, months. Too long.

They were way overdue for another visit, Cecil thought, as he and Muck peered through the stripper's curtains while she sat on the edge of her bed in a white terrycloth bathrobe that barely concealed her glorious thighs and muff as she applied blood-red polish to her toenails.

A couple engaged in *flagrante* in the room next to this one could clearly be heard not only by Lana Da Bottom, who did not react in any noticeable way to it presently, but by the bishop and his deacon—and so drawn, they moved on to that window sill.

Had to be henna-haired Stella Martel, known in porn circles and the strip club circuit as *Stunning* Stella Storm; sure, why not?—who changed her hair color from week to week, it seemed. Last time they saw her parading her snapper on McCoy's stage and humping the brass pole, her hair had been reddish-brown, week before that it was vagina pink, two weeks prior to that it had been electric blue. So who knew what it was lately—furthermore, who gave a damn, so long as they glimpsed that body. Only there didn't seem to be any chance there, because Stella was under the sheet (for the most part) with some guy; and she was screaming, moaning, tossing that same reddish-brown head of hair from side to side in an almost exaggerated way, evidently due to what the asshole down there between her thighs was doing to her with his able tongue.

The peepers watched with bated breath. Didn't matter to them if she were acting it or not, didn't matter if the jerk-off with her was just another john and paying for his pussy. Instead, what bothered them, what was frustrating as hell for them was that they could not see enough of what was exactly taking place.

Was all the gasping and writhing on Stella's part nothing more than practiced fakery? Probably—not that it mattered, because it worked away on them, got to them; it was too much to bear. Bitch was a convincing faker; they all were. Practice made perfect.

The Peeping Toms returned to Da Bottom's window in time to see her react to the hot sex going on in Stella's room by grabbing a foot-long vibrator from her dresser drawer, plopping back on her bed and gradually guiding it down toward the dark patch of hair between her thighs.

There was no mistaking the steady hum made by the vibrator, in spite of the noise coming from Stella's place, as the brunette seemed to hold it against the roof of her cunt. Problem was, most of this could only be guessed at by the peeping duo, as quite a bit of the action was blocked by Lana's thigh, as she had her leg bent in an upside down V. Still, it was clearly obvious what had taken place next: they knew she was inserting it into her moist cunt, giving her cooter a nice workout, probably shifting it up toward the clit and leaving it there for the needed duration, massaging it where it mattered the most.

Bitch was getting off, fucking her own pussy, as only a woman knew how to do—well, most women; with most of them it was like this, unless the guy had the patience to spend the time and tongue a ho in this laborious manner.

Didn't matter to him what a bitch wanted. Not at all. Only thing Biggs was ever concerned with was that he got his—any way he could.

Get yours, to the utmost—and then dispose of them, like a sack of garbage. Because, when you came down to it, that's what whores were: sacks of trash. Sluts, bitches, bimbos, prostitutes, ball-busting, useless sperm receptacles. And this particular sperm-receptacle's moans were beginning to increase in volume. You bet; not unlike Stella Martel's next window over.

Da Bottom had her head arched back, her neck was up, sticking out this way; even her shoulders were up, off the bed. The sounds she made were undecipherable. There was a bit of everything thrown in: gasps, sighs, moans, screams; deep-throated something or other. Only thing that mattered, that was evident: bitch was erupting like a volcano. Over and over and over again.

Marvin gripped the wrought iron bars on the window. Yanked like a wild man. This was too much. He was desperate to pull the bars off, if at all possible, jump inside the room, leap on top of the stripper and give her the ride of her life.

In his mind, what that vibrator was doin' for her was nothing compared to the way he could get her off. Vibrators ain't shit, thought Marvin. Ain't nothin' but a mothafuckin' fake Jones. What the ho be needin' is a real man with a real dick—right in her. What he would do is shove that vibrator up her shitter, while he fucked the shit out of her cunt. Yo. Ho be needin' man meat. What I got.

He kept gripping the bars and was, no doubt, about to do something about it. Biggs saw it, understood it, easily related to it, but shoved Muck back, away from the window in time to restrain him and stop him from attempting something that would have got them not only noticed, but bagged and thrown in jail.

"We have to wait, Free Ride. It's just a matter of time."

"Fuck on that waitin' boo-shit. I be tired of waitin'. My Jones can't wait. My Jones be wantin' some trim right now."

"Settle down."

Marvin cursed under his breath. "Them hoe' needs to be raped. They be wantin' it. You know them hoe' be rape deprive'. Lookit that shit. Look what they be doin'. They know we out here watchin'. You know they knows it. Makin' all that noise and actin' like don't nobody know' about it."

Biggs aimed his index finger at him. Pointed it right in his face. Laid down the riot act: *Calm down, or else.* Marvin had no choice. Nodded his head. He gripped his groin inside his trousers: stiff. Like that big, black flashlight Bigg' own—an' like' to beat the retard' wiff.

# CHAPTER 42

**They were back at the window, watching in contained silence, as both Stella and Lana's moans grew more frantic.**

There was no disagreeing with Marvin: Biggs had wanted to bust in on the bitches as much as Marvin had, bust in on them the way Richard Speck had done years ago in Chicago; tie all of them up. Butcher the lame john, then rape and sodomize the whores; stab them a few million times, slit their throats—and leave them to stew in their own juice.

*Yes yes yes.* Let them stew in their own blood and excreta.

He'd wanted it; he'd ached for it. Only now was not the time.

"We don't want to wake up the neighborhood by doing something stupid—and to break in on these cunts here would definitely set them off screaming and firing that gun. I know these loud-mouthed sperm-guzzlers, believe you me. That certainly would be a stupid thing for us to do."

Both women emitted what sounded like loud, yelping sounds, followed by sounds you could not hear: subdued, nearly silent. When this happened, Lana's body had arched one final time, stiffened; she stayed this way for one lingering moment, then dramatically went limp. She had kept her eyes closed for this last, precious phase of it.

The following happened, just as Biggs expected it would: his Caddy alarm went off. Made him wonder what took them this long.

He withdrew the pepper spray from the holder on his belt. Handed it to Marvin. They stepped away from the window and walked in the direction of the alley in back. Biggs paused as they reached the gate. Held the clicker out. Marvin took it. Didn't quite get why.

"Ain't you goin' after the mofo wiff yo piece?"

"Don't be stupid. Go kill the alarm instead."

Marvin didn't exactly understand what was going on, but went ahead. The car alarm stopped wailing at last. Biggs remained standing by the side of the gate, peering at the other end of the gangway—as familiar-sounding footsteps approached from the front of the building.

The silhouettes were easy to make out and proved him right: ex-con junkie "Glassy" and his bosom bud, sometime *Pachuko*, Felix Monk.

The fools skulked down the gangway to about Pearleen Bell's window. Lingered there. Figures. Desperate for drugs. Looking for trouble. Deliberately tripped his alarm as a distraction and to help persuade him to vacate the area.

Muck was back at the gate. Asked who he thought could've been messin' wiff the *Cadillac*. Biggs's chin-gestured in the zeroes' direction.

"Kick they ass, then. Take 'em out. You packin'. Yo."

"If they want the window, they can have it."

Biggs had no use for a confrontation. Felt like paying the former cheerleader a visit anyway, before she turned in for the night. Then afterwards it would be on to the Bordello of Fear and seeing to it that everything was copacetic over there. Then what? Time permitting, they'd probably take a drive over to the *CASBAH HIDEAWAY* to catch the pole dancers to their thing. After all, it was Halloween. For a good month now, the owner of the venue had been promising his customers one hell of a show come Halloween night. Well, this was it. Time had come. Something told Biggs this particular show was not to be missed. Fact was, Peach LaBelle was great no matter what night of the week she was on, but for this particular night, Biggs knew the second-to-none prick-teaser would go out of her way to make the males in the audience cream in their panties; hoes, too.

The bishop and his deacon walked to the *Cadillac,* and drove off as unobtrusively as they had pulled up.

# CHAPTER 43

**Ruse worked.** Every time. Footsteps grew louder, sloppier. Jesus "Ace" Ortiz and his co-conspirator Felix Monk walked up to Pearleen Bell's window.

Ace was the emaciated one with the crude prison tats up and down both sides of his neck. Various x-ed names of various ex-girlfriends made up some of those tats: Luz, Rosa, Blanca. Had a runny nose and bright blue left eye made of glass. The good eye was dark brown. The junkie was in his late thirties. Appeared closer to sixty. Due to heavy and constant use of meth in the past was missing teeth in the front: two upper, one lower. Off crank lately. Swore he'd never use again. Couldn't afford to lose what remained of his rotting choppers. Besides, his drug of choice was scag. He'd tried just about anything and everything he could get his hands on that would get him high, leave his brain buzzing and on fire: E, LSD, PCP, weed, model glue, crank, crack, booze. You name it, he'd been on it.

But yes, it came down to bump and junk, preferably the latter.

Ortiz was due for a bath these days. Hadn't had a shower in weeks, maybe a month or so. Haircut. He'd been wearing the same threadbare shirt and pants for months. Not that there was never coin to clean up and buy skins, get his ears lowered. Money came his way through all sorts of scams and rip-offs, break-ins—but it was squandered on dope and booze, getting that jolt, losing himself in it. Nothing beat a good hit off of some fly shit. Best thing about being above ground.

The twenty-two-year-old quasi *pachuko* with Ortiz was one Felix Jose Monk. In draped khakis, white T-shirt and stretch belt. Had on his feet canvas boat shoes decorated with neighborhood initials for *Varrio Nuevo Chumino.* His head gear consisted of a red bandana, tied low, to practically below the brows, and dark shades.

Did some time for petty offenses over the years: like trying to break into a pay phone, attempting to haul off a bubblegum machine from a hoagie joint in broad daylight during store hours, mistaking a sperm bank for a blood bank and breaking in to steal *Kool-Aid* and cookies; boosting chrome wheels and car stereos. Felix did not do nearly as much dope as Ortiz (would never mainline anything or huff glue) but wouldn't turn down a joint or a snort of blow, if and when available.


What really cracked Meth Mouth up about Felix right now was that slick and shiny little shopping bag with the fancy Beverly Hills logo on it that Felix got his hands on by breaking into a Mercedes out there in Encino earlier and was now carrying like a trick-or-treatin' little mothafuckah. Had some candy in it to make it look real: *Gummi Bears, M&Ms, Toostie Rolls, Kit Kat bars* and *Candy Corn.*

"Halloween night," he had claimed. "Looks better, don't it? Gives me a legit reason to go knockin on the ho's door."

"Huh?"

"*Trick or Treat*, man."

"Like Finger Lickin' Flinger."

"No way, dude. Like me."

Meth Mouth reached inside his friend's hoity-toity shopping bag and grabbed a fistful of mini Reese's peanut butter cups.

"What the fuck, homes? Need the candy to make it look like I'm on the level over here."

"Gotta eat somethin' sometime', less I pass out."

Meth Mouth jammed the goodies in his shirt pocket. Raised the paper sack in his hands (the bottom of which was lined with something a whole lot more potent than candy) to his mouth. Saw to it he had the opening pressed tightly round his lips and nose. Cupped it this way, using both hands—and proceeded to huff. Held it. And held it. Huffed again. Some more. Couldn't get enough.

Felix glanced at him. Shook his head. His boy "Glassy" was about to fry his brains some more with the fuckin' model glue. Let him. His life. Monk was busy eyeing Peaches LaBelle. Christ, *chucha* was unbelievable. Ace was watching, too, now, as Peaches reached for the vial in her purse. This was what Meth Mouth was after. Made him wonder how much toot and crack the bitch actually had hidden away in her place. These exotic stripper *prostituta* types made great bank showing off their *culo*, and spent most of what they earned on getting high, or else they had other ways to pull in the bucks: traded sex for drugs. They had ways, they always had ways, long as they was willing to suck dick or spread them knees. Lots of 'em did hardcore porn. Six hundred bucks per scene (or better, way better—when they did gang-bangs and anal).

Easy money. *Putas* had ways. When guys like him and Felix had to work their fingers to the bone for the crumbs they usually ended up with.

Ace found himself cursing through clenched teeth, out of frustration more than anything. On top of all that, he felt it coming on: bowel movement. Last thing he needed or wanted to have to deal with. Only hoped he could control it long enough to get what they had come for and that he didn't crap his pants. Sometimes it happened. It happened too often. Motherfuck. It was the junk. He was sick. Glue was okay, and that's all it was. Did the trick. Kept the monkey under control for a while, and if not entirely satisfied, at least calmed the fucker down some.

He had the sniff, sniffles. Wiped his nose on his sleeve. Nudged Felix. Offered the glue. Felix shook his head. Unable to take his eyes off the peeler. What he wanted right about now couldn't be found inside a paper sack.

"Fuckin' deadbeat. What do you want? *Wicky stick?* Ain't got no *wicky stick.*"

Felix didn't care what he was called. Kept eyeing the black goddess as she held the gold lamé cape she had been working on at the sewing machine. Pearleen had the cape just above that enormous bosom. Stood in front of the full-length mirror hanging from the closet door to get some idea how it would look on her, how and if to what extent it favored her figure. She knew that it would. Was a definite plus. But every woman needed all the assurance she could get, and now she was there.

She swayed her hips, ever so slightly, from side-to-side to the loud soul music playin'. *I just want to get next to you. . . .* Sounded like that Green dude. What was his name? Went from bein' a pop star to bein' some kind of preacher down there in the South.

She stuck her behind out. Then thrust her pelvis forward, simulating the sex act—and she did it again and again, grinding it to the max, as she knew this is what drew the male customers wild, and enough women, too.

# CHAPTER 44

**Felix Monk was beside himself.** Desperate for it. He also knew he would never get any, not with Peaches LaBelle. Woman was one of the untouchables. It drove him nuts with desire, nearly pissing him off. Here was a chick who stripped for a living, took her clothes off in front of peeps, got them all horny and shit, excited, had them creaming in their pants practically, and she wouldn't have sex with them. Well, unless. Depended. You had to be rich. Money and cars.

Rumor had it she did one hardcore flick years before. Was under age. Hadn't turned eighteen yet. Used fake ID. Hardcore. Video. Sucking and fucking. Money shot in her face. Peaches LaBelle. *The Untouchable.*

Nobody knew for sure. Flick was banned. Disappeared. *Chocha* was a "minor" at the time; underage. Illegal—and so was her movie.

Yeah, they all did it. Put out for cash. Why a regular guy could hardly get him some. Had to resort to peepin'. Peepin' was a crime. So was having to go without pussy. At least it should be. Yeah, make them *putas* give you pussy when you needed some. The way it ought to be, as far as he saw it. Never even heard of nobody getting any with Peaches LaBelle; no regular dude, anyway. Except maybe that one rich dude, the porn studio owner she'd dated that time a while back, but nothing since, and it didn't make any sense to him. Didn't figure. How could somebody be so full of sex— she was sex, built to fuck, built to be licked and eaten and screwed—and yet you couldn't get near her.

Ace punched him on the shoulder. He could care less about Peaches LaBelle and her body. Yeah, she looked all right, but so did a whole bunch of other cooters out there, so what?

"You fucked one you fucked 'em all," Ace said under his breath. "Who gives a shit? Pussy is pussy is pussy. You seen one *chocha* you seen them all, man. Yeah, she got curves all right. Nice tits and ass, long legs. Good enough to eat. Probably tastes better than a *Snickers* candy bar. Fact is, you licked one snapper you licked all of 'em. Seen one, seen the rest. Pee-hole and asshole and a mind just as fucked as everybody else."

"Keep it down, man."

"Fuck you. We come here with a plan—and it's time to push on that plan, Felix my man, before I shit my pants—and quit lookin' at all that beaver and *culo* like you ain't never seen it before, like you ain't never had any. I know you ain't no cherry—or am I wrong?"

"Get off it, Ace."

Felix kept his peepers on the gorgeous high yellow. Sure is tall, he thought, tall and beautiful, one of the most beautiful women his eyes had ever seen; and he had never gone for them black women, neither, but this one was something else. She coulda been Miss America, he thought, if she wanted to be.

Ace punched his shoulder for the second time. Got his homie's attention and dropped a plastic bag full of rings and bracelets, couple of ladies' watches into his fancy bag. It was cheap stuff, for the most part, but it was enough for the diversion. The good stuff, *quality merch* they had gotten from robbing graves, breaking into funeral parlors and ripping off stiffs (and any other way they could get their hands on gold) was kept to be sold to people in the neighborhood for jack. These here strippers seldom had any real bread, not that they didn't make any—they made a pile in tips and doing videos, but most was spent on crack, rent, shoes; some on clothes.

Ortiz pointed at the cheapjack jewelry items in his homie's shopping bag, then shoved him in the direction of the front of the building and go knock on the door to the bitches' apartment. Meanwhile, Ace wasted no time going to work with the chisel in his hand, jabbing away at the brittle stucco, forcing chunks of the stuff to break off, and eventually loosening the wrought iron bars just below the window sill and hoped that soul crap she had goin' on the record player disguised enough of it.

# CHAPTER 45

**Pretty soon Monk could be heard knocking on the apartment door.** Ortiz saw Peaches put on a long robe, grab a handful of mini candy bars, plus a couple of passes to her show for later that evening. She also held a dollar or two in her fist. Okay, so she don't be a total heartless bitch; not one hundred percent, anyway, like the rest of 'em. Porn hoes was cold-blooded. No fuckin' heart, or else if they had 'em a heart it was made of cast iron. Known for it. And the minute she walked across her room and stepped into the hallway to answer the door across it, Ortiz gripped the bars, and with all his body weight behind it, began to yank and twist this way and that, back and forth, until eventually the bolts on top gave and he was able to free the whole thing up.

Ortiz saw the ho drop the candy in his buddy Felix's trick-or- treat bag, then offer him the paper money. Heard her say: "You hungry?"

Then his asshole homie came back with: *"Not for food."* And lost out on the dollars. Right there. Mothafuckah ain't never gonna learn: hoes like her don't ever give up that pussy when you acted like a wuss. Got to be a man; show balls. Confidence. Like you got the world by the balls, even if you didn't. Had to act it; all of them got by this way. All of them showbiz turds got by this way. Faked it. Every day; every time. *Fake it 'till you make it.* What was the use? Felix was a born loser. Look at him. Just look at 'im. Enough to make a grown man weep. If he, Ace, acted like that he never woulda got any pee hole, ever. None. Gotta act like you don't give a shit if you never got any. All the time. Indifferent to it. Like pussy was the last thing on your pussy-hungry mind.

It drove Ortiz crazy, seein' what was taking place. Homie was doing his best to endear himself to the black stripper now, which was a waste of fuckin' time. That shit don't play with a hot ho like Peachy. Then, finally, his bud got down to showin' her the other items in his shiny shopping bag, doing his best at last to keep her occupied, to keep her attention solely on him and the worthless trinkets he had for sale.

That's it, Felix, Ortiz thought. Gimme time. Only fool still had his shades on and that do-rag over his eyes. Take the shades off, *pendejo.* Raise the do-rag some. It don't matter that's it Halloween, man. *Chochas* gotta see who they're talking to. *Fool had his mind on how to cop a feel, when he should be concentrating on how to cop blow.*

Finally took the dark shades off.

"Was about to give you a couple of bucks to go buy yourself somethin' to eat," Ace heard her say. "But you tryin' to sell this cheap shit to me ain't nothin' but an insult. You ain't never goin' to get anywhere this way, don't you know that? That worthless crap there ain't even good enough to be flushed away down my toilet, 'cause all it would do is jam up the works and cost us plenty to call the plumber up."

"Miss Peach, still open to acceptin' the paper money."

"You got nerve; all of you immature wannabe petty thugs got nerve."

"It was offered, Miss Pearleen."

"Now it ain't."

All I need is some time, homeboy, thought Ace. And crawled in through the window as quietly as he knew how. He could see Peaches, arms akimbo, shaking her head. She didn't appear to be remotely interested in what Monk was sheepishly offering. Had no time for him or his lame bullshit.

*Keep her busy*, Ortiz said to himself, while praying to *Jesus Cristo* that he didn't take a dump in his boxers. *Show her the other shit I gave you. The better shit. Anything, but keep her busy. I'm so close now.*

He could swear Felix was blushing, showing his nerves. All caused by the high yellow's looks. Only Ace Ortiz didn't give a damn about any of that.

*Forget her culo, man. Don't fall apart on me now, simple mothafuckah.*

# CHAPTER 46

**Ortiz advanced another two feet.** But progress, true progress, was close to impossible since Peaches was standing sideways now and he was worried about her peripheral vision. Not only that, he could hear Felix babbling about how he thought she was the most beautiful exotic dancer he'd ever known. Period. Ever. Black, white, Chinese. She had them all beat. And if he had the money he'd never miss a single show.

*Knock it off, fool*, Ortiz thought. She gets that line twenty thousand times a day. Let her see something else. Broads like jewelry. Give her jewelry. Monk was dumb enough to ask for a date. Practically begging. Stupid asshole.

Ortiz could hear the woman turn his buddy down cold, the same way she had turned the homie down in the past—by telling him she was busy.

"You're always busy."

"You're right."

"And popular."

"Better than the other."

"Wouldn't know," said Felix.

Monk showed her some of the other items he had. She shook her head impatiently. Who knew where the items came from. Woman wanted nothing to do with any of it. Been around.

"Would your roommates be interested?"

Peaches said she didn't think so.

Ortiz was sweating. Undecided. He was well aware if he didn't get to the purse before she did that it could be all she wrote. If La Belle of the Ball got to her gun before he did that she would not hesitate to use it. Then he wondered if it made any difference to him? All you got to do is get that toot, Ace. That's what you're here for.

He rose to his hands and knees. Made a sudden, clumsy dash for the purse. Only Peaches proved far quicker than the wasted junkie in leaping back inside her room and getting her hands on the *Sterling .25 automatic.*

The shots she fired at the spinning, fleeing Ace Ortiz seemed to coincide with gas emissions, if not equally as loud, close enough, that emanated from Ace's rear end.

He dove for the open window, losing control of his bowels at this precise moment. There was nothing to be done, as the excreta ran down both legs inside his trousers. What angered Ortiz was not so much the accident in his pants, but the fact he hadn't been able to get his hands on the bitch's purse.

Peaches, having lost the one, spun to face the other. Squeezed off a shot at Felix Monk, who scrambled for cover. Rolled out the door and disappeared into the night.

*"Lowlife motherfuckers. You don't ever fuck with Pearleen Bell."*

Pearleen's roommates, including the guy with Stella, ran out of their respective rooms to see what was going on.

"*Ace,*" hissed Peachy. "*Dirty, one-eyed bastard.*"

# CHAPTER 47

**If the stacked and exotic-looking eighteen-year-old former high school cheerleader, Olivia Duarte, looked fantastic in her cheerleading outfit in all those blowups on Biggs's dresser mirror and walls, she looked even more so now sitting on the edge of her bed in her pink teddy talking on the phone to her boyfriend Rudy Perez, whose picture she had her wallet open to.** Two years older than Olivia, Rudy Perez was a handsome hunk with dark eyes and hair—and possessed a zest and a kind of flair about him that Cecil Biggs knew he lacked to draw someone like Olivia Duarte to him—without resorting to his usual means—and he despised the Perez kid for it. His resentment went deep enough to foster images of Cecil, in his Trusty face and cleaver in hand, going at the kid, who was full of life, until all life had left him—as he watched the scene transpire through his night vision glasses from a backyard garage roof to the left of the Duarte family domicile. He and Marvin were lying on their bellies, taking it in.

Muck kept asking to use the binoculars so that he'd have an excuse to take the mask off for a while, and Cecil kept telling him to forget it. But then Muck would yank back the lower half in order to catch some fresh air and Biggs would tell him to pull the goddamned thing back down over his face.

Liv Duarte was certainly another one of those stunning prick-teasers that Biggs could never get enough of. She had it without trying. She had it—and someone else, that punk Perez (more than likely) was going to put his pecker in it one day. Envy ate away at him. He was kicking himself for not having abducted her that time he broke into her room. He had molested her in her sleep, massaged and licked her pussy, even finger-fucked her, although not to the extent that her hymen was ruptured. Left her a virgin. Filched undergarments, the cheerleading skirt.

Her room had been on the first floor back then, in the rear. Now she was on this second floor and those windows down there had bars on them.

Too many homes in this part of the Valley had barred windows these days. What were you going to do? Citizenry had to protect itself against home invasions. Who could blame them? He had installed bars on the windows of his own church for this same reason, had he not?

Biggs eased the binoculars away from her for a moment to take in parts of the room, the framed family photos on the end table, more on her neat white dresser, photos of her taken during her cheerleading days as well as during the two seasons she had spent playing right field on the high school softball team (two seasons of outdoor workouts and games that Cecil Biggs seldom missed).

There were photos of Mr. and Mrs. Duarte, Olivia's three sisters, and a sixteen-year-old brother named Carlos. There were other photos of birthday parties and Christmases, photos taken when she was a little girl hugging a fluffy stuffed animal or doll. Those same stuffed animals and dolls were in evidence throughout the room where everything was in its proper place—all so very neat and meticulous.

Biggs was amused by it. The urge was never far away, the impulse to destroy anything that reminded him of what he never had as a youngster, that reminded him of a stolen childhood fraught with pain and misery.

"A very tidy and bright young lady. . . . Four years, baby. Four years of waiting and fantasizing. Four long years. . . ."

"Four year' too long, if you aks me."

"Keep your voice down."

Cecil reminded him that sound carried easier as well as further at night. Made no sense to let her become aware of their whereabouts and hear them, the way they were able to hear what she was saying to the punk on the phone.

"I can't just tell them we want to be engaged, Rudy. You don't understand. I have to wait for the right time to approach my family about this."

Muck tried again to reach for the binoculars in Biggs's hands. There was no way the bishop would allow that to happen. He kept ogling the former cheerleader and rubbing his crotch. There was a loud knock on her door.

"Who's that you're talking to on the phone, Livia?" It was Yolanda, Olivia's older sister by four years and no less delectable. Biggs and Marvin were able to make her out through the hallway window curtain as she stood there with her ear pressed against the door. Broad was both: snoop as well as eavesdropper. Kind of shot the myth to hell: Duarte kids were raised with values and principles.

"Just a friend—"

"I bet. You can tell Rudy Perez we're onto his little tricks around here and that he can stop bothering you."

*"Why don't you lighten up, Yolanda. You're not my mother."*

"Don't make me talk to the folks about this, Liv. You know damn well where they stand on the subject."

"You better not be screening my calls, *sister*." Olivia slammed down the receiver and turned out the light.

"Show's over." Biggs lowered the field glasses. "Let's go see what's shakin' at the *Casbah*."

# CHAPTER 48

Parking lot to Fritz McCoy's CASBAH HIDEAWAY– Cabaret & Nightclub was filling up nicely, with more than a few party-goers sporting their Halloween best—or worst; depended how you looked

**at it.** Made Brother Trusty, in his favorite alter ego persona, feel right at home for a change. And Muck? Couldn't stop whining about the rancid reeking Porky Pig mask he was tired of wearin' for no good reason.

"Halloween be boo-shit anyway. All these old mothafuckahs actin' like Wilbur Flinger."

In order to shut the punk up, Biggs yanked the damned thing off of him, that unfortunately resulted in tearing a section somewhere in the back. Biggs cursed under his breath. These things were always tough and tedious to sew together. Marvin had been eager to grouse about something else again, when Biggs shoved him in the direction of the canopied front entrance and the line of people waiting to get in. There seemed to be a vetting process in progress: folks had to pass muster first. A six-foot-five Afro-American in Ali Baba pants and vest with powerful arms that sported tats of Malcolm X and Reverend Martin Luther King gave everyone the once-over to make sure they were not excessively wasted on drugs or booze before allowing entry.

Once inside the foyer, you paused at the cashier's counter where a cover was paid and the back of your hand "branded" with a rubber stamp, whereby you proceeded on to the next phase: another weightlifter/bodybuilder type with impressive arms and chest, thick neck and shaved head wearing a similar type of getup as the guy out front, double-checking your hand for the blue ink silhouette of a tom sitting up on its hind end.

This guy was Hispanic. Not friendly looking at all. An earring in the shape of a gold cross dangled from one ear. The tattoo on his torso was that of Cesar Chavez.

# CHAPTER 49

**Biggs had had to fork over twenty bucks to cover his and Muck's entry fee.** That hadn't made him feel good at all. The two drink minimum (each) he would soon be required to pay for in addition felt like a stab in the heart. It killed him inside.

He paused there, had Marvin do the same, to allow their eyes to adjust to the low-key lighting and were soon approached by a waitress. Cecil ordered two bottles of beer for the perpetually broke sidekick, two Ginger Ales for himself. Bitch was gone with her plastic smile and exaggerated shake of the hips.

Place was packed. Stage, with its red velvet curtains, was to the right and there was a skinny comic up there delivering jokes. Far wall and the wall he and Marvin stood against had painted likenesses of icons from music and film: James Brown, Aretha, Etta James, B.B. King, Billie Holiday, Bessie Smith, Little Richard, Jerry Lee Lewis, Elvis Presley, Gene Pitney, Gene McDaniel, Roy Orbison, Barbara Lewis, Sarah Vaughan, Dinah Washington, Big Mama Thornton; there was Sidney Poitier, James Dean, John Wayne, Richard Pryor, Donna Summer, Diana Ross, tv's *Fugitive* David Janssen, Charles Bronson, Edward G. Robinson (in his *Little Caesar* derby and three-piece suit).

Over at the far left and that entire back wall was taken up by the bar, bar stools, dining tables—with not a single vacant stool or chair in sight. The tables themselves in that area, as well as the far part of the nightclub and floor Biggs and Marvin stood on, was a good foot higher than the dance floor (located in the center of all this), so that the patrons had a clear view of the stage no matter where they happened to be seated or standing. There were handrails as a safety measure and to protect the owner against lawsuit-happy patrons.

There wasn't an empty seat in sight, nor one foot of available dance floor space. Waitresses were constantly forced to elbow their way through the crowd balancing trays of drinks in order to reach their destinations.

Among other things, Casbah Hideaway was known for its steaks and baked potatoes, fried chicken, burgers and french fries. "The Hideaway" was also famous for its variety of home-based sauces: steak and barbecue; *Kickin' Ketchup*; mustard and mayo; various salad dressings.

Then there were the drinks: Casbah Hideaway's version of *Coco Loco*: dumped into a coconut shell, two ounces each of tequila, vodka, gin, Grenadine, and 150 proof Mexican rum—filled with ice and coconut water.

Variety of others: Pina Coladas, Margaritas, Daiquiris, Martinis and "flirtinies," Mint Juleps, Mai Tais.


There was a huge popcorn machine in the center of the dance floor. That was free. It was always popping. All anyone who wanted popcorn had to do was grab a paper sack, reach inside the plexiglass enclosure for the scoop and shovel the popcorn in. It was buttered, too. Real butter. None of that imitation crap. Fritz McCoy's customers mattered to him. All else he charged an arm and a leg for.


Marvin couldn't wait. Nudged Cecil in the ribs. Wanted his share of popcorn. Would be nice to have something to chew on other than that nasty food Greta make. Biggs nodded the go-ahead, then followed himself. Why not? Look at the cover he had to pay. McCoy was an A-1 gouger. Bastard and pimp.

It was tough to get to the popper, though. Seems everyone had to come out this night. Yeah, well; it was Halloween. Many a table, if not quite all, sported a jack-o'-lantern with a glowing candle inside that enhanced the festive tone, as did cardboard cutouts of broom-straddling witches in black conical hats and attire that dangled from wires above the revelers' heads. People on the dance floor were not dancing, either, presently, instead stood around impatiently taking in the goofy-looking stand-up on stage. Like Cecil Biggs, they were here primarily for the dancers, strippers; the girls. Tits and ass. Pussy. Audience, for the most part, consisted of working stiffs who favored their women on the voluptuous side. They were truck drivers, plumbers, house painters, studio grips, assistant directors, bit players, ditch diggers, brick layers, ice cream vendors, *7-Eleven* store clerks, factory workers.

What pulled them in, more or less, was the ebony bombshell named Pearleen Bell, better known by her showbiz moniker as Peaches LaBelle, not that the other dancers did not have their share of fans in attendance. Problem was the ball-busting diva, who was the featured act, was not on stage yet—neither were any of the other T & A beauties, instead the lame-o opener was a dorky-looking, raunchy white guy who called himself Manic Jello. Fit the Halloween motif, no doubt.

Effeminate and skeletal, this was Manic. Dark hair cut Page Boy style. Checked pants too short. Then you had the purple socks that were not of the same shade of purple; green blazer, pink shirt (with too many buttons that needed buttoning up.) All of it loud, and none of it matching up with anything else.

His chest hair was probably store-bought and had been pasted on. On his feet he wore black combat boots that weren't properly laced. It was possible he had stuffed balled socks inside his crotch.

The man's appearance was downright baffling. People never knew if they were being put on, or if this was truly how imbalanced this character was in real life.

However, if he had anything, he had timing. Jello's was a dry delivery; he never cracked a smile—and the raunch was served with a deadpan face that drew more than a few chuckles. Trouble was the restless crowd had no time for the pathetic loser or his *shtick*. They wanted one thing and one thing only: LaBelle's wide hips and narrow waist; they wanted her muscular thighs and to-die-for caboose, not to mention those mouth-watering double-E naturals with the thick nipples.

The pelting began soon enough: eggs, pocket change, popcorn, fries, chicken legs. Someone pitched a partially-consumed steak, the comic's face clearly the intended bull's-eye. The thrower could not have been more pleased when he saw it smack Manic on the kisser. Not one to pass up a free meal, the put upon stand-up held on to the T-bone. Took a bite, after he'd recovered.

"Say what you will, the buffet's what I like best about the Casbah. All you can eat—for the same low price."

"Your ass gonna be fed wood if you don't get off the stage, *queer mothafuckah.*"

"Is that love or is that love?"

A black punk in his twenties scrambled past the beefy Ali Baba bouncers standing guard at the foot of the stage, jumped up on stage, and ran up to the comedian and cold-cocked him. Was about to face the audience to take, what he was convinced, was a well-deserved bow, and was dragged off by security.

# CHAPTER 50

**Stage band, SweatBone, went into their version of *Take Five.*** Not that they were able to equal Paul Desmond and Dave Brubeck's original, still, the tune did what it was supposed to: calmed the rowdy crowd.

A black MC in a spiffy electric blue suit and slicked back Chuck Berry hair stepped up to the mic.

"You know exactly who I mean when I say: Mama got major junk in her trunk. Gonna make your jaw hit the floor and your jones hard as a lead pipe; diva gonna make you squirm like a worm and growl like a tiger. She gonna have you droolin' like a fool; leave you sweatin' like that monk what ain't had him a taste of trim in such a long time dude was about to have a mothafuckin' meltdown. I wouldn't lie to you. To hell with this vow of celibacy, is exactly what he said when he laid eyes on a magazine spread of this fine lady that I'm talking about. Dude busted out of the monastery the other day just to be here. That's right: he's here tonight. Promised the homie I wouldn't point him out; give him my word of honor I'd spare him the embarrassment. Let him enjoy the show *incognito*. He *had* to be here. It was either that, or have a nervous breakdown—like that fool Manic Jello; only difference being Jello's falling apart because he ain't had a *chubby* in his skinny *culo* in the last twenty-four hours. That's right: I said it. Fuck all that political correctness bullshit. You heard me. This ain't a fag-friendly venue. They got enough of their own fag joints to go to—and need to stay there, because that's where sissies belong. Them motherfuckers hate, HATE these women that the rest of us love and would gladly die for: big tits and wide hips. Leggy babes with the *grande culo.* You know what I'm talking about. Yes, you do. And as far as Manic Jello is concerned, dude just got escorted to a wagon by some serious-looking gentlemen in white coats. Anyway, enough about that punk and his kind. Frankly, I don't know who booked him. Claimed he was straight. Maybe he is. Who gives a damn? Got a super great lady about to come out here and entertain you folks. You know who I mean."

He waited for the applause to die down. SweatBone switched to *Harlem Nocturne,* hitting it hard and heavy. Diva deserved the biggest intro they had in them, per the owner's emphatic instructions. "The one, the only: LaBelle of the Ball: Peaches LaBelle!"

Crowd went nuts.

"'Bout time you brung the pussy out!"

"Got wood just thinking about that ho!"

Curtains in back of the MC parted and he made himself scarce.


Fog rose up from the stage floor. When it thinned out there she stood: the goddess herself. In high heels, fishnets, black spandex mini skirt, metallic gold, mid-thigh raincoat—and a shimmering gold bustier under the raincoat that she only allowed brief glimpses of (for now).

The stripper made a minor adjustment to the mic part of the wireless headset as she strolled about halfway toward the foot of the stage, swinging those hips with each and every step that she took. Paused there, arms akimbo. She owned not only the venue and the lust-filled crowd who came to see her, but the entire galaxy and everything in it—and she knew it.

The band turned up the heat a notch or two. There wasn't a Stan Getz or Buddy Rich or Barney Kessel among them, not that any of it mattered, not to the crowd; they played loud and had energy and easily segued into what had become the stripper's most recent signature tune: *HOTTER THAN A HOT FUDGE SUNDAE* (And Just As Delicious).

*Ooh Baby, sometimes I like to tease . . .*
*Ooh Baby, sometimes I like to please . . .*

*Lover-Boy, say you love me a whole lot . . .*
*Lover-Boy, I'll show you what I got . . .*

Line hit home. Cabaret crowd went ballistic. Wanting her to follow through. She knew what she was doing. Work them; have them beg for every piece of clothing you peel off. With her right hand, she reached the top of her zipper on the raincoat. Held it there.

And held it. Grinning, teasing.

They hooted and hollered for her to start discarding the outfit, and not stop until the entire getup was gone.

Peaches would not have any of that right now. She would not be rushed.

"Good things come to those who wait."

Peeler had a way of sighing lasciviously into the mic like some bronze version of Marilyn Monroe—only hotter, way hotter. What this Amazon possessed the vastly overrated Marilyn couldn't touch.

"Been waitin' a lifetime, baby. That long enough for you?"

"Was it worth it?"

"You bet your sweet bucket seat."

She tugged on the zipper to about a third of the way down. Stopped, turned, so that her backside was to the audience. Hiked up the raincoat, exposing inviting hips inside that ever-so-tight-to-bursting spandex skirt. The hips floated from side to side, as the band played on, underscoring her every move. Although obviously no Bix Beiderbecke, the horn player blasted that horn with a lot of heart. Even the legendary cornet player, were he alive and had not tragically passed at twenty-eight back in 1931, might have been moved enough to take notice.

She turned again. Tugged at the zipper. Down it went. All the way. Got out of the slick raincoat. Held it out in her hand so that it dangled from her fingertips. Was about to drop it there on the floor, when a couple of dwarfs, miniature replicas of the tip bowl bouncers, in that they were attired like them, hurried out from stage right, carrying a stretcher with the stripper's gold lamé cape laid out on it like some still and silent anaconda.

They lowered the litter. One of the dwarfs reached up for the raincoat and placed it on the stretcher. They picked up the cape; lifted it toward her. The stripper pretended to refuse to take it—and continued to sing the tune she had paid Petunia Roscoe to pen especially for her:

*Sweetie-pie, please don't be mad at me . .*
*if all them other boys like what they see . . .*

*Can't explain; it's all in vain . . .*
*Don't you see?*

*All I ever wanted to be . . .*
*was unassuming lil' ol' me . . .*

She accepted the cape. As a way of thanking them, leaned down and offered them an opportunity to kiss her on the face, pointing flamboyantly with index fingers that they plant a peck on either cheek. The pouting dwarfs were not inclined. They were interested in kissing something else instead. She shook a finger at them; admonishing: naughty, naughty.

Giving in finally to their insistence, she turned, sticking her rear out toward the audience. Swung one forefinger, then the other at either buttock. Held them there. Ear-to-ear grins appeared on the dwarves' faces, as they stood on either side of her and each planted a kiss on his half of her behind.

They straightened, while smoke wafted from beneath their turbans and out their ears, up through their collars.

The stripper turned, facing the audience, with a look of exaggerated shock on her face. Watched as the dwarfs lifted their turbans, while down below artificial penises stood at attention. More steam followed—and both dwarfs, clutching at their hearts in mock pain, staggered in place, and fell flat on their backs.

Oh my, did I cause that?—said the expression on the stripper's face, while two hotties in stiletto heels and short, tight Red Cross nurse's uniforms rushed out. Rolled the mini-men onto the stretcher and carried them away.

The stripper recovered from having witnessed the dwarves and their "heart-attack" stunts. Adjusted the cape, making certain her goodies were good and covered.

*They say I'm too much . . .*
*Gotta have your touch . . .*

*It's plain to see . . .*
*nothing else works for me . . .*

She swayed those hips from where she stood in place, hard, out to one wing of the stage, then the other.

Paused long enough to turn, raised the cape and shifted from one leg to the other, one hip to the other. This is what they were here for: hips and thighs; her long legs, the gyrating pelvis.

When she turned, facing them, leaned forward to give a good glimpse of what was inside that bra. Any man would have gladly given up a month's worth of paychecks to be able to get his lips around those nipples, then go south for a taste of that juicy quiff and butt hole.

Paper money was dropped into the bowl. She winked to the donors. Crossed her arms, concealing the forty-four-inch bust again with the cape. She turned her back to the crowd, spread the cape, raising it high enough to showcase her killer caboose.

The swaying started anew, and she stayed with it. The crowd encouraged her to the point she felt a strong need to please, in spite of what her attitude was about stripping in a joint like this. It was not a Paris stage, or some fancy Vegas showroom. Still, she was wanted. These were ass-men. Men who knew and appreciated the sight of a great rear end. A lot of brothers and Hispanic males, some whites, mostly European white guys, went nuts over a wide ass with a narrow waist.

This was her type of crowd. She was not only admired for her bosom, but her behind as well.

A lot of white boys in America only tended to go for tits, the bigger the better. Didn't seem to matter to them if they were fake, either. Didn't bother them if the woman didn't have good legs or even any kind of shapely derriere.

She never understood it. Too many strippers had toothpick legs and a boney ass, ugly tattoos and piercings; it was baffling—and yet too many hillbilly types like Roscoe didn't seem to be bothered by it, so long as the woman had the huge "knockers." Wasn't put off if the chick was fat, had varicose veins and a cellulite keister even—so long as she had "major jugs."

Well, what she had was all real: front *and* back. Including hair. Would never consider wearing a wig, false eyelashes, or contacts. No reason for it. That was for chicks who had to continually "improve on" what wasn't there to begin with.

Bottom line: these were her kind of people, men who valued a woman with her unique measurements. The idea was to please her admirers to the best of her ability and she put much effort into doing so. Sure, she would have preferred being in London or some other part of Europe as a member of an extravagant musical review. It would happen. She had to bide her time.

She gyrated some more. Did slow pumping of the air with the pelvis. When she turned to face them, the cape was over the bustier and the 38 EE cups within the bra part. She froze, a hip aimed at the audience. She had a thumb and index finger on the zipper of her skirt and began the slow descent with it. Paused halfway down. Went further.

Had the zipper nearly all the way down, then slowly, gradually, in uber tease fashion, pulled it back up. Took her hand off the zipper and waved an index finger back and forth at them for being not only naughty, but wanting to corrupt her in much the same way.

Moans and groans followed that drew a smile from her.

"My my, you are a *nasty bunch*, aren't you?"

Wolf whistles and hoots ensued.

"Take me home, baby."

"Gimme a peek at that *whisker box.*"

"Casbah Hideaway is full of *horndogs* tonight."

"You breakin' my heart, mama."

*"ASS TO DIE FOR."*

She turned again, giving them her backside. Went for the zipper once more. And this time, even though she drew it out for all it was worth, she stayed with it all the way and the spandex mini skirt dropped to the stage, revealing black bikini panties and garter belt. She kicked the skirt confidently to one side, and bent over to give them a better view of what they craved.

One of the dwarfs ran out, picked up the skirt, and made a clumsy effort to cover up her behind with it, and was soon hauled away by his diminutive pal, who dragged him off stage right.

*You know your body leaves me . . .*
*craving for more . . .*
*It's only you I do this for . . .*

She danced, accentuating every move. Covered her body with the cape, then opened it wide enough to reveal what there was. . . .

At some point her hand went to a side zipper on the bustier. Did a slow tug downward, and the bustier came off, leaving her in bra and panties, fishnets and garter belt.

The dwarf was back out again, attempting to cover her up. The other dwarf came chasing after the first. Yanked him away. Had to punch him out and knock him on his butt to stop him, then with the bustier draped over the knocked out dwarf's face, grabbed him by the wrists and dragged him off stage.

It was time for the bra to go. She had teased and tortured them enough with it. While clutching the cape closed over her bosom and the rest of that part of her body in her left hand, she undid the bra beneath with her other hand, withdrew it, held it above her head and spun it and sent it flying into the same part of the stage the mini men had disappeared off to earlier.

By the time she opened up the cape and revealed the unencumbered tits, the crowd was in hooter heaven. There was something there to please all of them: breast men; leg men; men who liked their women with *personality and looks*. What LaBelle of the Ball was about.

The fact that her nipples had those heart-shaped pasties over them did not seem to bother her salivating audience any. They were seeing what they needed to see: full and thick, all-natural 44 Fs, hanging freely, inviting, begging to be sucked and fondled. If only that were possible. Where was the legendary Russ Meyer to see this? Where was the incorrigible tit man? More than a few fans of his flicks wondered about that. Meyer knew how to cast his films. No silicone, no babes with pretzel thin chicken legs or skeletal posteriors, off-putting tattoos and disgusting tongue bars.

Peaches leaned over. Shook her torso from side-to-side, letting them take in her wondrous mammaries as they hung there to be admired by the crowd. She turned, bent over so that her hands were on either ankle, then she ran them slowly up her legs, and back down again. When they slid back up it was inside her thighs that they did so, and over her buttocks and outer hips.

*"Mothafuckin' ho is hot! SHHHIIIIYETTT!"*

She rose, facing them. Perched her right hand on her right hip. Hooked her thumb into the waistband of her panties, ran it back and forth, grinning at the crowd, teasing.

"Don't tell me you'd like to see the panties go next?"

Marvin Muck felt a need to participate. Yelled back for her to do it. *"YEAH, BABY!"*

"You can't be that nasty."

Others in the audience continued to do the same: shouting encouragement. Practically pleading with her to reveal everything.

"Show me some *pussy*, mama!"

"You don't really want them to come off. Or need I ask?"

They shouted back in the affirmative. Just as she was evidently about to yank the black panties off, she had that cape over the front of her, and teased them further: *should they go, or shouldn't they?* She toyed with them. The band played, spanking her butt. The magic hips swayed from one end of the Cabaret stage to the other.

"I want to hear you beg me to take them off."

They did. It was not loud enough as far as she was concerned.

"Do they come off?"

"YES!"

"Or do they stay on?"

"NO!"

"I can't hear you."

The response pleased her this time. She yanked the panties off, tearing the Velcro strips that held them together at opposite hips, raised them high into the air, and spun them above her head, then flung them at the maddened crowd. Men fought over them. The grateful winner, a horn-rimmed glasses-wearing brother from Hollywood, held them to his nose, huffing as though his life depended on it.

"I can hop the perch now. Don't nothing be better."

Peachy pulled the cape back for a moment, revealing the G-string, and the crowd showed their appreciation. More money was dropped into the glass bowl.

The stripper unfastened the cape, bunched the ends into either hand and ran the cape up between her legs, against her crotch. Up and down the cape went, rubbing against the mound that was her cunt. Biggs and Marvin watched in awe. Fought their way to get right up to the stage. There was more to come. Jaws were hanging.

The featured peeler covered up with the cape. Let them all drool and go nuts with desire. This was the trick that so many girls didn't get: the power is in *your* hands, not theirs. You controlled the situation, manipulated their hunger for it; intensified their desire by making them go insane with need.

*Naughty as can be . . .*
*Only you can do this to me . . .*

*Because your body leaves me craving for more . . .*
*It's only you I do this for . . .*

She happened to look down at the section of crowd directly beyond the foot of the stage for the time being, and Cecil Omar Biggs—with that disturbing clown makeup on his face that he was partial to—like so many males in the lust-filled, rowdy audience, was convinced Peaches LaBelle's obscenely suggestive gestures were aimed at no one but him.

He believed it enough to slip an envelope to Marvin to place inside the glass tip bowl. Took some doing on Marvin's part, in that first he had to get past the two steroid-inflated bruisers with crossed arms and Ali Baba outfits and convey his intentions. They didn't want anyone rushing the stage, like that guy earlier who had assaulted Manic Jello.


Muck paid no mind to the fixed frowns and the shit they wore: turned up pointed shoes, harem pants, turbans, and rhinestone-studded vests that showcased biceps thicker than his neck.

Sissies ain't all that, thought Base. Could prob'ly kick they fag ass if he had to. Wouldn't do it, though. Now don't be the time. Don't be wantin' to piss Bigg' off, neither. Waved to Peachy. Made sure she saw him drop the envelope in the bowl that had lots of cash in it by now.


No matter how intensely the strippers happened to be into their routine, they rarely missed the amount that was dropped into the tip bowl or by whom and were always prepared to wink a thank-you or flash a grateful smile. LaBelle was no exception.

She nodded. Spun around. Swung the cape aside, showcasing the tush and the brown butt crack within, not entirely concealed by the thong part of the G-string.

She turned once again, facing the crowd, revealing the tits—with nothing more than those heart-shaped pasties over the areola and nipples.

Other men dropped bills in with phone numbers attached and the name of the girl they were interested in. Quite a few wanted Peaches, not that they ever would get their hands on her or their peckers in her. All was not lost, though. The luckier ones would soon be visiting some of the other girls in one of the back parlors with a sign on the door that read: **Kismet Room — Members Only. PRIVATE.**

Pearleen never did like playing that game, never would—to the disappointment of many. She did follow the wink with a come-hither smile (first to Marvin, then to Cecil—whose money she knew this to be). Not that Muck needed the encouragement.

*"TAKE IT OFF! TAKE IT OFF, PEACH! TAKE IT ALL OFF!"*

Instead, she sang:

> *You know I'm a wildcat in bed, baby,*
> *sex-machine supreme . . .*

Sound of her voice, combined with the lyrics, tended to increase the crowd's existing frenzy.

> *You've got hot moves, baby . . .*
> *that make me scream . . .*
> *and holler for more . . .*
> *Let me be yo nasty little ho . . .*

Unlike the other girls, Peaches did it all without need of a brass pole. She had so much natural rhythm that a brass pole would only have hindered her ability to go all out and showcase just what she was able to do with hips and pelvis, not to mention the heavy knockers that hung there like undiscovered natural wonders of the world, which only her audience would soon be privy to gawk at at length.

Strippers like Dione "Divine" Aragon and Stunning Stella Storm, who lacked genuine rhythm, and who truly were only marginally capable as dancers, usually clung to the pole as an in dispensable prop, and did a variety of moves to it, with it, in close proximity of it: humped it, stroked it, licked it as though flicking a massive shaft to orgasm; ran their butts up and down against it—and did lots of swinging from it and around it.

The reality of it was the entertainment-hungry audience didn't seem to mind, so long as the woman was a hottie and went all out to please with all the salacious moves that she could muster. Peaches was the top-shelf, no question, but there was room for many types—and that niche was filled by the other peelers.

What helped, made a difference, even when the girls were far from impressive dancers, they, to a one, knew how to grind it out, make that luscious mound move; and when they stuck the backside out, to reveal glimpses of butt crack and beaver (thong not withstanding) . . . that was all it took to get the gawkers to start stomping their feet like a herd of buffalo and let go with wolf whistles and shouts of approval.

Pussy still made the world go round; pussy and tits, butt crack and hips. This was what they came to see. Get high, maybe get blown or receive a hand job in the Kismet Room, or else if they arrived with a date, it was step out in the parking lot for more toot and hot sex in the backseat of a car, that is, if they couldn't wait to get home, or to the motel room.

Peach wouldn't go near a brass pole. Let McCoy know it when he hired her. Brass pole was nothing more than a crutch. Truth was she had them eating out of the palm of her hand on her own; truth was if the males in the audience, as well as more than a few women, could have had it their way, they would have been eating out something else. And if the stern-faced, two-legged guard dogs in their Pepe La Moco outfits weren't stationed at the foot of the stage to prevent people from charging it, who knew what might have taken place?

# CHAPTER 51

**It was time to do away with the cape completely and reveal the tits in their full and optimum glory—sans interruption and/or further psychological torment from here on out.**

There was also the rest of her down there: bonus to top all bonuses: G-string, fishnets and garter belt, high heels.

Crowd loved it. The ebony peeler's wondrous hangers were unencumbered by any sort of actual clothing finally, with the exception of the nipples, which had those heart-shaped pasties over them. Leave something to the imagination.

She turned. Showing more of the backside, while letting the cape dangle from the fingertips of her right hand. Dwarfs ran out and carried it off as if in possession of something holy and precious—and maybe it was.

Peach faced them once more, would never cup the breasts, but did the next best thing; in fact, had just as great an impact as if she had: caressed the areas under the breasts, as well as around, then pushed in from either side against her bosom, hence not only pressing the naturals together this way, but lifting them upwards and leaving the crowd transfixed, practically gasping.

The following motion may have been awkward for other girls of her size to accomplish, but not for Peachy. She was graceful, perfect example of fluidity and control, as she arched her shoulders back, and lowered her head down toward the stage floor, so that her presently out-stretched arms and fingers touched it and she eased the crown of her head back this way, so that it, too, rested against the stage and her glorious mammaries were pulled back by gravity to either side of her torso.

Now that she no longer required her hands for support, she lifted them from the floor and swung them in dream-like slo-mo fashion against either hip and inched them ever-so-gradually down toward her outer, then inner thighs and began to caress the outline of the patch of cloth over the swollen mound that was the most-prized, if not priceless, part of her anatomy.

Her delicate and feminine fingers remained down there, along the perimeter of the mound and she began with gentle and deliberate thrusts, pumping the air this way.

She may not have been driving the universe to orgasm, but she certainly was goading the ever-willing crowd in this direction.

What it was about, what it was they had come for. Forget their nine-to-fives for a while, back rent, car insurance that was due, physical and emotional ailments, auto repair bills, money owed the dentist, money owed the ex-wife or some Gardena loan shark, phone bill that had yet to be paid the phone company—and all the other crap that pulled you down. You came here, saw a fantasy woman like Peaches LaBelle roll around on stage in simulated throes of ecstasy and all the weight on your shoulders, all that everyday strife that stressed you out during the week dissipated like a puff of smoke.

The ebony goddess knew well enough and was clever enough not to make them wild, frantic thrusts, instead slow and controlled—and she stayed with it, squeezing every precious ounce out of every move and moan until she had the crowd stomping their feet to the point the Ali Babas on either side of the giant tip glass began to show signs of apprehension. If the crowd turned into a mob and suddenly decided to lose control, they knew in their anabolically inflated arms and pecs that there wouldn't be a damned thing they could do about it.

Fortunately, it didn't happen. Audience was having a good time. Nothing out of the ordinary going on, no signs of an actual, impending riot. Crowd was crazy/vociferous, but not insanely out of control. Some wildness was not only to be expected, but had to be *accepted*. They paid their cash to cut loose a little, let their hair down. Had earned the right.

Bouncers' foreheads glistened with perspiration, but they maintained. Let it go.

Marvin was yelling. *"DO IT, SUGAR-BUSH! DO IT!"* Crowd joined in, echoing same.

*"HOW MUCH, BABY? HOW MUCH YOU CHARGE TO LET ME PARK MY MUSTANG IN YOUR GARAGE?"*

*"LIKE TO PUT MY CUBAN MISSILE UP THAT BITCH'S CULO, NO SHIT!"*

*I just want to be your nasty,*
*one and only true ho . . .*

*Ooh baby, baby . . .*
*Sometimes I like to tease . . .*
*Ooh baby, baby . . .*
*It's only you I love to please . . .*

She wouldn't remove the G-string, which they clamored she do. In fact, she couldn't, even if she had wanted to, which she didn't. This was not that type of club, nor was it legal. Never mind that a lot more went on elsewhere in the back that she wanted no part of or wanted to think about.

Peachy did the next best thing, that in all reality, quite possibly worked far better on a psychological level. By caressing her inner thighs, and sitting up, she pushed her breasts together as she had before, gingerly running the tips of her fingers over the presently-hardened nipples behind the pasties, while keeping her eyes closed.

She may as well have been pleasuring herself. What the crowd did not know, would never be aware of, as far as she was concerned, she would have been terrific with or without them being there simply because she was good at what she did because she had to be. It was a job, a job she knew how to be very effective at.

She tilted her head back, sighing, gently thrusting her pelvis, her crotch deliberately aimed at the crowd; and then she rolled over on her belly, lifted her behind in order to give them yet another view of it.

She had been around long enough to know the slightest sign of the *culo* (aka butt crack) drew a lot of men insane with desire, as much if not more so, as seeing coochie. There was a need to taste, lick, worship a well-built woman's behind and bury their nose and mouth into the elusive crack within. She knew, was absolutely aware of the value of what she possessed.

The pumping of the buttocks continued. She was leaning forward on all fours. Lifted her belly off the floor some more, her chest as well—to showcase the full hangers as they dangled there, cock-stiffening and beyond their reach. She swung them, up and down, back and forth—rubbing the nipples (within the pasties) against the polished floor of the stage.

It was empowering. All the way. This never escaped her. The fact that they couldn't have her breasts, her pussy and behind. Drove them nuts with need. She understood the psychology of it easily enough. Been wise to it since childhood. Older men had plied her with candy and cash begging for a peek at her "cookie." Some of them had been clearly pathetic. Too often that's what they were. How needy they acted. The more they craved what was hers, the less she was inclined to give it up. She didn't come cheap; couldn't be bought that way, either (unless she were inclined, and she rarely was). When it happened, the rare times that it did, it was on her terms, strictly.

Some day she would want to settle down. Start a family. Maybe. Only bringing a kid into this world and what giving birth did to a woman's body, the way it devastated a woman's figure, was no laughing matter. Not only the weight gain. That was the least of it. Weakened teeth and postpartum depression. Labor was agony. More often than not. Breasts developed stretch marks and went into permanent sag mode, so did the stomach. Not to mention other side effects.

She snapped out of it. Reminded herself to stay focused on what she was doing. Keep the audience wanting, keep them drooling. Couldn't deny that deep down she did get a charge out of it. Power she had over them was exhilarating. Wouldn't have surprised her if some had begun to masturbate; wouldn't have been shocked if they had their hands down there, playing *"pocket pool."*

She was familiar with the expression from having overheard military types use it. Pocket pool. Let them. So long as they didn't go near her.

She engaged in some additional pumping; and (only slightly) exaggerated sighing, as she despised fakery of any sort.

She turned on her back for more of the same: the gentle rubbing of and around the breasts, and then her right hand gradually slid down in the region of her upper thighs and her hips increased their pumping motion with each thrust and LaBelle of the Ball's steadily increasing sexual state kept building and reaching its peak and she released a moan to top off the previous ones, and then she collapsed against the stage. Absolutely spent. Lights faded to black. Curtains were drawn.

The crowd cheered, wanting more. Always wanting more. They could never get enough of Peaches LaBelle. Applause grew. Was not about to die down. Spotlight came back on. Curtains parted. The high yellow stood there, upstage. Took a few steps down the center of the stage, swaying those million dollar hips. Paused, took her bows. Blew a kiss to the crowd.

As before, fog materialized from above somewhere, as well as the stage floor, and by the time it cleared, so had the stripper. Curtains were drawn closed to ever-greater applause, not that it yielded an encore. There would be no "extras," not with Ms. LaBelle. "Always leave them wanting more," someone had said to her when she first started in this business. It was advice she had taken to heart.

Leave them panting for more. Always, leave them in a state of perpetual hunger, and keep your fee up there. No compromise. Only McCoy was far from generous when it came to taking care of the talent. Sure, he paid—when his arm was twisted, and he had no choice. Or else he came around when he was after something, the lech. Greasy slob was known for it. Plied the girls with gifts and promises, when he was intent on getting his.

SweatBone slipped into *Booker T & The MGs' Melting Pot* in order to give the audience a chance to cool down and recover, catch their collective breath and wipe their brows.

# CHAPTER 52

**By the time the curtain parted fifteen minutes later, the band was into a lively version of *Recado Bossa Nova*.** Fog materialized up from the stage that formed a circle approximately fourteen feet in diameter in an area roughly in the center of it and this same portion of the stage rose by about a foot, followed by three rising brass poles six feet in height, positioned evenly apart. There was the unmoving form of a single female stationed per pole in quasi-silhouette, eyes downcast, as still as statues. The three women were attired in vinyl, mid-thigh raincoats and pumps that matched each woman's particular hair color.

The fog dissipated by degrees and the round pedestal began to rotate like a slow-crawling carousel and the curvaceous bodies inside those slick raincoats took their time "waking" as it did, with the crimson-hued spotlight presently showcasing the brass pole in the foreground and the raven-haired dancer in the black raincoat whose stage name the regulars knew to be Lana Da Bottom.

The carousel paused momentarily, as it would for each girl in turn, before moving on.

Lana didn't "seem" to be doing much, merely stood in place, gently swaying those hips—and yet she did exactly what she needed to.

There wouldn't be a whole lot to take off here, other than the raincoat itself (that would be discarded eventually).

The gyrations were lazy and deliberate. You didn't knock yourself out right away and expend your energy within a short span of time. No need to rush. Only newcomers worked themselves into a frenzy and ran out of steam before they were supposed to.

She moved what she had in the thigh and hip area. It soon became obvious (to those who had never feasted eyes on her until now) there was quite the figure within that shiny raincoat. And once it came off, on her third trip around on the rotating platform, after she had done her share of teasing prick and beaver alike, and tossed it off to the side, it was evident why the Latina was called "Da Bottom."

Although not quite in the same league as LaBelle, not that many were, Lana possessed a dynamic figure and had nothing to be ashamed of. Tits and curves were all there. Long legs and that voluptuous behind. No fat on her. In tip-top shape. Pasties over the nipples, patch of cloth (that was part of the G-string) over the sacred bush. In heels. No fishnets or garter belt.

She knew it for a fact: if not for Pearl, she'd have been the main act here. She had rhythm most strippers could only dream of. Was LaBelle's equal when it came to having command of her body.

She had her hands on either side of the pole, and she ran them ever-so-gradually up, up, up . . . and down . . . down, as if stroking a massive brass erection. Below tended to accentuate what was happening above: she had her pelvis giving the pole slow and deliberate thrusts. If she were accomplished at anything, this had to be it: fucking. She knew how to please a man and wanted the audience to know it.

Although, for the most part by now, the crowd on the dance floor were engaged in just that: dancing, every so often more than a few of the males would stop to take in what Lana was into up there on that carousel and yell out approval.

The stage rotated, and Da Bottom stayed with what she was doing, in partial shadow or not, as one of the other dancers was eased into the rose-hued spotlight and became prominent. The carousel slowed to a stop at this point. It was Stella Storm's turn, the henna-haired babe in the fire-engine red raincoat. Built well enough. Lacking genuine rhythm. This was also true. Not that it mattered to the horndogs. She had her share of fans in the audience, and did what she was supposed to to deliver. Her admirers were here to see her in person. Knew her from the hardcore vids she did. Porn starlet was second-to-none when it came to giving head in all those fuck-fests she did on tape. Seeing her live was a treat and a real thrill. Men loved her. Didn't make a bit of difference to them that she couldn't dance worth a damn or that better than 50 percent of the video titles she was in were with women.

The disk-shaped pedestal moved again, resuming its slow crawl until the spotlight was on Dione Divine. Color of her heels and raincoat was a shade of platinum and as bright as a Dutch van Gogh sunflower that not only complemented but enhanced the natural, sunny waves of her own breathtaking locks. Marvin liked her well enough. Couldn't help it when his eyes caught sight of something else he could be interested in: off-stage and a lot closer, possibly approachable, and he made every effort to make eye contact with a good-looking black hostess with violet contacts and a wig with auburn highlights who was not impressed in the least and was not shy about letting him know it.

This did not keep Muck from leaning in conspiratorially, while hustling his crotch. Had a need to whisper in her ear.

"I be packin' enough for two white mens, or three of them Oriental. You be the judge."

As far as the woman was concerned, he was as disgusting as they come and made certain he got the message with a look that said as much.

"Yo, *sugah-bush*. Know why your pussy be close to your asshole? When a ho like you get' drunk you can be carried like a six-pack."

"That stupid joke, if you can call it that, is older than the smelly rags you got on." The hostess proceeded to go about her business.

"Skunk pussy ho."

Marvin grabbed her by the arm, only to be held back by Biggs in time to prevent a scene from developing. Biggs glared at him, hard, without saying anything, then let go.

"Why we can't get a real drink, Cecil? Taste of hooch. Anything. Bottle of *Michelob. Colt .45*. Take the edge off."

Biggs was no longer looking at him. "I want us both to stay sober."

"Heard what the bitch said about my skins? Ain't nothing but a low ho waitin' table' in a jive joint and she got nerve to dis somebody."

"Settle down."

"I feel like gettin' tight, man. This ain't right. See everybody else in here gettin' down, gettin' high—gettin' ready to do the *funky-monkey*."

"You just had two beers."

"Two don't do nothin'. Don't *even* do nothin'."

Biggs glared at him. "Got any idea what this is costing me?"

"What chu care? You rich."

Cecil handed him another envelope. Only this one was folded-over and had a plastic baggy in it. Muck stuck it in his pants.

"As soon as Lana Da Bottom and her cute friends finish their number, I want you to go say *how-do* in their dressing room. Got it? Like we planned."

"Like we plan'?"

*"Yeah, asshole. Like we planned."*

"Got you, homes. What chu want me to say to 'em this time, Brotha Trusty?"

"We discussed this already."

"Right. I know what chu mean."

"You better. That shit is not free. *I want you to remember that.* Use it sparingly."

Marvin responded with a quizzical look, but then immediately nodded his head when he saw the expression on Biggs's face that clearly said to get it together.

"Sure thang, Cecil. I could take care of it."

Muck walked off toward the rear of the club.

# CHAPTER 53

**The strippers' dressing room was oblong and disheveled.** Left wall was a series of vanities with makeup counter and stools. Closet and john were on the right. Shower stalls were at the far end, also on the right.

Dione Aragon's lanky husband cradled their eight-month-old daughter Clarissa in his arms (who would not stop crying). The infant did not want the pacifier he wished she would accept. Dione had lit a smoke and was in her bathrobe and desperately craved a chance to unwind.

The baby continued to wave its arms and claw at her daddy's *Stray Cats T*, tugging on his collar-length hair and droopy mustache.

"She's hungry, honey."

"I know that, Danny. I was hoping to take a shower first. I'm real sweaty. I could use a break."

Danny nodded. "Sorry."

Dione kissed her husband on the cheek. She stuck the smoke in her husband's mouth and took the baby in her arms. She parted her robe and guided a breast inside the kid's mouth. The baby stopped crying.

"Thank God," quipped Lana Sepulveda."Ain't no place for kids. Really."

Dione and her husband exchanged silent glances, but said nothing. It would have been out of place for them to object. Circumstances prevailed. It had been a hard two months of day-to-day living, two months of struggle to put enough money together to get their Chevy repaired and think about heading back home. Their number one priority was to get out of Southern California and return to Bakersfield, their home town.

"Why don't you cool it, Lana," suggested Pearleen Bell.

Lana "Da Bottom" and Stella "Storm" Martel lit up *Virginia Slims* and proceeded to empty the huge tip glass loaded with paper money and change on the makeup counter and began to count out the pile that clearly represented a small fortune.

Lana Sepulveda held up Cecil Biggs's white envelope, flashing the hundred dollar bill she found inside for all to see.

"Motherfucker is loaded. Hundred dollars. Didn't have to fuck him or suck him off, either. Makes you wonder what the fool would pay for sex these days, inflation being what it is. Should charge him inflation rates for sure."

"You said it," Stella said. "I'd like to get my hands on his credit cards.

Make him take me *shopping* on *Rodeo Drive*."

"Keep wishing," said Pearleen Bell. Although the money was just as important to her, she did not take any real pleasure in handling it or even counting it out like Lana and Stella were doing right now. Pearleen's attitude was: she needed money for life's necessities; to get by and possibly get somewhere with her stage act. That's all money ever meant to her. Have a nice little place to live, maybe by the beach somewhere. Maybe a garden to tend, grow her own vegetables, have a cat. . . . She loved animals. Only they were not allowed where she was staying with the others. It was also true, money got you certain other things: toot now and then, when you needed it.

She kept a close eye on the cash as they divvied it up, making sure that Dione Aragon, who was preoccupied with her baby, did not get shortchanged.

Dressing room door banged open and no one jumped higher than Lana, who had half-expected her mother to barge in, demanding the usual: her "share of the cash."

Mrs. Sepulveda had had a couple of drinks, as was her custom, and walked in with three young boys in tow. The youngest being eight years old, the oldest no more than eleven. Lana's mother could not have been more than thirty-eight herself. Easily appeared years older.

She wasted no time reaching for the greenbacks in her daughter's hands.

"What do you do with all your welfare money, Ma?" exploded Lana, and snatched the money back.

"I got obligations," her mother shouted, waving various utility bills in her hand. "I got mouths to feed."

"If you used contraceptives once in a while you wouldn't have so many goddamn kids to support. I got rent; I got bills, too. You think my roommates would let me stay in the apartment if I didn't come up with my share of the rent every month? Ask them, Ma. Go on, ask them. Be real, will you."

"How many times do I have to explain about the Catholic Church and the pill?" her mother said. "Pope is against the pill. What do you want me to do about it?"

"Take it up with the Pope," said Lana. "I don't want to hear it." She shook her head. Got another smoke going. She counted out a few five dollar bills and singles. Shoved them in her mother's face. "Be happy. Now leave me the fuck alone."

While this was going on, Pearleen handed a box of See's chocolate candy to the youngest of Mrs. Sepulveda's boys.

"What do you say?" Mrs. Sepulveda said to her son. "Well, what is it? You know better than that. You have been taught better."

All three boys were thanking Pearleen just as a peroxide blond with a bad complexion stuck her head in the door.

"Ms. LaBelle," the woman said to Pearleen Bell, "Mr. McCoy wants to see *YOU* in his office."

"What's he want now?"

"As if you didn't know," Lana remarked facetiously.

"Mine is not to question," said the messenger, "merely to deliver the message." And she was gone.

"Man's in love with you, Pearl honey," Stella said.

"Make life easier for yourself and go for it. Got a *Sugar Daddy* waiting to be made," said Lana.

*"I am so sick of his bullshit."* Pearleen got into her trench coat. *"Why is it I'm the one gets harassed all the time?"*

"You be nice to the gentleman now, he'll be nice to you."

Pearleen Bell shot Lana a scowl. Held it. Grabbed her purse, and left the dressing room.

"If looks could kill," snickered Lana. "Bitch could at least buy herself a sense of humor with all the bucks she rakes in."

# CHAPTER 54

**A black tom named Ahmed had his snout buried in a can of tuna on a corner of the Cabaret owner's desk.** Framed photos (featuring suspect autographs) of football greats Jim Brown, Fred "The Hammer" Williamson, actor Billy Dee Williams, comics George Wallace and Rodney Dangerfield; poster from the film *CAR WASH* signed by Richard Pryor, George Carlin, and other cast members hung from wood-paneled office walls.

There was a movie poster from *Lady Sings the Blues*, posters and/or flyers from appearances by Willie Dixon from years ago at various Euro venues, of Howlin' Wolf and Robert Johnson, Duke Ellington and his orchestra, Count Basie; baseball figures Hank Aaron, Willy Mays, Jackie Robinson; boxers Mohammad Ali, Tommy "Hit Man" Hearns, Evander Holyfield, Joe Frazier.

Fritz McCoy, not so much as tall, but large, sat in a black leather swivel behind the massive desk sucking on a Cuban cigar. He had a three-piece pin-striped suit on, white shirt with the top buttons unbuttoned that revealed several gold chains. The sausage-like fingers sported too many rings; the wristwatch easily retailed at ten grand.

The suit he wore was far from second-rate, not that it mattered much or did anything for his looks and general appearance. The stogie puffing Casbah owner could have been attired in a custom-tailored outfit with a fourteen-hundred-dollar price tag and it still would have looked like it had been purchased at a Lankershim Boulevard thrift store for under three sawbucks.

McCoy's jet black hair was styled in a pompadour and kept this way with a generous amount of pomade, and he was sweating a little more than was usual for him in this air-conditioned office, sweating and carefully running a comb through his perfectly coiffed hair that didn't need it, making certain all the same that every single marcelled strand was in place before LaBelle of the Ball appeared.

He put the comb away. The unwanted, excess grease across the top of his brow and ears he dabbed at with a white handkerchief.

He wiped his hands when he was done and stuffed the handkerchief back into the breast pocket of his suit jacket.


There was a knock on his door.

"Please do come in."

Office door opened, and Pearleen Bell walked in. An unlit cigarette dangled from her lips and she was rummaging inside her purse for a light.

McCoy asked her to close the door. She did that. When she turned, she found the owner tossing a small, pink-ribboned box her way. Even though thrown off guard, she caught it.

"I don't accept gifts. We had an understanding."

"You make my customers happy. That makes me happy. They can't get enough of you."

"That's what it's about, isn't it?"

"Token of my appreciation. Take a look inside. Go on."

She lifted the lid. There was what appeared to be a gold-plated lighter in there. Inscription read:


To: P.B.

Classiest lady

I know.

In gratitude,

Fritz

The ever-familiar logo, to those who frequented the Casbah Hideaway, of Ahmed in black silhouette sitting up on his hind quarters occupied the lower right corner.

She lit her cigarette.

"Nice. Unfortunately, I can't accept it."

As she leaned forward to place the lighter on his desk, she noticed the rails of cocaine on a hand-held mirror and a razorblade next to it on a section of his desk to the left of her left arm. The big tom continued to devour the tuna at the opposite end. She would have liked to have been able to pet the cat, her love of all animals emotionally pulled her in that direction. But she would not. Had to restrain herself. Getting too familiar with a creep like McCoy, on any level, was not a good idea. The other thing was: the dope tugged at her. The need for it. How do you pretend that you don't want it?

She knew that McCoy knew what was going on and that there was no point trying to con her way out.

She didn't bother.

"Keep it. Please. It's the least I can do. You earned it."

"I did, didn't I? That's not the problem. The problem is when people, club owners, do you favors, they expect favors in return. I don't play that game."

"No strings. Got my word. Nobody's forcing you to do anything you don't want to."

"So long as we're straight on it."

Pearl knew better, though. A snake in the grass was a snake in the grass. Repulsive dog was after something; they were all after something. No matter what they said, no matter how hard they worked at pretending that they weren't.

She dropped the lighter in her purse. Zipped it closed.

McCoy puffed on his expensive cigar. Probably bigger than his dick, she thought. Always smelled like horse manure, too.

She thanked him for the gift. Ached for the rails of blow on his desk. Fought the fight. To resist. They both knew it. To be sharing the same space with the lech made her less than comfortable. Pigs like this were always making passes, always making life so much tougher than it had to be.

# CHAPTER 55

**She dragged on her cigarette.** Waited for him to talk. Only he didn't. "If there's nothing else, Mr. McCoy, I'd like to get back."

The club owner tapped ash into the ashtray.

"You been shakin' that fine booty in my establishment for close to a year now—and I still get turned on watching you do your act. Not coming on; all I'm saying it's rare for me to react to one of my dancers this way. Girls come and girls go. Seen one/seen them all. Funny thing is, every one of them thinks they're special, unique—and hardly ever are. This is not a come-on, Pearleen. Strictly meant as a compliment."

"I understand."

McCoy indicated the cocaine.

"Help yourself."

Truth was she would have huffed the powder the second her eyes had zeroed in on it, only with this type of slob the price was always too high.

"What do I got to do? *Fuck you?* That's it, isn't it?"

"Not like you to be vulgar."

"That's what you're after, isn't it? In spite of what you insisted a minute ago." And she saw him attempt to flash that unappealing wolfish grin he'd been testing out on her from day one. Degenerates were the same. Give you a job and act like they own you. Body and soul. Nasty old fool.

"Come see my new Jacuzzi. You're not obligated. No strings. I give you my word."

*"I explained myself when I took this job, Mr. McCoy. We were clear on it: I'm not a prostitute. I'm paid to dance. Nothing more. I don't fuck your customers, your associates—or the club's owner. Men like you, too many men like you, expect me to put out. I don't do that shit. I'm a professional dancer and get paid to dance, on a stage, and nothing additional."*

If there was too much of the gutter in her outburst she didn't give a damn at this point, because the situation had called for it. If you acted meek and respectful and "proper" with these slimy bastards they took advantage of it; they were all over you then. Treated you like dirt. She wasn't about to let them trample what remained of her self-esteem. *I'll be courteous and respectful and treat people like human beings when they treat me the same way, but when all they are after is that other thing, when all they know how to do is treat you like a tramp because of your circumstances and are forced to work places like this, what they'll get is the gutter thrown right back at them.*

She straightened. Stood there and waited. *You want to fire me? Go ahead, fatso; fire me.* I can get a job taking my clothes off anywhere. Town's full of places like this. The only reason she was still in LA doing all this and not in Vegas was because she needed to save up enough money, buy a better car, improve her wardrobe, continue to refine her act and she would definitely be headed for Vegas and other big towns, maybe even Paris. Why the hell not? She might go to Paris. Josephine Baker did. All she had to do was get a passport, put together a nest egg.

She waited for him to respond. *Say something, you pig. Didn't expect me to throw your crap right back at you, did you?*

"No need to get uptight, baby. You're a professional, I'm a professional." McCoy indicated the coke again. "Help yourself. That's my way of showing appreciation for the crowds you draw. They like you, no doubt about it."

"As long as we understand each other."

Pearleen walked over to the desk, bent down and snorted up the cocaine with a tooter. Up one nostril, then the other. Blow was great. She held the mirror up. Flicked her nose with the tip of her index finger. "I appreciate being appreciated."

"Your mama and step-daddy's been calling again, pleading with me to try to talk you into moving back home."

"They can go to hell."

"That ain't nice."

*"You want nice, Mr. McCoy?"*

Pearleen proceeded to remove body makeup from her arms, left ankle, right ankle, revealing a series of old and not-so-old scars and bruises.

*"Here's a nice scar they left me with to remember them by; and here's another one, and another one—from when I was younger and couldn't defend myself. They want me to move back in with them for one reason: so they can keep draining me financially, the way Lana's mother keeps draining Lana. Only Mrs. Sepulveda is a saint compared to my mother and stepfather. So I'll tell you what, Mr. Fritz McCoy: You live your life your way and I will live my life my way—and we'll just keep my parents out of it."*

She turned to leave. Paused at the door. "I want to thank you again for the toot."

And she was gone. Had closed the door behind her at least.

McCoy puffed on his stogie.

"You'll come around, bitch. . . . Just like the others, just like all the others."

The notion made him chuckle. Ahmed leapt onto his lap, seeking attention. Fritz rubbed the back of the cat's neck.

# CHAPTER 56

**On the other side of that same office door Pearleen had taken a minute to regain her equilibrium, compose herself.** The tough broad act she had just pulled off in there with the disgusting slob had not been easy and had taken a lot out of her. Then, too, her eyes had begun to well because she knew that this cocaine business was beginning to rule and ruin her life. Fact was the only reason she worked at a place like this was because of her need for blow. She could have easily been playing a fancy Reno or Vegas showroom by now. She had the height. Had the figure. Was attractive enough, and she was a damned good dancer—as good as any of those Las Vegas showgirls.

But it was the goddamned dope. And she had done it again: taken the fat creep's toot, snorted it; and every time afterwards had promised that that would be the last time. Would never do it again. McCoy was getting to her. Little by little, bit by bit.

She'd been huffing his powder, as well as Cecil's and Marvin's and anyone else's she could get her hands on; spent most of her earnings on it, but kept telling herself she wasn't hooked.

Deny, deny; deny it. Keep denying it to yourself. Keep bullshitting yourself, Pearleen. Keep saying you're not addicted; you're no coke-head. You won't sleep with some low dog just because you have a need for dope. Not you. That's not you. You won't stoop to that level. You won't do it. You can't. . . .

# CHAPTER 57

**Pearleen Bell returned to the dressing room.** Lana and her mother were still going at it, matching one another decibel for decibel.

"Who are you shouting at? This is your mother you're talking to. I know what you waste your money on. I know. Don't tell *me* fairy tales."

Pearleen settled on a stool in a corner to the left of the door, away from most of the ruckus. She sat there at the vanity looking at nothing, dragged on a butt, and made every effort to tune out the fighting. It took a good deal of hard concentration to accomplish this.

Mrs. Sepulveda was glaring at the girls, giving them the piercing once-over, the pointing, accusing finger.

"All of you in here, with the possible exception of Pearl, squander your income on dope. Drugs. What a waste."

"And you blow all the cash you get from Lana on booze and Bingo parlors, Mrs. Sepulveda," said Stella Martel out of the side of her mouth.

"You stay out of this," Lana's mother said to the stripper.

"You already got most of my money, Ma. Told you before: a percentage of it goes to musicians and bouncers. Ain't all ours to keep."

"How much?"

"Why don't you just leave? That's 'how much.' Take the kids out of here. They don't belong in here. This is a ladies' dressing room, not a nursery."

"Tell it to the parents of that baby." Lana's mother was pointing at Dione, who continued to nurse her daughter.

"I'm sick and tired of you doing this to me. You're draining me. I work hard for every dime I get. Do you think I enjoy taking my clothes off in front of all those strangers out there?"

"More than you care to admit," Pearleen said under her breath, and dragged on her cigarette without ever looking at them.

Lana hadn't cared for the remark. Allowed it to pass. She had her mother to deal with.

"Why don't you get a husband who'll stick around long enough to support them brats, Ma? You got to stop having kids, Ma. It ain't my fault you got so many kids."

"I can take care of my little ones. Don't you worry about that, missy."

"Surprised you ain't brung the rest of them over. Treat this place like a nursery. Want me to get shit-canned? This is not a nursery; it's no place for kids. No, Dione's not supposed to have her baby in here. At least she works here. She has a reason to be here. On the other hand, you don't. Get it?"

Mrs. Sepulveda did not say anything just then and shook her head. She was looking at her daughter, at the other strippers. Took it all in the way she had just a moment ago.

She seemed saddened by the whole situation: shoddy dressing room, sleazy atmosphere of the strip club and the kind of lowlifes who frequented places like this. It saddened and depressed her.

"God help you. God help you. You're destroying yourselves with drugs, with this kind of nowhere life. You think you got your looks forever? Gonna stay young and beautiful forever? Men will throw themselves at you; give you their money? It goes. It all goes. Quicker than you think. A few fast years, all of a sudden you're pushing forty, don't look so hot no more."

"Thanks for the sermon, Ma. Now I won't have to go to church this week."

"It wouldn't hurt if you did."

"At least I know enough to use birth control, don't I, Ma?"

Mrs. Sepulveda collected her youngsters, and was out the door.

"Can you believe that shit? Spent all her good years living it up—and now she's coming down on me for trying to live my own life? Too much."

"I like your mother. She's right. This sucks."

"Yeah? You can have her. You got no idea what she's really like. Try living with her—then come and talk to me about how right she is, Pearl." Lana withdrew money from her bathrobe that she had withheld from her mother.

"Barely got enough to score some rocks, pay off some bills. Woman drives me absolutely fucking nuts." She stuffed the money in her purse. Shed the bathrobe and stepped into a shower stall. Stella got out of her own robe as well and opted for a shower next to Lana's.

"I'm thinking of quitting."

"And do what, Pearl?" Stella said. "And go where?"

"Vegas. Maybe try to get hired on *Solid Gold.*"

"Yeah. Sure," Lana said. "Pipe dream."

"McCoy's constantly on my back. I don't know how much longer I can take it."

"I can take it as long as the tips keep coming."

"I told you guys about Vegas," said Stella. "You get busted doing toot and you are out on your ass. They don't want their talent fooling with dope."

"It's too fucking strict out there," Lana seconded. "At least with Fritz he don't give a shit about that 'cause he's into it himself—so long as you're cool about it. Speaking of dope, I wonder what Cecil's flunky will come in here with this time. I hope it's super fly shit whatever it is."

"There's no way I'm going back to that smelly old house," said Pearleen. She was enamored with the baby and wondered if she'd be able to hold her for a while once Dione was done breast-feeding her.

"Of course you can," said Dione.

"What was that, Pearl?" Lana yelled out from the shower. "You can't wait to go back for another visit to that smelly old house?"

"Not me. No more. Who needs it?"

"Where have I heard that before? Reverend Stinky knows exactly what he's doing. Gives Marvin enough to get us interested—then he'll say: If you *want* more of the same come on over to the bishop's *cribby* and do a private strip for the dude. He'll give you all the dope you can hack."

"I'm with Pearl," said Stella. "I'm not going back—unless absolutely necessary."

"We'll see about that," Lana said, stepping out of the shower.

# CHAPTER 58

**There was nothing resembling anything close to a real knock on the dressing room door when it opened and Muck walked in with a stupid grin on his face.** Dione was finishing up breast-feeding her baby and Marvin's grin widened.

"That chile got all the luck in the world."

Dione was quick to shove the exposed breast back inside her robe, only it hadn't been quick enough as far as her husband Danny was concerned. His wife glanced at him with a shrug: What was she supposed to have done? Maybe Marvin behaved like a jerk because he just happened to be one. He'd entered the dressing room practically unannounced. Hadn't even given anyone a chance to cover themselves up. Yes, she also knew it was no place for a child. They had to bear up under the circumstances.

As she said she would, she let Pearleen hold Clarissa, then stepped into a shower herself, all the while keeping an eye on the room so that she wouldn't miss out on what might be taking place with Marvin and whatever he may have brought with him.

Marvin had moved close enough to the showers to catch enough bare skin now and then through the clear plastic shower curtains as she and Stella lathered up in their respective stalls.

The other strippers were, in fact, aware of what Muck was up to but did not make a fuss, as he very often brought "goodies" with him, even if he did smell nearly as bad as Biggs himself, and dressed even worse.

"How all you fine hoe' like the jack Brotha Muck left in the bowl for my bitches?"

"Bullshit," Lana said, drying herself off with a towel. "That was the man's own cash you dropped in the tip glass. Everyone knows you don't have a pot to piss in, *Free Ride.* "Cause if you did, you wouldn't be wearing them clothes. Lookit them kicks. Like a senior citizen."

Marvin looked down. It was nothing more than a knee-jerk reaction. He'd heard it all before. When he looked back up he was grinning anyway.

"Yeah? Well, this be one 'senile citizen' wiff somethin' special all you womens is gonna be jumpin' for joy. 'Sides, how you know I ain't savin' up all my bread to open up my own nightclub? How you know that? Gonna get me a real class joint. Hire all the best lookin' bitches LA ever seen. Make *twiced* the bank you makin' now workin' for that ugly nigga what ain't got a dick no bigger than my pussy finger. Got it all figured out, me. Up here. An' you ain't got to fuck no mens 'less you feel like it. An' we split the coin so all of us be real happy wiff the arrangement all around."

"Another one with a pipe dream," Lana quipped. "I'd like to know what you're on, *'Brotha Muck,'* what you've been smokin'."

"Don't jive us, Marvin," said Stella, stepping out of the shower herself. Grabbed a towel. "We don't have time for your *'boo-shit.'* "

*"No boo-shit.* Why come I don't spend my coin on bling and wardrobe. All that be later."

He reached inside his pocket and pulled out the folded-over envelope, then the Ziploc baggy with enough crack to make the women stop giving him a hard time and go for crack pipes that they each owned and kept handy in purses that were never far from their reach.

"It ain't what I been smokin'. More like what I'm about to." Bitches be searchin' for they glass stem' and be ready to play the game, thought Marvin. They all be singin' a different tune all of a sudden.

Lana was quickest to move. He watched her dump the contents of her purse onto the vanity counter and dig out a red box cutter. Had a few of them. Different colors: black, red, white. Aluminum. The kind with the single edge blade.

All of these hoe' got somethin' to hurt a dude wiff. Like Omar always be sayin': never trust no ho, 'specially a ghetto ho. An' they was that.

He watched her attempt to scrape out the bowl with the blade. Only the blade was too wide. She was back to rummaging through the pile of items on the counter: lipstick, nail polish, mirror, eyeliner, coins, *Tampons*.

Settled on a nail file. Scraped the bowl out and placed a new screen in. She was itching to get her hands on the *Ziploc* baggy. Marvin held it back. Beyond her reach.

"Just one thing."

"Asshole. What's the catch this time?"

"Catch? Yo, why you *raggin', Stella*?"

"You heard her. What are you after this time? I don't do anal."

"You done it, *shuga-bush*. Seen the video, Lana. You take Jones in yo back door."

"You couldn't afford it."

"Be that way. Only I ain't even here for that. I be yo friend, you know that. Best friend you bitches got."

"So are we hittin' it, or what?"

"Yo, we gonna hit this shit, Stella."

Marvin dangled the rocks before their hungry eyes. They wanted it, and were practically willing to do just about anything for it. Pearl was the only one who remained reserved. She craved the dope as much as the others, no matter what she had stated a moment ago, but would not let it show. Her high, from McCoy's toot, was winding down. If she could have extended it by hitting the rocks a couple of times would have been real nice.

She didn't say much. Waited to see how the thing would evolve. She played with the baby. Kissed her on the forehead.

"Only the dude *aksed* me if you was all willin' to come back to the *cribby*. Get acquainted. *You know.*"

"What did I tell you? Fuckers always gotta be after something."

"Only fair, ain't it? When you dance on McCoy' stage you get paid, *Lana DaBottom*. When you dance in Cecil' livin' room you get paid, too. Crack don't be free. Dude pay' for it outta his own pocket."

"How do we know rocks are any good?"

"'Cause I be tellin' you this be some great jellybean', Lana. Had me some back at the cribby the other day. You know Cecil don't never buy no weak dope. All the dope he get be some *fly shit*. Blow, smack, crank, crack. Name it. All be quality."

# CHAPTER 59

**Danny Aragon, who had stood by the door all the while, saw what was about to take place in back of the dressing room and decided he'd like to be part of it.** Why not? Just a hit or two. Wouldn't hurt. LA can get you down. This was a way to stay up.

"Sorry, Brotha. Bitches only, I mean *womens only*. Don't be enough here to go around."

Clearly disappointed, Danny collected his infant daughter and left the room.

"That was uncalled for. It was rude."

"One way of lookin' at it, Peachy. All I can do is what my homie tell' me to do. Anyway, fuck Danny. He don't pay for this shit. Crack don't grow on no tree. *Aks* Cecil about that. Dude be *remindin'* me all the time."

The strippers had gathered round him, with the exception of Dione. Rest of them never give a damn about Danny anyway. Peach don't neither. Only like' to act like she do. Marvin knew it. Had the sly smile going. Man was in charge. Like Iceberg. King of all pimp'.

"Wait for me, you guys." Dione was shampooing her hair and some of it had ended up in her eyes. She had stuck her head out, squinting, straining to make out what was going on. Marvin had the charm working overtime.

"Not to worry, sugar-bush. My main man Cecil got you covered. Dude say if you womens want to smoke the *nugget'* you gonna havta come to the cribby and put on a show. Only be right. Don't it?"

Dione's eyes were burning and she needed to rinse the soap out of them and ducked back in the shower.

"Not a problem," Lana said. "Only don't tell me there's no catch—because there always is."

Rocks were in the pipe. She got her torch going. Had a long blast, as was her custom. Held the smoke in her lungs, then released it slowly. This was her way of going for the fullest effect.


Pipe was passed around to Stella and Peachy. By the time it reached Marvin there wasn't much left to smoke. He sucked on it all the same, burning down the 'due.

"I don't mind. Only you ain't right to keep sayin' there be a catch all the time. There don't be no catch. Never been. You got bump and whatnot, weed an' crack—and whatnot, last time you all was at the house—and what about them other time' Stella and Lana and them other hoe' what ain't here no more—and all that great shit: ludes, Scotty, base?"

"Sure. We dance for the dickhead. If the rest of them nuggets are as good as this."

Her friends nodded in agreement.

"Buncha funny-ass bitches. You smokin' this fine dope and got nerve to say: *Now, if the rest of that shit be as good.* . . . How many time' I got to prove it?"

He chuckled. "You can trust the deacon. Deacon Muck ain't gonna come around with nothin' but the best for all you fine stone bitches—'cause you deserves the best. That simple. How it all work'."

"Wait for me," Dione kept beseeching from the shower. Only Lana had already scraped out her bowl. Stuck a fresh screen in using the end of what looked like part of a chopstick. Added the new rocks. She had the torch going in no time, firing up the rocks. Stayed with it until she had the lot crinkling to her satisfaction.

She hit it, and passed the stem on to Stella Martel. Stella's system was to go for short hits. Did a couple, then a third, before Pearleen held her hand out and opted for Lana's way: taking a long, deep blast, and leaned back against the vanity counter.

Not wanting them to smoke it all up before he'd had his share, Muck pulled up a stool, got his hands on the stem and had a lasting, hard hit. Nothing like it in the world. The only way to top it would be to have one of the bitches suck his joint. Take his Johnson out and go to town on it. Only he didn't know if he could make them do it. Risked getting busted by McCoy and kicked out for good. Did it matter? He was willing to take that chance.

"How 'bout it?"

"What?"

"Do me, Lana. Suck my dick, while I be suckin' on this here pipe."

"Ain't happening."

"Could go for a Double Master Blaster, me."

"Not here, not now."

"How about you, Stella? Ain't none a y'all my friend?"

"You heard her."

"Scotty be *fly* this time. Fuckin' rocket fuel."

Puttin' up wiff Omar and his boo-shit was worf it when you got to smoke fly crack like this. Marvin's brain felt like it was on fire. Sizzling. Be a cool way to burn. Go up in flame'.

# CHAPTER 60

**Stem was passed around, and in no time the crack was down to residue as before.** Lana sucked on it anyway. Wasn't much to get. The strippers eyed the rest of what remained in the baggy. Muck had it out. Baiting them. Was reluctant to go through with it.

"Bishop ain't gonna like it if we do it up. Got to save some for the party, ain't we?"

"Because you didn't get your dick blown, so you have to play your fucking game."

"Ain't like that, Lana."

"Sure it is."

Stella had sidled up and was rubbing the inside of his thigh. Had her hand gently moving back and forth, just about near his groin. Massaged the area enough to be effective. It was working. Marvin fought the urge to want to get off. No chance.

"We can have that party right now. If you want. . . ."

"You got no idea what Omar be like. Dude got him a temper. Tight wiff his coin and dope. I got to do what the dude *aksed* me. Get you womens to come back to the cribby and do a show on his little bitty stage like he say. You ain't got to do the dude if you don't want, just do a show. Do yo act."

Stella continued the gentle rubbing. Stayed clear of the crotch. Got near it, but not on it. She was quite the prick-teaser.

Muck handed the baggy over and watched Lana Sepulveda stuff what was left of the "gravel" down into the bowl of her pipe. Fired up the torch. Hit the glo long and hard, as before, to her friends' dismay.

Pearleen Bell had her hand on the stem quickly enough and went for the longest of hits this time. Passed the stem back to Lana. Only when Stella objected with a "hey" did Lana place the stem in Stella's mouth long enough for her to go for her few quick hits. Stella did this, all the while being kind to Marvin's inner thigh.

Lana Sepulveda was back on it. Had her typical long blast, and passed it on to Pearleen. By the time Pearleen Bell had hers there was not much left for Muck to take in. He sucked on it all the same. Didn't seem to care—so long as he got Stella to blow him. Only he wished she would *get wiff it*. Follow through. All the ho be doin' is teasing his joint.

He unzipped his fly to help her along, and was about to unleash "the package" for that "Double Master Blaster" he was way over due. Only Stella stopped him in time. Ceased what she had been doing with her hand, too. Ended all of it. Had her reason. The other strippers were quick to back her.

"If Fritz catches us we'll get shit-canned for sure."

"Yo." Marvin was practically pleading. "Y'all can't leave me like this. Gonna give me *blue balls*."

"Better you with blue balls, than what would happen to us."

"Pearl's telling the truth about Fritz. It pisses him off that he can't get any of us to do him. Not a good idea to mix business with pleasure."

"Now you tell me that, Lana? Now? After you done give me the blue balls."

"You're blaming us because you walk around with a guided missile 24/7? How is that our fault?"

"You play wiff my Johnson, *Stella 'Storm' Martel*, got it all good and hard, then say it don't be yo fault? Whose fault do it be, then? Mine? I don't be walkin' in here wiff hard meat."

"No?" said Lana. "That thing of yours never goes down."

Frustrated as hell, Marvin had little choice but to shove his groin back inside his pants. There was somethin' he coulda done, though. Rape the hoe'. Make the bitches suck his dick anyway—and risk going back to jail—

for a long time. Rapin' bitches got you more time than was worf it, 'specially if you got caught.

Instead, he zipped up.

The strippers were after more crack. It don't never be enough for them. Just like Omar say. Sometime' that mofo know' what he be talkin' about.

"There don't be no more. What do I look like? *Pusher?* You know I don't be pushin.' All I got is what I brung; what the mofo gimme." Lest they forget: "Well don't be dry. Where there be *'Hope,'* there be *dope.* Back at the cribby. How about we decide what time you womens is comin' by for a real party? We together on that? Yo."

Now that they were where they needed to be, and there was no more to be had, they were no longer interested in "Deacon Muck" or anything that he had to say. Lana didn't care that he didn't like it, either. Let it be known.

"Seeing your 'hero,' *BROTHA TRUSTY,* cut a chicken's head off the last time we were there, because that was the only way he could get it up, wasn't exactly a pleasant sight. Didn't exactly endear him to us."

"If that don't beat all. You done smoke' the dope and now you sayin' you ain't comin'?"

"It's the chicken killing. Cutting heads off chicken to get his dick up."

"He don't do that no more. Cecil ain't like that. That was that one time he put that chicken down. His dick was nappin' 'cause of the medication. He ain't loco or nothin'. Dude get depress'. He ain't ice' no yardbird in a long time. Got my word on it. I ain't lyin'."

As far as the strippers were concerned, the discussion was over. They wanted this loser to go away and let them be.


A beefy, blond-haired lady who wore her hair in a style that resembled a flattop walked in carrying a gym bag in one hand and a portable folding table in the other. Woman was in gray sweats and built like a sumo wrestler. The blond whiskers above her upper lip were visible enough to pass for a mustache.

"Hello, Frederika," one of the strippers said. Frederika grunted. Walked in the back and began to set up. Unzipped her bag, withdrew a boom box, towel, containers of body oils and placed them on the vanity counter.

"Yo. I don't hear nobody sayin' nothin' *to me.*"

Marvin Muck made little effort to conceal his frustration. The strippers suddenly became very good at appearing preoccupied. Lana couldn't wait to lie on her belly on the massage table for the rubdown that Frederika was quite the expert at evidently.

Pearleen wanted to step in the shower, and needed Marvin to leave before she made her move. After she reminded him that it was not a good time for what he was after and that he needed to vacate their space, she considered skipping the shower altogether, getting into her street clothes and walking out of the club for good. Did she have the nerve to do it? Did she dare walk away from a steady, money-making gig like this?

Frederika, the Swiss masseuse, punched a button on her boom box and soothing New Age-type music filled the dressing room.

"We'll make it some other day, handsome. We have a second show to do. It's our chance to rest up and prepare. You have no idea how much performing on stage takes out of you."

"*Second show?* Since when, Lana?"

"It's a weekend night. It's always that way. You know that."

"Said the man don't be killin' no more chicken. You ain't got to worry about that. He keep' them *Foghorn Leghorn* around for fresh egg' and to make chicken soup. Dude be watchin' his health. Them croaker at the VA told him he better."

"We get it. All right? *All right, Marvin?* Forget the chicken. It's got nothing to do with that."

Marvin didn't know what to believe at this point. Mack Daddy wannabe hadn't liked the way he had been out-slicked, but he had his own buzz going and he did not want to throw a tantrum that might've wrecked anything with the strippers in the future, scared them off completely.

Deacon had his smile going again. The smile was back.

"Cool, shuga-bush. No problem. Sure do enjoy your company. You know you got two of the biggest fan' in the world in Omar an' me. We sure love to watch you all move around on that stage. Ain't nothin' Hoss wouldn't give if you was to do some of them fancy move' in his livin' room. My homeboy, Brotha Trusty sure know' how to appreciate real talent."

He thanked them profusely, released a series of farts—that he didn't seem to be aware of, or else didn't care—and left.

Pearleen shook her head, and reached for a can of air freshener. "Low-class a-hole."


The only one who may have been unhappy about Marvin doing a disappearing act was Dione, who had stepped out of the shower, with water dripping from hair and body, looking for her share of something that was long gone.

# CHAPTER 61

**Biggs was waiting for his deacon in the hallway outside the men's room door when Marvin ambled by in that contrived inner city hood way that he had, even though he was about as familiar with that world as he was with seasoned, tough-as-nails pimps and their street-hardened whores.** He had the walk down, hand and chin gestures, way of sounding like a gangster rapper-cum-hustler, it still only added up to him being nothing more than another wannabe Iceberg. Biggs didn't let it bother him. More-often-than-not, it didn't, unless he was having an off day to begin with, unless something or someone, society at large, put him in a foul mood, and then it didn't take much at all to trigger the ever-present, below-the-surface, simmering rage.

He was already stressed at having had his haunted house business shut down, not to mention being annoyed with himself at having given up a Ben Franklin and two Alexander Hamiltons without any assurance whatsoever that the cunts would even want to stop by his place later. Parting with money had always been painful for him, especially a considerable amount such as this.

"What about it?"

"What about what?" Still out of it from the dope, Marvin wanted nothing more than to be left alone and not be fucked with.

"In here." Biggs shoved him inside the men's room. "I want to talk to you."

There were a couple of Mexicans standing at the urinals relieving themselves.

"Are they coming over? What happened back there?"

"Said they was busy."

Muck found the third degree he was being given clearly amusing and was oblivious to Biggs's surfacing anger.

The bishop waited for the Mexicans to leave, got both his hands on the nearest stall door and yanked it off the hinges and dropped it down on the floor to brace against the men's room door and the stall—only it was short by a couple of feet. He turned, zeroed in on a cabinet on the wall, its doors locked. He pulled the cabinet out of the wall and dropped it between the door he had lying flat on the tile floor and the stall itself, thus preventing anyone who might wish to enter the restroom from being able to.

He spun in Marvin's direction, slapped him hard enough to send the tinted sunglasses flying. Muck heard them hit the far wall of the restroom and drop to the floor. Hadn't cared for it obviously, yet not able, or was inclined, to turn off the stupid grin entirely.

"What the fuck, Dawg? Yo."

Biggs gripped him by the collar and threw him inside the doorless stall with all his might and jammed the Mag under his chin. Marvin was no longer amused by anything.

"Told you, Brotha: they say they was busy. Got a second show to do."

"Bullshit."

"Lana be the one. She don't like seein' you ice a chicken to get yo Jones up."

"You motherfucker. That's a side effect caused by the meds. They know that. I can't be the only one who suffers from periodic impotence due to anti-depressants. You were conned. Plain and simple. Conned."

"I explained about the med'. That you don't be killin' no chicken these day'."

"Even if I did, what's it to them? They're a bunch of whores and well paid to do what whores do. They don't have the right to question me and my methods of dealing with impotence."

"Peach said some other time; she would do it some other time. They all tol' me that. What can I do about it if they want to drop by the cribby some other time?"

"What do you got left? Let's see it."

"What do you mean what do I got left? I give it to 'em like you said."

"You smoked the bait? You were supposed to entice them with it. *You smoked the bait?*" Biggs slammed him against the wall. "You're not only fucking with the wrong man, but you're fucking with the wrong Man of the Cloth, asshole. I don't give you the goddamn shit so you can have a good time. I told you in plain English over and over: If they don't want to come out to the house, you do not let them smoke all of it. Give them a taste. That's eighty bucks worth of C they smoked. Eighty. Plus the hundred dollar tip that went into that bowl for them. Almost two hundred dollars—not including cover charge and drinks—and for what? The tip alone should have been plenty. You were supposed to reel them in with the other shit."

"I tried, Cecil. Swear it. Tried to do what you tol' me. They all laugh at me in there. Said I be wearin' *'Senile Citizen'* skins."

"*'Senile Citizen'?*"

"What they was sayin'."

"You got blown. That's what happened. You get 'sucked off' and I get 'screwed.'"

"They rubbed my Jones. Stella had her hand on my leg—and was rubbin' it. Made my dick hard, too."

"Wait a minute, instead of getting laid, you got played."

"Better than nothin', ain't it?"

"What's better than nothing? Blue Balls? As opposed to what? Getting your rocks off?"

"Said if McCoy saw them doin' me they would all get shit-can'. Piss' him off that Peach an' them, Dione an' them other two, Lana and Stella, won't give the nigga some pussy."

"Bullshit. That's a line they fed you. You got played, plain and simple. They practically have a whore house going on in there. He's got parlors next to his office where the sluts give head 24/7. Head and hand jobs. Gets his rocks by watching through a peep hole. Evidently everyone knows it but you." Biggs paused to collect himself. Had to. The excitement and stress wouldn't do his health much good.

"They're right. *You are senile.*"

"If I can't do it, you the one should."

"No, I'm no good with the sweet-talk. That's why I let you hang around me, punk. Only you're not pulling your weight these days. You're supposed to be the Pussy Magnet, the slick, smooth-talking Mack Daddy with the broads, remember? You got the walk down, got the jive down— truth is you never spent a day in the inner city in your life. Never set foot in Compton or South Central."

"Delivered phone book' door-to-door for a week in South Central one time. Do it count?"

Biggs glared at him. One day, truly, he would enjoy tearing him to pieces. Strap him to the butcher's block and sever his limbs with the *Black & Decker*. One day.

"I done my share of time. Cain't nobody claim different."

"I know all about the foster homes, orphanages—and none of it adds up to being a South Central gang-banger, or even an East LA *cholo*."

"Was never my game plan. Graveyard' be full of gang-banger'. Puttin' a bunch of bitches together and gettin' 'em out there to work the track was the plan."

"That's the plan?"

"Was always the plan. From the start—"

Biggs jammed the barrel inside the deacon's mouth. "Bite down on it, bitch. Do it."

Marvin did that. Biggs's hands reached for Marvin's ears. Held them this way as if he intended to tear them both off. Stared at him for a long moment.

"You're mistaking kindness for weakness here, punk, and I don't like it. I don't like being taken advantage of. Hear?"

Marvin nodded his head. Snot and sweat dripped from his upper lip. Seemed to be out of excuses. Biggs withdrew the Mag from his mouth. Wiped the barrel against Marvin's shirt. Re-holstered it. He walked over to a sink to wash his face. Marvin stayed put in the stall. Thought it be a good idea to stay there.

"When I was a kid people were always mistaking my kindness for weakness."

Biggs shoved the cabinet and the stall door out of the way, and walked out of the men's room.

"Hardly believe that." Marvin made it out of the stall to wash up at the sink. "Man never heard of kindness. Mothafuckah be crazy. Should get me a piece and blow his fuckin' head off, me."

A drunk staggered out of a stall at the far end and gave Marvin a real start. The man was black, in his fifties, in a rumpled dark suit and stained white shirt and red tie. He was grumbling about something as he stooped to pick up Marvin's rose-tinted glasses, and walked over to the sink next to the one Marvin was using. He handed him the shades without looking at him.

"Thanks. Yo."

Muck checked the sunglasses to see what shape they were in. Lenses were intact. Muck put them on. Adjusted them in the mirror.

The drunk washed his hands under the tap.

"You a fuckin' Oreo cookie, man."

Marvin's reaction was immediate and furious. He spun in the drunk's direction and punched him in the belly twice. Watched him double up, about to vomit. Lifted him by the collar.

"Who you callin' *'Oreo,'* wino? I'll tear both of your eye' out. *Call me a fuckin' Oreo.*"

The drunk, paralyzed with fear, could not offer up a verbal response. Saliva, mixed-in with bile, oozed down his chin.

"Don't no wino go there wiff me. Hear what I said, *nigga?*"

Marvin removed his shades. Head butted the man. Saw his melon bounce against the wall, and he slid to the floor. Muck took the time to kick him about the jaw with everything that he had.

"Don't nobody go there wiff me, ever. I ain't no *Oreo.* Never been. You the onliest *'Oreo''* round here, *mothafuckah.*"

The drunk at his feet was squirming, dealing with a serious attack of dry heaves. For all intents and purposes, was oblivious to the rest of it.

Marvin let it go. Didn't need another *'boo-shit rap'* added to his existing rap sheet. Not only that, peeps was entering the crapper and he needed to get the hell out. He walked out of there. Did feel better about having worked the big mouth over, but not much.

# CHAPTER 62

**He rechecked the shades for damage.** Put them on and elbowed his way through the crowded hallway, the thick cigarette smoke and unmistakable reefer aroma. Bummed a smoke from a skinny black skank with orange hair. Ugly as sin. Now that sayin' describe this *ho* to a *T.*

Marvin shoved his way past other sweaty bodies that reeked of cheap perfume and aftershave as he reached the main dance floor and finally made it toward the exit.

"Gonna take longer to get the bitches interested again. Meanwhile, the man be blowin' bank on dope and he don't like that—so you best get yo slick ass in gear, Base." I can take care of my end, Marvin told himself. Only we got to work together on this thang. "Try tellin' that to the crazy mofo."

The deacon made it outside. The parking lot was a sea of cars and not as well lit as it should have been, but there was enough light for him to make out Brotha Trusty standing out there by his *Caddy* in the middle of it all obviously eyeing the females standing outside the entrance smoking cigarettes and chatting with other females or guys trying to pick them up. Then he saw Cecil make a sharp arm gesture for him to hurry up and get his behind over to the *Cadillac* before bending in himself.

Not all that pleased with his lame performance in the dressing room, Marvin Muck was not inclined to pick up his pace as he walked in the direction of the sedan.

Dude was gonna mess wiff him some more. Couldn't even enjoy bein' high from the crack he fired up wiff the hoes. Gettin' a *.357 Magnum* shoved in his mouf and damn near losing both his ear' ain't made him feel too good, neither. On top of that, some old drunk nigga he never seen in his life had the nerve to call him *'Oreo'*—and he also knew that deep down he could have tried harder, worked the bitches a little better. Ain't tried hard enough. Wasn't smart what he done in there. Wanted to see all that tang again, up close, too, real *nekkid* and stripping and doin' a lap dance for nobody but his partner Cecil and him, right there in the livin' room— all their clothes off, shakin' that fine booty and them beaver' so close you could prob'ly stick yo tongue out an' taste 'em.

That' the way it was gonna be—and it will be, he was sure of it, only it took time. Bitches was there not that long ago, and they be comin' 'round again. Watch. These dopefiend' ain't no different from all the rest. They actin' like they be too good—but they all the same. They be comin' around in time, you just got to wait. Problem was that mofo sittin' in that red *Cadillac* over there don't like waitin', don't like havin' to spend his Benjamins on dope while the waitin' be goin' on.

He wished he could get his hand' on Peach LaBelle. Ho was the best, and the hardest to get prob'ly, after Livia Duarte. The other' wouldn't be so tough, 'specially not Lana Da Bottom. Strawberry got the rep for puttin' out long as the price be right, and sometime you could sweet talk Stella Storm to go that way, too. 'Sho nuff. Stella don't be no easy lay like Lana, leastways she be actin' like it, sayin' shit like, "I got to like the man first." Yo, so long as the dude come across wiff the coin' an' toot. *Well, I be a likable Daddy*, Marvin Muck thought. An' the rest? We get to it. Yo. An' what about Dione? What be her problem? Dione be loyal to Danny and they baby, but she like' to get high as much as any ho. It be a fucked up society of doper and sex fiend. You just had to get yo share of good time', yo share of what was out there; yo share of vagina and dope; yo cut of the pie while you wuz alive—an' the rest don't matter. Don't nothin' else matter, he said to himself, while approaching the Caddy, as a familiar-sounding female voice called his name from somewhere in back of him. He turned to take a look. It was Dione Aragon. Running after him.

"What's your hurry, Marvin? How about a hit? If you still got any left. Never did get my share. I was in the shower while everyone else got high, got theirs. Ain't fair."

# CHAPTER 63

**Bishop Cecil O. Biggs took the opportunity to flip toggles that disengaged his lights, all of them: to include headlights, parking lights, dash and dome light, brake lights and license plate lights.**

Yes, the windows were tinted. Play it safe anyway. Wondered if he had time to hop out and switch the plates for the bogus ones behind them? No. Not now. Biggs had had front and rear plates rigged so that it was possible to swap them for stolen ones with the greatest of ease and without need of a screwdriver. He had the same setup in place with the plates on the cargo van that he used from time to time. The only risk involved when using fake plates came when you got pulled over by the rollers, *if one got pulled over*. Because then you were fucked. Unless you had a piece handy and could deal with the problem. Unfortunately no plan was one hundred percent foolproof. The only time he used fake plates was when he trolled the streets at night for fresh meat and as a hedge against eyewitnesses.

He remained seated. There was no time to get out and fool with the rear plate, not that he knew for certain what was about to go down. One fact was indisputable: the adrenaline was kicking in. The mere thought of abducting one of these bitches caused his groin to stir in his trousers.

He turned his head and could see them through his rear right window. Adjusted his rearview mirror so that he wouldn't have to keep craning his neck and observed them this way.

Marvin had his arm around Danny's hot wife and that insincere smile of his was working overtime as he guided the woman toward the Caddy's rear door. Bishop could hear him lay it on, thick and heavy.

"All right, sugah-bush. No problem. We can take care of that. Plenty of super fly bump left. You know you in luck wiff Mack Daddy Muck. Gonna take care of his favorite honey right now."

Deacon had the back door open, and steered her into the seat. Promptly got in himself and shut the door. Was smooth and discreet when he pressed down on the interior door lock lever with his elbow.

"Hi ya, Dione." Biggs handed her a joint. "You were just fantastic tonight."

"Thank you." Dione got her clean fingers on the dirty reefer. Toked. "Got any *Kibbles n' Bits*? I can pay."

"Baby, yo greedy friend' dun smoked all that fine dope I brung wiff me. There be more where it come from, plenty more. Ain't that right, *Brotha Trusty*?"

"Oh yeah. It's there all right." And while Biggs was saying this and while the young woman continued to suck on the joint, Biggs was reaching down under his seat. Got his hand on a blackjack and whirled so quickly and efficiently with it that Dione Aragon never knew what knocked her out as Brother Trusty gave her a hard whack above the eyes that literally fractured her skull and left a deep indentation in her forehead. The evil clown followed up with another whack, and the bulbous end of the sap hammered into her right cheekbone and eye socket with a squishing, crunching sound. It was a blow that left a good deal of that side of her face shattered and jammed the eye far enough inside the socket so that it looked like a hole full of dark red gooey mush.

The woman's body slumped down in the seat.

"Dione?" There was a male voice calling the vic's name from somewhere in back of them. Biggs looked up, while his partner spun around in the back seat. Danny Aragon, having emerged from the Casbah's side entrance with the eight-month-old baby crying in his arms, was looking for his wife.

He paused briefly to shove the pacifier in his daughter's mouth and then appeared to be headed in the direction of the *Cadillac*. He was making his way through the many parked cars in the poorly lighted lot, wondering what happened, how she could've vanished so quickly? Danny was fairly certain that had been her a moment ago standing in the middle of the lot, but he had been so preoccupied with trying to make it past the party types without bumping into any of them with the baby, and then there had been that hassle with the bouncer who had admonished him for bringing a kid around when he knew that under no circumstances did the owner allow his employees to have their underage children anywhere near his place of business, that when Danny had turned his head again, Dione was disappeared. Gone.

He continued to call her name as he drifted closer to the *Cadillac*.

"Get him over here."

"How?"

*"Do it. He probably saw her get in with you. Get his doomed ass over here before he walks back and lets somebody know. Get him over here now."*

# CHAPTER 64

**Marvin Muck hopped out of the *Cadillac.*** Called out to the woman's husband. While he did that, Biggs was wiping the blood from the stripper's face. Propped her up just a bit to make it seem that she was merely slouching from the high; she had a buzz on and was "nodding."

Biggs had his fingers around the *Magnum* butt now and waited for young hubby to get in the car.

Soon enough the back door opened. Danny stuck his head in. The pacifier dropped from the infant's mouth and she started in on another jag. Noise was unnerving. Doubled the pressure to get Danny Aragon inside the vehicle.

*Keep your composure*, Cecil reminded himself. *Calm. Collected.* Whatever you do, do not lose it. Not here. Not now. You cannot afford to miscalculate.

"Come on in, man. Your better half's doing fine, flying high. Check her out. Just took a couple of good hits off of some great shit."

The baby carried on. Biggs could feel perspiration all across his forehead. Armpits were soaking wet. Down there, too, balls were sweaty and itched. All he wanted to do was see the baby shut the fuck up.

*Shut it. Smash it. Kill it. Kill the kid.* End the noise. But you got to get the fucking Papa in first. Keep smiling. Stay at ease. Part of his nervousness, unease, adrenaline—brought about by what was about to take place.

Get in, punk. *Your fate is sealed.* It's only a matter of time.

Danny Aragon took a look around and could not see much in the poorly-illuminated backseat. Could not even tell if that was his wife exactly sitting over there against the far door.

"Ain't you got any light in this fine ride, bro?"

"Fuse is out. Been meaning to replace it. You know how it is."

Danny Aragon nodded. Bent in finally with the kid. Marvin wasted no time himself, and slid in behind him. Helped him in, so to speak. Made certain the door was locked. Biggs spun around at about the same time. Leveled the *Magnum* at Danny's face. Cocked the hammer.

*"Not a word. Don't even blink."*

Biggs gestured to drop the noisy toddler on the floor. Danny did as told: lowered his daughter to the space at his feet. Biggs handed Muck a pair of handcuffs. Watched as Muck was about to cuff the husband's wrists in front of him.

"No. Behind his back."

"He ain't goin' no place."

*"Behind his back."*

The order was carried out. Danny Aragon's wrists were pulled in back of him and the cuffs clamped on.

*"You do it right?"*

"Got them on there tight as could be."

Biggs reached back with the blackjack and gave Danny a series of blows across the side of his face and skull that knocked him unconscious.

The baby's cries seemed to intensify, if anything, and it made it unbearable for the Caddy owner now, absolutely unbearable. Biggs leaned over the backrest once more, pulled himself over it in order to be able to get at the baby and swung down hard—and suddenly it got real quiet inside the car.

"That's how you take care of that."

Biggs looked up, checking the club's entrance, making sure that no one else wanted any part of the *Cadillac*, nor its occupants.

Marvin sat speechless in the backseat, staring at the floor and the silent bundle inside the pink blanket with the ever-spreading dark stain in the area where the presently still infant's head was.

*"Hey!* Hand me the purse."

Muck did that. Biggs dropped it in his medical bag. Reminded Muck to get Danny's wallet and search his pockets for whatever else there was to be found. The wallet was handed over.

Biggs opened it to see what was in there. Wad of greenbacks. Now was not the time to start counting. He wouldn't. Dropped the wallet in. Muck handed over keys, wad of crumpled banknotes and coins. Pack of smokes.

All of it, with the exception of the smokes, was dropped in the bag. Bishop handed the smokes back to Marvin, with a warning not to smoke them in his presence.

"Should hit the road, man."

"Get the wedding bands. Any and all other rings and watches. Earrings. Get her earrings."

This was accomplished in rapid succession. Handed over to the man and dumped into the black leather medical bag.

"Not bad. Not bad at all for a single night's take."

Biggs snapped the bag shut, turned the key in the ignition, and slowly pulled out of the parking space. When he looked up in his rearview he noticed that Muck had stuck a butt between his lips.

"What did I just say? Did I not just tell you not to light up around me? Especially not in the *Cadillac*."

"See me light up?"

"You were going to."

"Fuck I was. That be one gone baby, Cecil."

"No shit. Kid's better off. Look what it had for parents. *Dirt*. Won't have to worry about life's many little disappointments now, will she? Wished they had done me the favor when I was born. Should have strangled me—or something—or strangled my parents. Psychos weren't fit to raise pigeons."

"In the dressin' room back there I was sayin' how that must be the luckiest baby in the world 'cause she was suckin' on her mama' big titty— wished I was suckin' on that big titty myself instead—and now that baby ain't lucky no more, is it?"

"I told you: *It's better off.* Get your act together. We're not out of the woods yet. It's on your head the way this whole thing got messy. If you'd have done what you were supposed to and not given the whores all that dope in there it wouldn't have turned out like this. Fuck it. No use crying over spilt milk. Don't lose your head now, Base. Are you with me, partner—or what?"

Marvin nodded. "I be wiff you, Cecil. You know that. Yo."

Sure you are, thought Biggs. You better be. He scratched his crotch absentmindedly and his lips twisted into a nervous smile as he guided the Caddy slowly through the crowded parking lot, passing arriving cars with obnoxious revelers.

"That's what I like to hear, Marvin." Biggs inched the big car into the street finally and turned the lights on. "Makes me feel better to know who's on my side—and who isn't. It helps clarify things."

"I be on your side, Brotha. All I be wantin' was some pussy. Vagina. Went in there thinkin' we was gonna get them hoe' to come out to the cribby and take they panty off and shit. We was gonna party, do the nasty. Didn't figure we was gonna off no baby. . . ."

"What of it, goddammit? It happened, and it's over with. Get used to it."

"I be gettin' used to it."

"We'll have to dump the kid before Dione comes to, otherwise she's liable to freak to the point it might spoil the party I've got planned for her. Are you with me?"

"Said I be wiff you, Brotha."

"All the way?"

"All the way. You know my motto: blood don't bother me, long as it don't be mine."

Biggs said nothing. Checked his mirrors to make certain they were not being tailed, that no rollers were in back of them for any reason. He adjusted the volume on the police scanner. Concentrated on the road ahead. Did his best to leave the city as efficiently as possible without violating traffic laws that would get them pulled over, and headed out toward a section of Angeles Crest that was sure to be deserted this time of night.

# CHAPTER 65

**Biggs left the main highway, got on a bridle path, and took that deep into the mountains.**

Hundred foot sycamores as well as equally tall maples and even taller pine tended to block out the chrome-like, bluish glow generated by the almost-there full moon above—and the deeper they got into the trees, the less glow they had to work with, forcing Biggs to use his headlights periodically.

They reached a clearing. Cecil dimmed his lights. Drove across. He parked the *Cadillac* in a grove of live oak. There was a slope on the right. He engaged a lever that rolled Marvin's window down. Told him to pitch the bundle.

"Bundle? What 'bundle'? I ain't touchin' no dead kid. I ain't no baby killa, me."

"Who said you did anything? Pitch it out the window so we can get a move on. Do it before they come to."

Marvin Muck shook his head. "Fuck that."

Biggs got out. Had the back door open on Marvin's side. Told him to get in the front. "Wait. Hand me the kid first."

Marvin stared at him without saying anything. "You know I have a bad back. It doesn't take much."

"Fuck that noise."

Marvin got out and sat in the front.

"Useless, worthless, retard asshole."

Biggs reached down for the dead infant in the pink blanket. It occurred to him that Sassy favored the color pink and that he just might like to have something this nice and fuzzy. Why not? Why throw it away and leave this much evidence behind?

And the kid?—if left out here? Would eventually be mangled and devoured by scavengers. He yanked up on the blanket and the small body rolled off onto the floor.

Biggs held the blanket up and shone his Maglite on it. Noticed blood stains here and there. Poured a liberal amount of water on it to dilute the blood. Wrung the blanket to squeeze the blood and water out. Fanned it out for a closer look and tossed it inside the trunk. The trouble he went to for the ungrateful geeks. Not that all were ungrateful. Enough of them were.

He returned to the backseat, picked the "bundle" up and carried it to the edge of the slope. Tossed it. The way it came down, hit the ground, bounced a couple of times, and rolled toward the bottom, reminded him of the way Charlotte Yvonne did her own share of bouncing before she came to rest at the ditch digger's feet and jackhammer. Flashbacks wouldn't let you be. What it came down to. No matter what type of activity you happened to be involved in, no matter how many years had passed. Whether you were asleep or wide awake—the flashbacks constantly pecked at your psyche.

He returned to the car. Drove another seventy, eighty feet. Climbed out.

# CHAPTER 66

**Danny Aragon was coming to.** His wife Dione was having a fit of some kind. Her good eye, the left eye, and that side of her face kept twitching. It was the fractured skull that caused it, no doubt—not to mention pure and paralyzing fear induced by staring death in the face—*and that's what they were both doing right about now: having a little tete-a-tete with death.*

*"Please, Cecil. Don't hurt us no more."*

Trusty ignored her. They had to get a move on it.

"Get with it, Deacon. Get the shovel out of the back. Hurry up."

Marvin took his time getting out of the car.

"Where you want me to start diggin'?"

"Bottom of that slope looks familiar."

Biggs pressed the trunk release inside the glove compartment. Marvin got his hands on a shovel and made the slow, cautious descent down the grassy incline that was fairly slippery. Didn't take long for him to lose his footing and balance and down he went, hard, rolling, and did not stop until he landed on an old and warped, oblong-shaped sheet of plywood that had been camouflaged with branches and dirt.

"This is no time to be taking a nap."

"I don't be takin' no nap, me."

Muck cursed, and picked himself up, picked the shovel up. Wedged the tip under the plywood and shoved it aside, and went about modifying the shallow hole in the ground to accommodate someone of Danny Aragon's size and height.

The ominous sounds of an owl hooting from one of those trees up there and the nerve-wracking noise the cicadas were making, among other bugs and animals, possibly coyotes or possum, did not help his anxiety any.

He looked up to see if Cecil was still watching. He wasn't. Couldn't see where he was. Gone back to the Caddy to mess wiff the ho.

"All right, get the job done."

Marvin was talking to himself to help steady his nerves. "There be work to do and some fuckin' to be got." He could hear Danny and his wife up there on the ridge trying to talk their way out of the fix they were in.

Marvin didn't much care what Biggs did to the punk, not really, so long as they could both get a taste of his old lady. Now, to ice a dude like Danny don't be his idea. Only what could he do? Let it take place, is what. Don't be the first time. Bigg' say can't leave a witness. Danny be a witness. Now, to waste that *trim* would make no kinda sense. That would bother him—if that be what Omar got on his mind to do.

She did look good. Look' fine. Even wiff that fucked up eyeball she still be a fine piece of pussy. Only you know Omar ain't gonna let you have none of that, unless he don't want it no more hisself. Might let you have some, then. Yo. Real Sloppy Second'—if not that, could be Thrillin' Third'.

## CHAPTER 67

**Marvin shook his head.** Glanced back up at the top. That be one crazy, baby-killin' mothafuckah up there, that Brotha Trusty. One psycho mofo. He could hear more pleading, *victim' aksking to be spared.*

"What did we ever do to you, Mr. Biggs? Why are we being treated this way?"

"Let's just say I didn't care for the way you were raising the kid, Danny. Or something like it. Ignorant assholes like you should never be allowed to have offspring."

*"My baby's back there at the club, Cecil."* It was Dione this time, half-choking on tears, not able to fully comprehend the reason behind the nightmare. Why was it happening to her and her husband? What had they done to be punished this way? And there was every indication that the situation would only get worse.

*"I love my baby.... I just want to get back to my baby.... I'm worried about my little girl.... Can't you just take us back? Take us back and leave us and we'll forget any of this ever happened. You can do that, can't you?"*

"We're at the point of no return, so knock it off with the unrealistic notions."

Biggs held the *.357* in his right hand. Walked around to Danny's door and pulled him out by the cuffs. He dragged him away from the Caddy and over to the edge of the incline. Danny Aragon was far from being a willing participant in the program. Struggled. Attempted to rise. Cecil smacked him once against the back of the head with the *Magnum* that was like a hammer blow that forced Dione's hubby to drop to his knees, where Cecil wanted him.

"You about ready down there, Brother Marvin?"

"This be hard work, man."

"Hurry it up." Biggs held the barrel end against the base of Danny's skull. "Make it deep enough to keep scavengers from tampering with the body."

*"Please, don't."* Danny was back at it again. Sobbing. *"Please. . . ."*

"What's happening down there? I'm getting tired of waiting."

"And I be gettin' tired of diggin'. Seem' to me waitin' be a whole lot easier than diggin'."

"The hole was fucking dug already. All you had to do was enlarge it, make it a little deeper to keep animals from getting at the body."

Marvin said nothing. Did his work. Kept his head down. There was time' it was the best thing to do, else he could find hisself in the ground wiff the stiff. Never can tell. Didn't think Cecil would do him like that, him bein' a big help to him. Never could tell, though; never was sure about it.

What he gonna do wiffout me? Wiff that fucked up back and the 'roid burnin' up his asshole? He best not try no shit. 'Cause if he do, I'm gone, me. Drop a dime on his crazy ass.

# CHAPTER 68

**Dione's young husband continued to plead for his life.** Cecil was, in fact, just a little weary of it. He stepped in front of the man and whipped him across the face with the *.357* and watched Danny land on his side. Part of his upper lip and nose torn off by the blow. He was spitting blood and chipped teeth, coughing and sobbing uncontrollably.

*"Quit your fakin', boy.* Take it like a man. If the bitch wants to whimper, that's a different story there. You're supposed to be a man. Take it like a man. What did you expect? To live forever? No matter how much crack

and weed you cocksuckers got off me it was never enough. Here's where the party ends and the piper is paid. Get it, boy? So don't whimper and don't pray to god because 'god' won't hear you and 'He' won't save you."

Biggs paused to take another look down at what was going on with Muck. Aimed his Maglite at him. Free Ride had stopped digging and had stepped to the side of the hole, awaiting approval.

"Looks deep enough from where I'm standing."

Biggs ordered the victim to sit up. Made certain that he still faced the gully. He stood directly behind Dione's husband, held the muzzle at the base of his head, waited, turned to see if Dione was taking it in. He knew that she would be. His eyes were back on the *Magnum.* Lowered it. Returned to the Caddy to tape her mouth shut, then made it to the rear. Dug around under the blue tarp for a fourteen-by-fourteen-inch sheet of metal approximately one quarter inch thick with a sheet of plywood on either side glued to it. There was a bolt in each of the corners to further ensure that it all held together like it was supposed to under the most challenging circumstances. Biggs had painted red targets on both sides with a perfectly formed bull's-eye in the center. If stopped and questioned, he was ready to claim the board had been created for shooting practice— which in fact it was, never mind that his idea of practice differed from other people's—and the pocks in the wood, cracks and scars, would back it, or so he reasoned. And if it failed to convince the rollers? Too bad, because the board's real purpose was that it made it easier to locate the slugs afterwards. Sometimes the slugs penetrated both wood and metal, not very often, sometimes, depended on the caliber used (as well as type of ammo).

Whatever the result, whether the lead was retained, or ended up in the soil, it made it far easier to dig out when the shooting was over and spared him enough aggravation to make it worth the effort by making it a little more difficult for forensics to figure out what had caused what. Less evidence, that's all; less to trace back to whoever did the deed.

Nothing was ever one hundred percent foolproof, although precautions such as this did make it more of a task for those whose job it was to track down and hinder types like him from having their fun and living life the way they chose.

He returned to where Danny waited, on his knees, facing the gully below. Blood and mucus oozed from his nose and mouth.

Trusty the Clown smacked him against the back of the head with the heavy board and watched him tumble down toward the grave, where his upper half, conveniently enough, ended up.

Biggs made his way down. Had Marvin turn the victim on his back. Told him to shove the rest of him in there. Handed him the bull's-eye.

"Prep him for his dirt nap."

Marvin placed the board directly under the victim's head, and stepped away. Cecil O. looked back at the ridge. Told Marvin to get up there and drag the bitch out of the car and to make certain that she saw what was about to take place.

"Toss one of those empty water jugs down while you're up there."

Muck had a pretty good idea what that meant. Made him queasy in the belly. No pretending it didn't.

"Ho gonna freak. Gonna be hard to control later."

"Or she just might be *easier* to control later."

There was no recourse but to obey the order. Muck found the empty plastic jug inside the trunk and flung it down in Cecil's general direction. Carried Dione Aragon out and lowered her close enough to the edge so that there was no doubt that she would be able to view the proceedings.

Biggs knelt beside the male victim. Held the barrel near to his face, said nothing. Watched Danny Aragon's lips tremble and twitch and the tears flow. There was something about the worthless punk a-hole that made Biggs want to savor every millisecond. Payback was sweet. Doing unto others was far sweeter than the FBI ever knew. All those experts who were convinced they had guys like him figured. They interviewed countless serial killers, or so they liked to claim . . . and knew exactly what made them tick. . . . What a laugh.

He uncapped the jug. Had his switchblade out. Clicked the release mechanism. Shiny stainless steel blade and hilt. A marvel of German engineering, durable. He had smuggled it out from when he was stationed there and kept it over the years. Quality like this was something you cherished and wanted to hold on to, unlike that piece of crap of a knife made in Mexico that Ortiz liked to wave around in people's faces to show what a badass he was.

But that was Ortiz. He had some other punk here to deal with. To cut him in the neck would serve his purpose, so long as he did not go anywhere near the carotid artery. Slicing into the carotid would cause the victim's blood to spray and the bag-of-manure to expire before he'd had a chance to nuke his brains while he was still breathing and aware of his surroundings. You always wanted them to be fully aware of what was going on before they "egressed."


Cecil cut into his neck, away from the crucial artery, and the blood flowed to the point he was able to capture enough of it via the plastic jug for his eventual purpose.

Biggs recapped the jug and set it aside. He rose. Jammed earplugs in his ears. Aimed the *Magnum* at Danny Aragon's face. The look of utter and absolutely paralyzing fear gave him wood. He was close to creaming in his pants from this alone. Wouldn't allow it. Not now. Not here.

He squeezed the trigger and watched as the back of the beaner's skull exploded. Blowback was the icing on the cake: brains and blood, gristle and bone punched out both ears, nose, and mouth. Who could ask for more? The act had nearly caused him to climax. In fact, his groin had first begun to stir way back in the parking lot, while in the Caddy and the initial throes of violence, and gone down periodically; had risen a degree and also given up the battle.

Presently what he had was a full blown erection. Let the profilers contemplate that one.

Dione was groaning and carrying on up there at the top of the slope, calling Jesus' name and moaning a muffled *"NO!"* over and over again through the duct tape. It may not have been original, but it was genuine. Seemed to mean every bit of it. Was rapidly working herself into a state of exhaustion, if she did not temper it some.

Biggs yelled up at Marvin to come on down. Muck complied. Left her gasping there through the gag and twisting about on the ground, while he scrambled down to where the body was.

"He dead. You gettin' good at this."

"Yeah? He's not dead enough."

Marvin got the point. Was about to lift the dead man's head in order to retrieve the plywood square and take a look at the bull's-eye to see how close Trusty Lusty had come this time, instead he knew enough to jump back.

The bishop stood over Dione's dead husband. Aimed the barrel low. Squeezed off a second shot, and watched the rest of the head disintegrate into so many bloody chunks of brain and matted hair.

Biggs resumed standing in place. Needing to savor every detail. Memories were made of this. He took the plugs out of his ears.

"He dead enough now? Yo."

"Get the board. Make sure both slugs were contained by it."

Marvin was about to wipe the mess off the board against the dead man's clothing when Biggs stopped him in time.

"Wood particles can be used as evidence later."

Biggs told him to take fifty steps or so and wipe the board against grass and dry leaves. Marvin did that and brought it back.

"Bull's-eye."

"Both?"

"Can't hardly tell. One for sure. Ain't got all the mess off."

Biggs angled it for better viewing. Couldn't tell where the other bullet had hit. Marvin was right: one bull's-eye for certain. The other slug was iffy. Missed by two inches, in fact. Made him wonder if this was a bad omen. Never made him feel good to miscalculate by this much.

"See it?"

"Don't worry about it." Biggs tossed him the key to the handcuffs. "Get the bracelets. Throw dirt on him."

Soon it was over with.

"What chu want to do wiff the other plywood? The large one?"

"Can't very well take it with us in the Caddy. Drag it sixty feet out and leave it."

This was done.

# CHAPTER 69

**Biggs picked up the jug with the blood and they climbed to the top of the slope, where a terrified, hysterical Dione Aragon was on her side and appeared to be gagging on vomit.**

Biggs peeled the gag off. He took the plywood square with the bull's-eye, did some more swiping of it against the ground. Saw to it that it was free and clear of blood and hair, brains and bone fragments belonging to Danny Aragon. Did his best under the circumstances. Further cleansing would take place later.

He sprayed the board with enzyme and poured rubbing alcohol over both sides and slid it under the blue tarp in the trunk, under the metal chest.

"She's choking on puke. I don't want it on my interior."

Dione was clearly gagging, in that vomit emanated from her mouth and nasal passages.

"What chu be sayin'?"

"I'm saying she better not expire."

"What do I do? I don't want barf on me."

Biggs walked back to where the woman was sitting on the ground, head bent over, heaving, choking on chunks. He gave her back several whacks with an open palm. It helped, but not in any significant way.

"Blow your nose. Blow it. Blow your nose, cunt, before I blow your brains out."

Vomit oozed from her nostrils. She made the effort as ordered. Cleared the nasal passages to some small degree.

"Get your fingers in there and unclog her throat."

Marvin hadn't cared for the idea.

"Do it now."

The woman continued to choke, gasping. Mucus and vomit dripped from nose and mouth. Finally Marvin did as ordered. Didn't want to see the ho suffer. He'd wanted to rape them all, but no way did he like seein' this kind of shit go down. Rape never hurt no ho. Beatin' on 'em and killin' 'em did nobody no good.

He stuck a couple of his long, bony fingers inside her mouth and cleared the blockage. Got the vomit out of there, possibly skinned a knuckle on her teeth.

Biggs held out the box of *Kleenex* for him. Watched as Marvin yanked a handful to wipe her mouth and chin with. Wiped his fingers free of blood and whatnot, snot and vomit, while he was at it.

"What I don't be doin' for the *Church of Retard and Dope*."

"That's good enough. Shit costs money."

"Yo. Everything be costin' coin' these day'."

Marvin was about to toss the used tissues when Biggs stopped him from doing this as well. Had a plastic trash bag open and waiting for the refuse. Muck dropped it in.

Biggs uncapped the jug with the tap water and poured it over the gasping, convulsing victim's face. Muck was grousing about something again.

"What now?"

"You givin' her tap water?"

"Beats barf, don't it?"

"She don't be good enough for *Hawaiian Punch*?"

Biggs said nothing. Poured the water.

"Surprised you ain't give her the blood in the jug."

"I would, except there isn't enough to go around. I have better use for her hubby's plasma." Biggs saw to it that some of the water reached her mouth. A coughing seizure appeared to overtake her.

"Quit your fakin', cunt."

He slapped her across the face a couple of times. They were moderately hard slaps to get her to settle down. He had Marvin pick her up in his arms and carry her back to the *Cadillac* and dump her in the backseat. Biggs unsnapped the strap on the black medical bag. Dug around in there until he found what he wanted: dark wig, lipstick, blush-on, black eyeliner; container of *Tylenol*.

He shoved three rapid release gels in her mouth. Poured tap water down her throat to help chase the gels down. He recapped the container and returned it to the black medical bag.

"Aspirin? You givin' the ho aspirin? Ho got both: head and eye fucked up and you be givin' her aspirin?"

"It's *Tylenol*, dummy. *Extra-strength*. Unless you're willing to take her place, I suggest you stop running your mouth."

# CHAPTER 70

**Biggs applied the cherry red lipstick to her mouth, blush-on to her cheeks, eyeliner to the good eye.** Affixed the wig over her bloody blond locks and he was good to go. Clown climbed on board and ripped her clothes off. What he couldn't tear with his bare hands he cut away with his switchblade.

*"Like Ecstasy, bitch? I've got your Ecstasy right here."*

He had his fly unzipped and his stiffening tool in his right hand. "Do you know how much I spent on that shit? Do you have any idea? Did you give a fuck? Hell, no. You didn't. *But you will. You better be good."*

He slid his hand between her moist thighs. Handed Marvin the Maglite.

"Shine it on her cunt."

Marvin did that. He liked what he was seeing and wanted in on the action.

"When do I get me some, Dawg?"

"Shut up." Biggs noticed it. "She pissed her panties. Another one. Lookit all that urine on my upholstery. This is a new *Cadillac*, bitch." Suddenly he found himself not minding. "That's all right. I like it."

"Coulda been worse." Marvin rubbed himself inside his trousers as he spoke. "She coulda shit all over the new Caddy seat."

"Forget it. Nothing the matter with a little urine between friends."

"Easy for you to say. 'Cause Marvin here be the clean-up nigga."

Biggs parted the woman's legs and slipped his groin inside and began stroking.

"I was beginning to wonder if it was all worth it, taking a crazy chance like that in McCoy's parking lot. Sometimes you just have to do what you have to do."

"That be right." Marvin was muttering to himself; he was nodding his head and muttering. Had his member out and was full-on masturbating. "Man got to do what he got to do."

"Yeah, Dolly."

Biggs stroked. Held her tighter. Dug his hands under her buttocks and held her up, toward him, pressing her pelvis against his this way. He probed with his middle finger. Found her rectum and slid it in. Followed up with a second finger inside her anus. It was dry going. Uncapped the jug with the blood. Stuck his fingers inside the spout and turned the jug over so that enough of the red stuff covered his fingers. Lowered the jug and reinserted the same fingers inside her. The lubing effort was not necessarily for her benefit, but his. A smooth ride was far more preferable than a dry hump.

He withdrew his groin from her vagina and slid it inside her butt crack. He stayed with it for another two minutes or so. Stroked. Felt the explosion nearing and paused long enough to postpone it. Didn't want to blow his load just yet. Resumed stroking for a while longer. Warned her to get ready to suck the poison out of him.

"Get ready to suck the meds out, bitch. All that shit they put in me over the years—all those toxins they pumped into me that only managed to exacerbate my condition."

Trusty withdrew from her rectum, and shoved his cock deep inside her mouth and unloaded with a gasp. Held on tight until he was completely spent, and got up.

# CHAPTER 71

**Outside the Caddy, Marvin was finishing up himself.** Pushed his groin back inside his baggy jeans and zipped up.

"That's enough for the time being." Clown wiped his brow. "Whew. All right. There's more where that came from. Plenty more. We've got to get you back to the house. Yeah. You'll do just fine, as long as you don't go passing out on me all the time—because then we'll just have to dispose of you like your old man. Got it? Stay alert and healthy for ol' Trusty."

Biggs was out of the backseat, zipping up and getting behind the steering wheel.

"How about some for me?"

"Later. There better not be any of your sperm on my rear bumper, Marvin. That's all I've got to say about that." Biggs started the Caddy engine. "I want to get back before dawn. Get her into the chest."

Marvin cursed. Pulled the girl out of the backseat and yanked her by the arm toward the trunk. Had the trunk open, and was lifting the suitcase-shaped, metal chest out and placing it on the ground. Biggs noticed it from where he sat, and thought: What the fuck? He hopped out. Stopped Muck from creating twice the work and taking twice the time.

"No. Leave the fucking chest in the trunk, and then force the *henpecker* in there. Less lifting, less effort."

"If you say so."

The chest was tossed back in by the sidekick. There he was trying to get the victim to stand in it, or whatever it was he was attempting that galled Biggs further. He shoved Muck out of the way, grabbed the female by the neck and pushed her down into the suitcase. Forced her in, on her side, into something resembling the fetal position. He tried closing the lid and could not quite manage. Parts of her prevented it. Shoulder and head, in the hip area. He punched away until he had that problem solved.

"We don't have all fucking night, heifer."

He lifted the lid now. Indicated the foot and a half length of hose, one end of which had a mouthpiece on it that resembled something used by scuba divers. The other end ran through a hole the size of a quarter, or a mite smaller, in the side, between the two nylon cord handles.

He pulled the hose out. Had Marvin hold it to his mouth and blow through it to make certain there were no obstructions, then had him find a stick long enough to poke through.

Marvin located a twig. Handed it to Biggs, and he ran it through. Hose was clear.

"How come you always be messin' wiff that shit, Brotha? Ain't nothin' in that hose. I done that last time."

Biggs ran the twig back and forth inside the hose. He finished with it. Satisfied. Ran one end of the hose through the hole in the chest, and stuck the mouthpiece in the victim's jaw.

"I suggest that you do not let the mouthpiece slip out of your kisser. That's your sole connection to life—between now and our destination. Lack of oxygen could result in your untimely demise—and we wouldn't want that."

They brought the lid down. It took some doing, but they managed to close it. Flipped the clasps in place. Slammed the trunk shut.

"That's how it's done."

Biggs got in behind the wheel. Muck got in on the other side.

"I want to keep her around as long as possible. That's why I take the time to fool with the tubing. Victims need air—just like you and me and everyone else. You want a piece of that, don't you?"

"Said I did."

"We have to take certain precautions. Keep her alive until she's of no use to us. I think I cracked her skull pretty good with that sap. She won't last long anyway. We'll hold on to her for as long as we can—until something else comes along."

"Yo. Until we get our hand' on LaBelle of da Ball."

"I dream about that. A day doesn't go by that I don't think about Pearleen Bell and Olivia Duarte. Olivia's older sister is not bad, either."

Biggs drove through the clearing. Found his way back to the bridle path, and took that toward the highway. Less than two hours later they were pulling up to the gate.

# CHAPTER 72

**The gray prefab house to the right of Biggs's church did not have any of its lights on but that did not mean that the Roscoes, Marty and his wife Petunia, whose domicile this happened to be, were both sound asleep.**

The dogs had taken turns yelping, waking the woman, while her husband slept like a log, snoring away, as usual.

Petunia was full-figured, as some liked to call a certain type of woman built in this fashion. She was a couple of years past forty, stood a shade under five foot four inches. Mrs. Roscoe was not known for her calm demeanor, instead her "claim-to-fame" and/or "infamy," depending on the individual making the observation, were her enormous "udders," that her husband rarely failed to boast about, measured a good forty-four inches. Triple E.

The Boston terrier, Darcy, had first barked about something, then the Lhasa apso named Ziggy had followed suit, and created enough of a ruckus between them to cause Petunia to remain fully awake.

She had heard Biggs pull up in that boat of a car, and she had rushed to the living room curtains to steal a peek. Saw Marvin hop out to unlock Biggs's front gate and the *Brougham* pull into the driveway and disappear behind the church as Biggs drove it on to his backyard.

Marvin had locked the gate back up, and hurried on foot to meet up with the bishop back there.

Petunia found herself practically running through the house, across the carpeted bedroom floor, to get to the rear porch door. Was careful to open it and the screen door as quietly as possible. Chewing on her lower lip nervously, she had tiptoed across the porch and cautiously climbed down the stoop. Made every effort to stay silent as she snuck up to the picket fence to peer through a crack.


She saw Biggs, in that hideous clown makeup, and his sidekick, the one he referred to as "Deacon," reach inside the trunk for a large, suitcase-type metal chest and carry it inside the church through the rear door.

After a while, Biggs reappeared and made certain the Caddy doors were locked, closed the trunk quietly enough, clicked on the car alarm, and hurried back inside his church.


Petunia looked at the watch on her wrist. It was twelve past four. She returned to bed, sliding in beside her husband.

She had wanted to tell him that Biggs and Marvin were at it again, that they were hauling that chest around. *Something* was not right, she felt like telling Marty—only Marty snored on. That was usually his response to most of these suspicious sightings that she felt like discussing, going over with him.

"I wonder what those two creeps could be up to? Every time I see them they're either carrying something out of that house to one of his fancy cars, or else it's the other way around: carrying something from either the *Cadillac* or the *Rolls-Royce into* the house. . . ."

Her husband coughed. Turned on his side. The snoring did not stop.

"Marty?"

"Hmmm?"

"Marty, you're snoring."

# CHAPTER 73

**Biggs and Marvin carried the suitcase into the basement and lowered it near the pit.** The bishop had Marvin stay put and not do anything while he walked in the direction of the Geek Room with the baby blanket.

Biggs parted the small curtain over the Judas window. Idiot box was on, flickering. Some of the geeks were awake and watching, or asleep, or just plain staring off into space. One of the generic geek males in a lower bunk picked his nose, another one was squatting over a honey bucket. Goodfellow, the diaper-wearer, had his hands inside the diaper and he was fondling his privates.

Biggs unlocked the door. Sassy, in his bunk, left row, lower berth, was doing the usual: lying on his belly and grinding his forehead back and forth against the metal frame. Some blood was visible along the brow and 'neath the hairline of the scalp he had on.

"Knock it off, Sassounian. Better stop it, or it's electroconvulsive therapy time again—an extra helping of it. Plus a week in Siberia. Get me?"

Sassounian stopped what he had been doing, although he took his sweet time about it.

"Atta girl, Sassy. Got something for you." Biggs held the blanket out to him. "*Pink.* You like pink, right? You love the color pink."

Sassounian took the blanket in his hands with the taped fingertips and gently rubbed it against his cheek. His eyes appeared to be misting, only Biggs could not be certain due to lack of light and the flickering images produced by the black-and-white television. Not that it made any difference.

"You're quite welcome, you know."

Biggs stepped out. Locked the door back up. Drew the curtain closed over the Judas window, and walked back to where Muck waited with the metal chest by the pit in the floor.

"Shouldn't a brung that blanket back. 'Cause now, every time I see it gonna remind me of what we done to the kid. . . ."

"Guess what? I don't want to hear about it. It's over and done with. Whacking that kid is no different from you helping me ice those two cunts who were turning tricks for you on Hollywood Boulevard."

"Wasn't none of my idea to ice them hoe'. You put them in the kettle. Said peep' gotta eat."

Biggs was not interested in any of it. Proceeded to undo the clasps on the chest. Lifted the lid open, and watched Dione Aragon shoot out with a great deal of frantic energy bordering on hysteria, anguish, loud gasps for fresh air, air that her (supposedly) long-deprived lungs could not get enough of.

Why was she acting up? There was no real reason, that Biggs could see. Why did she have to carry on like this? Unless it was more fakery, which *vics* very often were likely to indulge in. She'd had access to the breathing tube, and she was among the living, for the time being. So what was up?

"Quit your fakin'." His advice to her. The tears that flowed did so from that one good eye that she had left.

"Ho should be happy to be out of the suitcase." Marvin was trying to get back on Cecil's good side. "Instead she still be carryin' on."

"Please don't make me get back in the chest. It's so difficult to breathe in there."

"Is it? It's a miracle that you didn't asphyxiate."

She nodded her head. "I thought for sure I would suffocate. I can't take being locked up like that. Please."

"You had access to air. You had the hose to breathe through. Did I not warn you not to let the mouthpiece slip out of your mouth?"

She continued to shake. Biggs let her. Knew that she would have to settle down eventually. Enough blood had flowed out from the eye wound and that side of her head during the trip that it left quite a bit of her face covered in it. Her message came through loud and clear with all the quaking and nervousness, that she would rather endure anything, anything at all, than be forced back into the metal trunk.

"No one is going to put you back in it. So take it easy."

Biggs remained amused by her behavior, Marvin less so. Bishop reminded him to keep one hand on her cuffs, in case she got the bright idea to take off up the staircase and they'd have to do a repeat of what had gone down with the Klopp cunt.

"Yo, where the ho gonna go? Door upstairs be locked. Front door be locked. Back door be locked. Like a fuckin' crack house in here. Where she gonna go?"

*"Hold on to her."*

# CHAPTER 74

**While the bishop was unlocking the door over the pit, Marvin Muck took the opportunity to run his other hand up between Dione's thighs.** Ran it across her belly. Felt her breasts.

Biggs lifted the door open. Shined his flashlight down at the murky water. Must have wakened a few flies, or else they were drawn to the sores and smell of fresh blood, because they were buzzing again. Not what he needed.

Small chunks of something or other floated on the water's surface. There was an item that resembled a hard-boiled egg, only considerably smaller—or was it an eyeball? Against the far edge. Portion of a tongue, several teeth, bridgework, along the top edge. Fragments of bone, partial fingers.

Dione's good eye took it in. It made it nearly impossible to calm down under the circumstances.

There was a young woman in the pit. Hair and face swathed in grime and blood. Terri Denise Klopp was the victim who'd showered Marvin's discolored, less-than-appealing face with ammonia a while back. Hardly the "feisty" one presently. Happened with all of them eventually, thought Biggs.

Her eyes were closed, and remained that way even after Cecil prodded at her with his foot to see if she were at all alive. Her wrists had been handcuffed behind her back and she appeared to be "frozen" in that awkward position against the upper right hand corner of the pit.

He prodded. It became obvious soon enough, when he saw her blink, that she was indeed alive. She may not have been full of pep, *joie de vivre*, not entirely the life of the party—but she was blinking and she was breathing.

Dione Aragon's mental state was fragile at best at this point, her desperation not easy to rein in.

Biggs kicked at the woman in the pit. Not to hurt or punish, but to determine how much life there was left in her, and a rat appeared out of nowhere: more-than-likely surfaced from the depths of the pit, scurried up and over his shit-kicker boot, across the victim's practically motionless shoulder, made it to the top of her head and promptly bounced off into the darkness and disappeared.

Dione Aragon's own head was shaking from side to side and she was practically retching. It had to do with the stench, the rat, the pit, and the bits and pieces in it, not to mention the woman in the water and the suffering she must have endured. This was nothing less than a dungeon of depravity that she had been brought to.

What had it been for? Drugs? Getting high? Why'd she have to get high? Why did she have to accept drugs from Cecil and Marvin?

They had lured her with drugs, baited her with tips, with money—to use to buy her and Danny's drugs with. And Danny was dead now; he was dead. . . .

Where was Clarissa? What had they done to her sweet little angelic baby?

Tears rolled down from her good eye. She had been blinded in the other eye. Probably sustained a skull fracture. Only they didn't seem to care. They were cold-blooded and brutal, and didn't care what they did to people.

We never should have left Bakersfield. Should never have driven down to LA. It was Danny. Wanted to visit a high school friend. Score some good weed at a great rate. Great deal, easy money, he had told her. Had convinced her to go along. They could come out with enough to put a down payment on a house of their own. Get out from under the roof of her mom and her overbearing boyfriend.

They'd ripped Danny off. Took their money, their hard-earned money. Left them broke with their broken-down used car. No way to get back. . . . If only they had never left home. . . . If only they had stayed away from LA.

The regrets piled on. It was too late for it. But she could not stop thinking, could not keep the images from appearing and flashing inside her aching head. She was in so much fear that her teeth rattled. There was no way to stop it.

Biggs bent down. Turned Terri Denise Klopp around and unlocked the cuffs on her wrists, then recuffed them in front of her. He rose. Pushed

Marvin away from Dione. Rechecked her handcuffs. Uncuffed one of her wrists, held them in front of her and clamped the cuff back on.

He advised her to compose herself.

"I don't want any over-the-top, needless screaming and carrying on. Ordinarily I don't mind the noise; you can be feisty all you want—basement is practically sound-proof. Windows have boards on them: inside and out. Thing of it is, some sound probably travels and my neighbors like to bitch and moan at the slightest excuse. They have nothing better to do. That's how neighbors are. Busybodies. Bunch of grousers. Like that professional ballbuster Petunia Roscoe. Lives in the shack to the right of us. Has to stick her nose in other people's business constantly."

"Yo, you right about that, Cecil. Petunia be nosy."

"Chunky pit bull cunt gets on my nerves, as you may have guessed. Even more so than the black couple who live to the left of here. Then you've got the limping curmudgeon across the street. Medal of Honor winner. World War II hero. World War II pain-in-the-ass is more like it."

"An' Finger Lickin' Flinger. That be another one."

Cecil did not want to discuss Wilburn Claude, Lloyd Dicker's raw-egg-sucking grandson; he had other things on his mind. Like the business at hand. Noticed that Dione Aragon's good eye kept looking down at the nasty water in the pit and its contents and then back up at him. All it managed to do was amuse him.

"Don't concern yourself with the pit. It's not in your immediate future—nor will it be—unless you rile me. Pit Therapy is a form of punishment we resort to when certain individuals get out of line, break the rules." He indicated Terri Denise Klopp down there in the oblong-shaped hole in the floor. "Strumpet made life difficult for us. Splashed ammonia in Marvin's face."

"Sho did. Had no cause. Coulda been my bottom ho, too, 'cept she done her Mack Daddy wrong."

# CHAPTER 75

**Somehow, Dione was able to steady her nerves and calm down.** There was an inner voice that urged her to settle down, and that maybe, just maybe by settling down she would be able to keep from angering her captors further and that her chances of surviving what was happening to her might be better. She didn't know; had no way of knowing. The woman in the pit had undoubtedly caused them trouble and this was her punishment. She would go the other way; she would cooperate. She would. She would do her best.

Dione looked at Biggs. Waited for him to make a decision. Was she supposed to get down there? Something caused a ripple in the water that drew her attention: a second rat swam across at the other end, climbed out, and scampered out of sight. These rats were large and well-fed. Scary looking.

"Rodents."

Biggs detached the key to the Fun Room, and had Marvin retrieve a metal collar with the loops on the sides, the same type the victim in the pit had on her neck.

"Best get used to them. If there's one thing we've got plenty of around here, it's rodents. All type. Kept a cat for that very reason. The Ripper. Hated to see the mice and whatnot get into the food supply—but the cat, a black male, a big one, called him the Ripper, just up and disappeared a few months back and we haven't seen him since. Still got plenty of cans of his favorite cat food left. He'll either show up, or we just might have to go out and pick up another feline to do battle with the vermin."

"I be for that."

Marvin had returned with the collar. Handed it to Biggs. Cecil unlocked the lock on the hasp, opened the collar, secured it and closed it around Dione's neck. He flipped the hasp in place, slipped the lock through and locked it.

"Long as he don't be messin' wiff my homie'. My homie' pet don't even be safe around them dirty sewer rat' . Prob'ly it was Norbert ate the Ripper. Fuckin' Norbert. 'Less it was Rutherford. Before he run off."

"Or your pets ganged up on him."

Biggs closed the door over the pit. Locked the lock. He escorted Dione to the Mattress Room. Marvin followed.

"Yo, thought you said I could have me a piece, Cecil."

"Later."

Biggs unlocked the door to the Mattress Room. There was a long chain that hung from a beam in the ceiling. That end had been wrapped around the six-by-six beam and held together with a lock, the other end was long enough so that it not only touched the cement floor, but also allowed for plenty of slack.

Biggs produced a second, larger lock, and ran it through the metal collar on her neck and the end of the bicycle chain, thus the victim had plenty of room to move about freely, although her wrists were cuffed and she was connected to the chain from the ceiling via the iron collar.

There was a jug of drinking water, ten-gallon paint can to go in, a roll of toilet paper. There were mattresses, soiled, to be sure: grime and blood and urine-stained. A rickety coffee table, a half-eaten loaf of white bread, a half-empty jar of peanut butter. Couple of dog biscuits. There was a bare bulb up above, but could only be turned on by a flip of the switch outside the door.

"Be back in a minute. Don't go anywhere."

When he returned he had latex gloves on his hands and he was holding a generic greeting card, stamped envelope, piece of paper with what seemed like writing on it, a pen.

He placed the items on the coffee table. Had her pick up the pen and write in the card what was on the piece of paper. Knowing that her parents were divorced and that she and her mother were close, Biggs had her write:

Dear Mom,
We are in rehab. The plan is to save up enough
for a down payment on a house before we go
back. We are well. Don't worry.
Love,
Dione

He had her seal the envelope using her own saliva, then picked it up, the pen, his handwritten version of the greeting.

"Don't damage my furniture. Paid good money for it. It's used and old and not in the best of condition; it still cost plenty."

"Yo. You buys that cheap shit at a garage sale in Van Nuy'."

The bishop gestured that the fool leave. A befuddled Muck stepped out, bugged about something. Cecil Omar did likewise, and locked the door on his way out. Muck followed him to the walk-in cooler-cum-Abattoir.

"Thought you said I could have me some, Cecil."

"Did I? Not right now."

# CHAPTER 76

**Biggs unlocked the lock on the chain, unraveled the chain, opened the door, and went in.**

"We've got work to do."

Bishop looked down at the two metal chests containing viscera and limbs. The stench could not be denied, even to these two—who were around it 24/7.

Muck had his sleeve over his mouth. Biggs was having a bit of a hard time with it himself. Ordinarily he thrived on the miasma, ordinarily—only there were a host of other, undesirable odors that added to the stench:

lime, disinfectant, rodent poison, cat excrement, human waste, that crept in from the basement john, the Geek Cell—as well as other places.

What could you do?

Biggs handed Marvin a spade and had him scoop up what was on the floor: all that mess, the loose stuff Norbert had spilled the other day, and dump as much of it as possible into one of the chests. The rest, considerable chunks and limbs, were left in the other.

"There are times I genuinely wonder if Mr. Fimple is worth keeping."

"He the one done it."

"Can't reason with the stubborn bastard. Does no good to try, either."

They got the unsavory mess off the floor. Closed the lid on the metal chest and snapped it shut.

"Dump it in the furnace, Cecil? That the plan?"

"No. We can't. Too soon to use that furnace again. Asshole neighbors, like old Lloyd Dicker across the street, are complaining about the odor. That's what Finger Lickin' was doing in the backyard the other day: sniffing around; on orders from the old man."

"Lloyd Dicker? Fuck Lloyd Dicker. Dump all this shit in the furnace anyway. What do we care? They can't prove nothin'."

"How often do I have to go into it? We can't keep using the incinerator, not every time. It's a little more work this other way, but it's still a whole lot better than having North Hollywood PD snooping around—and I'm getting a little tired of Marty Roscoe's mutts trying to dig their way into the basement every time we toss something in the fire. I'm not even exactly sure how they can tell where the smell is coming from, but they can."

"Your show, Trusty. I be deacon. You the Bishop, my man. Yo."

"Grab that mop over there. Get that crap off the floor. Mop it up. Get the blood out of the corners."

Marvin did that. Worked on the corner to the left of the door. Cecil had him push the bucket and mop out and rinse them in the john bathtub.

"Pour some water in the bucket and then dump it in the crapper. Flush it away. Rinse the mop out thoroughly. We'll leave it and the bucket in the Fun Room."

They both stepped out and Biggs locked the door to the Abattoir.

"Ain't we gonna get rid of the shit that be in the suitcase?"

"Later. My back can't take anymore of this activity. Besides, staff and board members deserve some breakfast, don't you think?"

"They be eatin' all the time."

"I should be hitting the sack pretty soon, too."

Muck pushed the bucket in the direction of the john, while Biggs headed to the Fun Room, and waited for him there.

Muck made it. Shoved the bucket with the mop in it into the Fun Room, and Cecil locked it back up.

"You sure you want them geek' up on the first floor? That mean' somebody got to carry granny wiff the anal wart' up the stair' in her wheelchair."

"Get Greta to help you with her, or else Big T. Round them up. Let's go. It's inhuman to keep them cooped up down here all the time without exposing them to some light and showing them how life should be lived."

Muck did a double take.

"Go get them."

# CHAPTER 77

They had the lot of them gathered in the kitchen on the first floor and seated at the table: Goodfellow, Big T., Ionesco, Sassounian, Betty Lou Rutterschmidt and her adopted daughter Mildred Elizabeth, Patience McDaniel, Greta "The Leaper" Otto, some others—with one obvious exception: Mr. Norbert Fimple, who Biggs felt deserved a few more days in Siberia and would be fed later.

He had Greta pass *Pop-Tarts* around and fill tumblers with *Kool-Aid*.

Biggs had cleaned up, washed the clown face off and changed into cleaner clothes. He sat at the head of the table, at the wall-of-pennies side. Like Doc Holiday, liked having his back to the wall. Wild Bill Hickok usually did, too. The one time he didn't, "Broken Nose Jack" McCall walked up from behind with his gun drawn and put one in Mr. Hickok's head.

Cecil sipped his cherry soda and ate a *Ding Dong*. Had the *Wall Street Journal* open and would from time to time glance up at his "*schutzstaffel.*" What a bunch, what a wondrous cadre of hopeless cases.

"May I ask something, Bishop Biggs?"

Biggs lifted his eyes.

"Ask."

"Nothing."

"What is it? Speak up, Cabbie. You're among friends here—Commie infiltrator."

"Red sumbitch," sighed Big T. under his breath.

"Why we have *Kool-Aid* for breakfast and *Pop-Tart* all the time? I don't understand. Why not regular breakfast with eggs and sausage, bacon? Orange juice and coffee? Cereal and milk? Like all human in the world?"

"You had that in Russia?" said Big T. "Lyin' sack of sheep dung."

"Want *Fruit Loops?*" said Biggs. "That it? Like that hillbilly next door?"

"I don't understand. What is *Fruit Loop?* I don't know."

"You going to pay for this fancy breakfast that you're suggesting?"

"I ask only. And, no, I do not drive taxi no more. That was shit job I do for short time. *Fuck the taxi; I fuck the taxi.*"

"Calm down and eat your *Pop-Tart* and drink your *Kool-Aid.* It's either that, or dog biscuit treats."

"I do what you say, *Tovarich.* You are the boss."

"Never trust no *Commie Pinko sumbitch*, is what I always tell folk."

Muck was eyeing the box of *Pop-tarts* that Greta held in her hand. "Still be hungry."

Biggs nodded in Greta's direction, giving the okay. She refilled Muck's tumbler from a pitcher. Stuck her hand inside the Pop-Tart box and looked at Biggs and waited for him to tell her how many exactly to give him.

"Two. Give him two."

She did that. Sat back down to eat her own and sip her *Kool-Aid*. Muck requested hooch instead of the lame-ass *Kool-Aid*.

"*Kool-Aid* be for kids."

Biggs ignored him. Read the *Wall Street Journal*. His stock was up. Across the board. He'd made some astute decisions over the years. There was money to be made, so long as you knew what you were doing. It took brains and it took know-how—and Biggs felt he had both to spare.

"When you gonna read the *Bible* to us again, Bishop Biggs?" Mildred Elizabeth wanted to know. "Mother likes to hear you read scripture. It relaxes her."

"Won't be long now. We're having flyers printed up and they'll be passed out throughout the neighborhood. We'll have a fair amount of worshippers, I imagine, like we used to do—before I got swamped with chores and various obligations. I'll give a sermon. We'll have gospel music—like before—that is, if *Mademoiselle* Rutterschmidt would honor us with her exquisite ability on the organ."

Betty Lou Rutterschmidt looked up from that huge *Bible* on her lap. "It would be my pleasure, Bishop Biggs."

"How's that, Mildred?"

Mildred hadn't heard, or maybe she had. Her way of responding was to run that inordinately long tongue of hers over the gray whiskers across her upper lip and then shift it down toward that dark and large wart between her lower lip and chin.

She had a habit of doing something else that Biggs did not quite care for: she rubbed the thumb on her right hand against the little finger on the same hand. A nervous, compulsive condition that she had little or no control over.

He knew it. Still, it did not make it any easier to tolerate.

"You drive me nuts with the fingers, Mildred. And quit playing with the wart. Stop licking it. Leave it alone. Leave-the-wart-a-lone. Eat up. Hurry it up."

# CHAPTER 78

**Less than a quarter mile east of Biggs's compound, eight-year-old Monica Duarte was screaming in her sleep.** Even after her older sister Olivia came running into the youngster's room and did what she could to console her, the nightmare in the little girl's mind's eye did not immediately leave her.

Monica's body shook as she clung to the older sister.

"Take it easy, baby. . . . Everything is all right, Monica. I'm here for you. I'm right here."

"*I dreamed that something awful happened to you, Livia. The boogeyman was after you.*"

"It's all right now. . . ."

"You kept trying to run away from the boogeyman, Livia . . . but you couldn't get away. You couldn't get away. You kept trying to get away. You were running down this dark alley and he kept coming after you. I heard you screaming for help, Livia. You were scared. I wanted to help you. I could see you were so scared but I couldn't help you. I just cried when he came after you, Livia. I wanted to help you. I was crying and screaming as loud as I could so maybe someone could get us help. Nobody came to help, Livia. Nobody wanted to help us; there was nobody there to help . . . in the dark. . . ."

"Everything is fine now, Monica. . . . You just had a bad dream, that's all. Just a bad dream."

"But it was re*al; it was just like being there. I could see everything.*"

Olivia reached down for the younger girl's doll that had fallen to the floor and held it out to her. Monica did not waste time wrapping her arms around it. A tall, attractive woman in her early forties walked in. Sarah Duarte had the same large almond eyes as her girls, same wavy, lengthy, auburn locks.

Olivia stood up.

"Another nightmare."

"It's those horror movies you kids keep renting. I said it would come to this. She's too young to be exposed to that junk."

"I'm not the one who lets her watch those movies, Mom."

Sarah Duarte sat on the edge of the girl's bed. Held her youngest in her arms. Monica had settled down quite a bit by now. "You rent them."

"Your son Carlos rents them. Your sixteen-year-old son rents all the horror movies, the worst he can find, the really violent ones. Why can't you and Dad talk to him about it if you're both so concerned?"

"That's enough."

Mrs. Duarte gently rubbed the tears away from the eight-year-old's eyes. She brushed the hair from her face and massaged her temples.

"Are you all right, honey?"

The youngster had closed her eyes and she was nodding her head.

Olivia left the room to take a shower and dress for work.

# CHAPTER 79

It was still dark out as Rudy Perez and his brother Monroe, four years his senior, zigzagged down the quiet street in their pickup truck loaded down with rolled up *LA Times*. Monroe did the driving, while Rudy did the expert flinging from the back, able to aim and throw with both hands simultaneously.

Sighted in on a couple of doors on his right. Pitched the papers and knew they would land where they were supposed to without having to look.

His brother shifted gears. Zipped to the other side of the street. Rudy repeated the process: flinging two more papers, and they continued on this way without a hitch.

Years of doing it made it look easy, years of rising at three or four in the morning for the route, of hustling to make a dollar, hustling to get that early morning gig out of the way. Because for Rudy, afterwards, it was on to Marty and Petunia Roscoe's to take their two dogs for a walk, and for "Roe" it was off to his job at Big Tony's auto body shop. After finishing up with the dogs, Rudy would hurry on back home to repair cars in their driveway. He felt guilty about having dropped out of high school in his third year; he and his brother both felt guilt over it, but Rudy was stubborn about it; had felt a need to contribute financially for the time being, and Roe, not wanting to be pushy, and knowing how stubborn his younger brother could be, had gone along with it, under one condition: that at some point Rudy would return to school, not only for his high school diploma, but maybe consider college. If not college, not everyone *had to* go to college and be part of the white collar work force, blue collar was just fine, so long as he took courses to familiarize himself with today's heavily computerized car engines. That was the agreement.

For the time being, the answer was to stay busy, earn money in order to keep the bank from foreclosing on the house; the only way they knew to keep their grandparents from ending up in some shabby retirement home, or worse.

So they worked; did their best. Stayed busy. It kept them out of trouble. They had no one to rely on but themselves. It was down to that. Rudy and Roe. But that was okay. They didn't mind. Nothing was free in this world. Their father had taught them that. Now gone. Both gone. Mother and father. Rest their souls. It was up to the brothers to see to it that their grandparents did not end up on the street.

Rudy's girlfriend Olivia was on his mind as he continued to hurl papers from the truck bed, wanting to get this morning's run over with in order to race on over to the Roscoes, pick up the dogs, and make it to his girlfriend's and walk her to her job at the diner. He couldn't think of a better way to start a day.

# CHAPTER 80

**Olivia toweled herself off, combed her hair out.** She got into her brown server's dress and walked to the kitchen. She poured milk into a saucer for the family cat, a white Ragamuffin with blue eyes that they called Angelina.

# CHAPTER 81

**The Perez brothers neared the end of their route.** Rudy pitched the last of the newspapers three doors down from the Roscoe residence and Roe kicked the accelerator and came to a screeching halt in front of Marty's house.

Rudy hopped out. Smiling ear-to-ear. Kept looking at his watch. The older brother shook his head. Forever amused by it.

"One of these days you'll break your neck just to spend two minutes with that Duarte chick."

"Yeah? My neck."

"Little Sister gonna do like Big Sister done, kid. Gonna tear your heart to pieces."

Rudy laughed.

"Won't be so funny when it happens. I worry about you."

"You keep forgetting Olivia is not Yolanda."

"They're sisters. Same family. Them Duartes are all alike. She's stringing you along, Rudy."

"That's okay. I think you're wrong about her."

"I hope you're right." Monroe drove off. "Later."


Rudy climbed the stoop to Marty and Petunia Roscoe's front porch. Knocked. It took a while. Eventually a sleepy-eyed, thirty-nine-year-old burly type with a streaked, Rod Stewart shag cut appeared in his boxers. Pumped up biceps and strong shoulders; trunk-like legs—the result of all that weightlifting that he did. Fit as a fiddle, just about, all around—with the exception of the belly and the wide backside, the result of too much beer and his addiction to *Fruit Loops*. Roscoe couldn't get enough of either one. Although this morning his mind was not on beer or cereal, all he wanted was to return to bed. Could barely keep his eyelids open as he stuck the leather leashes in Rudy's face.

Rudy greeted the man, grabbed the straps. Watched Ziggy and Darcy scamper out, eager for their morning jaunt. They tugged away. Roscoe had ducked back inside and had the door closed before the dogs cleared the porch. Rudy got his hand on the pooper-scooper in time, and they were off.


Dogs didn't need to be shown in which direction they were headed. Pretty soon Rudy was running ahead of them, leading the way all the same. The need to get to his girl's house in a hurry was there. The sooner they got to it, the more time he would have to spend with her.

As usual, Ziggy, the Lhasa apso, even though heavier of the two dogs by about ten pounds, and older by several years, was somehow still able to keep up a lot easier than the nine-year-old Boston terrier.


Rudy kept them moving as fast as he thought they could possibly go without getting them too exhausted. It never took long, though, because pretty soon it became evident both dogs were struggling to keep up. He realized he needed to ease up and did so.

Can't run these poor things ragged. Sure, he wanted to spend time with Liv, but not at the risk of the dogs dropping dead on him. Slow down. Slow it down some.

Couple of blocks later, and he was there. The goal was to sneak up without being spotted by her or her family, hide behind the topiary, and leap at her from behind and fold his arms around her waist and lift her clean off the ground and tell her how much he loved her and that he could hardly stand living without her.

He had an incredibly strong desire this morning to get a good whiff of her, to inhale that wonderful smell of her and that intoxicating perfume that she liked to use—and he thought he would steal a couple of kisses while he was at it, too. Why not? Only he'd have to be careful she didn't get upset by it. Olivia didn't go for any of this boyfriend-girlfriend business so close to where she lived.

# CHAPTER 82

**Olivia reached for a cashmere sweater and tied the sleeves round her waist.** She tossed Ayn Rand's *The Fountainhead* in her purse, took the flight of stairs down to the first floor, and saw to it the front door was locked on her way out.

She walked down the narrow concrete path, past the manicured hedges and lawn, rose bushes. It was still early dawn, the temperature tolerable, and in about an hour or two the stifling Valley heat would be upon them. Bringing the sweater hadn't really made much sense, but she liked to wear it on the job because it made her feel "safer"; the sweater was loose enough to make her larger-than-average bust less noticeable and did not draw as much attention from the customers at the diner, not that she was personally bothered by the size of her thirty-eight-inch bosom; it was merely a way to curtail comments from certain uncouth types who came to eat at Mr. Jessup's diner.

She turned right on the sidewalk, passed a second row of hedges, when a male figure bounded at her from behind and swung a pair of arms around her middle and gave her a hard squeeze. This was followed by a kiss on the neck. Of course by then she realized who it was. She looked down and the Lhasa apso and the smaller Boston terrier were not far behind on leashes, and neither was Rudy Perez's *English Leather*. She'd gotten used to the cologne; in fact, liked it. It was this other thing that she felt quite uncomfortable with.

Rudy was not paying much attention to her reaction.

"Good morning, beautiful."

Still had his arms about her waist. Olivia broke free of the embrace, and did it as gently as she knew how. Granted, the way he liked to sneak up on her had to be pretty childish, if you thought about it—but even that was not as bothersome as the possibility of being discovered by her parents in this type of situation—especially with Rudy Perez. Those were her circumstances, circumstances she constantly had to be mindful of, like it or not.

How would she have explained what was going on? She put an end to the hugging, and walked on. Rudy and Co. followed.

"What's the matter? Did I scare you? God, you look great."

"One of these days my parents will see us and I'll really be in trouble."

"Well, good morning to you, too."

"I mean it, Rudy. I'm having enough to deal with from Yolanda as it is. She knows something is going on. She's suspicious."

"Whose fault is that, Livia? I keep telling you to just level with your family. Tell them the truth. It usually works for me."

"How do you tell someone 'the truth' if they don't want to hear it? If they refuse to listen?"

"Don't waste your time then, is my answer. Like I said before: we can always elope. That would really make them happy—"

"Rudy—"

"I know, I know: these things take time. That's what you keep saying. They don't even know me but they hate me. Right? That's terrific."

Maybe there was a way to change the subject. Olivia glanced down at the happy campers: tails wagging, thrilled to be out. Well, Ziggy's tail was wagging, the other one didn't have much of one.

"Don't you ever get embarrassed walking those dogs?"

Rudy shrugged. "What do I care what people think? I like to keep busy and my family can use the money. It's an easy fifteen bucks a week. You want anything in this world, you gotta work for it. What my father used to say."

"Those are Marty Roscoe's dogs, am I right? I never see Mr. Roscoe walking his own dogs. Doesn't it make you feel just a little silly at your age? He's using you if all you're getting is fifteen dollars a week, Rudy. It's a joke."

"It's not a joke to me. What does anybody care? It's my business, ain't it?"

"Don't say ain't."

"God, you sound like every English teacher I ever had when you say that. I hate it when you correct me as much as teachers hate hearing the word ain't."

"You are hopeless. Really, Rudy."

"Hopelessly in love with a girl named Olivia Duarte who *ain't* got the guts to tell her parents she's at least dating a *fabuloso* guy with prospects, real prospects; the way I see it."

"I will talk to them, Rudy."

"Right. One of these days. Which could mean anything: a year from now, or five years from now. Who knows? Meanwhile, I'm not getting any younger."

"Poor baby. Going on twenty. That's really old."

"Twenty-one in three months. A buddy of mine got married at eighteen—and another friend got hitched who wasn't even eighteen."

"Yeah? That's not smart, if you ask me. Bet they got their girlfriends 'in trouble.'"

"Pregnant? They didn't get married 'cause they got their women pregnant. They got married 'cause they were in love. Try explaining that to your mother and father—especially your sister."

They reached a corner, and a large black woman wearing the same type of brown Polyester dress as Olivia joined them. Bertha Lenier gave them both a cheerful greeting, and all three people and the two dogs continued on.

# CHAPTER 83

**They heard the rattling, noisy muffler long before the familiar, ugly junk heap appeared, fouling up the already foul Valley air.** The pesky duo in the multi-colored wreck, namely Ace Ortiz and his bosom buddy Felix Monk, were about the last two unfunny jokers in the world anyone in the group wanted to see. In addition, the dogs carried on enough to the extent their opinion of the scamming backsliders was even less than what the humans thought of them.

The *pachuko* with the red bandana across his forehead double-parked the Toyota long enough for Ace to stagger out in a stupor, nearly going down—but not quite. Ace held on to the door for support. Heavy sweat poured from his face and neck as he walked over to the group. Ortiz had something to say, as well as something to peddle. He was desperate and in sorry shape, as usual: a pathetic, emaciated mess.

He looked at Rudy and the leashes in his hand and the barking dogs at the end of those leashes.

"What kind of bread you make walking them dirty pooches for that lazy redneck, anyway? Gotta be makin' a mint, bustin' your ass like you're doin'."

"Grave robbing again, Ace?"

"Hey, you ain't even funny. But it's an idea."

Ortiz culled a handful of rings and watches that he had in a clear plastic bag. Held them out for Rudy and Olivia and the other waitress to see.

"Lookee-here. This is quality merchandise, baby. Give you my best discount."

"No, thanks."

Ace was looking at Bertha. Giving her the attention now. "How about you, pretty mama?"

"Why don't you get yourself cleaned up? Get a job."

"Why don't *you* drop a hundred pounds and you just might be able to get yourself a real man?"

"Like you?"

"You got it."

Bertha dug a hand inside her purse. When it came back out it had a *.22* in it. She was not shy about sticking it in the junkie's face, either, nor was she shy about breaking wind—and did so: releasing several loud farts. No one thought there was anything remotely comical about it. Least of all Ace Ortiz.

"I shoulda expected that."

"Always askin' for it, ain't you?"

"It only looks that way." Ortiz wanted no part of the double-deuce, or the gas, and took a step back. "Lookee-here, Bertha: I don't want no trouble, mama. Just trying to make a buck."

"Sure could use you some manners in your technique." Bertha's gun went back in her purse.

"Slim is always looking for a dishwasher/short order cook," Olivia said.

"He's too good to wash dishes. Ain't you, *Mr. Ace Ortiz?* Too cool, fool."

"Too cool for Slim's greasy spoon. How about it, Rudy? Buy your number one girl a nice engagement ring, man? Lookit this: fourteen karat gold, homes. Can't beat it. Show your baby how much you love her."

"She knows how I feel. I don't buy hot rings, or watches."

"Told you, brother, *merch* ain't *'hot.'* It may look *'hot,'* 'cause it's *quality*, is what it is. Me and my partner's legit, everybody knows that. We're clean. Give you a bill of sale, even, and a *life-time guarantee*. You ain't happy with it, trade it in for something else, no extra charge. Lookit that look of pure devotion your kind-hearted baby's givin' you, man. Ain't you got no romance in your soul, Perez? Tell him, Olivia. Dude's got to start acting like a real man. Ain't that right? Makin' all that jack walkin' them dogs for that good-for-nothing Arkie and too tight to spend any of it on your lady. Just don't seem right."

All of them turned another corner, Monk trailing along in that noisy, beat-up junk heap, staying with them. They were on Biggs's block.

# CHAPTER 84

Biggs's *Cadillac* idled in his driveway, as the bishop sat in the front seat with the sidekick, waiting and watching the group through his windshield.

When Olivia and the others walked past his place, heading north, Marvin was quick to hop out of the car to unlock the front gate, waited for Cecil to pull out to the curb, locked the gate up the way he always did, and was back in the front seat.

Biggs turned left onto the street, trailing the group at a deliberately slow pace, his hungry eyes on Olivia Duarte, those out-of-this-world legs and that fine ass those out-of-this-world legs led to under that brown server's dress. He was just about salivating the way he always did when he saw her, as well as when he laid eyes on any woman who looked like this and was built this way.

And it was safe to keep staring, the lightly tinted windows made it possible by providing anonymity: he and Marvin could see out, Rudy & Co. could not see in; they were not able to see Biggs's hanging jaw and those haunting, deep-set eyes that ached with regret, regret triggered by images in his head of that night he crawled in through her first floor bedroom window, before her family (soon after) got wise and moved her up higher and made it impossible to get near her.

He had knocked her out with chloroform (to make certain she remained immobile), fondled her, eaten her cunt and asshole out, finger fucked her. That had been the extent of it. Should have carried her out. Would have been so easy.

It bothered him still. It always would. Regret was a bitch.

"I'd like some more of that."

"Like to stick my tongue up Big Bertha' booty myself."

"Who cares about her, dipstick? I'm talking about the Duarte whore."

"Can forget about that one. Got lucky that time. Her family be watchin' that bitch like a hawk. She don't get high, don't hardly ever go clubbin'. I know about that ho. All she do is study and work. Virgin vagina. She be clean."

I've been keeping an eye on her for years, thought Biggs, and this punk is going to tell me about her?

"Luck had nothing to do with it."

"You know Perez be goin' batshit 'cause he can't get none. Been tryin' for months now. His time be runnin' out, too. Ho gettin' ready to go to college, maybe out of state. So if you want that piece of chicken you ain't got much time left."

"That's what I like about you, Marvin—your positive attitude."

Biggs took his eyes off of Olivia's rear for a moment and looked at the goofball sitting next to him.

"Haven't you learned anything by now? If you want something you go after it. You think about how to accomplish your goal; you think that it can be done—have yourself convinced, absolutely convinced that it's doable—as opposed to impossible. Nothing is impossible. *Nothing.* Don't ever trap yourself into thinking that way. It's self-defeating. You won't ever get anywhere like that, Free Ride. I didn't get this *Cadillac* and the *Rolls*, the *Rolex* worth big bucks, the house, and everything else that I have, by being negative. No one out there is any better than you." Biggs stopped himself. Reconsidered what he'd just said. "Maybe some are. *Yeah*. In your case. Some would have to be." Indicated Olivia Duarte. "That piece of ass, as fine as she may be, is in reality no better or worse than any other piece of ass out there. She's not beyond reach."

Marvin was nodding his head. Agreeing.

"You know what you be talkin' about, Cecil. Why I dig hangin' wiff you. I be learnin'."

"You're learning shit."

Biggs's eyes were back on the group. He kept the *Cadillac* rolling and was careful not to be too obvious about what he was doing, and yet he needed to get closer. She did look fine.

Ace would not take no for an answer and kept pressing Rudy to buy something from him.

"I'm not going for it, Ortiz. I need my money for other things."

"Can't you see I'm in a bad way, homes? I need my shit, a line. . . . I got bargain basement prices for top-notch, super quality, over-the-counter merchandise here."

Rudy kept wanting to move away every time Ace shoved his cheap-jack crap at him and was getting pretty disgusted by now.

"Don't you ever get tired of shooting that garbage in your veins?"

"Lookee-here, I wouldn't talk if I was you. You're the chump who walks dogs for chump change. How *small time* can you get? Ace Ortiz wouldn't be caught dead carryin' a *pooper-scooper* or *scrubbing greasy plates. No way in hell.*"

# CHAPTER 85

Ace was just about making a spectacle of himself: shaking his head, jabbing a bony thumb in his chest.

*"I don't wash dishes. I ain't no sud-buster."*

"Slim got other jobs open: bus boy, fry cook, waiter."

"Fry cook, Bertha? What's it pay?"

"Minimum wage to start. And you get a fifty cent raise in six months. Don't sound too shabby to me for a part-time job."

"I'm gonna blow my rep for a lousy three-fifty an hour? You gotta be out of your mind, ma'am. 'Sides, you know the dude would never hire me. Got a plan to talk to Harold Crust—see if I can hook up with him. Pullin' in tips; makin' money hand-over-fist."

"Shinin' shoes? Who you jivin'?"

"Shinin' kicks and eyeballin' chicks. What's wrong with it?"

"You talkin' out of your bee-hind, is what's wrong with it." Bertha happened to look in Biggs's direction just then. Ace caught sight of the shiny hooptie himself: Biggs in his crawling *Cadillac*. All it took to unnerve the needy hype.

*"What the hell is your problem, man?"*

The *Cadillac* stopped. The group stared at the hard to read ominous shadows behind the tinted windows without ever expecting a response. They all knew that the driver of the *Brougham* ought to be left alone—all, that is, except Jesus Ortiz. Rudy suggested he cool it.

Ortiz wouldn't hear of it. Hadn't been doing too good lately, hadn't been able to unload any of his trinkets, and he was pretty desperate for a fix, some toot, just about anything that would provide him with a good enough buzz.

*"Hey, you! In the Cadillac! Pendejo! I'm talking to you! How come you always watching somebody? How come you always so creepy? Gonna step on you good one of these days!"*

"Leave the man be. Could be the reason he don't want to talk to nobody is because the devil stuck another cookie in his throat."

Meth Mouth looked at her. What in hell was "Godzilla" talking about now?

"The devil what?"

"You heard: Shoved a cookie in his throat. What I remember 'bout him; what the papers said years ago and on tv, when he got sent up to that place: *Camarillo*. Gave a note to the police. Said he couldn't talk no more 'cause the devil stuck a cookie in his throat."

"What'd I tell you? Didn't I tell you he's *loco*? Didn't I? I know what I'm talking about."

"Fed his victims dog biscuit treats, bread, and oatmeal. But he's good these days, got his head on right. Got himself a church, got religion. He's a pastor—and you should treat the man with respect. Took Marvin off the street and made him deacon, too. Cecil's a man of god these days. He got a right to live his life."

"That don't give them the right to creep, Big Mama. They creep. I see 'em all the time, at night, *creepin'*. Why's he gotta follow us? I don't like him around, or Deacon Moron."

Ace was back facing the *Cadillac*, moving toward it.

"Hey, you! With the cookie stuck in your throat! *Yeah, you!* I got this feeling the Devil musta shoved something else in your mouth, and in your *culo*, too!"

The *Cadillac* was rolling again. Picked up speed as it passed them. Ace Ortiz was in the street waving obscene gestures after it.

"I got your *cookie! Right here!* Give you two cookies for the price of one: *my balls, a pair of balls! Huevos!*"

The *Cadillac* drove off, disappearing down the street. Ace Ortiz couldn't shut it off, going full force. *"Hey, I'm talking to you! HEY, YOU! MARICON! Come back here!"* And he topped all the wild waving with a final, lewd arm gesture. Thoroughly worked up and beside himself. Monkey on his ass craved to be fed. Made him nuts, a loon.

# CHAPTER 86

**Olivia hadn't liked any of it; she hadn't cared for being bothered by a known druggie like Ace Ortiz and his druggie friend Felix Monk.** She just wanted to get to her job.

"It's not worth getting upset over—"

*"Who's upset? I ain't 'upset.' I might be pissed, but I ain't 'upset.' I'm cool. I don't let a douche like that get to me."*

"Hey, Ace, he's one of our customers. Me and my brother wash and wax his cars and do some other things for the man."

"I don't give a shit about your psycho customers, Rudy; okay? Guy's a *fucking geek*. Not only is he a *fucking geek and a creep*, but he's an *asshole*. I'm the one should be driving a *Caddy* like that."

"Sure thing, Ace."

"How about if you shut your *pie-hole*, Felix?"

Ace walked over to the junker of a car and had Felix slide to the passenger side. Got in. They drove off. The rattling, rumbling muffler leaving a gray, choking cloud of exhaust fumes in its wake.

"I guarantee you that boy gets shot one of these days. You just can't talk to folks that way. Got no manners, no class. That boy got no respect for nobody, least of all hisself. Fool with junk, end up junk."

Rudy couldn't agree more.

Bertha glanced at her watch.

"Come on, girl. We best get on to the diner before Slim throws a fit 'cause we late for the early breakfast rush."

Rudy hugged and kissed his girlfriend, and watched her hurry off down the sidewalk with Big Bertha Lenier.

He stood there awhile, his eyes on his sweetie. Could be that crazy junkie's got something there, could be he was making some sense after all. He should have bought Olivia a ring, some kind of ring at least. Only he would go about it the right way. He would go to a legit jewelry store and buy her the real McCoy. Nothing hot and cheap like the crap Ace carried around with him. And although he may have been kidding when he made that remark about the grave-robbing, it really was not all that far-fetched to imagine someone like Jesus Ortiz doing something that sick. A user will stoop to any level to get his dope.

There had been reports that grave robbing was up again. Desperate people will do desperate things—and if Ortiz isn't desperate, he thought, who is?

Rudy turned, and walked to Marty Roscoe's to return the dogs. Could be Olivia had been right about the mutts, though; could be he could do without it. Hell, it was silly, just a little. Only nobody understood when you were trying to do something with your life, when you wanted to accomplish a goal. Only his brother Roe got it because he was part of that goal, part of the dream to open up their own shop, a shop that would be named in honor of their father Gil, rest his soul. So yeah, he could keep walking these dogs a while longer. What else did he have to do this early every morning right after the paper route?

He said good morning to sleepy-eyed Marty Roscoe still in his underwear and that spare tire of Roscoe's hanging out over the top of the elastic band. Now that was usually a funny sight. Marty Roscoe had muscles everywhere, big arms, barrel of a chest, tree trunks for legs, larger and stronger than average wrists and forearms, he'd supposed, but he also had a belly from all that *cervesa* he liked to guzzle while watching wrestling on tv. So what good did the weight-lifting do him, Rudy wondered, if he had a big gut like that? It hadn't made any sense to him. Then thought: So what? It's none of my business anyway. I just hope that never happens to me. I hope I never get like that.

Rudy handed over the leashes, left the pooper-scooper on the porch, and hurried back home in order to get to work repairing cars that sat in his family's driveway.

# CHAPTER 87

## Tuesday, 8:05 a.m.

**Driving through Pacoima was some ordeal, especially on a day when the mercury was determined to reach triple digits and nearly succeeding.**

It was hot and clammy and the smog, that gray haze that the Valley wouldn't be the Valley without, if not dense enough to obscure the stucco barrio dwellings in Biggs's and Marvin's relative vicinity, at least a great deal of those two blocks off in any direction they happened to look were.

Pollution was a concern, and Biggs knew it couldn't be good for his health, but he had the windows down all the same. Kept the AC off in order to conserve fuel.


Sweat poured from the bishop and his partner the deacon as they drove up Van Nuys Boulevard. Marvin R. Muck wiped his neck and bare chest with a balled-up black T-shirt.

"Gotta be at least a hunnerd."

"I don't want to hear it." The heat and smog had caused Cecil's head to ache again. "Keep your eyes peeled for that Mexican market where we picked up the live chicken."

"What kind of sense do it make to buy a *Cadillac* when you don't even be usin' the A/C?"

"You trying to be smart?"

"Smart? I ain't smart. Just be *aksking*."

"Soup bones. . . . Soup bones. . . ."

Biggs noticed the familiar large white paper signs with red lettering in the Mexican-type grocery store window that contained ads for *chorizo*, on sale, hamburger, pork chops—and other meats and sundry.

He pulled up in front. Had Marvin remain behind to guard the Caddy, and went in. When he stepped back out he had a full shopping bag in one hand, while holding a paper cup in the other. He handed the cup to

Marvin, who took a sip—and made a face.

"*Water?* Tap water. Warm, too."

Biggs walked to the back of the car. "Know what you are? Ungrateful."

"How about you? Bet you anything, if I had me coin to bet, you had yo'self a nice, cold *Hawaiian Punch* in there. Drank it fast, too, to keep me from gettin' some. Got nerve to give me water—from a store be owned by wetback'. Messican water kill' peep', is what it do. Make 'em shit 'till they die."

"You're wrong."

"I ain't wrong about nothin'."

"It wasn't *Hawaiian Punch,* it was *Hi-C.*"

"Coulda bought me one."

"You don't like *Hi-C.*"

"Coulda bought me some hooch. Yo."

"Nest needs feathering. Feathering requires money and takes precedence over all else."

"Like one goddamn bottle of hooch would keep you from puttin' feather in yo nest."

"If you're done bitching, how about hitting the trunk release."

Marvin did that, and joined Cecil in the back and watched him place the shopping bag next to the metal chest. Didn't fail to notice how cautious he was not to tip over the plastic jug of blood he had hidden away inside a crevice. Marvin suspected what the jug meant: dude was gonna do some more of that nasty shit when they got to where they was goin'. He said nothing about it. It was best not to. For the time being.

"We got dead dog' hangin' in the walk-in. Coulda used 'em, 'stead of droppin' good coin on soup bone'."

"Greta needs to skin them."

"Kick her ass. Make her do it. Coulda bought me a bottle of *Ripple* wiff the bread you spent on soup bone."

"They don't make it anymore."

"They make *Boone' Farm*; they still be makin' *Night Train, Cold Duck, T-Bird, Mad Dog. Mad Dog* be some good shit. Be like *Ripple.* One bottle knock a dude on his ass—if he don't be careful."

Having lived with a stepfather who had been addicted to rotgut and recalling the nightmare his childhood had been because of it, Cecil had next-to-zero tolerance when it came to listening to Marvin run his mouth about it.

Beads of sweat rolled down his neck. Didn't do much good to wipe, either, because the sweat kept on coming. Pacoima, this time of year, with its smog and heat, was hell on earth. Had to be. There was no need to believe in anything like the afterlife, netherworld, Hades, hell below—because hell was above ground. All you had to do was take a look around. At least having been able to get his hands on the soup bones made him feel better about the trip and the task; not a whole great deal, but enough. Mix the animal bones with the Homo sapiens ones inside the chest and it just might be enough of a diversion to throw the coroner's creeps off, should the limbs ever be discovered.

Never a sure thing, nothing was, but at least it was a way to hedge his bets.

He clenched his butt cheeks to suppress a fart. Slammed the trunk shut, and got behind the wheel. Marvin had got in on his side already and was pouring some of the water that was in the cup over his head and upper chest.

"Messican water give folk the runnin' shit'. That be a fac'."

"How do you figure it's Mexican water? We're in America, not Tijuana. Might look like Tijuana, but it's not. It's America. So far. For the time being."

Biggs pulled away from the curb, causing Marvin to spill water onto the upholstered seat. Marvin realized what he'd done and begrudgingly wiped about the area where he sat with his balled-up T.

Biggs dug into a pocket. Produced a can of *Hi-C*. Held it out to Muck (with the slightest trace of a grin). Muck went for it fast enough. Cracked it. Gulped quite a bit of the *Hi-C* down.

*"Yeah."*

"Not bad for 'cat piss'."

"Sometime you the best, other time' you like the rest."

"I'm certainly not one for manners, except in the presence of the congregation, decorum and all, when in the company of fresh meat we're trying to lure—but it would be nice to hear 'thank you' once in a while. It wouldn't solve anything, wouldn't make much difference, because the world would still be a pile of fecal matter, but it would be nice to know one is appreciated by one's colleagues and/or associates."

"Do my share. Pull weight. That be my way of sayin' you *Da Man*."

Marvin had the can back to his mouth. Finished it off. Tossed the empty out the window.

"You're quite welcome, Brother Free Ride."

"Man, you know my homie on the Boulevard call me *'Base.'* What they knowed me by."

"Free Base/Free Ride—what's the difference? Doesn't change the fact you're a bona fide, free-loading bottom-feeder."

"Yeah?"

"You just tossed money out the window, which proves my point."

"Wanna go back and get it?"

The idiocy never ended. Biggs punched in a funk tune on the FM dial. Thought of the Jolly Dolly out there in Lopez Canyon, lying in sweet repose, waiting for him. Wrists cuffed behind her back. The experience had been so gratifying and left him with such a lasting rush that he'd forgotten to take the handcuffs with him. Handcuffs did not come cheap—and there was no point leaving them with the victim.

At Gladstone Avenue, Biggs made a left, and they drove to Lopez Canyon Road.

# CHAPTER 88

**It was serene in this part of the Valley—no buses, cars, or people— just a lot of trees and hills on both sides of the two-lane blacktop (save for a retirement compound for the elderly that they passed on their left as they headed deeper into the Canyon).** That was, for the most part, about the only sign of "life" out here. This obviously explained why it was such a favorite dump site not only for him and his associate, but for other anti-social types as well over the years. The area was just about secluded enough and convenient enough for discarding a body or two— or, in this case, a load of putrefied parts.

He and Marvin had been out this way before, dumped a couple of bodies in this neck of the Valley a while back. It was relatively safe out here, only you had to make sure that you parked your car off the paved road and out of sight, that you parked it in the thick brush and low-lying trees in case the occasional motorist drove by, in case the dreaded mailman passed in his US Postal Jeep to deliver mail to the retirement home (as he did so once a day coming down from Glenhaven Memorial Park and the few residences north of it). Only the distance between the memorial park and the retirement compound was so vast and the terrain so varied—a mile or so north of the retirement home the area changed from trees and lush green undergrowth to practically barren, rocky hills—that at times was used by the National Guard for maneuvers and war games. No war games now. Nothing to worry about. If you drove deep enough into the brush (to park and/or carry out your task), you were fine. Concealment guaranteed.

Biggs stayed north, passing a dog carcass by the side of the road, and then a dead rattlesnake in the middle of the hot pavement.

The bishop pulled over. Got into a pair of latex gloves. Walked to the shoulder where he picked up a rock and dropped it on the snake's head.

"Why you went and did that? Snake be dead."

"A dead snake can still bite an hour after its demise."

"Ain't never heard of it."

Bishop had the flunky grab a plastic garbage bag and hold it open. Cecil tossed the snake in there. Had Marvin grab a fresh bag and the same was done with the canine carcass, with Muck grumbling and cursing the entire time.

"Don't nobody wiff a *Cadillac* stop to pick up roadkill."

"You see roadkill. I see grub. Greta can do wonders with these."

"Yo, the only wonder be I don't get them runnin' shit' more than I do. Get 'em enough, too."

"Don't see why. Should be used to it by now."

Biggs closed the trunk and got back in the car.

"I ain't never gettin' used to it, me."

Marvin climbed in on the other side.

The bishop and his deacon rolled until a familiar clearing appeared on their left. Biggs pulled off the road and drove across bumpy undergrowth, past a pile of concrete chunks someone had evidently dumped a while back, years before, past a more recently discarded large pile of trash. They kept going until they reached brush and tall weeds, trees, and Biggs stopped the Caddy.

There was an incline that would have taken them down into a dry creek bed lined with pebbles and rocks the size of cantaloupes or larger. Biggs didn't feel it was worth driving into and risk scarring the paint job. No. He would park the *Brougham* where they were behind the brush.

He turned his head to take a look back there at the two-lane blacktop to make sure that they were far enough away and concealed to the point they wouldn't be spotted by anyone who happened to drive by. Where they were would have to do.

# CHAPTER 89

**Biggs and Marvin got out and worked on dragging the heavy chest out of the trunk.** They each grabbed a rope handle, pulled, lifted, and Cecil's back froze him up as a sharp shaft of pain traveled the length of his spine to the base of his skull.

*"Christ."*

Biggs let go of the nylon rope handle and leaned against the side of the *Cadillac*. It was his damned back again.

"You all right, homie?"

Biggs did not say anything and remained motionless for a while. Son of a bitch, it hurt.

"If it isn't the fucking head, it's the fucking back. Or the fucking rectum."

Marvin was able to drag the custom-crafted suitcase out of the trunk on his own. Lowered it in the soft sand. Biggs tried moving his upper body from side to side, and then bending forward, touching his shins, maybe his toes, with his fingertips—and it felt better. It shouldn't have, but it did. He would be okay, so long as he did not make any sudden moves and took it easy.

He reached for a shovel inside the trunk and looked at Marvin, who was busy covering his nose and mouth with his T-shirt, trying to block out the over-powering odor coming from the chest. Biggs handed him the shovel.

"Get to it."

"Still say we coulda just dumped it all in the fuckin' fire, Cecil."

"I told you before: We can't burn everything. The odor gets in the air, and travels. Not to mention: This way I don't have to listen to you grouse at having to scrape all the ash off inside the furnace. You complain enough, as it is."

Marvin R. Muck tried to hurry up and get the hole dug, but the stench was getting to be too much to take and he had to jump back a few yards, take a deep breath, and return to the task at hand.

*"Goddamn. That be some nasty smellin' shit."*

"So hurry it up and get the hole dug. The sooner we get it done, the sooner we get the hell out of here and get something to eat."

"I be for dat."

Marvin resumed digging, really putting some muscle into it. As soon as the top layer had been cleared, he reached firm soil and stayed with it, sweating heavily as he worked that shovel.

"You're doing fine, Marvin."

Dude be talkin' to me, thought Marvin, but I know where his mind really be at. Jug of blood. He glanced back at the mofo half-a-nigga givin' him the compliment. Shit. That blood be nasty in that jug, but that don't never stop him before.

Marvin was right. Biggs knew it. Suspected what the punk was thinking, not that it mattered, because there was no way to keep his thoughts off of that plastic jug sitting inside the trunk.

Why'd you bring it if you're not going to do anything with it? I will. My back still hurts. And he couldn't stop thinking of the blood and the young cunt it had come from, a young cunt named Pamela Alice Phelps, whom he had bludgeoned to death on top of that ridge the last time he was here. He wondered if the blood was too cruddy at this point for consumption? Blood had a way of turning dark and nasty over time.

Marvin noticed him looking in the direction.

"You be thinkin' 'bout that ho Alice, ain't you?"

"How'd you guess?"

"Guess nothin'. Man, I can see yo' dick be gettin' hard inside yo' trouser'; an' you ain't brung that jug of her blood out here for no reason, Cecil. Bet you anything you can't keep away from her."

"We have to get moving. You got the hole dug?"

The hole seemed deep enough now and large enough for all the contents in the chest to be dumped in. Biggs gave him a hand unfastening the lid. They each grabbed a handle, slowly tilted the chest, and the entrails and blood, scalp chunks, noses, forearms and feet—all of it, slid down into the hole in the ground. Muck had turned his head away all the while. Tried to keep it that way.

"This be the part that don't be fun. Be like work."

Remains filled up the depression rapidly, and now the stuff had piled up and it appeared to be higher than the surface.

"Have to make the pit deeper and larger. Thought you knew your shit by now."

"I knows my shit."

"Get that shovel."

Marvin reached for the shovel, and went about enlarging the hole.

"Thought I had it figured right. One thing be for sure: ground gonna soak all that blood right up; and what the ground don't get and what don't rot, you know them coyote' gonna dig up and feed on."

"Depredation is exactly what you don't want to happen. You don't want animals dragging body parts all over the canyon and maybe dropping limbs on the road or maybe right in front of that retirement home back there."

"Guess you right, Cecil."

"It's too good a place for dumping all this shit to let somebody start snooping around and maybe cause the rollers to get suspicious. One of my favorite burial sites, you could say. Like to keep it that way."

# CHAPTER 90

**The depression was large enough now and the pile seemed to recede down into it.** Marvin had the shovel on top of the heap and pressed down on it. Couple of the bigger bones were still sticking out more than they should have been and he gave them a good whack and some of the blood spattered him across the face. Muck wiped at the blood with the back of his hand and then licked that right off.

"Hate the smell. Be likin' the taste."

Except Biggs knew he was faking.

"Don't be stupid. You're eating dirt."

Bishop watched him cough, spit it out, and cough some more. Cecil waited. Deacon ran his sleeve across his mouth and face. Cursed.

"You done?"

Marvin nodded.

"Get the shopping bag."

Marvin walked to the Caddy trunk, reached inside with both hands to grab what he presumed was a package of soup bones, instead what he came up with was a large and bloody boar's head with major fangs. And there were two others under it. He froze that instant, cursing up a storm. Dropped the head back in. *Goddamn, Trusty.*

He was leaning over, away from the Caddy trunk, about to vomit. *"Mothafuck."*

"What's your problem?"

"How many of these fuckin' things we need, Cecil?"

"Not your concern."

"An' what about the coin them fuckin' Parfrey head' be costin'? You got three of 'em in there, man. Three fuckin' Porky Pig head'. Waste of bank. What chu gonna do wiff 'em? Ain't we got enough of them mask' back at the crib?"

"Bring the bones over. We need to get going."

Muck wiped vomit from his chin. Carried the shopping bag over.

"Take the bones out."

Marvin stood there, looking at him.

"You hard of hearing? My back's acting up."

Muck shook his head. Turned his head away, then reached down. Came up with one of the bloody and vicious heads. It was immensely gross. He couldn't stand to look at it.

"Don't lay it in the dirt. And I can't have it touching the ground—at all."

"What chu want me to do, man?"

"How about if you shove it up your crybaby ass, punk?"

"Fuck you, clown."

Biggs drew his Mag. Held it in Muck's face, and waited. Marvin's eyes shifted nervously from side to side, while a series of farts escaped his rectum. Biggs released the hammer, re-holstered the weapon and walked to the Caddy. Was back with that blue plastic tarp. There was a patch of weeds and grass near there and he spread the tarp over it.

"Lower the heads on the tarp. Don't drop them. *Lower them. Gently.* I don't want them damaged."

Marvin carried the head over, his face turned away, grimacing. Leaned over carefully, cautiously, and lowered the head to just about on the tarp, then, misjudging, dropped it when he had it inches above it. He cursed to himself.

Biggs let it go.

"Now, get the other two. Don't drop them. I don't want the Parfrey heads soiled and/or damaged. We don't disrespect the Parfrey heads. Ever."

"Fuckin' one pig head be like any other. All of them be the same to me. But you keep callin' all of them *Parfrey*." Marvin proceeded, until he had completed the task. Was relieved. Quite. Wiped his forehead.

"Get the bones."

Marvin reached down for the bones wrapped in wax paper. Handed the package to Biggs. Bishop tore it open. Dumped the soup bones on top of the human remains in the hole. Grabbed a shovel and stirred things up a bit, mixed things up. This way you hoped no one would be the wiser. He knew there were no guarantees, but at least he made the effort. It was worth that.

"Cover it up."

Both men shoveled dirt and sand on top. Cecil's pain remained, although not as intense presently. He would tolerate it. What choice did he have? The hole got covered up, and Biggs had the deacon place some large rocks on top of the dirt for good measure.

"Make sure you got all that blood off the shovel."

Muck ran it through grass and dry leaves along the bank of the wash and then began slamming the shovel indiscriminately. Biggs had been "slicing sand" with his.

"What's the point? You won't accomplish anything that way. Run it through sand like I'm doing with mine. Pay attention. You might learn something."

"Yo. I like learnin'."

Did as told. Dug the shovel into the sand a few times. Turned it over, and did it again, giving both sides equal time. Biggs examined the shovels for traces of blood, hair, and other bits of DNA. Enough blood was visible to make him go for the water jug in the trunk. He had Marvin hold his shovel out while he poured tap water over it. Had him turn it over and did it again. The same procedure was followed with the other shovel.

"Look' like you got it all off."

"DNA is not as easy to get rid of as you think. Can't always be spotted with the naked eye. Should pour ammonia on them both to make sure— only it always fouls up the trunk."

"You sho don't be wantin' that."

Hearing Marvin say it was enough to convince Biggs to change his mind. Better to be safe than sorry.

He had Muck get the jug. Ammonia was poured liberally over one shovel, and then the other. They were both shoved between thick layers of old newspapers in the trunk. He had Marvin tilt the chest while he rinsed the inside of it with water. Poured ammonia over it as well. Inside and out. Handles, too. Wiped it clean with a towel. The tarp was folded over the "Parfrey heads" and placed inside the chest, and the chest was returned to the trunk.

It was then that Biggs hesitated, not able to turn away from the plastic jug that had blood in it sitting snuggly inside a corner on his right.

He cursed under his breath. Reached for it. Grabbed the battered case that contained the makeup kit, grabbed the entrenching tool.

"What I said? Man got wood."

"Shut up, and pay attention to the police scanner. Hear anything. Let me know right away."

"You the boss, Hoss."

Biggs was no more partial to being called "Hoss" than he was to being called Omar, but he was anxious to get going. Hurried back across the sand and climbed the ridge, losing his footing intermittently in the loose dirt and small rocks in his desperation to get to level ground up there.

A lizard, five inches in length, appeared out of nowhere. Froze up among the poison ivy and weeds, wild flowers, to give him the quick once-over, and just as suddenly fled out of sight.

He pushed on. Reached the top. Noticed an area that may have been used (post dumping of this Jolly Dolly) as a ritual site by quasi Satan-worshipping types, in that pentagrams, inverted crosses, double-bladed inverted axes, black mass indicators and other symbols of this nature were in evidence, carved into barks of trees, as well as painted on various rocks on the ground that had been formed into a circle approximately nine feet in diameter. What it actually meant he didn't know, nor did he care. The only reason it perturbed him at all is that this particular spot used to be his for dumping, exclusively.

He looked about, searching out with his eyes for the grave he had buried the body in almost four weeks ago, and while doing so could easily feel the sensation in his loins. There was no use trying to prevent the arousal phase. It was happening. Fine, so long as it didn't happen too rapidly and resulted in premature ejaculation.

"Pearly Girlie, Jolly Dolly . . . where art thou?" Where the hell was she? "Where did I plant your ass?"

Punk was right. No denying it. The need was there. The need. Goddamn Muck, and all the rest of them. Didn't get it. They never would.

# CHAPTER 91

**He paused.** Had to. Things did not look right. It had been too long. Lowered the jug and makeup case. He reached in his pocket. Withdrew a stack of *Polaroid* shots wrapped in clear plastic. Some were of the McVictim he was desperate to see again, the others were of the gravesite— in an attempt to gain perspective that would make sense and yield the answer. It didn't work. There was but one thing to do: select a sturdy enough stick or rod and start probing the earth with it. He went about it with bated breath, literally, hoping that premature *spooge* would not occur to taint and lessen the thrill.

Alas, the excitement increased so rapidly that he wondered if he would be able to have control over any of it.

I can't shoot my wad now, without seeing the body first and making it look right. Her makeup needed to be done. Appearance meant a lot. Can't let it happen. Don't allow it. Stay focused. Concentration is everything.


He poked at the earth, driving the stick in every conceivable patch of ground that he could think of, before his loins erupted and the spooge was for naught.

He stopped. Looked around. Where hadn't he driven the damned stick into the ground? Where was left? Couldn't tell. Went over the stack of *Polaroids* again. Ones on top were of the area, the rest were of the body, the whore: Before and After shots. He didn't dare gaze too long at the post kill images from fear that he would climax right where he stood.

It was back to the *Polaroids* of the area itself. He recalled having left markers, three stones: one about the size of a Crenshaw melon, the others no larger than your average grapefruit—only they were not in sight, to be seen anywhere. Covered in leaves? Removed by someone? Human or animal? Couldn't tell. Maybe those Devil worshipping assholes had been here tampering, doing their ritual and needed stones for it? Couldn't be certain.

There was nothing to do but probe with the stick some more and hope to get lucky. Once, twice, three times . . . with zero results.

It wasn't until about another two dozen times of driving the stick down into the soil did he feel it bump against something solid. Missy? About time. It was. He tossed the stick aside, grabbed the entrenching tool and fervently scraped leaves, twigs, and dead weeds aside, rocks.

Scooped the top layer away. Did the same with moist soil underneath. And there it was: the corpse. Waiting to be unearthed. And unearth it he would. Careful now, though. Don't disrupt to any great length, don't disturb.

The storm that had pummeled the Valley a few days back had brought the vermin out en masse: fibrillating night crawlers (anywhere from a couple of inches to a foot long), dozens of them, inch-long grub worms (and other invertebrates) feasted on his Jolly Dolly: slugs, slow worms (that were not worms at all, but legless lizards), beetles (full grown, and the other, in their infancy stage as grubs) centipedes, pocket gopher or two, what he perceived were pill bugs and sow bugs, voles, and a nine-inch mole with a mouthful of night-crawlers, while flesh-eating birds circled overhead, after a piece of his Pearly Girlie, without ever requesting or having been granted consent by him.

The flying scavengers were far easier to deal with than the underground type, who were everywhere: either burrowing into the soil and/or digging deep inside the corpse through various and varied body cavities: sockets (and what was left of the eyes; his own fault there, should have harvested them when he had the chance), nose, mouth, vagina, and rectum, desperate to escape the ultra violet rays of the sun. All of them, just about all of them, did what they could to avoid the harsh sunlight that these below ground, nocturnal creatures (with the exception of the fully matured beetles) had a justified fear of.

The stunned mole did an about-face, attempting to flee daylight and the dangers it surely foreshadowed and seek out the protective safety of the tunnel it had emerged from. Only Biggs was quicker. Whacked at it once with the entrenching tool, severing the creature in half. Flecks of blood sprayed his jacket front and upper brow.

Other rodents wasted no time scampering for cover, either below ground or off under leaves and weeds and brush.

Biggs had his gloves on and did what he could to scrape off the rest. If not all, quite a few grub worms and others of their ilk who crawled, or slithered away, inside the dead woman.

Some had been in and around her mouth. Not very many, since her throat had been stuffed with her very own underpants. There were things crawling in and around various dagger wounds, vagina, and rectum.

The parasites may have repulsed a loser like Marvin, and others like him, instead the sight had the opposite effect on the bishop: enhanced his arousal by increasing the intensity. Never failed. Mainstream squares were repulsed because they didn't get it, couldn't grasp it, never would. Then, too, you had the unmistakable odor of death, decay. Nothing opened up his sense of smell and invigorated him sexually like the miasma caused by decomposition.

Explain it to Joe *Lunchbucket* out there? Vinnie *Bagadonuts?* Never. Beyond their ability to comprehend. Not in a million years.

Drones worked shit jobs for slave wages because drones served that particular purpose and function and were never meant to rise above it, therefore could never fathom anything like the thrilling sight before him. McCunt. McBush. *"Mo betta than a Happy Meal at Mickey D"* as dufus Muck might utter—while ogling a live one.


The white vinyl gloves he had on were torn in places and needed to be replaced. He stashed them away inside the makeup case. Unlocked the cuffs on her wrists, and tossed them in the case as well. Got into a pair of fresh vinyl gloves before doing some more brushing away of dirt and assortment of worms. Well, the ones who had squirmed their way inside her rectum he wouldn't bother with, couldn't get to. Let them eat shit, what the hell. Nor could he do anything about the others, countless of them, slithering inside the dead whore's mouth, who had managed to get past her balled-up panties in there, as well as the vagina. In too deep.

And there were the flies, thousands of them, beetles flying about, wasps, mosquitoes—and other insects who felt a need to encroach on his Pearly Girlie.

Should run back to the Caddy and get the can of *Black Flag* for the flying bloodsuckers. No time. Bloodsuckers were annoying, more than anything. Didn't mind them gorging on the corpse, only their assault didn't stop there; they were taking bites out of *his* neck and face. Goddamn them. He swiped at the determined, impossible-to-reason-with sons of bitches. What else?

Forget them. Try to. His groin rigid. Near eruption. No, thought Biggs. Not yet. Can't shoot your load just yet. Put it off, keep putting it off, until after you've combed her hair, applied the lipstick and blush-on. He scrutinized the fingernail polish on her nails. Chipped. Far from clean. Parts of her nails were chipped as well. This wouldn't do. His mother, Charlotte Yvonne, may not have been the neatest whore who ever existed, but her makeup she never failed to keep up, nor were her fingernails ever-less-than attractive and impeccable. Cherry red was her favorite. Cherry red. Lips and fingernails. Toenails, too.

He reopened the makeup case. Did what he could with the nails. Brushed them with a manicurist's brush. Applied blood-red nail polish. Went to work on the hair next, at least attempted to, except the scalp slid off when he tried to adjust the head, position it straight while placing a rock under it for a pillow. The hair needed combing out; there was a certain way he needed it to be. Curling the hair would have made it perfect, the way he liked it, but there was no time and no place to plug in the curling iron out here, either. There was no use. The goddamned scalp shouldn't be sliding off. Water logged. That it? "Skin slippage." Could be, or else he was to blame for having made an incision all around at the time (had considered taking it with him to give to Sassounian to wear, but decided against it, out of respect for the victim).

There was no real reason to be one hundred percent without conscience, without a degree of some feeling and respect for the victims he slaughtered.

"Just say no. Say no no no. . . ." He recalled her pleading in this gentle manner during the assault. Well, he reasoned, if on the other hand, she had cried: Do it. Please do it. Kill me—he may have stopped himself. Sure. It was possible. Show fear and weakness and it fueled his rage. On the other hand, show that you feared nothing, that his menacing and deadly ways of committing homicide and various sundry atrocities were without impact, were not fear-inducing . . . and it defeated the intent and took the wind out of his sails. Something like it.


Biggs went about applying white powder to the face, blush-on to the cheeks. Had the stick of cherry-red lipstick in his hand needing to do her lips, only not easy to accomplish when the corpse had a pair of her panties jammed in her mouth.

He pushed down on the panties, shoving them out of the way and making it possible to apply the lipstick. Biggs was generous with it, seeing to it that the cherry-red overlapped plenty. He applied black eyeliner, penciled in exaggerated brows.

"My, my, what a pearly girlie you are. . . ."

Readjusted the scalp. Made a renewed effort to run a comb through the hair. Wasn't easy. Dirt was impossible to get rid of; blood was caked and too tough to do anything about.

He reached for the Polaroid camera. Aimed carefully, and took a series of shots. Once he was satisfied with the results, he placed these latest treasured pics inside the clear plastic bag with the others. Laid them under a false cardboard bottom inside the makeup case. Placed the tray that contained the various items of makeup on top. Closed the case and locked it. Biggs unzipped his fly, withdrew his groin and began to masturbate while guzzling blood from the jug in his other hand. It would not take him long to ejaculate. The sight of all those bones in the chest earlier, the blood, the dumping, and then throwing dirt over it to cover it up had kept him excited, caused him to have a strong desire for sex (as he had known it would). Muck had tried to be comical about it. What a fool. Just another thing that annoyed him about the low IQ retard.

He wondered if he performed orally on her if there might be a chance, albeit a slim one, to bring her back to life—so that he might bludgeon her to death all over again?

Deep down something told him that it was wishful thinking.

Cecil found himself placing his mouth on the genital area just the same, and badly wanted to chew on parts of her body. He bit into her buttocks repeatedly, then rubbed his penis against a thigh, while touching the breasts.

Some preferred them full of life, he preferred them struggling to hold on to life, then ultimately in this present state, under control. It's when they weren't breathing that they didn't give you any lip.

He turned the body on its side, the right hip side, drew a condom over his groin (not only as defense against worms and other parasites, but more importantly—should the body ever be discovered and gone over with a fine tooth comb by the coroner and his cretins, who by the way molested far more stiffs than he was ever able to get *his* hands on and his chubby in), poured some blood over the prophylactic and proceeded to sodomize the corpse.

There would be a tinge of regret later, mixed in with disgust. So be it, because the only thing that mattered at this moment was to shoot his load, and get off he did.

Could have been better. It was good enough. It was the condom, having to use a condom. He'd never cared for them much. What would he do with it? Didn't want to take it with. Had no choice. Sperm was DNA. Pubic hair? DNA.

He pulled the rubber off. Held it over the dead woman's face. Emptied the contents this way. Checked for stray pubic strands. Saw none. Even if he had, he still would have done the following: poured a touch/pinch of Tabasco sauce in, and tossed the condom aside. Let them knock themselves out testing for traces of DNA.

He chugged more blood, until he began to gag and was about to vomit. Blood didn't quite agree with his taste buds, although he believed it had to be good for his health.

The next thing had to happen, as it always did after dropping a load: there was no avoiding it, the need to urinate was there. And he did so over the body.

"I piss on your corpse."

It was said to no one, while he attempted to guzzle what remained of the blood inside the jug—and could not bring himself to do it.

# CHAPTER 92

**Goddammit, he felt sick, satisfied (somehow) but sick to his stomach.** There was no preempting the hollowness that ensued. It was the blood, it was post corpse molestation nausea that he could not exactly pinpoint or wanted to deal with. He had consumed too much blood; that's what it was. Made sense. Had allowed himself to get too worked up and excited.

Prior to coming out here he had determined to control that part of it— and he had failed. As always, *he had failed* and failed miserably.

Let it go. You'd brought that jug with her blood in it, didn't you? *What did you expect to happen?* Forget it. Drop it. There was no way to mask the feeling of disgust, no way to deny it. What made it worse, blood this old turned black and tasted way cruddy.

The nausea hung in there. One thing he could always count on. Some bile wound its way up. He was bending over to spit it out. Wiped his mouth. Turned the jug over the corpse and emptied the contents out, over the body in the shallow grave (where it undoubtedly belonged).

He wiped prints off the jug handle and spout, other parts. Rubbed it against dirt—and flung it. He zipped up. Using the entrenching tool, covered the body with dirt and leaves.

He hadn't wanted to deal with the latest development, and yet there was no putting it off. Just as a moment ago the urge to urinate had been there, now he had the need to defecate. There was no getting around it. Couldn't do much about the bowel movement he was experiencing.

He dug a hand inside the left pocket of his trousers to see if he might find something to wipe with: couple of old paper napkins, *Walgreens* and *Target* receipts. They would have to do.

He dropped his pants. Saw to it that he was positioned on top of the grave. Squatted. Did his business. It was a good one.

"I shit on your grave."

He wiped. Pulled his pants up. Guilt gnawed at him, as he knew it would. The price one paid.

Why'd you have to do it? Wasn't it enough that you owned her, body and soul? Sure. Man had to mark off what was his, didn't he? Animals did it all the time: dogs, cats, mountain lions. . . . All I did was to mark off what belongs to me. Nothing remotely disgusting about it, except the turmoil inside his head would not leave him be. Disgust, regret, remorse; hollow emptiness that had no bottom.

Pearly Girlie hadn't deserved to be shat on this way, even though, when you truly came down to it, they were nothing more than whores, worthless sperm receptacles who did not have a clue what it was about and spread their thighs and opened their mouths at first sight of money . . . or dope; notoriety.

Everything was upside down these days. They fucked for fame, attention, jack, dust—anything and everything—but the one thing that mattered above all else, the one thing he lacked in his life, that he was alien to (because the biggest whore in the universe hadn't possessed it herself, his mother, had shat on it herself), therefore did not pass it on to him (the way she was supposed to), whatever that element was that one required to be a "well-rounded" human.

Why? Why were they this way? Because twats didn't have any other way. They lived to whore, and whored to live. All of them. From Charlotte Yvonne, on. And those who worked hardest at pretending not to be this way, like Pearleen Bell and Olivia Duarte, and others like them, were, in fact, far worse, the worst. Smelly sluts with gamey pissers.

That's exactly why this particular Pearly Girlie, Jolly Dolly, had needed to be whizzed on, and her grave dumped on.

He gathered up enough rocks, some the size of eggplants or small melons, and placed them at the end where the head was.

Not certain why he did this. Out of respect, a degree of it, a small degree of it, or to keep animals from disturbing it.

Whatever the motive, he hoped scavengers wouldn't tamper with it. There was also the issue of footprints. Piggies had ways of making casts. He went about destroying any and all signs that could be traced back to him, and made it down the ridge to the *Cadillac*.

# CHAPTER 93

**Bishop and his deacon climbed in the car. Biggs drove it to the edge of the road.** Shut the engine off. Sat there. Considered letting Muck take care of the tracks. Then thought better of it.

Want something done? Want anything done right, especially something as important as this—you had to do it yourself.

He got out. Found a fresh branch. Walked back to where the limbs and bones were buried and went about eliminating any and all signs that they had ever been in the area. Some of it was no fun, in that he had to stoop to get at the tracks left by the tires all the way back to where the *Cadillac* sat parked by the road.

He told Marvin to step out. Handed him the branch with instructions to do the same once he pulled the car onto the blacktop. Muck did as told—to the best of his ability—while Biggs watched him from the driver's seat. Muck finished up. Tossed the branch, and got in. Serial killer and his apprentice drove off.

In spite of the mixed feelings Biggs had had to cope with on the ridge, there was no denying the underlying euphoria that stayed with him, a euphoria fueled by the fetid odor that lingered in his nostrils long after he and Marvin were gone from the dump site.

Biggs thought he was hungry and said so. Gargled with *Listerine*, and spat the mouthwash out the window.

"You hungry, Base?"

"Hear my belly cryin' out for food, Omar. Just cryin' out for some good eatin'. Yo."

Cecil Omar Biggs looked at the other man.

"Keep calling me 'Omar' you won't get shit."

They were south-bound on Laurel Canyon Boulevard soon enough, making their way back toward North Hollywood.

# CHAPTER 94

**It was five minutes past ten and the morning rush at Jessup's Family Diner had come and gone.** This was the lull before the lunch hour crowd filled up the place. Vester "Slim" Jessup, the lanky fifty-year-old African-American who owned the eatery, was in the kitchen in the back helping scrub some of the larger pans that were too enormous for the automated dishwasher to handle, and he was scrubbing them now in the trough-like sink while he had the time before the next wave of customers appeared.

Big Bertha sat at the far end of the counter taking in a coffee break and a smoke. Olivia helped out with what orders there were. She walked over to where Pearleen Bell sat at a table with her two friends Stella Martel and Lana Sepulveda, saw to it that they were taken care of, let some of their snide remarks about her and the whole Duarte family being square and squeaky clean wash right off, and was back behind the counter when Rudy Perez walked in.

Rudy wanted to talk.

Olivia tried to tell him that she was the only one presently working, since Bertha was still on her break.

*"Can you please stop for just one minute?* There's something I'd like to say to you."

"I can't, Rudy. Slim watches his employees like a hawk. Besides, we're busy."

"Huh?" His brows raised, Rudy looked about the nearly empty diner. "You call this busy?"

Olivia walked away, but then had a change of heart. Smiled, and walked back. She planted her elbows on the counter in front of him and cupped her gorgeous face in her open palms.

"What is it? What's so important that you absolutely have to talk to me?"

Rudy's right hand slid across the counter toward her, obviously concealing something underneath. When he lifted his hand there was a small, square-shaped red felt box there.

"What's this?"

"Open it."

Olivia hesitated. Opened the box to find a heart-shaped diamond ring.

"It's beautiful, Rudy."

"Yep."

"Where did you get the money?"

Rudy shrugged.

"Your shop money, Rudy. What will your brother say?"

"I don't know. I'll just tell him the truth: I spent some money on a ring for the girl I want to marry."

Olivia looked at the engagement ring, clearly overwhelmed by the gesture. She felt, at first, she wanted to try it on her finger, instead decided against it.

"I can't accept this, Rudy."

"Sure you can. We're engaged."

"Rudy, I can't. My parents—"

"You're looking at the real thing: fourteen karat with a real diamond. And I got it in a real jewelry store, and not off Jesus Ortiz."

Olivia held the ring in her hand. Slid it on her finger.

"It's gorgeous. Thank you."

She leaned over and kissed him on the cheek. About time, Rudy thought.

"The only thing left to do is tell your parents."

Olivia did not appear remotely thrilled at the prospect.

"Come on, Livia. After six months we should at least have the guts to tell them the way things are."

# CHAPTER 95

At the strippers' table, in a section of the diner to the left of the entrance as you walked in, Pearl Bell was clearing her throat to alert her stripper pals that "Moneybags" was pulling up outside in his *Cadillac.* "Mr. Moneybags" and his sidekick Deacon Marvin "Free Base" Muck.

The roommates watched as Biggs and Marvin, wearing ball caps with God's #1 embroidered across the front, with Biggs lugging that oversized *Bible* with him, climbed out of the luxury car and entered the faux coach diner. Muck was known for having a habit of tugging, then cupping his crotch. Today was no exception. He was at it. Big Bertha Lenier noticed it herself. Couldn't help but look. She'd taken a moment from what she'd been doing behind the counter to fire up a smoke and took it in.

"Fool is always playing with hisself. Like nobody else got one of them."

Biggs paused inside the entrance, with lap dog Marvin standing to the left of him, eyeing the trim on his side of the diner. Bishop was taking a moment to decide where he wanted to sit.

"Look' like a ho convention over there."

"Ho convention?"

Biggs turned his head in the direction of the strippers, while his eyes sought out and lingered on what appeared to be a shiny gold lighter that Pearleen Bell was lighting up with. He thought he might like to get his hands on it someday.

"Be lookin' that way to me."

"About as valid an observation as any."

Biggs let the cigarette lighter go for the time being, and decided on a quiet section on his right, away from the yakking twats. The observant flunky followed him to a red booth by the window. It didn't take long for Biggs's eyes to take in Olivia Duarte and the way she was chatting it up with Rudy Perez and admiring a ring he'd obviously just presented her with.

What was punk Perez doing wasting his time on something he truly did not have the nerve to go after? What the hell was he doing buying her a ring for? A cunt like that, a young, healthy, robust number like that didn't need a ring, a ring she could get anytime, anywhere. What she needed was to be taken, raped. Plain and simple. And put out of her misery afterwards. They were all miserable, every single female, every damned single cunt—and needed to be put out of their dilemma. Only a dumb pissant like Rudy Perez didn't get it. *Too young and too stupid.* Lack of perception. It took a higher IQ and a far more sophisticated intellect to comprehend what was going on with the female of the species.

*Cut her loose, boy. Let her up for air. Let the young bitch do her nothing job. Let her come over here and lick my balls, or at least take my order. Give it up, punk.*

Biggs continued to eye the two of them still talking at the counter. Olivia seemed concerned now that her boss Slim Jessup may be watching and not liking her slacking this way and that perhaps she ought to be getting back to work and taking care of the customers, earning her pay.

"Okay, I'm leaving. I know you're *busy*. See you tonight?"

"I can't get away, Rudy."

"Tomorrow night, then?"

Olivia said nothing.

"Please?"

She smiled. Gave him a nod. Rudy leaned over to give her a parting kiss, and headed toward the exit. When he spotted Biggs and Marvin R. Muck sitting in their booth, he decided a word was in order concerning what had transpired earlier that morning—if for no other reason but courtesy. He walked over.

"Excuse me, sir." Biggs looked up from the menu in his hands. "Mr. Biggs, ah, about this morning—I just want to apologize. Ace gets crazy like that sometimes. He likes to shoot his mouth off."

"Been doin' a lot of that crank, I bet. Shit'll fuck up yo head every time."

"Don't worry about it, Rudy." Even as he spoke, Cecil Biggs's eyes were back on Olivia Duarte: moving around, leaning over now and then to pick up something, or as she reached up to grab a pie or a slice of cake up on the pie shelf inside the glass case on the wall behind the counter, and this caused the hem of her dress to go up, revealing plenty of thigh and the occasional flash of pink underpants. Biggs and Marvin were getting an eyeful, and Rudy Perez was not aware of any of it.

"No harm done."

"Thought I'd apologize, you being one of our regulars and everything."

Rudy turned, gave Olivia one last wave, and was out the door and practically collided with Marty Roscoe and his loaded-down bicycle outside the diner entrance.

"Hi, Marty/so long, Marty."

"Pussy-whipped. Got to be. Only thing what makes a man act that squirrelly."

# CHAPTER 96

**Marty Roscoe chained his bike to the handicapped sign on the sidewalk, walked inside, and slid his wide backside onto a stool at the counter.** There was an issue of the *LA Times* and Roscoe picked it up for something to do; more accurately, to use as a prop to hide behind as he checked out the poontang.

First thing Roscoe noticed was Pearleen Bell and her friends. Those short skirts had a tendency to reveal plenty of flank when a woman sat in a chair wearing that stuff: black fishnets, black stiletto heels. They were in back of him, sitting at a table to his left.

Since he couldn't very well keep craning his head to keep ogling and risk getting called out on it by the strippers, he did the next best thing: stared hard into the mirror on the wall in front of him, above the back counter and pie rack and assorted shelving.

Sure know how to make you want it, he thought. Would have paid for it right now if he had the money. Lana Da Bottom had quoted him two hundred bucks for a roll with her. Half hour. He was thinking about it. He'd have to bust his ass making every swap meet and yard sale this month to afford her, and he was going to have to save up the money without his wife getting wind of it.

While Roscoe turned his head this way and that so that he might get a better view of all that leg there was to see in the mirror on the wall above the bread case and toaster, Biggs had his peepers on Olivia Duarte, who was at his table now with the order.

She placed a plate of fries in front of a disbelieving Marvin Muck. Biggs had had the urge for their popular cheese and mushroom omelette with green peppers, sautéed onions—hold the bacon bits—and this is what was on the table before him.

Marvin kept staring at his own measly fries and then at the appetizing omelette on Biggs's plate. Biggs didn't give a damn. His own eyes were on a large black fly buzzing around against the windowpane above his left shoulder presently.

The fly stayed in the center of the window by some handprints/smudge marks, and then buzzed on up toward the top of the glass and then moved off toward that corner.

Biggs watched the fly and thought about wanting to reach up there and grab it. He wanted to tear its wings off, one wing at a time, and then let it jerk around on its back like that with its spindly legs going crazy, like he used to do as a kid in that tenement. The fly brought forth yet another memory, far from pleasant one, in the wannabe shrink's office at the VA Hospital.

Marvin ate a French fry. Biggs got a forkful of omelette in his mouth, savoring the taste as he chewed, and then washed it down with coffee.

"That's what I call an omelette. About the only thing they know how to make here that's any good."

His flunky stuck another fry in his mouth.

"I had better to eat in the fuckin' bughouse."

"You've got to start earning your keep, Deacon."

"Already be underweight."

"You can have my leftovers."

"The way it always be. I want to be on top sometime and give some other mofo *my* leftover, me."

"You get fed, you get laid, and got a roof over your head. You never had it so good—*'Free Ride.'*"

Marvin emptied the cream container into his coffee mug. Added packs of sugar to that.

"Don't nothin' be 'free' in this world. Could be worse. Could be eatin' mustard sandwich or mayo—or diggin' in garbage can'. Done it all the time; ate food out of dumpster' in back of fast food an' supermarket'. Kept me alive. Yo."

# CHAPTER 97

**Vester Jessup, commonly known as "Slim" by the regulars, served Marty Roscoe the cheeseburger and *Coke* he had ordered.** Roscoe lowered the *LA Times* and bit into the juicy burger.

"You gonna be wantin' any *Fruit Loops* today, Marty?"

"Not today."

"How's the better half?"

"Working."

"How's life treating you, Marty?"

"Can't complain long as the wife keeps working. She's assistant manager now, makes more money. Says ever since she married me her luck's been getting better and better. What can I say? I brung her good fortune."

"You'll take all the credit you can get."

"I ain't arguin' if she wants to think that. Nag you to death anyway. Why encourage them?"

Slim grinned and shook his head, and every time he did so or smiled wide enough to reveal a mouth loaded with bright yellow nuggets, Cecil Biggs made it a point to catch the glitter from where he sat in his booth. Five of them. Three in the upper jaw, two in the lower. *Gold.* To Biggs, those gold teeth represented money, money to buy crack with for the sluts, nose candy cash—and he was looking at a man with a kisser full of cash just itching to be at one with his *slush fund*. Right there. Where everyone could see them choppers.

He couldn't figure why people wanted gold teeth to begin with, because in most cases when you croaked, the undertaker, or some greasy grave robber like Jesus Ortiz or Tulio Pedroza, who ran the cemetery where his parents were buried out there in the Altadena foothills, came along and yanked all that gold right out of your mouth. Nazis did it. They were notorious for it. What's more, Jessup had some gold on his fingers. That watch had to be worth something. Big Bertha had gold, too. Not as much as the diner owner had in his jaw, but enough. Woman was partial to rings. All types. Rings on her fat fingers more than made up for what she didn't have in her mouth. Assuming they were worth anything to begin with. They had to be. Vain beast like that.

Slim picked up on what Marty Roscoe was trying to get a better look at in the mirror: Lana and Stella showing plenty of leg, too much so.

"Lookit that haunch. *Lord have mercy.*"

Pearleen and her friends were well aware of the attention they usually drew, and not only from Slim and Marty. Lana was loving it.

"Roscoe can't afford my time, baby. Man ain't even got a real job. Got his wife supporting his lazy ass."

Stella Martel glanced in the redneck's direction. "She must be a stupid old woman to let somebody like that freeload."

"It ain't none of my business, honey, long as Marty Roscoe don't waste my time with his jive. See him drooling?"

Slim Jessup and Marty Roscoe could hear the girls laugh at that.

Olivia returned to refresh Cecil's and Marvin's coffee mugs. Bishop slid a fifty dollar bill her way.

"Will that cover the divas' tab?"

Olivia was certain that it would. "That's more than enough for what they ordered, sir."

"That's all right. You keep the rest."

"Thank you."

Olivia was back at the cash register to ring it up.


Marvin Muck had watched the Ulysses S. Grant disappear and it had made him angry enough. Bigg' like' to lay that green on everybody but him.

*"What about me?"*

"What about you? If you'd have been born with a cunt between your legs things might have gone better for you."

"You think so?"

Biggs added cream to his coffee, a pack or two of sugar, and stirred. "Probably not."

He could see Olivia walk over to Pearleen and her leggy friends to give them the good news: Their check had been taken care of.

The ebony beauty looked up, as did Lana and Stella. They waved *Thank Yous* in Cecil's direction. Biggs acknowledged with a brief, quick nod, and was back concentrating on his yet unfinished omelette. Marvin, on the other hand, was eating up the attention the girls were sending their way and waved right back. Had a big, toothy grin for them.

"*Mamita.* Peach LaBelle. *Yeah.*"

# CHAPTER 98

**Slim Jessup slid Marty Roscoe's second cheeseburger in front of him.** Redneck still had the newspaper in his hand and looked at it periodically, when he wasn't stealing glances at the strippers.

"There's enough crime and everything else in the paper every day to make you wonder what in hell's going on. I try not to read it, Marty; try not to watch the news. It's depressing."

"People will do just about anything for money."

Jessup nodded. "Lie, cheat, kidnap, murder . . ."

"And fuck."

"You said it."

"Got to have a *Cadillac* now days, Slim, just to get near a piece of ass." Marty Roscoe jerked his thumb in Biggs's direction. "Didn't always used to be that way. Got to have a *Fleetwood Brougham*—fully loaded."

"That old bicycle you got, Marty, ain't gonna impress them much."

"You're right about that, Mr. Jessup. Peaches LaBelle sure makes my dick hard. She was born to shag."

"Pricey, though."

"Last time I paid for a piece of ass, if you didn't count 'Nam, was when I rented a tux seven years ago to marry the old lady. She wanted to see me in a tux when we got hitched so I rented one. Cummerbund; the works. Ain't paid for gash since."

"Heard that. Peaches don't put out, from what I get. Likes to show it off. Look, but don't touch—unless she wants you to touch. The kind of show she does you ain't got to touch to get your rocks off, man."

"You better believe it. Gotta be one of the hottest chicks I ever seen. Fact is, I ain't never seen nobody move on a stage the way she does. Jesus. And them others with her? They don't just suck dick. Them whores siphon the chowder right out; drain the nutsack dry. Can hardly stand on your feet by the time they're done with you."

"That good, huh?"

Marty shook his head. "Unbelievable. Worth every cent. Good ol' boy could go broke gettin' head all the time. Can't help it, though. You get so used to it. Want it all the time."

"You got that taken care of, Marty. Bein' married."

"Yeah. But she don't do it like she used to. Got to nearly beg for it. Wasn't like that before we got hitched. She couldn't get enough. Hell, they're all like that, these days. That's how they reel you in. Get you to marry 'em. Blow jobs 24/7. And then they ration it out. Want a taste of beaver? Gotta take the garbage out. Itchin' to have your knob polished? Your nutsack and asshole licked? Gotta repair the backyard fence. Eager for some corn-hole action? Give the dogs a bath—and if you do a good enough job, only then will I consider taking care of *your* needs. Marriage ain't nothing but a trap. For fools and losers, is what I always say. Try tellin' Rudy and them other young bucks around here. Won't listen. Think they know it all, when in fact they don't know shit. *Wet behind the ears.* Man can get more pussy by not being married. Especially in Porn Valley. Why I decided to stay out here. Roadied for Willie and them: Jennings, Cash, Jerry Lee. Roadies get the poontang. Overflow. Whatever the talent can't handle—and they can only handle so much. What a life. But it took its toll. Travelin' did. Roach-infested motel rooms and bad food. Missed home cookin'. Decided to stay put when I met Petunia. We was in town with Jerry Lee. Jerry Lee was doin' a gig at the *Palomino*. Petunia come up. Was tryin' to get her songs seen. Hooked her up with some people I knew." Marty took a good bite of the burger. "Why I moved out from Flat Rock. Pussy capitol of the world is right here. *Poontang Paradise.* Only you gotta pay. Pussy ain't cheap here. They got wind of how valuable that money-maker is, got smart—and greedy—and they charge an arm and a leg, damned near. Man's got to find all kinds of ways to earn money to pay for his pussy. And these porn bitches? All they got to do is spread them ass cheeks, or the beaver, and the gold pours in. Drive *Beemers* and *Benzos*—lot of 'em do—unless they spend it on dope. And me? Well, you know about that." Marty chewed his food. "Fuck it. Bicycle gets me around. So long as I keep them baskets full of rotary dialers, all that shit—for the studios to buy and put in their movies."

Slim decided he had to walk away. Marty Roscoe was talking way too loud and using foul language.

"Marty; listen to me, Marty. This is a family diner. We got to keep it kosher. Ain't right to be using graphic language like that. Customers come in here with their kids."

"I understand, Slim." Marty looked around. "Sorry. You know how it is: get all worked up whenever we discuss poon."

Slim grabbed a bottle of ketchup, salt and pepper shakers that needed refilling and walked off. Shouldn't have been talking to Marty Roscoe to begin with. Big Mouth didn't know when to keep it down. Worse than that, most of what he said was bullshit anyway.

# CHAPTER 99

**Bertha's break was over and she rejoined Olivia behind the counter; helped get more coffee ready and other things for the noon bunch.** She glanced in Cecil Biggs's direction and was discreet with comments regarding Mr. Smelly. "Bigg' got odor to him like a pile of used socks."

"How do you know that?"

"I ain't got to serve the man every time to know what the man smell' like. Used socks; *dirty old pile of used socks.*"

"More like the inside of a cat's butt."

The large woman did a double take. Bertha wasn't sure she had heard right. Did that come out of Livia's mouth? Wasn't like her. She looked at Olivia, who was grinning, then shot a glance in the direction of Pearleen Bell and her friends.

"Lemme guess where you pick up language like that." Bertha kept indicating the strippers' table. The expression said she was taken aback by this.

Olivia remained amused. Shrugged off Big Bertha's reaction and walked to the other end of the counter to refill a customer's coffee mug.

Biggs and Marvin finished their food and walked outside to the *Cadillac.* Pretty soon Lana was running out after them. The bishop was already sitting inside his car when the dark-haired stripper caught up with his deacon as he reached for the door handle on the passenger side.

"Wait up, handsome."

Marvin turned, giving her the big grin. Now she want' it. Hard up for bump and she gonna gimme the come-on.

"What do you say we party it up? The girls are in the mood."

"That be funny. Now you in the mood? How about what happen' the other night in the dressin' room? After all you hoe' done smoked all that good dope and got Trusty all pissed off, on my ass?"

"You know we couldn't leave, baby."

"Don't boo-shit the boo-shitter, hear?"

"Forget it, then. All right? Fuck it."

"Hold on now. I ain't said nothin' like that. I just don't like peep' jerkin' my chain, is all, sugah-bush. If you on the level wiff me—I be on the level wiff you. Be a two-way street, baby. All I be sayin' here. Don't like bein' played for no suckah, *Ms. Lana Da Bottom*. Can you dig that?"

"Heard you the first time. Do we party, or not? Talk to the rev."

"I ain't got to talk to the man. I know what the man want'. You say you womens ready to party—that mean all the womens? Includin' Livia?"

"You know that bitch is squeaky clean. She don't ever want to do nothing, just like her older sister. Went to high school with her. Same shit. Ask Peaches. Couple of squares raised by squares. What can I tell you?"

"Too bad. 'Cause my main man the bishop over there go for that Chicana. Got the thang for her. Like' long hair and dark meat. No shit. Remind' him of the Filipino lady he was in love with. My main man dig that dark meat, not that Livia be all that dark. Man' mama was *Creole*. He like' that type: dark hair, dark eye'; an' he like' them yellow ho."

"Well, shit, what do you want me to do? We can't get her. I'm half-Mexican. You don't think my hair's dark enough?"

"As far as I be concern', you jus' fine, sugar-bush. Ain't me wiff the problem."

"What about Peachy? He likes Peachy."

"Like her myself. More than I can say."

"Let's party, then."

"Let me check wiff the bishop first." Marvin opened the passenger side door. Was about to speak to Cecil.

"Get in. I don't want her to hear."

Marvin hopped in. Closed the door.

"What do you think, Cecil? They want to get high, do the thang."

Biggs was looking straight ahead, through the windshield, and could see Marty Roscoe unchaining his bike.

"It's no good. Too many witnesses."

"Come on, Cecil."

"Use your fucking head. The dope is the bait. Why waste all that dope when we can't do anything with them right now?"

"Can get to know them better."

"*Know them?* I know all there is to know about cum-guzzlers like that."

"Let them sit in the *Cadillac* for a minnit. They get off on it. New car smell make' 'em hot."

"What makes them *'hot'* . . . is *cold, hard cash—and drugs.*"

"That be yo last word on it?"

Biggs waited. Nodded his consent at last.

"Call them over."

# CHAPTER 100

**Marvin stepped out.** Waved to Lana and her peeler pals. It did not take them long to climb in the backseat and were practically demanding to get high. Biggs produced a joint that appeared odder than the usual in some way that they couldn't quite place.

"Got something special here for you."

"What is it?" said Stella.

"*Jim Jones,*" explained Marvin. "Got toot in it, dipped in dust."

"PCP?" said Lana. "Fucking cool."

"Super fly shit," said Marvin. "Blow the top of your head right off." And he couldn't wait to get his share of it. Biggs shook his head. "No way."

Passed it on to the strippers. Marvin began to curse and make a general fuss.

"Be like that. Only next time you be needin' *my* help to lift somethin' HEAVY, don't be lookin' *my* way, *Bro-tha Trusty.*"

"Let him have a toke," Biggs said to the women. Marvin was thrilled. Had a long one, then passed it back to them. Rested his head back. Didn't care for the time being where he was or who he was or anything like that. You got high and the world went away; everything that be fucked up about life, being alive, disappeared.

Cecil looked at him, despising his weakness, despising all of them for it. He stared straight ahead. Martin Thurman Roscoe could still be seen in front of the diner fiddling with his back tire, inflating it with a bicycle pump.

The girls noticed that Biggs was not joining in and wondered about it, although there hardly was call for it; they knew the man was on antidepressants.

"Doctor's orders. They got me on stuff to deal with the occasional funk that settles in."

Now Stella and Lana were readily admitting that they understood; they'd been on meds (as so many of their friends have) from time to time over the years themselves.

"My mother is on *Zoloft,*" Lana confessed.

"*Zoloft?*" said Biggs. "I know about *Zoloft.* They had me on *Thorazine* and some other shit, *Paxil.* Not a good idea to do dope or alcohol when you're on meds."

"Marvin over here promised us there won't be any chickens killed, either," said Lana "Da Bottom" Sepulveda. "Are we straight on that? Otherwise I can't go along. I don't like seein' animals get killed for no real reason. I know you can get it up without having to cut a poor chicken's head off."

"That's behind me. A man shouldn't have to harm a feather on a chicken to get an erection. It's mind over matter. What it really comes down to."

"Good," said Lana.

"I'll second that," said Stella. Pearleen Bell was in agreement on the topic, but said nothing.

The *Jim Jones* was smoked down, further small talk continued, but their minds were so blown that they made little sense; all they knew was that they wanted to get back outside where the air smelled better. They thanked Mr. B. and the sidekick. All said that they ought to get together soon, and climbed out, tried to, as Stella lost her balance, tripped, and went down and had to be helped up by her friends. Biggs wasted no time in starting the motor up and pulling out of the parking lot, and the *Cadillac* was gone in the gray noon haze.

# CHAPTER 101

**Roscoe looked up.** He was through inflating his tire. Dropped the pump in one of the baskets in the back and walked up to Pearleen and her voluptuous friends standing next to her off-white '77 *Mustang* with the sunroof and the many dings and dents that made the car look something like an eyesore. Not as bad as that beater Ortiz and Felix tooled around in, still . . . There was no real reason for a *Mustang* such as this to look so shoddy.

Marty pointed out to the owner that her car needed a paint job and that he knew where she could have it done at a reasonable price. He couldn't help leering as he said it.

"I ain't got the means to paint it myself, but sure can fill in the cracks. Can let the Perez brothers do the rest. It'd be worth it, I think. Car like that."

Pearleen let it pass. The fool couldn't stop ogling. He asked about the song his wife had written for her, and how it was working out.

"I hear you're using it in your act."

"Why wouldn't I be using it in my act? That's why I paid her to write it for me."

"I hear crowds are diggin' it."

"It's a winner. Tell Petunia to write me another."

"I sure will. She'll be glad to hear it; only she's gonna want more than a hundred bucks for the next one—unless we can work something out."

"Just like fatso McCoy. Always on the make."

"Can you blame me? I mean, you got some hot body there."

"Does that give you the right to treat me like a piece of meat?"

"Ain't no need to put on airs with me, honey pie. I know what all you chicks is like. This is *Porn Valley*. You'll do anything for blow. Got to the point a good ole boy has to pay through the nose just to get laid, just to get him some poon."

"How we live is none of your business, is it, Roscoe? I fuck who I want to fuck—and if you don't like it, *tough shit*."

"Tell him, Lana," Stella urged.

"Why do men have to be such assholes all the time? Why can't you ever grow up?"

"All I know is Biggs and that 8-ball he runs with is dangerous. Got some loose screws, if you get the picture."

"Why don't you let us worry about that?" Pearleen was not glaring at him, although she came close.

"You're just jealous because the man's got the *Cadillac* and all you got is that old bicycle." Lana was back at it. Needed to remind him. He was asking for it. "Baskets fulla worthless junk. Fucking jealous. I told you: two hundred bucks if you want some, otherwise stay the hell out of my life."

The other girls were laughing now.

"We'll see who laughs last. Biggs kidnapped a Puerto Rican chick a few years back. You know the one. Did hardcore. *Loco* Biggs kept her locked up in a coffin—"

"Mona Please?" Stella knew her. So did the others. Nothing new there. "Mistress Mona? Bitch was into rough sex and shit. Her scene. Dumb cunt had it comin' to her. Still does it, too. Into whips and leather. Likes it rough. Fuck her. Probably it was her idea to let Biggs do that to her. DA got her to lie about Cecil 'cause they were after him. IRS don't like him for having that church and not paying his taxes. Fuck them; fuck the government. Always giving people a hard time."

"He's a nutcake. He was convicted in '78, did a nickel in the bughouse. People I know seen him in the West LA VA more than once, talkin' to shrinks, gettin' his medication. Seen him myself over here in the Valley VA. He don't usually use this hospital 'cause he don't want folks in the neighborhood to be reminded that he's unstable. Always was, always will be."

"What were *you* doin' there?" Lana hadn't been able to deny the urge to give back as good as the jerk was dishing out. *Chauvinist.* "Getting *your* meds?"

Stella was eager to back her. "Make me sick. Live off your wife like a suitcase pimp. Bastard. You're worse than a pimp. She supports your fat *culo*, while you're riding around on a bicycle fucking with garage sales. Sorry asshole. Get a job. Quit living off your wife."

Roscoe did what he could to keep a calm exterior. If he truly pissed them off, he'd never get any beaver later, no matter what he'd be willing to pay.

"The reason I was at the VA is because somebody give me VD. Good thing I caught it in time. Could've wrecked my marriage. Some chicks just don't give a shit."

"You're a liar," they snapped back.

"We take care of ourselves." Stella Martel made sure the thick-skulled hillbilly got the message. "Have regular checkups. The industry demands it. You are a fucking liar to insinuate that it was one of us you got it from. *Redneck rube loser.*"

"Like I said before," Lana said, "eat your heart out, Roscoe. The man owns that new *Cadillac*, owns a *Rolls-Royce*, that house he lives in—all legal. He's a licensed bishop, and his house is a legitimate church—and nobody, not you, not the IRS, not the North Hollywood PD can change that—"

"Yeah? What kind of church can it be when he's got porn chicks over there all the time, doin' drugs and who knows what else?"

"How about if you and your wife start minding your own business for a change?" Pearleen Bell had had it. The redneck was pissing her off. "I get so tired of all this crap. Why do people have to be so goddamn nosy?"

"All I'm saying is he's a nutjob. Attempted suicide a bunch of times."

"I wish you'd commit suicide," said Lana, drawing sniggers from her pals.

"You don't know his mental history."

"Like we know yours?"

"Burns his dick with cigarettes."

"How would he do that?" Stella wanted to know. "When the man don't even smoke?"

Marty Roscoe shook his head. It was hopeless.

"Just make sure you bring a condom when you come to see me, Roscoe, and the two hundred bucks."

They walked off.

"Tell you what, how about if I wrap that two hundred dollars of my hard-earned money right around my dick and jerk off with it, Lana? I'd rather do that than let you bitches have it. *I work for my money*, and I don't mean on my knees, neither. I do my share; always did my share. My wife ain't no hooker (that I know of). You got no right to say shit like that. I ain't no pimp. You got no right to compare what I do to make a dollar to what a pimp does."

He waved at the air with an open palm, as if swatting a flying insect that wasn't worth bothering with, after all.

*"Buncha crack whores."*

# CHAPTER 102

**"I believe it's time to take the Party Wagon out for a run," said Biggs to his partner the Deacon Marvin R. Muck, and jammed *Gummi Bears* and lemon drops in his mouth.** Marvin held his hand out and Biggs shook a few lemon drops out of the bag for him.

"Lemon drop' be good." Marvin R. dumped them down the gullet.

"I like lemon drops. Lemon drops are good. I like trolling for pussy a lot better."

Marvin looked up. Noticed they were heading back to the church.

"Yo. Why we goin' home?"

"I think we can use the catatonic's help this time around."

Biggs crunched lemon drops in his mouth. Ground them down. "At this rate I won't have any teeth left before long. Too much sugar, sweets. Not good for your health."

Marvin was shaking his head. "Cata—what? The mental retard? Bitch only be in the way, man."

Biggs looked at him. "I know what I'm doing. It looks better if you got a girlie with you. It can only help."

"You sayin' I ain't good enough to bring the bitches in by myself?"

"I want Patience on the scene. Work in tandem. Cunts will trust to go with someone like her a lot quicker than they will a guy working alone."

"*Tandem?* I don't be likin' the sound of it."

"Who gives a shit what you like?"

Marvin shrugged. "The way it always be."

"What always 'be'?"

"Fuck it. Do it your way."

"I intend to."

# CHAPTER 103

**They pulled up to the church.** Marvin hopped out to unlock the gate and Biggs drove the Caddy through. They went inside.

Patience was cleaned up, given cleaner clothes to wear, and soon enough the three of them were in the Caddy driving north to the secret garage where Biggs kept the Party Wagon, a *Ford Econoline 500* cargo van without seats in the back that he preferred to do his trolling in and sometimes the actual torture and killing in.

Two miles prior to reaching the garage, Biggs had Marvin get in the backseat with her, and hunch down on the floor.

"Make sure she keeps her head out of sight. Both of you: keep your heads down until I tell you otherwise."

Biggs drove down an alley. Stopped at a roll-up garage door with peeling gray paint. Hopped out. Unlocked it. Yanked up on the roll-up and drove the Caddy in. It wasn't until he had pulled down on the door that he gave the both of them permission to lift their heads, step out of the *Cadillac,* and climb in the *Econoline.*

"Hate bein' wiff the retard. Ho don't never be sayin' nothin' but I'm cold, I'm cold. Be summertime all the time and 'tard be cold."

"Don't worry about it. Hunker down in the van until I tell you different. Both of you."

"Again?"

"You know the routine. It's for your own good."

Marvin did as instructed. Made sure Patience complied as well. Biggs reached down on the roll-up handle and yanked up on it to reopen it. He got in the Party Wagon and backed it out.

The sidekick was grumbling.

"Right. Be for my own good. I get it now. Why we got to play Dick Tracy an' shit."

"Anything happens and we get busted, the less you know the better off you'll be. It's that simple."

Biggs cleared the garage door. Hopped back out to pull it down.

Locked the handle. He was in the driver's seat. Tearing down the alley. He could hear Marvin talking to the almost there catatonic.

"See, why we be doin' all this: if po-leece ever aks us, you don't never be knowin' nothin' 'cause you never seen nothin'. Don't know where the garage be or nothin'. None a dat. Hear no evil shit, see no evil shit. Somethin' like dat."

"Marvin?"

"Yeah, boss?"

"You're wasting your time with her."

"Could be. She don't be gettin' none of it. Why I said why bring the 'tard wiff us? She don't be no good no way."

Biggs pulled the van into the parking lot of a vacant antique furniture store. Switched both front and rear plates. Got back in.

"You can come up now."

"That be more like it."

# CHAPTER 104

**They were on the Hollywood Freeway, heading south, through Hollywood, past Downtown LA.** Soon enough Biggs had them on the Long Beach Freeway, taking the Firestone off- ramp, the City of South Gate. He pulled into a *Target* parking lot.

It was Saturday afternoon, plenty of cars around, plenty of shoppers, especially younger ones, female type, the kind Biggs was interested in.

Patience was sitting on the floor in the back, shivering, staring at the bright sun that shone through the windshield. Having had Marvin clean her up for the occasion had been a smart move. She looked presentable. They'd washed her face, combed her hair out and given her those acceptable clothes to wear. Never mind that they were clothes they had gotten off previous victims; they looked nice enough on her. They had even sprayed her armpits and crotch with deodorant in an effort to mask her body odor, and on top of that, had her gargle with mouthwash.

"Listen up, Marvin, you better make goddamned sure the zombie doesn't get lost in the crowd, make sure she doesn't drift off on her own."

"I got you, Cecil."

"You choose. You know what I like, and then step back, keep your distance, and let Patience do the rest."

"Patience could do the rest. Got it."

"You sure about that?"

"Prob'ly."

Biggs reached down for the bottle of mouthwash in his black bag. "Hand it to her. She better gargle some more. The only thing she'll draw with that breath is bugs."

Marvin moved to the back. Had the woman gargle. When she was through, she spit it out inside the van.

"*Not in here.* You were supposed to spit it outside. Out there. Not in here."

"Want her to do some more?"

"No; that's enough." Biggs looked at Patience. "Are you listening to all this?"

"Can you please turn the heat up?"

"Bullshit. How can you be cold when it's eighty-five degrees outside? It's all in your head."

"I'm cold; that's all I know. I'm freezing."

"I told you she be gone. Head ain't right. Got to tell her everything 'bout fifty time'—and she still don't be gettin' it."

"Yeah? Almost as bad as you."

Cecil handed her a joint.

"You know what you're supposed to say, right? So we don't have to go over it again. We're doing what we did before, right? Remember? Your friend's got more weed in the van; great shit: weed, toot, 'ludes, crystal meth, hillbilly heroin, and some other goodies. And your friend's prices are reasonable. They won't get gouged; your friend is not a gouger. Got all that, Patience?"

Patience said nothing. Stared at the sun through the glass as though wanting to reach out to it. Needing its warmth.

"You got all that, bitch, or do I have to give you another beating right here in the van? Say something."

Patience McDaniel remained silent. Biggs started to get out of his seat and Patience nodded her head.

"My friend's prices are reasonable."

Biggs sat back down. He looked at Marvin. "Keep a close eye on her. Understand?"

Marvin said he did. Biggs gave him a joint. "If you latch onto something really good and it looks like it won't take, you got them on the hook but it looks like they may slip away, use that; move in and use that other joint. Do what you have to, but get them to the Party Wagon. Stay away from couples if you can. I don't want to deal with anyone too big if I don't have to. A young cunt by herself would be ideal, even two together is okay."

"I got you, Cecil."

"You got all that? Are you listening?"

"I be listenin'."

"You won't fuck up on me?"

"I won't fuck up on you."

"I don't want you wasting good dope on some chunky fifty-year-old lizard butt hag with dentures and thick ankles."

"I ain't gonna do that to you, Cecil. I know what you like."

Biggs was looking at Patience again. "And you—listen up. You so much as try to take off or tip the assholes off or do anything stupid and your punishment will be far worse than anything you can imagine. Do what you're told and do what you did before. You got that?"

Patience stared in silence. The bishop was forced to get out of his seat again. He grabbed her by the shoulders and shook her this way.

"I said you got that?"

"Yes. I got that."

"Then get with it. Go on. Take off." Remembered something. A detail they'd overlooked. Biggs dug his hand back into the black bag. Slapped a fake stash on Marvin's face that fairly concealed the discolored area above the upper lip and nostrils. Tossed him a black ball cap with the purple, sweat-stained bill. Patience was handed a brown wig with long, blond and auburn streaks in it. She held it in her hands, staring. Did nothing with it.

"Get it on her."

Marvin did so. Leaving the wig askew.

"Want something done right? Do it yourself."

Biggs made the proper adjustment so that the wig did not appear to be a wig and served its intended purpose. He handed her a pair of sunglasses with rose-tinted lenses. It was appropriate. The way she saw the world. At least she did not require help putting the shades on.

Cecil opened the back door for her.

"Go for it."

Marvin heaved the side door open and stepped down. Biggs waited to see if he had enough sense to close the damn door without being reminded. This time he did. Slid the door back into place and even walked around to the back and helped Patience climb down. Just like a real gentleman. Water carrier exhibited enough intelligence to close this door as well.

What do you know, thought Biggs. It always made life easier when things went the way they were supposed to, no matter how minor or seemingly insignificant.

# CHAPTER 105

**He checked to make sure his guns were loaded.** He'd brought a *9mm* with him, as well as the *.357 Magnum* this time. There was the *Mossman 500* shotgun that he kept in the oblong box just in case.

He had plenty of handcuffs, a tire iron, claw hammer, baseball bat, two bottles of chloroform, shovels, a pickaxe, blankets. It was all there in the van, and he had a tough time controlling his rising excitement. Thoughts of what was about to (possibly) take place had the adrenaline pumping.

It always had this effect on him, the excitement of it, element of danger. There was always that chance that something might go wrong, that the goofy black woman would screw up, that she might draw a couple to the Party Wagon and that he might discover that one of them was a gigantic male who would not be easy to control.

The chances you took. But it felt good. He checked his hair in the side mirror. Thought to pull the small handheld mirror from the black bag that he kept in there as it came in handy the times he was around hookers and other sluts who used it for cutting out rails. Now he was holding it up at the back of his head, near the top, checking on the area where the hair was thinning.

Was there a *bald spot* developing back there? Didn't want to admit it. He was losing hair up near the top back there where he'd had the bar code tattooed years before. The bar code and the series of numbers directly under it were becoming, if only faintly, visible.

Maybe he ought to just cut it all off? Shave the head like he used to, even though there would then be no way to conceal the dent in his forehead, at least not to his satisfaction. The white cap he at times wore with the God's #1 black script across the front helped to some extent, it was true, but it wasn't always appropriate to wear, either—such as now. It would have been absolutely inappropriate for the present situation. Inappropriate and hypocritical. Selling weed and wearing head gear that praised a deity, never mind that this deity never existed—just as none of them ever existed.

Fact remained: damned dent spooked some of them. Made him look less attractive to the cunts, even with the tinted reading glasses he usually wore that helped detract some of the negative vibes caused by the deformed temple.

He put the hand mirror away. Picked up the hairbrush and brushed his hair down on top, brushed it back around the ears.

Yeah. He looked all right, considering. Being on mood elevators and dealing with flashbacks. Years of it. Considering.

He took the reading glasses off. That's all they were. Bifocals to be sure, technically speaking, although the upper half (or better) of the lenses was plain glass and tinted for a reason: he liked the fact his eyes were not easy to detect during the day by the enemy the times he had to interact with them.

And the lower part? The lower third, that is? He had a difficult time reading without them. Sight was still pretty damned good; he could see and do just about anything without the glasses, except when it came to reading the newspaper and all those books he kept around the house.

It was all the reading, no doubt, decades of it, the strain on the eyes that contributed. Reading shit like *Mein Kampf* that caused it, and more shit like *Capital* by Karl Marx that added to it. You realized, as you grew older, that most books were a waste of time and did nothing for you.

He wiped the lenses with *Kleenex*. Wiped sweat from his brow, and put the glasses back on. Then got the sudden notion to apply the Trusty makeup. Should help with the cover.

There was nothing to do but sit and wait now. Got the *Bushnell* field glasses out and watched Patience and Marvin approach a young redhead as she unlocked her car. That one did not take. The redhead had shaken her head. Not interested.

She would have filled the bill, Biggs thought. Nice body—but wrong pick on Marvin's part, because the woman did not look like she did dope and he didn't care for red hair.

Get a doper. Don't waste time on the others. Sniff out a doper, Free Ride. Get me a doper, a user. Get a *cokehead,* or *pothead*; a *pill popper*— and stay away from red hair.

He kept the binoculars trained on the action for another twenty, twenty-five minutes and could see a young couple in jeans and Beatles Tshirts walking along with Patience.

The kid and his girlfriend had blond hair. And the kid seemed very anxious, in a hurry. Apparently he could not wait to get his hands on some more of that fine weed.

Biggs readied himself. Futzed around with the radio dial, hoping for some shitty Beatles tune. He preferred anything to the "Fab Four" and their overrated bubblegum tripe, any group at all: Boxtops, *Butthole Surfers, Squirrel Nut Zippers, Echo & the Bunnymen, Hootie & the Blowfish, Monkees, Steppenwolf, Three Dog Night, ZZ Top, Rammstein, Dr. Hook, Dr. John, Judas Priest, Metallica, Guns N' Roses, Black Sabbath, Black Flag, Stones, Temptations, Commodores, Jackie Wilson, Wilson Picket, Bobby "Boris" Pickett, Earth, Wind & Fire, Kinks, Sausage Links*—didn't matter— anyone but the Beatles. For now, he wanted a mop-tops tune, and got nowhere. Instead, he happened upon something about a dead skunk in the middle of the road and that it was stinking to high heaven on one of the MOR stations by accident and decided to leave it on for the hell of it, sat back down and pretended to be reading the horoscope in the *LA Weekly* and waited for the easy meat to get in his van.

# CHAPTER 106

**Biggs could not believe his good fortune when he saw what Patience showed up with at the *Econoline's* back door.** The couple looked much better than he could have hoped.

They were from Georgia, visiting relatives in Cerritos. They were healthy and friendly and wanted to get high, and they kept saying what a nice man Cecil was and what a cool lady his girlfriend Patience was.

"Lost my job at the haunted house: *Lizzy Borden's Bordello of Fear.* Cutbacks due to drop in ticket sales." He flashed a glossie of the original

Parfrey. "Crucial part of the act. Claimed there was no money in their budget to feed a '*hog*'. We were unceremoniously let go. Otherwise I wouldn't even consider taking money for this stuff. Need cash for gas. That's what it is, so I can keep looking for work. It's tough, especially when you have a black fiancée. You know how racist some folks can be. Her brother there? He's not able to work. Has a problem with authority figures. Sorry to be charging you."

The guy and his girlfriend didn't mind. Handed Biggs some bills. Climbed in the van. They got another joint going.

Patience had remained outside and shut the door on them, as previously instructed. The Southern Belle's boyfriend had a question, as Cecil thought he might.

"So where's the real dope?"

"I'm looking at him."

Biggs drew the *.357 Magnum.* Patience and Marvin hustled into the van through the door on the passenger side. Closed it. Biggs handed Marvin a pair of handcuffs and watched him scramble in the back to where the guy sat, yanked his wrists behind him and clamped the cuffs on like a pro. There were times Marvin came in handy.

"Anyone else with them? Anyone see you bring them to the van?"

"Not that I know of, Cecil."

Biggs just about winced at mention of his name, not that it actually mattered, the McVictims weren't going to live long enough to tell anyone about any of it. Biggs tossed him a second pair of cuffs for the Southern Belle. Marvin did his job well. The deacon was learning. About time.

Biggs reached down for a bottle of chloroform and a terry-cloth towel. Handed them to Marvin. Muck poured chloroform onto the towel, and was about to bury the kid's nose and mouth in it—only the kid struggled enough so that it made it difficult.

Biggs cursed under his breath. Marvin was fucking up, just when he thought he might be getting his act together. And then, adding to the confusion and hassle, the girl started screaming. On impulse, Biggs jumped out of his seat and clamped his hand over her mouth. The girl bit down on his index finger and Trusty Lusty backhanded her. Tossed the tire iron to Marvin.

"Hit a grand slam off his skull."

Marvin Muck gripped the tire iron. Hesitated to follow through. Had to be told again.

"Hit the motherfucker. Are you deaf?"

Marvin turned his head away, and struck the girl's boyfriend across the face with the tire iron. Kid went down. Blood flowed from his nose and mouth.

"Encore."

Marvin looked away. "I be in this for pussy, man. I ain't no killa."

"I won't tell you again."

Marvin waited. Cursed some more. Smacked the kid across the left side of his jaw. For all intents and purposes, the vic was out.

"Now do the chloroform."

"Why? Shit could fuck up his liver. Tol' me so yo'self. Chloroform be some bad shit."

"His liver? You're worried about his liver? At a time like this? *Fuck his liver.*"

Marvin pressed the towel against the victim's mouth and nostrils. Kept it there. Made sure the boyfriend wouldn't be waking up for a while. Biggs tossed him the duct tape. Watched Marvin fumble with it, tear a strip off the roll and slap it over the unlucky sucker's mouth.

"Now get her."

Marvin looked at him.

"What?"

"Do a 'grand slam' or . . ."

"No, just the towel."

Marvin pressed the towel to her kisser until she, too, lost consciousness. Biggs recapped the chloroform bottle and returned it to the black medical satchel.

He reached inside for a white plastic bag and held it open for Marvin to toss the towel in. Biggs folded the bag over twice and shoved it under the mattress. Went through the vic's purse. Found the usual: lipstick, makeup, sanitary napkins and Tampons, prophylactics, pocket calculator, keys, zit cream, loose change, and what amounted to eighteen dollars in paper money.

He pocketed the bills, and dumped the rest of it inside the black bag. When he looked up, Marvin was going through the kid's pockets. Held up a wad of receipts, the usual junk: packet of *Trojans*, house and car keys, a few nickels and dimes; crumpled up singles adding up to twelve dollars.

"Get his wallet."

Muck did that. Handed it over. He also dug up a pack of smokes and matches, and was about to light up.

"Not in here. You know I can't take cigarette smoke. Shit causes cancer."

Seeing that he had no choice, Muck put the butt away. Biggs unfolded the kid's billfold. Found twenty-six bucks in there. Pocketed the bills, and dropped the wallet into the medical bag.

"Get the jewelry, watches. See what you can find."

Marvin undid the boyfriend's wristwatch, as well as the belle's gold necklace, the *Bulova* on her wrist, and a ring that looked far from expensive.

Biggs had the deacon place it all in his open palm. Cecil O. looked the items over. Decided Marvin could keep the cheap Timex he got off the punk. He dropped the rest of the items into the medical satchel, feeling less than thrilled with the meager take.

What did you expect to find in South Gate? This wasn't Beverly Hills, and it wasn't the Palisades. While Biggs mumbled and grumbled, Muck took the opportunity to run his hands over the unconscious woman's breasts. Slid a hand inside her T, squeezed some more, then ran his right hand down inside her blue jeans.

"What do you think you're doing? Get your hands off her. *Tape her mouth.*"

Marvin did that.

"Finish searching the punk."

"Just done it."

"You look inside his boots?"

"What for?"

"Do it."

Marvin attempted to pry his fingers inside one of the snake skin boots on the kid's foot. Biggs shook his head.

"Pull them off."

Marvin did, and a pocketknife dropped out. He picked it up. Unfolded it. The blade was sharp and three inches in length.

"Yo. Good thing we took a look inside them kicks, no shit."

Biggs said nothing. Held his hand out. Marvin placed the knife in it.

"I got no protection."

"From what?"

"Never mind. At least I got me a *Timex* watch. Yo. Them *Timex* got a reputation." He held it close to his ear to see if he could hear it ticking in there. Yeah. Wristwatch was ticking. *Timex* was known for that. *Tick tick tick.*

Cecil ignored the rest of it. Turned the key in the ignition, and drove the van out of the shopping mall parking lot. It isn't over yet, the bishop kept telling himself, as they moved slowly past cars and shoppers on foot, kids. Biggs kept looking this way and that, tense, making sure there was no one running after them, shouting for him to stop because he, Biggs, had their son or brother or sister or uncle (or whatnot) in his panel truck with him.

Nothing of the sort happened. And he kept going. Pulled out on Garfield Avenue. When he reached Firestone Boulevard, he turned left. Got on the Long Beach Freeway and headed north.

"Do the boots fit you?"

"They be too small."

"How do you know?"

"I can tell."

"Try them on."

"Wear size thirteen. Yo. These don't be thirteen."

"Do it."

"All right, man, if it make' you happy."

Marvin attempted to get a boot on. It wasn't working. His feet were too long and large. "They be too tight, like I said." Tossed them to the side. "Could be they more yo size, Dawg."

Biggs let it pass. Kept turning his head, looking back at what lay quietly inside the Party Wagon. It was impossible for him to contain his excitement.

*What a catch.*

Young bitch would do just fine. Too bad she had blond hair, though. He preferred them with dark hair, dark eyes.

All you're doing is nitpicking. Too late for that. Be happy with what you got—and what you got is still a catch and will do just fine.

She was five-six, maybe thirty-six- or thirty-seven-inch tits. D cup. Nice ass. Yeah, she would do. Her boyfriend, on the other hand, he saw as being totally unworthy of her. Thin punk was but five-eleven, pimply faced, sickly. Shaggy dishwater blond hair.

For a brief moment Cecil wondered what a cunt like this, hot piece of ass that she was, saw in a kid with a bad complexion like that. Where they came from, he supposed, bitches were not too particular. What the hell did any of that matter now? He would have his fun pretty soon, and could hardly wait.

# CHAPTER 107

**Night had fallen by the time they reached the part of the San Gabriel Mountains that Biggs wanted.** He turned off the paved highway and drove up a winding dirt road. The deeper they traveled into the woods, the bumpier the ride got.

"How far we goin', Cee?"

"Until we reach the spot."

"How can you tell? I can't, me."

Biggs drove another hundred yards and killed the motor. Looked at the couple on the mattress. Wide awake now. The kid's nostrils, mouth and chin were covered with crusted blood. Tears flowed freely from his eyes. That whack with the crowbar must have busted a blood vessel or two because his eyes had a red glow to them, something like Cecil's own eyes when he was engaged in slaughtering McVics. The girl's soft sobs were hardly audible due to the gag.

Biggs took his shirt off. Turned the girl over on her back. Ripped the duct tape off her face and kissed her on the neck, avoiding the mouth and chloroform odor. He rolled that Beatles T-shirt back far enough to expose her full breasts. It was then Biggs realized that Patience was also in the van with them. He got up and took the black woman outside. Found a tree about thirty feet from there. Had her hug it and slapped cuffs on her wrists. He returned to the cargo van and got on top of the blond from Georgia.

"Are you going to kill us?"

Biggs almost felt like laughing, but not quite. "You don't have to concern yourself with that. That's the last thing you want to concern yourself with."

"Please don't do this. . . . Please. . . ."

He asked the boyfriend what size pants he wore. Marvin removed the tape from the kid's mouth so he could answer.

"Thirty-two waist."

"Will that fit you?"

Flunky nodded his head. "Guess so. Yo."

"Take his pants off, then. What are you waiting for? An invitation?"

# CHAPTER 108

**Marvin R. Muck proceeded to relieve the kid of his jeans.** Undid the top button, unzipped the fly and pulled them all the way down, leaving the victim in white jockey underwear.

While Marvin did that, Cecil was busy applying makeup to the girl's face: dark, arching brows; heavy, black eyeliner. Plenty of rouge for the cheeks, and more than was adequate of that red lipstick to her mouth.

"Every whore should have that whore look."

Laid the lipstick on there, overlapping, as before with the other. He then topped it all off by fitting a black wig over her own ash blond locks.

Once finished with this phase of it, he reached for the switchblade. Made certain cuts into the cloth of her jeans, and yanked them off. The young blond's black panties were moist with urine. He freed her of those. Held them to his nose and huffed. Held the undergarment out to Marvin and the sidekick did the same.

"Smell' like good, clean vagina to me."

"*Please* . . . I'll do . . ."

"I'm sure you will."

"Take all the money we got. Have about two hundred dollars between us. . . . Please take it. . . ."

"Already got yo bread, punk. Never found no two hunnerd dolla'."

"Entire lot added up to about twenty-six and change."

"Inside my sock. The right one. There's money there."

"I won't even ask how you managed to overlook it, Base."

Muck pulled the sock off without saying anything. Knew he had fucked up—again. Turned the sock inside out. There was a hundred twenty in twenties and tens. Marvin plucked the money and handed it over to Biggs, who stuffed it in his wallet. Muck checked the other sock and found nothing in it.

"We can get more."

"How much more?"

"Hundreds."

Biggs looked at him. Said nothing.

"Maybe eight hundred dollars. In her aunt's house. It's our money. You can have all of it."

Biggs decided he didn't want to hear another word about it. Pulled his own pants down. Rubbed himself for a while. Spread the girl's legs, and drove his groin in.

Muck had unzipped his own fly and was stroking his massive erection. He'd maneuvered himself over the victim's face and was trying to slip meat in her mouth.

"Get off of her. She's mine. Let the punk blow you."

"That be queer shit, Dawg. I ain't queer, me. That be fuckin' queer shit."

"Suit yourself. If he sucks you off, how does that make *you* queer?"

Marvin cursed. Didn't like the idea of it.

"That be the kind of shit went down in reform school and bug bin: fag punk' suckin' and fuckin', playin' grab-ass. I don't be likin' it." He needed to get off, only it was no use. The mothafuckah wouldn't let him have none, least way' not right now. If he wait' he would get his chance at Sloppy Second'—or Thrillin' Third, but that be later. He be wantin' in on some tang right now, not a week from now. His dick couldn't wait that long.

Biggs had his hands under the blond's buttocks. Held her up like that as he continued to stroke himself. He probed with a finger and slid it inside her rectum, just as he had that time with Dione Aragon. Different bitch/same method.

So long as it worked for him. He pushed his finger all the way in. After a while he withdrew it, then stuck it in his mouth and worked it like a *Popsicle*.

Suddenly, he grabbed a handful of the girl's hair, yanked her up, toward his erection, and ejaculated on her face. Forced his organ inside her mouth and ordered her to finish him off. He wanted his knob polished.

"Lick my cum, bitch. Lick it. Lap it up with fervor. Yeah. Do it right. Polish the knob. Suck the *toxins* out. Siphon the *poison* out."

She finished him off and he rolled off of her. Dipped his hand into the *Little Playmate Ultra Cooler* full of crushed ice. He withdrew a can of *Hawaiian Punch. Fruit Juice Red.*

Had several long pulls. Marvin asked for a can of the "cat piss" for himself. Biggs let him have his instead.

"Drain it. And start enlarging the hole."

"How big?"

"How big do you think?"

"For both of them?"

"No. Just the 'bumpkin.'"

Marvin finished off the *Hawaiian Punch*, grabbed a shovel and scooted out the open back door. He looked around for the rectangular sheet of weathered plywood that they had left over the shallow grave a while back. As before, they had tossed brush and weeds, rocks and dirt on top of the plywood and it was not easy to locate.

He discovered it eventually. Dug a hand under one end of it and flipped the plywood over and out of the way.

Enlarging the grave and having to make it deeper, as usual, required work—not that in and of itself was unusual, as there was always work that was required of him. Problem was Marvin wanted pussy so bad his balls hurt.

# CHAPTER 109

**In another ten minutes Biggs was ready for seconds.** He flipped the girl over on her stomach, propped her rear end up so that she was on her knees now, face down against the blood-stained, grimy mattress.

He stroked his groin some more, watched it harden, and slid it inside the woman's vagina. Biggs had shut his eyes this time as he did this.

*"I want it to last. We'll make it last. . . ."*


It was sudden, although not entirely unexpected, when the boyfriend rolled out toward the open back door, landed on his side on the ground outside, scrambled to his feet and made a break for it. The kid took off into the dark woods.

Marvin looked up, saw Cecil shove his erection back inside his fly, grab the Maglite and withdraw the *.357*, and hop out of the van after him.

"Stay here. Keep an eye on her."

"Yo. Keep my eye on her all right."

Muck dropped the shovel and was in the van, and did not waste time jamming his groin inside the woman's mouth.

He discovered soon enough that she wasn't very good at it. Not many bitches knew how to suck dick; they had to be taught. Only there was no time for dick sucking lessons here. Besides, it didn't matter. The act alone of seeing her lick it was thrilling enough.

He slid the entire ten inches in and out. Watched her gasp and gag. Too bad. He liked it this way. Make the bitch choke on it.

"Suck it, ho. Suck the big black Jones, white trash ho. . . ."

He withdrew it for a bit. Let her catch her breath. He was grinning. "See, that fuckin' clown ain't shit. Got hisself a weird lookin' sissy-ass *weenie*. Got them scar' and shit on it; that black mole right on the head what look' fuckin' *nasty*, if you aks me."


He stroked himself. Hurried about it. Needed to blast cum before Omar got back and put a stop to it—and maybe kicked his ass. A-hole Omar.

He jammed it back in there. She was getting better at it, not gagging and carrying on as much. Yeah. Suckin' it. He helped her with it by sliding it inside and out. Tried pushing it down as far as it would go once again. She had a hard time breathing. It pissed him off.

"Do it, ho."

He withdrew, nervous about it all. Cecil gonna be back any minute. Fuck. He rubbed the massive head of his groin, and it happened: spurted sperm inside her open jaw. Filling it plenty. Yo. Be like *buttermilk.* All that white cum filling up the inside of her throat and jaw.

There was nothing else to see: no teeth or tonsils or even tongue practically. It was all a big load of *sour cream* or *yogurt.* Yeah. *Yogurt by Marvin Muck.* You got it. And it felt good.

He zipped up. Dug his hand inside the cooler and grabbed a cold *Butterfinger* candy bar. Jumped out of the van. Took his time biting into the candy bar while resting an elbow on top of the shovel handle.

There was always a way to beat the dude at his own game. All you had to do was be patient, take your time and wait for opportunity.

He heard voices, or was it just Omar talking not far from there? Caught up wiff the punk by now. Serve' the punk right. Shouldn't a took off that way. Don't matter. Wouldn't work out for him nohow. Clown gonna cap his ass no matter what.

# CHAPTER 110

**It didn't take much or very long for Biggs to catch up to the** boyfriend. The kid's wounds hadn't allowed him to get very far. He'd kept fainting and faltering, and by the time he was finally able to rise to his knees from the last blackout, he was staring directly into the barrel of Cecil's *Colt "Python."*

"Now that was a cowardly thing to do: abandon your little girlfriend that way."

Biggs smacked him across the mouth with the revolver and watched the kid go down, spitting several teeth, bits of lower lip.

Biggs shined the Maglite on the kid's face. There was blood in and around his mouth.

"Get up."

The kid struggled to make it and did not have the strength.

"*Quit your fakin', boy*. Get your dead ass up. *Heard what I said, boy?*" It was all done in his best John Joseph impression. When the kid still failed to do as ordered, Biggs reached down, snatched him by the cuffs and yanked up, hard. Pointed him in the direction of the Party Wagon. Half-pushed/half-carried him along this way.

# CHAPTER 111

**For all of Marvin's (seeming) toil and sweat, all he had to show for it was nothing more than a slight improvement on the shallow grave that they had dug the last time they were out here.** On top of that, a cigarette dangled from his lips while he lazily shoveled a measly portion of dirt out.

Cigarette smoke was something Biggs had detested from the time he was a child being around J.J. and the old lady, who were heavy smokers. The smoke caused his belly to cramp and gave him headaches, and it didn't matter that they were in the outdoors. Cigarette smoke and the smell and taste of rotgut: two things he hated about as much as he hated anything else when it came to being alive. But he let him drag on the butt; the backslider had to have something to make him happy. Never mind that he was close to useless.

Biggs let the fool go, and took a long, hard look at the girl. Could not be certain that anything was amiss.

Had the asshole been molesting his piece while he was gone? He couldn't tell. There weren't any telltale signs he was aware of. When he turned his head back to look at Marvin, the freeloading retard continued to go about his business with that shovel in his hands as though nothing out of the ordinary had gone on while he'd been off chasing down the kid. Could be he was being paranoid. It was possible. Wouldn't be the first time.

Hole was hardly deep enough. It would do. Biggs gestured at the poor excuse for a grave.

"Get down there."

The boyfriend managed a couple of unsteady steps. It was the best he was able. Tears poured. Snot and blood traveled down his chin. The more anguish of this nature Biggs witnessed, the more he relished it. What it was about. What he lived for.

"Please. Don't. Please. . . ."

"Lie down in the grave."

The kid hesitated, his blood-filled eyes imploring to be spared.

*"Do it—if you want your girlfriend to live."*

The kid did as told. Slipped and fell on his side. Cecil glanced back at the van and noticed that the female vic had gone out again. He climbed back in. Shook the girlfriend and slapped her several times hard enough to bring her to.

*"Get him in there. I want him on his back looking up at me."*

Marvin bent down. Dragged the kid over until his upper body was in the grave. Did the same with the kid's legs and feet.

"In here, Marvin. Make sure she doesn't miss out on any of the fun." Trusty scrambled over to where the shallow grave was, while Base climbed into the van.

Although he had both his arms on the woman's shoulders, she was still able to keep her face turned away from what was about to transpire. Cecil glared at him.

"Can't you do anything right?"

"What now?"

"I want her to see it. Every bit of it."

Marvin clamped her jaw in his hand and forced it in the bishop's direction.

"How that be, Cecil?"

Biggs said nothing. Continued to glare. Finally nodded, and was back focusing on the girl's whimpering male companion.

*"Jesus, no,"* the kid's girlfriend cried from the van. "Jesus help us. . . . *Please have mercy. . . . Please. . . .*"

"How's He going to do that? When He couldn't even help himself? Where was He when I begged to be spared and delivered? *Where was He for me, bitch?*" Biggs stood over the shallow grave. Aimed the *.357* at the kid's battered face. The vagina continued to invoke her "Savior's" name to the point it was beginning to rub him the wrong way. Just a touch.

"*Shove Jesus.*" Biggs glared in her direction. "*Buddha, Krishna,* and the rest of them while you're at it."

She wailed on.

"Shut her up. My concentration is being disrupted here. The key is focus. I'd like to be able to focus on what I'm doing."

"Ho be loud."

"Make her eat dirt if you have to."

Muck was uncertain what that meant.

"You heard. Feed her dirt. Make her eat dirt. But shut her up."

The sidekick was out of the van, scooping up a fistful of dirt mixed-in with grass and pine needles and leaves. Proceeded to jam the works into the victim's mouth. That muffled her to the point that it was manageable.

Biggs re-aimed the *Magnum* at the kid's face.

"Now get the bull's- eye."

The "bull's-eye" he had Muck retrieve from underneath the blankets in the van was similar to the version used on Danny Aragon, in that it was approximately a fourteen-by-fourteen inch, quarter-inch-thick sheet of stainless steel sandwiched between two pieces of plywood of equal size and had all been cemented with glue, as well as bolted together, to withstand Cecil Biggs's notion of "target practice."

As with the other board, both sides of this one contained a painted on, perfectly-centered bull's-eye. Marvin had it placed under the boyfriend's head in no time. Biggs's itchy trigger finger went the next step. Marvin did jump back in time. Blowback was something to witness: brains and blood punched out both ears and nose, while a good chunk of the back of the skull exploded.

Biggs fired a second shot. *Coup de grace.* There wasn't much of the head to look at after that. The girlfriend was out for the time being. It was just as well. Made no difference at this point. Party was over.

Biggs gestured with his head for Marvin to get on with the follow-up. The body was rolled on its side, the mess scraped off the plywood with the shovel. Held the board at an angle that favored the glow given off by the moon to see if he could make out the location of the slugs, or if they had penetrated the board.

None. Board had contained them both. *Bull's-eye.* Both slugs this time. Seemed that way.

Marvin handed the board to Biggs to take a look at, make sure. Biggs nodded. Hitting the bull's-eye was always a crap shoot and seldom easy. Took practice, lots of practice, so when it happened there was a strong sense of accomplishment.


The board was returned to the van and concealed under the layer of blankets and tarp on the bottom. Biggs would pry the bullets out later, at his own convenience, and dispose of them. Had to remind Marvin to remove the dirt from the girlie's jaw.

"Wouldn't want her to expire before her time."

Muck took care of it. Held his ear against the woman's chest.

"Ho ain't dead. That I can tell, me."

"Get his cuffs off."

Biggs handed him the key. Marvin did that. Tossed them back. Cuffs and key. Biggs reloaded the *Magnum.*

"Throw dirt on him."

"What about the big plywood board?"

"We'll take it with us."

While Muck busied himself covering up the body, Bishop Biggs busied himself in his own way: got in the van in order to conclude what he started earlier with the blond in the brunette wig.

# CHAPTER 112

**Cecil O. was feeling hungry and wanted to get something to eat; he also wanted to get back to the house before dawn.** The blond was going to have to be carried through the back door and he just didn't want to make it any easier for his nosy neighbors; did not want to give them further reason to talk more shit behind his back. They wagged their tongues enough as it was.

The blond was forced down into the same custom-crafted suitcase used for Dione Aragon. As before, the tube was double-checked to make certain that no pebbles, dirt, leaves, encrusted blood or vomit remained to make the intake of oxygen an issue.

Biggs stuck the mouthpiece in her mouth, ran the other end through the hole between the nylon cord handles, and the lid was slammed down several times before it stayed down. The clasps were flipped in place. Victim was good to go—and she was not about to go anywhere that her abductors did not want her to.

Handcuffs were taken off of Patience McDaniel's wrists and she was escorted back to the cargo van.

Biggs sat in the driver's seat eating a glazed doughnut and considered killing the retarded black woman. Why not? Was she even worth keeping around? He'd needed her from time to time to attract/lure others like the young couple, cunts Marvin otherwise did not have much success with; and if he did away with Patience he would only be forced to go back to the nut house and recruit another nut like her—and it would be the same trying bullshit all over again, having to break the new one in the same way. It was never easy. All you had to do to be reminded was take a look at the hassle the diaper-wearing Goodfellow deviate from one of the Dakotas was putting him through.

Olin Goodfellow. Aka *"Swine Vomit."* What Greta Otto had named him. Pinned that tag on him ever since she found out that Goodfellow had been in and out of bug bins all over the damn Midwest and West Coast for molesting farm animals. Gave pigs a bad name. Certainly did a pig like Parfrey.

Well, you had to keep extra retards on hand. No choice. In case some up and dropped dead, or committed suicide, or just could not take the juice in the pit that they had coming to them on occasion—for not obeying rules and regulations. So the extra loon now and then was nothing more than a backup 'tard. Backup.

At least Patience did not talk much, didn't seem to care or notice what was actually happening to her, nor around her.

She was just too far out of it 99.9% of the time, the bishop concluded, and that was the only thing that kept him from ultimately putting a bullet in her head.

He ate his glazed doughnut and looked at her as she sat across from him just staring at nothing in front of her, at the darkness; staring, lost, shivering. Saying nothing. Christ, Biggs thought. I hope I never get that fucking bad. There had been times in the past he had acted like it to get over. Faked it. I'd rather be dead than live like that, than actually be that way.

*Look at her. Unbelievable.* All she talks about is being *cold*. Doesn't ask for food, or want sex or anything else, unlike the other rejects who made up his staff and board.

He wondered if maybe a hard prick in her asshole might solve her problems. Yeah. Only she didn't do anything for him. Too bad. Patience was unattractive. Ugly duckling was mentally defective. Too much so even for him.

Biggs came close to cracking a smile. Shook his head. He turned to look at Marvin. Gestured in Patience's direction. Marvin shrugged his shoulders. Had other things on his mind.

"How about we get something to eat, Cecil? I'm hungry. All that hard work make' me hungry."

"There's always jambalaya at the house."

Biggs started the van up and turned it around. Steered it back down the dirt road toward the paved highway.

"I'm sick of that shit. Sick of it. Sick of Greta' cookin', too. Bitch burn' everything all the time. Cause me abdominal pain."

"I want to give my broker a call from the house."

As much as Biggs wanted to stop at a *Jack-in-the-Crack*, or some other fast food joint to pick up a cheeseburger and a milk shake, he would not do so—because then that might have meant having to buy Marvin R. and even Patience something to eat as well. He did not feel like spending a dime more than he had to. Money spent on dope was something else. That was different.

Had to be done. The way he saw it. Money spent on drugs was *bait money, slush fund*; cash he kept on hand, set aside for dope and dildos, chloroform, handcuffs, chains, chainsaws, ice picks, lumber for building coffins and all those other torture contraptions (tools of the trade). That was different. Money well spent. Not that he liked to spend anything at all, but it had to be done.

# CHAPTER 113

**Biggs found a secluded spot at an all-night gas station.** Changed the plates back. He had Marvin and Patience hunker down in the rear of the van, facing away from the windshield, prior to continuing on to the residential neighborhood where he rented the two-car garage.

He guided the Party Wagon north on Laurel Canyon Boulevard. When he got to Strathern, he made a left. There was a new strip mall on his right that he drove past. He reached Vantage Avenue and made a right turn. Stayed north beyond the rear parking to the strip mall until he neared the alley entrance on the right side. He turned into it. Drove a hundred feet. Made a left at the main alley. This alley served his needs perfectly. Nothing but high brick walls and chain-link fences with rising ivy on his left-hand side all the way down to the end of the block. Garages were on his right, the east side. Couldn't have picked a better area to rent one.

He drove another hundred yards and stopped the van. Looked both ways, always, before unlocking the garage door. Gripped the handle and yanked up on the roll-up. Biggs got back in the van and eased it in next to the *Cadillac*. Marvin Muck and Patience McDaniel were allowed to disembark from the Party Wagon only after he had pulled the garage door down.

He and Marvin quickly carried the suitcase into the backseat of the Caddy. Biggs had the black woman climb in the trunk. Patience complied without a peep. That's what he liked about her. Never gave him any grief. "Catatonic" was right. She was an inch away from it. Bishop then told Marvin to join her to keep her company.

"Shit, man. Yo. I'm suppose' to be Deacon, Cecil. I get the phobia in there."

"It's a large trunk. What are you complaining about? It's a *Cadillac* trunk. First class all the way when you travel with Trusty."

"I know it be a *Cadillac*, Cecil. I get them cold sweat' in it, man. How 'bout I wear the hoodie an' stay in the front wiff you and keep my head down? Be the same."

*"Get your chickenshit ass in there, goddammit.* It's only for five fucking minutes."

Marvin was about to relent and crawl inside the trunk. "All right. Yo. I'll do it, me. Don't be the first time."

"I know you will." Biggs shook his head. "More trouble than you're worth."

It was obvious soon enough to both what a tight squeeze it would be. Biggs grabbed him by the arm and shoved him toward the front instead. Slammed the trunk shut. Marvin looked at him.

"Get in the front seat. What are you waiting for? Pull the hood over your head. Get on the floor."

"Know the rest. Ain't got to tell me *twiced.* Keep my head down 'till you say different."

Biggs pulled the garage door up and backed the *Brougham* into the alley. No cars drove through. No one in sight. All was fine. In that regard. He pulled the roll-up down. Made double-certain that it was locked before getting back in the Caddy and driving off.

Few minutes later, near the corner of Saticoy and Vineland, he pulled the *Cadillac* into the back of a gas station. Pressed the trunk release. He got out. Lifted the trunk open and instructed Patience to squeeze into the backseat next to the suitcase. He closed the trunk and got behind the steering wheel. Marvin was still grumbling about something.

"Now that the ho be in the backseat, take the hoodie off?"

Cecil yanked it off for him. Told the deacon to sit up. Biggs chin-gestured in Patience's direction. Docile as usual.

"See? Never complains. Didn't matter to her that she had to spend a few minutes in the trunk."

"Yo. You try it sometime, Omar. See how you like it."

Biggs's right hand snapped out like a cobra going for a lethal strike. He gripped Marvin R. Muck by the Adam's apple, his fingers digging in like a vice, applying pressure.

"When I ask you to do something, pissant . . ."

Marvin gasped. Unable to get a word out.

"I told you before, don't ever call me *Omar.* I don't like it. I don't like the memories that go with it."

Marvin made some more desperate sounds in his throat.

"I let you sit up here because I'm reasonable. I'll go so far as to say I take pride in it; and also because it appeared a bit crowded with her back there. Only next time I say jump, motherfucker—you don't say but one thing: How high? I call the shots, run the show. Got it?"

Marvin nodded his head. "Yeah, Hoss."

"Then say it. Let me hear you say it."

Marvin tried to speak, but the other's grip was too tight and made it difficult. Biggs let him go.

"You the boss, Hoss. I ain't got no problem wiff it."

Cecil watched him go through a coughing fit of some kind. Probably imagined, more than anything. Exaggerated.

"Knock it off."

"How we gonna stay partner', if you be pissed every time I don't agree wiff you, man? Ain't right. Yo."

"You think I'm pissed? Do you really believe I was pissed just then?"

"Maybe not."

Biggs looked at him. Glanced in the direction of the suitcase.

"Anyway, what's there to be pissed off about, Free Ride? We got goods in the car, don't we? We got goods, pussy on the hoof, don't we?"

"We sure do, Omar—I mean Cecil. Sorry, Hoss. We sure got the good'. Pussy on the hoof."

"That's right."

Biggs started the engine, and rejoined the Vineland traffic. They were headed south, south toward home and a dopamine-generated rush.

# CHAPTER 114

Biggs waited for Marvin to unlock the front gate and drove on in and stopped just inside the yard to make certain the gate was locked back up properly and Muck tossed the key back to him. Once that was done, Biggs continued to the rear of the house. Backed the Caddy to the door.

Had Patience get out of the car while he waited for Muck to walk back there.

Patience McDaniel did her usual: stood in place, staring off into space. He was tempted to take a look at what she was fixated on, and stopped himself in time. Nothing she ever stared at was worth bothering with. It was the way she went about it, so thoroughly focused, that had you believing that whatever it was she was looking at no one else had ever seen before, or ever would.

Only it was a crock. Because she stared at nothing, ever, that mattered.

Muck was dragging his ass. Made it back. Biggs and his Man Friday each grabbed a nylon cord handle and hauled the heavy suitcase out of the backseat and lugged it inside the hallway. Cecil called the woman in. Patience would have stayed out there the rest of the night, gazing at the stars, if he hadn't.

The back door was locked.

# CHAPTER 115

**Petunia Roscoe had heard the *Cadillac* pull up and soon she was out of bed and dragging a chair across the bedroom carpet to the rear porch door.** She climbed the chair and was straining through a crack in the curtains over the glass portion of the door to see what was going on with Pastor Stinky and his *aide-de-camp*. Only she couldn't make anything out. It was too dark back there.

She whispered Marty's name from where she stood on the chair, hoping to wake him and let him know that they were at it again, for what good it did. Marty Roscoe's typical response was to continue snoring. He just didn't give a damn. What would she have told him anyway? What *were*

Biggs and the light-skinned negro up to? Nothing that she could tell.

It all seemed fishy somehow, sinister. The Sinister Minister. How fitting. Hardly enough. Had that evil clown makeup on again. She had no real proof that anything out of the ordinary was taking place, and yet deep down something told her that it certainly was. Then you had the odd-looking chest. Always. These things appeared to be made out of wood, or metal, and were in the shape and size of a large *Samsonite* suitcase, maybe larger. Yes, it was larger, considerably. Had some type of rope handles on the sides. And, on top, where the average suitcase had a single handle, their "suitcase" had two. Rope handles. There was that length of "tubing," looked like tubing, sticking out between the handles on that same side of the chest.

Furthermore, why did this activity most always take place under cover of night? She also knew that loud music and noise, boisterous festivities and whatnot, very often followed. That was the routine with the Sinister Minister and his demented deacon.

She looked at her husband. Dead to the world. What would have been the use? He was on his back, scratching his testicles, and snoring like a thousand-pound hog.

That's what had kept her awake: her husband's snoring. Seven years of it and she was just about at her wits' end. Maybe they ought to reconsider sleeping in separate rooms—even if it meant having Marty sleep on the sofa in the front room, which would not have made either of them happy, to tell the truth. Then, too, she was used to sleeping and sharing the same bed with him.

To be fair, the snoring hadn't always been an issue, had not always been this bad. It sure seemed to get worse lately.

She returned to bed, shook him awake, and told him to knock it off.

"Was I snoring again? I didn't know I was snoring, babe. Sorry."

"You never used to snore, Marty. Not like this. I don't sleep much these days. Those creeps are at it again, Marty. It's just a matter of time before the music starts up. And it's three o'clock in the morning."

Roscoe said nothing. Sound asleep again. So quickly. His favorite activity (or should it be non-activity?), and chasing skirts. If not necessarily snoring this time, he was wheezing. They were wheezing sounds.

Petunia looked at him. Rolled her eyes. "What's the use? Talking to myself, as usual."

# CHAPTER 116

**The African-American couple, Harold Crust and his wife Fay, who lived in the modest wood and stucco house on Biggs's left, had a bedroom window that faced the bishop's backyard.** Although Biggs's rear door could not be viewed entirely from it, enough could be seen in order to basically determine the activity going on with Biggs and his sidekick—if and when anything was going on back there.

Short and wiry, fifty-two-year-old Harold Crust had been lying in bed, risen and taken a look through the curtains, and returned to bed intent on getting some shuteye in spite of the televangelist blaring from the color set that his wife had going in the living room, to no avail.

It was no use. And yet, he knew it, couldn't deny it: it wasn't the tv so much as the craving for a smoke and a drink, a shot (double, preferably) of something strong.

He'd been lying there, fantasizing about how good it would feel to fire up a cigarette and have a taste of whiskey, when he heard the *Cadillac* pull up a moment ago and then watched Biggs—in that scary-ass clown shit on his face—and that dumb young nigga Marvin through a thin crack in the curtains unload a suitcase or some kind of chest out of the trunk of the *Cadillac* and lug it inside the church. Not only was the suitcase large in appearance, but must have been pretty damned heavy the way it took the both of them to lift and carry it on in. He didn't need a telegram from Western Union to tell him what would happen next: Party Time in Bishop Biggs's "sacred" Church of Re-Newed Hope would soon follow. That's what those rude and crude sons of bitches usually did; the shouting and music blasting always happened afterwards.

Call Valley PD again? What for? He'd complained to the rollers too often already about it all, had discussed it with Fay, who didn't seem to be bothered by it nearly half as much as he was: woman was wrapped up in all that tv evangelist crap, but had in fact talked to Marty and his wife Petunia and Petunia had tried calling the police herself to at least force Biggs to knock off the racket, bring it down to a tolerable level. It hadn't done any good. In four months the rollers had only showed up one time in a black-and-white, but Biggs had been alerted somehow, or his intuition told him to turn it down, and the noise had stopped before the cops arrived, and that had been the end of it (that time). The noise had died down to nothing, for a few days or so, a week, and then the same bullshit had started right up again. The racket wouldn't have bothered Harold as much as it did, frankly, if only the strange cats would strictly do it during daytime hours while people was up and about, at work. Why cause all that ruckus at night and in the early hours of the morning when people got to sleep? When working folks got to rest up so they can make it in to their job and earn a living?

I'll tell you why: Man got bread up the yin-yang. Don't have to get up early five, six days a week to make a dollar, that's why.

Trouble was, you couldn't reason with somebody like that. Dude got plenty money. Loaded. Owns that big house with the big front yard, two-car garage in back, never mind that he don't spend a whole lotta time on upkeep; owns a *Rolls-Royce*—even if it's only a '72, it's still a badass *Rolls*, and that brand new *Cadillac*.

Don't work like most folks; he don't have to. When you got pockets full of dough. Stays up all night raising hell. Plays that disco, plays funk, rock-n-roll. There's times he even leaves gospel on—that still don't make the clown look like any preacher he ever knew. Not only that—there was that damned stench comin' outta his house not long ago.

Smelled awful, like burning flesh. . . . Christ, what a thing to say. The idea made his skin crawl. Woulda never even thought it until Old Lloyd Dicker from across the street suggested it smelled like that: death. Dead bodies. Flesh being burned. What Mr. Dicker said.

All he knew it just smelled bad. Couldn't tell what it was. Lord, it stank. Stayed that way. Off and on. Just when you thought it was gone—it came back. Keeps comin' back. And Marty's wife had agreed with him, too. Petunia been trying to get Fay to go on over there and talk to Mr. Biggs about it, at least try to see the inside of his "church"—and Harold hadn't felt comfortable with that at all, didn't care for the looks of that Bishop Biggs. But that big-mouth Petunia Roscoe kept saying that Fay could do it easy because she was religious and watching them Christian programs on tee-vee all the time, and that if she was to go knock on Biggs's front door that he would let her in with open arms because, as she saw it, "Fay and Biggs got so much in common"—and they could all figure out what the hell was going on in there. Was it a real church like the bishop claims, or was it something else?

For a while there it seemed to be. A few years back. And why come he was so picky about who was allowed inside from the neighborhood? Why couldn't Petunia go in? *Why wouldn't Biggs and Marvin let her in to say a prayer?*

Biggs had told her that only those selective few who truly had the faith were allowed to join his parish. Had to do with security, too. Said they been getting death threats. Had to be a bunch of bull. What else? Who knew what to believe?

"Please turn the television down, Fay. I gotta get my rest."

Volume was lowered some. It was still too loud far as Harold was concerned.

# CHAPTER 117

**Biggs and Marvin carried the chest down into the basement.** Lowered it next to the pit. They undid the clasps, and lifted the lid open and watched the girl pop out hysterically, gasping for air the way Dione and others before her had, even though she'd clearly had access to the breathing tube. But it was okay. Biggs found it amusing when they carried on.

"What's your name, girlie?"

"Dixie Osgood."

He liked that, too. Dixie. He'd never known a "Dixie" before.


The bishop unlocked the door over the pit, opened it, to reveal the victim below. Terri Denise Klopp. Hardly treading water.

"This is what happens to bitches who cause me grief. We call it Pit Therapy around here."

"Them hole' there? In the door? Dude be runnin' hot wire through them hole' in case them victim don't be gettin' the message."

Biggs closed the door. Locked it. Indicated the steel entrance to the cooler in the distance, by the bookshelves and play area.

"Now, should you end up in there—for whatever infraction—that's pretty much it. End of the line."

Biggs yanked the girl up by the handcuffs and dragged her over to the door to the Mattress Room, where Dione was heard from, sobbing, pleading to be let out. Biggs got the door unlocked and shoved her in, and stiffened like a statue. Grimaced. Didn't dare budge.

"What do it be, Trusty? Yo."

"My back. *Son of a bitch.*" And Biggs could not move one inch without experiencing severe pain. He leaned against the doorjamb this way. Held on for support, gasping. *Fuck.* Why was this happening to him now? The victim scrambled past him. Made it out of the room and ran up the stairs and started wailing and pounding on the locked door.

Dione was heard from as well, wanting to be let out, released. All Biggs could do at this point was turn his head and look up at the girl from

Georgia hammering at the basement door with her fists. He had his *Magnum* in his hand. Movement of any rapidity was out of the question. Still, something needed to be done. Commotion by the heifer was not good for his psychological well-being.

"What do you want me to do wiff her, Hoss?"

*"What do you think? Bring her back down."*

All Biggs could do was sigh and shake his head in frustration. Muck climbed the stairs with his arms open, the idea being that he would wrap them around her waist once he got close enough and carry her down. Only the victim kicked out at him. Tried for his groin. Missing, crying, shouting. She did her best to fight him off, keep him at bay. It worked for a while.

Marvin dove for her legs, and yanked on them this way, pulling her down the flight of stairs to the cement floor of the basement. The victim was in no shape to do much after that. Marvin was groggy enough himself.

"Do you see now why I keep this place tighter than a virgin's pee hole?" Biggs was recovering. "Keeps this type of nuisance down to a minimum." A grin crossed his face. He still had to be careful how he moved. Anything sudden, and the pain would be back; the unpredictable nerves that ran up and down his spine were sure to let him know it.

Easy does it. Nothing sudden. Got to be a slipped disk. Wrenched back. Something like it.

He walked to the part of the basement on the Roscoe side, stopping at the Abattoir door. Unlocked the lock that hung from the chain and unwound the chain.

"Cunt has balls. Can't say that I don't entirely appreciate it. Feisty."

"Sho is."

Muck shook off the cobwebs in his head. Began to rub his hand between the victim's upper thighs.

"We'll see just how *'feisty'* she really is. Bring her over here."

Marvin carried the young woman to the walk-in.

"Yo. Put the ho on the hook, Cecil?"

"You sound eager."

"I ain't eager. Only be *akskin'*."

"No. Not yet."

The idea what may have been inside the cooler might have terrified the woman a moment ago, only now she was getting an eyeful of the real thing: the stench, a degree or two stronger than what her nostrils had been exposed to heretofore; the hanging, bleeding bodies, the animal carcasses dangling from hooks in the ceiling, the eyeless skulls lined up along a top-tiered wire shelf, and began convulsing, heaving uncontrollably.

Biggs motioned to the wall on the left. "Chain the strumpet to the wall. Over there. In the corner." Was close to chuckling to himself for using the word "strumpet." Hell, his word of choice to describe them was "whore," "bitch," "cunt," "slut." All meant the same, as far as he was concerned, but did use *"strumpet"* and/or *"harlot"* from time-to-time for Betty Lou Rutterschmidt's benefit. Prune-faced Betty Lou got a real charge from hearing the word spoken by others and uttered it often enough herself.

"When do I get me a piece of this one, Cecil?"

"Do it, asshole."

Muck did as ordered.

"Only it don't be my fault when the ho end up like a *Popsicle* Finger Lickin' always be suckin' on."

"Not likely she'll end up a Popsicle." Biggs tossed him a key. "Go in the Storage Room and get a blanket." Marvin was about to do as ordered. Biggs stopped him. Instead had him free her from the chain and had him walk her out of there and to the pit in the floor.

Biggs stepped out of the Abattoir, wrapped the chain around the handle, being cautious about it, as his spine continued to give him intermittent reminders that anything sudden could force him to freeze up again.

He snapped the lock into place. Dixie's wrists were cuffed behind her back, and she was dropped in the water in the pit with the other victim.

The door was closed over them, and locked.

# CHAPTER 118

**Biggs returned to the Mattress Room.** Addressed Dione "Divine" Aragon from where he stood in the doorway: "The next step for you is the pit. There's just about enough room in there for another one. It wouldn't be easy, but I believe we could squeeze you in—pack you tight—like sardines." A pregnant pause followed. "I don't want to hear a peep out of you. I don't want you climbing up on the coffee table. It's flimsy and is liable to break. I can't keep wasting hard-earned money on second-rate furniture that McVictims feel they can destroy whenever they feel like it. Are we clear on that?"

Dione looked at him without saying anything. Tears rolled down from the good eye. She wiped away. "You don't have the right to keep people locked up like animals. That poor girl you're keeping in that pit out there is dying. Don't you get it? She's dying."

"She's faking."

"They'll get you. Sooner or later, the police will get you for what you're doing. You can't keep people locked up like slaves."

"Marvin is a proponent of that, actually: slavery. Mack Daddy Muck would like us to start our very own *Rent-A-Bush* service."

"What have you done with my baby?"

"Let me remind you again: That coffee table cost me money. There is nothing to be gained by climbing up on it and banging on the boards that cover the window. Nothing."

Marvin showed at the door with a paper bag that contained peroxide, gauze and *Band-Aids, Tampons;* balls of white cotton.

"What do you think you're doing?"

"A dead ho don't do nobody no good."

Biggs held his hand out. Muck placed the bag in it.

"The key." Muck handed him the storage room key. Biggs redirected his attention to the victim. "You should count your blessings."

She didn't say a word. Her expression said enough.

"Look, we all have our problems. I've dealt with a fucked up back for years. Hemorrhoids, migraines, depression. Not to mention childhood-related flashbacks. What the fuck do you want from me? Whoever said life was going to be a bed of tulips? What the hick used to say to my mother. 'Tulips,' not roses."

"I want to go home."

"Yeah, well, I wanted to kill the asshole who brought me up . . . and never got the chance. . . ."

He left the peroxide and the rest of it with her. Checked to make sure the water jug had fresh water in it. Saw that there was enough toilet paper around. Had Marvin take the chamber pot and dump it in the john, and bring it back.

Biggs locked the door to the Mattress Room on their way out.

"Ho be hurt."

They climbed the stairs to the first floor.

"Which ho?"

"Divine ho. Dione. Got her eye fucked up."

"Been taken care of. What else am I supposed to do? Bring a doctor in here? Wouldn't work anyway. Doctors don't make house calls these days."

"Ho got damage. Can't make no kinda bank wiff a ho got a messed up face like that."

Biggs stopped at the top to unlock the door. Turned his head to look at the other one. "Isn't it about time you came to your senses and realized that the life of a Mack Daddy just isn't in the cards for you? First of all, you have to be super sharp—up here—to even control these bitches. It takes a lot more than having a dick the size of a zucchini."

"Lot of them hoe' be likin' it. Dude can control a ho wiff his dick, if he got him a big dick. All it take'."

"Bullshit. A smart dealer never gets high on his supply, a clever pimp never shags his stable. If you want to have control over a bitch these days you have to put the fear in her, let her know you're willing to cause her serious pain in order to keep her in line—not only that, but are ready and able to dismember her and her twat friends whenever you fucking feel like it."

"Rent-A-Bush be a good way to make bank. Got to admit that."

"Yeah, it would be a good way to end up back in a padded room up at *Atascadero*—or on a cold slab and a toe tag."

He unlocked the door. Waited for Marvin to walk past, then locked it back up. Biggs wanted to be by himself and told Marvin to get lost.

Muck shrugged. "Be that way, homes." Made it to his room. Biggs walked down the hallway. Unlocked his bedroom door. Entered. Closed and locked it behind him.

# CHAPTER 119

**He needed to unwind and hoped the pain in his lower back would go away and let him be.** All he could do was wait it out.

He shoved one of his favorite videos into the combo TV/VCR. Fluffed a couple of pillows against the headboard and took great caution and care to stretch out on the bed.

The low-budget, Z-grade color flick came on. Something about a dark-haired wench from the big city moving to an isolated cabin in the sticks— real bright of her—to sketch and paint nature scenes and keep a journal of her progress. A real nature lover and bird watcher, who went around with a pair of field glasses observing various species of birds in this lush, seemingly tranquil habitat taking photos of a vast array of flora and fauna and general scenery/serenity of and by a gently flowing clear water stream nearby.

None of this interested him much: not the warblers, nor nature scenes. What engaged his interest (and gripped his nut-sack) was the way this bimbo was assaulted by a group of pee-hole craving swine farmers. Brutalized and fucked. Left for dead. Only the dark-haired "city heifer," a label J.J. had been partial to (and used at every opportunity regarding every bitch he laid eyes on, especially Charlotte Yvonne) unfortunately didn't die. They left her for dead—but did not take the time to make certain that she was, in fact, no longer among the living. Just as he had failed to do with the dominatrix. They would pay, no doubt, just as he had paid.

The twat recovered (as one might have expected she would) and proceeded to seek sweet vengeance by going after the white trash hillbilly scum, dispatching them one by one.


He ate four *Ding Dongs* and two *Butterfinger* candy bars. Washed it all down with *Hawaiian Punch. Fruit Juice Red.* Ejected the tape and watched something about some deranged killing a-hole who wore a hockey mask and chopped his victims up with a machete. Amusing stuff.

Horny "camp counselors" appear at a summer camp by a lake in order to get things in tip-top shape before the kiddies showed for the summer and the camp's official opening.

This was the general premise. Only the antisocial type in the hockey mask and the machete for an equalizer had an agenda of his own: To lop off a few heads and limbs with that stainless steel whacker before the youngsters arrived.


It was entertaining to see these generic, two-dimensional, irritating camp counselors turned into screaming, weeping, helpless vics pissing their panties.

The thing that was always missing for him (and stuck out like a sledged and swollen thumb) was the fact the killer didn't rape the cunts. *Before or After.* Wouldn't have mattered: *either/or.* . . . The sex was missing. How can that be? So strange and obvious and unrealistic. Sex and violence went hand in hand. Like love and hatred. Like gore and spooge. Life and death.


He should have fucked them, slashed their clothes to ribbons and sodomized them, made them blow him—and then, only then—carved them up to his satisfaction and taken his sweet time about it.

Hurt them, rape them, torture and discard them. . . .

What do you expect? This was excreted by the Tinsel Factory. Suspension of disbelief. Sissies made these movies. Liberal queers without balls created these celluloid fantasies in order to turn a quick buck, without ever being interested in the way it was in the real world.

They didn't make horror films. They made comedies with corn syrup and red food coloring. It was done with trick photography and cheesy effects.

# CHAPTER 120

**He shoved another movie in.** Watched favored parts and stroked himself.

A young slit in a pair of short shorts enters the crazed killer's house in search of her boyfriend. Dumbshit boyfriend had entered a moment earlier seeking the owner/resident in order to "borrow gas." She takes a cautious look around, sniffs out the odoriferous air and decides it's time to vamoose—just as the killer freako (wearing a mask of human skin) appears from a loud, sliding and shiny aluminum door at the other end of the hallway and gives chase. Short Shorts screams at the top of her lungs. Makes a mad dash for the front door. Gets as far as the threshold and is snatched up by the beefy psycho.

Biggs wondered if the filmmakers got the idea for the skin mask from reading about Nazi uber SS cunt Ilse Koch, who had an endearing habit of selecting male prisoners whose tats she admired and would then have the unfortunate prisoners put to death and had their tattoos sliced out and framed. Real nice of her.

Ilse also had the somewhat unconventional and peculiar (to some) habit of having lamp shades made from human skin; and there were other things that she did with it. It was also said she favored shrunken human heads that she used as paper weights. A heartless bitch after his own heart, thought Cecil.

Too bad they didn't take her, after she was hung post Nuremberg trial, carved her up and flushed her away like so much sewage. He envied the fuckers for what they were able to get away with. The lot of them.

There was also dorky, grave-robbing Eddie Gein, who had the habit of prancing about in the moonlight in a suit fashioned from human *chamois*. Filmmakers may have gotten the idea from hearing about him. It was possible.

He replayed the moment. The fat *fucktoid* appears, nearly causing the young wench to shit her shorts. She makes the feeble attempt to flee this Mansion of Nihilism, and gets about as far as the front entrance, makes it past the screen door—in time for *lardo* to clamp his massive arms about her waist and carry her back inside this dwelling of dread and doom. And the city heifer is hung on a hook in the kitchen.

Biggs came close to laughing. Almost. Laughter was alien. Always would be. It was close enough for him. His back was all right again. That's what mattered.

Chop 'em up, make them feel pain, make them squirm. Strike out, strike fast, strike hard. It was entertainment at its best.

He replayed the scene. Couldn't get enough of it. Liked to hear the sound made by the hook as it penetrated the bitch's spine. You could never make them suffer to the extent that they had made him suffer. Couldn't come close. If you captured a million cunts and burned them alive—it still wouldn't come close to paying them back for all the suffering they had caused him over the years.

"Let the bimbo hang like that for a while."

Bishop stroked himself lightly, massaging the helmet, but would not go all the way with it. Restraint was called for here. He would save it for later. It always felt better with the real thing.

He stopped the film. Channel surfed until he happened upon an episode of *Leave It to Beaver*. Now there's a name for home-spun family entertainment. Amusing stuff. Had nothing remotely to do with reality and the way things truly were.

June Cleaver. Talk about a fictional character. Pure make-believe. And then, of course, the other lie: Mr. Cleaver. Good ol' Ward. Patient. Understanding. More so even than Patience McDaniel—in that Ward was clearly clear-headed, while Patience, it could safely be suggested, was slightly confused.

What a dad.

He switched channels and came upon another scene from a world he had never known: More make-believe. *Father Knows Best*. Everyone seemed sane here. Reasonable. Made him (almost) chuckle. Daddy knew best. J.J. was best at being brutal.

Stayed with the comedy for a while. Moved on to the *Donna Reed Show*. Beautifully coiffed. Impeccably attired. Groomed. Family lived in a nice, clean, organized home. No rats or roaches or dog crap in sight. Nothing was out of place, not so much as a single pubic hair on anyone's precious groin. Furthermore, no one was required to eat dog food, no one was humiliated or cuffed or had wine bottles pitched at them for wetting the bed.

He kept watching, on the verge of chuckling to himself. You never saw Donna Reed running down some busy city street in broad daylight without any clothes on and urine pouring out of her hairy muff like a waterfall. Not this wife and mother. You never saw June Cleaver hop on the hood of a parked LAPD car, hike up her dress and take a major dump, then hop off with a satisfied grin on her overly made-up face as though she'd just given a grateful homeless bum a *Mickey D's Happy Meal*. Not Mrs. Cleaver. Not Ward Cleaver's sane and pleasant and dutiful better half.

He kept watching and half-grinning to himself. Recalled, as a kid, while viewing these blatantly bogus scenarios, and believing it all at the time, how much he wished he could have been a part of a family like the ones he saw on television. Recalled, praying secretly, under the covers in his bed, to be taken away from his parents in order to be adopted by someone like June and Ward Cleaver, by someone like Robert Young and Jane Wyatt, by Donna Reed and her easy going tv show spouse, better yet: a sweet and sane couple like his friends Flora and Truly Turnbull. He would have loved it. Prayed for it to take place. Confessed as much to them both. Even after Mrs. Turnbull had passed away when her ticker finally gave out, he had begged Mr. Turnbull to take him in permanently, adopt him. Cried and pleaded, and so had the old man—cried, because he had not been able to; city wouldn't let him. Established laws made it not only impossible, but absolutely unthinkable.

Charlotte and the redneck had been unwilling to give up their favorite punching bag.

"Mr. Turnbull, sir, you see how good I am with Parfrey. You don't see how much I love you both? You're not able to drive, sir, to get to the market. I don't mind doing the shopping for you. You know I don't. You got that catheter in you and the tube that runs down to that plastic bag strapped to your leg. You need me, Trusty. You need me. You need me as much as I need you and Parfrey both. I don't mind taking the city bus; or walking. I would walk miles for you."

Images were there, easily triggered, as they always would be; had imposed themselves over the bullshit on the screen.

The old man had been dealing with BPH, enlarged prostate. Couldn't pass urine without medical help. And they had stuck a tube in his penis at the VA; tube was attached to a hose that ran down the side of his right leg to where a urinary drainage bag had been secured. Urine would flow through the hose down into the plastic bag until it filled up and had to be drained. Cecil never had to actually assist with any of this, but knew of it from the old man, who had patiently explained what his troubles were and why he limped when he walked and why it was difficult for him to leave his house and take his pet for a walk or buy groceries or do much of anything that required physical stamina. Cecil easily understood. He may have been repulsed by it initially, but he surely understood what a big help he was to his friend and was always glad to support him anyway he could, as a way of repaying the kindness he and his gentle wife had shown him all the times he had nowhere to go or hide away from the unpredictable loonies he was stuck to live with that had been nothing short of a toxic nightmare for him; that Biggs, even then, at that young age, had been aware enough to know, would leave him scarred forever.

He was fucked, and there was no way out. That was when the cutting had started; anything sharp he could get his hands on: glass shard, knife, can opener; didn't matter. What stopped it was Charlotte and the redneck wanting to blame Mr. Turnbull for it.

Finally, it was Mr. Turnbull making him promise to cease and desist; that life was worth living, after all. Even though he had lost his darling Flora, he still could not see suicide as a way out, even though existence without her would never be the same for him or even Parfrey, their darling pet hog.

"Life is a miracle," Trusty would often remind him. "Life is precious. Don't you dare harm yourself that way. It hurts me, son." The old man had wept. "Not only does it hurt *me*, but you can see how sad it makes *Parfrey*." And he had been right: Parfrey did appear forlorn at the time, all the while nuzzling up to Cecil. It was then he had given the old gent his word that he would stop hurting himself. And they had sealed the deal with gingersnaps and milk.

Cecil recalled the hog liking the gingersnaps as much as he ever did. Seeing him eat out of his hand had brought a smile to his face. Trusty had been smiling too. He had wiped his tears with the back of his shaky hand and hugged them both.

"You're my only dad, Mr. Turnbull. You'll always be my true Daddy."

"I love you, boy. I couldn't love you anymore if you were mine biologically. That is the Lord's truth." Cecil O. had buried his face in the old man's chest, and fought hard not to start weeping again. Trusty had rubbed the back of his head, promised him that everything would turn out all right. There was nothing to worry about. No reason to give up hope.

"You're in my will, lad. Haunted house is yours as soon as you're of age. As well as all that Flora and I own that is of any value and worth. This house here, my coin and stamp collection." He gave him the name of the attorney to see when he turned eighteen. "Do you think you can remember the name, lad?" Cecil had nodded his head. The old man had reached for the thick phone book, opened the Yellow Pages, and pointed to the listed law firm and their prominent ad. He had circled the ad with a sharpie, and had Cecil repeat the name.

Cecil had looked up at him."What would I do with a haunted house, Mr. Turnbull?"

"Beside the point, son. You'll know when the time comes. Run it, or simply have someone run it for you. Pursue whatever you wish, but it's always nice to have a plan-B, something to fall back on. A well-managed and creative haunted house will never go out of style, especially around here. We're in *Loony Tunes Land*, son. That's a fact. No need to I remind you. Know it better than I do, Cecil. Folks will never tire of the harmless jolt that made-to-order fear induces, and fear is with us from day one. Real fear. True fear. For every single one of us. From birth to death. Just the way it is. Doesn't mean that there isn't much else to appreciate while being above ground, that there isn't love and happiness and all those other wonderful things. Remember that." He had paused, before stating the rest: "Anyway, do with it as you wish. Coin collection is worth a pretty penny; quite a bit of it is. Not so much some of that paper money from the civil war, but the rare coins, silver dollars. Worth a small fortune." He had added: "Let's not concern ourselves with it now. There'll be time for that later."

"What I want is for you to get well, Trusty. Get them to take that bag off your leg, so you can walk without hurting and be able to go to the bathroom like everybody else."

"Eventually, lad. Eventually. No need to fret. Most important thing to remember is never to give up hope: in me, or yourself. Because I'm not. I got faith in us both, lad. . . ."

He'd noticed the man wincing from time to time when he moved about, or even when sitting still or lying in his bed. He'd watched him open his jaw as though about to scream or give out a loud roar, only they were silent screams and soundless roars. He never made a sound during these moments. Never shed a tear. It was his way of dealing with the pain caused by having a tube inside his urinary tract. Cecil, having been a young kid and not known much about it other than what the old gent told him, inquired if it was hard to take. How uncomfortable and intense.

"Only when I pass water; or if I move suddenly. Primarily it's the other: when I have to go and have no control over it and urine flows through the tube in there, inside of me, and down through the hose, then it feels like a bunch of angry bees trapped in there and trying like hell to get out, stinging the inside of my groin the entire time. So don't you be alarmed when you see me hopping about, grimacing for a minute or so, 'cause that's what it is, son. Passing water. It's a tad uncomfortable, but I'll get through it. My point earlier being: we don't give up on the wonders of being alive and all the great joys this world has to offer just because we have a challenge or two tossed our way. We get through things, son; we get through quite a lot. Survivors; that's what we are. You and I, Cecil. We know how to survive. And it's worth it. It certainly is. Don't let anyone tell you different, young man."

What he loved about him. The man never spoke down to him. Didn't treat him like a child who didn't know shit from Shinola. That was the original Trusty Lusty; the Real McCoy. Mr. Truly Turnbull.

Well, it never did happen. Adoption was no option. Not for him. Escape was mere fantasy. What he got, instead, was what fate had stuck him with; what he got, instead, while watching shows like this these days, was vague (initially) images, appearing in his mind's eye, of his mother taking him around to various funerals as a kid. He was four, five, maybe six, not much was clear, but there were many funerals, people they had not been related to in any way, people who were not even acquaintances—no matter, because to his mother it was on a par with a religious ritual, a ritual he could never fathom to this day. Not only were funerals in general a waste of time, but why appear at a stranger's funeral? And they had all been strangers. Total strangers. What sense did it make? What did she get out of it?—other than the cut-rate for the occasional blow job she performed behind some tree or bramble or tombstone while he stood in front as lookout?

The funerals alone had left him with a sense of dread, and then the cheap sex acts she thrived on and could never get enough of. Dread. It had been dread, started out as dread—of the scene. Constant reminder of death. All it was. She was drawn to it: the morbid and gutter sex with geezers. Had dragged him from cemetery to cemetery to stare at coffins being lowered into the earth, men and women in black attire shedding crocodile tears, when some of the males weren't way in back of the pack being serviced by his loony mother.

June Cleaver? Yes. This was the "June Cleaver" he knew, the real June Cleaver. Nympho tramp who sucked tubesteak for chump change.

Why was it coming back to him now? What did it mean? He didn't need it. Could have done without it. It had to be Mrs. Cleaver, the Beave's perfect mom.

June Lockhart was another one who fucked with his head. These women weren't real. They were patient and understanding; they . . . they were "human, nice. . . ." They were everything his own mother wasn't. These people, these tv/Hollywood parents represented everything that he never had, everything that had nothing, zip, zero, to do with what his childhood had been like, what his reality was like.

Then, too, sometimes the sex triggered it. He shook it off. All of it. Funerals, priests, old men unzipping their flies and shoving their peckers into the whore's insatiable mouth; images of the whore, his mother, running down East LA streets stark naked, urinating in public; images of John Joseph holding a gun to his temple and waiting for what was bound to happen next: Cecil wetting his pants, and John Joseph would then pull the trigger, revealing that the gun had been empty all along.

J.J. would laugh out loud afterwards, pull on a bottle of rotgut or beer, would unfasten his leather belt and beat him with the buckle end for the mess he'd made on the living room carpet. Shoved his face in it for the encore. Pleasant memories. Could never tune them out entirely. You tried. Year after year. But they only managed to haunt him—time and time again. Refused to stay buried—like all those stiffs they witnessed get put down, lowered.

Biggs shut his eyes tight. Shook his head a few times. Squeezed his temples. Needed to let it all go. Forced it to disappear. If not completely, at least by about eighty-five percent. Best he could do, as once again, he focused on what was happening on the tv screen.

He flipped channels and settled on *My Three Sons*. Fred McMurray. What an easy-going gent. Reminded him of *Captain Kangaroo*.

Pleasant. Good-humored. Kind. They were kind. All of these fuckers— from A to Z—were kind, and it was this kindness, this seeming kindness that fanned the flames of his enduring and ever-lasting, absolute rage— and made him think about the captives in his dungeon, and this had his groin swelling again, gave him a certified chubby.

It was kindness that killed the real Trusty. It was kindness that ultimately caused Mr. Turnbull's demise. Kindness equaled weakness— and he would deal with it as he had always dealt with it (ever since becoming aware that life/existence/the world) was a lie. All of it. *Lie*. And would deal with it in his own way.

He cupped his testicles. They were large. Hairy and large. A man should have big balls—and his were that. Although his cock was far from it, the way that half a halfwit Marvin's was; it was thick enough and a bit larger than your average dick. If the average cock was five inches, he had an inch more than the average schmuck out there.

It was plenty. Sure, he should be the one with a pole on him like Muck's got, but what the hell—that was all the idiot had. Had no money or even a bank account; didn't have a car or his smarts. Shit-for-brains had exactly that: *shit-for-brains.*

He squeezed the base of his groin. Proud of it. The head turned a reddish purple. *Ready to shoot juice again. Yeah. Ready to blast cum all over those sluts down there.*

He looked at the *Rolex* on his right wrist. Not five a.m. even. Still too early to party. The neighbors were sure to gripe. Shoeshine man wasn't getting enough shuteye in order to make it in to his shoeshine stand and pretend to be peppy and full of life. Lack of pep hurt him in the pocketbook. Too bad. Tragic maybe. He couldn't wait and didn't care. The pain had not entirely left him, but enough had and was presently manageable.

*Fuck them all.*
Let them gripe.
It's a free country, isn't it?
Last time he checked.

# CHAPTER 121

## Thursday Morning

**Biggs was in the basement.** Had his rubber boots on, yellow slicker, hard hat with light on top, goggles, flashlight. He had Marvin Muck go in the Fun Room and bring the fifty-foot electrical extension cord out and plug it in the socket in the wall. Biggs was cautious to hold the two exposed wires not only in separate hands, but well apart.

He was on elbows and knees on the door over the pit, right eye glued to a hole the size of a silver dollar somewhere near the center, checking out the victims below: Terri Denise Klopp and Dixie Osgood.

Brunette-haired, nineteen-year-old Terri remained motionless, head hung down, eyes closed, floating in the water at about chin level. He and Marvin had nabbed this one in that Valencia parking lot one evening. Was a checker at *Lumber City*. Cunt was tall, large-boned, and blue-eyed. Had blond hair until Cecil had her dye it a dark brown, bordering on brunette, and she had expressed a fondness for grass and nose candy. *Dust. Toot. Blow.* What else was new? They had picked her up a little over a month ago and she had been kept in the pit (for most of that time) as punishment for kicking Biggs in the groin once and for throwing ammonia in Muck's face, not to mention the two escape attempts, between beatings and sexual abuse, and she had lost a considerable amount of weight due to her own stubbornness and outright refusal to eat the jambalaya that she was offered. And now here she was, pulling another stunt, and he was about tired of her. Out of patience, especially if she were faking it.

"Time to make room for fresh pussy."

Took a gander at the other heifer. From Georgia. Southern Belle. Seemed to be doing okay. At least she wasn't trying to con him.

Biggs took the exposed wire in his left hand and ran it through one of several other holes and stuck it in the water, while searching out the metal collar on Terri's neck by the wire in his right hand. It wasn't easy getting to the collar. Took some effort and strong sense of purpose.

Finally, once he connected, saw the hint of a spark or two; he stayed with it and witnessed her do a *spaz-like number*, in that she jerked about as the others before her had.

A grin appeared on Cecil's face. He had known it all along: the Klopp cunt had been faking it. Too bad. Made no difference now. He'd had his fill of her. Besides, if he waited any longer there would hardly be any meat left on her bones to even feed Marvin's fancy rats.

He looked up at Muck.

"How do you like that? Was I right? I know these bitches."

"Ho should know better by now. Trusty got the IQ. Cain't hardly outsmart Trusty."

Biggs suspected Base was being a wise-ass. Let it go. Was back with his eye to the hole in the door, playing around with the wire in his right hand. The wire eventually scraped against the metal collar on the victim's neck and the sparks flew. The bitch bounced around some more down there. Screamed out. Begging.

"You're CTD, cunt." Biggs withdrew the wire. *"She's Circling the Drain."* Didn't want her to die just yet. Had Marvin pull the cord out of the wall. To keep shocking her would have finished her off too quickly. Dixie seemed in shock herself—from merely having witnessed what the other went through. That worked for him. Let them get the message. Kept them in line. Kept them from scheming.

He unlocked the door over the pit, lifted it open. Told Muck to haul Terri out of there and carry her to the Fun Room. Biggs swung the door back over the pit. Hooked the lock through the hasp, but did not lock it.

As hurt and confused as she was, Terri Denise Klopp surmised what awaited her was far worse—and she was not a willing participant. Did not wish to go anywhere, let alone to a section of the dungeon Cecil Biggs referred to as the *"Fun Room."*

Muck dragged her in. Biggs followed. Took over. Grabbed her by the cuffs. On the cement floor was that free-standing copper Victorian era type of slipper style bathtub with claw feet that had been bolted into the floor. The brass, rim-mounted gooseneck spout and hand shower rose up from the middle of the same side of the tub that the door to the room was on and hung over the tub this way. The tub was heavily dented and scarred and stained with grime and crud consisting of bits of skin and hair strands and scalp, stray tooth or two, enough fresh and not-so-fresh blood from previous torture sessions with previous victims. He saw to it that the rubber stopper was in place, the drain sealed tight.

"You sure ho be *CTD*, Cecil?"

"Do your part."

Biggs indicated the customized torture board that hung from hooks in that section of the wall to the left of the metal cabinet. Devoid of hinges or knob, the torture board had been fashioned from a solid wood conventional door and featured six eyebolts that had been screwed into it: two at top corners, two at approximately the halfway point, and the remaining couple at bottom corners. Heavy-duty sections of nylon rope dangled from each eyebolt. In addition to the rope restraints, handcuffs had been secured next to the eyebolts at the top. There was a shackle each at near the bottom corners. Locked to a corner eyebolt was a bicycle chain, the other end of which was secured to one of the tub's claw feet.

Across the back of the torture board, a foot from the top, were three iron hoops that made it possible to hang the door in this manner from the trio of iron hooks in the wall.

"I said she's CTD, and she's CTD."

Not that Marvin was thrilled. Waste of good tang. Ho still had her some good tang left. Mothafuckin' *Vagina Killa* gonna do what he gonna do. Kept it to himself. Instead, mentioned about the chain. "Gonna have to unlock it, if I was to take the door down."

Cecil did that for him. Muck placed the heavy and cumbersome torture board directly over the tub lengthwise, the end with the cuffs over the backrest (that was situated on the same side of the room that the cabinet was on).

The woman had not stopped resisting. Refused to accept her fate.

"Get out of the way."

Biggs shoved Marvin aside. Reached inside the gray metal cabinet for a claw hammer. Marvin stepped back. No choice. Winced, as Cecil gave the woman a shot to the head with the hammer. Another shot to the face settled her down.

"That's how that's done." Biggs proceeded to lay the quivering *Lumber City* checker across the torture board. "I want her on her belly."

The deacon gave him a hand with her. Muck shackled her ankles at one end, while Biggs was at the other end of the board handcuffing the victim's wrists to either corner.

Sometimes cuffing cunts and assholes was simpler, quicker, especially when the victim did not have thick wrists to cause problems. This one certainly didn't. The hammer blows to the noggin had dazed her enough, and yet there she was, like so many before her, unwilling and/or unable to come to terms with her fate: Thrusting that bare ass from side to side, up and down—and all other ways. Twisted her wrists, yanked, did what she could to jerk her legs and feet about at the other end. None of it would do her much good. Blood oozed from her face.

"Now get that cunt Dixie in here. I want her to see who runs the show."

"Just seen you shock this ho. Don't it be enough?"

"No, it don't be enough."

Marvin was about to step through the door to carry out the order.

"Hey. What do you say?"

Marvin stopped. Looked at him.

"Hate the Sin, Not the Sinner."

Marvin shook his head. Said *"Shit"* to himself. "You the boss, Hoss."

"Say it."

"Hate the Sin, Not the Sinner."

"What's being accomplished here?"

"Filthy ho gettin' they punishment."

"No, not 'ho.' *Fornicator.* Go on. Get her."

# CHAPTER 122

**Marvin walked to the pit.** Mumbled something about "filthy fornicatin' ho bein' punished by the Lord" while removing the lock. Thought to add: "Hate the Sin, Not the Sinner" line. Heard Betty Lou and her daughter Mildred Elizabeth echo same from within the Geek Cell.

He lifted the door open. Helped Dixie Osgood climb up, out of the water. Held onto her handcuffed wrists in back while he closed the door over the pit and made sure it was locked.

Dixie Osgood was shivering, cold. Bitch be scared, too. Marvin thought he had something he could warm her up wiff. Sho nuff. Truck load of hot fuckin' chowder. Only there don't be no time to mess wiff her now. Cecil be waitin'.

He brought her to the Fun Room. A ball-gag was shoved in her mouth by the bishop, who saw to it that the leather strap in the back was good and tight. He un-cuffed one of her wrists and secured the free handcuff to a chain in the wall to the right of the door as you entered. He tossed Marvin a couple of keys.

"Now, go to the Mattress Room and bring Dione 'Divine' in here."

"I could *tap* some of this here *PAWG*, me. Put some hard meat in her ass."

"Get Dione."

Marvin Muck left the room.

# CHAPTER 123

**Biggs had his groin out and was stroking himself.** Ran his tongue over his upper and then lower lip, while focusing on Terri Denise Klopp's grimy buttocks. He eyed Dixie Osgood briefly, took in the bloodshot eyes, the tears that cascaded down her face, accompanied by muffled sounds she made through the ball-gag.

Ordinarily he would have done away with the gag. He preferred the noise, histrionics, screaming, violent shaking, and pleading. It was too early in the day for it, he'd supposed. Besides, Terri Denise Klopp was making plenty enough noise on her own. He hadn't bothered to gag her.

A struggling, defiant Dione Aragon was yanked inside the Workshop-cum-Fun Room.

"Ho was standin' on the coffee table. Bangin' on the board on the window wiff her fist, carryin' on an' shit."

"That right?"

"Broke the coffee table, too. Can't trust no ho. Only ain't no reason to smoke her ass. Ho got good tang left, even wiff that fucked up eye."

Seeing what was being done to the victim secured to the tub, Dione could not help the following: urine trickled down her leg, as it did down Dixie Osgood's. Fear brought it on, perpetual fear.

"Bring her over here."

Marvin dragged the victim to where the bishop stood. Turned over the two keys.

"I foresee Pit Therapy in your future. Get me? You had your warning and were aware of the consequences. You can't be trusted. Trust is everything. Trust."

"Heard that, ho? Trust be everything wiff Trusty Lusty."


Biggs unlocked the cuff on one of Dione's wrists. Backhanded her, hard, so that she staggered back, reeling against Dixie Osgood.

"Handcuff her to the other cunt."

While Marvin carried out the order, Biggs picked up a bucket. Slid the torture board away from the side of the tub that the spout was on. Filled the bucket with water. He walked back to the handcuffed duo. Swung the bucket so that about one third splashed Dixie Osgood, another third Dione Aragon.

"We like our victims clean, don't we, Free Ride?"

"Clean tang, dirty tang—make' no difference to me."

Biggs stood over Terri Denise Klopp, splashing what remained of the water on her backside, and was able to get more than enough of the grime and residue from the pit off. He reached for a jar of clear lube in the cabinet. Shoved a good dollop into her rectum. Tossed the jar to Marvin. Marvin stood there, looking at him.

"Lube Dixie Osgood's asshole."

Marvin remained standing. Unsure he heard right.

"You want to bang that butt, don't you?"

Marvin nodded his head. "You the boss, Cecil."

"Get it. I want to see that black python fill her tight asshole, want to see the cunt scream out in pain while you pound that rectum."

The sidekick didn't need to be told again. Went about the lubing business. Got plenty inside the woman. He had his fully erect groin out. Applied a degree of the lotion to the large head and about half of the shaft. He had the woman face the wall.

"Spread your ass cheeks, Dixie," Biggs said from where he stood. He had his own member out, and reminded Marvin to remove the ball-gag from her mouth. Marvin complied.

Biggs said: "Spread your asshole for the man."

She did.

"Yo. Brotha Muck doin' the Black Attack thang here, the Funky Monkey."

"How about if you spare us the play-by-play commentary," said Biggs, as they proceeded to sodomize the captives. Biggs unloaded inside his captive's rectum, while instructing Marvin, once again, to dump in his bitch's mouth. "Have her gag on your prick. Give her the mother of all lodes. Hose her face. Let her drown in ball juice."

Free Ride followed suit. No problem. This was cool by him. It was times like this bein' 'round Bigg' was the best. Rapin' ho', gettin' trim. I don't never be tired of trim.

Even though Biggs was through with his piece, had shoved his groin back inside his fly and zipped up, he stood there squeezing himself while watching Marvin Muck fuck the shit out of the cunt's shitter.

Man knew how to fuck. Had to hand it to him. Loser was useless in every other way, but he sure knew how to bang his bitches. Too bad he didn't have his length or circumference. Made him feel damned inadequate witnessing the action.

"Cream in her mouth. You ready to pop?"

"I could pop, me."

The victim was gasping, struggling against it. Marvin withdrew at that moment, spun her around and jammed his member in her gaping jaw. Shot a load. It was plentiful. Filling her mouth. Some of it overlapped and began to ooze out, and Marvin rubbed the head of his cock up against her face, shoving the cream back into her mouth, all of it. *Man said let her drown in ball juice.*

"Sink or swim, ho. Be mo' betta than a *Happy Meal* at *Mickey D.* Yeah; that be real good."

"Zip up. Come here. Turn this one over."

Marvin snapped out of his daze. Zipped his fly up and staggered over.

"I want her on her back. I want her to see what's coming up."

Marvin had had to bend over to reach the far edge of the torture board with his right hand, while gripping the edge against his waist with his left. He was about to flip the board this way, without a thought to releasing the victim first.

"What are you doing?"

The sidekick looked at him. *"Said to turn the ho over."*

"That must have been some piece of ass, because apparently it wiped out what few brain cells you had left. Don't turn the board over with her *cuffed to it.* Let go of the board. *Uncuff* her."

"What wiff?"

Biggs unlocked the handcuffs himself, the shackles. Stepped back.

"Now turn her over. Not the board, her only."

Marvin did this. Handcuffed her back up: legs spread apart, ankles secured to separate corners. Same was accomplished at the other end with her wrists.

"That's fine. I'm damned proud of you."

"Yo. Ain't got to be proud."

"What are you grousing about now? What is it?"

"Coulda had these hoe' makin' us some jack. Had our own ho business—"

"Yeah, like you had that time pimping out those two underage cunts on Hollywood Boulevard for crystal meth. Coupla bucks here, coupla bucks there. You're small time. Always will be."

"Coulda had us somethin' better. Call it *Rent-A-Ho*, or *Rent-A-Bush*. Outcall. Be listed in Beverly Hill' *Yellow Page'* as dinner date'. I knowed some brothas be makin' nothin' but *bank* doin' it that way. Them rich Hollywood mofo be payin' top dolla for tang."

"Rent-A-Bush, huh? Rent-A-Ho? Are you for real? Know how fast you'd get busted? This isn't 50's LA. Lookit how they nailed the Hollywood Madam."

"Don't matter. I ain't no Hollywood Madam. Got the touch, me."

"Sure you do. Everything you touch turns to excreta."

"Say what?"

"Forget it."

# CHAPTER 124

**Terri Denise Klopp was coming to.** Her vision returned in time to see Cecil Omar Biggs don a stained apron and pick up a *Black & Decker* chainsaw with an eighteen-inch blade.

Blood continued to flow from the gashes in her head, down the end of the torture board at her feet and into the tub or onto the floor. Cecil adjusted the door so that most of the blood would flow into the tub. The woman had regained her senses to the point that she was able to jerk about and implore to be spared.

*"PLEASE, DON'T! PLEASE! NNNOOOOOOO! PLEASE, DON'T!"* She was in and out of it, the head wounds causing her vision to blur even now as the buzz of the chainsaw in Biggs's hands made it clearly obvious what was about to happen to her.

Biggs was happy about that. Had Muck tear a strip of duct tape off a roll and stand by with it. Biggs brought the *Black & Decker* blade down against the side of the woman's neck and allowed it to carve in above the collar bone, away from the carotid artery, and watched blood appear and flow. Some of it ending up on the floor of the Fun Room, leaving him in dismay. He wanted her blood inside the tub. He had plans for it.

Dixie and Dione found it impossible to take. The shaking and screaming started. Retching followed. Dione dropped, passing out. Dixie was there soon enough herself.

"Turn up the stereo. Do it."

The stereo was on the top shelf in the metal cabinet. Marvin popped a Run DMC cassette in and cranked the volume up. Full blast.

"Turn that *shit* off. You know I hate rap. Put Little Richard on, or James Brown. I want to hear some James Brown. Rick James or Rammstein would do."

"Take it easy, home'. Got it under control. Yo." Muck stuck a James Brown cassette into the cassette player. James Brown, the *Godfather of Soul,* was feeling good and said so.


As far as Cecil was concerned, the next step would be much tougher to pull off, but he needed the spatter to be pronounced and was not willing to stop until he accomplished it. He moved the blade away from this area of the neck and raised it a bit higher, holding it inches away from the carotid artery. Reminded Marvin once again that he would have to slap the duct tape on her not long after the cut, or else they risked losing her altogether. That would be too soon and too easy for this particular ballbuster. He didn't want her dead, only bleeding. Then he decided against it for the time being. Biggs positioned the chainsaw blade down there at her feet. Pressed the blade against the toes on the woman's right foot. The blade cut through bone like a hot knife slicing through shortening. Toes dropped off. First the big, then the rest. He did the same with the other foot: one toe at a time. Watched as the woman jerked around, screaming with everything she had. The copper tub had quite a bit of her blood in it by now. It was great. Biggs's cock was definitely in the process of reaching a state of arousal. Man, he might have to stop to go again. Meds weren't getting in the way this time.

Sometimes that shit made it impossible to reach erection mode. Well, not here, not now. No way. The blood excited him beyond his dreams. *This cunt is fantastic.*

He was back at the end where her head was. Couldn't help himself. If you wanted *spatter*, if you craved true and real and *fabulous spatter*, no place was better than the *neck*. Right up against her neck. Inched the spinning teeth ever closer. More wailing and twisting on her part, more blood flowed into the tub. It was fine, but hardly enough. The neck; you had to go for the neck. Not to kill, not to sever the head, but to see the red spray and the vic denote abject terror. Grim Reaper was knocking on her door. Fear of the Grim Reaper was second to none. Joy to witness. His erection was holding up nicely as a result.

"You ready?"

Muck shook his head. All he was good for. Being negative. Never mind the punk, thought Biggs. Can't let anything spoil your fun. He lowered, then ever-so-cautiously pressed the saw blade against her neck. The metal teeth cut into the carotid. Spray was wondrous. Blood all over his hard hat, goggles and face, walls and floor of the Fun Room. He licked some of it off his lips. His taste buds didn't care for it. Too bad. Blood was good for you.

*"Seal it. Stop it. Plug it up."*

Marvin was clumsy, but managed. Stop-gap. It would do.

*Christ, why hadn't he shown the brass to live out his fantasies years before? Go all out? Should have/could have. Repression was not healthy. Could have been the greatest, the best serial Slaughter King of them all. Yes, had killed now and then, here and there, but never gone all out like he was doing now.*

*Fuck chubby Gacy* and *Mama's Boy Eddie Gein; fuck that queer Corona, fuck that transvestite Norman Bates.* Losers and retards. He could have been better. He was better. Straight, too. A man. That set him apart right there. Liked his pussy straight. No dressing up in funny women's clothing like Ed Wood, no wearing of silk panties and high heels, no matter what J.J.

*tried* to turn him into. No. None of that shit for Cecil O. Biggs. But that was all right. He would catch up. There was time. *Brother Trusty* would help him get there. Haunted house was taking in plenty until the lawsuits shut him down. For the time bing. No matter. He would be the biggest and baddest of them all. None of these cocksuckers had his brains, his IQ. Manson was a dumb-shit no-class hillbilly like Marty Roscoe. None of them could touch the Bishop. They didn't have his guts or his smarts; his cunning and panache. That's funny, though, he thought: Got plenty of guts around here, for sure. I'm worth half a million, at least, own my own two-story chamber of horrors, a *Rolls* and a *Cad*, money in the bank and cash stashed away that nobody knows about. Satan is a drag queen, and J.C. never existed. The pentagram is for queers and other degenerates.

He stood back, wanting to take it all in, just wanting to watch. What would he do next? His groin grew inside his trousers, and this was something he could not continue to ignore. He lowered the chainsaw. Shut it off.

"Get these two bitches out of here. I think they got the message. I want to be alone for a while. I want it quiet. A man can't hear himself think anymore."

"Mattress Room?"

"Huh?"

"Take the hoe' to the Mattress Room?"

"No. Dione Divine earned herself time in the pit. The other one goes in the Abattoir."

"Southern Belle?"

"Dixie Osgood, the Southern Belle. Yes."

"Ho could end up like ice in there."

"You said before."

"Could be a crowd in there. You know you got them two other hoe' hangin' on hook': Connie Higgin' and the fit ho. Sandra Hargrove, or somethin' like that."

"*Harcourt. Sandra Harcourt.* Aerobics instructor."

"That be the one."

"Chain her to the wall in there, then. Put a metal collar on her, a chain leash."

Muck grabbed a metal collar from the cabinet, a leash. Attached them to the victim using the proper size lock.

"Go in the clothes closet and pick up a blanket. Give it to her."

"Bangin' pussy be cold as *ice cube'* don't be no fun."

"On second thought, it's too early to have her succumb. She's got mileage left. Forget the blanket. Find her something modest to wear, instead. Turn her over to Miss Betty. She'll know how to deal with her—without taking her out."

"That be worst yet."

"Never happy, never satisfied. That's you."

"That evil granny gonna do a number on her. Young ho don't be good for nobody, then. You know Betty hate' good-lookin' young bitches like this."

"She earned Miss Betty's wrath when she ran up those stairs. I have to have trust. I expect loyalty. These cunts can't wait to turn on you the minute you let your guard down."

Muck saw that there was no point discussing anything anyway. The bishop detached the required keys from the carabiner and tossed them to the flunky, who in turn escorted the hysterical victims out of the Fun Room.

# CHAPTER 125

**Biggs got out of his gear and clothes.** Shut the music off. Closed the door. Released the helpless Terri Denise Klopp from the torture board and lifted the board to one side so that she slid into her own blood in the tub.

He was erect, self-loathing and all. He was too sharp to believe it was anything else, and yet there was no way around it. He craved it, needed to "bathe" in it. There was no going back once you crossed over—and he had crossed over a long, long time ago.

Not entirely all of his doing, either. He'd been shoved into it. You take a man's self-worth away, his self-esteem . . . and what do you have left? This is what's left. . . . What I'm doing right now. Payback. Paying them back for what they put *me* through.

"I want to wallow . . . in rivers of blood. Wade and wallow in it. . . . Drown in it. . . . Sink in it. . . . The only way the hollowness can be filled, the only way the void can be made whole again. . . ."

He knew that last part was BS as he even said it. You can't explain it away, quit trying to camouflage it. Stop lying to yourself. You want to get your rocks off. The best way to do it is the way you're going about it. . . .

He didn't fuck her. Not this time. Jerked it instead. Masturbated. Using her blood. In the tub with her. Jerked it, and spurted all over her.

There was no denying that same, not unfamiliar feeling of disgust, feeling of revulsion and self-loathing crept through him afterwards. . . . He didn't like it. Didn't care having to deal with it.

As if that weren't bothersome enough, a voice, in the distance (sounding a great deal like John Joseph) yelled something about him being a no-good half-a-whore's son; something about spending way too much time at that "pervert Bullturd's" place. Then he'd say: "How much the clown give ya this time?" Snatch the money before Cecil had even had a chance to take it out of his pocket. Backhanded him, hard. Of course there was that other thing. Words were clear now. Too clear.

*"Pissed your panties again! Lookit what you done to the bed, Pissy! No good little son of a bitch! Lookit the mattress! Soaked through and through! Stained! Another brand new rebuilt mattress shot! Ruined! You think rebuilt mattresses grow on trees? Is that what you think? You must, because you keep doin' it! Can't piss in the latrine like everybody else! What makes you so special that you can't get out of bed to do your pissin' in the latrine like the rest of us? Is the clown fuckin' you? What's causing it, ain't it? Gotta be. Is he? If he is, we need*

*to see more money from him!"*

Juicer Joe. Surely. The sound of the buzzing flies not that far off, either. Juicer couldn't wait to punish him for every infraction: imagined or real. Instead of talking to him like a human being. No way to explain the reason he continued to wet the bed is because he lived in perpetual fear of being beaten.

Forget it. How are you going to reason with a dogcatcher who brought dogs home and molested them? Forced him to do the same. Assaulted him if he didn't. Reason with someone like that? I don't think so.

Juicer Joe was inside his skull. Always—and forever. Would never be able to shake that warped billy motherfucker. Shouting, raging, waving the liquor bottle. Threatening to turn one of the hounds on him for what he "done" to the bed. Whipped Cecil's face with the dog leash. *"Another mattress what ain't no good now! I'll kill you one of these days, Pissy! Beat you to death! I will! You and that old heifer, both! For not scooping you out of that smelly twat of hers when I told her to!"* Enjoyed shoving Cecil's face in it.

Biggs did his best to tune the voice out. Was not able.

He climbed out of the tub. Carried the still breathing, whimpering victim to the chopping block, and reached for the *Black & Decker* once again. That's how you dealt with all of it: with a hard and heavy whack of the saw.

# CHAPTER 126

**"No use trying to sleep."** Harold got up. "Noise is too damn much. Dude just don't care about nobody. He don't care if people ain't gettin' no sleep because of all that racket he's makin' over there. What the hell is he doin', anyway? Cuttin' lumber this early in the mornin'? Man's crazy. Gotta be.

*Playin' that screamin' motherfucker James Brown all the time."*

Harold Crust shook his head. Looked at his wristwatch. It was 5:00 a.m. Might as well stay up now. The tv evangelist in the front room continued to ask for money. It was times like this Harold felt like taking his gun and putting a bullet or two right into the screen, right into the idiot box. But he knew he could never do that to his wife. He only wished she would show him some mercy and keep the set turned down low. Would it ever happen? They'd argued over it over the years. Claimed she couldn't hear unless the volume was turned up.

He walked to the living room. Saw that Fay was asleep in her recliner, as usual, and that damned Delonzo curled up and dozing on her lap. Never cared for him. Big-ass gray with the nasty copper eyes. Fay had saved him from being put down at the animal shelter a couple of years back. Mean mother didn't waste any time making himself right at home, either.

Harold had wanted him out. Didn't care for him. Didn't like cats, period. Tolerated him for Fay's sake.

Cat had detected his presence and opened his eyes and gave him, what clearly appeared to be, a dirty look. Son of a bitch Delonzo been acting like he was the one paying the mortgage ever since Fay brung him home. And there was a lot to him, too. Weighed about twenty, twenty-five pounds. Built like a dog. Damned near. Had a massive head. Broad shoulders. About as big as Roscoe's Boston terrier. Maybe bigger. Yeah. Gotta be. Made him nervous, too, sometime. Sheddin' all that fur. Come spring and summer. Was a real job gettin' all that cat hair off the carpet and furniture. Then you had the odor, cat shit, puke. And Fay went and got attached. "To be and live like a true Christian, you have to be kind now and then, Harold. Delonzo been abandoned. Lookin' for love and affection."

Not to mention all that tuna he could never get enough of and was costing them both more than he cared to think about.

Well, you did for your spouse. You did things to get along and because you loved your woman.

Delonzo annoyed him about as much as the tv still going, even though Fay was dozing. TV preachers maybe spent thirty minutes preaching, then would spend twice or three times as long pleading for donations, asking people to dig into their billfolds and make the preaching possible.

Only what was the point if she couldn't hear it and was not even awake? She always liked to do that. Why you got to leave the tee-vee on if you gonna fall asleep, woman? Harold felt like saying to her, but didn't. Wouldn't. Stopped himself in time. She put up with my crap all these years, he thought, it's time I put up with some of hers.

He stood there, hardly aware that he was running the tips of his fingers down the center of his chest, feeling the open-heart surgery scar. His fingers drifted to the left of the area, doing the same over the mound about the shape and size of a large coin. Did it to ensure that the pacemaker was doing its job, not that running his fingertips along the various reminders of the two surgeries determined anything. It was habit, more than anything. Habit. Just like a good shot, or more, of Jack Daniels had been habit, just like a snort of some prime toot now and then had been habit. But all that was in the past, history: toot, 'ludes, booze, hustlin' pool. Not only staying up at all hours of the night and then making it in to the shoeshine stand the next morning, but there were times, plenty of times, when he'd gone two or three days even, without sleep, and still worked the stand shining kicks like he was made of iron. Hell. You ain't no party animal no more, man. You a fifty-two-year-old dude what's gonna be takin' it easy from now on and forever. Remember that.

He noticed that his wife's blanket had slid off and was at her feet. He picked the blanket up, fanned it out. Harold made a psst sound in order to get Delonzo to move off. He did so, but not before he'd given him the nastiest of looks with those deep copper eyes and bared his fangs. Acting like he owned the place and was head of the household.

Harold preferred dogs any day to cats, but what were you going to do? Animals were a nuisance, pretty much. Ate and crapped and left your home a mess. Leave it. You did things for your better half; you did things to get along. He owed her, owed her a whole lot.

Harold draped the blanket over his missus so that it covered her up to about the collar bone. He clicked the remote to shut the television off and stepped into the kitchen. Fought the old craving.

"Sure could use a shot of Jack right now."

Noticed Fay's reproving eyes open. She had the remote in her hand and was clicking the tee-vee back on.

"You know what the doctor said, Harold. You ain't got liquor hid in this here house?"

"Yeah, I know what all them quacks said. No, I ain't got nothin' stashed no place. Wish I did." He reached in the refrigerator for the pitcher of ice water and poured some into a tumbler. Drank it down. Hating the taste of it.

"Don't you ever get tired of hearing them lies, Fay? Don't you ever get tired of them phony *Bible-thumpers* asking for money all the time?"

Fay had closed her eyes. Said nothing.

"They live in mansions like kings and queens, while the rest of us struggle to get by."

"Be grateful for what you have."

"Oh, I am—grateful we live in this rat-trap, can hardly make mortgage, eatin' franks and beans. I love it. Sure do. Can nobody claim I ain't grateful."

Harold wiped his mouth with the back of his hand. Pulled his boxers up. Looked down at the bony legs.

"I used to have some great legs, didn't I? Used to have strong legs. Lookit me now: *Toothpicks.* Skinny legs and a big belly. Seems all my weight shifted from my ass to my belly. Muscle gone from my arms and shoulders and just settled down into my belly—and I don't eat like I used to; used to eat like a horse, too." Then he said: "Sorry SOB is at it again."

"Say what, Harold?"

"You can't hear it 'cause you got the tv on. I'm tired of calling the Man on him, tired of the Man not wantin' to do nothin' about it."

"Get your rest, Harold. Go to bed."

"What I been trying to do all night: Go to bed. Hell, it's time to go to work—will be in an hour or so."

"You need your rest, Harold."

"Coming with, or you gonna spend your entire life in that chair?"

"I want to hear this."

"You heard it all a million times by now, Fay." Harold shook his head. "Them con men ain't gonna tell you nothin' you ain't heard before. They ain't gettin' no more of my money. I work hard for every dollar I make. Let them grifters go out there and shine shoes for a livin', see how they like it."

He walked back to the bedroom.

# CHAPTER 127

**Biggs lifted the buzzing chainsaw.** Carefully laid the blade down across Terri Denise Klopp's neck without cutting into it, then raised it again. He would have to pay heed to caution here, or else risk doing serious damage to the butcher's block. He lowered the spinning blade down to within one inch of the victim's neck, held it there, without so much as touching skin. The erection he experienced was the ready-made bonus. Might cum a third time if things went well enough. You just had to draw it out and make them suffer. This one hadn't suffered enough. None of them knew what true suffering was. How could they, when they were the cause? You had to prolong it, keep it going for as long as possible—without them opting for the *death rattle* as a way out, and depriving you of your pleasure and lust for blood.

Sweat poured down his face. Little by little, bit by bit, he applied enough pressure, guided the blade down, a spot above the strip of duct tape, watched it sink inside her neck, cutting the flesh open. He took his time. No need to rush. Savor it. Draw it out. Make the bitches pay. The blade sank deeper, parting the cut, slicing through the carotid and other veins, and the blood began to gush and spray in perfect unison with his orgasm below.

He continued to cut into the neck, ever mindful not to do anything to the table, perhaps only scratching the top; felt the teeth touch it, nibble at it, and the head was severed and rolled off and landed onto the floor below. The teeth inside her bloody jaw continued to chatter even then, the eyes blinking. Hens did it. Blood poured from her upper torso where her head used to be. He held the chainsaw vertically, started in at about the middle of her torso and began the slow, gradual cutting down the center of it, between the tits, on down through where the belly button was, below it, toward the lifeless vic's pelvis. The blade sliced into her vagina. Cleared it. He released the trigger. Shut the chainsaw off. Picked up a circular saw and attempted to cut her down into smaller pieces. Chunks of flesh, skin, and whatnot got caught up inside the upper blade guard and elsewhere and sprayed him as well to the extent that it made it nearly impossible a task. These things were made for cutting wood, not gristle and flesh.

He lowered the circular saw, stepped into the tub and washed himself off with the hand shower. Held it above his head, rinsing the blood and bits of flesh and bone shards out of his hair, armpits and groin region. He tended to his asshole and scrotum. Dried off. Dressed. Slipped into the slicker, and picked up the cleaver. He beckoned Marvin Muck back into the room, and proceeded to do the rest of his chopping with the cleaver, taking every opportunity here to separate the meaty parts from bone; did the same with the legs and buttocks, and had the deacon toss them accordingly into four galvanized buckets on the floor.

It didn't take long for Marvin and his way-too-sensitive nose to start botching things up by tossing meat in with the bones; and then, too, he was dumping entrails in there with the good meat.

Biggs had to remind him to pay a little more attention to what he was doing, not that it always worked. The room had turned into something resembling a gruesome nightmare: blood and viscera, arms, legs, feet—not to mention excreta. It was too much for Free Base. He'd been in it for the tang, pussy, gettin' over; pimping out bitches for dope and dough. He didn't mind rapin' them hoe', neither, taking that bush or cornhole when his dick be hard. But this . . . this be somethin' else. Mofo Bigg' should be in the bug bin.

"That be some strange shit."

"The fuck is the matter with you now? Sight of blood bother you? That it, *Slim?*"

"Yo. Blood don't bother me—long as it don't be mine."

# CHAPTER 128

## Same Day, Early Dawn

**Petunia peered through a crack in the drawn bedroom curtains.** It wasn't mere curiosity that caused her to behave this way; no, it was more than that. Her nerves couldn't take the pandemonium that had been coming from Biggs's place, all that strange noise, and it made her angry and she stayed angry.

Roscoe was sound asleep in their bed, snoring as usual. His wife looked at him and shook her head. Dead to the world. The house could have been on fire and he wouldn't know it; for that matter, all of San Fernando Valley could have been ablaze and oblivious Marty would have snored right through it.

Work a minimum amount, drink like a fish and sleep like a hog and chase those young bimbos in their clinging skirts every chance you get.

The racket across the way persisted and Petunia was back at the window trying to make out what the hell was going on, peering through the curtains. She was exhausted and needed sleep and was convinced Biggs was one inconsiderate jerk.

"Marty?"

Roscoe chortled like the true swine that she knew him to be.

"Hear that, Marty?"

"Hear what?" Roscoe hardly stirred.

"*Hear what?* Are you falling apart like Harold now?"

"Let me sleep, woman."

"Can't you hear that, for crying out loud? What's it sound like to you?"

Roscoe's eyes stayed closed. He was scratching his buttocks. "I don't know."

"What time is it?"

"Time to give your husband a blow job, woman."

"Idiot."

His wife shook her head. It was then the ruckus ended. It was quiet. Petunia remained standing at the window. Still. Waited for it to start up again. It didn't. It was too good to be true. It was nice and quiet. Bastard's probably too spent to party anymore. Those orgies must take a lot out of you.

She walked over to the bed and slid under the covers.

# CHAPTER 129

**Inside Biggs's Fun Room things were, in fact, relatively calm now.** It was clean-up time, time to get the hose out and get rid of the evidence: chunks of meat and bone, loose teeth, hair clumps, toes, intestines, torso halves, hacked off arms and other limbs.

There was the woman's head with the scalp gone, while a few feet away lay what remained of the rest of the body. There was blood everywhere; too much of it really. Other than it being one big mess, he hated to see so much blood go to waste. Truly did. And that head. What was it doing on the floor?

Trophies were to be handled with care. He'd gotten careless in the whole euphoria of it. Picked up the head. Placed it inside the metal cabinet. He would boil it in water later to get the flesh off. Make it look real nice. Paint it gray and find a place for it on the special shelf in the cooler with the other skulls, or maybe on top of the safe in his bedroom.

Probably safer that way. No way Mr. Fimple would be able to break into his bedroom the way he'd been able to break into the cooler from time to time. He gave Marvin the key to unlock the spigot out there by the pit, gave him one end of the hose. Told him to hook it up and turn the water on full blast.

Biggs went over the contents in the various buckets one more time to make certain anything with a decent amount of meat on it was separated from the rest and tossed into the proper bucket.

Marvin was back.

Biggs aimed the hose nozzle at the walls and began spraying. Did his best with it. Paused spraying long enough to have Marvin pick up the push broom and brush down the walls, cabinet, butcher's block and floor.

"Get with it."

As expected, Marvin's effort was half-assed.

"Get the lead out. This is the price we pay for the fun we have around here."

Muck did what he was supposed to. Didn't give it his all; never gave anything one hundred percent, other than when it was time to rape the whores. It would do. Biggs had him step back. Blasted the walls some more with water. Guided all the bits and pieces in a single pile in the center of the cement floor. Stopped spraying. Tossed some more of the limbs with potential, that Greta could use, into the designated bucket, while Marvin shoveled the rest into the remaining three.

"Grab the bucket with the meat and take it to the walk-in."

"Door be locked."

"I know door *'be locked.'* I didn't say to go inside, did I?"

"Could be you did."

"Could be you got shit in your ears."

"Could be 'cause you be playin' that loud mothafuckin' disco all the fuckin' time."

"You done exaggerating?"

"Didn't know I was, me."

"Come back for two more. Go on."

Marvin carried the bucket out, and was back shortly. Biggs grabbed the lighter of the three, left the remaining two for Muck to deal with, and they hauled them out. Biggs unlocked the door to the walk-in, dumped the meat in the one bucket in the freezer, stepped back out and locked the door back up.

They were inside the Furnace Room. Bishop unlatched the incinerator gate. Opened it, lifted the bucket loaded with bowels and other entrails and waste and dumped it in there. Try as he might, the odor was not particularly easy to ignore. Muck made a face, too. Stench was a bitch. It worried the bishop; it was a concern. Not Marvin's reaction to it, nor even his, but the repercussions it might result in eventually throughout the hood.


Marvin tossed the contents of one of his buckets in, then the other. Biggs had left the gate open. Stood there watching it all burn: cartilage, hair, entrails—and whatnot—watched it go up in smoke. There was no denying it left him with a certain satisfaction, gave him a feeling of victory, accomplishment: He had triumphed, they had not.

Their loss, his victory. Proof was in the smoke. There it was: End of the line. He savored moments such as this, always would—for the human race, all of the assholes of the world, deserved to end up in this manner: Fried. To end up wafting in smoke, or else streaming down into the grease trap as sludge. There was plenty of that: sludge, fat. And it was *yellow*. Human fat was *yellow*. One did not realize how much of it a body contained until you cremated a few of them.

Although it was a moment clearly to be relished, they always were, he could not disavow the concern: What problems would the odor cause for him again? Smoke carried it a fair distance. People had made comments in the past.

Some of the a-hole neighbors were sure to notice and make comments regarding this current disposal effort. Made him nervous. Edgy. Did it anyway, though, didn't you? Wasn't up to driving all the way out to Lopez Canyon every time he had some refuse to unload. Let the neighbors cluck. They weren't exactly smart enough to add it all up. They can grumble all they want, talk shit behind his back. Not a single one was clever enough to figure anything out.

"We can't keep using the furnace."

Muck looked at him.

"Be easy this way, don't it? Ain't got to dig no grave, ain't got to carry all that nasty, smelly shit out to some wood and bury it. Smell' up the car, too. I be the one got to clean up. Exactly be why them hoez give me a hard time, 'cause my wardrobe got that smell like the undertaker."

"Don't you understand? It takes two hours and change to cremate a body. Assholes like Lloyd Dicker are starting to gripe about the odor."

"Fuck 'em. Let 'em gripe. Odor don't be nothin' new. There be all kind' of odor, ain't there? Why this odor got to be more *nasty* or any *worst* than odor in they own cribby? They own cribby smell like the city dump. That be a fac'. All of Valley, includin' LA smell like that, if you *aks* me."

"Then I have to listen to you whine when I ask you to scrape ash inside the furnace and clean out the grease trap." Biggs knew Marvin wouldn't have a comeback for it, and he didn't.

"All I know Lloyd Dicker got to stop puttin' his tired weenie where it don't belong. What I thank."

Biggs stared at the purple flames inside the furnace. Watched all of it, with the exception of some of the larger bones, burn down to a crispy nothingness, down to ash, a pile of ashes. He would have to remind himself to have Marvin pull the bones out later and crush them with the sledge. It was just better that way. No need to make it possible for some wild animal to dig anything up out there in Lopez Canyon that resembled a human bone, or should they discard the remnants elsewhere, why risk anyone discovering anything that may have been part of a *Homo sapiens* once?

Biggs found himself grinning just then.

"She sure put up a struggle. Didn't want to go, didn't want to die. Kept saying: I don't want to die. Please don't kill me." He replayed the precise moment in his mind's eye. "The more she pleaded, the more I liked it. She kept screaming and beseeching; fighting, kicking, trying to bargain, didn't want to give up the ghost—and the more she carried on the more I kept trying to convince her that, hell, we all have to go sometime."

"That be the trouf."

"We all got to go sometime, and her time had come a little earlier than she expected, but so what? She needed to accept it, that's all. When death comes calling you should give in to it. I know I would. What's fair in this world? No one beats death. No one. That's just the way it is."

"I ain't goin' against what you say, Trusty. Kinda feel like it was a waste of good vagina myself, good trim."

"I love it when they put up a fight, though. She was a good fuck, too. Got my rocks off thrice. She was good. Maybe I shouldn't have finished her off right away. Could be you're right. I could have held onto her a while longer, gotten some more mileage out of her."

"Kinda what I be thinkin', Brotha Trusty. Waste of pussy."

"Killing them off causes problems when it comes to disposing of bones, parts we can't use—then again, the best way to get off is to torture them and then chop them up. Not to mention: Dead bitches tell no tales. She was getting to be too thin anyway. Not much meat left on her."

## **CHAPTER 130**

**The temperature had dropped down to about eighty-two degrees and it was sunny and just about great weather, as far as Rudy Perez was concerned, to be working on cars in his family's driveway and earning money.** And that's exactly what he was doing this Monday afternoon, proudly finishing up his latest effort: a battered *'84 Yugo GV hatchback.* He'd had the hood up, engine idling. He was wiping handprints off parts of the grill and other areas with a rag while listening for telltale signs that something might be amiss. Heard none.

Just as he decided he was pleased with himself and did some more wiping down with the cloth, the car's owner, a disheveled, pot-bellied thirty-year-old Chico Mancini rode up on a kid's bike. A Santana tune blasted from the boom box that dangled freely from the handlebar.

Mancini greeted him in his usual, boisterous manner. Asked how it was going.

Rudy slammed the hood shut.

"Fine. So far."

"You da man."

Mancini tossed the boom box in the front seat. Pulled the keys out of the ignition and had the hatchback unlocked in quick succession. Tossed the K-Mart bike in there. Jammed some paper money in Rudy's shirt pocket and jumped in the front seat. Turned the key. Raced the engine. The grin on his face said he was satisfied. While Mancini was doing that, Rudy had the bills out, counting. Wad was light a ten-spot.

"I thought we agreed on forty bucks, Chico."

"Are you sure, Homie? 'Cause all I got is what's there."

"We agreed on forty. I spent money on parts, Chico. There's labor. Not to mention gas to and from the junk yard—"

"I'll make it up to you next time, Rudy. That's a promise."

"Like my dad used to say: *You can hit me, just don't shit me.*"

"You got my word. Keep the thirty. *Por favor?*"

Mancini revved the motor. Junk heap never sounded better. He fiddled with the radio until he found the same tune that played on the boom box. Left it on. Something about somebody's pots and pans not being clean. Turned up the volume.

"You're the best. You and your family. I mean it. You saved my life. I couldn't get to my nine-to-five without wheels. You know how it is: no money, no honey. If you ain't got wheels you can't run your old lady to the hospital in her time of need."

"Your old lady? Which one? And what for?"

"You a funny guy. You know which one: My main girl. Looks like it's gonna be twins this time, too. Glad it's finally gonna be over. Woman's eatin' me out of house and home. Having a hard time keeping food in the refrigerator. Seems like I'm always loading it up—and it don't never stay full for long. *Mamacita's* addicted to Rocky Road ice cream and sauerkraut. I must be out of my mind, man. Got four young ones right now. Two in the oven makes it half a dozen. Doc says it's two boys. They got a way of figurin' these things out. If it's true, gonna name 'em after you and Roe— just for the hell of it."

"You don't have to do that."

"I know we don't. Me and Luz want to name 'em after you dudes. The least we can do. After all you and Monroe and your daddy, rest his soul, done for me and my family over the years."

"Okay if I let my brother know?"

"No problem. Only it might be better if we sprung it on him after she delivers, after we brung the babies over for Monroe and your grandparents to see 'em—and surprise them. If you know what I mean."

Olivia Duarte walked up the driveway. Kissed Rudy on the cheek.

"What I like to see. Lovebirds being affectionate. Makes me happy; makes me feel good inside."

Rudy looked at Chico. "Later." To hell with it. He didn't feel like haggling over ten bucks with Mancini right now. Besides, he was happy that his girl was here.

"He saved my life." Chico was still grinning and nodding his head, pointing at Rudy again. "You saved my life. I ain't bullshittin', either.

Saved my ass. I'll get back to you. That's a guarantee, homeboy."

The *Yugo* backed out of the driveway, and Chico Mancini was gone. Rudy stood there, shaking his head. And he couldn't help it, he was smiling.

"What?"

"His wife's expecting."

"Again?"

"Twins this time."

"They can hardly keep the kids they have now clothed and fed."

"Wouldn't it be funny, though, if the father turned out to be somebody else?"

"I swear I don't get you sometimes."

"Mancini's got kids from Van Nuys to East LA—and I'm talking about some of these women being married, or got boyfriends—and the husbands and boyfriends don't have a clue."

"That's amusing to you?"

"Sort of."

"That would be amusing to a man—"

"Now wait a minute. Chicks are always saying how they want a guy with a sense of humor—"

"How much did he gyp you out of this time, Rudy?"

"Not much."

"How much is 'not much?'"

"Ten bucks."

"Why do you let him do that to you?"

"I didn't let him do anything. He's just a sharpie."

"I bet."

"You heard him: Saved his life. No money/no honey. And he's naming his twins after me and Roe."

Olivia pursed her lips, and was not able to suppress a grin. She made a fist and playfully drove it into her boyfriend's right shoulder.

"Wise guy. *No money/no honey.* Should kick your butt for allowing yourself to be such an easy mark."

"Yeah?"

"Yeah."

"Who got yelled at by Slim for letting bums walk in off the street and con you out of free meals?"

"One time. Two months ago—when I was still new on the job. No one's conned me out of *anything* lately."

Rudy locked his arms around her waist and pulled her into the house through the side door—and neither of them had been aware of Biggs sitting across the street in his *Rolls*, watching them. A second after Rudy and his girl entered the house, Biggs started the *Rolls-Royce* and drove off.

# CHAPTER 131

**Rudy was in the bathroom hurrying to wash his face and hands in order to get back to Olivia who waited for him in the living room.**

He dried off, slapped English Leather on his face and armpits, got some on both sides of his neck and came out.

Olivia was sitting on the sofa and looking at the aquarium directly behind it. She gazed at the *cichlids*. Had never really cared for this type of fish, and yet there was something that fascinated due to their obvious predatory nature. The cichlids were dark and mean-looking and chunky, about five inches in length. There were four of them in the medium-sized tank. She kept looking at them, the way they swam around like they had a chip on their shoulder and wanted to "kick butt," anyone's butt, not unlike so many of those doped up hooligans throughout the neighborhood. Olivia also knew now that she was here she was sure Rudy would pull the same stunt he always liked to pull: Would come up with a plastic bag full of water with maybe five or six tiny goldfish in it and feed the goldfish to the cichlids in the tank. And the way it usually went the harmless goldfish would try to hide behind the artificial seaweed in the tank, attempt to hide behind the skull-shaped tank ornament sitting on the bottom in the pebbles—but as often was the case, the cichlids eventually crept up to the goldfish and gobbled them right up; every single one of them, every single time.

"I've got a surprise for you."

Rudy was hiding something behind his back. Probably the goldfish. Olivia shook her head.

"Little boys have to be little boys, don't they?"

"I ain't so little where it counts."

"All right. Let's see the goldfish, Rudy."

Rudy held up the plastic bag with the goldfish. He moved to the tank with glee and dropped several goldfish down in it and waited for the nasty, all-business cichlids to react.

The cichlids had a system that never failed: they moved around in the water with what seemed like genuine indifference, taking their sweet time, in order to throw the goldfish off guard. Gradually, and in time, having gotten close enough to the intended prey, the larger fish would gobble up the goldfish.

Soon the goldfish in the tank were gone. Olivia did not necessarily need to witness what was going on; in fact, she did not want to see any of it. Rudy, on the other hand, continued to be amused by her reaction, and dropped the remaining two goldfish in.

"Look, you take everything so serious. What's the big deal? I only paid a buck a piece for them."

Olivia had risen to her feet and walked to the other side of the room where Rudy's grandparents dozed in rocking chairs next to a radio tuned to a Mexican station. There was a tv console in that corner in front of them and next to it a birdcage with a cockatiel named *Papo*. Olivia handpicked several sunflower seeds from a glass jar that sat on a bookshelf to the left of the birdcage. She fed the sunflower seeds to the cockatiel.

"Hey, that's life. Dog-eat-dog."

Rudy was still chuckling about the whole thing.

"That's really profound."

"Maybe I'm not trying to be *'profound.'* Hey, you know the family next door gimme the tank before they moved. The jerky kid lost interest in the fish, wouldn't feed 'em, so they give 'em to me. What am I supposed to do? Flush them away? Come on."

Olivia said nothing.

"What do you think sharks eat? And whales? And seals and eels? They eat other fish. What's gross about that? What do eagles eat? What do tigers eat and lions eat? What do coyotes eat, and jackals? All of them—they eat other animals. Maybe it's gross—but it's life. People eat cattle, pork, turkey meat; dogs eat horse meat. Some people even eat people. Ever heard of cannibals?"

"Stop."

"All right, all right. Quit being so squeamish, quit trying to make me feel guilty."

"Just wish you didn't have to enjoy it so much."

"I told you, Olivia: They have to be fed goldfish once in a while. I didn't make them that way—God did." He smiled. "Why don't you come on over here and sit down? You don't have to worry about the goldfish— they're all gone anyway."

Olivia was back at the sofa and Rudy did not waste any time pulling her down by the hand and maneuvering himself on top. Olivia made what looked like an effort to get him off of her; she kept looking at his grandparents dozing in their rockers.

"Don't worry about them. If they can't hear Papo and the stereo, they ain't gonna hear us. Take my word for it. It's their nap time. Like I told you—every day like clockwork. The Mexican ballads remind them of Cuernavaca, where they were both born. Put them to sleep. They love it. They ain't gonna hear us." And then he began to unbutton her blouse— one button at a time. Olivia resisted, but Rudy would not let up until he had every single button undone. He parted the blouse and had to stop and take a real good look at the pink brassiere and all that it contained. He wrapped his hands around both cups, and squeezed nervously. He kissed her on the lips, and then his mouth traveled upwards to her forehead, dropped down to her eyes, kissing them both . . . and his lips made their slow descent back down toward Olivia's open mouth and those moist, ever-so-moist and warm *fuchsia* lips. . . .

His tongue slid inside her mouth, sought out her warm breath, circled the tip of her own trembling tongue and their lips locked, parted briefly, and connected again as they continued to kiss.

Rudy got up, discarded his own shirt, and was back on top of her again, getting Olivia's brassiere unhooked, taking it off, removing it and then just held her full breasts in his hands like that and looked and gazed and then lowered his face down against them, rubbing the nipples against his cheeks and nose, rubbing them against his lips and his lips parted and took in a hardened nipple and sucked, and he did the same with the other nipple, totally lost in the moment, wanting Olivia more than anything right now, wanting to tear her jeans off and go down on her, wanting to part her legs and taste her down there and possibly get his own pants undone in time and slide it in. . . .

Would she let him? How far would he get this time? *I've got to try*, he thought. *Have to. I want it. I want you, Livia. I want to make love to you, Livia; I want it more than anything I've ever wanted in my whole life.*

And Olivia Duarte held onto him. She liked it, for sure, but she also knew just how far she would permit Rudy to go . . . and both were completely unaware of the pair of haunting, dark eyes that stared at them, peeped at them through the parted curtains in the open window and screen on the other side of the fish tank, as Cecil Omar Biggs ogled and scrutinized their every move.

# CHAPTER 132

**Fuck her, you pathetic salsa-chugging, taco-scarfing bastard.** *What the hell are you waiting for? Fuck her brains out. Tear her clothes off, and ram your cock in her. Give it to her good and hard. That's what she's here for. Fuck her, you punk. Give it to her, you goddamned faggot. Alpha, never omega. Slap the shit out of her and fuck her. Punch her in the stomach and bend her over and take her asshole. Jam cock up her shitter, punk. Do it.* And should Granny and Grandpa wake up? Easy. Slit their throats, and resume raping the cunt until you've had your fill—and then dump all three in a shallow grave in the backyard.

Biggs kept hoping and watching, but knew it would never happen. Found it impossible not to get caught up in it. His own desire neared a state he might not be able to control.

He could feel his own member inside his boxers stir, the tip of his groin moist. There was plenty of juice in his loins now, all that ball juice just waiting to erupt.

What the hell was this young fag Perez doing wasting time like this?

Let her put a lip-lock on your cock, boy. Let those lips suck on your balls. . . . Do it . . . do it. . . . Shove her face down on your prick. Jam cock and balls in her mouth until she gags on it. Fill her whore's mouth with a heavy load of cum. Do it. But it was not happening fast enough for Biggs. He'd have taken care of things a lot differently.

*You bet.*

# CHAPTER 133

**Rudy's moves consisted of nervousness and obvious inexperience, but he wanted her desperately and kept trying.** Got her jeans off finally and Olivia was down to her silk pink panties, when suddenly she decided to put a stop to the whole thing. She'd had enough. Rudy reached for the panties again, and she brushed his hand off.

"Please, Olivia. . . ."

"No."

Rudy made another effort to get the undergarment off. He clung to her buttocks with the palms of his hands, lifted her up some that way, pressed his own body against her and held her. Pressed some more. Olivia pushed him off with both hands, and the look on her face said she meant it.

"I am not getting pregnant."

"We're engaged, Liv."

"I don't care. I'm still not getting knocked up."

"Come on. . . ."

"Is that why you gave me the ring, Rudy?"

"Of course not. You know better than that."

He zipped his pants up, and this was done carefully, as his testicles were clearly aching. Olivia had pretty much gotten all her clothes back on.

"Thank God that I do know better. I've got college to think of. Career, plans, responsibilities—"

Just then Rudy could not resist. Indicated the erection inside his trousers.

"What about your responsibility to me?"

"Funny, Rudy. Real funny."

"Actually, it's real painful."

"Look, getting knocked up is just not part of my plans right now."

"So we'll get married. What's the big deal? Get on the pill. How many times do I have to say it?"

"I can't do that to my parents."

"They don't have to know."

"Just like a man. As long as you get what you want, that's all that matters."

"I said I'd marry you. Don't you want that?"

"It's too soon, too fast."

"We've been together six months now—"

"More like five."

"What's the difference? Five, six—what's the damned difference? We can get married. You love me, don't you?"

"I told you it would be a while before I could break it to my family. They don't even know you gave me the ring. I can't get married. I have to get my education out of the way—"

"You can't even tell them I gave you a lousy ring? I don't get it. Monroe was right. They control you like a puppet. You got to do what they want you to do. It doesn't matter how *you* feel, does it?"

"It will take time, that's all. There is no need to rush into anything."

Both remained unaware of the Peeping Tom observing them through the screen over the open window.

"All right. Forget it."

"Don't pout."

"Hey, I don't *pout*, okay? You're something else, you know that? I don't mean just you, either—women in general. What am I supposed to do now? If you didn't like me to get all worked up you shouldn't let it happen."

A kind of smile appeared on Olivia's face. She couldn't help it.

"What did *I* do?"

"Nothing."

"Sorry."

"I bet you are."

Rudy walked to the kitchen to get a beer. He asked if she wanted one. She didn't. Rudy cracked a can open, pulled on it, and he was back in the living room, shaking his head, fighting the pain that persisted in his sack.

"Damned if you do, and damned if you don't. If you don't make a pass you're a faggot right away—and when you do make a pass and try to get somewhere all you get is a bad case of blue balls." He took a couple of steps in the direction of the sofa and it seemed to get worse for him.

"Damn, I'm in pain. I can't walk."

"You're cussing again."

"You're all heart."

"Sorry. I didn't mean for it to happen, Rudy."

Rudy pulled on his can. He was trying to chuckle in spite of the condition he was in.

"You really are funny. Just because somebody don't cuss that don't make him any better than the rest of us. That's bull. I know a lot of creeps who don't cuss and they're still creeps. And I know guys who cuss all the time, use filthy, dirty language all the time—talk about *foul-mouth*—and they're some of the best people you'd ever want to know. They got heart and they got real soul—"

"Yeah?"

"Yeah."

"Yeah?"

*"Yeah."*

"Like who?" Olivia knew what his answer would be.

"Like my brother."

"It's still a bad habit."

"Could be—but how come you always got to change the man? Why is it chicks always do that? What makes you always think that's what we want?"

"Maybe that's what you need and don't know it."

"Where do you get these pearls of wisdom? From your sister? I got a message for her—"

It was then that Biggs made his presence known through the side door. He was standing in the kitchen with a VCR in his hands and had given Rudy and his girl a real, if unpleasant start.

# CHAPTER 134

**"How'd you get in here?"**

"Kitchen door was open."

Rudy cleared his throat. Rose to his feet with a wince. Hell, the pain in his genitals was just as intense as it had been a moment ago and the safest thing to do was not move too much, not that it made any difference, actually; the pain stayed with you whether you budged or not.

"I mean, ain't it polite to knock first?"

"I did knock. For some reason you didn't hear me."

"I bet," Olivia said in a vaguely audible tone.

Biggs's intense eyes, for the most part, had remained on Rudy's girlfriend. He was speaking to Rudy, but he had his eyes on Olivia Duarte. "I'd like you and your brother to take a look at this VCR."

"What's wrong with it?"

Biggs' peepers were back on Rudy momentarily.

"You're asking me? Tape got stuck. Had to yank it out. Now it won't function. Could be there's a strip way in the back that jammed up the works."

"Can you leave it on the kitchen table? We'll take a look at it."

Cecil Biggs stood there, waiting; had resumed staring at Olivia Duarte, and was waiting. Wouldn't say a word.

"I don't mean right now, Mr. Biggs. We'll open it up and take a look first chance we get."

Biggs gave him a slow nod. Lowered the VCR onto the kitchen table. There was distinct hesitancy to his next motion. He turned, and walked back out.

"He never knocked. That's a lie. He's a peeper, Rudy. He was spying on us."

"He's a customer. When will I see you?"

She didn't say. Instead nudged him. Indicated with chin and eyes that someone was back, standing in his kitchen. Rudy turned his head. Could not believe the audacity of the guy.

"Mr. Bugs, I mean Biggs, sorry. I'm really sorry."

"I've been called worse."

"Like I just said: We got cars to repair. We'll get to the VCR when we can. My brother works a full-time job—"

"This isn't about the piece of shit VCR. That's been settled. Like you to take a look at the Caddy."

"Your *Cadillac*? What's the matter with it?"

"You want my business, or do I find somebody else?"

"I'll be right out."

Biggs hesitated, as before. Continued to stare at Rudy's honey, and stepped outside.

# CHAPTER 135

**Olivia's body shook, as if overcome by a sudden attack of the chills.** The cause? Cecil Biggs's creeping around.

"Oh, come on. He isn't that bad. Sure, he's weird, so are a lot of other people around here."

"I can't help it. That's twice he walked in on us without making a sound. Like a ghost; like some apparition. Suddenly he was just there, in the kitchen, standing there, watching us. That's all I need: For word to get out."

"Word to get out about what? Never mind. You didn't answer my question: When will I see you?"

"I wish you would reconsider going back to school, Rudy."

"You're not going to start that again?" Then carefully, gingerly, so as not to disturb the groin region and add to his discomfort, Rudy moved toward the window and craned his head enough to peer through the parted curtains to see what Biggs was up to (if anything). The bishop had his *Cadillac* parked in the driveway and was leaning against it. Had a clear plastic bag of candy in his hand and was popping what looked like lemon drops in his mouth.

Rudy sat back down. Olivia pressed on. "Just think about it. It would make life so much easier. I wouldn't have to keep sneaking around like this. I feel like a criminal or something. I just don't like doing this to my family. I don't like the situation—"

"Hey, can't you understand? It's the one thing I'm really good at: Working on cars. You know my brother and me want to open up our own shop. What's so terrible about being a car mechanic?"

"What happens when I leave for college and we grow apart?"

"To me that doesn't make any sense, Liv—because you're not even leaving the state."

"It happened to Roe and Yolanda, didn't it? And who knows? *I could be leaving the state.*"

"Your folks got that kind of money? To send you to some out-of-state university? I didn't know teachers made that kind of jack."

"They don't have that kind of *'jack.'* What if I were awarded a scholarship—"

"You've been holding out on me. You got a scholarship. Where to? Is it out of state?"

"I'm not saying. You're missing the whole point, anyway."

"Listen to me: People don't fall out of love or *'grow apart'* unless they want it to happen *and let it happen.* That's what my grandmother says, and she should know. If you got the real thing you don't split up, no matter what happens."

Olivia sighed. She'd been trying to get her message across and it clearly was not working. Get an education. That's what the whole thing came down to. That's exactly what her family had been saying to her and to tell any young man out there interested in her and her sisters that he would have to appreciate that whole attitude and mindset.

"They wish you were better educated."

"Why? How would it change things? I can read, I can write. I know I'm not some a-hole. I treat you right, don't I?"

"The foul language has got to go, Rudy."

"Why would I want to go to some college and waste four years of my life studying subjects I don't give a damn about when I could be making good money here? Saving up money to open up a business of our own. It doesn't make sense to me."

"Maybe you're right. Only I just wish, just once, you didn't have to be so stubborn about understanding and possibly seeing things from someone else's point of view."

"*Yeah? Someone else is going to tell me what's right for Rudy Perez? Your parents know what's better for me than me? How do they figure that?*"

"I give up. I have to go."

"When will I see you again?"

"I'm not sure, Rudy. Week, maybe two—"

"Come on. Don't be like that. Please?"

"Stop by the diner—"

"Not like that. When can I *see* you?"

"I never know that far in advance what my days off are going to be. It's up to Slim and Bertha. I work when they need me; take off when they don't—"

"Just give me two minutes. Let me find out what he wants." Rudy kissed her and walked outside to the Caddy.

# CHAPTER 136

**"Good looking woman. Filipino?"**

"We're engaged to be married."

Rudy really did not want to look at those damned weird eyes any longer than he had to. Eye contact was there, but it was brief when it happened.

"She ain't Filipino."

"I know about marriage. Filipino nurse married me a while back so she could stay on in the country. When she found it convenient to do so, she filed a civil suit claiming mental anguish. Right out of the blue. *Mental anguish.* A perfectly good marriage was discarded for no real reason."

Rudy nodded his head. Had no idea what the guy was talking about, nor was he interested in the man's personal life.

He popped the *Cadillac* hood and was looking at the engine and wanting to get this conversation over with as quickly as possible. Biggs's overwhelming body odor did not make things any easier, either.

Rudy glanced back toward the open living room window. His girl was on her feet, brushing her hair out. He just wanted to get back in there and try to smooth some feathers he had undoubtedly ruffled.

"Sorry to hear it. My girl was born in the States, so were her parents. She's American."

"I wonder why she looks Filipino to me. . . ."

Rudy wondered why the guy kept at it. You know she ain't Filipino. Why you got to keep asking?

"What's wrong with the car?"

"Needs a tune-up. Oil change. Fan belt is starting to show wear-and-tear."

Rudy bent his head in. Looked down at the fan belt again. Not really in need of replacement. The fan belt was okay.

Well, he thought to himself, if the guy wants a tune-up, the oil changed, and a new fan belt, do it then. Do what the man wants. It's his money. That's what you're in business for.

Rudy withdrew the dipstick. Oil was, in fact, dirty.

"You must do a hell of a lot of driving."

"I get around."

"I'll have it ready for you tomorrow. I won't be able to get to it today."

"Can you wash it instead?"

"Instead? You mean in addition to the tune-up?"

"No. Give it a wash and wax. I'll take it to the dealership for the rest." And he walked away.

"Yessir." A dismayed Rudy Perez asked about the keys. Saw Biggs stop. Turned to look at him.

"What do you need the keys for?"

"Interior. Don't you want the interior vacuumed? Can't clean the inside without the key."

"Interior's clean enough." Biggs walked on. Suddenly did an about-face. Returned to his car. Unlocked the door on the driver's side, and got in. "When I stop by to pick up the VCR. You can wash it then." He closed the door and drove off.

Rudy stood there a moment, his eyes on the *Cadillac* as it disappeared down the block. Forget trying to add it up about *Brother Trusty*, quit trying to figure that guy out—because it will get you nowhere.

He knew one thing, knew it for a fact: Dude gave him the *heebie-jeebies*. That was about all the arithmetic he got out of it.

# CHAPTER 137

**Rudy walked back.** Re-entered through the kitchen door. Olivia was through with her hair. Dropped the brush in her purse and snapped it shut.

"Could be you're right about Biggs. Christ, he smells."

"I noticed it *even from here*."

"Anyway, I don't want to talk about him." He had other things on his mind: Like wanting to wrap his arms around her waist—and it did not take. Olivia did not like it and would not allow it. Not now. There had been too much left unresolved.

"So where were we?"

Olivia pursed her lips. "My family is concerned, that's all."

"I appreciate that. Only do me a favor? I could do with a little less. Okay? No offense—but less concern, and a little more affection would be nice. If you might just get that message across to your wonderful people."

Two of Olivia's sisters appeared at the open door: Yolanda, who was the oldest of the girls, and Carla, who was four years Olivia's junior.

"What is this? Neighborhood *7-Eleven*? Nobody believes in knocking anymore. Whatever happened to that famous Duarte upbringing I've heard so much about? I'm shocked, actually." Rudy Perez may have been kidding, but he meant a good deal of it.

"Livia, Dad wants you at the dinner table." Yolanda's sultry, dark eyes were all business. Carla, the youngest of the Duarte girls, would one day grow up to be equally as exotic-looking as Yolanda and Olivia.

"Give us five minutes—"

*"Dad says right now, Liv."*

Rudy pulled on his beer. Chuckled.

"Say hi to 'Dad' for me, Yolanda, when you see him. Tell him the Perez Family appreciates his concern—"

Olivia wanted to keep him from going any further in that tone.

"Rudy, don't—"

"She spies on you, and we're supposed to just take it?"

"Stay out of this, Rudy."

Yolanda stepped away from the door. The other sisters followed suit. Rudy was not far behind them as they crossed the street to their station wagon. He was not about to relent. To hell with it. It annoyed him that Yolanda would have the nerve to behave in this manner. It's to be expected, Rudy. That's right. She'd treated Roe the same way. You saw the way she dumped on him and walked away, didn't you? The way the whole Duarte family had ganged up on his brother.

They were doing it to *him* now, and they were putting pressure on Olivia, pulling her strings just like a marionette. Who the hell were *they* to tell him how to live his life? What the hell was the matter with being a car mechanic? That had been his dad's whole life before he'd died. *Cars*. He'd worked on cars and supported his family that way. His mother had been happy with that. Had seen no problem at all. Grandpa had had his own garage down in TJ, raised his family on the money he made. What the hell was the matter with everybody in this crazy town?

Olivia's parents were a couple of high school teachers—so what was so great about that? Teachers didn't make great money. Mechanics made more money than teachers—at least the good mechanics did. A good mechanic made decent money. *Damned right.*

"What are you going to do? Talk behind my back?" He slipped into an effeminate-sounding voice, wringing his hands and shaking his head in mock hopelessness. "That Rudy Perez ain't nothing but a high school dropout. He just ain't good enough."

"It's a fact, isn't it? *You are a dropout—and quite possibly illiterate.*"

Rudy dropped the falsetto. He was through kidding around with this bitch.

"Illiterate? I got As and Bs in school. You call that *illiterate*? Ever heard of Dostoevsky? Read 'em. Charles Dickens? Read him. Henry Miller? Read 'em. Even Shakespeare. Read enough of him to know he ain't all that. Ever heard of Gabriel Garcia Márquez? You might have. *One Thousand Years of Solitude*? Read the whole damned thing in a week. Leslie Marmon Silko? Read her *Ceremony* and *The Turquoise Ledge* both. *Ooh. There.* Who's the *real dummy*? Guess what else? Nobody forced me to look these peeps up, either. Found them on my own just because I enjoy reading and I like to fill myself with knowledge. Period. Knowledge is education; education is information and how we behave and treat others, is it not? I talk the way I do sometimes to put people like you on—only you're the one not bright enough to get it. *Get it?* No, you *'ain't'* got it."

Yolanda's sisters had climbed in the station wagon. She got in herself and slammed the door shut. Made certain the window was all the way up.

Rudy stood in front of the grill and was not about to let her go anywhere until he'd had his say. There was a car parked in back of her and no way for Yolanda to pull out of the spot.

"Know what, Yolanda? I wasn't about to let you get to me. Only right now I don't really care what you think. Me and my brother worked hard to keep our grandparents out of the poor house. Had to bust our butts. That don't account for much with your family, does it? You can all go to hell. My brother had to quit college and go to work to keep the bank from taking the house. We're not asking for pity; we do all right. We get by. We got plans to open our own shop and that's what we're going to do, and if that isn't good enough for your family, that's just too bad. I got nothing *at all* against higher learning—only right now we need money. If later on I feel like taking some night classes to improve my education, that's my business and nobody is going to *force me.* Especially not you, Yolanda. *Tell that to your daddy.*"

Yolanda sat shaking her head and could not believe that Olivia would want to be involved with somebody like this. Olivia was concerned, too, now that it would all get back to their parents. It would do nothing but create more tension at home, more pressure to stop seeing Rudy Perez.

Monroe pulled up in his beat-up pickup truck. Swung it into his family's driveway and got out with a six-pack that he carried in a paper sack.

He crossed the street to the station wagon. Tugged Rudy away from the front of it, not that he had to apply any real force; gentle persuasion did the trick. Rudy had been prepared to relent on his own at this point anyway.

"Take it easy, will you, kid?" All the while Roe did his best not to look in Yolanda's direction. He was not going to look at her. It hurt enough just being so close. Could not stop himself entirely from merely stealing a glance, nothing more than a glance. All it did was bring back the pain. So damned fast, too. Just a quick look. That one look.

How long has it been now? Close to three years? Close to three years later and she still did that to him by showing her face.

Yolanda's response was a hard glare. She started the engine and stepped on the accelerator. Tires squealed and the station wagon took off down the street. Roe's eyes stayed on her. Watched as the station wagon turned a corner at the end of the block, and she was gone.

"Why does she have to come around here? Why? Why can't she stay away?" Roe was looking at his brother. "I don't go by their place, do I? I'm the guy who was told to stay away. '*Keep away from our daughter.*' And I have been. Only *she* keeps finding excuses to come around here.

Goddamned women. They know it's these little things, man, that get you, that tear your insides up."

# CHAPTER 138

**He walked Rudy back to the house.** They entered through the side entrance, stepping into the kitchen. Sat at the table.

"I do okay. That's a fact, Rudy. I do just fine—as long as my eyes don't see that woman, long as I don't get to look at that beautiful face with a heart of cement." Roe came close to cursing. Wouldn't do it around the house. Out of respect for the grandparents. Rudy was the same. Never claimed to be perfect, either. You respected your elders and people you loved. "That's what a woman like that has—heart of stone. Cement, man. A rock."

He reached inside the paper sack for a beer and placed it in front of his brother. Dug back in for a can for himself. Cracked the top. Had a pull.

"You think I'm stupid?"

"No way. She say you're illiterate? That's one of her favorites. If you don't have a university degree you're a bozo with room temperature IQ. She was always correcting my grammar. Screw 'em. I talk the way I talk because the guys at the shop talk this way. If I threw fifty dollar words at them I'd be accused of being a blowhard and a pompous jerk—and they'd be right. Guys who are sticklers when it comes to grammar are usually sissies, anyway. Can't get it up. Bookworms. Dorks. Well, not all. Usually. Present company excluded. She'll find out. You're not stupid, Rudy. Fact is, you're pretty smart. You're a mechanic. Well, you know about as much as a certified mechanic. Come pretty close. That takes intelligence. Don't let anyone tell you different."

Rudy cracked the ring on his beer. Took a pull.

"Ever have regrets you dropped out of college, Roe?"

Monroe got up to grab a bag of spicy hot chips from the cupboard, and sat back down. He tore the top off.

"No. Why should I? Besides, had no choice. I like working with my hands, getting into the grease and dirt. Some folks are put off by it, repulsed. Not me. Not Dad, either. Rest his soul. I like working for a living, as opposed to having to wear a prissy, starched white shirt and a tie to some office job and dealing with office politics and backstabbers."

He held the bag of chips out for his brother to take a few. Stuck a chip in his own mouth. Swallowed beer.

"Look, you're going back for your GED eventually. That's a given. That you want to do. I'm not pushing; I know how stubborn you can be. Just telling you. As far as college: Up to you. Try it. If you want. Find out for yourself. *Because you want to*—and not because some chick is after you to do it in order to bring the big paycheck home so she can have more *pesos* to squander. Government's no different: the more they tax, the more they spend. Always going broke, always crying for more."

Rudy cracked a smile. Roe was glad he was at least able to do that.

"Think I'm kidding? The way it is. The more you bring in, the more they spend." He shook his head. Irritated by all of it. Life in SoCal. "People like the Duartes always have to make it look like you're nothing if you're *blue collar*. It's *BS*. Be proud of your blue collar roots, I always say. Like Dad. May he rest in peace. Where would we all be without someone to repair cars, build houses, fix the plumbing, pave driveways, trim trees, stock supermarket shelves, deliver bread to delis, operate street sweepers, repair traffic lights and fill pot holes?" He ate a chip. Pulled from his can. "The other thing is: Your biggest thieves have always been white collar S.O.Bs. Remember that. It's cliche. Well worth repeating. We forget too often. The most destructive lowlifes, ones who hurt all of us more than any other type of criminal—have always been *white collar weasels*."

Rudy nodded his head. Knew his brother was telling it like it is. Gave him the truth. Still. There was the ache in his heart to be dealt with.

"I can't help it. I love her, Roe—even though she's trying to walk all over me."

"They will do it every time—if you let them."

"I get sick and tired of her and her family trying to change me. What are we supposed to do? Let Grandma and Grandpa stay in some roach-infested rest home after everything they've done for us? Why can't they understand?"

"Don't worry about it. That's exactly why things didn't work out between Landa and me. Too much pressure. Always pushing. Her folks were always saying she should be marrying a *professional man,* white collar type: doctor, lawyer; 'somebody important.' Hell, doctors and lawyers are some of the most corrupt people out there. Six, seven hundred dollars just to have your teeth cleaned. Step into a dental office to have your teeth cleaned, just to have them cleaned. I guarantee you you won't be in that chair two minutes before he tries to convince you to have thousands of dollars worth of dental work done. Corruption. That's what I'm talking about. *White collar crime.* Crooked politicians and doctors who are nothing more than butchers in disguise. Doing open-heart surgery on people who don't even need it. That is the God's truth. Lookit that poor SOB Harold Crust. They stuck a pacemaker in him even though he didn't need one. Had a great insurance policy at the time, so they talked him into it and cut him open."

"Are you serious about Mr. Crust?"

"Hell, yes. Think I'm saying all this just to hear myself talk? Some coked-up Beverly Hills quack not only conned him to have the open-heart surgery, but later on managed to convince him he needed a pacemaker on top. I found out the other day. Mr. Crust tries to keep it under wraps. Too embarrassed to admit he was hoodwinked. Wasn't his fault. Who can blame him? He's not the only one it was done to. Happens all the time."

"Why didn't he get a second opinion? Dad always said to get a second opinion."

Roe had another pull of beer. Ran the back of his hand back and forth across his mouth. "He did get a *second opinion.* After the butcher cut him open. Poor guy thought he was on his last gasp and had no choice. Found out later that this doctor he trusted had left him on the operating table in the middle of surgery to make a run to his bank across the street to cash a check, then zips on over to his dealer's on Burton Way to *score blow. Far-fetched?* Don't think it happens? *It happens. "*

"During surgery?"

*"What I'm saying. "*

"How can they?"

"Had abdominal pains long after the surgery was over and done with. Didn't figure. Harold did some nosing around, probing; asked questions. Found out the same quack had vomited on another patient."

"You're making me sick."

"Wait a minute. They told him to go away. It was all in his head. Mr. Crust got himself legal help. Forced the hospital to X-ray his chest. Guess what they discovered in there?"

"Wristwatch?"

"Not even close. *Dentures.*"

"That's really disgusting."

"It's more than that: It's *unconscionable.* Quack was so high he wasn't even aware that his teeth were missing, until he got home that evening and his wife pointed it out to him."

"His wife did?"

"Was a druggie herself. User."

"Same doctor who operated on Harold?"

"One and the same. Looked into his history. He'd been leaving things like gauze and tweezers, towels, guide wires in patients' necks, pelvises, abdomens."

"What kind of doctor does that? I hope he got busted."

"Oh, he's through. Finished. Harold has a lawsuit going against the hospital. *White Collar Crime.* Bad Apples. Don't misunderstand: Not saying all doctors are like that, just like not all car repair shops are on the up-and-up. Some are downright sleazy, cutthroat. Got rotten apples in every field. But generally speaking: White collar law-breakers get away with a lot more than anyone else. Haven't even touched on arms dealers and pharmaceutical corporations—and don't want to go there. *White collar.* You try and explain that to the Duartes. They don't want to hear it.

What they want is someone with *'class'* for their perfect girls. The white collar and the three-piece suit. *'Breeding.'* Whatever that means. I have a three-piece suit somewhere around here. Only wear it when I have to. I don't mind dressing up when the occasion calls for it. But to wear a suit and tie as some kind of disguise to get over, like so many of them out there? Forget it. Not interested. They aren't fooling me."

"I never stepped out on that girl, Roe. Not once in the time I've known her. I hardly even flirt with other chicks I see out there. I treat her right. Always treat her right."

"I know that. You don't have to convince me. I wouldn't blame Livia so much. It's her family, friends, putting ideas in her head. People are like that. Always jealous when you got a good thing going and they don't."

"You're probably right. Only I can't take much more. I don't deserve it."

"Hey, you're damned right you don't deserve it."

Roe drained his can. Cracked open another. Took a long pull. "My advice is *bail* while you're still in one piece." He looked at his brother. Rudy wasn't saying anything at the moment. On the verge of tears more than likely.

*"Easier said than done."* Roe thought he ought to say something uplifting at this point. Hated to see Rudy suffer this way. "Who knows? She might even come around when she finally realizes that my kid brother is just too good to pass up."

"You think it's possible?"

"With women you never know. Anything is possible. She might say to hell with what her family wants and decide for herself. *Never know.* You have to cheer up."

Rudy nodded his head. Felt that the older sibling was right about quite a bit of it. He walked to his room in the back to get the thing he'd been working on for close to a week now. It was only a cardboard sign presently and he'd used crayons and magic marker, but it would give Monroe a pretty good idea what the finished, professionally made sign would finally look like—if he liked it.

Rudy reappeared with it in the living room and held it in such a way so that Roe could not see what the words were. Flipped it, revealing the front that read:

## GIL PEREZ & SONS
## AUTO REPAIR & BODY WORK

The younger brother couldn't help it, and glanced at the mantle above the fireplace and the framed photos that lined it. Some of the photos were of their parents taken years before at their wedding, others were of aunts and uncles, cousins; others still of their dad, former marine, looking sharp and handsome in his Dress Blues. Next to this one was a picture of Roe: Like their dad, in his Marine uniform.

There were a couple of snapshots of their dad in Vietnam standing beside a Jeep he had been working on in the company motor pool, another of their father and his unit, along with the commanding officer, standing outside the barracks.

"Dad's name's gotta be part of the sign."

Monroe slapped his hands together.

"You're definitely on the right track now, Bro. Exactly what I'm talking about. We can't lose sight of our dream—*and the Duarte sisters are not getting in our way.*"

The grandparents stirred in their rocking chairs. Grandfather Neto had his handkerchief out and blew his nose.

"What do you think, Grandpa? *Gil Perez & Sons.*"

The silver-haired old guy looked at the sign for a moment. Clearly moved by the gesture. He approved with a wink.

"*Bueno*, Rudy. *Bueno.*"

"We're on our way. Just a while longer—you'll see—before we start raking in the bucks."

"Nobody is stopping us, Rudy. Remember that. *Nobody.*"

# CHAPTER 139

**Diner facade was a *faux* railroad coach and faced a vast parking lot with scores of shops and a variety of businesses on either side.** To the left, on commercial real estate about the length of a city block, were a supermarket, video store, baby shop, florist, toy store, weight gym, et al. On the right: among others, music store, futon retailer, pet shop, hair salon, stationary store, insurance office, kosher market, and a tanning salon, where a tan was the last thing anyone who entered here was after. It was known to more than a few regulars of the diner: If you yearned to have your "manhood massaged" after consuming one of Jessup's famous omelettes, *Foxy's Health Spa & Tanning Salon* was the place to go—and that Mr. Vester Jessup, although silent about it, owned controlling interest.

Sun was setting. Deacon Marvin R. Muck and Bishop Cecil O. Biggs were sitting in the latter's *Cadillac* that idled in the lot where the duo had a good, clear view of the eatery's front entrance and could see Rudy Perez sitting at the counter trying to make time with the Duarte bitch.

Let him, thought Biggs. He won't get anywhere. Too soft. Feckless. There was a bright red neon sign in the window to the right of the door that was meant to remind one and all that it was ***TIME TO EAT!***

Cecil's mind was not on food or eating, but the narrow street to the left of the railroad car—on the other side of which were located all those other shops. It was that street that ran through there for about two hundred or so feet to the main drag that was a concern, should he ever be tempted to snatch Olivia Duarte right there in the diner. You also had the added problem: the very same street crossed the alley in back of the diner and ran the entire length of the mall on the left, as well as on the right, where it ended at a relatively busy boulevard.

Say he pulled the van up to the loading dock of the greasy spoon, the dread was that a vehicle of some sort, delivery, whatnot, might drive through just as he and Marvin were in the process of doing some loading of their own.

How did one get around an obstacle like that? If you tried it at night you risked being nailed by a patrol car or roving security, if done during the day . . . you had garbage pickups or delivery trucks driving up and down the alley routinely.

What was the answer? Was there a solution? Grabbing a bitch and carrying her out through the front was clearly out of the question. . . .

What were you left with, wondered Biggs. Late evening/early evening? Slaughter Slim, and whoever else got in the way: Tuco, the cook, Bertha, whoever. Didn't matter. So long as you got your hands on the Duarte cunt. Carry her out in a laundry bag. There was risk involved. There always would be. Nothing was risk-free. That added to it, too. Added to the thrill.

The greater the risk, the more intense the rush. Would it ever be worth it? So long as you got away with it. Pearleen and her slutty friends were supposed to be in there convincing Olivia Duarte to take a ride with them over to his place. He'd promised them a good time, enough crack to smoke. On the other hand, what if they failed? And even if they didn't, he wouldn't be able to keep her indefinitely. What was left? What was the alternative? How many times have you asked yourself that already?

The glowing, yellow block letters on the roof declared:

## VESTER JESSUP'S FAMILY DINER

"How they gonna get that Duarte gash to go wiff them?" Marvin played with an unlit cigarette between his fingertips. He held a book of matches in his left hand. Lacked the nerve to fire up. Suspected Cecil would throw a fit if he so much as attempted it.

"That's their problem. They'll figure out a way if they want the dope."

"An' they gonna get her to take her panties off once they get her to the cribby?"

Biggs's response was a sigh. Hardly audible.

"Man, your attitude is all wrong. Let's take it one step at a time, one step at a time."

Alley rats Ace and Felix rolled up in their bucket, a rattling pile of junk on four wheels missing hub caps.

Bishop shifted into "D," and guided the *Cadillac* out of there.

# CHAPTER 140

**Olivia Duarte did such a fine job of ignoring Rudy Perez, who sat at the counter, that he may as well have been the Invisible Man.** He followed her with his eyes, wanting to make amends for that scene the other day in his family's living room and could not get to first base. What had made it doubly impossible to get anywhere were those loud-mouthed, interfering strippers. It was bad enough to have to swallow your pride and eat crow, but no man worth his salt could lower himself and expose his soft side when others were watching and taking pleasure in it. Well, thank God for small favors, because right now, for the time being, the three: Stella Martel, Lana Sepulveda, and Pearleen Bell were in the women's john—probably bangin' rails—and he did his best to form words in his head before getting them out, wanting to say the right thing the right way before the busybodies stepped out to hear everything and made it downright impossible.

Olivia kept finding things to do, hardly giving him a glance. *Invisible Man* was right. Meanwhile, those loudmouthed chicks were in the bathroom and would be out soon enough and he could forget about patching it up with Olivia with them around and listening to all that was said.

It left him frustrated. Ate him up inside. Why did love have to hurt so much? There had been girls in the past, girls who'd been way more interested in him than he had been in them; and if they had felt like carrying on and threatened to walk, he always shrugged, said: Go ahead. It's a free country. Do what you want. You go your way, I'll go mine. No strings, no problems.

Only this was way different here; this mattered, went deep—and because it mattered it took all his power away; wouldn't let him be himself. Left him frustrated, antsy—and sometimes that frustration turned to anger. Only you best not show anger here. Anger ain't gonna get it this time, won't work. Anger will only work against you. Got to be patient, cool and patient. Girl has a right to be herself, to have her own identity.

How many minutes did he have left to put the right words together before the chattering witches stepped out of the restroom?

He hated being stressed out this way. What it did to him. Caused him to get stressed. Felt a mild pain in his chest. Anxiety attack. Last thing of all he wanted.

# CHAPTER 141

**Inside the women's john, Stella Martel and Lana Sepulveda were agreeing what a bitch and a genuine pain-in-the-ass Olivia Duarte was because she had refused to take a ride with them in Cecil's *Cadillac* the week before, not to mention the other times they had invited her to visit the man's place with them and she had turned them down flat.**

*"Stuck up ho."*

"Don't make much sense, does it?" said Lana.

"You two shouldn't be so hard on her," Pearleen said.

"She's a *phony*," Stella said. "I know a *phony* when I see one. All she had to do was go with us so we could score some more of this great dope from the man. Nobody asked her to *suck his dick*."

"You did everything but ask her to do that," said Lana with a chuckle.

The approach used on Olivia this evening had been different. Simple. Easy. After Lana had apologized to the Duarte girl for having made all those cutting remarks in the past about her and the whole Duarte family being holier-than-thou, and after Pearleen had fervently explained: "I went to school with your sister Yolanda. We always got along. You know that. Ask her. You never heard me put you down. I never had anything against your family. Always wished my family was as close." She meant it. "What the girls wanted was to give you a ride home—that is, if you needed a ride. Since we're going your way anyway."

Olivia had told Pearleen Bell—in front of Rudy Perez—that if her sister showed up late that she would be glad to take them up on their offer. And this had given the strippers the assurance they had been looking for. If Olivia did not at least stop by Cecil's place, there probably would be no dope for them this time. Biggs had been after them for too long to bring Olivia with. Olivia wouldn't have to disrobe for him, she wouldn't have to have sex with him, or do anything really, other than show up, be there with them.

Lana had quickly got on the pay phone outside the bathroom door and dialed the Duarte home number, and in her best Big Bertha Lenier voice, or someone "in authority," told Olivia's brother Carlos at the other end that his sister would be getting off work a little later than usual this evening and to let Yolanda know. Yolanda was on the phone before she was able to get off and demanded to speak to Olivia.

"Can't get to the phone. She's working," Lana had told her, and hung up. The next call she made was to *Valley Cab*. And that had taken care of that.

Meanwhile, Pearleen had stayed at the front counter to explain to Olivia her life-long dream of hoping to make it in Vegas someday like Lola Falana and Ann-Margret had done, like Susan Anton and others, but before she could get anywhere near those fancy Las Vegas showrooms she would have to pay her dues by working venues like *McCoy's Casbah*

*Hideaway,* not to mention that costumes cost money (even when she designed and made most of them herself). She was saving up for it, trying very hard, and the only reason she even considered spending any time at all with Biggs was because he gave them all free toot.

"But I'm working on kicking. Not that I'm hooked or anything like that. It's just that I need it every once in a while for a quick pick-me-up. It really helps me deal with all those creepy men in the audience when I'm on stage. You don't know how difficult it is to have to take your clothes off like that with practically every part of your body exposed. There's times I'm so ashamed of myself I can't even look in the mirror."

"Like I told you and your friends, Pearleen, if my sister is not here by the time I'm ready to leave you can drop me off." And Olivia had walked away to tend to the remaining customers.

Rudy Perez had picked up on quite a bit of the conversation and hadn't liked any of it. Olivia had avoided his gaze whenever he made the effort to draw her attention, to say something, get a word out.

# CHAPTER 142

**The strippers remained in the ladies' room primping themselves for the "filthy rich" bishop and his "raggedy-looking" flunky.** They were applying lipstick and perfume; made sure their hair looked right and were all in agreement on one thing: the toot had been used up way too fast.

"Just how dumb can that girl be?" said Stella.

"Who cares?" said Lana. "All I know is if her sister don't show on time Olivia gets a ride with us—and that's all it takes to make Cecil happy. She rides with us and we get high at Pastor Stinky's *'cribby'*—"

"And drop her off like we promised," said Pearl.

"Yeah," shrugged Lana. *"After we're through doing up the man's dope."*

"Biggs sure got that odor to him," Stella said, while adjusting her bra.

She pushed her breasts together to deepen the cleavage, not that she needed to do anything of the sort.

"Tell me something I don't know, girlfriend," Lana quipped. "You ain't spending time with the man because you like his looks. That house he lives in smells way worse than the john in the *Kismet Room*. But I don't give a shit; at least you'll see me act like I don't give a shit."

"We *definitely* have to get them both in the shower before we do anything else with them," Stella said.

# CHAPTER 143

**Olivia was preparing to close up the diner.** She lowered the blinds, then yanked on a cord to flip the slats closed. She turned out the overhead lights.

Bertha was behind the counter doing her share. Rudy Perez continued with the overtures. Olivia was not making it easy for him.

The customers at the counter amounted to Ace Ortiz and his buddy Felix Monk; and sitting on Ace's left an older gent finishing up his burger and fries on a plate before him.

Ace and Felix sipped *Cokes*. While Ortiz worked on a mouthful of *Chuckles*, his partner ate a glazed doughnut.

Ortiz had one of his watches out, nestled in a white handkerchief that he kept polishing the gold band with.

He figured he had a potential mooch on his left, and there was another possible mark, American Indian type, on the far side of his homie Felix.

The white gent on Ace's left saw what was about to take place and thought he'd do a little preemptive number.

"If you're hungry, I'll buy you a burger. Only I ain't buying no piece of crap watch from you."

Ortiz nodded his head. Popped more *Chuckles* in his mouth.

"Can you spare a *square?*"

The man shook a butt out from a pack of *Marlboros* and held it out. Ortiz took it. Lit up.

"How about one for later?"

The man had stuck the pack back in his shirt pocket. Spoke without turning in Ortiz's direction. "You're out of bounds."

"I'd do the same for you."

"I believe you're out of line."

"How do you mean?"

Unbeknownst to Ortiz, Pearleen had walked up from behind, gripped a hunk of his hair in her left hand and spun him around. She got in his face, and sent her right fist into his nose. Continued to hold him up by the hair in order to keep him from toppling over in pain.

"Just a sample of what you got coming to you for damaging the bars on my bedroom window, *motherfucker*, and causing everybody problems in general."

"I'm not looking for trouble, Ms. Bell. Besides, you got me at a disadvantage at the moment."

"Don't I?"

"I was so out of it that night I had no idea what my homie Felix was gettin' us into."

*"Me?"* said Felix.

"You're an *asshole*, Ortiz." Pearleen's tone was low enough so others couldn't hear. "And so is your dorky friend over there." She had her face right up against the addict's. It was too close, actually—because his breath made her ill. "I won't miss next time. There's more where that came from. *Later.*"

She let him go, and returned to the ladies' room to wash her hands.

"And I'll be ready for you, bitch," said Ortiz to no one. "Lucky for you I'm in the middle of conducting business." He happened to glance at Felix who had a stupid smirk on his face. Ortiz flipped him the bird. "Right here, *pendejo.*"

"What's that for?"

Ortiz gestured for him to shut up. He didn't want to hear it—whatever it was. Pulled a handful of napkins from the dispenser. Wiped sweat from his brow. Monkey needed feeding and wouldn't take no for an answer. Had to do something about it. Didn't matter that a displeased Slim Jessup was probably monitoring everything through the fry cook's window from the kitchen, either. Wasn't sure of that. Too self-conscious to look in the direction to see if he was.

When he finally did glance over there, he was relieved that Slim had his eyes on Rudy Perez instead. Didn't seem to like that love-sick Romeo was bothering Livia, who should have been paying more attention to taking care of his customers.

Even Ortiz could hear what was going on. Perez couldn't get over that his 'honey Liv' might actually ride with the exotic dancers and felt a strong urge to voice his opinion on it.

"I can't believe that you're going with them."

"If my sister is late. *Yes, I will.* I've got a ride with Pearleen and her friends, Rudy. You heard right. If Yolanda is not here by the time I'm ready to leave."

"How can she be *'on time'* with the hours Slim keeps? *'Sunup to Sundown?'*"

"Take it up with Mr. Jessup."

"I thought you had better sense than to hang with that crowd?"

The remark stopped Olivia cold in her tracks.

"I get it from Bertha, I get it from my boss, my nosy sisters and my brother; I get it from my parents. Now *you're* going to tell me what to do?"

"All right. I'm sorry."

"I am tired of being treated this way."

"I know that, Olivia, and I apologize. Only my brother was right about Lana and them: They're a bunch of losers. I can't help it. The way I feel. They are tramps, cokeheads, strippers—"

"They have to make a living just like everybody else, Rudy. They do the best they can. You don't know anything about them, so stop judging."

"I know enough. Everybody knows about them."

"People do the best they can. It's real easy to judge."

"Tell me about it."

She knew what he meant, only would not give him the satisfaction. Instead, what Olivia made sure he saw was a look of sheer exasperation.

"What sense does it make for Stella to change her hair color every week?"

"Meaning what? Why should that bother you? Better yet, why should it bother anyone what a woman does with her hair and general appearance?"

"She's unstable. They're all like that. *Mixed up*. Against family and marriage. All they ever think about is getting high. It's a wonder their noses haven't dropped off from all the blow they do."

"At least they don't stick them where they don't belong."

"People die from blow. How can you expect me to say anything good about that?" He glanced in Ace Ortiz and Felix Monk's direction. "Nobody's forcing them to do it, either. They do it because they're irresponsible, and because all they care about is having a good time. *Yeah, baby; where's the next party? Pass the tooter. Gimme the spike.*"

"If you're bothered, why keep coming around? Nobody's forcing you to keep coming around, are they?"

"You said it: Nobody's forcing me. Could be my brother's right: All I'm doing is making a fool of myself." He shook his head. "Funny, I didn't think you were like Yolanda. Didn't think it; refused to believe you were a heart-breaker. My brother paid, though, didn't he? Fell for the wrong girl. And now it's my turn to pay for making the same dumb move."

Olivia flashed him a second helping of that expression that said she clearly had had enough, and walked away to grab a plate at the other end of the counter.

"Sure. Picking up someone's dirty plate is more important than keeping a relationship from falling apart."

# CHAPTER 144

As far as Ace Ortiz was concerned, Rudy Perez's matters of the heart
was soap opera drivel. He had a *suckah* on the line. That's what it was
about. Bait worked. All he had to do was reel him in. He'd done it before.
Lots of times. So long as you don't hit the geezer up for anymore butts.

"Watch ain't cheap." Ortiz spoke out of the side of his mouth. Buffed
the watch with that white handkerchief that had the timepiece gleaming;
like gold. "I don't deal in inferior goods, my brother—and it ain't about
grub. I got mine." Ortiz held up the *Chuckles*. Pointed to the *Snickers* in
his shirt pocket. "Food is overrated." He bit off a couple of *Chuckles*
squares. Did what he could to chew with what teeth he had left. He sipped
from his giant cup of *Coke* through a straw. Ortiz looked around
nervously, surveying the diner. Slim appeared busy back there inside the
kitchen, at least he hoped so. Although you never knew with Jessup. Never
missed a thing with them sharp peepers. Had warned him before not to be
peddling goods in his diner. That was a while back. So long as he was cool
about it, thought Ortiz, what did it hurt?

"What do you say, *amigo*? All I'm asking is twenty-five bucks for a
watch that's worth at least a hundred."

The old man ignored him. Rose to pay his check. Ortiz cursed under
his breath. Sweat poured down his face. All he needed was a couple of
balloons to set him straight: one of *chiva*, one of *blow*. He'd be all right for
a while. Felt the sickness within, churning his guts up inside of him. There
was Ex in the car. Not much. Some. What else? Not much of anything
else. Maybe a can of warm beer underneath all that shit somewhere that
Felix liked to collect. Had to unload the fucking watch. Should ask for
twenty. He'd be able to buy a *balloon* at least. Get the other on credit.

Told Felix to clear the stool and sit on the other side of him, so he could
*"bond"* with the Native American who sat on Felix's right.

"Lookee-here." Ace Ortiz resorted to a hushed tone this time. Held the
watch out in a discreet manner. "Hundred dollar timepiece that I'm letting
go for twenty. *Two sawbucks*. Can use the bread to buy my woman a gift.

Just had twins. How about it, chief?"

The Native American looked at him with a look of pure disdain. Called out the diner owner's name.

"No offense, Mr. Jessup, but I don't come here to be harassed by some hype hard-up for a fix. I come for coffee and pie. That's it. I like to eat my pie in peace."

He threw some bills on the counter, and walked out.


Slim Jessup made it over. Grabbed Ortiz by the scruff and guided him out the front entrance; with a convincing enough shove at the end that helped the junkie along.

"Stay out, or I drop a dime on your funky ass."

"What I do wrong?" Ortiz was practically in Jessup's face. "It ain't like I was eatin' what somebody left on their plate, man—like some peeps do. I paid for my *Coke.* I'm a paying customer. You ain't right."

"I warned you about *soliciting* in my place of business. This is a family diner, not a junky hangout. You and your scruffy pal do not peddle stolen merchandise in my place, hear?"

Ortiz's immediate reaction was to spit in the man's face. Slim Jessup hauled off and cold-cocked the junkie and walked back inside, wiping his face with the back of his sleeve.

He gestured to Felix to get out and join his pal outside. As Monk walked past, the owner took the opportunity to kick him in the rear hard enough to send him hurling through the door and sprawling on his belly.

Slim Jessup looked at his hands: some of the soft drink had got on them and his clothes. He wiped a piece of the *Chuckles* candy from his shirt collar. There was a bit, particle, something, stuck to his hand. It was not until he took a closer look did he realize that it was a tooth. One of Glassy's. Had to be. Left Jessup thoroughly disgusted.

He returned to the kitchen to clean himself off.

# CHAPTER 145

**Rudy Perez, still at the counter, hadn't given up on reaching Olivia—only it was not easy to talk to someone when they had their back turned to you most of the time.**

"Had it coming to them." Rudy tossed it out there—and got no reaction from her. He tried again. "I can understand you being angry with me because of what I said to Landa, and I apologize for it. But I don't get why you're sticking up for the cokeheads."

"Get off my case, Rudy. All I'm doing is getting a ride home."

"Why can't you go with me? I can call us a cab, or my brother can pick us up. I came here to apologize—"

She spun to face him. "You're rushing me; you're pushing. I can't be engaged. We never discussed it. You decide what's right for us and then tell me about it and expect me to like it. That's not what being with someone is all about."

"I didn't mean for it to look that way. Just trying to do the right thing, that's all."

"I can't be *rushed*, Rudy. I don't need the pressure."

"What are you saying?"

"If you want to know the truth, *I just don't feel like being with you right now*."

And she resumed cleaning the counter. Pearleen Bell and her friends emerged from the ladies' room. They looked great, every single one of them: beautiful, sexy. They should be in a Hollywood movie, Rudy thought—and hated them all just then, because deep down he knew what they really were. Maybe Olivia had been right about Pearleen not being as bad as the others, but they used drugs; they were, in fact, tramps. There was no other word for them, and now they were trying real hard to get their filthy rotten hooks in his girlfriend.

*Buncha dirty sluts*, Rudy thought. That's what his look said.

Lana shook her head. Made a tsk tsk sound.

"Poor baby. Having another spat with your girlfriend?"

"Matter of fact, you're right."

"Welcome to the club."

# CHAPTER 146

**Olivia looked up from where she was to see that the sun had set and there was no Yolanda.** Her sister knew diner hours were sunup to sunset.

She bid good night to Slim and Bertha, clocked out, and walked outside with Pearleen Bell and friends.

"I just want a ride home. I can't go anywhere else with you."

Lana said: "Gonna be a *goody-two-shoes* all your life, Olivia?"

Rudy took it in. Watched as they stood out there in front of the diner waiting for their taxi. It ate him up. There was nothing he could do about it but take it.

Slim walked up. On the other side of the counter, doing something. When he spoke, the words jarred him out of his world of pain, although not for long.

"My man Rudy Perez. The fine ones are always like that: Bustin' your chops. More trouble than they're worth. Get yourself an older woman, one that ain't as good lookin', who won't be playing them kind of games with you. Older woman knows how to treat a man. Easier to please, too."

"I don't want no older woman. Because I got the one I want: That's the one I love and want to marry." On that, Rudy walked out himself.

# CHAPTER 147

**A geezer in worn clothing approached Ace Ortiz for a handout in the parking lot.**

"Spare some change, Mister Ace? I ain't had a beer or nothin' in I don't know how long."

"What's your name, old timer?" Ace asked him, between pulls from a can of cheap beer.

"Henry Apsche."

"*Harry Apeshit?* Hell kind of name is that?"

"No, no; not ape shit, sir. Apsche."

"Lookee-here, brother. I'll give it to you plain and straight: My asshole bleeds for you, *Mr. Harry Apeshit*. Write it down. *On a piece of paper. Keep it in your pocket.* So you can remember not to fuck with me in the future." Then the parolee hurried on over to Rudy Perez with the intention of selling him a piece of jewelry, possibly something for his girl who was giving him so much grief. He guzzled the remaining brew, then tossed the can aside.

Rudy didn't wish to be bothered. His eyes remained focused on Olivia as she got in the cab with the others. Ace Ortiz stayed with him, insisting he should at least take a look at the ring he held in his hand.

"Guaranteed to bring her back, Rudy. Lookee-here—" He yanked on Rudy's sleeve. Rudy spun in his direction and sent a hard fist into Ace Ortiz's jaw. Ortiz staggered back, a mite stunned, and landed on his backside and dropped the ring in the process. That's three times he'd been punched in fairly quick succession, in a relatively short period of time. He'd had enough. Cursing, the former con rose to his feet, drawing a switchblade.

"*Ace,*" his buddy Felix called out, collecting the empty beer can. "*No, man.*"

"Stay out of this, Felix," said Ortiz, his unwavering gaze fixed on Rudy Perez. "I'm gonna step on you, suckah." Ace promised, making circular motions with the switchblade in his hand, all the while taking slow, cautious steps toward an equally angry Rudy Perez who would not be frightened off.

"*Step on you real good.* Shoulda done this to that nigger bitch inside the diner for ambushin' my ass when I wasn't even lookin'. Sambo Slim was watchin', and I couldn't. Now, we ain't inside, are we, motherfucker? Want to try that again?" He spit on the ground, making it a point to look his opponent in the eye while doing so. The ex-con tossed the knife in the air, above his own head, then swiftly snatched it by the hilt as it dropped back down, so that the blade pointed downward, thus giving him the added advantage of being able to use both fists to punch with, as well as the ability of slashing with the fist that held the switchblade.

"*Gonna stick you just like I done to that darkie punk in the slam. Teach you some respect. Done my time. Paid a lifetime of dues to let a bitch like you get away with it. Gonna slice-and-dice your sorry ass real good, suckah.*"

"People want to be left alone, Ace. Only you're too stupid to get it—"

"*Still gonna cut you, bitch—*"

"That's all you know, isn't it, Ortiz? Cut 'em up and rip 'em off. Mug them, beat them, scam them. It's easier than having to work for your money. The original short-cut man."

"You heard."

Right then both had little choice but to jump back, out of the way, to make room for Rudy's brother Monroe, as he sped onto the lot in his pickup truck and brought it to a skidding halt between them. Monroe hopped out with a ball bat. Glared at Ortiz who glared back.

"This ain't none of your business."

"I'm making it my business, Ace."

"You're a tough guy with that *lumber* in your hands, Roe."

"About as tough as you with that steel going up against someone who would never stoop so low as to even think about carrying something like that."

"I need it to protect myself from assholes like you."

As Roe was about to respond, thinking: This is dumb and there is no point to it, the panhandler staggered over toward Ace Ortiz, holding up the ring the ex-con had dropped a moment ago.

"Here you are, Mister Ace. I believe this is yours."

Ortiz pocketed the ring. Walked away.

"Just a quarter, Mister Ace? If you could spare a quarter? Somebody? I'm dry."

The junkie spit on the ground. Reached inside the Toyota for a beer. Pulled on it. Monroe walked to the other side of his truck where his younger brother stood and was now leaning against it, watching as the cab with his girl and those skanks in it pulled out of the lot finally.

"It's a losing battle, kid. A lot of pain. Let the heartbreaker do what she wants. Let her go."

"What am I supposed to do? *Give up like you did?* You just gave up on Yolanda. You didn't even make any real effort to stay with her."

"Yeah? *You're wrong, Rudy.* Nothing is worth a lifetime of hassle and bullshit from in-laws who never wanted you to marry their *'precious'* daughter to begin with."

"Maybe it's not for them to say, maybe Olivia and me's got something to say about it."

"If you think she's going to go against her family, you're more naive than I figured—"

"Why don't you stop playing the *big brother*, Monroe, and start minding your own business."

"I care about you, all right? That's what brothers are supposed to do." Monroe had his arm round Rudy's shoulder in a consoling way, hating to see his younger brother's eyes well. "Hey, come on. Let's go home. We'll get a couple of six-packs."

"*Get drunk.* That's the *answer* to everything, huh, Roe? Dad never drank, Grandpa never drank. How come you gotta be a *boozer?*"

And Rudy tore away from his brother and walked on out of the parking lot by himself.

Monroe remained behind, stood there like that, fully aware what his brother was going through, wished there was something he could do or say—and the truth of it was, no matter what anybody said to you at a time like this, it just didn't matter, didn't help, when all you wanted and needed was to be with your girl.

It was also true he never drank until Yolanda dumped him. Beer helped him forget. It didn't always work, but somehow managed to make it easier to deal with the pain of losing the woman you had given your heart to.

He turned and noticed Ace and his sidekick leaning against their multi-colored wreck pulling on generic beers and smirking about something in a self-satisfied way. Coupla real "tough guys."

Losers. Two complete washouts with nothing for a future. Monroe got in his pickup truck, and pulled up beside them.

*"You congenital assholes so much as touch my brother . . . Swear to God, I'll bust you up."*

He glared at them a moment. "Now, you can *chuckle* all you want, about anything you want—but that's a guarantee you can take to the bank."

He drove off the lot.

# CHAPTER 148

**Taxi driver was partial to Oldies.** Something called "96 Tears" by *Question Mark & the Mysterians* blasted the interior of his cab.

There was plenty of chatter and laughs, and the girls did their best to alleviate the Duarte girl's nervousness and apprehension. Pearleen sat in the front with the driver. Lana and Stella sat on either side of Olivia in the back.

"I just want to get home. I can't go anywhere else with you."

Stella Martel shot Olivia a look that was less-than-friendly.

"That Miss Goody-Two-Shoes act gets old fast, kid."

"Wet blanket," Lana said. "I told you, didn't I?"

"Drop it, you guys," said Pearleen Bell.

Stella lit a joint. Toked. Passed it on to Lana.

Stella said: "Still a virgin, ain't you, Olivia?" Then she laughed. "She don't part them knees for nobody—"

Lana was chuckling, shaking her head. She looked at Olivia Duarte sitting next to her. "Right," Lana said. "She don't spread 'em for nobody, until Rudy Perez pins her down one time and gets his, whether you like it or not, girlfriend. That's the way it is. You're gonna learn about men. Am I right, Stella?"

Stella readily agreed with a nod of her head. Got the reefer back. Allowed Pearleen a toke and then finished it off herself.

Lana "Da Bottom" Sepulveda was looking at the ring on Olivia's finger that Rudy had given her. "That engagement ring don't mean nothing. All it does is makes it easier for them to get laid when they feel like it. Soon as they get what they want, they're gone, and so is the wedding."

"How do you know so much, big mouth?" Olivia finally said.

"Because it happened to her—" Pearleen said.

"Half a dozen times, at least." Stella laughed out loud.

"No way. Happened *twice*. Big deal." Lana looked at Olivia. "You'll find out about life. You'll see, girl. Men are after *one thing*. That ring don't mean nothing. Not a damned thing."

"Why don't you get off her case. Both of you. She doesn't need to hear that."

"Oh yes, she does, Pearl," Lana countered. "Them's the hard facts of the way it is, girlfriend. The more you know how things are, the better off you are. All you got to do is take one look at what happened to my mother. Ain't pretty, is it?"

Soon they were approaching the block Biggs lived on. The cab slowed.

"I just want to get home."

Pearleen had Olivia convinced that they would drop her off as soon as they picked up something Cecil was holding for them, something he had promised them a while back. And then Pearleen Bell went into another explanation why she needed "the stuff," that it helped give her a boost, that it was free, that it was just this one time and that she was ready to quit.

"Cecil loves our act, honey. Why he does it."

The cab stopped in front of Biggs's Church of Re-Newed Hope. The strippers climbed out. A hesitant Olivia Duarte did likewise.

The driver was paid, tipped less than the customary 10% by Pearleen, and all four women watched the unhappy cabby take off and disappear down the poorly lighted street.

Olivia felt a shiver race up her spine. What now? It was too dark and too dangerous to walk the rest of the way home. If that were not enough to weigh her down, she realized that she did not have her purse. *Her purse was missing*. The cab driver had taken off with her purse.

Pearleen Bell picked up on her nervousness and gave her a friendly pat on the shoulder.

"It's a *church*. You ain't got nothing to worry about. Man let all them homeless in over the years. What you got that worried look on your face for? Relax, girl."

"It isn't that. I left my purse in the cab."

"All Cecil's got to do is make a phone call. Your purse ain't goin' nowhere."

# CHAPTER 149

**The gate had been left unlocked, and they walked through.** Biggs was at the front door to greet them. He did his best to project a smile, but the lifeless eyes were not smiling. Cecil Biggs's peepers did not look at people, they looked *through* them.

The women were invited inside. They entered, and the door was closed behind them. Pearleen mentioned that the cabbie had taken off with Olivia's purse, and she wondered if Cecil might give the cab company a call.

"No problem. As soon as we get you ladies situated."

"What'd I tell you?" said Pearleen to the Duarte girl.

"I hear you're considering going off to college, Olivia," Biggs said to her in the hallway, as he proceeded to unlock a door on his right. "While I can relate to your desire to leave the nest and see what new adventures await out there in the great beyond, you might want to consider taking a second look at the first-rate universities we have right here in good ol' Southern California."

He had the door opened and led his guests into the living room-cum-entertainment den.

"Welcome to the *United Christian Church of Recycled Hope*," deadpanned Biggs. If anyone found the line amusing they didn't show it. Nothing had changed, according to those who had been here in the past: worn carpeting, cracks in the walls, peeling wallpaper; old futon and leather studded recliner against the far wall, the Roscoe side; black *Naugahyde* sofa against the front, street side; battered dresser with a large mirror to the immediate left as they entered.

A combination television-VCR sat atop the dresser with a stack or two of videos having to do with Christ and the Resurrection.

There was a bookshelf of sorts to the left of the dresser, consisting of cinder blocks and warped boards that had been painted in bright pastels that did not match either in width, length, or color, that were loaded down with volumes on Christianity, and further videos having to do with the Prince of Peace and the "inevitable" Second Coming.

J.C., crucifixes, porcelain figurines of various characters from His era lined the top shelf—and all of it, with the exception of the books, covered in a layer of dust.

To the left of the bookshelf that occupied the corner, was a moderately small stage and a burgundy velvet curtain that hung from the ceiling above it.

The wall connected to this one was almost entirely covered in one-foot square, self-adhesive mirror tiles. To the right a bit was a closet door. A good section of this wall had nothing blocking the mirror tiles, should

Biggs have a yen to watch himself while he enjoyed the various trysts with paid-for-hookers and/or victims.

More bookshelves throughout the room occupied every available nook and cranny. The titles were there to point out/confirm/underscore (lest anyone be so bold as to challenge his IQ), Cecil's unique and far-reaching genius. The bookshelves were bulging with titles by and/or on Stephen Hawking, Einstein, Darwin, Plato, Socrates, Aristotle, Kierkegaard, Heidegger, Schopenhauer, Nietzsche, Hegel, Machiavelli, Sartre, Marx, Shakespeare, De Sade, Foucault, Derrida, Freud, Jung; a book or two on the *US Constitution* and the *Bill of Rights*; law books, and a volume entitled *Penal Code of California*, Peace Officers Abridged Edition.

There was a hard-bound, thick volume entitled *The Encyclopedia of Crime*; books on pyramids in Egypt, the *Aztecs*, oil drilling in Alaska, pythons in the Amazon, crocks in the Florida everglades, sharks off the coast of Australia; anthropologists Margaret Meade and Louis Leakey; naturalist Diane Fossey's tome entitled *Gorillas in the Mist*.

The bookshelves practically reached the ceiling, with books on just about every subject under the sun: books on celebrities, prize fighters and wrestlers; generals like George Patton, Nazi Rommel, Eisenhower; illusionists like Houdini and others of his stature; books on film directors like D.W. Griffin, Ingmar Bergman, Roberto Rossellini, Abel Gance, Fritz Lang; political heavyweights Ronald Reagan, George Washington, Ben Franklin, Abe Lincoln, Harry Truman, John Adams, Thomas Jefferson, Ulysses S. Grant, Woodrow Wilson, Franklin Roosevelt, James Madison, JFK; books on Churchill, Maggie Thatcher, Genghis Khan, Ho Chi Minh, Alexander the Great, Julius Caesar, Hitler, Stalin, Nazi death camp sadist Ilse Koch, *SS Kommandant* at *Auschwitz* Rudolph Hess (and others), as well as several titles by those who survived said Nazi death camps; all the major wars and battles since the beginning of civilization; inventors like Nikola Tesla, Edison, and others. History books, books on biology, *Scientology*, hunting and fishing, embalming and the undertaking trade, the universe, and medical books, and books on mental health (as well as mental illness—and so-called cures).

It was all there. Biggs, at one time or another, had read them all. And not a single name behind these volumes, be it male or female, be it *pole-smoker* or *muff-diving dyke*, did he feel had anything on him or what he knew to be his superior intellect.

"What, no *Walt Whitman?*" one of the women asked.

"No," he said, while shoving a religious epic into the VCR with the sound turned down low. "Absolutely not."

Truth was he had very little use for poets and poetry; truth was poets were useless sacks of sniveling snot.

What was it that drunken Irishman said? *Rage against the dying of the light?* Rummy got it wrong. It should be, instead, while jamming hard bone into a victim's mouth, instead of raging against this and that, there's nothing like shoving all that rage in their throat, after the rage had been rammed into their *shitter* first. Topped off, of course, by the *coup-de-grace*: some righteous slicing and dicing; better yet, partial strangulation during copulation and/or *fellatio*, to be followed by some insanely gratifying cutlery mayhem.

That was the only kind of "rage" he ever got anything out of. This explained why he did not want poetry contaminating his library. Poetry was nothing more than a stream of *excreta* drizzling out of some so-called poet's asshole—and when it came to *drizzling excreta*, he preferred seeing it *drizzle* out of a petrified bitch's rectum after she'd been fed *Ex-Lax* and beer.

Since there was more to life and the world than books and slaughter and porn, more to life than abducting victims and torturing them, sodomizing and carving them up into chunks to be tossed into Greta Otto's kettle to be turned into jambalaya, he let his walls do the talking to prove it.

Blowups of televangelists of the likes of Billy Graham, Gene Scott, Jimmy Swaggart, Robert Schuller, and others, had been tacked to walls in an obvious, although less-than-successful, attempt to conceal cracks as well as hold down the faded wallpaper.

Among the *Bible*-thumpers who decorated the walls, were also a few motion picture posters from epics like *The Ten Commandments*, *The Robe*, *Ben-Hur*, *The Greatest Story Ever Told*, others. And up, above, in the corners, cobwebs with dead moths and flies.

# CHAPTER 150

**The women worked to conceal the disappointment and general feeling of disgust that they felt by now.** Man had money and was this religious type, supposedly, head of his own little "house of prayer," and yet basically existed like a piggy in his private little pigsty. And then there was that off-putting odor, the odor; it could not be ignored—and yet they did their best to do just that.

"Yeah," Lana "Da Bottom" said, "it's medical school for that *Chicana*. She's going to be a brain surgeon. No lie."

"Actually," Olivia said, unperturbed, "I'd like to be a foreign correspondent for a cable network or news publication."

"Nothing the matter with that at all," Biggs said.

"For a whole year girlfriend was going around telling everybody how she was going to be a brain surgeon, just because she seen some woman brain surgeon interviewed by Barbara WaWa on 20/20," Lana said. "You think that's all there is to it, Olivia? What you see on tee-vee? If it was that easy every *Tom, Dick, and Harriet* would be all over it."

Biggs spoke in a relaxed tone. "I'm a registered practical nurse myself, Liv, you know? You might look into it. The money is not bad at all. Of course, I got a leg up, so to speak, by being in the army, where I received medical training. Once I got out I enrolled in a practical nursing program that lasted a year, followed by a six-month internship at a general hospital. Well worth it; being able to help people that way. I do miss it. Yearn to return to it—if only it were possible. These days most of my time is consumed by the church: running it, tending to countless details and issues, overseeing staff and aiding/assisting members of the congregation. Keeps me fairly busy. I'm convinced neurosurgery is certainly a worthwhile goal for someone to pursue. Tough, but not impossible, if you have the stomach for it. Personally, I don't have the stomach to cut into someone's skull and tinker around in there. I just don't have the nerves of steel something like that would require."

"God, that's gross," Stella said. "Couldn't we talk about something else?"

"Of course," Biggs said with a smile. "Like what else?"

"*What else?*" said Stella. "The *rank odor*, for one. That's what else. What's up with the *stench*, Bishop?"

"Oh that," said Biggs, reaching inside the mini fridge that was situated between the wall covered in mirror squares and that end of the futon. The mini fridge was stocked to capacity with beer and sodas. He passed them around for those who were interested, and for others, like Marvin Ritalin Muck, who grabbed a beer, but preferred to toke, better yet, to do blow, Biggs had rolled joints on hand. He was saving the hard drugs for later. He saved the expensive dope for his guests, in order to get his money's worth. You didn't dole out the nose candy until the time was right and you felt you'd get what *you* wanted in return. *Quid-pro-quo.* Something like it. He cracked open a can of soda for himself. Reached in back of the futon where the stereo sat on a shelf between stacks of books, explaining: "Had a cat once—The Ripper—and a German shepherd we called Rutherford. They didn't exactly get along. We're certain Rutherford killed The Ripper, then ran off. As a result, we have the carcass of a dead feline in the basement somewhere. Odor has a way of wafting."

"Why not take the body out?" said Stella. "The dead cat, I mean, and get rid of it?"

"We would, if we could pinpoint the location. We have a staff member, Norbert Fimple, who may have stashed it away somewhere." Biggs thought to pause here. "Please don't ask me why. It's one perplexing dilemma we have yet to resolve, obviously."

Marvin had taken it upon himself to begin spraying the room with disinfectant in order to get the women to stop complaining about the smell. Biggs looked at him. Told him to stop it. "All you're doing is making it worse."

Marvin stopped with a shrug.

"What then?"

Biggs found a bottle of inexpensive cologne on the bookshelf. Got enough of it on the tips of his index and middle finger, and then dabbed at the area just below the nostrils. Did the same for the women. He took the rest of the bottle and splashed the ceiling and walls with it. Solved the odor problem. Pretty much. For the time being. Only now, Stella "Storm" Martel was bitching about the place smelling like cheap aftershave. Some people were hard to please. "Storm" was a good moniker for her, as she was always stirring up trouble.

"You know, I have often said to Marvin: Some people like to complain about *everything*, while others never complain about *anything*."

"You're absolutely right about that, honey," said Stella. "Negative people are a turn-off; real pain in the ass. Exactly why I never had any patience being around them."

"Amen."

On that, Biggs cranked up a sexy tune by Barry White. White sang loud enough to rattle the shutters. That was fine with Biggs, the way he liked it. All seemed pleased with the choice in music, reefer and beer, all that is, except Olivia Duarte, who passed on everything, including the soda. She was determined not to accept anything to eat, drink, or smoke in this place. That was not for her.

Be patient long enough for Pearleen and her loose pals to do their thing and get out of here. She needed to get home. It was then Cecil Biggs produced (a la some great illusionist like Copperfield) a black leather men's purse that contained a vial mirror, straw with gold trim, and a clear plastic baggy with the powder. Devil's dandruff. Dumped a small mound of it on the glass-topped coffee table. Pearleen Bell wasted no time locating a super market discount card in her purse and began chopping at the cocaine with it, cutting out six equal rails-plus, in that there was enough left over for the deacon, as well Olivia, should she have wished to change her mind about partaking.

The strippers dug up their own tooters and snorted away. Pearleen banged a rail up one nostril, then the other. Life was good. Definitely worth living. With a little help from the neighborhood "Bishop" named Cecil O. Biggs.

"Tell me something, Peach," spoke the host. "Is there any truth to the rumor?"

"What rumor is that?" said Pearleen, dabbing at the white flecks about the septum, as well as either side of it.

"That you did hardcore at one time?"

"Porn?" She looked at him now.

"Yes. Porn. Hardcore porn."

"Not hardcore. I wouldn't do hardcore. Did a couple of soft porn-type videos, though. I was the only one in them. Needed the money."

"Word is you did a hardcore video once. I'm not judging; don't misunderstand. I'd like to see it. Would pay money to get my hands on it."

"People like to spread rumors. They can believe whatever the hell they want. They like to talk shit behind my back because they're jealous. That's what it comes down to: jealousy."

"I understand. I've dealt with it practically my entire life."

The hottest stripper, by far, of them all, was eager to change the subject—and what better way than to jump up in the center of the living room and begin a slow dance number.

Although she took nothing off initially, the choreography was considerably erotic as she moved nice and easy, swaying those bountiful hips, grinding the pelvis, teasing the hell out of Cecil Biggs and his crony Marvin Muck, and even drawing enough interest from Lana Sepulveda and Stella Martel. Pearleen Bell, aka Peaches LaBelle, was second-to-none when it came to this sort of thing; making men, even enough women, stare with a deep hunger within for something they could not even begin to describe or pinpoint—only there was no denying that it was there: indefinable, ephemeral, and mesmerizing to all those who witnessed it.

What Pearleen had could not be taught. It was a quality that one was born with.

They watched. In awe. Cecil O. Biggs and Marvin R. Muck had lust in their eyes and rape on their minds. Rape. Rape the hoez. Sodomize the sluts. All of them had it coming.

# CHAPTER 151

**Eventually, gradually, the black stripper began to discard items of clothing.** Olivia was quite embarrassed and felt out of place. She hadn't been brought up this way. She knew it wasn't right to be so quick to judge, but these people were different, had different morals, or at least their ideas of morality conflicted with the way she had been raised. Biggs called this place, this house, a church. What kind of "church" was it? They used dope, drank alcohol—and now a woman was taking her clothes off in front of others.

She had always known Cecil to be eccentric, everyone knew him to be "off the wall," weird; sure, he had money and the luxury cars—he was a weird one, only what was taking place in front of her was too much and out of line.

Biggs turned the lights down low. Switched on red lamps. Changed the record for a slower, smoother tune. Noticed the look on Olivia's face. Pearleen Bell continued to shed a few things.

# CHAPTER 152

**"We're a free-wheeling parish here, Olivia," explained Biggs.** "There's no need to be nervous. We adhere to our own rules and guidelines, our own Code of Conduct, so to speak. Sex is not thought of as a dirty activity in here the way it is out there. Every single member of the United Christian Church of Re-Newed Hope is indeed moral. It's just that we have our own ideas, beliefs—if you will—of morality, so please don't misconstrue what you see here. Our attitude, my attitude, is that sex is to be enjoyed, have fun with, and not thought of as repulsive and spoken of in hushed tones in darkened rooms.

"Intimacy is, after all, a beautiful thing. God's gift to us for all the indignities and suffering we endure on a daily basis. From womb to tomb. Sex is there to give us a break, that much-needed release from the grind that life very often is."

That was all fine and dandy, thought Olivia, for *others*, and wondered when he would make that phone call regarding her purse. She brought it up again.

"Soon," said Biggs. "Soon."

When he glanced down at the glass-topped table it was obvious enough that cokehead Marvin had *snouted* it clean. Could have easily gone for more. Looked like.

Biggs pushed him aside. Came up with the plastic *Ziploc* baggy and carefully tapped out enough for a rail or two. Produced a tooter. Gestured in Olivia's direction to take it and snort up. Olivia steadfastly declined. Wanted none of it.

Lana managed to get her arm around the presently seated bishop's neck, tongued his ear, while squeezing his groin inside his trousers—then just as swiftly as she managed this maneuver, she swooped down to where the bag with the dope was and shook some more out to add to what was already on the table.

Biggs eyed her with great dismay, although he did not move to stop her, as she not only extended the rails considerably, but made them way too fat. And before the other women could get in on it, before Marvin could move and get a piece of the action as well, Lana Sepulveda wasted no time huffing the lines like a Hoover vacuum: up one nasal passage, then the other.

She liked that so much she was back nibbling the bishop's upper chest and neck. Stella was not happy with what she just witnessed Da Bottom pull and she was not reluctant to show it.

*"Greedy bitch,"* she hissed. *"I hope your nose falls off."*

Pearleen was shaking her head as well.

"Pulls that shit a lot. That's Lana for you."

"You know you ain't right, Lana," grumbled Muck. "Was enough candy right there went up yo nose for everybody in this cribby to get fucked up on."

Unbeknownst to Lana, one of her nostrils had begun to bleed. Stella reached inside her own purse for a Kleenex, and held it out to the rude bitch to take. Lana wadded enough for a tiny ball and stuffed it in her nose.

"Serves you right, *'girlfriend,'*" said Stella Martel.

Lana wasn't interested and didn't care. She had seen Stella do the same damned thing herself lots of times. Couldn't be helped. The only thing that bothered her about it was the nosebleed. Too much huffing did it. Crack and base were preferable for this reason. Nosebleeds and sores was the price one paid.


She worked away on the bishop. Had her tongue in and around his ear, while slowly running her left hand along his left thigh.

Biggs was in heaven. Three hot bitches high on blow—in his place. This was life. Took a lot of money to pull off, too. If only Tillie Marie could have been a little more flexible. She could have been part of all this. And Honesto . . . Kid would have been raised the way a kid should be raised.

"Where's the *glo*, Rev?" said Lana. "Toot is great, but it's destroying my sinuses."

Stella had her crack pipe out and was readily agreeing. Crack was the thing he should have had them on to begin with, thought Biggs, before Lana snorted all those rails. Could have saved a few bucks. "Jellybeans" were easier to dole out. Less "waste" involved.

Cecil decided he wanted to enjoy the moment and not respond right away. *Take your time*, he thought. Let them sweat it.

The hand that the Latina had on his thigh had moved up higher and was on his crotch, massaging it gently and with great skill. She was certain she felt the "helmet" budge.

"Let's crack it up, Cecil. Blow is fucking up my nose."

Biggs, not unhappy to oblige, produced the baggy with the rocks. She moved, wanting to grab the baggy that he held beyond her reach in his right hand. He held the baggy back, above his head. He hadn't liked the way she had made the powder disappear a moment ago and was determined not to let the same happen again. Pushy broads were always out to dominate the situation. Not if he had anything to say about it. You never, ever allowed a twat to control a cock and a pair of balls.

He withdrew a rock from the baggy and handed it to Stella, who jammed it in her pipe. Had her torch out and going. She took short puffs. Pearleen stopped her dance routine long enough to nail her share of the crack. Got her hits, so did Marvin, and only then did they permit Lana to do her thing: Take that extended hit she was known for. Long and deep. She held it. Released it gradually. And loving it. She rested her head back against the futon, slumping back, enjoying the high, and soon enough was back to working on Biggs and making him feel good all over again.

She had her right hand massaging the back of his neck, while her other hand was back over his crotch, until it was time to pass the stem again and her turn to hit it.

Before they knew it, the glo was gone.

"So where do you keep the rest of your stash, Cecil?" asked Stella Martel. "Got it hidden away pretty good, I imagine."

"Where *you'll* never find it."

"Kidding aside," said Lana. "Come on. You can tell us."

"What kind of fool do you take me for?"

"How do you know it's safe?" said Stella. "How do you know someone like Glassy Ortiz won't try to break in one night to get his hands on it?"

"I wouldn't worry about it."

The strippers were anxious to get the pipe going again. No matter how much they snorted, or how much they smoked, it seemed to Biggs, it was never enough. Something like his addiction to porn and violence, he supposed. Sex and torture. Only difference was, and it was quite a big difference, the dope they consumed tended to deplete his pocketbook.

He was reluctant to abide. At least played it this way, for the moment. Let them "encourage" me, he thought.

"Why we're here, ain't it?" whispered Lana in his ear. "Not entirely for this reason, but it is part of it, after all—ain't it?"

"That's the main reason, as far as I'm concerned," spoke out Stella. "Here to get fucked up."

"To smoke some crack," said Pearleen Bell. "Or I'm out of here." She stopped moving. Stood there, arms on her hips. "Call a cab, then."

"Easy now," said Biggs. "This party's just getting started." And let Lana have the baggy and what remained in it. She fetched her own pipe from her purse, and stuffed the rocks in. Had her torch going. Resorted to her typical, drawn out hit.

Stella snatched the stem from her and did her thing. Short puffs, but enough of them; then kept going and would not have stopped if Pearleen had not stepped in and taken it away from her.

"Goddamn you," said Pearleen Bell. "Now you're behaving like Lana." She managed a good hit, and handed the pipe to Marvin.

"So you're not telling us how much shit you got on hand or where it is, that it?" said Lana. "I understand. Just trying to decide if it's worth hanging around and for how long. The idea is we stay so long as there's dope to smoke. Once the dope is gone, so are we."

"Let me put it to you this way, I'm not dumb enough to keep enough drugs on the property in order to get busted for pushing."

"Pushing?" said Stella. "No one's accusing you of pushing."

"I have enough to keep all of you happy for a while, but not enough to make it possible for Valley PD to put me away long enough to disrupt my life."

Muck held on to the stem and smoked the residue down. Once again. It was gone. In such a short time. And they wanted more. Wanted to keep their highs alive. As far as Biggs was concerned, it was no different from rolling up a twenty dollar bill, or a fifty, and putting a match to it.

The dopefiends wanted more.

"In a while."

Lana had his shirt unbuttoned and got it off of him. Was not at all surprised to see that he had his bulletproof vest on. Paranoid fuck never left his bedroom without it. She resumed the rubbing and kissing, the nibbling. He wasn't hard down there, yet. Eventually, she was certain, he would be. Took him longer than most men. But she'd get him there. Persistence was the key.

Biggs handed her a rock that he'd palmed in his hand. Lana grabbed the stem and stuffed the rock in. Sucked on the stem and was not about to relinquish it until she had the crack smoked down to nothing.

Stella leaned in; with her left hand snatched the pipe away from her, while with her right she grabbed a good hunk of Lana's thick mane and yanked it hard enough to pull the stripper not only away from Biggs, but cause her to tumble down off the futon.

Lana Sepulveda's retaliation was swift and strong, once she recovered, and flailed away at Stella's face with her balled up fists. Then just as suddenly as it began, it stopped. Lana's hands and wrists must have been aching, because she was no longer throwing punches. And she should have left it there, but she didn't feel like it, and spit at the other woman.

Stella wiped her face, cursed "cunt" or something to the effect, and had both her hands back on Lana's long hair and pulled and yanked with all her might until she had the Latina on the ratty carpet, and they rolled back and forth this way to Biggs's and Marvin's utter delight. They had a catfight taking place right before their very eyes—and it was a kick to see. Both thought so.

Pearleen Bell didn't. And got down between them and separated them and was not only strong and forceful enough to spread them apart, but stop it.

"Look at you," said Pearleen. "Should be ashamed of yourselves."

"Ho caused it by hogging the stem," said Stella.

"I don't need you to tell me how to smoke dope, *bitch,*" shouted Lana Sepulveda.

"Grow up," said Stella. "Learn to share. You're not the only one here who wants to keep her high going."

*"Oh, fuck you."*

And it was about to start again. Pearleen intervened, pushing Stella back.

Biggs stood up. He was grinning and holding up another baggy with some rocks in it.

"Grab your pipe," he said to Lana. "Follow me to the hallway john."

Eagerly so, she did, taking her purse with her—and flipped Stella the bird as she followed Cecil out of the living room. Stella shrugged Pearleen off of her. Was on her hands and knees carefully going over the carpet in search of rock crumbs that may have ended up down there.

Pearleen was back on her feet, dancing. She was bobbing her head and smiling, determined to work her way back to feeling the way she felt before the fight broke out. It was free dope, and these dumb-asses didn't even know how to enjoy it and have a good time. That wouldn't be her. She was here to party—and that's exactly what she was doing.

# CHAPTER 153

**Stella's quest paid off: She discovered a rock the size of a kernel of corn, then another under the coffee table.** She jammed them into her own pipe and was on the futon smoking. Marvin joined her soon enough, sitting down on her right.

They shared. He was grateful.

Stella waved the pipe in Pearleen's direction, who shook her head. Did not want any at the moment; she was doing fine, moving to the music.

"How about you, *sugar-bush*?" said Marvin to Olivia Duarte, knowing that she would turn them down, and did. Wouldn't go near drugs, especially something as addictive as rock cocaine.

Both Stella and Marvin shrugged their shoulders.

"Stupid bitch has no idea what she's missing," Stella whispered in Marvin's ear. The rocks in the pipe were smoked down, and she placed both of her hands on the back of Muck's neck and began to massage and knead the width of the nape, just as she had done back at the club's dressing room, the last time he stopped by to visit. This was how they were able to get over. Men were simple. Most times didn't even have to have sex with them. Make them feel important. Stroke their ego and you didn't have to stroke their dick. Usually.

Olivia could not stand much more. Got up and stepped into the hallway.

# CHAPTER 154

**A fully clothed Lana Sepulveda emerged from the john rubbing the wetness out of her hair with a towel.** Biggs soon followed, doing the same, running a towel over his head and face. Noticed Olivia Duarte standing in the foyer area befuddled and confused, nervous and uncomfortable, and thought to let her know about the altar and Prayer Hall on the second floor.

"You're welcome to go up."

"What denomination is your church?"

"What denomination would you *like it to be?*"

"I only wondered . . ."

"I apologize. We are non-denominational."

She decided to take him up on his offer to visit the upstairs.

"By the way, according to the cab driver . . . there was never any purse left in his cab when he dropped you off."

"I had my purse with me when I got in that cab, Mr. Biggs."

"All I can tell you is what I was told."

As she climbed the stairs on her way up, she heard Lana whisper something to him and laugh. They entered the living room and closed the door behind them.

Olivia continued on, pausing now and then, taking in the coins that lined the walls and ceiling, the paper money. There was a sign that caught her eye:


## SEEK
## AND YE SHALL RECEIVE


Receive what? Drugs? Perversion and general degeneracy? It made her shudder. She'd been so stupid to allow herself to get stuck in this situation. Part of it had been to spite Rudy, part of it had to do with knowing it would irritate Yolanda—and now she had to ride it out until Pearleen and her nutty friends were ready to leave.

She reached the upstairs hallway. Doors to rooms were on the right. She entered the first one. The altar/Prayer Room was basically twice the size of the living room downstairs, and had been transformed into a hall for sermons/weddings/various celebrations and worship, with benches and folding chairs lined up in rows like pews in a church. There was an elevated dais to her right, the street side, the altar with a huge crucifix behind it. She took in the lectern. It wasn't much: wooden fruit crates stacked three high, the cross on the crates nothing more than a couple of splintered pickets someone had nailed together. There was no denying it underscored the creepiness.

Church?

Denominational or not, a church should be neat and clean and have a sense of wonder and holiness about it. This was far from it. *Decrepit* and *dingy* were a couple of words that came to mind. Not to mention that odor that dogged you no matter what part of this place you happened to be in. True enough, it wasn't as overwhelming as it had been on the first floor, but it was strong enough. If she had remained in that living room down there another second she would have surely started gagging.

Olivia crossed herself. It was habit. Walked toward a black woman attired in a dark monk's robe sitting in one of the folding chairs in the front row. The woman had a tough to ignore case of the shivers. In this warm weather? And seemed out of it in other ways: was off someplace by herself as she stared at the crucifix, past it, more than likely; only there was nothing to stare at beyond the crucifix but wooden shutters over windows with the iron crossbars.

That was the other odd thing about the place: these inside shutters with crossbars on them and locks. What for? What was the purpose? Security measure? Or to prevent suicide attempts? To keep anyone from jumping? Didn't know. It creeped her out.

Olivia walked over. Said hi to the woman.

*"It's cold in here."* Patience McDaniel never turned her head or moved her eyes away from whatever it was she was focused on.

# CHAPTER 155

**Marvin R. Muck felt like the luckiest Mack Daddy-wannabe around.** Stella's terms of endearment and affection had progressed to her actually unzipping his fly and taking his groin out and fondling him with her experienced and knowing fingers. The strokes had him full mast in hardly no time at all.

Biggs, who sat on the same futon with Lana to the left of them, glanced in Marvin's direction from time to time with a degree of envy he was not able to conceal no matter how much he tried. Muck was not only becoming stiff, the halfwit almost had *"twiced"* as much as he did down there.

But then he turned away, and his eyes were back on Pearleen in the center of the room and the incredible evolving show she continued to put on for anyone wishing to ogle and obsorb.

Lana had Cecil's penis in her hand, caressing the helmet—for what good it did. He'd shot his load in the bathroom and there was no way he was going to be able to get off again this soon, not unless it involved additional blood or violence or both. She knew it well enough. Part of it, too, had to do with the meds.

It didn't matter, though. She wasn't stroking his weenie, but his ego. Twisted jerk was lucky to have that, especially after what he'd put her through in the john just so he could get off. She had to put it behind her. One of the other chicks better go with him next time. She would see to that. Better believe it. Let Stella deal with it. See how *she* likes it.

Her eyes, for the most part now, were on Pearleen, as were everyone else's. Why not? There was always a step or two to be learned from the bitch, ripped off, to be used in her own routine. If she could. As capable a dancer as she knew herself to be, she had to admit Pearl was better. And "Stunning" Stella Storm? No competition there. Nearly as awful as Dione. Made her wonder what had happened to her, too. Small town hick chick just up and took off.

Didn't matter, did it? That was the business they were in. Dancers came and went. And one of the most popular the Valley had ever seen was doing her thing for them right now.

Pearleen Bell, aka Peaches LaBelle, aka *LaBelle of the Ball,* among others, proceeded to mesmerize her audience. Had *Trusty the Clown* and *Bozo Deacon*, no doubt, taking in every gyration with bated breath.

She possessed not only the innate ability to grind her pelvis and sway her hips in time to the beat, but the exquisite intuition to squeeze the most out of every salacious move of her outstanding body.

She pivoted so that all eyes were on that fantastic behind and legs as she gave the rump slow, controlled rotations, and then slid her open palms down and over her buttocks, and when she turned, her hands were moving up along the inside of her upper thighs, inching toward the black panties and the mound of pubic hair within.

She had had to shave off quite a bit of her bush for her act, otherwise it would have been impossible to wear a G-string on stage, only Pearleen did not always take all the hair off because she did not like to, didn't like this area to be entirely devoid of fur, and she had also discovered over the years that men, a lot of men, liked *bush* in *that area*, that the sight of it excited them.

Her hands continued to slide up toward the mound . . . as her hips continued to gyrate and then her pelvis began its rhythmic pumping.

She had taken most of her clothes off by now and was down to the black bra and the panties, garter belt, fishnets, and black spike heels, and Biggs and Marvin could not get enough. Proof was there: Muck was like a steel rod down there, baton; Biggs, alas, far from anywhere near it. Not that Lana was giving up, though. Played with the hair on his chest that she was able to get to above the Kevlar, the lean belly below it, planting moist kisses and running her soft hands up and down the unwilling member.

Biggs was enjoying himself, in spite of his stubborn penis. What the hell? That was some incredible blast-off he'd experienced in the john— and there would be others to come. He had the ways and means. He only wished he had *the means* of handling the one upstairs. Up there. In the

Prayer Hall: Olivia Duarte. Wished he had the nerve to lock her in and keep her from leaving—ever. And the rest of them. Had that unlucky bitch Dione down in the cellar, and three more potential slave sluts here within reach.

Well, Pearleen was here. She was doing it, too. Had been costly. He had lusted after her for so long, and here she was in his place again doing a strip for him the way she had done a few months back and that had made him want her all the more.

Maybe not this time. Not this trip. The coke was working its magic on her. Bitch was hooked, like her dopefiend pals, no doubt —and he knew how it would all go pretty soon. Any day now the ebony beauty would be putting out, sexing him, giving him whatever he wanted, just so she could get her nose candy and crack. And as obvious it all was to him, the fact that he would be getting it eventually, for sure, it was real tough being patient, trying to feign patience, trying to pretend that blow jobs and shags (courtesy of Lana Da Bottom, and others) would suffice for the time being.

Still, it was goddamned near impossible to act like everything was all right and normal when you had a couple of super hot and untouchable pieces of ass like Livia Duarte and Pearl Bell right in your own home, within reach—within such easy reach. It was one of the toughest things he'd had to do and live through. He wondered how long before he snapped and pursued his lust for blood and need for violence? How long before he grabbed Lana's head and started punching her face in? What he'd put her through in the crapper a moment ago was nothing more than a primer and had whetted his appetite for the real thing.

"Feels good, baby. Feels real good."

*Stay in control, you must stay in control.* Everything is fine. It really is, Lusty. *Copacetic* is the word you're searching for. Enjoy yourself.

You've got a great looking slut fondling your cock for the second time around, and another drop-dead gorgeous bitch taking her clothes off right in front of your eyes, right under your roof. Pearleen Bell. *Prick-teaser nonpareil.* Just don't let things get out of hand. Do not lose control. Don't spoil it.

Meanwhile, over on his right, Mack Daddy Muck was as stiff as a billy.

# CHAPTER 156

**Stella continued to stroke the deacon.** Looked like Muck was close to blasting. His eyes shut tight, the jaw clenched.

*"Yawza."*

"I don't want to see cum on my carpet."

Muck placed his large hands on the back of Stella's head and guided her toward him, while at the same time driving his groin up into her mouth, exploding.

Stella hadn't cared for it, but it was too late. Deed was done. Marvin was smiling ear-to-ear. Stella claimed she had to use the john, rinse her mouth out.

"No," said Muck.

"Want me to *pee* right here, Base?"

"It would be something to see," said Biggs.

"What?"

"Open your mouth, Deacon."

"Fuck that. I don't let no crack ho piss in *my* mouf."

Biggs grinned. Let it go.

Stella left the living room and stepped into the hallway and was trying to figure out where the rest of the bishop's stash could possibly be. Tested several doors, only to find them locked. She tried another down toward the rear door, on the right. Kitchen door.

Opened it.

There was a long dining table and a large, demented-looking individual balancing himself on a chair, careful not to fall off, while attempting, with a wooden spoon in his hand, to whack away at one of two birdcages up there that hung from the ceiling.

There was no mistaking the clanging of metal, silverware and whatnot, bolts and washers, who knew?—that came from somewhere in the big man's belly with every missing swipe that he made.

The best he could accomplish, it seemed, was to rap the bottom of the cage, from time to time, causing the cage to swing from side to side and bang against the other one, that made the chickens inside them nervous and panicky, had them clucking wildly.

There could have been more than two chickens up there; she couldn't tell exactly. The cage he rapped at had that one in it. Whole thing was odd. Reverend Stinky and his weird ass way of doing things.

She saw the man take a hard, wild swing, whack the cage with plenty of force that sent it banging against the other cage, bounce back against the arm with the spoon with enough impact behind it so that it caused him to lose his balance and sent him to the floor.

The man recovered, noticed that there was someone else present, rose to his feet and sat in the chair and went at the stew in the bowl before him, without so much as ever acknowledging the intruder.

Norbert Fimple shoveled spoonfuls into his heavy jowls. Stella stared at the character with the eyeglasses taped to his forehead with a Band-Aid, the stained clothing, the scars on his face, the swollen lower lip and matted, greasy short hair that needed washing and a trim around the ears. Whoever had given him the haircut had failed to get the areas behind the ears. Must have been done by somebody half blind or just didn't give a shit.

He never looked at her, or even in her direction. Never once looked up at the chickens, either. He ate. The glazed, practically lifeless eyeballs looked at nothing.

Stella's focus shifted to the gas range in back of the beefy male, and the kettle sitting on top. There was a stainless steel meat grinder bolted down to the kitchen counter to the left of the sink; what appeared to be traces of ground up hamburger in and around the five-inch-by-six-inch hopper opening. There were palm and fingerprints on the wood hand crank and other parts of the grinder.

There was a tube-shaped sausage stuffer/jerky maker beside it. This item, too, had various prints on it, various traces of ground up meat.

Next to this was what looked like a heavy duty, commercial type of patty press. Like the grinder, this appliance was bolted to the counter. On the far side of the sink was a slicer, the type used for slicing roast beef, with what appeared to be a seven-inch steel blade.

Then she took notice of the refrigerators. Two of them. Large. Admirals. Doors chained up, with heavy duty padlocks hanging. On the refrigerator farthest from her was what appeared to be a recipe for making frankfurters. In bold, black marker, she could make out certain hand-printed headers:

**INGREDIENTS FOR 25 LBS.** Various ingredients followed, then the second header:

## GRINDING & MIXING

Following the instructions, another header:

## SMOKING & COOKING

Then:

## CHILLING

Lastly:

## EMULSIFYING INSTRUCTIONS

Stated to grind the meat up and mix in the required seasonings. Okay. Nothing particularly oddball there. Quite a few people made their own wieners and ground up meat in their homes, so why shouldn't *this* wiener?

Sitting on the floor, against the far wall, with its door open wide, was what looked like a smokehouse. Stainless steel. Three feet high. About a foot-and-a-half wide—and maybe just as deep. Newly purchased. Chrome-plated shelves for jerky. Hardwood dowels to hang sausage from. Sawdust pan. Next to it a white freezer. Oblong in shape, like a casket, only twice as tall.

Her eyes wandered up. Not unimpressed by what she saw. Wall was covered in pennies. The entire wall, from one end to the other, from floor to ceiling, decorated with copper pennies. The time and effort it must have taken. Made about as much sense as stuffing your own sausage. Pastor Stinky cut corners at every turn—in order to be able to stick money to walls, buy fancy rides and dope; tip big time.

What did you expect? Had never been in his kitchen before. Whatever it was she had expected wasn't this.

Felt like taking a look in the freezer. Had a need to. Would've been too easy for Cecil to stash anything in there. Was worth a try.

Sweaty slob acted like she wasn't there. Wouldn't look at her. No problem. She walked in back of him, past the refrigerators, crossing the kitchen to the other side. Took a gander inside the smokehouse (to satisfy her curiosity). Nothing in it. Door wouldn't have been left open if there had been.

Got her hands on the freezer lid. Lid was locked. Wouldn't budge. She looked at the big man with the double chins. Didn't want to. There were things you did to get your dope. *Mook* was as disgusting as they come. Obese degenerate. And he smelled.

"Can you open this for me, baby? I'm not interested in eating your food. Got a different kind of hunger."

The man ate. Stared straight ahead.

"He got any goodies in here? Where's the key?"

She may as well have been talking to one of the chickens. Frustration was a bitch, especially the kind that mounted. Cupboards would have been a good place to hide dope. All had locks on them. Refrigerators, too, would have been a good place to keep stuff in. Why else tie cycle chains around them? Had to be more than groceries in there.

"You're strong enough to break a chain. Break a chain for me, sweetie. I'll give you anything you want. . . . You can break the locks off the cupboards at least for me, can't you?"

It wasn't working. Asexual fuck wasn't normal. She would have had any other man panting for pussy by now. Stella walked back to where she had been standing before. Her eyes on the slob eating the slop. Those glasses taped to his face was the kicker. The imbecile had actually taken a single *Band-Aid* and stuck it vertically to the bridge of his nose. Held the glasses in place this way. If hardly. It was a long *Band-Aid* that ran from practically the tip of his nose, up the bridge, over that section of the glasses, and halfway up his forehead. Had to be a *mook*.

Cecil did say he had taken in some imbalanced homeless people to help them out. That was his business. Only the stench made Stella Martel want to turn right back out and leave. But she didn't. She was determined to get her hands on Biggs's stash. Why they had made the effort to come here. Had to get a lot more than what they saw in the living room for having to put up with Cecil and Marvin and their bullshit. Had to do it, too, while that dumb Mexican slut Lana was busy doing Creep #1.

She placed a hand on the back of Norbert's neck and rubbed gently. Men liked this. All went for it. She knew the tricks. Get them to relax, whisper sweet nothings in their ear—and watch them open up, reveal their innermost thoughts and secrets. Gullible creatures that they were. Worked every time. Not that any of them had anything to say that she was remotely interested in.

She soon had both hands working his upper back, rubbing, kneading the stressed out, knotted muscles she knew to be there, and was convinced would help in obtaining what she needed.

"Tell me where Cecil keeps his stash, baby. I'll make you feel good. In fact, I'll do better than that: I'll make it the thrill of a lifetime. . . ."

Norbert belched, and shoveled a spoonful of the jambalaya into his mouth. Paused suddenly, not chewing or doing anything, but enjoying the wonderful effect her magical fingers were having on him. Stella had leaned her head in, no closer than she had to, to be sure, as the man smelled something awful; she had the smile going, about as genuine as her interest in him—but that didn't matter, as far as she was concerned. She was about to get lucky. Could be. Might just be this smelly, sub-normal chauvinist would be able to provide her with enough information to point her in the right direction.

Norbert's features did not betray the slightest trace of an expression, as he stayed with his otherworldly stare, then without warning, spat out the entire load of stew he'd been holding back in his mouth, covering her face practically and leaving her gasping.

Stella spun away. Felt like throwing up. Swiped at some of it with her hands. One of the fragments that she swiped at appeared to be a thumbnail, a female thumbnail at that—but her vision having been greatly impaired by stew juice and growing anger, that it did not entirely register. Instead, rage kicked in at having all that unwanted debris on her, that on instinct she considered locking her hands together and maybe delivering a hammer-like blow against the back of this bastard's neck—or even punching him in the face, but that would have only resulted being left with sore fists. She reconsidered. Thought of something far better, as well as more practical: grabbed one of the metal chairs and swung it against the back of the slob's head that knocked Norbert's dentures out of his mouth and sent his face plopping hard into the bowl of slop before him.

# CHAPTER 157

**She left the kitchen in a hurry after that.** Made it to the bathroom down the hallway to wash the mess from her face.

Wiped it off. There was a distinct odor here as well. She paused, looked around. Noticed traces of blood along the edge of the tub; spots up and down the plastic shower curtain.

She drew the curtain back—and there it was: feathers. Blood. The sick fuck had murdered another chicken. Just couldn't stay away from it. Couldn't get his pathetic dick up without killing a harmless chicken. It disgusted her.

She rinsed her mouth out and sat on the toilet.

Look on the bright side: at least Lana was the one who'd had to deal with it; Lana was the one who'd been in the bathtub when he offed the chicken. Too bad. Somebody had to do it.

She washed her face some more. Looked around for a clean towel. In here? Didn't trust the towels hanging on the rack and resorted to wiping her face with her hands.

"What a sicko. What a sick, degenerate creep. This whole place gives me the willies." Couldn't shake what had gone down in the kitchen with the slob. Images stayed with her.

She was talking to herself and didn't care. "I have to get my hands on Stinky's stash. He's got to have shit hidden in the house somewhere. I know he does. No matter what he says."

Could be in that freezer in the kitchen, she thought. Only there was no way to get into the freezer or the refrigerators, or the cupboards even. Pry the lid on the freezer open? How? Refrigerators had chains on them. Cupboards had locks—top and bottom. Even if she were able to figure out how to get the slob out of there, there wouldn't be a way to deal with all the chains and locks and the locked freezer lid. It made her nuts.


She was out in the hallway again. Stood there. Taking in the various doors and trying to determine which ones she hadn't tried to open. There was that one to Marvin's room that she may have overlooked, and the one directly across the way from the kitchen. Wondered where it led to?

She moved in the direction. On edge was how she felt. Antsy. She heard a door open down at the other end of the hall, toward the rear. It was the kitchen door. The imbalanced giant who had given her the slop shower was emerging. Someone seemed to be shoving him.

Cecil? It was Cecil. She ducked behind the wall in the foyer area, for what good it did. Busted. Knew it. Heard them walk about halfway toward her and stop. When she peered from behind the wall she could no longer see where they were. There was an alcove where the door to the basement was.

Had to be where they were.

"Shame on you, Stella." It was Biggs. Spoke from where he stood at the door to the basement. "Really. Sneaking around like that."

"Sneaking around?" Stella Martel stepped out in full view. "Why would I be?"

"Not you."

"Frustrated." She walked toward where the two males stood. "That's what it is. I'm one frustrated chick right now. Can't get the square bitch to participate. You saw the way she acted in the living room, like she's better than everyone else. Was on my way upstairs to see if I can reason with her. Don't know if it'll do any good."

Biggs nodded. "Olivia?"

"Who else? She's a cunt. They're cunts in that family: males, females. All of them."

"I wouldn't be so hard on her."

"Of course not. Because you're holding all the cards."

"Speaking of cards. Will you excuse me while I escort my good friend Norbert downstairs to the play room where a poker game is waiting? His peers refuse to commence without him."

"Poker? He doesn't look like he'd know how to tie a shoelace without help."

"That's a bit harsh, don't you think?"

"Maybe it is. Sorry. While you're at it, see if you can get him to give up the dead cat. Odor is sickening."

"Do you hear that, Norbert?"

Mr. Fimple's response was a belch, followed by a series of gas emissions.

"I think I better go up there and try to talk some sense into the diva."

Biggs nodded with one of his chilling, patented grins this time. Waited for Stella to walk back down the hallway toward the front. It wasn't until he heard her begin to climb the stairs that would take her to the second floor did Biggs unlock the door to the basement. Had Mr. Fimple step through, and locked it back up.

He walked down the hallway toward the rear. Reached a door on his left, across the way from the kitchen. Let himself in. He locked it back up. As before, ascended the stairs to the second floor.

# CHAPTER 158

**As Stella Martel climbed the stairwell to the second floor, she could not help but notice, as did Olivia Duarte earlier, that Biggs had lined various parts of both walls with pennies and nickels, even quarters.**

The quarters were up near the ceiling and too far for anyone to reach. It was like that wall in the kitchen.

And then, way up there, on the ceiling itself, she realized that the fool had taped dollar bills. Actual money. He had dollar bills taped to the ceiling. Why? Some appeared to be from the Civil War. Old. Ancient. What was the point to any of it? To conceal the aging and discolored paint job? What sense did it make?

It made the kind of sense he wanted it to make: show people you're loaded. Impress the always broke motherfuckers with your wealth.

*Idiot* was right. Only *rich idiot* was closer to the truth.

And he had that fat ugly dick with the mole on the knob. At least they'd always been able to talk that dumb Mexican bitch Lana Sepulveda to screw him, instead of her and Pearl having to do it.

Definitely looked like he'd cut a chicken's head off down there in the hallway bathtub. She was sure to hear about it from Da Bottom eventually. Watch her whine about it first chance she gets.

Well, as far as Stella was concerned, she'd done *her* share by doing Deacon Moron. Fucked him and sucked his big dick more than once in the past. The thing about Marvin that made her half enjoy it was the asshole was hung like a pumpernickel baguette.

She didn't particularly enjoy fucking most men, but at least with Marvin she usually got off, whether it was intentional on his part or not. Truth was she preferred women, preferred going down on pussy, and one of these days she might even be able to convince "LaBelle of the Ball" to let her eat her out. That was something she'd been fantasizing about for some time now—but Pearl was straight and she had to be careful how she went about approaching her to let her taste that luscious muff.

She reached the second floor hallway. Dug around inside her handbag and withdrew a purse. She held the purse behind her back and walked up to a door on her right. Went in.

Olivia was sitting in the front row next to a shivering figure in a monk's robe with a hoodie on. Another one, thought Stella. Biggs seemed to be the Pied Piper to the mental defectives of Porn Valley.

This person, sitting in a chair on Olivia's left, who turned out to be a woman, turned her head, looking in Stella's direction.

"Can you please turn up the heat? Please?"

"We don't have much time left." Stella walked toward them. *"Where's the nose candy?"*

Patience McDaniel turned away. Resumed staring at whatever she had been staring at: empty space. Said nothing else.

"Great," said Stella to herself. Held the purse out. Said to Olivia: "Cecil said to ask if this is familiar to you."

"You know the purse belongs to me," said Olivia, taking it. "Where was it?"

"Good question. Must have slipped between the futon cushions."

"In his living room?"

Stella nodded. "If that's where the futon is."

"Not possible. I didn't have it with me when I stepped out of the cab."

Olivia looked inside the wallet. "I had eighty dollars in here. My money's missing."

"Is this the thanks I get for being a Good Samaritan?"

"Thief."

"Watch it."

"You got your grubby hands on my purse while we were in the backseat of that cab and stuck it in your handbag."

"You better watch it. I don't appreciate being accused of stealing."

"One of you did it. And took my money."

"Prove it." There was silence. Stella Martel pointed at Patience McDaniel. "What's wrong with this one?"

"It's quite cold in here," said Patience McDaniel without looking at anyone.

"No, it's not," said Stella.

"Hey, Stella," said Olivia. "Why don't you leave her alone?"

"Why don't you butt out?" Stella Martel countered. "Make me sick. Trying to act so pure all the time. You make me want to puke. What do you think we come here for? Use your head."

"I just want to get out of this place and I want to go home. My family must be worried about me."

"I don't give a shit about any of that. Nobody made you come with us. You're here now and you've got to wait until we're done with our business."

"Yeah? *What business would that be?*"

"*What do you think?*" Stella glared at her. Was annoyed that Olivia had the nerve to glare back; neither of them aware that Cecil Biggs was ensconced in a closet in the *Bible* Room in back of them, observing through a two-way mirror what was going on, as well as monitoring what was being said with aid of audio gear via a perforation in the wall.

# CHAPTER 159

**Downstairs in the pit in the basement, Dione had decided to give floating on her back a try in order to give her legs a rest.** She had been able to cling to either edge with her fingers and float this way with her mouth and chin above the murky, crud-infested water.

She could hear the deviates growling, making strange yelps and other sounds. One of them was even trying to unfasten the door above her. Could hear that easily enough, although the lack of light made it nearly impossible to visually make out much of anything through the holes in the door.

Maybe it was the thin one in the cowboy hat and jockstrap who looked like an underfed undertaker, the one they called "Big Tex," in those worn snakeskin boots with the big toe sticking out of one of them. She wasn't certain. Her head throbbed too much from the concussion and she knew for a fact that she was blind in one eye. But even that could have been acceptable to her just as long as she had a chance to live.

If only she could last long enough, survive long enough to get some medical attention. Someone, somewhere was sure to help her; someone was bound to catch these maniacs and stop them. *Someone is going to stop them*, she kept assuring herself. *Someone will. I know it.* There's families, people out there in this neighborhood. Someone is going to get suspicious about Biggs and that psycho Marvin he runs with and they will call the police and everything will be fine, everything will get taken care of.

She thought of her husband Danny and their little girl Clarissa and tears began to flow; she couldn't help it, tears formed in her good eye and flowed down into the water.

Danny is probably worried sick and has no idea what's happened with me. All he knows is that I stepped outside. I don't even think he saw me get in the evil clown's *Cadillac*. I'm not sure Danny saw anything. And then she regained enough of her senses and she wept because she realized that they had killed Danny right in front of her. They had taken him out of the backseat, had that hole dug in the ground and made Danny lie in it and Cecil had shot her husband in the face.

She couldn't help sobbing.

"Danny, Danny . . . Somebody has got to help me. . . ." Through the hole in the center of the door, and several other holes, she caught glimpses of the cowboy hat that indicated she had been right: "Big Tex" was the one trying to undo the hasp that would release her, at least get her out of the pit.

"We're here for you, little darlin'. You just show a bit more patience."

"Please help me."

"Doin' my best, little darlin'; doin' my doggone best."

# CHAPTER 160

**Stella doubted she could talk the square bitch into doing anything.** Had to keep trying. If only Biggs hadn't found her out in the hallway she might have been able to get into a room or two.

Then it dawned on her: What if the stash was hidden away in the living room? Right there, in front of their noses. *Hidden in plain sight.*

Goddamn him. What was all the work for? Guzzling Marvin's sperm. Not to mention time wasted. And this Duarte cunt refuses to get it. Effort invested by having to put up with two dickheads and their tired bullshit. Took way too much energy to con these jerks and stroke their fragile male egos—to get what in return? Bowl of disgusting mulligan stew in your face? A slop bath. What it had felt like. All because they were after some dope to get high for a while and not have to put up with any of the other crap men liked to have done to them. Wanted to have their balls and asshole licked; wanted you to swallow. Loads of it. Had almost been talked into pissing in Marvin's mouth. Come to think of it: she might have enjoyed that. What the assholes deserved. Tinkle on them. Golden showers. What they deserved and all were good for. More than one Hollywood asshole had asked her to shit on him, studio heads mostly.

Executives. Liked being pissed and shit on. The shitting was where she drew the line. She didn't shit on tricks. Maybe she should have, though. About all most of them rated.

She cursed again, because there was nowhere else left for her to go. Cecil was downstairs, and she couldn't risk getting busted by him again. Couldn't be seen roaming the hallway. If she had to, could claim a need to use the bathroom again. If she was forced to. As a last resort. How often would that excuse work anyway? Marvin and Cecil were dumb, but not that dumb. Should have left her hairbrush in the john. Use it as an excuse to return to it later. It was lame, to be sure—but if all else failed . . .

Place was an asylum. Fuck calling it a "church." It was full of loons. Why Cecil kept most of them out of sight. Probably more screwed up than the chick with the constant chills and the gorilla she ran into in the kitchen.

Seems Roscoe had a point. Hick had a point. Why let him know it? Best way, the only way to deal with men was to always keep them guessing, off balance. Make them feel insecure.

She didn't want to, but kept looking at the way the black woman continued to shake and shiver. Was staring at the floor now. Lost for good.

"Look, Olivia. You're right. It was rude of me. The lady is clearly troubled. Ran into another one, a man, down there in Cecil's kitchen. Did one of those raspberry numbers right in my face. He had a mouth full of stew when he did it. Sprayed me full on with stew. You can understand why I'm not a happy camper right now."

"Why don't you kindly go downstairs and tell your friends to hurry up whatever it is they have to do so we can clear out?"

"Why don't you stop acting like a nun and come down with me. Leave this nutty chick up here by herself. She doesn't need you to hold her hand. She's just another one of his batty lemmings. The man is really interested in you. You have no idea how valuable that is: to have a man of means like that crazy about you. You can get anything out of him that you want, anything. That's better than all the rest of those pathetic losers at Slim's trying to get into your panties. At least Stinky's loaded. He'll give us all the blow we want if you'll just be nice to him. You don't have to fuck him. You can be kind to the man; take some of your clothes off—"

"Are you out of your mind?"

"I ain't the one *out of my mind*. You don't have to fuck the annoying asshole. Just put on a show like Pearl is doing. It won't kill you. You never made out with that loser Rudy Perez by now? What are you acting so precious for? You never let Rudy feel you up? He never touched you? Who are you kidding? He's just another horndog. At least this motherfucker here is loaded. You don't have to put out. Lana took care of that already. Got him off. Looks like the imbecile had to kill a chicken to get it up, but he got it up. Tub's full of chicken feathers down there. Should see it. Chicken feathers and blood. What a nut." Stella dropped her tone a couple of notches. Added conspiratorially, desperate for it to do the trick: "Why don't you do it as a favor for your friends? Don't your friends mean anything to you?"

Olivia said nothing. Didn't even want to look at her. She finally understood: all the talk she'd heard over the years about Stella and the others was probably true. She didn't want any part of it.

"There is no hope for you. I'm so sorry I got in the cab with you. If anyone's a loser, it's you—and the rest of that amoral pack you run with."

"You stupid bitch." Stella slapped her, hard. "It's free toot. All you got to do is take your clothes off. Show him your tits. What's the big deal? You show them to Rudy, don't you? Dog walker got to see them."

It took Olivia a second or two to recover from the blow, and when she did she struck back equally as hard, if not harder, and Stella Martel found herself knocked out of the chair by a punch that sent her to the floor with a bloody lip.

"Don't you *ever* put your hands on me."

# CHAPTER 161

**In a part of the basement, at either times known as the Bunk Room or the Geek Cell, the "confused ones" were in a world of their own, preoccupied with various foibles and/or notions.** Dione Aragon's dilemma mattered little, if at all. The harlot was in the pit because it was her fate, a harlot's fate. And that unreliable, back-stabbing, no-account from Texas was out there attempting to pry that door loose, for who knew what for, and would only end up paying the price himself. The way it always happened, thought Betty Lou Rutterschmidt, who sat in her wheelchair and had that huge *Bible* of hers open and resting on her lap as she strained to read passages with the aid of the flashlight Bishop had been kind enough to let her have.

She was just inside the door, over in the right-hand corner, in a small area of the Geek Cell that was devoid of bunks. Her lips moved while she read, at times saying the words in a low, bordering on reverential whisper, so as not to wake her adopted daughter, sixty-seven-year-old Mildred Elizabeth, who slept on a thin mattress at her feet. Mildred, Mildred. Could have slept in her bunk, instead chose to stay close to dear old mom, as usual.

Miss Betty, as she was at times addressed, concentrated with all that she had, in order to glean the most out of what she read, even though she must have read the *Bible,* all the way through, more than a dozen times over the years, each reading having rendered new insights and reinvigorated her devotion to the Lord. The other reason for her fierce concentration and focus was in order to keep from losing her temper and doing something she might regret later, at what was taking place with the fools in the other bunks, especially the one they called "Swine Vomit," Olin Goodfellow, who, no doubt, was doing something disgusting underneath that blanket of his. Bag of waste gave hogs a bad name. Surely did.

The old woman's suspicions were far from inaccurate. Goodfellow was indeed lying in his bunk, lower berth, right side, in the middle there, and he had his hands down inside his diaper, fondling himself, while a nature film featuring bison unfolded up on the black-and-white television screen on a shelf near the ceiling.

He didn't seem to give a damn what his bunkmates were up to, didn't matter to him that Lawrence "Sassy" Sassounian was making a fuss by banging his forehead against the steel frame of his bunk, trying to draw attention to himself, as usual.

Sassy's problems and frustrations, figured Sassy, were far greater than anyone else's—and he was intent on reminding those around him at all times.

Sassounian still had that gamey scalp on with the long hair and barrette that Cecil had given him and he was lying on his belly and banging and rubbing the upper part of his face against the hard edge of the frame just above his pillow, agitating an earlier laceration until blood began to appear and oozed down. Some of the blood crawled close enough past his mouth that made it possible for him to get at with his tongue, what Sassy seemed to have been looking forward to. His fingers and toes had been heavily bandaged by the bishop and would not have been worth the effort to bother with. This, however, was different. Blood. Readily available.

The Rumanian, Julian "Red Menace" Ionesco, did what he could to carry out his part of the agreement he'd made with Sassy, which was: If he hurt him bad enough, caused him enough harm (and possibly made him bleed to the best of his ability), that Sassy would give him the pink blanket.

True enough, Ionesco had been eyeing that blanket that Sassy presently had wrapped about his neck ever since Bishop had given it to him. The blanket was pink, "pink," and should have been given to the Rumanian. Did Big Tex not give him the name "Pinko Punisher?"

Ionesco's bunk was in the upper berth, directly across the way. So as not to disturb Greta any more than was called for, so as not to draw her attention and ire, Ionesco quietly slid himself down off his bed and was attempting to reach with his right foot a part of Sassy's anatomy with it, any part, so long as the Pinko Punisher could inflict pain, break a finger or arm, a toe, anything, something—that would please him and Sassy both—and he kept kicking his foot out there trying to connect, all the while glancing in Greta's direction and doing his best so that she did not get wind of what was going on. The mean *fraulein* with those large buttocks and black leather German boots was powerful enough to cripple a man, break a man's back—or pee pee—and he wasn't in the mood for that sort of thing at the moment.

No, sir. He preferred it when he was the one doing the breaking and causing *others* to feel pain. Like Cecil always said. Besides, he stood to receive that beautiful baby blanket.


Sassy had stretched his own leg out there toward the one Julian was kicking out with.

Julian continued to keep an eye on Greta who was up there in the top berth across the way, in a bunk at the television end. He could hear her singing some silly song Cecil played from time to time. Had no idea what it meant, what the words were about, but went something like: *Flat foot floogie with the floy floy . . .*

Idiot American song, thought Ionesco. He never heard anyone sing anything this ridiculous in Europe in his whole life. *Flat foot floogie with the floy floy . . .* How can somebody make such a song? What is this "*floy floy*"?

Forget Greta. Let her keep singing. You sing, Sister *Kurva*, with the big buttocks. Yes. Sing, *Kurva. Ja ja.*


At last, the Pinko Punisher was able to connect. Made contact with Lawrence's left foot and kept kicking at it and kicking, stomping on it with his own heel that he was able to smash the other man's toes to the point that blood was beginning to show through the gauze—and this had made them both happy: the one relished meting out pain, while the other enjoyed being on the receiving end.

Greta Otto, The Leaper, still singing up there in her bunk, was adjusting the Cupid mask on her face in order to better see what was taking place down below at the other end. Were the pigs going at it again? Molesting one another? Wouldn't be surprised.

When she looked down, in Goodfellow's direction, she noticed that Swine Vomit still had his hands inside his diaper. It was annoying to her, no matter what he did, or what any of the male drips did, was annoying, but at least he wasn't anywhere near the pit and attempting to peer through the holes in the door and bothering the victim for the time being. The cowboy was. She knew it. Would wait to see what Cecil did to him. If he did nothing, she would handle it herself. He'd be tougher to manage than Swine Vomit, for sure. She'd have to ponder on it, before taking action.

She turned away. Her eyes back on the tee-vee screen that she had no interest in watching. She was singing that song again, the floy floy song, the flat foot floogie with the floy floy song. Had no real idea what it meant, but she sang it, repeated the words over and over again.

Now that the blanket was to be handed over, per their agreement, Ionesco reached for it only to discover that the other individual was unwilling to follow through on his part of the bargain. Blanket was his. It had been given to him by the bishop and was his to keep—and a tug-of-war ensued; the battling loons tugged at either end, refusing to concede.

Greta Otto, The Leaper, now humming softly up there in her bunk, had taken the Cupid mask off her face in order to better observe what was taking place below her. Let them claw at each other, she thought. The male was a lower form of life that the world certainly would have been better off without.

She turned her head; her attention back on the buffoonery with the bison. She hated nature shows. Shows with hyenas and lions, crocks. They were always devouring one another. Just like the dorks below, fighting over a blanket. What did they need with a blanket? Made no sense. She wished they'd kill each other and get it over with.

Only it went on. They would never kill each other—and that's what grated on her. Hissing and cursing. Over what?

She slid down from her berth. Stood in the aisle. The sight of her disfigured features probably unsettled them both, but not to the point they were willing to stop bickering—until they saw the blade. It was a paring knife.

Nowhere near as sharp as she would have liked. It would do the job. And then some. She stabbed at the blanket that made the trouble-makers cower, but not to the extent they were willing to give up anything.

She thrust the blade into the pink blanket repeatedly, watched as a tear developed at the top and others below it, watched as the dueling male drips tugged with all their might to retain what they each believed was their share of said blanket, and ripped it right down the middle.

Greta spit at the Rumanian, then at the other faggot, did an about-face, and paused at Swine Vomit's bunk. She held the tip of her blade about an inch away from Olin Goodfellow's left eyeball.

"Take your hands out of your diaper, pervert." Goodfellow had no choice, as he saw it, but to do as ordered. "Keep them both where I can see them—or else. I'll do to you what Cecil does to the victims—even if it means Pit Therapy for me."

"Please. You are making me wet myself."

*"Oh, shut up."*

Greta drove a hard elbow into Goodfellow's jaw. She stood there a while, watched him whimper and wheeze, then made it back up to her berth.

Miss Betty was relieved Greta had stepped in and taken care of that bit of nonsense, although not all the commotion was being caused by those in the Bunk Room. Not by a long shot. No, Lord. Big Tex was out there by the pit, trying to pry that door off, grunting and cursing; and they all knew that Big T. was begging for a beating, or worse: could easily end up in the pit himself, with "shock therapy" for a bonus.

There he was, though: part-time bronc-buster from Texas, or so he claimed, in that worn Stetson, clawing at that door over the pit.

They knew Big T. was aching to be punished, because Bishop had good cause for leaving that "fornicating sinner" in that water-filled hole in the floor. What it meant was Cecil Biggs did not want her disturbed, did not want anyone to go near her—for any reason. And yet, there he was—that big dumb cowboy from Ft. Worth, that cadaverous-looking cement truck driver from the Lone Star State wanting to get that heavy door removed so he could get at that noisy, one-eyed harlot who didn't know how to keep her big mouth shut.

She was down in the water because she had it coming and should be left alone.

# CHAPTER 162

**The music upstairs seemed to get louder, increased in volume, and Dione Aragon thought for sure she had heard other voices, familiar voices, sounds, through the floorboards above, sounds and voices that also filtered faintly through the bottom of the door up there at the top of the basement stairs.**

There were other people on the first floor besides Cecil and Marvin and one or two of these imbalanced individuals, couldn't tell exactly, who made up this crazy church; there were clearly other girls up there in the other rooms, moving about, dancing, it seemed; it surely seemed someone was moving on their feet up there above them on the first floor, dancing to a heavy bass beat.

Dione Aragon made every effort to urge the cowboy to hurry up. Even if she had to go through with what he wanted, within reason, of course, as she was not quite certain what that would be at this point, she was willing—that would free her and get her out of this hell and make it possible to be reunited with her baby girl. If she were pulled out of this nightmare she would take her Clarissa with her, Dear Lord; she would take her baby and she would hurry back home to Bakersfield. She would get out of LA, clear out of Southern California and never come back. If only the one intent on helping her would get on with it. She heard him say something, talking.

"Now me, I ain't like them others in here. They're just waitin' for you to up and die—so they can eat you."

"Please help me, Big Tex. Please help me get out of here."

"Big Tex is doin' his very best, little darlin'. We'll get you took care of. Got my word. And when a Texan gives his word, why that's as good as it gets. Ain't a soul in this country, ain't a soul in this entire world what defines dignity and honor better than a bronc-bustin' Texas cowhand."

# CHAPTER 163

Bishop Cecil Omar Biggs's next door neighbor Petunia Roscoe was sitting at her piano in the dining area of the living room trying to compose a song and she was not getting anywhere and it simply drove her nuts because the noise coming from Biggs's "church" was wreaking havoc with her concentration.

Her husband Marty, on the other hand, was in the kitchen with a fly swatter and he was having the time of his life.

He would whack a moth or a fly with the swatter and watch it drop to the floor and say to the Boston terrier: "Get the *bug*, Darcy. Get the *bug*." Incredibly enough, the little dog knew what he was talking about and those paws would patter across the kitchen linoleum in search of the moth or fly that had just dropped and the dog would lap it up in an instant. The Boston terrier loved eating spiders, moths, flies, and Marty Roscoe enjoyed watching the dog get excited at the prospect of getting more.

Petunia's husband swatted a couple of flies near the kitchen sink, scraped them off the counter and watched Darcy eat them up as soon as they hit the floor.

"That's right, Darcy. Get the *bug*. Get the *bug*, little girl." And then he would cross to the other side of the kitchen where the table sat and tease her by pretending he'd just killed another one of those pesky flies just to see the little dog's paws run after the imaginary insect.

Ziggy, the Lhasa apso, on the other hand, was lying on her belly on the living room carpet nearby, watching and wondering what all the commotion was about.

"That's a nine-year-old dog," Petunia said, clearly irritated. "You're running her ragged."

"No, I'm not. She's having fun. Can't believe how smart she is. She knows exactly what I'm talking about when I say *get the bug*. See the way she looks up? Never saw a dog what loves to eat flies like she does."

"That's disgusting."

Marty smacked another fly on the refrigerator door and watched the dog lap at it before it even hit the floor. Roscoe stood there chuckling and shaking his head.

"See that?"

Petunia didn't have time for it. Rose from her piano to peer through the living room curtains.

"He's running a slut house next door."

"Oh, I wouldn't say that."

"Well, I would. He's got those sluts from the *Casbah* in there again and that makes it a *slut house*. That's exactly what Peaches LaBelle and those other bimbos she runs around with are, you know: *sluts*. Nothing but a bunch of *immoral sluts*."

"One day you'll say the wrong thing to the wrong creep."

"At least I have the courage to speak my mind."

"You'll mouth off to the wrong psycho and then it will be too late. Sometimes it's smarter not to say anything at all."

She turned away from her curtains long enough to give Marty one of her angry looks he was well familiar with by now. "When was the last time you heeded your own advice?"

"Forget it, all right? There's no point trying to reason with you."

"Don't start that again."

"All I'm saying is careful how you talk to him. If he's running a 'slut house' next door that's his damned problem. Only I wouldn't say anything to his face about it."

"You wouldn't. I would."

"You're never satisfied until you got yourself all worked up. Always the same thing. Like a broken record."

"Don't you have any sympathy for me? I can't take the noise; I can't work like this."

"It's a free country, Petunia. Why is it acceptable for you to tickle the ivories and not acceptable for him to play his music?"

"Whose side are you on? Why does it have to be so loud?"

"I don't know why it has to be so loud and I don't care."

Petunia opened the front door and stuck her head out.

"Now Rudy Perez is out there. I wonder what's going on?"

"Could be he got religion."

"This late at night?"

"The Good Lord don't mind what time it is, woman. Man can be Saved anytime. Day or night."

"You know you're full of it, don't you?"

Roscoe had a grin on his face. Couldn't help it. She turned to look at him.

*"You do this just to annoy me."*

# CHAPTER 164

**Rudy Perez had fortified himself with a forty ouncer and was outside Biggs's church, shaking the gate and kicking at it, raising Cain, wanting to know what the hell was going on inside, wanting to see his girl, wanting in; only no one was listening, or maybe no one could hear him because the music was beyond loud.**

A pair of car headlights coming up from his left drew his attention briefly. Harold Crust had pulled up in his old Falcon. Parked it in his driveway, and walked over.

"How-do, Rudy?"

Rudy greeted him with a nod. Was about the best he could do. His mind was set on getting inside that house there. What kind of preacher was this Biggs anyway? What kind of preacher runs around with dopefiends and lap dancers? What kind of sense did any of it make? That was the point. It made no sense.

Harold Crust cleared his throat.

"Think you or your brother might find some time this weekend to take a look at my car? Runs kinda rough lately."

"Sure. Just bring it by, Mr. Crust."

Rudy was about to climb over Biggs's front gate. Harold Crust did not think it was such a good idea, at that.

"Man could get shot. Mr. Biggs packs heat. Seen it with my own eyes."

"I need to talk to somebody in there."

"Suit yourself."

Harold Crust walked away. He climbed his front porch steps. Stood there, searching for the key, when the door opened, and his wife Fay greeted him. Harold went in, turned to close the door behind him, paused there, taking into account that beat-up bucket with Ace Ortiz and his flaky buddy creeping along down the street. Rudy noticed them, too, as they crawled right on past him.

"Those two are always up to no good," said Harold to himself, and closed the door behind him.

Rudy paused, considered Harold's words of warning, and decided to scale the gate just the same. He reached the front door and started kicking and pounding on it until Marvin R. Muck opened it.

"Where's Olivia Duarte?"

Marvin did not answer him, turned, and had Rudy Perez follow him up the stairs to the Prayer Room. Showed him in.

Livia was still there, sitting next to the shivering black woman. Marvin left the room.


The first thing Rudy had picked up on was the odor; the weird, sickening kind of stench that did not agree with him.

Biggs usually reeked anyway, but this was far worse. Nearly impossible to take. What the hell was it? Dead cats? That's what it smelled like, dead cats and ammonia cleaner.

It was strong stuff whatever it was.

Olivia turned, and was not at all pleased at seeing him here. Undoubtedly he'd been following her. She hadn't cared for it at all. She was old enough to take care of herself, and besides, if she had needed somebody to watch over her there was her family. That was plenty. More than enough. She did not need Rudy Perez to start telling her how to live her life. Who did he think he was? *He buys you a ring and starts acting like he owns you.*

Patience saw this as yet another opportunity to put in her (by now familiar) request: "Mister, could you please, *please* turn up the heat?"

Rudy did not know how to respond. Was this woman all right? He didn't know. Didn't care about turning up the heat in this house. He didn't live here. Just wanted to take Olivia with him and leave. That was it.

"I don't appreciate being followed by you."

Rudy could not believe what he was hearing.

"What are you saying, Liv? I was worried."

"You've got a big problem, Rudy: *Jealousy.*"

"Jealousy? You've been watching the soaps again, or maybe you've been hanging around Peaches LaBelle and her friends too long. Those people are so screwed up they don't know what normal is. I love you and I worry about you."

"I'm fine."

Rudy took her by the arm. "Good. Let's get out of here."

Olivia saw to it to break free. "I don't appreciate being man-handled."

"What do *you* appreciate? You want to stay here? Is that what you want?"

There was silence. Neither of them spoke.

# CHAPTER 165

**Downstairs, in the living room, Pearleen had worked up quite a sweat, and since Biggs and Marvin were still absent, she decided to give herself a well-deserved break and sat down.**

The lack of love between Stella and Lana continued to be evident. The way Lana saw it, Stella should have been able to come up with something. Instead, she had returned empty-handed and had the nerve to pretend to be interested in Cecil's and Marvin's whereabouts, asking where they were, just so she wouldn't have to listen to her go over what she'd had to put up with in the john with Reverend Odor and his less-than-conventional approach to sex. There had been a chicken, and blood—and choking and shit. And as far as Lana was concerned, her anger was more than justified.

"I provide you with a distraction, keep him occupied—and you come back with excuses. You didn't look hard enough. What the whole problem is right there."

"How the hell would you know? Every goddamn door I tried was locked, except the door to the kitchen—and guess what I found in there? Should make you real happy: birdcages hanging from the ceiling, with chickens in them. That's right. And one of Cecil's evil simpletons standing on a chair trying to beat at them with a wooden spoon. Until he fell off. Psycho fell right off, then noticed me. Got his fat ass up and sat in that chair like I wasn't even there. Ate slop from a bowl—with a dead stare like he was the only one in the room. Just like that black woman upstairs. Same thing. *Fucking bipolar loons.* Only his staring wasn't the problem; that didn't bother me. Half expected it. Didn't expect to have my face sprayed with that pig slop he ate. Hear me? Hear what I'm saying? Demented asshole sprayed me with slop and you got some nerve trying to claim I didn't try hard enough. *'Brother Trusty'* keeps the rooms *locked.* I tried my best; tried real hard to talk that square Duarte bitch to come down at least, just spend some time with him, take a few of her clothes off for the man. She wouldn't do it; refuses to even discuss it. *Effing cunt.* Had to slap her, too. Who does she think she is to disrespect me."

Pearleen did not want to believe what she just heard.

"Let me get this straight: *you hit Olivia?*"

"You heard me."

"You—slapped—her?"

"Bitch fought back. Only I got the first one in."

"What gives you the right? We should be grateful that she decided to come with us in the first place. She didn't have to do anything, period."

"I don't want to hear that *'boo-shit'.* We coulda got the man's stash. Got him to give us some to take with. Stuck up cunt won't play the game. Won't help out."

"You just better keep your hands off that girl, Stella."

"Or what?"

"Or you deal with me."

Lana was glaring at them both. "I'm the one's got every right to be pissed. If you want to know the truth. I'm the one had to do it all, had to get that creep off. I didn't see none of you suckin' his ugly fat dick. Did I now?"

Pearleen and Stella exchanged glances and had to laugh. Lana hated them for it.

"You think that's funny? I don't think any of it is funny. I do the dirty work and you two think it's fucking hilarious. I didn't see either of *you* go down on him, did I now?"

"You saw me give Marvin a hand job, then give him a BJ."

"So what? That ain't shit. I sucked Cecil's dick and then had to fuck the dude—that's work. Fucker got rough, too. You know he likes that rough shit. Choked me in the shower. Choked the shit out of me and still couldn't get it up."

Pearl looked at her.

"Why did you take it? Why let him do that to you?"

"Maybe she secretly likes it."

"Fuck you, Stella. Nobody likes that shit."

"Some do. Ask Mona Payne."

"Drop dead, bitch," said Lana Sepulveda. To Pearleen Bell, she said: "You know why I took it; you both know why. Had to let him—if he was to ever get off. *Sick a-hole.* Had one of his chickens running around in the tub, too. Strangling me half to death wasn't good enough for him, didn't do it for him. It wasn't until he cut the chicken's head off and the blood sprayed him that he was able to get his weenie up."

"You got him to shoot his load," said Stella. "Like a real pro. Should be proud."

Lana rubbed her neck to ease the stiffness. She held up the hand mirror to check for bruises. "I warned Marvin about that chicken business. I told him I didn't want to see any chickens get killed. Shit is way the fuck out there."

"You're holding up fairly well," said Pearleen. "All things considered." Obviously fought to keep a grin from breaking through. Lana caught on and her anger resurfaced.

"All this is amusing to you. That's it, isn't it? One big joke. What I want to know is: How come you don't ever do some of the down-and-dirty work, *'Ms. LaBelle of da Ball'*? That's what I want to know."

"Because, Lana honey, it just ain't my thang, that's all. And you done well. We all got high, good and high, didn't we? And I know that you both know I did my share; always do. You wouldn't have got nowhere without my act."

"I got somewhere all right. My mother's gonna freak when she sees the bruise marks on my neck. Doesn't take much for her to go ballistic, either."

"I hope he apologized at least," quipped Stella.

"You're about as funny as Phyllis Diller—and if you don't watch it you could end up looking like her."

"He should have apologized—"

"Told you before: Fuck off, Stella. Just shut your unfunny, anchovy smelling hole—unless you want to see me do to you what he did to me." To Pearleen, Lana said: "Weird-ass did say he was sorry. Blamed it on 'force of habit.'"

"*Force of habit?* Maybe we ought to get one of McCoy's Ali Baba bouncers to do a little *force of habit* on his butt."

"That's what he claimed. That was his reason. Force of habit. And the nose bleed."

"Wait a minute."

"Can you believe that? Picked me because my nose was bleeding. The sight of blood did it. Exactly why he cut the chicken."

"Most men are fucked in the head," said Stella. "Should know as much by now. Where are they, anyway? Where's the sadist?"

"Said something about having to make sure that his board of directors had their tea and pastries," said Pearleen.

"Tea and pastries?" said Lana. "Where's *our* tea and pastries?"

"What about Marvin?" asked Stella.

"Stepped out," said Pearleen.

"I can see that," said Stella.

"Maybe he's in the closet," suggested Lana, pointing at the closet door. "Spying on us through one of those mirrors—to make sure we don't *steal* any of these *stolen* library books." Even as she said it, she had a hardcover of Truman Capote's *In Cold Blood* in her hands. She may have only been joking about the closet and Marvin hiding out in it. Stella tried the closet door all the same. It was locked.

"Marvin? You in there?"

"What are you doing?" said Pearl. "There's nobody in that closet. I think he had to use the john."

"Why would Cecil want to keep this door locked?"

"To keep dopefiends like you from stealing his dope," said Lana, and shoved the book back onto the shelf in back of the futon. She still could not get over the fact Cecil had chosen her because of the nose bleed. It was creepy, too creepy, even for her.

"You know as well as I do," said Pearl, "what keeps getting us into these situations: dope."

"Could be you're right, Peachy," said Lana. "Rehab may be the way—eventually. One day."

She dug around inside her leather purse. Came up with a pack of smokes. Extracted one of the butts. It looked ordinary enough, and it was, except the tip end had been filled with cocaine.

"Until then, what do you say we do up some *Cocoa Puffs?*"

Pearleen was shaking her head. That grin that she fought to suppress earlier was shining through this time; every bit of it. Stella's reaction was basically the same.

"You know she's right, Lana. All we're doing is fucking up our lives with this shit."

"Sure we are. And you can't wait to get in on this so you can keep your high alive."

Lana dragged on the cigarette. It was a long one, as usual, then passed it on to Pearleen. Pearleen had hers. Offered it to Stella Martel, who did not refuse. It went on in this fashion until the butt was smoked down.

# CHAPTER 166

**Things were getting loud again in the Prayer Room.** Biggs was at the two-way mirror eyeing Rudy and his ballbuster. It bothered him that he hadn't taken the time to walk Mr. Fimple to the Geek Room and chain him to his bunk, to be on the safe side. Mr. Fimple would be roaming now, possibly getting into trouble. Wouldn't put it past him. Didn't matter how often you shocked the son of a bitch, either, or stuck him in Siberia. Who else had been left out beside Big Tex and Norbert Fimple? Couldn't even recall locking the door to the Geek Room. Thinking about it made it difficult to stay focused on what was taking place before him, the latest development: Rudy Perez. If the notion of capturing Olivia and keeping her here was one he had toyed with, along with holding onto her exotic dancer friends, that notion had been shattered now by Rudy's presence.

There were just too damn many people in the church now, too many others who probably knew that they were here. There was nothing left to do but watch as Rudy Perez and his virginal girlfriend continued to battle it out.

"If this is any indication what being married is going to be like, I don't want it."

"You don't know what you want."

"I know exactly what I want, Rudy—"

"Good for you. Do you know who you're starting to sound like to me? Those tired, old, lesbian libber types. You know the kind: with the *mustache and hairy legs*—that no man would be interested in in the first place. *'Women'* like that, with their attitude, are *disgusting*."

"Don't push me, Rudy."

"I worry about you and this is the thanks I get?"

"Thank you. All right? I am old enough to take care of myself. If you weren't so blind and stubborn you'd see that you and I have some serious problems to work out—"

"Truth is we don't have any problems—"

*"Truth is you don't get it."*

"*I do get it.* Exactly. We're getting along fine, just great—only your sister and your family put ideas in your head. Your whole family's been against me from the beginning."

And Rudy proceeded to mimic the following: "*If you and Rudy ain't got no problems—make some up.*" He dropped that to continue in his normal tone of voice. "There's your excuse to have a fight and break up. I'm wise to you, Livia. You want to play that game? Go right ahead—only don't come blaming the split on me. You don't want me? Fine. There's lots of chicks out there who'd be real glad to have a guy like me. That's right. You got the *scoop.* I'm not about to let you or your family try to put me down. No way. My bro warned me about you. You're doing exactly what your sister did to him."

"That isn't true. You have no right to say those things to me, Rudy. No right at all."

Maybe he felt a twinge of remorse. He didn't know. Didn't want to think that maybe it was possible he came on too strong. All he wanted was to take Olivia with him and get out of the smelly house.

"I'm leaving. Are you coming with me?"

"If that's how you feel, why did you get involved?"

"You're the one who kept bringing your family's station wagon around for tuneups and repairs; not that I minded, you know. Don't get me wrong there. Only I wasn't the one who started coming around *your* house, remember? That definitely would have been a *no-no*; am I right? The way your family is?" He asked again: "*Are you coming?*"

Rudy reached the door. Waited. Olivia was intent on getting the ring he'd given her off her finger.

"What're you doing?"

"*Here. Take this with you.*"

"*No. You take it. And shove it.*"

He was out of there. She could hear him go down the stairs. Make it outside.

# CHAPTER 167

**No sooner did Rudy vault the gate, coming down over the other side, losing his footing and landing awkwardly, did Ortiz swing down with his beer bottle.** Rudy ducked in time and drove a fist into the junkie's belly. Spun around for something to defend himself with before Ortiz reached for either that switchblade he owned, or a gun.

Harold Crust's picket fence was in back of him a bit, on his left. He pried a picket off. Stood there facing the user. Felix had also crossed the street, approaching them, and he was holding something. Possibly a weapon; he wasn't sure.

So it was two against one once again—and all he had was the useless picket to defend himself with. Being involved with Olivia had caused him nothing but pain. The Duartes did nothing but cause his family a bunch of grief. Was it even worth it? Right now he wasn't so sure that it was.

"I ain't gonna waste you, asshole. Just cut you up a little to pay back for that bullshit you and your brother pulled in front of Slim's."

"Live and let live, Ace."

"Sure. Now that Roe ain't here to do your fightin' for you."

"I had nothing to do with you getting 86'd. Take it up with Mr. Jessup. That's between you and Mr. Jessup."

"Not what this is about—and you know it. Made me look bad, punk."

"It never did take much, Ace."

"You gonna pay."

Ortiz drew the switchblade. Clicking the blade into place.

"I'm no fighter. I don't want to fight you."

"Shoulda thought of that before, bitch."

"Me and my brother were taught not to look for trouble. We were also taught not to take crap off trouble-makers like you."

Harold Crust's front door opened and Harold stepped out on his porch. His right hand was down at his side, but it was plain that it held a gun.

"You don't want to see me raise my hand, Mr. Ortiz. Because if I do, the gun in it goes off—in your direction."

Ortiz stood there, undecided.

"A while back you asked if I'd let you work with me, rent a chair to make a few bucks.... Said I was willing to try it.... Been in your moccasins, and willing to give a man a break ... but you've got to stop carrying on like this."

Ortiz pressed a button on the hilt in his hand, and the blade retracted.

"Go on about your business, Rudy."

Rudy nodded, and walked off. Ortiz spat on the sidewalk. Stood there shaking his head. Harold Crust re-entered his place, and closed the door behind him.

# CHAPTER 168

**Olivia wiped her tears with a handkerchief.** After a while, she slid the ring back on her finger. Marvin Muck walked in the same door Rudy had gone out a moment ago.

"Sorry, sugah-bush. Couldn't help but overhear what you two was sayin' you be talkin' so loud. Know what, baby? That jive mothah ain't good enough to lick *sweat* off yo *fine booty. That be the bottom line.*"

"I want to leave. Where's Pearleen?"

"Pearleen? Don't know no Pearleen, me."

"Peaches."

"Peach? Peach be takin' a shower. Said she was, 'till she seen them chicken feather' in the baf'room an' tub. Could be she change' her mind. Who care' 'bout Peach an' them dopefiend' anyway? I be worried 'bout you instead, *sugah-bush*. What yo hurry, baby? Ain't no need to be in no hurry."

He left the Prayer Hall.

# CHAPTER 169

**Biggs remained watching Olivia through the two-way in the back wall, and thought: What the hell?** Why not keep her here? So what if Rudy's a witness and later claims he saw her in here last? By the time I finished with Olivia Candida Duarte, it wouldn't matter who knew about it. Not only that, he'd have the dancers to do with as he pleased: *Pearleen and Stella and Lana*. Olivia and Pearleen would have been the Big Prize, though. Pearleen was still unwilling to put out, still playing hard to get. Bitch knew how to get him worked up, excited. It had cost him a lot. He'd spent big money on all that dope, but it had been worth it—and if he locked them in the church right now he could have his fun without having to pay another dime for it, for a few days, maybe weeks, until someone got wise and started to look for them in his place. It was a risk worth taking.

Why the hell not? Could always get rid of the bodies afterwards. Even if punk Rudy Perez were to go around telling the whole neighborhood he had seen Olivia and the others in here before they disappeared, so what? What would that do to him? What kind of tight spot would it put him in and would he be able to work out of it?

Sure; why not? He'd have the dead bitches disposed of by then. Before he did that, however, he'd have each victim sign a greeting card and seal the envelope with her own saliva. DNA.

The greeting cards would say that all was well and not to sweat it. He would mail the cards from Vegas, while paying a visit to his fence out there and the guy he bought most of his drugs from.

Sounded like a viable plan to him. One worth pursuing. Question was: Did he dare? Risk losing everything he'd worked so hard over the years to achieve?

Biggs had his eye up against the two-way mirror and he couldn't stop looking, imagining, wondering what Olivia looked like under all that clothing, how big her tits were, what kind of shape her ass had, her thighs, pussy—and how long it would take him to beat her into submission, absolute compliancy, and force her and teach her how to lick his cock and balls and asshole.

That's what he thought about now, as he eyed her through the opening. What sort of tricks could he come up with to humiliate her? Could he have anything new up his sleeve? Improve on all the other games and tortures he'd used in the past on the others?

What would he make her do? He felt like going in there right now and holding a dagger blade to her throat and tearing her clothes off and fucking her right in front of the Holy Cross—just lay her down like that with that dagger against her throat, or maybe the dagger would be right up against her ass, or cunt, while he forced her to suck him off . . . with the catatonic in attendance.

The possibilities were incredible. And this kind of thinking only gave him another erection, and caused his cock to continue pulsating as he squeezed it in his fist.

He wondered if he had it in him to go again this soon? The Sepulveda cunt had drained him pretty good in the john. It didn't matter. He was hard.

Christ, he wanted her. Look at that untainted innocence—untouched beauty, unlicked pussy—pink and clean inside and fresh smelling. Even her asshole probably smelled like fresh spring flowers in the morning. Now that was purity . . . that was youth. . . . A clean, young thing like that, ripe, waiting to be taken . . . and dirtied up.

## CHAPTER 170

**Stella was in the hallway again, trying for the kitchen door for a second go, at least she wanted it to appear that way in case Biggs or one of his geeks walked up on her and she'd use being hungry as an excuse for snooping.** Just looking for something to eat. Got the munchies. She looked about. When no one showed and the coast looked clear, she let go of the doorknob. Took a few careful and quiet steps down the hallway toward the front.

She paused at the door that led to the basement and thought she heard noise, someone scream, a woman—but she could not be certain.

She turned the doorknob.

This door, too, was locked—and then Marvin Muck appeared at the opposite end by the front entrance, having descended the stairs from the above floor, or possibly having exited the living room.

"What chu be doin' over there, sugar-bush?"

Stella smiled at him. "Looking for the bathroom, handsome. Gotta go again."

"You know where the crapper be. You was just in there."

"That last hit of crack Cecil gave us did a real number. Truth is, I can't tell where I am: upstairs, downstairs. Know what I mean? Fucked me up."

"Know exactly what you be sayin'. Told you *shit be fly.*"

Stella feigned wooziness. "I'm about to start gagging."

"Don't do it on the floor. Cecil don't be likin' it."

"What the hell is it, anyway? What's the odor? I'm about to puke."

"'Lizzy Borden' be the one. Ax killa Lizzy."

"Don't fuck with me, Marvin. My head's spinning as it is. *Lizzy Borden? Who slaughtered her parents back in the late eighteen hundreds? That Lizzy Borden?*"

Marvin chuckled, while hustling his nuts. He was always hustling his nuts.

"No, man. Greta was *pretendin'* to be related to the psycho bitch who offed her mamma and daddy. Usta work with Cecil at the haunted house. All the time. You know Cecil got that evil clown thing goin' on: *Trusty Lusty,* an' Greta would be all made up in her crazy-ass Lizzy part: nightgown and arms all covered in Technicolor blood. Was part of they act: to make like the ho be related to the real ax killa: *Lizzy Borden.* You know? *Trusty Lusty' Bordello of Fear.* Peeps ate it up. Paid good coin to see the show. You never been? Missed out, *sugah-bush—big time.*"

"Sounds like *boo-shit*."

"No boo-shit. The two of them put on a show was kick-ass. In Temple City. Peeps ate that shit up. Was lovin' it. We was on *Entertainment Tonight*. Surprised you ain't never heard."

"I may have. I don't know. Who's got time?"

"All I be sayin', Greta be her real name. Otto, Greta Otto. She the one. Do all the cookin'. Big ho burn everything all the time. Leaper ain't no real cook, but the ho got to pay her way; jus' like all the hoe' got to pay they way. She come close to killin' one of the member of the payin' public two time' too many. They was payin' customer'. Bigg' started lettin' the bitch do her psycho Lizzy act part-time again not long ago; on weekend', on account Greta love doin' it; puttin' fear in them peeps an' shit. But then, about a month ago, in fac', ho attacked two Messicans with a ax handle. No shit. They was employee of Cecil. You know, at the Bordello of Fear? Doin' janitoral, cleanin' the crapper', an' like that. Greta sent 'em both to the hospital for a few day'. Cracked they skull real nice. On account they was wantin' some pussy. Tried to rape the bitch. Greta don't play that shit. Don't like mens. Except she ain't had me yet. Anyway, reason bein' why rollers shut our haunted house down the other day. For the time bein'. Messicans be tryin' to sue Cecil; shakin' his ass down for bank. Look' that way. So, instead of lettin' Greta go; instead of cuttin' her loose, Cecil say she could stay on, bein' the cook. Dude got a heart. Let her go back to bein' the cook full time from now on, instead of workin' at the Bordello of Fear. Only ho can't cook, neither. That be *the whole truff an' nothin' but the truff.*"

"I thought Cecil said you had a dead cat somewhere in the basement."

"Yes, ma'am. Dat, too. Dead cat, dead rat'. Cecil' dead shepherd Rutherford, and some other dead shit down there that be causin' the odor."

"Thought he said the dog ran off."

"Yeah. Could be. Mostly though, it be caused by the cook: Greta Otto. *Leaper.*"

"Leaper?"

"What they call the ho in the paper."

"Why not fire the bitch, then? If she can't do the job. Replace her."

"Cecil say he ain't got the heart to can Greta. Big ho got her face all fucked up in a fire an' can't get no job out there. If you aks me, all that be a bunch of *boo-shit*. But we ain't got to talk about it."

He walked over. Kissed her neck in his own clumsy manner. Reached inside the T-shirt she had on to squeeze a breast or two. His hand then slid down toward the belly button, bent lower, reaching pubic hair, and beyond. Stella stayed with him for a while this way. Reciprocated by fondling his impressive groin. Felt it develop mass rapidly enough, and then told him to go and wait for her in the other room with Lana and Peaches, that she would join them all for the encore, as soon as she finished up in the john.

"'*Encore*'? Head was sure good. Don't it be 'bout time to give this nigga some pussy by now?"

"Have to *pee*, handsome."

"When the ho got to go, go wiff the ho."

"You're not going anywhere with me." Stella broke away. "I need my privacy."

"You private? That it? Take too long, and Mack Daddy Muck gonna come lookin' for yo *private* ass, sugah-bush."

Stella entered the john, closing the door in his face. Muck entered the utility room, pushed a sliding panel open and stepped into the closet. He sat in a folding chair, looking through a two-way mirror that gave him pretty much a full view of the living room.

# CHAPTER 171

**There were developments taking place in the basement.** With Norbert Fimple's help, Big Tex was able to break the lock right off the door that had kept Dione imprisoned in the pit. The bandage over her right eye was soggy from periodic exposure to water and the bacteria in it and the surrounding swelling had only gotten worse. Flies buzzed around overhead and would not leave her alone. Big Tex thought to give the naked, manic-looking woman a helping head. Enfolded his arms around her waist, pressing her chest hard against his, and hauled her out. Greta handed him a robe with a hoodie and the cowboy assisted Dione into it. Guided her over to the stairwell and sat her down on the steps near the bottom and watched her shoulders go up and down as she sobbed uncontrollably.

"Isn't anyone ever going to help us get out of here?"

Dione Aragon looked around at the others, who had emerged from the Bunk Room with glares of pure contempt for Big T.

There were rules to abide by, restrictions to be aware of—and the "part-time bronc-buster" was bound to bring down unspeakable doom upon their existence with his selfish behavior.

No one said a word. Dione looked up at the door at the top of the stairs.

"Maybe they can help us. There's somebody up there. Maybe they can help if we can let them know somehow that we're down here, that we need medical attention, that we need to be looked after, fed and given a chance to clean ourselves properly." She wept. "I think I've got lice in my hair. . . . Doesn't anyone want to do anything about getting out of here?"

As if on cue, there was the sound of the toilet flushing in the basement john and the deep-throated voice of Betty Lou Rutterschmidt uttering: *"There's your answer, you disease-ridden, filthy trollop."*

"I want—"

*"You want?"* said Betty Lou, who was pushed out of the john in her wheelchair by the ever-loyal Mildred Elizabeth. "It's about you, isn't it? Always about you. Self-centered, rotten slut. What *we want* is for you to button your lip and close up your vagina, harlot!" the ninety-two-year-old woman shrieked. *"I can smell a harlot a mile off . . . and to me you smell like a harlot!"*

"You're wrong. My God, you are so wrong. I'm married and have a little daughter named Clarissa."

*"What gives you the right to make that claim? When I should be the one!* There is no one kinder, more faithful and true; no one with more patience! What audacity for a strumpet. Don't waste your breath denying it! Look at you! Written all over your filthy whore's body! They run around like the wanton fornicators that they are and then have the unmitigated gall to deny it! *Whore!"*

*"I only worked in that night club because we needed money to get back home,"* Dione made every effort to explain to these people who were clearly unstable. What choice did she have?

"If my mother says you're a *whore*, then you're a *whore!"* Miss Betty Lou's sixty-seven-year-old daughter Mildred cackled. "There's the smell of the gutter tramp about you—and you can't deny that, bitch! You're being punished for it now! Take it, because you earned it! Brought it on yourself! That's what all this is about!"

"All I did was work as a dancer in a night club. I didn't do anything else. . . ."

"You did enough!" Miss Betty Lou said.

"We needed money to eat and take care of the baby. . . . We were trying to get back to Bakersfield. . . . We did nothing . . ."

Mildred, having borrowed the lengthy chain from Mama Betty Lou, ran up and whipped the chain at her; whipped her across the back as hard and viciously as she was able.

Greta, the Leaper, Otto, saw it and hadn't liked it. Stepped in, got both hands on the chain and wound it once about Mildred's neck and yanked back so vehemently on it that she practically had her off her feet. Greta stayed with it: yanking, then heaved her with enough force in "Mommy Dearest's" direction that Mildred, completely off-balance and backpedaling, collided against the organist in the wheelchair with such impact that she not only knocked her over, but ended up sprawled on the floor herself.

Greta retrieved the chain and decided to hold on to it. Remained standing there for the time being, taking in the wretched old prunes and their pathetic moaning and griping.

Any other time she may have sided with them, felt a sense of kinship. Not here, not now—not after the way she saw them badger someone who was nothing more than a victim, one of their own stuck in the mire.

It took Mildred a moment to recover. Once she was able, she lifted the wheelchair upright, then helped her mother get back into it. Attempted to, in her own clumsy way. She had failed to lock the wheels and the chair had rolled back, away from them, and left the mother standing on wobbly legs.

"Apply the brakes!" urged Betty Lou. "Lock the brakes in! Lock them in next time! *The brakes!*"

Mildred pulled the chair up. Did what she was supposed to with the levers down there.

"I am! You see me doing it!"

"You sure?"

"Yes!"

"Took you long enough."

This time Mildred Elizabeth was able to guide Betty Lou Rutterschmidt's bony body into the wheelchair without further ado. This did not stop the older woman from cursing up a storm, grumbling to herself. Incensed and exhausted, the last thing she needed was for Mildred to act like some kind of ding-a-ling by nodding and going along with everything she said, which, in fact, she was guilty of.

"I couldn't agree more. Fornicators got it coming to them. Every one. They'll fry. Down there. When they meet up with the Nefarious One."

"Oh shut up, Millie, and hand me my *Bible.*" Mildred did this. "My flashlight. Find it." It took some effort. The daughter managed to locate it. Handed it to her.

"Give me a push now."

"Where, Mother?"

"Where else? The crapper. Before I go in this wheelchair."

Betty Lou gestured with her left hand for Mildred to start pushing, then with the other pointed in the direction of the bathroom in the corner.

"I'm doing it. Only you just went. How can you go again?"

"What a question. I have to take a dump, you ninny. I have waited days for this bowel movement. Days. And it's finally taking place. Why should I have to explain anything? Isn't it enough that I have warts on my behind?"

"All right. So you have to go; and you see me doing my best." She gave the wheelchair a push, steering Betty Lou in the direction.

# CHAPTER 172

Dione rose to her feet and slowly climbed to the top of the staircase, lest she missed out on any other signs that might otherwise detract from what she needed so badly to believe—that her friends were in the house.

When she got there, she wasted no time banging on the door, begging to be let out, pleading for help. The voice she heard earlier had sounded like Stella, must have been, had to have been—and she called out Stella's name.

If that's Stella Martel out there, she thought, then the others might be with her. Lana and Pearleen. Could be they were with her. Got to be. Marvin was always trying to get them to come here and dance for Cecil. She knew that Stella and Lana had been here once or twice before, had gotten high with Biggs, danced for him and had sex with him for drugs and money (or both).

Marvin had always been after Pearleen to join them and Pearleen had usually turned them down. Most of the time. Could be that's who that other woman's voice had sounded like: her friend Pearleen Bell.

Maybe if she kept calling and making noise, one of the girls would hear and then they might go out and get help.

*They would have to; someone would have to go out and get help. The girls will eventually figure out what's going on in this place. I know they will. I have to keep trying.*

She also knew she risked getting sparked. She knew it well enough. So be it—even if it meant paying with her life.

Big T. looked up at her from where he stood at the bottom of the stairwell. Tilted his head to the left a bit, needing to see what was under the robe. Tried tilting to the other side. Generally poor lighting conditions always made something like this difficult.

"I wouldn't go on makin' all that fuss, little darlin'. Bishop is likely to hear ya and he just might get riled about it and raise hell with all of us later. You know darn well he's got that thing he calls Pit Therapy that he does as a way to keep folks in line. Pit Therapy. You seen it, darlin'. He don't just take somebody and shoves them in the water, neither, not the second time around. Why he got all that water in it. Enjoys stickin' live wires in there, enjoys seein' them sparks."

He indicated the metal collar round his neck. "What this is for. You know it. Why you want to carry on like you don't? Makes no kinda sense to me."

He paused. "Can't say as I blame the preacher for doin' it. Keeps troublemakers in line that way. Some folk can only be kept in line when you put a little fear in them. Harsh way of lookin' at it, I know that, but it sure is true; it is." He had no idea if he was getting through or not. "I can tell you right now, Pit Therapy ain't exactly my idea of a hootenanny."

Dione's desperation to seek help any way that she might, easily overruled the fear she may have felt, fear underscored by Big T.'s earnest words of warning. She called her friends' names until she was simply too weak to go on.

Big Tex shook his head, dreading the consequences all this racket and ruckus could easily result in. He'd be dealt with for sure if Biggs ever found out he'd helped the filly break out of the pit.

# CHAPTER 173

**Gospel numbers mixed-in with funk and rock played so loud it made it impossible for Stella to determine if she had heard a girl or woman, someone, screaming in the basement.** She had pressed her ear to the basement door and listened. Heard nothing. The music was too goddamned loud.

Where was the man's stash? Where was all that blow and crack she'd heard so much about hidden? Where was it? She knew that it had to be somewhere in the house—but where?

All the doors were locked. How the hell was she supposed to find anything like this? It was impossible. Lana had the nerve to accuse her of not trying hard enough. *She* out here doing what I'm doing?

Screw it. Marvin was waiting in the living room and there was no way she could keep roaming about. Let the Mex bitch and Peachy go snooping about and risk getting busted by the creep.

Yeah, let *them* get caught trying to steal the shit. Why should it be me? She'd already been busted by Biggs, and then by Marvin, and wasn't about to push it. Or was she?

If she got her hands on it first she could probably keep it all for herself and wouldn't have to share.

She walked to the bathroom in the hallway. Remembered to leave her hairbrush on the sink this time so that she would have a valid enough reason to scurry out of the living room later, should she decide to, and joined Lana and Pearleen.

"Where's Livia, Stel?"

"What difference does it make, Lana? Who cares? Probably still upstairs. She ain't going for it. Told you that already. Somehow she got it in her head that her virginity will actually mean something to the jerk she finally marries. What she don't know no matter who she hooks up with the asshole will have had his share of good times. What I want to know is: If the *'groom'* ain't gonna be *'clean and pure,'* why should the woman? Fucking double standard. Shouldn't both of them be virgins?"

Stella thought to ask about Marvin. Where was he?

"In the john."

"No, he ain't. I just come from the john."

Pearleen was of the opinion that they were both being too hard on the Duarte girl.

"Like hell I am. Square bitch tried to slap me down. Showed her all right."

"I think you're probably jealous that she's a virgin and got herself a guy who wants to marry her," Pearleen Bell suggested.

"Bullshit," Lana said. "How do you know that Rudy Perez and his brother ain't been with half the hoes in the Valley?"

"We gotta figure out a way to get our hands on some more rocks; to take with us for later—so we can get the hell out of this nasty house," Pearleen said. Stood in front of the section of the wall that was covered in mirror squares and applied a touch of magenta lipstick to her lips, unaware that one of the squares was a two-way mirror and that Cecil's right-hand man, Marvin Muck, was on the other side of this mirror in another room, a closet, that he had entered from the hallway via the utility/laundry room, and was keeping an eye on them—per the bishop's instructions.

"Hey," said Lana.

"What?" said Pearleen.

"How come there's no phone in here? Do you see a phone? I don't see a phone. There was a phone in this room last time we were here."

"To keep chicks like you from abusing the privilege."

"I don't like it. I know there was a phone in here."

"Keeps it under lock and key, like everything else. What do you expect from a paranoid schizophrenic?"

"Listen, you two. I know this sounds insane . . . but I heard screams when I was in the hallway. . . . Like a woman, you know, screaming. Through the basement door—and it sounded like Dione."

The other two stopped what they had been doing—and looked at her, not knowing what to think. Last thing they wanted to hear was something that would fuck up their highs.

# CHAPTER 174

The cowboy had climbed the basement stairs to where Dione was at the landing, had put his arms around her and tried to talk her into stopping the pounding and screaming, tried to convince her to keep it down, because, as he saw it, the noise would only cause to bring Bishop's wrath down on them all.

He'd managed to convince Dione to descend the stairs, only to have her break away from him and scramble back up.

"Don't you see? We have to get out of here. How can you go on living like this?"

And it crossed her mind that she could have been trying to reason with mentally unbalanced people; they clearly seemed to be. But even if they were nutty, how could they not want to get out of this smelly, dark hellhole of a basement? How could they not want to get out? It was way too dark when the small black-and-white set in the crazies' room was not on, and since Cecil Biggs kept the remote and controlled viewing hours, the set was not left on all the time, hence, the light it generated was limited. Depended on the mood Biggs happened to be in.

There was the nightlight that gave off a weak, hellish-red glow, the nightlight down there by the bookcase and patio table, only the wattage was so low it was hardly anything to speak of. About the only other source of light that they perceived came from the bottom of this basement door, light that filtered through from the hallway (when the light was on).

"*Ja ja.*" Julian Ionesco had positioned himself at the bottom of the stairwell. "He help us."

"*How did he help you? By keeping you imprisoned in this dungeon? By keeping me locked up in that pit?*"

"He help by taking us when hospital let everybody go. Many hospital people said we was free to leave and live with society—only we have no place to stay, no money, and sleep on sidewalk. *Ja, ja.* I sleep in cardboard box downtown near to city hall when Cecil help me. Same with others. He help everybody."

"He kills people. He's a *cannibal. Drinks blood.* He killed my husband."

"None of that makes any difference." It was not Ionesco this time. Someone else had joined the conversation. "Because the plague is coming."

"The plague?"

"Apocalypse," one of the crew said.

"He's a murderer, a killer. He murdered Danny, my husband. Just murdered him."

"Because your husband do something to Cecil to make him unhappy, make him angry," the Rumanian reasoned.

"Like you're doin' right now, little darlin'."

The one who looked like an underfed undertaker and went by Big Tex had followed her to the landing and was rubbing the back of her head and neck.

"Biggs ain't gonna be happy about it. Hate to say it, don't care to think it: could be you got discipline coming. Was bad enough for you to break out of the pit. Preacher must have a good reason for keepin' you in it. Your kind can't be counted on, can't be trusted. Preacher don't cotton to that. Could be you got discipline on the way."

*"Please understand. I just want us all to get help. . . . Look at my face. . . . Don't you think I need to be treated by a doctor? Look at me. Please, look at me. . . ."*

"I would, darlin'. Only there ain't hardly enough light right now for that sort of thing."

*"Don't you want to get out? Don't you miss the outside? The sun? Fresh air? I miss my baby girl. . . ."*

"I explain to you before: I miss Rumania. . . . I miss my country. Since my dear wife kick the can, or maybe she kick the bucket—not sure how to say—maybe yes: *kick the bucket;* since she die . . . I feel I cannot make it in America. . . . I don't have Dream no more. America only good if you have Dream; if you don't have Dream, America not so good. It is very good for people who have Dream. . . . The Big Dream die when my kind wife die. . . ."

His tone took a sudden, drastic turn. Man was at the end of his rope, and this whining blond prostitute up there by the door was the cause of it.

He had a light-colored scarf, or rag, something, was not easy for Dione to make out, tied around his neck the way one would a scarf. He wiped his brow with it. Dabbed at his eyes. Blew his nose into it.

"What you want me to do with your bullshit life? You think I worry about your *idiot eye*? I cannot see your idiot eye. Even if there was more light and I could see it very well, I still don't care about your *idiot eye*. You lose one eye, big deal. I lose *Mrs.!* First they take pancreas, they take spleen, they take gallbladder and intestine; they take so much intestine my dear wife she shit three time' every day. Every day; in the toilet, shitting, three time for two years—the cancer it come back, and finally they take the life. I lose my wife. Radiation and chemo. Day after day, week after week. She cry all the time because the pain is too much. She weep; how she weep. Can't eat; no appetite. Everything taste like metal when she eat little bit. Like paper. No flavor. Chemo do this. I can do nothing for her. We was married eighteen years. She is everything for me, do everything, taking care of me; she clean my shirt and she clean my shorts; press my pants and give me haircut. Trim the hair in my nose and hair in my ear. I ask her to take hair off my private part; I don't like gray hair on my private part. She say to me: No, Julian. Leave it like that. It is natural. Okay. Fine. Whatever make my dear wife happy I do. In Rumania we was happy. I was engineer. In America, in New York, and when we move to Los Angeles, I am force to be *taxi driver* and it is very difficult to be happy." He spit on the floor, hard. "All of the people in Beverly Hills do like that, if you are *taxi driver*. If you taxi driver in Beverly Hills you are *kaka, shit*. They tell me I am *shit*, because I drive taxicab and they are millionaire movie producer and eat steak at Dan Tana. Drink *slivovitz*. I know. I see all the time. You think I care what you cry about? You full of *kaka, nothing prostitute!* Miss Betty and daughter Mildred say it all! Say it right! What I do to you? I tell you: I gonna break your arm! This will make me feel good, very good—when I break your arm. I don't need your pussy, like Big Texas need it. What I need, what make me happy is when I hear snap; when your bone break like pretzel, like celery, and then *you will shit*. You will be in so much pain *you will shit—three times every day*. Like my dear wife."

He was spitting some more, unable, as well as unwilling, to contain his rage, and charged up the steps in order to get at her and do what he felt needed to be done. And in that brief moment was all it took for it to register in Dione Aragon's eye: the rag tied round his neck was part of a blanket, a pink blanket. He'd had a torn portion of it wrapped around his massive neck. Who knew where the rest of her baby's blanket was?

Proof? She had no proof. Only suspected. Had no choice but to add it up . . . about her darling girl.

She did the only thing she could do in defense: cowered at the impending assault, not that she needed to, as the foreigner was blocked by the cowboy, who cold-cocked him and sent the Red Menace right back down to land on his rear end at the bottom.

*"I break your arm for this, kurva from Texas."* Julian Ionesco promised, glaring up at them and waving a finger. *"You watch it. I give you one big guarantee. Ja ja."*

*"Ja ja*, yourself. What happened to all that *comrade* crap, then, *amigo?* Why you always sayin' *comrade this and comrade that*, Pinko Commie sumbitch? *Always knowed you was fulla horse manure."*

"You keep *kurva* away from door before she cause everybody big trouble. If she don't stop what she do Bishop gonna say 'You got discipline coming!' And then *'Siberia!'* to everybody. Everybody will pay. If I pay I gonna make you pay more, *American kaka! You are kaka; for sure you are kaka."* Ionesco turned, and staggered off, rubbing his jaw.


Dione was sitting on the floor of the landing, her back against the wall. She had her face buried in her trembling hands and she was sobbing. Big Tex sat beside her.

"It's all gonna be just fine, little darlin'. Yes, ma'am. You ain't got to pay no attention to him. You ain't no '*kurva.*' My wife was, I suspect— not you. I doubt, strongly doubt you're one of them."

And he proceeded to gently pull back the part of her robe that covered her feet. Ran his left hand over her ankles. As soon as she realized what was taking place, what it was he was after, Dione yanked the robe back, withdrawing into the corner.

*"What are you doing?"* She covered her feet back up. *"What the fuck are you doing?"*

"Everything is gonna be just fine, little darlin'."

Big Tex clamped his right hand across the back of her neck and pushed her face against the door, while his left hand lifted the robe all the way off.

Dione struggled, but it did nothing. She did not have enough strength and doubted she could fight him off. She screamed and fought to get him away from her, throw him off, but Big Tex was too big and strong. He held her face pressed against the door, while running his left hand up and down her grime-covered, wet legs; up her thighs, and then slid it under her buttocks. He parted her legs, freed his erection from his jockstrap, and rubbed his penis up against her. Gently rubbed it this way.

"We gonna get you out of here, little darlin'. You're right about that. We all want to get out, and one fine day we will. We surely will, not that I care for what's out there, not that I'm sure I'm ready to face it. Don't suppose any of us is, actually. We had our taste, plenty of it. Ain't nothin' better out there. All it is is different. But I understand: You want out. Don't care to be cooped up like a hen in a tight cage; like them chickens Bishop keeps in the kitchen in them canary cages that are just too damned tight for 'em. Now me, *tight* is something I ain't got nothin' against. No, ma'am. *Tight is good. Beaver or back door.* Don't matter. Now, my wife, she never give up that back door for me. Oh, she done give it up to my best friend, my best *amigo*. Silver-tongued devil was slick enough to get her to make that back door available. . . . *Open Sesame*, he said, and she damned well did. . . ."

Dione twisted her head away, and would not stop screaming.

"You want out of here? Why, we can do that; we can get you out—and we will. Only we got to do one thing at a time, that's all. One thing at a time. Do you have any idea how long it's been since I had me some of what you got there? Hate to tell you, that's all."

He had his right hand back over her mouth to stop all the noise she was making and prevent her from spoiling, what he was convinced, was and should be a romantic episode. If not that, at least a mindless, soulless screw—and there was nothing the matter with one of those from time to time. As he pointed out a moment ago: it had been a very long time for him, too.

"You just take it nice and easy. . . . We might as well enjoy this, little darlin'. That's the way Big Tex sees it. Enjoy while you can. 'Cause you know, they say life is short."

# CHAPTER 175

**"What denomination is your church?"**

*"What denomination would you like it to be?"*

"I only wondered . . ."

*"I apologize. We are non-denominational."*

The words seemed to be on instant replay inside her head. He was interested in porn tapes Peaches appeared in and had cocaine to entice her and her friends with. What kind of church allows this kind of behavior?

Non-denominational? More like non-religious and godless. She felt nervous and scared and had this fear of being locked up in the "Prayer Room," as Biggs called it, and not being permitted to leave. Olivia also knew that she needed to calm down, take it easy.

Look, everyone knows the guy to be an oddball, weird. Nothing new there. He was still a preacher, a man of God. And his church: United Christian Church of Re-Newed Hope is not the sort of parish she and her family would ever want to be a part of . . . that did not mean that it was necessarily evil and totally without merit. . . . They're different from the norm, that's all.

Take a deep breath. Let it out. There you go. . . . You're doing fine. . . .

She looked at Patience. Still sitting there in the front row staring up at the holy cross, the crucifix. Patience was shivering. It was warm in the large room and Olivia could not understand why Patience would be cold. Well, Patience is a bit unusual—different, like Biggs—but that is none of your business, Liv. Get to the door and get on home.

Olivia tried the door nearest her, the one she had entered through. Found it locked. She walked to the other door in back, on that same side of the room. This door, too, was locked.

*You're telling me I don't have the right to be nervous? I am nervous. You know it. More than nervous.*

"I just want to get out of here. I have to leave."

Biggs would make a good cult leader probably. He's always carrying that *Bible* around with him. Wears that hat that has God's #1 on it. Puts on a good pious front, doesn't he?—when he's away from here, doesn't he? I know better now. Having seen what I've seen. Who buys an ordinary-looking, creepy house like this and turns it into a so-called church, and then only allows certain people, mostly undesirables, to see the inside of his "church"? Who does that? A weird-ass would do that. Make that a couple of weird-asses named Biggs and Muck.

She pounded on the door. Hurried back to where the black woman sat.

"Look, I want to get out of here. Both doors are locked. What is going on?"

The black woman remained lost in her own world, her mind indeed somewhere else.

"Where would you go? It's cold out there."

*"I want to get out of here. I have to get home."*

It was evident to Olivia that she was not getting anywhere with this approach, and she hurried back to the door she had walked through originally, turned the knob. It opened this time.

Olivia scrambled down the flight of stairs. Reached the front entrance and hoped that it was not locked, so that she could keep right on going and scram out of the place.

Only the front door wouldn't open. Music blared from the living room intermixed with what sounded like screams or laughter coming from another part of the house, maybe the basement. She could not tell and didn't care, all she wanted to do was get outside, and panic set in.

Out of nowhere, it seemed, Cecil Biggs's left arm whisked past her face at lightning speed (as he planted his palm) against the front door just at about Olivia's eye level.

"I see your purse turned up. That pleases me."

She was way too spooked to get a word out in response to this, way too intimidated to let him know what she thought: that his druggie, light-fingered loser friends had taken a substantial amount of cash from her and that it angered her enough so that she wouldn't want to have anything to do with them ever again.

"As someone of note once noted, *there is nothing to fear but fear itself.*" A pregnant pause followed that felt like eternity: uncomfortable and nerve-wracking. "Burglaries are on the rise. Doors are kept locked as a precaution. We apologize if a staff member or two gave you a scare. They certainly didn't mean to."

"I need to get home."

Did it do any good to keep pointing it out? Olivia did not want to or was even able to look at those eyes of his that represented the opposite of anything positive and life affirming. Creep had always made her skin crawl. Being this close to him only made it far worse. She prayed that her knees wouldn't buckle. Swallowed hard. Throat was dry.

"For some reason you remind me of my ex-wife. She's from the Philippines."

"I'm not Filipino. My ancestors go back to Spain and Mexico, mostly Spain."

"My mother, rest her soul, had hair like that."

She'd heard it before. Too often. Hadn't liked it. What was she expected to respond with? Psycho was always talking a bunch of incoherent nonsense.

Door to the living room opened. Pearleen, Stella and Lana appeared.

At about the mid-point down the hallway, another door opened, and Marvin stepped out from a room on the bathroom side.

Biggs's eyes remained fixed on Olivia. He did his very best to appear relaxed and at ease—only it had the opposite effect on her.

"I called a cab for you."

He proceeded to unlock the front door. Took his sweet time about it, too. Finally had it open. Desperately needed fresh air—never mind that it was smog-tainted Valley air—wafted in like a gift from the gods.

There was a cab idling at the curb and Olivia ran to it. Jumped in the backseat and screamed at the driver to get going. Cecil Biggs's reaction was one of manufactured bemusement as he gave his head a mild shake.

"Told you that *stuck-up bitch* thinks she's too good to share a cab with us," said a pissed Lana to her stripper pals. Before her companions could react to the comment or attitude, the screams coming from the basement were much stronger and louder now and could be heard through the music. There was pounding on the basement door and Stella Martel found herself being drawn to it.

She walked to the door. Her name was being called. She was certain this time. Biggs saw it, reacted the only way he thought prudent: locked the front door for good measure.

"Like I said before," Stella Martel reminded her coke-addicted cohorts: "I'm either losing my mind, or that sounds like Dione Aragon crying for help."

# CHAPTER 176

**Down in Biggs's basement Dione had made every effort to stay loud and scream for deliverance, but having been so weak to begin with she had no energy to go on.** The Texan had held her down on the landing and sexually assaulted her, and now that he had dragged her back down to the bottom of the staircase and gotten his rest, he was forcing himself in her mouth again, slamming his long, carrot-shaped groin against her wounded face. Why don't they help me?

*"Help me, please. Help me."*

Big Tex laughed out loud. Rubbed his erect penis and tried to find her lips with it. Slid it in. Dione bit down on it as hard as she was able and the tall man pulled back with a groan.

Greta Otto moved up from behind as the cowboy stood leaning against the banister; she whirled that chain in her hands like a baton, moved another step, adding power and spin, and let the chain whip up between the cowboy's thighs.

The man howled like a wounded, wild beast. Reeled back, staggered, and dropped into the water in the pit. Enough mud and water and blood found its way inside his mouth and he continued to jerk around in there, wailing and cupping his precious, aching genitals in his hands, doing his best not to irritate or inflame further.

A moment later he spat the water back up and a rodent wiggled out with it and swam to safety. Greta, the all-powerful and in command, stood over him with the chain and gave him a good, solid whack across the face that shut him up.

Big Tex should have gone out, but didn't. At least he was no longer running his gums.

Greta covered Dione back up with the robe. Held her in her arms. Realized she had suffered a few cuts and bruises herself. Hand that she held the chain in was bleeding between thumb and forefinger. Right side of her neck was sore. There was pain there. Blood below the jawline. Must have accidentally whacked herself and not have been aware of it during all the punishment she was gleefully meting out.

"I'll be back. Big Sis will be back."

She rose. Retreated to the Bunk Room for balm and *Band-Aids.*

Someone was calling Dione's name. On the other side of the basement door up there. Dione was certain of it. A pair of hands clamped onto her. Kept her from climbing up. Had to be the "Pinko Punisher." Ionesco.

*It's Stella. Stella's calling me.*

"Stella! Stella, is that you? Stella? Please, help me! They raped me! I need my baby! Please, help me!"

# CHAPTER 177

**Stella Martel was on the opposite side of the basement door with her ear pressed against it, listening intently.** Biggs had his back to the front entrance as he stood there watching Stella and the other women react.

Lana glared at him.

"You just gonna stand there, or you gonna call us another cab, Cecil?"

Biggs said nothing.

"What are you doing, Stella?" Pearleen had her purse pressed against her waist. She could sense that something was not right with the bishop.

Biggs cleared his throat. "I suggest you move away from there, Stella. For your own safety. You've already had one encounter with Norbert, as I understand it. I guarantee you you wouldn't want another."

"Like I said, Pearl. Call me crazy, but I heard Dione's voice just then."

Stella straightened and was looking directly at Biggs, who remained at the other end of the hallway. *"You got Dione Aragon down there, don't you? That's what happened to her that night she 'disappeared' in McCoy's parking lot."*

Pearleen did not want to believe what Stella was implying. It wouldn't have made any sense to begin with. Why would Cecil have to kidnap anyone when all he had to do was flash his dope and money, and most women did what he asked. It was sad, but true. She, Pearleen Bell, was here, wasn't she? She hoped Stella's accusation were not true. Because if it were, that could mean trouble for the three of them as well now, big trouble. How would they get out of the place if Biggs did not want them to leave? How would they let the cops know that he had kidnapped Dione and held her prisoner in his basement?

Owner of the house cleared his throat.

"Got some of my people down there. Staff and board members. I had the basement turned into a large play den and living quarters for them. It's quite comfortable, actually. You saw me let one of them in earlier, the poker player named Norbert Fimple."

"The one who likes *dead cats*?" said Stella. *"That was Dione I heard,"* she insisted.

"Come off it, Stella," Lana said. "Get us that cab, Cecil. Where's the goddamn phone? I'll call the taxi myself."

Biggs stood his ground. Pearleen looked at Stella, and then her head turned slowly in Biggs's direction. Thank God she had her purse with her.

*Let him try something. I'll shoot if I have to*, she thought. *I don't want to shoot nobody, but I will do it to defend myself.* Let him try something. He's always been weird, hasn't he? But you never paid much attention to that; none of us did. Didn't want to heed our instincts. Get that toot; that's all that mattered. You were always pissed at the way that greasy slob McCoy came on to you, and look at you now.

*"Open this door if she's not down there,"* Stella demanded. *"Open the fucking door!"*

"If you insist." Biggs tossed the keys to Muck. "Unlock the door, Marvin. Show her she's imagining things."

The sidekick fumbled with the keys, searching for the one that would fit. Found it. Unlocked the door to the basement and left it wide open.

"Take a look for yo'self, you don't believe us."

Biggs held his hand up. "Toss the keys over here, Deacon."

Marvin did that. Biggs caught the keys. Reached for the light switch in the foyer and suddenly the hallway light went out, as did the light in the living room.

# CHAPTER 178

**Pearleen had her *Sterling .25 automatic* out of her purse.** It was too dark to see anything, let alone start firing.

Well, she had seven rounds to work with: six in the magazine, one in the chamber. No, it was never a smart thing to do, have a round in the chamber, she knew it, but this was the way she liked it whenever being around *low dogs* like *"Brotha Trusty"* and *"Brotha Muck."*

Lana had her purse with the cardboard cutters. Liked to keep a few on hand just to be on the safe side. People were always laughing and giving her a hard time about it. Lookit the situation they was in now. Cutters might come in handy, and she was glad she had them. They wasn't anything special: aluminum, with single edge blades. With the palm of your hand, you shoved to open, shoved to close. Easy to use and effective enough when used right. It took guts, too. She could cut them up if she had to. She hoped she didn't have to.

Lana nudged Stella. Handed her one.

"What am I supposed to do with this?"

"Slice peckers if you have to."

"Easier said than done."

*"Fuck you, then.* I don't give a shit what you do with it."

"I didn't mean it that way."

Lana was irritated to the point she just wanted to tell the other to close her trap, and was stopped by Dione, who could clearly be heard through the open basement door saying their names over and over again. Sounded like she was near the bottom of the staircase somewhere. Couldn't see her. Not enough light at all.

"It's all right, honey." Stella had ventured onto the landing. Forced her eyes to adjust to the weak bluish and red-toned light below. "We're gonna get you out of here."

"Where's my baby? How's my baby? Is my baby all right?"

Stella felt she had little choice at this point, other than to offer up a blatant lie. "She's fine." Adhering to caution, she began her descent.

Braved a few steps, and paused. "Clarissa is just fine. Come up the stairs. Meet me halfway, Dione. Can you do it?"

"Son of a bitch turned out the light."

"No shit, Lana," chuckled Marvin. "'Bout time you noticed."

"We want to get out of here, Biggs."

Pearleen gripped the *.25 auto* and would have walked in one or the other direction, only lack of light prevented anything of the sort. Besides, there was but one direction she was interested in heading: toward the front door.

"We know you got that piece on you, Peach." Marvin Muck stood inside his room and had the door open enough to be able to run his mouth. "Only you just gonna be wastin' all them caps, 'cause Dawg be wearin' the bulletproof, hot mama."

Biggs, having slipped into his own bedroom, cracked his door periodically to respond when he felt a need to. His advice to Muck at the moment was to shut up.

*"Let us out, Cecil. Let us out right now. People know we're here."*

"There it is: Tone of sheer desperation, just before total fear and panic set in and take over. I do enjoy it. Always have."

Pearleen aimed her gun in the direction of the front door, the last place she had seen Biggs standing. Squeezed off a shot. Hoped she hit the asshole. Didn't hear a grunt or anyone fall. Too bad.

"Let us the fuck out of here, Mr. Biggs. We all had some fun and now the party is over. Turn the lights back on and open the door. You don't want to go to jail over this. Let us out right now."

"You're wasting your breath, Ms. Bell. I like you and would like you to stay. You do things to me. But you know all this."

Lana Sepulveda was at the end of her rope. Could not stand this civilized back-and-forth bullshit any longer.

*"CUT US LOOSE, YOU CRAZY MOTHERFUCKER! YOU HEAR, MOTHERFUCKER? I SWEAR I WILL CUT THAT UGLY MOLE RIGHT OFF! THEN THE REST OF IT! I WANT THE FUCK OUT!"*
She had found her way to the front door and began pounding on it, to no

avail. "My mother knows I'm here, Cecil. I don't ever go no place without her knowing about it."

"Can't stand yo mama, ho. So don't you be layin' all that *boo-shit* on us. Them's fairy tale', ho; nothin' but fairy tale'."

Lana stood there momentarily, not certain which way to turn or where to go or what to do, while holding the cutter out in front of her. She decided it made more sense to stay with Peach and let her know she was walking back and not to aim that damned gun in her direction.

Dione was still crying for her baby girl down in the basement; and Miss Betty and her sixty-seven-year-old adopted daughter Mildred Elizabeth and Julian "Pinko Punisher" Ionesco, and some others down there with him, could not stop giggling.

# CHAPTER 179

**Biggs had his bedroom door open wide enough to stick his nose out.** Listened intently long enough to hear that Lana and LaBelle of the Ball were at the landing to the basement stairs and were scheming in voices too low for him to pick up. Couldn't quite make it out over the music. No matter; it wouldn't get them anywhere. Let them whisper, let them plan and connive. He still wanted the "strumpets" caught alive and stated thus from where he stood loud enough for the "cellar dwellers" to hear. He especially did not want to see any harm come to the high yellow whose stage moniker happened to be Peaches LaBelle. He closed his door. Wanted to go over the silencers. Thought the occasion was appropriate for one. Only a certain addle-brained wannabe procurer was tapping on the door and wasn't about to let up. Muck whispered his name. Insisted he see him.

"You hit?" Biggs was not inclined to open up even if he were. Fool had no business being in the hallway.

"Don't be that lucky, me."

"What is it?"

"Open the damn door, man. Heard Lana and Peach go down the basement stair'. *Peach don't be here.* Open the goddamn door and lemme say what I got to say."

Cecil flipped the switch on the wall, cutting out the light. Took his time opening the door. Cracked it just enough to point the barrel end of the *Magnum* in Marvin's shaken mug. Muck had evidently crawled over on hands and knees and was still down there on the floor, looking around nervously. Peach could be comin' back anytime.

Biggs looked up and down the hallway himself, making certain he was not being set up. By the time Marvin stopped twisting his head in every which direction, he realized he was staring at a piece.

"Who sent you?"

"Don't be doin' me like that, Dawg."

"What's your fucking problem? You hurt?"

"I don't be hurt."

"The fuck you on your knees for, then? Never, ever, for any reason, let a bitch bring you down to your knees."

Marvin rose. Stood flat against the wall—in case Peach snuck back in the hallway and let go with another cap.

"Spit it out."

"We ain't doin' nothin' but throwin' away some fine pussy here. *Why we always gotta ice the ho? Some of these ho be too hot to ice, Dawg.*"

Biggs lowered the gun at last. Flicked on a weak penlight. Was cautious with it.

"Did you not hear me order the geeks not to harm the cunts? Are you deaf?"

"You know you gonna cut 'em up." Marvin was using a lower tone here. "Sooner or later; they gonna be. That be yo *MO* all the time: *take 'em out.*"

"You risked getting *capped* just to tell me this?"

"They be some mighty fine piece of trim, Brotha Trusty. "

"Things die/things live. It doesn't mean much either way. No matter how you look at it, no matter how you live or what you do—we all end up in the ground sooner or later, so what's the difference if we help some of these Dollies get there a little sooner than they figured?"

"We ain't right to be doin' it. Suckin' my dick gimme cramp' in my neck and back."

"Vacate the hallway, *Rapo*. You'll be of no use to me or to the church if you get hit."

"You don't be gettin' my point: *Bitches be too good to chill, blood*."

"No, *you* don't get the point, *'blood'*: They have to be hacked-and-sacked. *They know too much*."

"They don't even be *CTD*. *They ain't circlin' no drain.*"

"Who's going to provide the *Pop-Tarts* and the *Kool-Aid*? *Dog biscuit treats*? You? Who's going to *clothe them*? *You*?"

"Do for them the way you done for them tard'."

"Why don't you stop straining before you short-circuit your brain?"

"*Sex slave*, Cecil. *Rent-A-Bush*."

Biggs eyed him without expression.

"We could have us a bunch of *sex slave'*, build us a *harem*, like the *A-Rab be doin'*; an' then we ain't got to get no more bitches for a while. Be smart that way, don't it? *The more bitches be missin', the more po-leece be lookin' for 'em—the more relative' be goin' crazy lookin' 'round for these bitches be missin'. So we grab less of them—but we can't do that if we slice and dice 'em every time.*"

"Like I told you before, *'Dawg,' if I want any shit out of you, I'll squeeze your scrawny neck.*"

Biggs slammed the door in the punk's face. He'd heard enough. Punk had pussy on the brain. Didn't matter to him that he risked losing his burgeoning empire if the bitches were allowed to live indefinitely.

What was it he had wanted to do before the bleeding-heart rapist interrupted him?

# CHAPTER 180

**Cecil O. gripped the suppressor-fitted *Walther P38*.** He'd fashioned the silencer himself from steel wool, Tornado Tube, plastic water bottle. He regretted not having tested it for safety and decided he did not want to risk having it blow up in his face.

He unscrewed the suppressor, and tossed it back in the drawer in the safe. He held on to the *P38*. His backup. With or without suppressor.

There were other sound moderators there that he'd fooled around with in his spare time: one he'd crafted out of PVC bushing, coupling and lawnmower muffler; he'd made another one with a section of twelve-inch aluminum tubing and CPVC bushing; and yet a third type he'd toyed with, twelve-by-one-and-a-quarter-inch chrome-plated plumbing tube, four-inch section of one-inch aluminum tubing and ballcock nut. All were either too cumbersome and/or unproven, and he wasn't going to risk anything going wrong.

He left them in the safe. Closed the door and spun the combination dial, making certain it was locked. The *.357* and the *Walther* backing it should do it. Gospel music blasted his home sweet home and he felt good enough about it to camouflage gun shots. Besides, he figured most of it would take place in the basement.


Biggs gripped the revolver. Stood in place. Motionless. Felt his heart pounding. Could hear it easily enough. He was sweating, too, but that was all right. He reached down with his free hand to squeeze the erection-in-progress inside his trousers.

Seldom failed. This sort of situation usually did that to him. Christ; it was great. Thrill of the hunt. What it came down to.

Couldn't figure it, and he didn't care how or why or any of it. Screw trying to reason it out. Made no difference how many times he'd tapped his nutsack here-to-fore, either.

Look, all you know is this: trapping something living, cornering it, tying it up and then cutting away at it bit-by-bit, be it a four-legged animal or the two-legged human kind (preferably the latter), did it for him. He fed off the victim's fear. Their fear and desperation made him stronger, gave him this immense, god-like power. At least left him feeling this way. Their panic-stricken screams and pleas gave him wood, made his cock pulsate with blood, and the blue and purple veins get bigger as his cock grew rigid and the blood surged through it.

He felt like nailing a piece of Pearleen Bell, getting a piece of her—not with a hammer and nails exactly just now, but instead with his prick. He didn't want to see her die just yet. The others didn't matter; he didn't care what happened with them.

Maybe Free Ride had something there, after all, maybe they ought to hold onto the cunts a while longer—but how long? People were sure to start missing them. That slob McCoy was sure to run his mouth because his top-of-the-line peelers had vanished on him, disappeared off the face of the earth. And sooner or later that Duarte cooze was sure to comment to someone about it; she would let it be known that she had last seen Pearleen Bell and her friends here—and then trouble-makers like Lloyd Dicker and others, Lana's mother, were likely to come sniffing around.

Not that he really gave a fuck. That was why Marvin's idea was off-the-wall. They couldn't keep all these bitches around. That was just out of the question, not that he wouldn't want to keep the high yellow here for a time.

Lana was to be used and discarded. Stella was a closet dyke who had given him the nose in the past, the cold shoulder, and he would enjoy dismembering that hot number as much as doing away with Lana "Da Bottom" Sepulveda.

And then it occurred to him the one way to diffuse the whole issue and prevent further snooping would be to latch onto Olivia Duarte—and he'd been after her for so long now, dreamt about her, had fantasized doing things to her—and all his plans to nab her the way he'd been able to nab all those others out in the open during the day (or at night) had not worked out.

It grated on him that he'd allowed her to leave. He'd had her in his grasp—and now she was out there again. Free as a bird.

Biggs made certain his bulletproof vest was secure and covered his chest and back adequately. Jammed an earplug in each ear. The plugs would protect the eardrums to the extent they required protection, while allowing him to hear well enough to function. He grabbed the shooting muffs just the same. Hung them round his neck. Reached for the dark glasses. He turned out the light. Stepped into the hallway.

Careful, Cecil. Your chest and back may be protected, the rest of you is not.

He took another step. There was a shot. Bullet thumped into one of the walls, or was it a door? Marvin had it wrong: Bitch was in the hallway firing that pea shooter. Peach may have been down in the basement a moment ago, gone down the stairs some. Was definitely on the first floor presently. He didn't mind the trapped ho using up her bullets, so long as he wasn't the one being shot at. He froze in his tracks, then ducked back into his room. Minute later, he opened the door a bit.

Dione was screaming in the basement. They were harrowing, high-pitched wails that would have made anyone's hair stand on end—but all it did was sweeten it for the bishop.

# CHAPTER 181

**Julian "Pinko Punisher" Ionesco fought off the Texan and the others.** Grabbed Dione around the waist and literally carried her down by the pit. "*Ja ja, kurva.* Every American woman *kurva.*" He threw her to the cement floor. Yanked on her left arm, placed it over the edge of the pit, and shut the door on it. Pressed down, hard, until her arm snapped. The woman twisted, jerked about frantically, for what good it did her. The Rumanian got hold of her other arm and repeated the process: shut the door on it at about the elbow. He moved her arm a notch, slammed the door on the forearm and broke it in half. Dione went out with a deep bellow, losing consciousness.

Stella Martel had stepped up from behind with her razor and slashed at the back of Ionesco's neck, cutting him sufficiently, but not enough to render him helpless. The heavy-set geek twisted away, swinging with the club in his hand.

*"Kurva. Ja ja, American kurva."*

Stella kicked him in the groin and watched and heard the man go down hard, reel back against the wooden stairs crying out in pain.

*"Dear Mother of God! Holy Mary Mother of God! I HURT! I HURT! HOLY MOTHER OF GOD!"*

Lana paused near the bottom of the basement stairs holding her cigarette lighter in her hand. She screamed to let Stella know that the freaky cowboy in the jockstrap was moving up from behind.

Stella spun in the Texan's direction and the man jumped back in time; he did not want any part of the cutter. He rolled, reaching Dione. Attempted to drag her away with him, to pull her down into the pit.

"I see I done made a grave mistake gettin' you out of there, didn't I?"

Stella kicked at the door and watched it slam down over the pit, preventing the cowboy from accomplishing his goal.

"WATCH HIM, STELLA!" Lana made her way to the end of the staircase. She had stowed the lighter and waved the box cutter around. "WATCH YOUR BACK!"

Betty and her daughter moved up from behind, the former wielding an ice pick, the latter had yanked one of her brogans off and swung it up and down like a hammer.

"COME ON, YOU BASTARD!" Stella screamed at the cowboy. Saw him try to kick at her with those boots he had on, and then attempted to leap on top of her.

Emerging from the Bunk Room, bandaged right hand and neck, Greta whirled her chain overhead and whacked the cowboy across the face with it. Stella rolled, regained her equilibrium, and slashed at the man's back and legs with the cutter.

The cowboy cursed, kicked at her wildly and finally ran off to disappear toward the front of the basement in the darkness.


Stella reached down to help Dione get to her feet and was unable to in time, as Miss Betty directed the wheelchair she was in right at her, toppling Stella once again and causing her to lose the cutter.

Mildred made shrieks as she pounded away at Stella with the shoe in her hand, missing Stella for the most part and smacking Dione Aragon across the face and chest, knocking her out cold.

Lana leapt over the Rumanian. Cocked her left arm, and sent a vicious fist into Mildred Elizabeth's face and the old woman fell on top of her mother, forcing the wheelchair to bounce back against the cooler door and both mother and adopted daughter went down, the wheelchair flipping on its side.

Stella had a sense of panic about her now. Pissed and frustrated. Couldn't see well enough in the poorly lighted cellar.

"I lost it. I lost it. I can't see where it landed."

"What, goddammit? What the hell is it?"

*"The cutter. I dropped it."*

"These fucking degenerates! We gotta get outta here. WE GOTTA MAKE IT."

"Where's Pearl? Where is she? We need her."

"Good question. I think she's gone back upstairs to bargain with Cecil and the idiot."

"How do we get outside? It's like Cybil Brand in here."

"I know one damned thing: we're in the basement. There's windows down here. All we got to do is bust one of these windows open. That's what we gotta do. Find something to do it with. If we try to go back upstairs he could shoot us. I'm not saying he would, I don't think he would—but he could."

"Do you think he might listen to reason? All he's guilty of so far is abduction. As far as I can tell—nobody's dead, Dione isn't dead. Hurt. She's definitely hurt, but alive. He would have to go to jail for keeping her against her will."

"Fine. What about Danny? Where's Danny?"

Lana had her lighter back out. Flicked it on. Carefully walked around a bit, while holding onto the cutter. She stopped, tripping on a dead rat and began to gag. Stella walked over, and was nauseous herself.

Dione moaned back to life. Cried out to them.

"The window in the bathroom at the other end of the basement. The window. Has a curtain over it. That's our best hope. . . . Down there in the corner. Windows are boarded up and got bars. At least you can climb up on the counter—and do something. . . . You can try. . . . Please. . . . Try. . . . Please. . . ." And she fainted again.

# CHAPTER 182

**Upstairs, on the first floor, Pearl fired another round.** Stood silently, and waited.

The commotion that had transpired down in the basement a moment ago had subsided a great deal and she had no idea what was taking place at this point. She was sure of one thing: she would have to be sparing with the bullets. She had used up three shots, four to go. Someone out there must have heard those shots. *I have to believe it. Olivia is sure to get them help.* She prayed she was right about that. *Police will be paying Cecil Biggs a visit pretty soon.*

She reached what was the kitchen door. Tried it. Saw that it was locked. So was the door directly across, as was the back. Could hear Biggs and

Marvin whispering at the other end of the hallway, and that left her no place to go but back down in the basement and join the others.

"Stella? Lana?"

"*What are you doing?* We can use you down here! We're outnumbered! Got us way outnumbered!"

"*Come on down!*" Lana seconded. "*Careful with that gun! Make the bullets count! She's right: We got us a bunch of crazy muthers down here, but we're all right! We're kicking ass! We're gonna bust out through a window in the john! Give us a hand!*"

Pearleen felt her way to the open basement door. Paused at the landing.

"All we want is to get out of here, Cecil. I don't want to shoot nobody. Just want to get out of here."

No one responded.

"Hear me, Biggs? *Brother Trusty?* Your neighbors musta heard some of this at least: gun shots, screaming. Rollers are on their way, Biggs. Think about it. I would if I was you. Livia's over there right about now telling them what she saw."

"I don't want to harm you. In fact, the deacon and I don't want to harm any of you ladies. You have to believe that. What would be the sense in it? We just want you to get all prettied up again and dance for us some more, that's all. I've got some great toot left and it's yours, yours and your girlfriends', or yours alone, if you like. I know how much you love this stuff, Peaches. That's why I went to all the trouble and risk to score for you, to get the best: *LSD, PCP, 'ludes, rock candy, Ecstasy*, you name it; *reefer, meth*. Spent good money, Peachy. Just to watch you dance. You're a beautiful dancer. Second to none."

"*Yeah? That why you locked your front door and won't let us leave?*"

"Like I tried to explain to Olivia Duarte a minute ago. Doors are kept locked due to an increase in crime in the area. Law-abiding types like Deacon Muck and myself have to protect ourselves, don't we? It only stands to reason. You know as well as I do that Valley PD can't provide adequate protection. Home invasions are commonplace these days. A man has a right to protect his life and valuables. You were a victim yourself recently, were you not?"

"Why did you have to kidnap Dione? What have you been doing to her?"

"Dione be all right, sugar-bush. All you got to do is talk to her. See for yo-self."

"She's just fine. Well, sort of. Took it hard when she found out hubby fled the coop for Bakersfield with baby and funds. Dione is tripping on *PCP*. As I said: it devastated her."

"You're lying, Cecil. You're lying; playing games. Only it won't work, Cecil."

"You know how badly you ache for toot, Peaches. Why torture yourself this way? Why deny yourself? Put that pea-shooter away and we can be friends again. You can do your fabulous LaBelle of the Ball number for us. How about it, Pearleen?"

Pearleen Bell said nothing. Swallowed hard. She wiped sweat from her brow, and proceeded down the basement stairs. She caught sight of Lana, or at least what she perceived was her silhouette.

"Watch yourself, Pearl. Fucker's got a whole mental ward down here. Buncha straitjacket candidates."

Mildred struggled to assist her mother back into the wheelchair. Did what she could to lift her up that way, and only managed to falter back, with the mother landing on top of her and the wheelchair on top of the mother.

"Stand the chair up first, dammit, daughter. Get the chair up first. And then give me a hand. The chair goes first, and *then* get me into it."

The daughter fought back, screeched like a wounded animal, and it was hopeless for her. "I did, Mother! I want to help you but you won't let me! You won't let me! I want to help! I don't know what you want me to do, Mother! I'm trying! It's too dark! It's too dark, Mother! Too dark to see!"

"Help me up, daughter! Stop sniveling, dammit! What's it matter that it's dark? You're legally blind!"

"I am not blind, Mother! *I am not blind!* You say I'm blind when that is not true!"

"You are *legally blind.* Don't argue with me. Damn you, daughter. Sure turned out to be some kind of helpless ninny."

# CHAPTER 183

**The daughter worked to get the wheelchair up against the cooler door and then helped lift her mother into it.**

"Men are such assholes. I want kids, lots of kids. My biological clock is running out."

"Mama, you got me." Mildred was at a loss as to what to do. What she truly needed and wanted was to hug her mother. Fear and nerves stopped her from following through.

"I want kids, lots of kids running around. But as I have pointed out many times in the past: men are such incorrigible rectums. Useless. Absolutely useless. Worthless." She recovered her icepick. Asked the daughter about her shoe. "Where is it? Bishop won't like it if you lost another."

"I don't know, Mother. I once had two. Now down to one."

"Oh, stop your sniveling, you perverted, over-the-hill floozie."

"Take that other shoe off your foot and prepare to thrash them with it for the Lord."

Mildred Elizabeth heeded the advice.

"Now all you have to do is point me in the direction of that harlot who assaulted us, the filthy slut who dared show her presence in this House of Worship, the Lord's House; the unwashed floozies dared taint this air what once was pure and holy. You can always tell when a heathen fornicator is present: they foul up the very air we breathe with their foul thoughts."

Lana Sepulveda had had her fill of the old hag. Far worse than her own mother even. "You've got a lot of nerve, you rancid old witch."

"You can always tell the direction heathen like you is headed—the same direction you come from, the same direction you're traveling directly to—and that could be only one place: the lower world. HADES. You come from it and will be going there shortly. Hades is the place for cheap strumpets like you. The lower region. And it will be my great pleasure to send you back to burn for all eternity!"

"You talk too much, you old bag of bones."

# CHAPTER 184

**Having dug her cigarette lighter out of her purse and used it for the limited illumination it provided, Pearleen was able to descend a few more steps, and paused.**

Ionesco was still in a lot of pain, but he was looking up at her, thinking of going after her, maybe tackling her; at least grabbing her feet. Could he make it that far up the flight of stairs? Although he was clearly aching, he negotiated a single step, and then another.

Pearleen trained her weapon on the slobbering slob.

"I'll cap your ugly ass. I will."

The Pinko Punisher's gaze remained fixed on her feet, wincing, considering the move all the same. It was tempting. He was willing to chance the risk.

"Don't make me smoke you."

"Ja ja, African *kurva*, you vill die; Ja ja, so vill I." The one-time Beverly Hills cabbie and former "Butler to the Stars" was intent on going for it. If he got shot, so be it. It would solve his problems.

Lana decided she'd attempt to solve her colleague Pearleen's dilemma by running up from behind and slashing the Rumanian across the buttocks a few times with her box cutter and watched the man roll back down the stairs and land on his head. Took him a moment to regain his senses and remind himself where he was. Soon enough he was reaching back with both hands in a futile effort to do something about his lacerated posterior. Alas, Ionesco's only recourse was to scurry away on hands and knees.

"That's how you deal with these insane fucks. The way I see it, we're stuck in a lunatic asylum—for the time being, anyway—and the only way to deal with these loons is to hit back, hit hard. We give them ten times as much grief as they try to put us through. Lookit what they did to Dione."

Dione "Divine" Aragon was coming back to again. Pearleen reached the bottom of the staircase. Dropped her lighter in her purse to save it for later use. Knelt down to help Dione sit up. Heard her yelp in agony when her arms were accidentally moved. Stella assisted.

"They broke both of her arms. I don't know what happened to her eye. It doesn't look good. She needs a doctor."

*"They killed Danny. My husband; they killed my husband. . . . In the woods. . . . Buried him in a shallow grave. They kept me in that pit because I tried to call for help from a cell they had me in. . . . I stood on a coffee table, this crappy coffee table . . . and for that . . . they . . . Help me. . . . Please help. . . . They'll . . . If we don't get out of here . . . I'm weak. . . . They starved me. . . . Forced me to eat dog food . . . mixed with . . . It had . . . it had . . . You don't understand. . . . They'll keep you around for a while . . . for kicks, so they can rape you; so they can torture . . . Please help me get out. I need my baby girl. . . . Clarissa . . . My little angel . . . Clarissa . . ."*

She passed out.

# CHAPTER 185

**Biggs was upstairs standing by the entrance to his basement and he was eating a *Butterfinger* candy bar and listening to what was being said by Dione and her pals.** He was satisfied with the way things had turned. They had the vics in one place, where he wanted them. That was fine. Made things a lot easier.

"What now, Cecil?"

"We wait."

"You heard them: they want to bust out that crapper window down there."

"Let them try."

"Let them try?"

"It's boarded up: inside and outside, both. Not to mention wire mesh and wrought iron bars. Three hopped up bitches can get past all that? Let them try."

"What chu call a Messican stand-off, ain't it?"

"Hardly. We don't have to do a damned thing—just leave them down there."

"I don't be getttin' it. You don't want some more of that vagina?"

"We starve them out. Let them go without food for two or three days. They'll come crawling out, begging for a *Pop-Tart* or *dog biscuit*—like the others, like all the others. It's relatively simple."

He would wait if he had to. Also thought of a way to have some fun with the trapped captives in the meantime. Biggs did a head gesture in the direction of Marvin's room. The sidekick understood all too well what it meant. Made him none too happy.

"I'll be in the basement."

Marvin shook his head, unwilling to go along with the unspoken request. "What chu gonna do, Brotha Trusty?"

"Do it, Brother Base. Make yourself useful. I'll be waiting downstairs."

Marvin did not want any part of what was on the man's mind, neither would he want any part of the bishop's wrath for refusing to go along with the program.

He entered his room.

Biggs made it down the stairwell with his Maglite. Headed toward the laundry area outside the john. The bitches had obviously decided to make their stand in the bathroom. He was at the door. Listening. The vaginas were whining about something. Vaginas were always groaning and moaning, bitching and pissing about something.

He looked about the area. Didn't like what he was not seeing: they had the *Maytag* dryer with them. Washer was untouched. Large playpen that contained clean clothes for the geeks was there. Noticed that both hampers were also gone. No doubt had them braced against the door.

He borrowed Betty Lou's icepick and poked it in the hole in the center of the doorknob to unlock it, for what good it did him. Door was no longer locked, true enough—only the cunts had it fortified to the point it kept him from being able to push it in.

# CHAPTER 186

**Inside the bathroom a degree of disappointment had washed over all three strippers.** They had the dryer and hampers lined up in a row, braced against the door—and were still about a foot and a half short. There was a utility cabinet below the sink. Pearleen thought to yank one of the utility cabinet doors off and placed it on the floor lengthwise, between the tub and the last hamper—so that it reinforced what they already had.

Not a one of them doubted that eventually Biggs and his goons would be able to force their way in. At least for now they figured they'd be able to buy some time with what they were able to do.

The other letdown had happened after Lana had climbed up on the counter, parted the curtain over the window, to discover that it was boarded up, not that it had made any difference actually, because you also had the pane, more planks and bars on the outside.

Pearleen gave Da Bottom a glare that clearly said: *Got any other bright ideas?*

"I knew about it. We all did." Lana climbed down. "All these windows got bars on them. It was still worth a look."

They heard Cecil Biggs, their captor, clear his throat on the other side of the john door.

"There's no real reason why we shouldn't be able to reach some sort of compromise, ladies. I offer you prime toot . . . in exchange for companionship. Doesn't sound unreasonable to me."

Pearleen shook her head at the women with her. They whispered to one another; they had to. Lana looked at the other two.

"What about it?"

Pearleen did not like it. "Companionship? What the fuck is that?"

*"What the fuck is what?* What do you think it is? It's an offer."

"Olivia Duarte will be getting help. We have to be patient."

Stella wished she could agree with Pearl. Wanted to. "You hope that *diva* is getting help."

Biggs let it be known he remained on the other side of that door. "Still awaiting your answer, ladies."

"What about it? He'll give us toot—"

"Don't be stupid, Lana. You know what they did to Dione. You heard what Dione said, how they took Danny out. *Probably killed the baby.*"

Lana faced the door. "What about that, Cecil?"

"Like I explained to your friend Pearl a moment ago upstairs. Dione practically had a nervous breakdown when she found out that hubs absconded with funds and baby and took off for the Central Valley. That's where they're from originally, isn't it? He hated LA, and couldn't wait to get out. Dione wanted to stay on; liked the money she was making as a peeler. Their big fight was over her wanting to do *porn*; the straw that broke the camel's back, so to speak. Her way of dealing with it was to trip out on PCP."

## CHAPTER 187

**Lana Sepulveda seemed willing to buy into it.** Pearleen shook her head. Could not believe how eager Lana and even the other chick were to accept the lame explanation.

"What's the pit for? *She was tortured in the pit.*" Pearl was talking to Lana and Stella. *"Look what was done to her."*

"I'd rather not have church staff *defecating* on my floor. And that's exactly what will start happening if you ladies refuse to vacate the john. Is that so difficult to comprehend?"

"Like this is the only bathroom in the house." Pearleen Bell wasn't buying. Said as much. "Why don't you answer the question, Biggs? What's the pit for?"

Biggs sighed on the other side of the door. "I'd rather not have them use the other johns. They tend to get sloppy—and then I'm the one who has to put up with Marvin's carping, because he's the one who usually does the cleaning up."

"What about the pit?" Lana was the one inquiring this time. "What's the purpose of the pit?"

"I was getting to that. There are times certain members of my staff get somewhat out of control, misbehave, and what we do, Marvin and I, simply on occasion, mind you, have them spend a certain amount of time in the hole. Nothing else. In fact, very often, usually, it seldom happens; we rarely need to put anyone in there, because by the pit merely being there, to where they are aware of it, they tend to behave—for the most part. And no one is hurt; there is no need to penalize."

"That still doesn't explain what was done to Dion."

"However, Ms. Bell, Marvin and I cannot be here, cannot watch over them *24/7*. It isn't possible. They were offended by what she does for a living, not to mention her craving for drugs—and they saw fit to 'discipline' her for it."

"What about the dope, Cecil?" Lana seemed to find it difficult to stay clear of the subject.

"I'm right here, Dolly."

"Let's see it. Let's see what you got."

To Pearl's utter and absolute dismay, Lana had the door unlocked. Cracked it about an inch, as that was about all that the fortification made possible, and stuck her right eye up against the opening. She was looking at it. It was no fantasy. Cecil was holding up a plastic baggy with enough rocks for all three of them to stay high on for hours. Let the other two know it. The salivating kicked in. Even so, Pearleen closed and locked the door. Someone had to be strong enough.

"Plenty here. And then some. All I ask is that you give up the gun—before someone is seriously hurt. Let's be civilized about this."

*"Bullshit."* Pearleen found herself whispering to the others. *"We can't be stupid. It's a con. We know too much."*

Lana tended to side with their captor and was back at it. Looked at her friends. "You can't blame him for what the retards did." Turned away from them. Faced the door. "Isn't that right, Cecil?"

"We only have so much control over them. They never should have been released and forced to fend for themselves, but Ronnie Reagan was looking for ways to trim the budget—and this is the result, unfortunately. I took them in. They were homeless, just about all of them were homeless. As far as those who hadn't been pushed out of the wards, they were about to be. I took them in, rather than have them face the elements, the harsh reality of coping with life on the streets without employment, food, or shelter." He needed to take a breather. The 'roids itched like a bitch. The only thing he dared was to scratch his rear in the vicinity of the rectum. It would have to do. The situation with the cunts wasn't helping the stress factor, either. "Now, don't get me wrong—I support Dutch all the way. Ronnie means well, I know that. But he needed to make himself and his people look good. Only I doubt he was aware of the absolute tragedy of his budget cuts."

Lana was readily agreeing. Practically taking the words out of Stella's mouth.

"See that? Cecil ain't the one. Why blame him? Nobody could control these crazy motherfuckers in here. Him and Marvin ain't nothing but sex addicts—like that's news to you." It was directed at Pearleen basically. Biggs continued his spiel on the other side of the door that separated the captives from their captor.

"Institutions across the nation suffered drastic budget cuts. The end result is what you see here. I did what I could to help out. Instead of being *commended*, I am being *condemned*. I don't get it. Then again, I suppose that's life."

# CHAPTER 188

**Pearleen Bell didn't like it**. Spoke in a low tone.

*"Fuck him."*

"He's *sex-crazed*." Stella was now trying to make her friend Pearl see the light. "Mood elevators make him crazy for sex. Like Lana said: ain't the first time. If these sex fiends didn't exist we'd all be out of work."

"I still say it's bullshit." Pearleen wanted the drugs as much as the others, but not if it meant risking their lives. "He can't be trusted. Marty Roscoe was right about him. That dumb hick horndog was right."

"I'm with Stella. Why don't you give him the gun?"

"Why don't you take it away from me, bitch?"

"I just might do that."

"Try it." Pearleen pointed the business end at the other woman's head. "You're so desperate for dope you don't even see the most obvious. *Trusty* is *schizo*; they all are. This gun may not give us much of a chance, but it's the only chance we have."

Stella was fed up with the bickering and told them both to knock it off."

"You two want to go out there? Go right ahead. You'll die for sure. Only chance we got at the moment is with this piece. We have to hold them off until help gets here."

Lana was up against that door again. "All you want is sex. Ain't that right, Cecil? You want sex, just like before. And we get that dope if we fuck you."

"You got it, Lana. You always were the realist. *Down-to-earth*. The thing I appreciate about you the most. Latin women know how to please a man. Look at Vanessa Del Rio. That's one amazing woman."

Pearleen was shaking her head. "You'll die. Why would he waste dope on you when he can have you anyway? He can do what he wants. Ain't nobody can hear us if we scream."

Stella reminded them they were done either way. "If we don't get out of this bathroom. It stinks in here."

"The whole place stinks. So what?"

"Mighty quiet on your side. What's your answer, ladies? What's going on, my friend Lana?"

"Pearleen has yet to make up her mind."

What followed was a hushed-toned, heated discussion between Biggs and Marvin that the trapped women could not quite figure out what it was about. All they were able to pick up on was that Biggs was *pro*, Marvin *against*. Biggs insisted that Marvin *do it*, and Marvin countered that he *couldn't*.

"What's the verdict, *mademoiselles?* Lana, can you help me out? Anything?"

"Ain't decided yet, Cecil."

"I see. Maybe this will help you make up your minds." And before the women knew it, or even had a chance to do something about it, he was shoving at the door again, pushing. Soon enough had it pried by an inch or two; then a little more—and a rat was guided through above the clothes dryer. The creature dove off the appliance, landing on the hard cement floor of the john, and proceeded to scramble from side to side in zigzag fashion.

The strippers were beside themselves, practically gagging, especially Lana and Stella, who were unable to contain their revulsion and keep from urinating on the spot.

"That be homie Youngblood." Marvin had stuck his snout in the crack. "You be nice to homie. He ain't gonna hurt nobody."

Pearleen slammed the door shut in his face.

"Shoot it!" Lana was the one doing the screaming. "Kill it, Pearleen! Do it!"

"No." Pearleen Bell was firm. She was also disgusted enough herself.

Someone had to have a degree of control here.

"We can't waste bullets."

She pushed the dryer back in place, so that it was against the bathroom door as before. She also adjusted the cabinet door that had been forced up, out of place and rendered ineffective by Cecil. **S**he pressed down on it so that it was flat again, the way they had it originally—and the fortification was back in place.

"Cap the rat, damn you!" It was Stella now, adding to the yelling. "We'll get rabies if it bites us!"

"You're nuts—both of you. It's a domestic rat." Pearleen took aim all the same just to shut them up. The rodent, clearly sensing its very existence was in danger, had sought refuge behind the toilet bowl. The strippers screamed for Pearl to get it over with.

Pearleen fired a shot. Hit the intended target. The resulting scene made all three women queasy in the belly as they watched the hairy, repulsive-looking thing quiver for several minutes, then expire.

"You satisfied?" Pearleen Bell found herself posing the question to the two dumb bitches she was stuck with in this nightmare. *"You happy?"*

They hadn't bothered to respond. Lana and Stella were relieved that the creature was no longer alive. That's what it had been about with them. Nothing more. However, on the other side of that door, to Marvin Muck, the story was entirely different. He could be heard cursing and arguing with Biggs about something else. What now?—the women wondered.

*"Shit, Hoss."*

# CHAPTER 189

**As before, the door was pushed in.** Forced open enough to shove another rat through. The women picked up on "MC Psycho" as being the moniker of this one. Biggs was snickering, didn't know how to laugh, but he could snicker, make noise with his lips and teeth. Something like tsk tsk. That's what it sounded like.

Pearleen took aim. Waited. Only this four-legged freak was quicker. Hit the ground running and took a different route. Hurried across the cement floor of the john, up the cabinet door that lay flat, braced against the tub, and leapt into the tub itself and wasted no time scaling its way up the frayed shower curtain.

*"GET HIM!"* Lana and Stella screamed in tandem. The rat had made it up to the shower rod, its life at stake, and, like its predecessor, seemed to sense it. Ran back and forth across that shower rod: from one end to the other.

Lana Sepulveda and Stella Martel shrieked loud enough at Pearleen to kill the goddamned filthy thing before it attacked them and gave them all something. Rats were ugly and nasty. Whether they were pets or not didn't matter. *Only good rat was a dead rat.*

Getting a bead on it was not going to be easy. Pearleen did her best. Aimed high. There was too much movement—and bullets were scarce. She fired. Was way off.

"Great. You missed."

*"You think you can do better, Lana?"*

"Give it to me. I'll show you how to use a gun."

"Get your own."

"Kill the goddamn rat, will you!"

And while this back-and-forth shouting match was going on, they failed to notice that a dark, purplish, molasses-like liquid appeared to soak through the hole made by the bullet in the drywall in back of the portable shower head in the wall on the right. The liquid temporarily collected in the hole, and dropped off, landing on the edge of the tub below.

*"CAN'T YOU SEE WHAT THEY'RE DOING? IT'S SO OBVIOUS!"*

"Kill the rat, or give me the piece!"

"Fuck you!"

Pearleen spun back to face the rat. Still up there on its perch, moving about, grinding its jaws. Bullets were too precious and too few to be frittered away.

She reached up at the shower curtain rod end above the tank, the rat was at the other end. Yanked hard on it, tearing it out of the wall, and a good chunk of the brittle drywall at the rat's end came with it. The rat went down, landing inside the tub. Scrambled to its feet. Attempted to claw its way out. Got nowhere; the tub way too slippery with slimy crud for traction. More of the purplish liquid (not unlike crude oil and/or molasses) appeared in the hole in the wall that the women were too preoccupied to notice at the moment; they had a rat to destroy. There wasn't a second to waste. Pearleen slid the worn curtain off the rod itself, and whacked away at the creature in the tub until it was dead.

# CHAPTER 190

**Stella was gagging in the corner, Lana damned near close to it, so was Pearleen, as tough as she appeared to make herself.** A bleeding rat with its crushed skull and torn open belly was not a pretty sight. The thing was too revolting to look at.

Shower curtain rod still in her possession, Pearleen thought she would brace it against the door, in order to further fortify what they already had on the floor with the dryer: two hampers and cabinet door. Only the rod was short by a foot. What else could they use it for? Weapon? Not many bullets remained. At least the rod was something, no match against what Biggs had, but at least it was something, something. . . . Desperation had you willing to try any damned, stupid thing—just about.

It didn't take long for Lana to comment, just as Pearleen Bell knew she'd have to open her big mouth.

"That won't do anything. What are you going to do with it?"

"Maybe I'll beat your ass with it."

"I want out of here! All they're after is some lovin'! Got a bad sex *jonze*. You heard him. Am I right, Cecil? You want to have some fun. You don't want to hurt nobody?"

Pearleen could not believe her ears. For a hit of crack this shallow chick was willing to jeopardize their lives.

"Don't you be shaking your head at me, bitch! I know the streets; I know what I'm talking about! There was no real reason to run in here and get the man all pissed off at us! No reason at all! All Trusty wants is to get laid!"

"How can you even think that way after what you told us was done to you upstairs in that john? After everything Dione told us? How can you be so gullible?"

"A little cooperation." Bishop was back with his spiel. "Understanding. Is that too much to ask after all the dope you ladies were provided with? After all the laughs we had? Is this reasonable behavior on your part? I hardly think so."

"There's no way to reason with this cunt, Cecil. I never had a real problem with you; it's this cunt Pearl!"

"You are being *naive!*" Pearleen was back in Lana's face. The animosity was clearly reaching a boiling point. In the time it had taken Stella to turn her head, staring blankly past Pearleen, at the wall behind her, wiped her eyes, her battling friends had each grabbed a handful of the other's hair and were about to start yanking. Stella's ensuing gasp and look in her eyes had managed not only to shut them up, but cause them to freeze up mid-action, and for the moment, had them forgetting about all that dope in Cecil Biggs's baggy on the other side of the bathroom door.

Stella Martel stared at the hole in the wall above the cracked and aging ceramic tile in back of Pearleen and the dark liquid that seemed to collect and dripped down into the tub.

She reached out with her index finger at last to touch one of the drops before it fell off. Held the blackish smear on her finger to her face. The shade of crimson it was had her convinced it had to be one thing.

# CHAPTER 191

**While Lana was back doing the balancing act on what was part of the vanity counter and attempting to loosen the planks off, Pearleen had torn the other door off the utility cabinet and was banging away at the wall below the drip, although to the right of the portion that was tiled.** She figured plasterboard would be easier to dig into than ceramic tile, not that it didn't require work. Her instinct was accurate, at least on that count.

She whacked away, cracking it in chunks and tearing them off by hand and tossing them at the floor. There was insulation: thick, cotton-like; wood slats that she had to shove aside, and more plasterboard.

Lana succeeded in yanking a couple of the bottom planks off the window that revealed the pane itself and the additional planks on the other side of it.

She proceeded to pry some of the planks off at the midsection and top, and a solid, battleship gray panel swung down from above the window and slammed shut into place over it that just about caused her to lose her footing.

She righted herself in time and took a closer look at the panel: one inch thick and *unbudgeable*. Rapped it with her knuckles. Possibly made of wood—or metal. Possibly both. Wood on the outside, maybe plywood—like a sheet of it on either side—with a thick sheet of metal in the middle.

"Twisted fuck."

Pearleen told her to forget the window. "How would we get the bars off?—even if you could get the other boards off on the outside."

"You heard Dione. Window is our best chance."

*"How would she know?"*

Pearleen decided it wasn't worth going on about. Lana Sepulveda wiped her brow, checked her forehead for blood where the panel may have nicked her.

She paused there this way, needing to put her thoughts together. What could be the answer to this situation they were caught up in? What would it take? She climbed down.

# CHAPTER 192

**Pearleen hammered away at the wall with a corner of the cabinet door and watched the opening widen.** More thick, cotton-like insulation had to be pulled out, more plasterboard chunks twisted and torn off. There was a gash that she was able to peer through. What she saw was not exactly encouraging; in fact, what all three were now looking at was far from hope-inducing or comforting: it was a view of the cell with the black-and-white tv and the bunk beds, that cell where the defectives spent most of their time in restless repose.

Lana stepped back. "Move to the left. Try digging to the left."

"I need you to tell me that?"

"It's dripping *over there.* Punch a hole below it. Wouldn't that make more sense?"

"It's ceramic tile. Lots harder to break up. That's why I thought I'd try this part of the wall first."

"You see where it got us."

"How about if you shut the hell up?"

Pearleen felt exhausted, but there was no way she would so much as consider quitting—even though they really had no idea what the purpose of it was. Yes, something that appeared to be blood had dripped down from inside somewhere. So what? What did it mean? *Crawl space?* Possibly. Then what? Place to hide out—and wait him out until Olivia showed with Valley PD.

She plowed away at the cracked and cruddy tile with the cabinet door about a foot to the left of their earlier effort, poking holes in it, chipping away at it. She paused for a second to look at Stella who was not doing much at all but standing there and watching her work. Neither was the other one, come to think of it. Big mouth who liked to give orders like a Marine sergeant.

"It would be nice if I could get some help over here. *Like sometime today.*"

Lana handed a plank to Stella and she and Pearleen attacked the wall in tandem. Lana did what she could herself from where she stood on the rim of the tub. Stabbed at the wall above their heads with one of the other planks.

The drywall came apart. There was the insulation material, pink and cotton-like—or maybe steel wool-like—some of it soggy with black blood, two-by-four and additional drywall on the other side.

Soon enough the hole they had created was enough to peer through. There was what seemed to be a narrow storage corridor with a low ceiling, the ceiling itself consisting of wooden pallets, above which was a crawl space.

# CHAPTER 193

**They banged away at the wall until the opening to the storage corridor was potentially large enough to crawl through.**

Lana was the first to attempt it. Got her left foot and then the rest of her leg and head through and something wet and sticky began to drip down on her. Blood or polluted water—or something else? It was like molasses or motor oil. Not certain. Wouldn't have made any difference. She paused there, unable to move any further. They hadn't made the opening wide enough.

She wiped at whatever the hell was on her face: dirt and stucco, and whatever the liquid was. Too dark to see clearly. Even with the aid of her cigarette lighter, it was too dark.

Pearleen asked what the problem was.

"What's it look like? I'm stuck. Can't see much, either."

Lana squeezed the rest of the way through the opening and had to remain stooped, practically in a crouch, as the ceiling was low.

She held the lighter up, and could make out box springs and old and smelly and stained mattresses propped against the wall on the right. There were odds and ends of furniture, broken, old: end tables, cocktail tables with missing or broken legs, damaged and ancient phones, cassette players, stacks of porn magazines and newspapers, stacks of black-and-white glossies of past and present strippers and porn starlets, stacks and stacks of VHS hardcore pornography.

The corridor was approximately three feet wide and hardly five feet high. If she raised her head any higher she risked banging it against the ceiling.

More of the liquid came down through cracks in the skids the ceiling was made up of. When she turned to tell the others what she encountered about the corridor and the crawl space above, more of the liquid landed on her, practically drenching her features. It soon became evident what it was.

Stella sighed, when she saw Lana turn to wave them on.

*"Blood. You've got blood all over your face."*

# CHAPTER 194

**Lana shrugged.** It took her a moment to recover and deal with it. She took a quick, deep breath. Released it. "I don't give a damn." She wiped her face. "We're getting the fuck out of here. Ain't no way that sicko is putting his hands on me again."

"I thought all they were after was some *'lovin'*, girlfriend. What's the harm in it?"

Lana's response to Pearl's dig was a hard glare and a middle finger, then let it go. Having to remain stooped was tough enough to deal with. She turned sideways to make room for the others to enter the space. Moved up some to make room for them. It was cramped and that tight in here.

More blood dripped down from cracks in the boards in the ceiling. Stella and Pearleen followed suit, climbed through the opening in the bathroom wall.

The storage corridor was packed with so much junk and whatnot that it was a real challenge to keep moving: folded blankets, towels, all types of mirrors, bags of doorknobs, boxes of locks, planks, plywood, sheets of metal, containers of generic laundry soap and bleach, *Liquid-Plumr*, rat poison and mouse traps. There were moments and stretches here when the only way to get past was to turn sideways, even then it was a struggle to make progress.

# CHAPTER 195

**They stayed close to Lana, moving along the corridor, and they could hear Biggs and Marvin back there banging away at the bathroom door, pounding away, doing their best to knock it in.**

The wall on their left was solid, professionally built, the wall on the right just as impossible, cinder blocks, what they could see of it past the furniture and junk, sheets of plasterboard, long planks left leaning haphazardly against it. Even if they could have kicked a hole in it somehow, penetrated it, it would have only taken them back into (generally) the same part of the basement they had just escaped from. What was the alternative? Had no answer, but kept rapping and/or kicking the wall on her left as she moved along it, hoping there was some sort of passageway they'd be able to take to freedom. Freak had a pit in his floor, secret storage corridor with all kinds of weird shit and junk, and a crawl space above. Would it be far-fetched to hope for a secret passage that would make escape possible?

So she alternated: either slapping at the wall with an open palm, or rapping at it with a hairbrush.

Pearleen suggested she keep moving.

"Yeah? Where to?"

"It don't figure." Stella was hunched over, looking about. "What's the purpose?"

"You're asking me? Ask the pervert. Ask him why he's got a pit in the floor full of water, ask him why he's got to kill chickens to get his pathetic dick up; while you're at it, ask him what's causing the stench and whose blood do I have on my face."

Pearleen did not bother reacting to this. "If we could find something to defend ourselves with, maybe something to pry the bars off one of the windows."

"Ain't seen but one window, and that was the window in the john—and I'm not about to go back there and havta deal with him and his army of psychos. Besides, you didn't see how thick that panel that come down over the window was. You'd have to pry that loose, get it off there, before you'd even have a chance at the bars on the outside."

She gave the wall on the left a kick out of sheer frustration. Nothing hollow. Cinder block wall.

Stella asked what she was doing.

"Hoping for a miracle. Everything's solid on this side. Was hoping for another corridor, secret storage space—to barricade ourselves in for a while. Like Pearl suggested: find something, anything, to fight with."

The others followed her lead: whacked at it with open palms. The only thing loose were some of the boards overhead, some of the pallets, and dirt and whatnot was beginning to trickle from above.

By now more and more of the dark "liquid" had begun to drizzle on them. Stella was in tears.

"More blood. Dear God. I've got blood on me."

"Don't worry about it."

"He's got a bunch of bodies stashed in the crawl space up there. Look at the blood."

"You don't know that, Stella, so knock it off!"

*"I know it's blood. It has to be."*

"Knock it off, damn you! I mean it. We have to show some balls if we want to get out of here."

"Lana's right." Pearleen did her best to keep from trembling. It was blood all right. Probably human. The limp female arm, covered in dry blood and dirt, that dropped down through a crack in the boards, dangling that way, only confirmed it.

One of the strippers, possibly Stella, accidentally bumped her head against a loose board and about a quart of crimson rained down on them, several pounds of entrails. Stella Martel was throwing up; the others practically there as well.

# CHAPTER 196

**They collected themselves.** Took some doing. They managed, and reached a fork in the corridor and were able to stand straight in this area. The ceiling here was as high as the ceiling in the john and rest of the basement.

On their left was a large sheet of dirty and warped plywood propped against the wall and held in place this way by a single cinder block on the floor. The right passageway led to a door—on the other side of which was the basement, no doubt.

Where was there left to go now? Move on straight ahead? Once again, the ceiling was low, no higher than five feet, the corridor about as wide as the one behind them. More stained box springs and mattresses, old furniture, sheets of weathered plywood, old Magnavox sets with cracked screens and bent rabbit ears, turntables without covers, blankets and towels with embroidered names of motel chains they were filched from; books, lots of books in cardboard boxes with the names on their spines of the various public libraries and universities they were stolen from.

This section of the corridor was just as dark as the one they had left in back of them. Lana still had her "torch," and Pearleen Bell had that gold cigarette lighter McCoy had given her in his office that time.

Lana's lighter had gone out. She flicked it, to no avail. Blood and grime had rendered it ineffective. She tossed it aside.

Pearleen's lighter was still functioning, no matter that the flickering flame was weak and provided far from sufficient illumination. Low on fluid by now? There was that possibility.

They shoved the piles and boxes of books out of the way, busted stereos and broken furniture and other junk, even a broken down, homemade coffin stained with crud and black blood.

There were things hanging from above, through the cracks in the crude, makeshift ceiling—and a couple of hundred pounds of putrefied limbs, a torso, and viscera poured down this time until they were drenched in it.

If the miasma that they had been exposed to earlier upstairs, as well as the other side of the basement and john had been sickening enough, this was far more potent and had them gagging and ultimately retching.

There was more debris raining down from above: teeth and eyeballs, tongues and fingers, rodents and night crawlers easily a foot long that they fought to get off of them. A headless corpse, possibly female, rotting, with enough rats clinging to it, dropped on them, followed by another—also with its head missing.

# CHAPTER 197

**Stella's panic got the best of her and she fainted.** Pearleen kept flicking her lighter in a dire need to produce a bit of light, and moved on ahead of Lana.

The ceiling, once again, was as high as the ceiling on the other side of the drywall, as high as the ceiling was in the bathroom. She rose. Stood straight.

There was a jail type cell at the other end and had a gate with wrought iron bars. Inside the cell was a cot against the left wall, above it a window, boarded up, like the window in the john. Looked like there was a panel above it, like the one back there in the bathroom. Just waiting to be triggered so that it would slam down over the window.

There was a mini refrigerator against the opposite wall, a potty, the kind a youngster might use. There were photographs taped to the wall above the mini fridge that she could not quite make out: of Biggs and someone. Woman possibly.

There were also vertical rows and rows of receipts taped to the wall.

Lana reached her. Stood there, taking in the jail cell and what was in it. She walked up to the gate to see if it would open—for the hell of it. There was a window up there, wasn't there? Maybe they could give this one a real try, force the bars off and bust out.

Gate was locked. There went that notion. And there was nothing for them to do but turn around.

Ducking down, they made it back to where that dirty sheet of plywood was. Stella was just coming to. Pearleen helped. Sat her on the cinder block. Then asked her to stand up.

"Please. Get off the cinder block."

Stella remained out of it. Groggy and dazed. Weak. Pearleen looked at Lana. "Something like this concrete cinder block is what I was talking about. If we could get inside that jail cell, push the refrigerator over to the window side—and shove the cinder block through the boards; bang away at the boards with it."

"How would you get in the cell? You saw the gate. Gate is locked."

"Use the cinder block the same way. Hit the bars, bend them back— and squeeze through. Then we work on the window."

They helped Stella get to her feet, and the plywood tipped over, revealing a door.

# CHAPTER 198

**Pearleen's lighter was too wet, too something.** The bile, blood, slime and grime prevented it from functioning.

She wiped the gunk off. Rubbed the lighter against her blouse. Flicked it endlessly. Until at last a tiny, weak flame materialized.

Once Stella had adequately recovered, Pearleen gave her the lighter with instructions to hold it up and keep it going, while she and Lana lifted the cinder block and smashed at the door with it repeatedly until it gave, and they had created a portal wide enough to squeeze through.

They had no idea where this would take them, where it led. It had to lead somewhere—possibly, hopefully somewhere to keep safe long enough to figure out what to do.

Pearleen Bell got her lighter back from Stella Martel, and held it out through the opening in the door. It was a tunnel. Looked like it. A crudely fashioned one. Tunnel floor was dirt and puddles and planks. There was the occasional cinder block with chains locked to them that seemed to disappear beneath the planks and dirt. Strange creatures moved about: cockroaches, worms, rats. Some dirt from above trickled down from spaces in the planks and two by sixes that was the ceiling. The support posts, staggered at three- to four-foot intervals, were either four by fours and/or two by sixes. The ceiling itself, at six feet, was about a foot higher than the storage corridor ceiling. The walls were an amalgam of sheetrock, two-foot-by-six-foot plywood panels as well as thick planks about six feet in length. Sections of either wall also appeared to consist of wooden pallets. The rectangular panels had what looked like an aluminum handle at each end.

They helped Stella go through, then joined her.

# CHAPTER 199

**In hard hats and goggles, Biggs and Marvin made considerable progress by utilizing Norbert Fimple's head (sans protective head gear) as a battering ram.** And when Norbert could no longer stand it, Sassounian was there to volunteer: banged his practically hairless noggin against the bathroom door on his own. Managed to get it unhinged, and promptly passed out. Additional muscle was required still, as the dryer not only needed to be pushed back, but shoved aside.

Biggs was the first to enter the john. Saw the damage that had been done to his window, the planks that had been pried off. Then there was the cabinet below that the bitches hadn't been able to leave alone. Had no respect whatsoever for other people's property.

He glanced to his right. Did a double take. Floor was a mess. Wall above the tub had sustained the worst and costliest damage of all. Tub had plenty of rubble in it: tile fragments, stucco, dirt, chunks of drywall, blood.

Earthworms crawled about. Various rodents and cockroaches. Only

Marvin failed to see any of his four-legged buddies among the debris. His primary concern.

"Where my homie'?"

"Your 'homie'? Fuck your homie."

Biggs surveyed the damage with his eyes and did not feel good about any of it. "It'll take some doing to repair all this."

"Them hoe' sure knows about the tunnel now."

"Figured that out all by yourself, did you, Brother Muck?"

Marvin's missing buddies were on his mind and he damned sure didn't feel like responding; only as he did, it surprised even him. "Yeah, I did. Ain't had no help that time neither, me."

There was a four by four partially sticking out of the hole in the wall that Cecil yanked loose and probed under the crud and debris in the tub with. Shoved a degree of it aside, revealing one of Muck's crushed rats. Marvin was beside himself.

"*Psycho?* Yo. That ain't you. Don't let it be you."

"Why name a pet after a sissy?" Biggs tabulated in his head the work and money it would take to fix things up. "Why 'Psycho'? Hollywood ditz is a sissy."

"That don't be why I give homie the name. Ain't never even seen *PSYCHO.*"

"You never saw *PSYCHO?*"

"Never did. Lame boo-shit anyway." Marvin didn't want to discuss it. Had something else on his mind. *"Yo. Don't be dead. Psycho; don't be gone."*

Biggs noticed something else behind the bowl. A tail? Rat's tail? Beneath stucco rubble and whatnot. Stepped past Muck and shoved the crud aside with the two-by-four, revealing Marvin Muck's other bosom buddy. Just as history as the one in the bathtub. Marvin was carrying on. All it did was irritate the bishop even more.

# CHAPTER 200

**Stella recovered, to the extent that full recovery was remotely possible.**
They had no real idea where the tunnel would take them. Garage maybe? It was worth a try. Little choice but to risk it.

They helped Stella up, and walked along the creaky boards, dodging foot-long, water and slime-soaked rats with crimson-covered, glistening snouts. The odor was suffocating. Seemed to be much worse than a moment ago: a potent combination of raw sewage and decay, rodent droppings mixed in with the nausea-inducing stench of rotting flesh and lime powder that appeared to have been sprinkled throughout.

Choking, they fought to keep from breathing at the longest stretches possible. Did not wish to take in air at all—and ultimately failed. You could not endure without needing oxygen at some point.

"We're trapped. We're done."

"Shut up, Stella. I warned you about that. You're making it worse."

"You didn't see the *meat grinder* and the *sausage stuffer*, you didn't see the *patty press* and the *meat slicer* in his kitchen—I did!"

Images flashed in her mind's eye and could not be suppressed. Nothing close to it. Bits and pieces of *"hamburger"* in and around the *hopper opening,* as well as on the wooden handle of the grinder and other parts of it. *Blood-red palm and fingerprints* on the grinder that would not let her be, that she could not make go away.

The slicer had had prints on it; patty press did, too. One of the stew *"bits"* that she had wiped from her face after the fat freak with the metal clanging in his belly had sprayed her full on, had resembled a *thumbnail.* She hadn't been certain of it at the time.

Things had changed since then. How they have changed. *A thumbnail.*

"We're stuck! They'll chop us up! You've seen it! It's a *slaughter house! Real one! Trusty's Bordello of Fear! They'll grind us up like hamburger!* What do you think that stench is! All those bodies! *Mutilated!* They were mutilated and stuffed inside these walls! All these walls got dead bodies in them! It's a house of death! Roscoe was right! He was right about Cecil! Serial killer! What he is! My God, Roscoe was so right. We shouldn't have laughed at him! He knew what he was talking about. He knew."

"You were the one who laughed at him," pointed out Pearleen Bell.

"That's right," seconded Lana "Da Bottom." "Next time you run into Marty why not comp him a *BJ* to make it up to him? How's that?"

Stella Martel shook her head at how idiotic and pointless she thought their comments were.

"Cecil's been in and out of psychopathic hospitals. He's sick; he's twisted. The asshole's sick, I tell you! He's sick! And we're trapped in this house of freaks and cannibals!"

"The next thing that comes out of your mouth better not be: *We're all going to die!* Because if it is, I'll kill you myself right now, bitch! I'll beat your stupid ass!"

*"I can't take this shit anymore! I can't!"*

"Oh, you'll take it." Lana Sepulveda spun in the other's direction. "I guarantee you you'll take it!" She slapped Stella Martel several times, hard, across the face and watched her stagger and go down: a sobbing, hysterical heap.

# CHAPTER 201

**Pearleen stepped in.** Had no choice. Grabbed Lana around the waist and pulled her off of the other woman. Now all three were sobbing.

"Stella. I'm sorry, Stella. I didn't mean to hit you, Stella. Forgive me. I am so very sorry."

Lana and Pearleen were soon holding one another tight and weeping against each other's shoulder. They separated. Helped Stella to her feet. Stella had wrapped her arms around them both. Made a frantic effort to hold on, needing to. Unable to let go.

It was clear now to Lana and Pearleen that their friend was no longer capable of rational thought.

"Look, Pearl, we're inside a tunnel. It has to lead somewhere. My guess is it will take us to the garage. What other purpose would a tunnel like this serve? What would be the point?"

"With somebody like Cecil, who dresses up like a sadistic clown and calls himself *Trusty Lusty*, who knows?"

"*It has to lead to his garage.* What better way to smuggle victims in and keep neighbors from finding out than by pulling into the garage with the victims in the trunk? All he's got to do is go through some secret trap door that takes him down here to the tunnel—and he's home-free. And the neighbors wouldn't know it."

"Let's just keep moving. Please, God, let there be a way out. Please . . . please . . . please. . . ."

Stella slipped, her feet gave way and she took Pearleen with her, with the latter staggering against the "wall" on the right and leaving a prominent crack along the center of the cruddy plywood panel, from one end to the other. Dirt drizzled down from the ceiling; one of the planks cracked at about the middle, breaking into two halves and swung down, dangling this way from either side of the ceiling above them.

Other chunks of soil and small rocks fell on them, threatening to bury them alive. The rectangular panel continued to crack, outwardly this time and on its own, with some force, and a body rolled from it and landed on the floor. Evidently a shelf had been built into the wall that the body had been kept in. It was a woman. Intact and alive, if only barely so. No clothes on her. Wrists had been cuffed behind her back. She wept.

"Miss Betty. . . . *What are you going to do to me, Miss Betty?* I had to . . . I had to . . . I just couldn't take it in there anymore. . . ."

"No, no." Pearleen did what she could to convey that they were not out to harm her in any way. "We're from out there, outside. We're not part of Biggs's depraved bunch."

"No way," Lana assured the half-mad, half-dead woman.

"Help me, then. Why don't you help me? Somebody . . . Somebody has got to help us. . . . Deliver us from this hell. . . . Mercy; just a touch of mercy. . . ."

Lana and Pearleen were near hysteria themselves, seemingly succumbing to the same state their friend Stella was in. More tears flowed. This new development froze them up, left them undecided as to what to do about the pain-wracked woman at their feet crying out for help one minute, then something else the next. She wanted to die.

"Kill me. I beg you, Miss Betty . . . Kill me. . . ."

Pearl tried again. Wanted to assure her that Miss Betty was not with them. "There's no Miss Betty here. Not in the tunnel—at this time. No way are we part of *Brother Trusty's* twisted followers. Understand?"

The woman may have caught on. Was beyond tears.

"My name is Helen Irene Sanchez. . . . Let my family know . . . what happened to me. My two sons . . . my parents. . . . Let them know. . . . Biggs forced me to get in his van at gun point in Culver City. . . . Cecil Omar Biggs and Marvin Ritalin Muck. Please tell my family. Now . . . end my pain. . . ."

Blood flowed from her mouth and upper thighs; a good deal of her toes had been chewed off. Rodents, no doubt.

"I can't do that." Pearleen choked back sobs. "Forgive me. I can't. . . ." She wiped hair and dirt away from the dying woman's face. . . .

"They kidnapped me five months ago." The woman spoke in a tone so low and weak she was hardly audible. "Now that I have told someone . . . I can . . . My family will know. . . . My family . . ." Mouth agape, eyes open, she said nothing more. Was still. After a moment, Pearleen pressed her ear against the woman's chest. Couldn't tell a thing. She felt her neck in search of a pulse.

"She's gone."

Pearl closed Helen Irene Sanchez'es eyes.

# **CHAPTER 202**

**They rose.** There was nothing else to do but keep going. It was not long before they heard other moans. It was obvious enough to them, these new, faintly heard cries for help came from behind the same wall, only further on. The illumination projected by the lighter in Pearleen's hand continued to decrease.

"Please let me out." Another female voice. Pleading. "Please, Miss Betty. . . . Bishop Biggs? Where are you? I'll be good. Do as you wish—in every way. I can be trusted. . . . *Trust is everything.* Trust and loyalty. Please let me out. . . ."

Pearleen tapped at the wood. Lana glared at her. "We have to get out of here! Pearl! We'll never make it if we keep stopping every two minutes!"

Pearleen's rapping of her knuckles led her to yet another plywood panel. She pulled on the handle that was there. Got nowhere. The panel was loose. There was a rail above, as well as along the bottom. She yanked the handle to the right and the rectangular panel slid open.

"We can't help nobody else until we help ourselves first, Pearleen, dammit!"

There was a crudely built coffin inside the wall that sat horizontally on a shelf. The victim trapped within could be heard whimpering, trying to speak.

"I'll be just the way you want me to be. My life as a strumpet is over, Miss Betty. . . . I promise. . . . Miss Betty. . . . Give me *The Word.* . . . I am so ready to accept *The Word.* . . . I'll be the best for you, Bishop Biggs. . . ."

"Another one. . . ." Lana shook her head. It was hard to take.

Pearleen searched for and found the latch on the lid. A padlock hung from it. Lana moved up and helped her out with it. They twisted the thing back and forth, yanked up and down on it until they had it off. They lifted the coffin lid. There was a woman lying inside the poorly constructed oblong box. Hands cuffed behind her back, same as the other one. She was not clothed. Her head remained ever-so-still, as she dared not move. Only her eyeballs shifted, to see who had come to deliver her from her mind-numbing predicament.

# CHAPTER 203

**"Is that you, Bishop Biggs?" wondered Dixie Osgood in a tone closer to plea than query, while her eyes adjusted to the flickering, weak light in Pearleen's hand.** It was more light than she was accustomed to.

Excreta stench was choking, unbearable. The ever-present cockroaches, practically as thick as thumbs, scrambled out of sight.

Pearleen and Lana dragged the homemade coffin out of the wall. Lowered it to the planks and dirt and mud that was the floor. They reached down to help the woman. Only she was not budging.

"Did Bishop Biggs send you?" Dixie was clearly concerned. Her eyes were welling.

Pearleen took pause. What was she supposed to say? The situation continued to make her ill to her stomach.

"Nobody sent us."

Lana urged the woman to get up. "We're getting out of this place."

Dixie Osgood shook her head. Was adamant. She did not wish to be touched or moved. Fear did this, fear of Cecil Omar Biggs, fear of his disciples, fear of what Biggs would do to her should he discover that she had been "bad," had gone and done something he had not approved of.

*"I can't. I can't. DON'T TOUCH ME! DON'T TOUCH ME! Bishop will punish me if I'm bad. He'll punish me. He'll tell Miss Betty to hurt me. He'll tell her to hurt me if he finds out."*

Lana's advice to Pearleen was to let her go. They did. The woman remained in the coffin.

"He'll know I betrayed him. Because you moved me. You moved the box. The bishop will know."

Lana DaBottom had had it up to here with the whole nightmarish circus of it.

*"FUCK HIM! So goddamn what!"*

Pearleen's tip to Lana was to take it easy. DaBottom wasn't interested.

"Tunnel takes us to the garage; am I right?"

"Please put me back where you found me. *Please . . .*"

"Leave her be."

# CHAPTER 204

**Pearleen rose.** They decided to keep moving forward. Lana soon followed. Passed her up, with Stella awkwardly hurling herself ahead of them both.

There was a sound, at the far end of the tunnel, above their heads somewhere: like a hatch or trap door maybe, lowered closed and locked into place, that resulted in the briefest flash of light. Was it that? Or nothing more than their impression of it? Before they'd had a chance to think it through, or arrive at anything resembling a conclusion, Stella Martel's next step triggered something like a bear trap and she released a sharp, anguished cry as the steel teeth of the thing dug into her right ankle.

The disorienting suddenness of it, coupled with indescribable pain, sent her staggering against the Latina, whose own left foot triggered another animal-type metal trap—and both women went down in agony.

Pearleen sought to help. Attempted to pry the traps loose and free them—and it could not be done. Furthermore, the traps were linked to chains that were in turn secured to cinder blocks buried beneath planks that made up the floor. Choking on tears, Pearleen knew she would have to leave the two of them where they were for the time being. She wondered what other surprises Biggs had rigged the tunnel with?

Rising to her feet, she held the butane lighter out in front of her and noticed now why Lana and Stella had not been able to spot the traps: they'd been concealed within carefully-constructed depressions in the floor and covered over with dark plastic trash bags.

She aimed the lighter directly at the floor, and ever-so-carefully, moved further along the tunnel. She reached a short, wooden stoop at the end. Looked up. Yes, indeed there was a portal up there. Trap door. Just as there was one to her left, in that side of the tunnel. Door was about half the size of your average door, both: in height and width. Appeared to be metal. Where did it lead? Another passageway? She grabbed the steel handle with both hands, and yanked hard. Didn't matter where the door lead to because it was solid and it was locked. Concluded immediately she was expending time and energy she could ill afford. She turned back toward the stoop and her eyes caught something else: a snake slithering down from the top step.

She fired once at the head, stopping it. It was not until she was able to get a closer look at the snake did she realize that the reptile had had its skull flattened by someone long before her bullet ever went through it.

Just more of the weirdo's games that made no sense. The bastard did get you to waste another one of your precious bullets, didn't he?

Pearleen proceeded to make it up the stoop, holding her breath, praying that she would be able to get out this way.

Slowly, taking one step at a time, she made it up. Held the gun out in front of her in both hands. She counted the steps. Eight steps to the door.

She was halfway there when the door creaked open, and a grinning Cecil Omar Biggs appeared, using a couple of male geeks, wearing bloody and disgusting hog masks with slobbering long tongues hanging out, as human shields.

Biggs held a gun in one hand, and the black, aircraft-aluminum Maglite in the other.

"Pearleen Bell. You didn't think it was going to be this easy, did you?"

Biggs prodded the retards to move down the steps—with a reminder not to harm her, only hold her.

"This is sick, Cecil. You can't go on. They'll get you. Sooner or later they'll get you."

"Meanwhile, I'm having the time of my life."

He shoved the men down after her. Pearleen emptied her gun into the psychos and watched them thrust themselves at her just the same, tumbling down to the bottom and taking her with in the process.

That was it for Cecil's goons in the repulsive hog masks. The wounded geeks were in too much pain to think about rising back up.

Pearleen Bell made it to her feet. Hurried in the opposite direction. She staggered over the coffin, the other dead woman. Found her way toward the opening, and got trapped inside the corridor—and was yanked out through the same hole in the bathroom wall by members of Cecil's "inner circle."

# CHAPTER 205

**Biggs was already there, waiting at the door to the john.**

"Look at the damage you did to the wall. My storage corridor is a disaster, the tunnel a mess. All this is going to cost time and money, lots of money. Not to mention hard work. I can't help but get annoyed when people come in here and think they can destroy my property."

He held the Maglite horizontally and whacked her across the belly with it. Pearleen doubled over. Went down.

"It's a simple fact, real estate that is not kept up automatically depreciates. Any moron will tell you that. Am I right, Brother Muck?"

"Yo, why you be lookin' at me? Don't be me put no hole in the wall."

Biggs's eyes were back on the stripper.

"You see, the plan is to eventually unload the house and relocate the United Christian Church of Re-Newed Hope to larger, more accommodating quarters. Possibly Temple City. I'm determined to get a decent price for the place."

He nodded to board members and staff to help her up. They managed.

"Only it makes it pretty difficult when someone like you feels you can come in here and start knocking holes in my walls. It's bad enough we have to keep an eye on Sassy and Mr. Fimple for this very same thing. I mean every time I turn my back, there they are, banging their heads against something: wall, door, staircase, other staff members, or members of the congregation. I don't care for it at all. Can stress a man out." And he let her have it again, right across the mid-section, that sent her sprawling back down. Where she belongs, thought Cecil. He would have preferred smacking her in the jaw, or face, neck—but then that might have impaired her ability to suck cock, which he had plans for her to do later.

"Remind me to give her a tetanus booster shot. Might have to give one to myself—to be on the safe side."

# CHAPTER 206

**Pearleen Bell was carried to the Mattress Room.** Leggings were clamped to her ankles that came with a foot and a half long chain between them, this then was attached via lock to a long chain that hung from an overhead pipe. Biggs saw to it that there was enough slack in the chain so that she would be able to lie down on any one of the soiled and ratty mattresses on the cement floor should she be inclined to do so at some point in the future. He held her wrists and handcuffed them in front of her.

Pearleen crawled to what she assumed to be the chamber pot. Found herself throwing up. The last blow to the belly and general decay and stench in the tunnel and here in this room had brought it on.

"As you may or may not have surmised, I don't like to see vomit on my floor. Use the bucket to shit in, piss in—puke in. It'll have to do for the time being. You'll eventually be allowed access to the john. You'll be provided with fresh tap water to drink, food to eat."

He had her purse with him and had already taken a look inside, not for the handgun, as he'd already found it, but for something else.

"Where's the lighter?"

"Good question."

"Gold, isn't it?"

"That's what Fritz claimed. It didn't look cheap."

"It wasn't. Where is it?"

"If I knew I'd tell you."

"Sure you would."


He needed to return to the tunnel. Wished he had invested in a biohazard suit. Money; it took money, though. Money was painful to part with. Now he had to face reentering the tunnel sans real protection from rats, roaches, worms—and all the other creepy-crawly, bacteria-carrying, flesh-eating parasites.

It had to be done. No way around it.

There was the floor-to-ceiling bookcase between the Furnace Room and walk-in cooler that would have to be pushed aside first. Though it was on steel casters, it still required muscle to accomplish. Not only that, he didn't like reminding the geeks that there was a door here that led to a tunnel—and the outside. Would any of them ever attempt to go this route just for the hell of it? He doubted it.

Had no choice but to follow through. Didn't feel like having to lug those two other bitches through the cluttered corridor and that hole in the bathroom wall.


Get it over with. Bookshelf was pushed to the side. Unlocked the fortified tunnel door, and went in with some of the able-bodied geeks to retrieve Lana "Da Bottom" Sepulveda and Stella "Storm" Martel. Couple of lame twats.

Mr. Fimple regarded Lana's bloody leg as she lay on the tunnel floor, rushed in, dropped to his knees to lap up her blood. It took great effort on Lana's part, fighting weakness and pain, but she managed to lift the hand she held the cutter in and swing with it so that the blade sliced the geek diagonally across the face. The geek dropped to the ground yowling. The others saw it and laughed.

Cecil Biggs could not move back in time himself as Lana Sepulveda shifted again, lashing him across the upper right thigh, inches from his groin.

The bishop grunted, stepping back. He lifted his flashlight and smashed it down against the side of the brunette's neck. He did it again. Watched the unconscious woman drop back.

*"Just for that, I've got a special treat in store for you, sweetheart."*

# CHAPTER 207

**"Ain't no use."**

Harold Crust rolled out of bed. Got into his bathrobe and peeked through his bedroom curtains for the fiftieth time. All that screaming and loud music and pounding was just too much to take. What on earth could the man be doing this late at night? Don't he ever sleep? What kind of church can that be? Church of Re-Newed Hope, he calls it. That's what the sign on Biggs's door said: *UNITED CHRISTIAN CHURCH OF RE-NEWED HOPE.* What bullshit. Church of *No Hope* is more like it. Sounds like a wild party goin' on over there, if you ask me. Listen to it.

All he wanted to do was get some rest. Lack of rest usually made him grumpy on the job. How you supposed to make tips if you grumpy? You always lose jack when you ain't cheerful. That was the truth. He'd been in the shoeshine business long enough to know that.

The regulars: postal workers, motorcycle cops, bus drivers, *Pep Boys* stock clerks, used car salesmen in the area, all those regulars who stopped by his stand to have their shoes polished mainly did so to say hello to him. That was it. They didn't need to have their kicks shined; they usually came by to have a nice chat with Harold 'cause Harold Crust was always up, easy to talk to, endearing.

Yeah, he'd heard folks say that about him. He was endearing. Nice guy to be around. And he felt pretty lousy right now. Needed something for his headache; sleeping pills would have been better, except he didn't like to take sleeping pills.

Sleep, rest, would have been perfect (without no kind of pill), but that strange, so-called preacher wouldn't let him sleep.

Try calling the rollers. When did that ever do any good?

He opened the bedroom door. Could hear the tv going in the living room. Fay had that all-night religious program on again. He shook his head. Didn't she ever get enough of that jive? He didn't have anything against religion. Considered himself a Christian, believed in God, always had—but these tv evangelists made him sick to his stomach.

Harold Crust couldn't stand the sight of them.

If only he could have had a shot of whiskey, half a shot even, that would have cured everything, made up for it all—a taste of *Jack Daniels*, a line of toot, a short one. He knew he wouldn't dare go near any of it, and yet he couldn't stop himself from wanting it, from thinking about it from time to time. Was it his fault? Was he to blame because his brain and body craved it? Was he?

Quacks had told him cocaine was the reason his blood pressure was in the crapper and why he needed the heart surgery. Only they wasn't done by a long shot. No sir. Stuck a pacemaker in him for the added bonus— to their pocketbook. Fucked him once with the surgery—and then fucked him again with the pacemaker. Said cocaine was the reason. *Blow*. He had known blow wasn't good for him; he had also known not everyone who fooled with toot had to have their heart operated on, either. But he had gone along. They had scared him enough. Said: Do it. Or risk dropping dead from a coronary. Cocaine had damaged his valves, they said, and booze. Heavy drinking. Fast women. Too much running around. Caught up with him. And they had also told him that he was lucky he hadn't destroyed the *mucus membranes* in his nose with the powder (which often happened with heavy users).

That was just it, he had done his best to explain: he hadn't been a heavy user. Had liked having a good time, true enough. Heavy user? Didn't think he rated. Not him. He'd done his share, he supposed. And Fay had tolerated it all this time, waited patiently for him to clean up his act. She had stuck to her *Bible* and religious programs on television, attended church every Sunday (a real church, and not the one next door, thank God. So far, anyway). Point being: she had stood by him, when so many women would have given him the boot. He loved that about her more than anything.

Woman was loyal to the bone. There just weren't that many left like her. He wished he remembered it more often.

# CHAPTER 208

**He reached the living room.** Saw Fay sitting in her recliner in front of the color tv—and she was writing out a check.

"We got any booze in the house?"

He saw it coming. Knew it would happen. The look she gave him was one of silent reproach. As far as she was concerned he wasn't funny. Harold poured himself a tumbler of ice water in the kitchen. Held it up to the light.

"Here it is. Shot of rye. No harm in pretending."

He popped two *Excedrin* in his mouth. Chased them down with the water in the tumbler.

"Lord, that's nasty."

"Why not go back on the cranberry juice? You liked it well enough."

"Got any idea how much sugar they put in that stuff, Fay? Always made me sick in my belly. Way worse than this nasty ol' tap water."

"Buy a filter. People I work for got one. Makes tap water taste better."

"Nothing can make this water taste better. Could be worth a try, I suppose."

"You need your rest, Harold. Should go back to bed."

"That man next door won't let me sleep. Sure got to be some kind of exclusive church Biggs is runnin' for loose women and dopefiends."

The set blared on in the living room, the clean-cut televangelist in black suit and tie, "as American as apple pie," continued to implore for donations. Harold pretended not to hear. That only got him so far.

*"Shearing the sheep, fleecing the flock."*

Knew it made no difference to Fay no matter what he said about them. Forget the televangelist. Can't win that battle. Instead, he leaned over the kitchen sink to peer through the crack in the window curtain above it, trying to figure the impossible: what in tarnation was going on in Bishop Cecil Omar Biggs's place?

Something furry and quite alive unexpectedly rubbed itself past his ankles that gave him a real start. If not a stroke exactly, close enough to it. Harold looked down. Should have known: *Delonzo.* Acting like a hotshot. Scowled for Harold's benefit, then leisurely walked off. Harold wished the cat would find the front door and keep right on going. Would never happen. Cat had it made here and knew it. Free grub, and didn't have to do nothing to earn it, either.

"They took us off the air in Dallas, took us off the air in Albuquerque, took us off the air in Tucson. Do you want the same to happen in Southern California? Do you? Is that what you want? If you don't want that to happen here you had better let me know that you don't, and you know there is only one way to do that. Donations pays bills, and we got more bills than we know what to do with, friends, enough bills to wallpaper this entire house, the Lord's House. We have bills up to our eyeballs. We are swimming in bills. It's a crying shame we got so many bills. *Send money, friends; send money.* Don't let them shut us down, don't let them take us off the air. If twenty dollars is the best that you can do, then send that twenty right now. And as for the rest of you: *I know that you can do better than that; I know that you can.*"

What with Biggs and that noise over there and the obnoxious tv hustler "selling" his *jive*, there just was no peace of mind to be had around here. And on top of all that, he had to put up with the cat making him jump whenever he took a step—in his own home, no less; making him feel like a stranger and giving him that Evil Eye every time he looked at him.

# CHAPTER 209

**Harold was back in the living room.** Saw the check on the coffee table.

"Woman, you know how many kicks I got to shine to make that kind of bread?"

"It's only twenty dollars, Harold."

"To you it's only twenty dollars—to me it's ten pair of dirty shoes. I'm driving without car insurance and you're giving money away?"

Fay's eyes stayed on the evangelist. Her *Bible* nearby.

"Don't make a fuss, Harold. Reverend Goodrum says they're going broke and won't be able to stay on the air if they can't pay their bills. They will be taken *off the air* if they can't meet their financial obligations, Harold."

"Yeah, you see me cryin', don't you? Those people are always going broke, Fay; always asking for more money—meanwhile, they're living in fancy mansions with gold crappers and driving luxury automobiles like Biggs over there, while people like us got to struggle just to make ends meet."

Unlike Marty Roscoe's wife Petunia, Fay Crust was naturally calm, collected. Not much phased her. There was a deep faith that seemed to keep her not only rooted, but guided her in the right direction and gave her strength. She knew the Lord would provide and there was no need to get excited about anything.

"You don't have to shout, Harold. No need to raise your voice. Be mindful of your pacemaker and your blood pressure."

"Trouble is I am mindful, too much so—on account someone's always reminding me."

"It's only twenty dollars, Harold, and it's for a good cause."

"You said."

Only twenty. Tell it to the hospital and the butcher he had the lawsuit goin' against. Might get them to hurry up and settle. Their ship was due. Any day now. Meanwhile, they had to go on living. Pay bills. Them twenty-dollar donations added up.

Harold was not entirely aware that he was at it again: running the tips of his fingers down the center of his chest, along the main heart surgery scar. He'd been doing it out of habit lately.

"If you ask me, all these televangelists should be lined up against the wall. That's right: put 'em up against a wall. Why not? They ain't nothing more than a bunch of bloodsuckers."

"Harold."

"Ought to be thrashed, at the least. I ain't kidding. There ain't no worse grifter on this earth. God knows what I'm talking about. I don't mind giving to a legitimate charity—"

Harold aimed a finger at the tailor-cut suit on the color screen that probably cost more than he earned in a month.

"That's just rip-off time—big time. Thievin' from the poor and elderly. Make the Mafia look like Boy Scouts."

Suddenly he made a gesture with his hands that said it was all hopeless anyway, and thought if it makes her feel better to give the twenty let her do it; let her be. Did her share around the place, did what she could to contribute. Working as a domestic down there in Bel Air for that movie producer and his family wasn't exactly easy, not at her age, even if she only did it part-time. Got a decent woman there. Leave her alone. Your beef ain't with her or even with the tee-vee preacher, but that rude Biggs crowd.

"Good night, Fay. I'm going back to bed. I got to get some rest if I plan to make any money tomorrow."

"Good night, hon."

His wife never turned away from the screen.

# CHAPTER 210

**There was a semblance of order in the basement for the time being.** Biggs used his experience as a practical nurse to tend to his cuts and bruises.

He took care of his people so long as their wounds were non-life threatening and did not require serious attention. Helped patch them up with Greta Otto's assistance. And the others? A different fate awaited them. By the time he got to Stella to pry the bear trap off her foot, half a dozen large rats had already converged on Helen Irene Sanchez, the dead victim, and were devouring her flesh.

Stella Martel was clearly in pain and practically beside herself.

"Brought it on yourself, didn't you, Girlie? What I gave just wasn't good enough for you bitches. Never enough. Always wanting more. Gave Mr. Fimple quite a headache when you clobbered him with that chair up there. Not only that . . . it's the general disrespect that I find more annoying than anything else."

He located her purse. Rifled through it. Pocketed the cash he found, most of which he presumed was Olivia's.

"Business before pleasure."

Had the geeks lift her up off the tunnel floor and summarily carry her into the cooler and hung her on a hook. Biggs checked her fingers for rings, wrists for bracelets, as she dangled. Relieved her of what he found. Took her wristwatch off, the gold cross that hung from her neck, earrings. Checked her feet for ankle bracelets. Discovered one on the ankle with all the lacerations. Had blood on it. Didn't matter. He helped himself to it.

# CHAPTER 211

**Before leaving the walk-in, he paused to turn the temperature up from thirty degrees to about thirty-five, so that she would not succumb to the cold as rapidly—and would stay alive longer.**

He stepped out of the cooler, closed the door and locked it. While a grieving Muck was in the backyard giving his dead rat pals a "proper" *adios*—not to mention wasting time and tears—Biggs returned to the tunnel and the oblong box the inconsiderate bitches had left on the floor.

He knelt beside the plywood coffin. Lifted the lid. Some of the rats who had been feasting on Helen Irene Sanchez a moment ago must have left her, and other rats from elsewhere must have joined the ones here, got in through gaps in the bottom and sides, but there were about four or five of them taking chunks out of Dixie's flesh. They were all over: face and neck, vagina and thighs. Since her wrists were cuffed behind her back, there wasn't much the victim could do other than move her head from side to side, kick out somewhat with her feet at the other end. Rats didn't give a damn; this was not about to deter them.

*"Bishop Biggs? Please . . . Can you stop them? Can you please, please stop them?"*

The way Biggs saw it: the rats were saving him ammo. Sons of bitches didn't care, were not bothered by the fact that he shined his flashlight on them. They were hungry, and food was at hand. Bellies needed to be fed—and fed they would be.

Cecil Biggs stood there, taking it in—as the whimpering went on. Her lips got chewed up and eyes. Blood ran from her groin region. Fuck, he came close to creaming in his trousers himself. He didn't care for rats, true enough, but there was no denying they provided a service, just as the woman would be providing Greta Otto's kettle with real meat.

He squeezed his groin. Hard. Like bamboo.

He lowered the lid over the rats and walked over to the stoop, the wooden steps that led to the trap door in the garage floor, relieved the severely wounded geeks of their Parfrey pig masks and put one slug apiece into their heads.

He shone the light on Lana Sepulveda. Super Latina. *Princess Likk Mi Azz*, among other aliases. Lying there. Conscious enough to keep the rats at bay—and barely at that. He would need a hand with her.

Remembered to take the shades off, the shooting muffs. Had the safety helmet where it belonged: on his head.

He climbed the stoop to the garage floor. Cracked open the large garage doors to see what was going on. Muck was on his hands and knees in the dirt, weeping over his rodents. A serial rapist dropping tears over some dead scavenging beasts. He'd pulled weeds, made a clearing, swept litter aside. Had even fashioned small crosses from twigs and *Popsicle* sticks as grave markers.

Biggs shook his head. They were rats. Fucking rats. Granted, not as low as humans, but they were RATS. *Rattus norvegicus*. He was distraught because a couple of mangy sewer dwellers bit the dust. Retard. Weren't they all?

He took the plugs out of his ears. Called him over.

"Need a hand."

Marvin looked up. Wiped his eyes.

"They was iced for nothing."

"They went down for the cause."

"Homie Snagglepuss and Homie Dizz be only ones I got left now."

"Pet shops are full of them. Rats are dime a dozen."

"They was my bud'."

"Life is a bitch. Speaking of bitches, I can use a hand with that Sepulveda cunt."

Marvin nodded his head. Entered the garage. Soon enough they were inside the tunnel freeing the semi-conscious Lana Sepulveda from the bear trap and carrying her to the Fun Room. She was placed on the workbench that resembled a modified butcher's block. Biggs had her legs spread apart and strapped the ankles down to opposite corners at that end; strapped the wrists down at her sides. He reached for the vanity case and began applying makeup to her face: dark pencil for the arched brows, eyeliner; blush-on for the cheeks. Heavy on the cherry-red lipstick for the mouth.

"Go get Snaggletooth."

"Why him? Why my favorite? Why not the other one?"

"Because he's the largest—and the toughest."

"What if he bite' the dust? What then?"

"We'll go back to the pet shop and buy more."

"He don't be the kind you can replace. Had him from the beginning; day one. Had him from the time I was hangin' on Hollywood Boulevard. Me and him go back."

"You said. I'm all broken up about it."

"Look it."

"Go get the ugly fucker."

"No, man. You ain't gonna do to MC Snagglepuss what you done to them other."

"Get the rat."

Biggs glared at him.

"What for? What chu gonna do?"

"You'll find out."

"Yo, you don't be givin' a fart 'bout nothin'. Didn't like it when your daddy took your hog an' dog out, but it be cool to do to my own."

"You have a point. I'll give you that much, even though I paid for all but the one. I'll do my best not to hurt Snaggletooth. How's that?"

"*'Snagglepuss'* be the name I give him."

Marvin cursed under his breath. Wiped his eyes and left to get the pet. Biggs shook his head: he was surrounded by halfwits and idiots.

He saw to it that the small curtain that hung over the Judas window was drawn so that the defectives wouldn't be able to get an eyeful of what was about to unfold inside the Fun Room. It wasn't that it mattered all that much to the bishop; it came down to him simply preferring to handle the situation in this manner. The geeks had enough to cope with as it was, why expose them to visuals that might cause further anxiety and/or excitement?

It occurred to him that there was one individual he felt should be here to witness this. Put her through it. See how she holds up. If she fails the test, at least her presence would only enhance the overall experience for him.

# CHAPTER 212

He stepped out to the Mattress Room across the way, and a moment later returned with the somewhat disorientated and still trembling Pearleen Bell. Her ankles were in shackles. He let her sit in a metal folding chair facing the butcher's block.

"I suggest you stay alert for this. Keep your eyes open. Don't turn away. I make myself clear?"

"Quite."

"We'll see. Brought this on yourself. *Like to party?* No problem. We're going to party—*my way.*"

"Why do I need to see this? I don't need to see this."

"You don't *ask* here—you *do.*"

He cut at Lana "Da Bottom's" clothing with his switchblade until he had it all off. A bucket of water was dumped on her to wash off grime and the like. Her wounds and lacerations were tended to with *Band-Aids* and a kerchief to prevent further loss of blood. Blood would be spilled, of course, but at his convenience and say-so. The rest of her was strapped down to the workbench: torso, hips, knees. Her head was lifted and a folded towel slid under to make her nice and comfy.

An oblong-shaped, crudely-constructed cage made from chicken wire had been fastened to the victim's upper thighs and crotch. The cage had been designed so that it contained a gate at each end. The gate that was pressed against her vagina had been created so that one could pull up on it to allow easy egress —as well as reentry. While the gate at the other end made these very same functions readily possible: entry and exit; it was the type that swung out.


Biggs went over the leather straps again that he had secured the woman to the butcher's block with to make sure there was no slack that would allow her to jerk her waist or pelvis and thighs in any way. The legs had been spread apart wide enough, the straps on the ankles good and tight.

The bishop also had an adjustable angle mirror present: twenty inches by sixty inches. On a chrome stand with casters. About a foot to the right of her right ankle, so that she would have access to a perfect view of what was being done to her down there between her legs, should she be interested—once she came to.

Marvin was back with his favorite pal MC Snagglepuss. The gate at the opposite end of the stripper's pelvis was opened, and the rat was transferred inside and the gate closed. Latch flipped in place.

"Make sure you got film in the *Polaroid*."

Marvin did that. Nodded his head. He did look concerned, not liking what Snagglepuss was about to be put through. No, he didn't like what was about to be done to the ho neither, although his primary concern was with his homie the rat and what the mental toll would be on him. Didn't like doin' this to his pet'. No way. None of it made him happy. Cecil be the one callin' him *rapo* and all that. He could live wiff it. 'Cause maybe he was. Rapin' them hoe' every chance he got. Only hurtin' his homie' be way out of line.

Biggs turned the volume up on the police scanner. Cracked a vial of smelling salts in half. Waved it under Da Bottom's nose. He pulled the goggles down over his eyes and reached for a chopstick. Marvin saw it and cursed.

"Watch your aim. I expect some great *Before and After* shots of this."

Marvin grumbled and shook his head. He was about to start weeping again.

"Are you a man or a crybaby? What the fuck is this? How will you be able to keep your hands steady to give me some good stills if you're bawling like a baby?"

"If you hurt him, I swear I'll never forgive you, Cecil. I swear it, home'. . . ."

# CHAPTER 213

**As Lana came to, she thought she heard or felt what sounded like a small cage being handled or fussed with somewhere below her waist.** Some kind of wire contraption had been fastened to her crotch. She couldn't tell what it was. What were they doing to her now? Where was she?

It took her a moment. She realized it soon enough: she was not dreaming it; it was not a dream, bad or otherwise, but actually happening. She noticed the mirror at this point, some kind of contraption, like an oblong-shaped birdcage, had been attached to her lower region. Saw exactly what the *hairy creature* with its long, thin tail was: *a rat*.

Biggs was grinning. Raised the gate at the vagina end. Prodded at the rat with the chopstick. He kept prodding and poking at it until the rodent found itself at the woman's vagina and began nibbling with its sharp teeth.

Lana's panic increased with each nanosecond. Shifted into full blown hysteria soon enough. The high yellow did her own share of wailing. Pearleen's tears surfaced, then flowed down either side of her nose. There was gasping and screaming—and then the rest of it: gagging and vomiting. Had her mouth leaning over her right shoulder and puked her guts out.

Biggs didn't care for it; didn't care for any of it: the way she carried on, nor the puke. She was failing him. Granted, it was entertaining to witness, and added to the thrill, but all in all he had hoped for something else: less emotion, and/or revulsion.

"That's enough now. You're overdoing it."

Pearleen was retching. Unable to stop. Her body quaked in the seat. Finally, the shakes were so bad that she fell over on the side the vomit was on: slipped off the chair and dropped into her own pool of vomit.

"Look what you've gone and done. I didn't expect this. I'm not sure what I expected, but it wasn't this. Not from a *tough-as-nails ballbuster like yourself.*"

Muck took a shot of her lying in the bile. Bishop did a hand gesture that said it was nothing more than a waste of film.

"Concentrate on the other one." His eyes were on Pearleen. "Like using me for my money and dope? Like fucking with my gender?"

Pearleen remained on her side, sobbing her heart out. Unable to stop.

"Knock it off. You're worse than Marvin. At least when he blubbers he has a legit reason: those rats are his 'homies.' In your case: I don't see how you can justify your display of emotion. You never could stand Da Bottom, and she never gave two shits for you, either."

# CHAPTER 214

**Marvin took his pictures, while Biggs guided the creature.** There was no other way to make the rat do what he needed it to: and that was to enter the cunt's cunt.

"You bet. Get inside, motherfucker. Eat the bitch's snatch."

The rat was reluctant to go in. Paused there at the opening. Began to nibble at her anus.

"Chew her asshole. Eat her shit-hole; and then, my furry friend, want you to crawl inside her pee-hole and do some more devouring."

Lana was all out screaming. The more she howled, the better Biggs liked it. No denying he was disappointed in Pearleen's reaction to the drama, although Sepulveda's histrionics more than compensated.

Lana may have been justified, in that she felt the sharp teeth of the rat chew bits of her anus and labia lips. Her privates were being consumed by the hungry creature. It liked blood, too. Lapped it up.

Biggs glanced at Marvin.

"Get me some close-ups of her face."

Marvin took a couple. Lowered the camera.

"You sure, home'? Film be costin' coin."

"That's why I watch the overhead—to have money for stuff like this."

Marvin moved around for a different angle. Biggs had eased up on the poking now that the rat had entered the wailing, jerking captive. She was able to twist her body to some extent, but not enough to shake the slimy, beastly thing out, not enough to prevent what was happening.

"I like the look on her face. Sheer panic. The beauty of it. Lookit the ballbuster. Who's got the power now, bitch?" Faced Pearleen. "See what you twats are made of finally? See what it comes down to? Yelps and fainting spells."

Marvin took a couple of shots of the expression on Lana's face: fear and panic. Madness; she was on the verge of slipping into madness.

Biggs enjoyed it for what it was worth. The rat had buried its way inside. Biggs let up on the prodding. There was no need to continue with it, no use for it at this point.

Somehow Snagglepuss had managed to make a full turnaround inside the woman and was now poking his head out, wondering if it was safe enough to re-emerge.

Biggs clouted it with the chopstick, not to hurt it in any way, but to ensure that the rat got the message: he wanted it inside the stripper's vagina; he wanted it in there to do as much damage as possible. The rat chewed away at the loose bits of flesh and blood, lapping it up.

The adjustable angle mirror was to Cecil's left, Lana's lower right. He looked at it. Repositioned it to make certain Lana was getting a good view of what was going on, what the ravenous animal was doing to her.

She felt the pain, to be sure, that was plain, but he also wanted her to get the full effect of the visual. Her face was a shade of deep crimson from all the screaming and shaking of her head. She was close to hoarse now and about to go out. Biggs didn't want that. The smelling salts helped, and he cracked another vial under her nose, then tossed a couple of keys to Marvin, and ordered him to pick up a bucket.

"Fill it with ice from the freezer in the walk-in cooler. Lock them both up when you're done. Bring the bucket back here. Don't forget to give up the keys when you get back. Don't forget to stay clear of the sodas and *Twinkies; Ding Dongs.*"

"Why you always got to say shit like that? Know how that make' me feel?"

"Do it."

Marvin put the camera down. Left the room with his bucket.

Biggs continued to wave the smelling salts under the victim's nose for full effect.

"Stay awake, bitch. Don't want you to miss out on any of the action. Stay awake. Keep your eyes open."

# CHAPTER 215

**Marvin had returned.** Was about to hand Cecil the bucket. Biggs wanted the keys instead. Both of the keys were handed over and Cecil slipped them back onto the carabiner. He had Marvin raise his arms and turn around, while giving him a cursory search. Didn't see his pockets bulging with *Twinkies* or anything else: no *sodas* or *Ding Dongs*.

"What chu be lookin' for?"

Biggs told him to stick the bucket in the tub and fill it with cold water. Marvin did that and handed the bucket back.

Cecil poured some of the ice cold water on the vic's face. Grabbed a chunk of ice and rubbed it over her eyes and temples.

"Don't go to sleep. This is no time to be taking a nap. . . ."

Marvin leaned in to see what he could make out of his buddy MC Snagglepuss. Lookit what Omar was makin' him do. Fuckin' tight-ass Omar don't care 'bout nothin'. Why come you be puttin' up wiff it? He gonna do to Snagglepuss what he done to them other'. You watch.

"Pick up the *Polaroid*."

"Ain't got to tell me *twiced*."

"I didn't."

Biggs placed the half-empty bucket under the butcher's block. Lana, sufficiently alert by now, was freaking at what the insatiable beast continued to do to her at the other end. What blood appeared at her vagina and anus the rat gobbled up quickly, chewed some more flesh surrounding Lana Sepulveda's vagina and was back to nibbling at the labia. The razor sharp teeth tore away at the loose flesh, ripped it out with uncanny skillfulness. Meanwhile, Biggs had unzipped his fly and forced his erection inside Lana's mouth.

"If you want me to let Snaggletooth out, baby, you'll have to give the best head of your life. Get some shots of this, Marvin. Better yet, give me the *Impulse*. I'll do it myself."

Lana did what she could, moved her mouth frantically, anything to get the animal out of her body and to stay alive.

Biggs took three or four pictures of the woman sucking his cock. His groin was so sensitive and his pleasure heightened to such a degree that he found himself unable to concentrate long enough to keep shooting. Besides, the steam inside his goggles had collected to such a degree that it made it impossible for him to see clearly.

He shoved the goggles back to the top of the hard hat. Handed the camera back to Marvin. Slid his groin in and out of Da Bottom's desperate mouth. It would be another considerable load—and it was.

He withdrew. Shot cum down in her throat, and then plenty as well over her lips, nose, and eyes. Biggs grunted, cursing. The climax had been one of the more intense for him.

It was all finally too much for the victim. She fainted on him again. Biggs decided to let her stay out this time.

He looked at Muck.

"That's enough, Base. Don't waste anymore film on this cunt. Shit's expensive. Ten bucks a pack."

# CHAPTER 216

**Muck did not need to be told a second time.** Returned the camera to the cabinet. He wanted to rescue his rat. Biggs sat in the folding chair. A break was in order. Nodded his head.

"Get Snaggletooth out of here. He did good. Real good."

Marvin unfastened the chicken wire cage. MC Snagglepuss was swathed in blood. Marvin scooped him out, nearly choking back tears at the condition his pal was in. He held him under the spout in the tub. Washed the blood and bits of flesh off. Dried him by wiping him down carefully with a dry cloth, and returned him to the birdcage and carried him out of the room.

Cecil stayed put in the chair, head tilted back, grinning. Didn't make sense to him at the way Marvin carried on over the creatures, at the way people in general got attached to things, to other people, animals, things. Made no sense at all.

He reached for his switchblade, a silver chalice. Even though blood swirled out of Lana Da Bottom where the rat had been (he didn't want that, no matter that Muck's meat-eaters were clean enough and there was no fear of contamination) and made, instead, an incision in the unconscious woman's forearm, and held the chalice so that the blood flowed into it.

About the only thing that made sense. Blood. Fresh blood kept you happy, healthy, and wise. Dracula was right. The healing elixir. Drink of the gods. Only I piss and shit on all the gods, as they do not exist, never did exist. The only thing that ever came close to the power, the feeling of being god-like, for a human, was when you had them chained up, at your mercy. The one who had the power over others was "god," the only "god." With a lower case "g." Even at that.

He taped down the incision to cut off the flow, keep it from being wasted, and emptied the chalice down his throat. Wiped his mouth with the back of his hand.

What a blow job. Well, sure, it was the look in her eyes. All that desperation, panic, fear; the hysterics. The mania. Cunt had a rat in her cunt and it freaked her into a state of absolute hysteria. Madness. Bitch was nutty to begin with; they all are, but certainly, it was safe to assume, was insane by now. Pushed over the edge.

Speaking of madness, Miss Betty could be heard delivering passages from the *Bible* outside the Fun Room door. She knew well enough to keep out unless given permission to enter.

*"Their deeds will not allow them to return to their God, for a spirit of harlotry is within them, And they do not know the* Lord."

"Amen, Sister Betty Lou." Biggs made it a point to be loud enough for the elderly woman to hear through the closed Fun Room door. He wiped sweat from his brow with a handkerchief.

"Trying to force Satan out of sinners is hard work."

"Nobody said it was going to be easy, Bishop Biggs. Let me in and I shall help."

"In a minute."

Biggs pulled the goggles down over his eyes. Marvin had returned with his four-legged *frer.* The deacon looked like he'd been shedding a few teardrops.

"What now?"

"He ain't right. He don't never be the same after that."

"I can always count on you to piss on my parade. Can't I?"

"Don't mean to. MC Snagglepuss be nervous and shit. Be movin' wiff a limp, too. Ate too much, for sure. Belly be bloated now. Should take him to a vet."

Biggs lifted his goggles. Pushed them back.

"You're kidding, right? A vet? You want to take a rat to the vet's?"

"If I had me the coin. Why not? I can't rightly tell what be the matter wiff him."

"You're too much."

Marvin held his rat to his chin, concerned and worried.

"Put the fucking rat down." Biggs lowered the goggles. "And let the geeks in. They want in on this. Can't say as I blame them, either."

Marvin had his pet back inside the original cage. Placed the cage on the floor. He paused at the door, wiping his eyes. Waited for further instructions. Biggs stripped the tape down from Lana's forearm, refilled his chalice and set it aside on a shelf. He then made an incision across the left side of her neck. Blood spurted.

"Let them in, Marvin."

The deacon did that. And the rest of the congregation, save for Greta and Patience, save for Swine Vomit and Brother Muck, rushed in, extending their mugs, wanting their share of the pouring crimson. Norbert Fimple simply positioned himself directly underneath the flowing fountain of blood with his mouth open wide and gobbled up what he could, choking and coughing, until he was shoved out of the way by the Rumanian.

Biggs reached for the chainsaw. Yanked on the starter handle. The blade whirred; and he cut Lana's head right off. Sassy Sassounian was there to catch it in his lap as it rolled off the table. Mr. Fimple had resumed his previous position: all he'd had to do was open his mouth wide, and more crimson showered his face and upper body, while Mildred Elizabeth and others struggled to get their share.

*"We put into the earth, so that there can be birth. Isn't that right, Mother?"*

Biggs felt a pat on the head was appropriate here, figuratively speaking. "Amen to that, Sister Mildred. Amen." While the one had earned his admiration, the other: Pearleen Bell, had managed to raise his ire. "Get your ass up, *henpecker*." Looked like she could have used a helping hand. He "assisted" by picking up the bucket and splashing her face and upper body with what remained of the ice water, and returned her to the Mattress Room. When he came back, Julian "Pinko Punisher" Ionesco was requesting to start breaking things.

"I wish to break the bones, Bishop Biggs. I needs it very much."

Biggs let him.

# CHAPTER 217

**Now that Lana had been decapitated and the rest of her limbs severed (the meat efficiently separated from thigh and calf bones, arms), now that the fun was over (having taken quite a bit out of him), Biggs felt a break was in order.**

He reached for the chalice he had left on the shelf. Sipped from it. He'd have to admit, if he were entirely honest with himself, that drinking human blood was not anything he did out of sheer enjoyment, for human blood did not taste very good at all. His taste buds never failed to remind him of the fact. Eating flesh, on the other hand, was a different matter. He did not have a problem with the way flesh tasted. You baked it or you fried it, at times boiled it, you added tenderizer, added this and the other—and it went down just fine. But the blood, the blood was something he consumed more out of a need to counterbalance all the junk food and candy he filled his body with on a daily basis, to counter the soda and *Hawaiian Punch* habit. Drinking human blood was one of the few positive things he did for his overall well-being.

Only because he was aware that Biggs's eyes were on him, did Marvin R. Muck take a cup and hold it under the headless torso for the red stuff to drizzle into.

He had half a cup. Raised it to his lips—and was (only) able to consume a fraction of it.

"That hole in the bathroom wall will have to be patched up. The window repaired. Only I'm too damned tired and not exactly in the mood."


The bishop and his deacon stood back and watched as the geeks went at what remained of Lana Sepulveda. Lawrence Sassounian had taken a claw hammer and begun removing the scalp with the forked end. He eagerly discarded his old scalp for the new one, picked up the hammer again and whacked away at the blood-covered skull with the claw end until the top caved in and the ensuing opening was adequate enough for him to reach inside and scoop brains out with his fingers and stuffed the pinkish-gray pudding-like substance into his mouth.

Norbert Fimple wanted in on this and fought to get his share.

"No class. In Europe you would not eat this way."

The Rumanian tossed them plastic spoons. Mr. Fimple dug inside the skull and scooped up brains. His arm shook so much and his eyeglasses were askew to such a degree that he could not quite get the spoonful in his mouth. Sassounian bent down, clamped his own jaw around the other's spoon and sucked the brains in.

"No class." Julian "Pinko Punisher" Ionesco insisted was his opinion of the evolving situation. "No class, no upbringing. Like *animal.* No respect for friendship. In Rumania you did not do this. Your family would beat you if you did not show *respect* and eat the proper way."

"Bullshit," Biggs said.

Miss Betty and Mildred Elizabeth had chopped a slice off one of dismembered Lana's thighs. Attempted to eat it raw this way. Added salt and pepper. It still lacked something. Adding to this dilemma: one of Miss Betty's fake teeth broke off. That did it.

"This meat ain't cooked. Teeth just ain't strong enough to eat it like this."

Big Tex had a suggestion: "What we ought to do is get a couple of them skewers. Stick some meat on them; tomatoes, onions, green peppers—and roast 'em. Make *kebobs.* Marinate the meat. Stick the works in the furnace. Maybe add tenderizer. What do you think, Bishop? Add *A-l Steak Sauce,* maybe *Tabasco.* What do you think of that, Bishop?"

Biggs agreed to go along with it. "Only we can't do too much of it that way. We'll let Greta cook up some of her stew, too. Maybe gumbo. How about that, Norbert?"

Norbert Fimple's expression seemed to say he more than approved. Big Tex picked up on it.

"'Course he's gonna like it. Lookit that grin. Man loves to eat. Speakin' of grub: the more we eat, the more we shit. Feel it comin' on. Gotta go take a dump. If all you good folk will excuse me." Big Tex left to use the john at the other end of the basement. *"Be right back, ya hear?"*

# CHAPTER 218

**Biggs searched the metal cabinet for the skewers.** Found one. Made it upstairs to the kitchen to dig up a couple more, as well as the required vegetables to make the kebobs.

He was back in no time. Had the chunks of meat and the veggies on the skewers, alternately, and the geeks followed him out to the Furnace Room. Biggs unlocked the door. Went in with the others. The furnace gate was opened, and he let the geeks, his *"schutzstaffel,"* stick the kebobs in there, over the flames, to roast. Reminded them to turn the kebobs over periodically so that the meat and onions, peppers, etc., roasted evenly.

They handled it okay. No problem there. About time they did something right without it turning into a major fiasco.

It wasn't long before they got restless and wanted to withdraw the skewers and start chowing down.

"Not yet. Doubt the meat is done." They heeded the bishop's advice, but not for long—because before he knew it, they had the kebobs out of the oven and were trying to get at them.

Stuff was too hot. Got dropped. Didn't prevent them from converging on the shish kebobs on the cement floor like jackals attacking carrion.

As expected, Mr. Fimple was the worst of the lot. Trouble was the kebobs were too hot for anyone to take an actual bite. Those who were foolhardy enough to attempt a nibble, or better, without waiting to give the food the proper time to cool, did so with great regret, burning lips and fingertips. Those who simply stood back and watched it happen, like Marvin, Cecil, and Miss Betty Rutterschmidt, could not stop jeering and chuckling.

Soon, though, the kebobs were cool enough, and they went at it, devouring the meat and vegetables like hungry beasts. By the time Leo Nix returned from the crapper he did not look too pleased with what was going on.

"Ain't nothin' left but skewers. Ain't right. Nobody gives a shit about nobody else around here. Used to be Church of Re-Newed Hope stood for something. You coulda left a bite for me. I gotta live, too. Damned Yankee buzzards. Butt-breath gutter trash. Ain't no hope for none of y'all in here. That's the Lord's truth."

# CHAPTER 219

**Marvin had had enough of all the "bughouse boo-shit" going on in the basement.** Had picked up the cage Snagglepuss was in and gone up the flight of stairs to his room on the first floor. He placed the cage on the threadbare carpet next to the grimy foam mattress, opened the gate to the cage and scooped the fancy rat up in his hands.

There were white socks lying about. Marvin picked one up and wiped his friend down some more. He stretched out on the mattress when he was done and held his pal to his chest.

Muck attempted to collect himself. There was no way to relax, no way to forget what Cecil had gone and done to his other pet'. *Mothafuckah.*

He'd raised them from the time they was small, and now they was gone. Buried back there among the weeds and trash in the backyard. Wasn't right. He didn't give a turd about much in this life, never had much and never would, *prob'ly*, but they was his buddies. . . . Tears rolled down the sides of his cheeks.

He tried to sleep. Had his eyes closed. Sleep wouldn't come.

Well, he opened one eye to check on Snagglepuss. Snagglepuss was doin' all right, resting up. Dozing, it seemed like. Grinding his teeth, though. As usual. Marvin rubbed the back of his friend's neck with his thumb. Did it gently.

"Yeah, worked you hard, didn't he? Wasn't my fault, homie. You seen me. Couldn't get the mofo to think of somethin' else to do."

He stopped rubbing his pet's neck, and held him in his cupped hands.

It took an hour or so of struggling to doze off, but it happened eventually, and Marvin slept.

# CHAPTER 220

**He didn't wake until after 3:00 p.m. the next afternoon.** Looked up. Snagglepuss had left the place on his chest and had entered his cage and was lapping up water from a tray.

No doubt about it, Muck's own belly was empty and he was thirsty. Needed to take a leak. There was no denying his pole was hard.

He rose. Opened his door. Stuck his head out into the hallway. It was quiet. Wondered where Cecil was and what he was up to? He walked to the john, urinated and returned to his room.

What was there to eat? He hated that dog food and ground up meat stew Greta be always makin'. Let the retard' eat that shit. Ain't my style. I could go for some real food, like that omelette Cecil got hisself at Slim'. Only that kinda meal take' jack, jack I ain't even got. If I had me a hot dog wiff onion' and mustard, now that could be real good, would taste real good. Yeah. And a super large *Coke*. Shit. Man ain't gonna gimme no coin to buy nothin'.

He looked at the two shelves consisting of four cinder blocks. Bottom shelf had on it a plate, bowl, some silverware. On the top shelf sat a jar of *Skippy* peanut butter, *creamy*, a half-eaten loaf of "day old" *Wonder Bread*. Day-old; what Cecil usually be buyin'. Day-old. Get' him a discount that way.

Day old would be all right, 'cept this bread was more like month old. Dry and hard. Moldy in places.

He took a slice out. Broke the moldy sections off. Tossed them into a corner. Reached for the butter knife. Opened the jar of peanut butter and scooped some out. Spread it on the slice. Took a bite. It was way too dry. He cursed.

"Mothafuckah almost be like a walking *ATM machine* and can't buy me no real food."

There was an unclean mug that hadn't been properly washed in weeks. He grabbed it. Walked out again to the john. Filled the mug with tap water, and returned to his room. Sat up on the mattress with his back against the wall, and chased the slice of peanut buttered bread with the tap water. Went down hard. He hated it. Maybe Greta Otto' stew was better after all. He didn't know, wasn't sure. He was sure of one thing: this peanut butter and hard bread was *boo-shit.*

# CHAPTER 221

**He ate what he could of it.** Stood in front of the full-length mirror on the closet door. Took his shirt off. Too fuckin' skinny these day'. No food. Losing too much weight. Gonna be lookin' somethin' like a skeleton pretty soon. Like that short nigga next door. All be Cecil' fault.

I can't eat what them retard' be eatin'. Can't be drinkin' all that blood neither, me.

He looked down. His dick was still hard. He thought about sneaking into the Mattress Room where Cecil had that hot ho Peach chained to the wall. Maybe get her to suck the *black mamba,* maybe shoot a full load in her mouf, fuck her in the ass and pussy.

Did he dare chance it? Cecil would be pissed as hell. Fuckin' Trusty Lusty. Gotta be his way, he say—or no way. Well, he did let him have some tang now and then. Sure did. Shaggin' Dixie was good, real nice, but he be needin' more pussy, always be needin' more.

Stella. What about Stella? Hangin' from that hook in the cooler. Was stupid of Cecil to do. Why let that bitch die a slow death like that?

Yeah, I know: ho be a cunt—but why let her die? Don't even make no kinda sense. If he tried to get some of that, Cecil would be on his ass for it, too.

Could lick his own dick. Only lickin' it make his neck stiff. Man could break his mothafuckin' neck that way. He could jerk it, play wiff hisself. Shit; it don't never feel as good as real tang.

What about Greta? The cook. How would he talk to the psycho ho? Never even seen what that big mama be lookin' like behind that mask she all the time got on. Do it matter? Not really. All that matter the ho got what he like': big ass—and a mouf for suckin' dick.


That six-inch-tall toy monk figure standing atop the tv caught his eye. He'd ripped it off at a magic shop down there on Hollywood Boulevard.

Bald-headed monk. Wiff a brown robe on, just like the kind Cecil like' to wear at his sermon', the kind he have them retard' wear while he be playin' the preacher up there in the Prayer Hall, readin' from the *Bible*.

He picked up the toy monk. Pressed down on the head with the palm of his hand and watched a stiffy spring right out through an opening in the robe. No shit. Hard-on. Monk wiff a hard-on. Woody. Woody the Monk. Folded arms across his chest.

He left his room. Walked to the basement door. Knew better than to turn the knob. Locked; it was locked. Fuckin' Trusty. Got to keep everything locked. What the fuck? I want that ho to blow me.

He knocked on Biggs's door.

"What do you want?"

"I want that big-ass ho Greta to suck my black dick. If that be cool wiff you."

"You want The Leaper to do what?"

"You be sayin' I can't?"

"I'm saying it's probably not a good idea."

Fuck that, thought Marvin.

"Need some trim, me."

"What's stopping you?"

"Basement door be locked, Cecil."

The door opened. Biggs was in his boxers, sleepy-eyed. He had the bullet-proof Kevlar vest on, the *.357* in the shoulder holster. Paranoid, thought Marvin. Mofo don't even take the vest off when he go to bed.

Biggs stepped into the hallway with the keys, and Marvin followed him to the basement door. Watched him unlock it. Asked him once again if it was all right "wiff" him if he got some from Greta.

"Entirely up to you. Only don't come crying to me if she hurts your feeble-minded, wannabe pimp ass."

Biggs opened the door. Marvin remained standing there.

"What else?"

"Yo. What chu gonna do wiff Peach?"

"What's it to you?"

"Like to have me some of that. Ho be hot."

"She's hot—and she's off limits. When you're done, or rather, when Greta's done with you—pound on the door loud enough for me to hear."

"Ain't got to tell me *twiced.*"

Marvin descended the stairs. Basement door was closed behind him. And locked.

# CHAPTER 222

**Marvin held the toy monk in his hands.** He'd teased the cook with it from time to time.

The less she liked being teased the more he was inclined to keep at it (so long as Cecil stayed out of his way and left him alone).

Well, you seen it: Cecil give you the *green light,* and he knowed what you be up to.

He stood there in the doorway to the Bunk Room. Greta was to his left, sitting by herself on the bare cement floor of the foyer-like area, her back to the wall. The small black-and-white tv up on the shelf was on.

About the only available light in here. Some of the other retards were in their beds, dozing or watching the tube or mumbling to themselves. He didn't care what they was up to or even where the rest of them was, so long as Betty Lou was not around with that big-ass *Bible* to beat on his Jones wiff. Prob'ly out there in the play area readin' her book. Thought he seen one or two of 'em out there by the bookcase where the red nightlight was. Good for her. He'd have to keep his eyes open and stay sharp.

His eyes were on Greta. Ho had her boots off and she was applying fingernail polish to her toes with her right hand. She was also quietly shedding tears underneath that mask, only Marvin was not aware of it, not that he would have given a damn or let it interfere with his immediate plans. Not able to help himself, he continued to stare at all that flank and heavy tits hanging under that gravy-stained black sweater. The negligee she wore under the sweater hardly covered the woman's muscular thighs.

This was a turn-on to him. Marvin had always gone in for thick thighs and a big ass. This was a *booty ho*. Large-boned. He wondered why Bigg' never made any real try to put turkey neck in her asshole.

Cecil had told him once why he didn't bother with the woman, but Muck had not believed a word of it. "She's too ugly, too unpredictable. Besides, she's staff. I don't mess with staff."

The explanation had not made any sense to him. Bitch looked just as good enough to do as any of the other hoe'. Dirty maybe, and that mask be freaky enough, as was the back of her head: the tufts of yellow hair consisted of clumps here and there. Grimy. Matted. There was bald spots, too.

Yeah, that was rank about her, for sure. The few times her ears was exposed he got to see that they didn't look anything like ears at all: balled up, wrinkled, twisted lump' of skin and cartilage with a small hole in the center to hear through.

"How about some company, *mamita?*"

# CHAPTER 223

**Marvin stepped in and sat down on her right.** Greta made angry, guttural sounds. Shook her head. She wanted to be left alone. She was obviously fuming under her breath, but Muck paid no attention to that as he placed that toy monk in front of his crossed legs on the cement.

He made sure she could see what was going on, and then pressed down on the monk's hairless dome and laughed when the toy figure's sexual organ stuck right out.

"Bigger than shit. What do you think of that, Greta? Like the way his woody be out there? Kind of make you hungry for the real thang, don't it?"

Greta continued to fume behind the mask; she was applying the nail polish and fuming. She simply wished to be left alone.

She made other sounds, in order to get her message across. She did not want to be bothered, especially not by some worthless male drip like Marvin Muck. More importantly, what the deacon did not know is that Greta held that paring knife in her other hand; it was that same blade she had stabbed at the pink blanket that time, the one Sassy and the Commie Ionesco had been in a tug-of-war over.

The blade itself was dull and measured a mere three inches (the only reason Cecil let her hold onto it), but since she did not have her deadly hobnailed *Gestapo* shit-kickers on to deal with this annoying pimp-wannabe, the blade was going to have to do.

"Still ain't convince' me, big mama, that you be likin' to lick slit mo better than suckin' dick. You be tryin' to act like you go for trim, big mama. I know deep down what you really want is turkey neck, man meat. See, my dick be like that Maglite Omar got: big and black. I got special ability, too, lotta them hoe' be *akskin'* to see me do all the time: Lick my own dick. Wanna see me do it? Huh, mamita?"

Marvin reached out and pulled her mask off and it was enough to make him hold back, look at her that way. The homeliness of her utterly deformed features simply turned his stomach. Christ.

"No wonder Cecil don't be wantin' to jump your pussy. Man, what happened to you? Somebody sho put the ugly stick to yo face, tall mama."

Greta stared at him now, her anger rising to a boiling point. The pus and sores and scabs; it was all there. That's what her face was made up of. The discoloration, too, was much worse than what Marvin thought he had to be concerned with with his own face below the nose, above the upper lip.

She may a been a good-looking woman onced. *Jesus Christ, who woulda guess?*

# CHAPTER 224

**Marvin couldn't stop shaking his head.** Moved away slowly. He didn't want any part of this, not with the mask off her face.

"Please, big booty mama, put Cupid back on, or get one of them brown paper bag' to put on yo face and I swear I will rape yo ass 'till we both drop, then. We can have us some good lovin'—but you got to cover up yo face, baby."

She attacked him just then. Clawed away at his face, raked her nails down his arms. She cut him with the blade and kept cutting and swinging with it until Marvin Muck, clutching the miniature monk in his hands, was able to kick out with his feet and somehow roll out of the room. Greta stayed right on top of him. Then, just as suddenly as she had made her first thrust, she stopped.

The rest of the geeks, some of whom were scattered throughout the basement and had observed quite a bit of it, found it far more entertaining than the usual crap they were used to seeing on tv.

Julian "Red Menace" Ionesco, who happened to be seated at the patio table, got a kick out of it himself, as did Cecil O., who had opened the basement door and was standing on the landing at the top of the staircase—having expected nothing short of what had transpired.

Patience McDaniel was the sole disinterested party here, as was her way. She sat on the hard cement, huddled against the locked door to the Furnace Room, not saying anything, not laughing, just shivering.


Ionesco stopped snickering long enough to get a rag and a few time-worn *Band-Aids* and give Marvin R. Muck a hand. Helped stop the bleeding. Wiped away blood. Applied *Band-Aids*.

"We support one another, *Tovarich*."

"That be one fucked-up, mixed-up ho. Goddamn dyke."

"Ja ja, *comrade*. Greta Otto is *uber fraulein*."

"Talk about ugly. I seen some ugly suckas in my time. She make' an ugly ol' ho like Mildred look hot. No shit."

"Greta set hair on fire one time. She splash acid on face another time. She have terrible experience with someone she love very much. She was beautiful woman before—"

"Yo. Didn't *aks* for her life story, *suckah*. So the lezzy bitch got dumped by one of her own kind. So what, man? That ain't cause to cut me like that."

"No, you do not understand, *comrade*. She love a man when she was young and very beautiful. She was pregnant with baby. Greta jump from three-story building, and the baby die. Greta attempt to commit suicide many time—"

"Maybe the bitch should try for number four. Yeah. My man who be talkin' funny: Four could be the magic number." Marvin extended four fingers for Greta's benefit. "*Yo, ho—try for numba fo'. Go up fo' next time. Hear me, ho? Yo lucky numba could be fo'.*"

"*Ja ja*, there was problem with Greta and her grandfather."

Marvin Muck had had enough of the accent, more than enough.

He stood up. Brushed the Pinko Punisher off of him.

"Can't take yo jive. Funny talkin' refugee mothafuckah. I been wiff Bigg' over a year and still ain't got used to that funny way of rappin' you got, egghead punk."

"I explain to you—"

*"YOU DON'T NEEDS TO BE EXPLAININ' NOTHIN' TO ME, FOOL! BUNCHA SMELLY-ASS, FLAKEY MOTHAFUCKAHS IN HERE!"*

Marvin walked. Spun in Greta's direction. Aimed a finger at her. "I'll get yo ass, ho, when you least *assept* it. You think I let shit like that slide? No way, bitch."

He negotiated the stairs. The door was open up there. Biggs was amused about something. Mothafuckah always be laughin' when I be the one in pain, thought Marvin.

"By the way, I'm missing a paring knife. I suspect Greta's the one who filched it."

"You *suspec'*?" Marvin held up his bandaged fingers. "You *'suspec'*?'"

"She does the cooking. Stands to reason she would be the one."

"Coulda tol' me."

Marvin reached the landing. Biggs closed the door behind him. Locked it.

"I did say I didn't think it was a good idea to bother her."

"Ain't said nothin' 'bout no shank."

Marvin walked to his room. Biggs handed him a bottle of peroxide, some cotton swabs and gauze. Fresh *Band-Aids*.

"I can't blame her for taking the knife. With Norbert and the others to deal with."

"I'll get her ass. She got my guarantee. Lizard butt white trash ho."

Marvin stripped off the less-than-clean *Band-Aids* the foreign dude had given him, swabbed his cuts with peroxide and applied new *Band-Aids* and gauze. Biggs handed him a roll of white medical tape to tape over the gauze. Muck did that.

"I need the Leaper for the work that she does around the place. Best thing to do is forget what happened—and stay clear of her."

Marvin cursed. "Still say you coulda let me know."

He reached inside the rat cage. Lifted Snagglepuss out. Gently rubbed the back of his pet's neck. The rat ground its jaws in that rhythmic fashion that rats have.

When Marvin looked back up, Biggs was no longer standing there, and could hear him walk down the hallway and open the door to his room.

Yeah, walk away, mofo, thought Marvin. Ain't no skin off yo ass.

# CHAPTER 225

**Downstairs, in the basement, Greta "The Leaper" Otto was lying in her bunk.** She had slipped the mask back on. Tears rolled down 'neath the plastic facade. Nothing made any sense. Life was one long ordeal.

When you were a young kid, a little girl, all you had wanted was to be happy, have a happy, perfect life, and if not entirely perfect, at least as perfect and happy as possible. . . . And then somehow, somewhere along the way it had all turned hellish and bleak. Your life has been a nightmare as far back as you can remember and stayed that way . . . a nightmare she was quite certain did not begin here in this dungeon, not here in this dark hellhole, the stench and slop, the mutilations that went on that she knew in her heart had to be wrong, but it went on just the same—but even that didn't matter because her own nightmare had begun years before, snuck up on her many years before.

If only she'd been able to kill herself back then, way back there when she'd had the courage and had felt she knew how to end the flashbacks, the ugly existence.

She stared at the blade in her hand, thought about suicide, but with a dull paring knife like this it never would work. She'd attempted suicide so often, cut herself so many times . . . and it never got her anywhere.

Maybe throwing herself in the furnace . . . or getting her hands on one of the bigger daggers, or just cutting her chest open with one of the chainsaws Cecil owns and letting her heart and insides spill out. That could be the way. Chainsaw or hatchet. Next time you get your hands on one or the other, should the opportunity present itself.

Do you want to die, Greta? Do you want to die? All you have to do is make Biggs angry enough and he'll do it for you. He would.

Don't you think that he would oblige? Wouldn't he want that? Insult him. Tell him what you think of him. But you tried that before and it hadn't worked. For some reason he did not want to kill you, for some reason he saw no point in doing harm to those who made up his staff and were members of the board. Even after the incidents with the paying customers at his haunted house; even after this, the most recent of disturbing encounters, with the Mexican janitors who had attempted to sexually assault you in the women's room. You'd beaten the shit out of them with an axe handle; in fact, made them vomit and piss themselves, cost them a few teeth—and Cecil hadn't gone after you; hadn't made you pay with a pound of your own flesh. DA's office had threatened to keep the business locked up until the claim was fully investigated and satisfactorily resolved. Cecil had been in a rage about it, to be sure, and had gone into some of the details; enough so to put fear in her, force her to mind her ways, supposedly. She had defied him; urged him to follow through on his threat to annihilate her, make her disappear; chop her up, fry and cook her, and feed her to church members—the same way he'd had her doing to victims he's been bringing in from the outside. But he hadn't laid a finger on her. *Not so much as a finger.* What was that about? Asshole gave a damn? Actually cared about us? Sure, to the extent he needed us. Take out a board member, and you've got to find another to take his or her place. All you had to do was take a look at that worthless degenerate Olin Goodfellow. Made her belly clench to so much as stand next to him. Slime-faced troll.

Go figure it out. I can't. I don't know what's going on. Just don't know. You should have castrated Marvin. That's exactly what you should have done to him, because now he'll be back to fuck with you for sure. Like these flies around here, creepy-crawlies and rodents. He's a rat-faced shit, and you can be sure he'll try something.

Well, she thought, I wish he would; I really wish he would try again because I'll be ready for him.

# CHAPTER 226

**It was a quarter past 4:OO a.m. when Ace Ortiz and Felix Monk decided to climb over Biggs's front yard fence.** Ortiz had had a harder time of it since his head hadn't had a chance to clear from the model glue and *MD 20/20* he'd had earlier, and getting punched in the belly by that sissy Rudy Perez hadn't helped, either.

They made it to the *Cadillac*. Ortiz let Felix hold the *.38*, while he produced a *slim jim* from inside his waist. Got his wire cutters out, a screwdriver. Got the door unlocked with the *slim jim* and the alarm started wailing and Ace Ortiz had it cut off eventually. Took him longer than he was happy with, but he got it done. Was inside shining his penlight at the cassette player in the dash, figuring how to extract it with the least amount of damage—the less damage the more money he'd be able to fence it for— and then he toyed with the idea of simply riding off in the *Caddy*, just driving off in it with Felix. Remembered that there was a chain-link fence, a locked gate. They'd have to knock it down with the *Caddy*; just drive over it. It could be done. Wondered if it was possible? How much damage would it do to the body and cost them in terms of how much they'd be able to get for it. Would it even be worth it?

Yeah, it would. Why not? Drive it down to the border and sell it to a bent TJ roller, or else take it to Bellflower and sell the thing for parts. They could do well with it. Why waste time fucking with the stereo?

That's when he heard his name being called by his partner. Biggs had snuck up on Felix with a baseball bat and a *.357 Magnum*. Had stuck the

Mag barrel in Monk's right ear and convinced him to relinquish the *.38*. At this point Muck emerged from around the corner of the house and took the slugger from Cecil.

Felix sensed what was about to take place and suddenly developed a bad case of the shakes. Felt the need to give his homie a heads-up; that the jig was up. It was over. They was busted by the man and fucked big time.

*"Ace."*

"Keep it down, *coño*."

*"Get out of that Cadillac, Ace."*

"What the—"

Ace turned his head in time to see Felix get his face pistol-whipped. Cecil's man Friday waited for Ace to step out of the *Brougham* and delivered the ball bat into his crotch. Followed that up with a whack across Ace's upper torso. Ace and Felix were both sprawled in the weeds, seeing stars and feeling a lot of pain. The blow to Ortiz's privates had him gasping and clutching his waist. Monk felt his jaw and knew three or four of his teeth were loose now.

# CHAPTER 227

**The bishop slipped on a pair of leather gloves and waited for Ortiz to stop carrying on, turned him over on his back and proceeded to punch him about the face methodically.** Gave him shots to the mouth and nose region, then worked on both eyes until his fist was just about too sore to keep punching. Took a moment to collect himself. Gave Ortiz's bad eye one good, final shot that sent the fake eyeball popping out of the socket.

Cecil found himself unable to resist: Picked up the glass marble and stuck it inside the semi-conscious junkie's mouth and clamped his jaw shut for him.

"Let's take them inside."

"Could be a bad idea, Dawg. *Yo.*"

"Since when do you do the thinking?"

"Since I seen that old nigga Harold Crust watchin' from his livin' room window."

Biggs turned his head. Sure enough, Crust was standing there at his window with the lights out and the shade up. It seemed he was pleased and gestured with his hand to indicate as much.

Biggs ignored him. Felt disappointed, if anything.

"Yo. We got us a fan across the street, too."

Lloyd Dicker's own lights were out. They were able to tell he had the curtains partially parted in his front room and he had his night vision glasses up.

Biggs had little choice. Had Marvin unlock the front gate instead, and they carried the ex-con and his buddy back to their junker where it sat parked at the curb in front of Dicker's place. Ace was dumped in the back seat that was littered with sardine cans, *Chuckles* wrappers and empty short dog bottles. Felix was dropped in the front.

Biggs and Marvin returned to the church. The gate was locked back up and they went inside.

# CHAPTER 228

A moment later Felix and Ace Ortiz were coming to: battered, bleeding, still dazed perhaps, but coming to slowly.

"What happened?" Felix was moaning. Unable to raise his head. "*Madre de Dios*, what happened?"

Ace Ortiz had the door open on his side and stuck his face out with a possible urge to vomit—and out rolled his fake eye instead. He cried out in pain.

"You amateur. You was the cover, fool. You was the cover. Now I gotta go out and hustle up another piece."

Felix continued to moan.

"Gonna cut that fruitcake's *cajones* right off. Stomp them down his throat. *That's how you deal with a maricon like that. Pendejo. Hijo de la gran puta. He's dead. He's dead. Him and that pimp loser he runs with. Dead.*" Ortiz paused to retch. "On my shit list. Rudy, too—and his brother."

"Don't forget Vester. You left out Vester."

"Don't know no *Vester.*"

"Slim . . ."

"Don't talk. Don't say a word. My head . . ."

"Panhandler. . . . One picked up the ring got knocked out of your hand. You don't want to let him off the hook."

"*Shut your culo*, Felix."

"I need a doctor. At least a bandage. Some aspirin." Felix struggled to sit up. Couldn't do it.

Ace wiped his mouth with the back of his torn sleeve. Crawled outside in a desperate search for his glass eye. Got a hand on it somehow and made every effort to pull himself up. Got as far as his knees. Tried some more. Made it to his feet. Lost his balance. Went down.

# CHAPTER 229

**Biggs was in the kitchen wiping blood and crud off the *.357* with a rag.** Marvin was there with him, wiping down the ball bat.

"Fucked them up pretty good, Cecil. They ain't comin' back. What they get for messin' wiff my bro' ride. Done 'em real good. Only I thank some of that puke got on me."

"Oh, they'll be back. Those two are gluttons for discipline—something like Mr. Fimple, and that Olin Goodfellow, the inbred swine molester. Then there's Sassounian."

"Yo. Could be you right. They keep comin' back. Don't never get nowhere, neither."

"All it takes, you would know this, you *pop the lock* in the door with a *slim-jim*; you use a *slam-hammer* to break and *extract* the ignition—in no time at all, seconds—only with a couple of rank amateurs like Ace and Felix it takes long enough to get nailed by the owner. Actually, pros don't bother with any of that. Too smart. Have access to keys. That's how that's done. Keys."

"They was tryin' to boost the stereo."

"Couldn't even do that."

"See, Ace got that eye that go the wrong way; *lazy*. That be why."

"Lazy? Like someone you know?"

"No, man. One eye be lookin' right at you, while the other one be checkin' out something way the fuck over there."

"Glass eye."

"Say what?"

"It's a glass eye. You weren't aware of that? That's why it appears weird. Why do you think they call him *'Glassy'*?"

"Don't know, me. Thought the dude was like Norbert Pimple: Ate glass."

"You didn't catch me feed it to him?"

"You did?"

"Norbert's name is *Fimple*, by the way. It's Norbert *Fimple*."

"What I said, ain't it? He the one be eatin' lightbulb'."

He handed the bat to Biggs. Rinsed out the rag in the sink and brushed the front of his flannel shirt down with it. Cecil grabbed the bucket and made it to his room. Returned the bat to its place in the closet, tossed the *.38* he got off the failed car thieves in a dresser drawer. He withdrew the *.357*, emptied the chambers and dropped the rounds in a breast pocket. Re-holstered the *Magnum*. He worked the combination on his safe. Got his hands on a *.380 auto*. Five round. It was a small handgun with a two-inch barrel. It would do. It was loaded, with a round in the chamber. He jammed it in his left jacket pocket.

Biggs slipped on a pair of latex gloves. There was a typical greeting card box with some items in it that he picked up and stuffed in his other pocket.

"Hate the sin, not the sinner." Talking to himself this way was nothing more than a reminder to bring along a *Bible*. Say the retards, the "righteous" ones in the group, got wind of what was going on, with what he was up to with the hot cunt. It just looked better when he had a *Bible* with him. Heathen fornicating strumpet was being aware of the *Good Book* and how J. Christ intended for us to live in this world rife with temptation and sin.

He grabbed the foot-long black flashlight that looked more like a baton than anything else. Stepped in the hallway. Locked his door back up. He crossed the hallway to the john to pick up a few additional things: first-aid kit in the cabinet under the sink, found a bottle of *Listerine* in the medicine cabinet above, bar of soap, sponge. Tossed the items in the bucket. Added a clean towel to the pile.

"Hate the sin, not the sinner." Was at it again while taking the hallway back to the kitchen. "One thing you can count on: those two pulling an encore."

# CHAPTER 230

**Biggs unlocked the lock that hung from the chain wrapped around one of the refrigerators.** Took a jug of cold water and placed it on the table. "They're like flies: can't help but fuck with people. Until you nail them, swat them out of existence."

He grabbed a wooden bowl from the cupboard, a ladle from the wire dish holder. Dipped the ladle into the kettle that sat inside the refrigerator a couple of times and emptied it into the fryer on the range.

Added one more ladleful and heated up the jambalaya. Stirred it in the fryer.

"Cold water and hot mulligan. You goin' downstairs to see that ho Peach?"

"She'll need food and something to drink. I'd like to keep her around for a while—breathing."

Biggs locked up the refrigerator and emptied the stew into the bowl. Turned the range off. He noticed that Marvin had taken the items out of the bucket and was presently holding the bucket under the tap and was about to fill it with water.

"Why do that when there's a spigot in the basement?"

"Don't rightly know."

Biggs had to remind him to put the crap back in the bucket.

"Grab the dog biscuits."

Marvin did.

"And the chow bowl."

Had him step into the hallway with it all. Biggs grabbed the plastic jug. Stepped into the hallway himself and locked the kitchen door behind him. He was reciting "Hate the sin, not the sinner" line as he walked to the basement door where the sidekick stood waiting.

Bishop unlocked it. Looked at him. *"Hate the sin, not the sinner."* It was stated with some resonance this time. Marvin did not seem to get it.

"Say it."

"Why come?"

"Say it, Deacon. Hate the sin, not the sinner."

"Whatever you say, Hoss. *Hate the sin, not the sinner.*"

They descended the stairs, all the while repeating the line. As they neared the bottom steps, Norbert Fimple could be heard making all sorts of nasty sounds, sounds that emanated from both: his rectum as well as his mouth.

Reaching the basement floor, Biggs aimed his light in the direction of the john. Crazy Norbert had left the door practically wide open as he sat on the throne, defecating and farting up a storm. Brought forth memories of Goodfellow behaving no differently the other day. No sense to close the door while they did their business. He didn't mind watching bitches take a dump, especially after he'd fed them *Ex-Lax* and beer, but this was not pleasant. Hearing it and seeing it. Not pleasant at all.

"Sound' like Norbert got the runnin' shit' again."

"That's what happens when you consume mice and cockroaches. Not to mention pulverized lightbulbs and raw meat. Not to mention all the silverware and who knows what else."

"Yo. He the one like' them lightbulb and mice. Dude be likin' them mice way more than the Ripper ever did."

"That's all right. He's learning. He can shit all he wants, so long as he does it in the john."

"Mothafuckah better not be gettin' no idea about eatin' my pet homie', neither."

Biggs handed him three double-A size rechargeable batteries to pass on to the *Bible-thumper* in the wheelchair. Reminded him to distribute the dog biscuit treats among the retards.

Muck proceeded to do so.

# CHAPTER 231

**The small black-and-white tv perched on a shelf high on the far wall in the Bunk Room hardly yielded enough light.** And that other, the blood-red nightlight in the play area to the right, the Roscoe side of the basement, with the steel round table and patio chairs bolted into the cement in front of the walk-in, wasn't much of an improvement. It was better than no light at all, he supposed. And *"Mademoiselle Betty?"* And that flashlight of hers? (A mini version of the impressive black horse cock Maglite that Cecil carried around with him) was used sparingly by her and usually aimed directly at the passage she happened to be immersed in in the oversized open *Bible* before her.

Just one more thing that annoyed the deacon: that the *"bag of bone"'* could have her own flashlight, and he couldn't.

He walked over to where the old ho was sittin' at the table and had her open *Bible* in front of her. No sooner did he drop the batteries in her lap, did Miss Betty start in on something that was troubling her.

*Yo*, thought Marvin, *everybody got they problem'*. He didn't want to hear it, and went about passing out the dog biscuit treats to the others.

# CHAPTER 232

**Having done an about-face, Biggs walked about thirty feet in back of the stairwell.** He was at the door to the Mattress Room and looking for the key to unlock it, when Muck rejoined him.

Biggs asked him if Mr. Fimple was done in the john, in case others had to go. He didn't particularly like seeing the geeks go in the honey buckets—or on the floor. Because that's what happened on occasion when they used the buckets: they missed the bucket and the waste hit the floor.

"Guess who moans about having to clean up after them?"

"Pimple? He done."

"You mean *Fimple*."

"What I said: *Fimple*. Be done shittin'. Only now he sittin' there. Can't make up his mind which hand to wipe wiff."

"He's conflicted. Who does that remind you of?"

"Wouldn't know, me. Don't know nobody like that dude—'cept Goodfellow an' them."

"You give *Mademoiselle Rutterschmidt* the batteries?"

"That remind' me: nasty ol' Mildred be suckin' on Leo Nix' carrot.

Back there by Siberia, in the dark—so don't nobody know they be doin' it."

"That's not what I asked."

"I give 'em to her. Old ho be complainin' about anal wart' again. Don't want to hear it, me. I ain't the croaker. Tol' her to go see Sassy. He the head Doc, ain't he? I don't know nothin' about no anal wart'. Never had 'em. Some peep' got 'em. I ain't sayin' who. I ain't one. Only look' like Sassy be kissin' Leo Nix *culo*—at the same time Mildred on the other side suckin' on that skinny dick."

"Not your concern."

"All I can say: if Greta catch 'em at it she gonna kick some ass. Betty Lou, too. Old ho hate' them queer chump' doin' that nasty shit."

"I have far more valid concerns to deal with: mortgage, food and light bill, car insurance. *Dog biscuits* don't grow on trees."

"Sassy ain't nothin' but a low-class sissy to be doin' that, if you aks me."

"Beats gnawing on your limbs. I'd much rather see him pole smoking, than chewing off his fingers."

"You right. 'Cause if you ain't got yo hand, how you gonna be able to wipe yo behind that way?"

Biggs shined his Maglite where the action was supposedly going on. It sure was. He didn't give a damn what the retards were up to. Let them stay preoccupied.

Over in the play area, Betty Lou was replacing the old batteries in her flashlight with the new. She had the old ones in the battery recharger and was fiddling with it.

He hoped she had it plugged in. Had previously reminded her that the recharger needed to be plugged into the socket in the wall for it to work.

He couldn't quite make out where the rest were: Greta and the others. Looked like they were in the Geek Room lying in their bunk beds. Watching the black-and-white tv.

"Let them be. Whatever makes them happy. See, that was something J.J. never could stand: people being happy; me smiling, hugging Parfrey, playing with him. Having fun. The old lady was jealous of the love I had for Mr. Turnbull and his hog."

"Yo. Hate the sin, not the sinner." And both could easily hear Betty Lou Rutterschmidt echo same.

Biggs unlocked the door to the Mattress Room. Went in.

# CHAPTER 233

**A startled Pearleen Bell sat up, huddled, on a mattress in a corner to his right.**

Biggs had Marvin bring in the first-aid kit, pussy plugs, and the other items and place them on that rickety coffee table that Dione Aragon had wrecked earlier and that he'd had Big Tex painstakingly reconstruct.

Probably would have made more sense to pick up another at a garage sale somewhere—or even dig one out of the storage corridor, although the corridor was a shambles, courtesy of Pearleen and friends.

You did your best to save a buck whenever possible. Besides, the feeble-minded ones should be pulling their weight, paying their way. Having Big T. mend broken furniture from time to time served that purpose.

"Now leave, Marvin."

"I wanna hang and watch, Cecil. Been wantin' to take a real good, up-close look at the hot trim a long time now. Yo."

"It's not what you think. Her cuts and bruises should be gone over."

"You ain't got to *boo-shit* me, Cecil. This be Marvin Muck you be talkin' to, Brotha."

Biggs detached a key from the carabiner on his belt. Handed it to him.

"Key to the tap. Fill the bucket, and then screw the hose on. Drag the nozzle end in here. Bring the lock back. I want you to turn the water on, then get yourself some sleep."

Marvin did the bit with the hose: had it screwed to the tap in the wall by the pit, then dragged the end with the sprayer handle into the Mattress

Room. Handed the lock and key over. Lingered. Not eager to leave.

"The water on?"

"Water be on."

"What are you standing around for? Go get yourself some shuteye. You like to complain about being tired."

"Like you: can't sleep. Had me a hard time gettin' to sleep all the time. Why all a them mofo had me on Ritalin an' shit."

"In that case, go keep an eye on the cars, then."

"Them *pepper belly* ain't dumb enough to be back right away. 'Sides, they be hurtin', more than likely. In a world of pain. They be lookin' for a croaker right now."

"You're about to piss me off. *Get me?*"

"All right, then. Ain't got to tell me *twiced, Brotha Trusty.* Ain't got to rag on me like you doin'. Only I thought we wuz partner', and we wuz supposta share like partner'. Bro' before hoe'. Somethin' like that."

"Never satisfied, are you? You had Dixie, the others."

"What about the basement door? Don't it be locked? You lock every damn door, every time."

Biggs stood there, glaring at the hopeless fool until he left the room.

# CHAPTER 234

**He faced Pearleen.** She had plenty of scrapes on both arms, neck, and a few on her face. There was enough blood on her legs; blood and grime. Practically a horrid sight. Nothing that a little soap and water, dab of peroxide, and a butterfly *Band-Aid* or two wouldn't fix.

There was no denying the sudden surge of annoyance that swept through him, nor could he put his finger on why exactly it was happening. Something about the way she sat there pressing a worn blanket against her chest and crotch.

It dawned on him: the false and blatant modesty of it. The whore showed off her privates to perfect strangers for a living, and here she was covering it up. *What hypocrisy.*

He yanked the blanket away. Ordered her to stand up. She did so, taking her sweet time. *Not here*, thought Biggs.

"When I give a command, you hop to it." To see that she got the message, he reached out with his right hand, gripped her by the throat—to the extent that she was gasping.

"Let's get one thing straight: We have rules around here—and I'm the one who makes them. The all-important rule is you do as I say. Fail to comply, disappoint me in any way—and the punishment will be severe. Do we understand one another?"

She may have been defiant initially. No longer. She was batting her eyes and made the effort to nod. His grip was powerful enough that he practically lifted her off the floor.

He held her this way, wanting the vic to absorb the words and allow the message to sink in—then just as suddenly let go and watched her fall back against the wall and drop to the mattress.

"I want you to get cleaned up. Are you thirsty?" It took her a moment to recover and catch her breath. She said she was.

"I thought you might be."

He handed her the *Listerine.*

"Gargle the vomit out of your mouth."

She did as told. Spit it out into the honey bucket. He handed her the jug with tap water. There was hesitation on her part, just as he had expected. Not that he could blame her.

"I don't poison my victims. That's for screwy murdering bitches without balls. It's nothing more than a cowardly way of taking someone's life. If I want to kill somebody I just do it, using my own tried-and-true methods. No poisoning of water or grub."

She drank from the jug. He waited for her to have her fill, then held the bowl of stew out. The stripper took a whiff. Wouldn't be interested.

"It's jambalaya. Perfectly nutritious."

Pearleen Bell wasn't about to change her mind.

"Suit yourself. If you don't eat you'll starve to death—not to mention your tits will eventually shrivel up and so will that great ass. What good would you be to me then?"

He shined the Maglite on her face. "You look weak as it is. Lack of food will do it every time. I know what I'm talking about."

He placed the bowl on the coffee table. Extracted the greeting card box from his jacket pocket. Handed it to her. Told her to open it, and take the items out: pen, generic greeting card, white envelope, postage stamp—and a sheet of paper with some writing on it. He asked her to read the writing.

Fritz,
A brief note to let you know I found work in
Sin City. The money is too good to pass up.
Lana and Stella are with me. We're checking
into rehab to get clean before we start the new
gig. We're not coming back.

Best wishes,
Pearleen

She looked up.

"What is it?"

"I wouldn't sign it that way."

"What way?"

"I never could stand him and his smelly cigars. Up yours, sounds more like me."

"It does at that. Only it's too harsh, in my opinion. Why not compromise and sign it simply: Pearleen?"

She nodded, and proceeded to transcribe the note onto the card. He had her insert it into the envelope and seal it with her own saliva, affix the stamp in the same manner: always using her own DNA. He had her address the envelope: writing down Las Vegas, NV as the place where it was being sent from.

# CHAPTER 235

**Biggs left the Mattress Room briefly, and was back, sans latex gloves.** He tore her blouse off, then the rest of her clothing. Wouldn't have done her much good anyway. Torn and stained with blood and grime. Left her in bra and black panties. Un-cuffed her wrists to allow her freedom to wash the crud and whatnot off.

He watched her run the sponge up and down one arm, then the other. She dipped it in the water in the bucket. Then Biggs got a better idea. Turned the hose on her. Sprayed her up and down. The cold water made her shake and shiver, but not for long—as it was summer and the water eventually turned lukewarm.

He released the sprayer handle. Had her resume the rest of her sponge bath.

"Get your face. You have stuff on your face."

She did that.

"Get your legs. We don't want to overlook those incredible legs."

She did as instructed, but was reluctant to go very high; in fact, refrained from cleaning her upper thighs. The false modesty was making a comeback. What bullshit. They spread that cunt at the drop of a fifty- or hundred-dollar bill, snort of toot, hit of crack, and here she was pretending to be a virgin who never had a cock in her hairy hole.

"Get those inner thighs, Pearleen baby. Upper thighs. Don't be bashful—because we know you're not. Not only is false modesty a waste of time, but it truly rubs me the wrong way."

She did that.

"I asked you once before: Did you ever appear in X-rated videos? Did you ever do hardcore?"

"One time. I needed money to rent a place, buy food. I was on my own."

"We all have our reasons when it comes to money. What name were you using at the time? What was your *nom de porn?*"

She washed herself down. Glanced up as she answered. "DeLyte."

"*Afrodesia DeLyte?* The name you used for the masturbation videos?"

She nodded.

"What happened to the video? Why is it impossible to find?"

"It was banned, I believe. I was sixteen at the time. It got back to the DA's office and the video was pulled from store shelves."

"What did you do in the video?" said Biggs, while gently rubbing his groin inside his trousers. Even though the erection wasn't happening just yet, there was a *tingle* in his *nutsack.* Something was going on down there. Something.

"Regular sex."

"What exactly was done? I want details."

"We did most of the usual positions."

"Yeah? What's your favorite?"

"On top. What they call cowgirl."

"You would. Like to be in control. Well, you relinquished all that once you stepped through my front door." He asked her if they did it doggy style. She said that they did.

"Show me. Get on the mattress . . . and show me."

The stripper was on hands and knees, her rear end stuck out, in the air.

"Move it. Let me see you move it. . . ."

She did some easy swaying of the hips, from side to side. Did some gentle thrusting. He continued to rub himself. Told her to get up, continue to clean her thighs and the rest of it. Pearleen rose.

"What else happened?"

"I gave him a blow job."

"Did he cum on your face?"

"On my tits."

"On your tits? Why not in your mouth or on your face? Those are the best money shots."

"I didn't want him to do it on my face . . . and said so."

"They were afraid of losing you, of having you walk out . . . so they capitulated. *Yellow-livered chickenshits.* Did you like it otherwise? You enjoy it? Did you like fucking on camera? In front of people?"

She cleared her throat. Did it again.

"I asked you . . ."

"It wasn't as bad as I thought it would be, once I got over my shyness. . . ."

"Your shyness? That's good. Was he black? White? What? What was he?"

"White. . . ."

"Was he hung?"

"He was. Yes. That doesn't always mean that they're good or are able to perform."

"How big was he?"

She lifted her hands to indicate a distance of about ten inches between them. "Like that."

"Eight? Ten inches?"

"Yes."

"Which? Eight inches or ten inches?"

"Ten, maybe. Possibly."

"How thick?"

"Thick."

"Did they have a *fluff girl* there? Did the guy have trouble getting it up?"

"Fluff girl? There was no fluff girl. He helped himself out. Used his own hand and baby oil. He was good to go after that."

"I don't get it. Why would a guy have trouble getting it up with a hot cunt like you? Was he queer or something? A sissy?"

"I don't know. There was a rumor that he did gay porn before he did that video with me. I couldn't say. He didn't seem gay to me. I didn't think about it. I did it for the money."

"I understand. We do a lot for money." He rubbed himself. Things were going on, taking shape. "He was able to keep it up?"

"Yes, he was."

"When he came, did he cum a lot? Was it a good pop shot?"

"Yes; he came quite a bit. There was lots of it. I didn't expect that much. It was a lot. There was a lot of it."

"What happened?"

"He rubbed it all over my boobs. . . ."

"And you had your face turned away. . . . Because you didn't want any to get anywhere near your mouth. Is that right?"

"Pretty much the way it happened."

"See how right I am? I know what I'm talking about. I know people, I know whores." He stared at her in silence. "Did he go down on you at all? Lick your butt?"

"He, ah, wouldn't do it at first. The director made him do it. The director yelled at him to do it—and then he did it."

"He yelled at him *to lick your ass?*"

"Yes. Because he wouldn't do it."

"Did you want him to do it?"

"I didn't care. It didn't matter to me. The whole thing was impersonal. There was no love involved, no emotion or feeling—on his part or mine. I wasn't there; my mind wasn't even there. My body was, but I wasn't. I did it to be paid . . . and wanted it to be over with."

"Don't talk to me about love. The bitch I was *discarded by* filed a restraining order against me. She's killing me financially with her alimony demands and child support for a kid who isn't even mine. So *fuck love. Love is a lie.* Love is a gold digger from the Philippines out to take me for all I'm worth. What I'd like to do is lure the slut and her little tyke . . . lure them to some isolated place, area, spot . . ." His features seemed to be turning a shade of crimson at this point. He paused. Pointed to his face. Was shaking his head. "See what the cunt does to me? Face is flushed. And it's no good, no good for me, my health." He collected himself. "Where were we?"

"He was yelled at by the director . . ."

"For not wanting to go *south.* Didn't want to go *downtown.*"

"Yes."

"Don't tell me you didn't enjoy it . . . when he finally got his tongue down there. . . ."

"I wasn't used to anyone licking my behind. . . . The other wasn't bad."

"That's all? Wasn't bad?"

"It was enjoyable. . . . Eventually. . . ."

"Were you told to lick *his* ass? Did they make you do it?"

"They told me to do it. I wouldn't. I was inexperienced . . . and couldn't. . . . I couldn't. . . ."

"What about lately?"

"Some people don't mind it. I'm old fashioned when it comes to sex. . . ."

"Sure. Except when there's *toot* in the mix. Then you and all the other whores will do anything. Isn't that right? *Toot, dust, weed, wicky sticks, crack.* . . ."

"Even then; it wasn't for me. . . ."

"It's time to grow up. Time to get with it. . . . Messy money shots and ass reaming is part of it. Slurping spooge, ATM: Ass-To-Mouth. . . . All part of it. Golden Showers; bitches pissing on each other. They say, in fact, bitches are nastier, way nastier than men. . . . I believe it. Only you want to think otherwise, to believe that it isn't true. Only we know that it is true. All of it."

She did a thing with her eyes: batted her lids. Seemed to be going along with it.

"Why wouldn't it be true? You leak every month. What could be more disgusting than that? Blood pours out of you the same way urine does: out of the same pee-hole. Blood and urine. And shit, huge big turds come out the other end. So it figures: you'd have to be far nastier than the male of the species. And on top of everything else: babies, newborn, are squeezed out of the same putrid hole. It's repulsive; it's sickening—and explains exactly why society, humans, are as fucked as we are. Why there was never any hope for us. We are all *fucked—thoroughly fucked.*"

She said nothing. Was not certain what to say. It was all right by him. Didn't need her to respond to it this time.

"Of course, when it comes to ass-banging, you want to use enough lube. Lube matters. Lube makes it happen. And when you have a *culo* built like yours, it's a crime not to fuck it. That's some amazing ass . . . amazing brown-eye. Tight brown-eye. Shapely butt cheeks. It would be a crime not to do anal with a turd-cutter like yours." His member down there seemed to be agreeing. "Of course, you're aware of it. . . . Showcase it during your stage act every chance you get."

Pearleen Bell stayed quiet.

"Why did you lie to me about doing the video that time? Why deny it?"

"It wasn't something I wanted to get around. I don't like porn. Even most of the girls who do videos only do it for the money. The dancing is different. I'm not ashamed of it. A girl has to make a living. I always enjoyed dancing. . . . I don't necessarily like working for someone like Fritz McCoy. That part isn't fun."

"But he provided enough drugs to keep you from leaving."

# CHAPTER 236

**Biggs propped the long, black Maglite against the first-aid kit on the coffee table so that it provided them with just the right amount of illumination: not too harsh in its brightness, but certainly adequate, and re-aimed the spray nozzle, spraying inside the bra and down there, over the panties.** Stuck the hose inside them, and blasted her rectum. Released his grip, and tossed the nozzle aside.

"What size is your bra?"

"Thirty-eight EE."

"Unfasten it. Take it off."

She did, and her enormous ebony tits dropped out, hanging there: a sight for Cecil to marvel at and follow through on a need and desire to cup in his hands, squeeze and fondle them.

He nibbled and licked without breaking skin and watched the woman's thick nipples begin to harden. He knew her dimensions by heart.

"What are your measurements?"

"Forty-four, twenty-nine, thirty-eight."

Her nipples were fully erect now. Biggs liked the effect he was having on her, and could feel movement in his trousers. Cock desired her cunt and tight brown asshole.

In the back of his mind there was no denying it: he wondered if he'd be able to make it all the way without the requisite choking and sundry forms of violence? He wanted to shake the idea of it. Wondered if he'd be able to? Couldn't tell. Wondered if his cock would continue rising—or fail him?

Biggs ached to fill her mouth with his groin, needing to spray cum in her mouth and cover that gorgeous face with it. Only for that to happen he had to be fully erect. The way it worked, the way nature had it set up. Nature had rules. No erection, no spraying of ball juice—and ultimately a waste of time and effort.


He pushed the negative thought away. He'd get hard, no matter what he had to do. He'd get hard and he would climax. Spray hot cum. *Spray the goo.*

He re-cuffed her wrists in front of her. Paused briefly to feel the soft, though wet, black silk panties, ran his hand across her buttocks, and then under, feeling the wet bush.

He liked pubic hair; it turned him on, and was happy that although she shaved down there, she'd had sense to leave enough of a "landing strip."

Hair on the cunt drove him nuts, even some hair in and around the butt hole did things to him. It was all good.

He tore the panties off, and was on his knees kissing the woman's inner thighs, licking, moving inside and up, teasing her privates with his hard-working, eager tongue. He asked her to sing her trademark tune, or at least hum it. He'd heard the song so often by now he could recite it by heart, and did so.

*"Let me be your nasty little whore . . . It's only you I do this for . . ."* They sang in tandem. Biggs did his best to accompany her, while at the same time parting her cheeks with his fingers and burying his tongue inside her butt crack and kept it there for a while. If heaven at all existed, this was it. His tongue was way up inside her bunghole. It was the best. Almost. Came close. Maybe about as good as carving them up, about as good as shoving a butcher knife deep into some cunt's neck and tits while he pumped the shitter or while cumming over the blood-drenched, squirming, screaming soon-to-be-dead whore.

He fought off the images, did his best. Fought off the impulse to fetch a machete and chop her dirty slut's skull off one bloody, bursting chunk at a time. Had to. Got to keep her around for a while. Not many twats built like her out there these days. Resist the impulse. *Got to.* The impulse was a beast and close to impossible to keep under control.

Cecil's busy tongue traveled south again, working toward the stripper's moist bush. . . . Cunt was in fear for her life, and there it was, impossible to deny: pussy juices flowed and flowed plenty. She was being taken by an unpredictable psycho fuck who did as he pleased with her. Helpless bitch was at his mercy. Explained it. Never been in a situation like this before. Probably always *in control,* turned her lovers into pliable, pussy-whipped, sorry excuses of the male species. The American male was scared, sissified and spineless, and rendered this way by a nation of overbearing ballbusters like Pearleen Bell, Petunia Roscoe, the Duarte sisters, and their ilk.

Cecil undid his pants. Let them drop. He parted the woman's bush, seeing to it that the thick hair that made up the landing strip around it was out of the way, and then slid his groin inside and stroked.

The intention was to take it easy at first, taking his good time with it. He had his mouth up and down the back of her neck, biting into her flesh and biting hard, leaving a series of pronounced, nearly blood-red hickeys all over it. Licked both ears, as the middle finger of his left hand found and slid down toward the center of the exotic dancer's powerful ass cheeks. Continued to slide it all the way inside her ever-so-tight crapper hole. It was more than evident she'd never had a man's hard cock in there. Too bad. Always a red flag you were dealing with one of them, the enemy: a just about worthless, man-hating, all-out controlling type of feminist wench. Those were about the best to carve up, best to torture and made to suffer, although for him, it felt pretty good to do any and all.

He drove the finger hard up against her, as hard as it would go, then added a second finger. The bitch winced. New to it.

"Around here, *bitches get fucked in the shitter* on a routine basis. I suggest you start getting used to it."

The wincing continued. He liked that. Wince, grunt, yelp, yowl, scream your head off even. It was all good, enhanced the thrill.

He was still sliding his cock in and out of her moist cunt, and he stayed with it. Take your time, Cecil reminded himself repeatedly. Make it last. Patience is a virtue—and makes for a greater blast to come. He'd wanted this to last forever. Goddamn; he'd watched this bitch in that strip joint strut her stuff so many times over the months, he'd spent countless nights and even afternoons and all that cash on overpriced cream sodas and purified water and on tips watching her lasciviously parade her tits and pussy and those impossibly great buttocks in front of all those poor bastards who'd been desperate for it—and he knew she had enjoyed driving them insane with desire, enjoyed doing it to the men as well women. A born prick-teaser, that's what Pearleen Bell was and all she could ever be. A true ball-buster with a body that just would not quit.

That she was—and he had her.

Ass-to-die for, tits that made your mouth water; beautifully-shaped perfect cunt and asshole that made your moose dick ache with desire. And he had her, to do with her as he wished, to fuck her any damn way that he pleased—and then, once he tired of her, which was bound to happen, it always did, he'd chop her up like all the others, like all the rest of that human garbage. But that would be later, much later, because this voluptuous fuck machine was just too good, way too goddamned good for him to even be thinking along those lines.

"I want to fuck you until I drop."

Biggs pulled out of her cunt. He had her bend over in order to be able to slide the ever-sensitive head of his penis into her open mouth. She took his groin in and was smart enough not to show resistance this time. Biggs hadn't even had to instruct her to wrap her handcuffed hands around his chubby as she began to work it like the natural-born cocksucker that all cunts were.

She took him out long enough to add plenty of saliva to the swollen head, flicked at it readily with her tireless tongue and then proceeded on to the shaft, up and down both sides.

He had her lick his balls. She sucked on each one, taking turns.

"Lick my *asshole*. I want to feel your tongue *deep in my asshole*. Do for me what I did for you. Lick my sweat; lick it. Worthless fucking whore. Be gentle. The 'roids demand it."

It didn't appear she was all that eager, but followed through just the same.

"Lick it like it's your last meal on earth. You're on death row. Warden just served you your last meal. Savor it. There might not be another."

Pearleen Bell complied. What choice did she have? Waited for the next command.

He had her take her tongue out of his butt and back working on his member. Goddamn, his loins were about to blast one of the heaviest loads ever. He was also grateful the meds hadn't fucked things up for him, hadn't caused him to prematurely ejaculate. It happened more often than he cared to think about. Fucking meds. Never knew what the side effects would be or even when it would happen. Sometimes he shit his trousers, other times his dick dripped. Never could predict what to expect, until after it happened.

For him, right at this moment, the pleasure was incomparable. He cursed to himself. Thought: She's too good to dismember. *I can't kill this cunt.* I'd be absolutely insane to kill her, ballbuster or not, man-hater or not, chip-on-her-shoulder feminist or not. Can't do it. Don't even think about it. No point to it. *You can't butcher a hot piece of ass like this.*

"You're the best, baby. You're the absolute best. Keep at it, baby. . . . Stay with it. . . . I'm getting ready to blast in your mouth. I'll blast a heavy load down your throat and on your face. Hear that, cunt? It's on the way. A milk wagon of white hot ball juice for you to gag on. It'll be the heaviest load you've ever had in your hungry street whore's mouth."

The more things Biggs uttered and the louder he uttered them the harder the woman worked. She did not always look up at him, up at the scarred, demented face—a glance now and then was enough. She was in control, if not of everything that had happened to her up to this point, at least she was in control of this very moment. She had him, she had this sick bastard where she wanted him. It was her one chance of staying alive, and she knew it more than anything, and she kept at it, doing a greater job of it than she had ever done before in her life because her very existence depended on it.

Biggs gave out one final scream, and then a much quieter sound of sorts that emerged from deep inside his throat. The woman was not letting up, as she continued to work it much easier now but worked it nonetheless, getting it all, drawing it deep inside her warm mouth.

Biggs had planted the palms of his hands on the back of her head, seeming to show gentleness strangely enough, just too spent to do anything else. He clung to her like this. Held her. Finally, there was no getting around it, being too sensitive down there right now, he had to withdraw from her mouth altogether. He let the stripper lick his fingers, all of them, one at a time, his palms, the back of his hands, and then he just kind of lowered himself down to the mattress and sat there with his back against the wall. Feeling drained, as well as at peace, or as close to peace as was possible for him. Biggs shut his eyes to savor the moment, to recoup and recharge his battery. This was just too good. He couldn't believe it. Why had he waited this long to get his hands on her? Why had it taken him this long to get to Pearleen Bell? But then he thought: What does that matter now? All that matters is that she's here, she's right here with me. She's mine to do with as I please.

Just think of all the fucking and sucking you've got to look forward to. . . . Think of it. Wouldn't have to keep on taking all those risks, at least for a while anyway. Think of it.

He reminded himself: it wasn't entirely up to him. It came down to the *urge*: to *destroy, torture, and butcher. Slice and dice/hack and sack. Consume. Devour. And shit them out afterwards.*

# CHAPTER 237

**His eyes were open now and he was looking right up at her, right up her hairy beaver, the glistening beads of sweat around it, the pearls of sweat on the small of her slick golden back and all that healthy golden ass.**

There was one thing on his mind just then: to get up and go for more. Get your rest, you need that, and then go again, and this time try for something else.

"Baby, I want to go for seconds. How about you? How do you feel about it?"

Pearl had managed to stifle what tears had been brewing inside her, and she had done a fine job of it, knowing that it would not have gotten her anywhere; on the contrary, it would have only made her predicament much worse. Tears and struggle only made matters worse. It wouldn't have changed anything. It wouldn't keep this sick bastard from doing what he intends on doing to me, she thought. She'd tried to fight her way out, hadn't she?—tried to fight these psycho geeks in here, all these crazy, psycho ward candidates and it had only made matters worse for her. It had only gotten her bruised and bloodied.

"Hear me talking to you? *Huh?*"

Pearleen Bell nodded her head. "Whatever you want, honey. That's what I'm here for, ain't it?"

"You have got the best lip-lock I have ever experienced in my entire life—and that is definitely a compliment."

"Thank you. I appreciate that."

"You better appreciate it. Because I don't grant many compliments. What do we do for an encore? What do we do this time? How do you want it?"

"Whatever you say, lover."

"Is that right? Whatever I say. . . . I like that."

Biggs wiped his forehead with his shirt. Took a drink from the jug and handed it to her. Pearleen had some water. Thanked him.

"It's a damn shame we couldn't have met years before. Yeah. . . . I was a little more stable back then . . . believe it or not. I was okay. I wasn't always this mixed-up. Truth is . . . the whole thing just got out of hand . . . with the buzzing in my head, the flies and flashbacks. . . . All of it. . . . I never thought my life would turn out this way. . . ."

Pearleen nodded her head as though she understood.

"I know what you mean."

He looked at her.

"I do. You expect things to turn out one way, the way you planned, the way you dreamed of wanting things to turn out. . . . Before you know it, you're stuck in a life and a rut so far removed from your goals and dreams that it don't seem like your life at all."

"You're right. That's how it happened. Things got out of hand. All of it. Out of hand. Then again, maybe they were supposed to. Could be you're right about the rut part. Could be I am in a rut—but what a rut to be in. Sure, my numbers could be better. I'd be lying if I said it didn't bother me. I'm working on it, though. 'Dreams and goals' don't happen overnight."

He studied her for a bit. Wasn't certain he cared for the way she clearly appeared to be scrutinizing his psyche with what he felt were carefully chosen words and phrases. What did she hope to gain? Upper hand? You never knew with a bitch.

"And here I am, and here you are. At least you're with me now. . . . Don't worry, nothing is forever. Nothing lasts. It isn't supposed to. That's life. About the only guarantee you get in this world: doom and demise. Taxes notwithstanding. We die. All of us. Fate. One-way road that always leads to a dead end. So don't lose sleep over any of that. It isn't worth worrying about. See, the smart ones know it's all a big con anyway, a trick."

Pearleen's lower lip was trembling now and she was well aware of it and could not do much to stop it. Her fear was showing through and it could be fatal for her. She collected herself. Swallowed hard.

"Am I going to be taken out?"

Biggs was looking at her again. Noticed her lip doing things. Twitching. "What have you got to be afraid of? Live for the moment."

"You're right. I didn't mean *by you*—I meant by the others."

"In here, no one makes a move *without my consent*—unless they want to spend time in the pit. I'll have to think about it. I can't make a decision like that right now. You don't expect me to be able to do that, do you? My mind is on something else at the moment. . . ."

And he gripped his semi-limp organ in his right hand. Held it like that. Stroked it a few times and watched it grow to its full size: all six inches of veiny, rigid, thick-rounded hunk of meat. He spit in his hand just then and ran it over the rather large mushroom-like head of his erection.

"Damn, that feels good."

No matter how she fought this time to hold back the tears, Pearleen Bell found herself losing the battle as a teardrop rolled down the right side of her face, the side Biggs could not see. Pearleen got rid of the teardrop by rubbing her face against her bare shoulder.

"Here." Biggs was looking up again. "Turn this way some."

Pearleen shifted so that her pelvis faced him and was just above his forehead.

"No. Move the other way. Right. Yeah, I want to be able to look up your ass. I want to see that tight asshole. I want to be able to look right up that beautiful bronze butt, baby. Yeah. . . ."

He continued to give himself slow strokes while looking up at the woman's glistening buttocks.

"Bend over some, Dolly. That's it, Pearly-Girlie. Bend over like that. Stick your ass out toward me."

Pearleen did as she was told. Biggs was up on his knees now with his tongue hanging out. He had both his hands on the woman's buttocks and began licking, running his tongue all over perspiring flesh. He planted kisses across the small of her back and down one cheek, across part of her vagina and rectum, across the other cheek and up again, and soon his tongue was back probing her cunt. The juice was still there; it was all wet inside and he extended his tongue as far as it would go, way in there; wiggled it around inside, brought it back out again, and ran it across the outer edge. Biggs found himself kissing her rectum, parted her legs some more and was moving back down toward that wet bush, the pubic hair, unable to get enough of it.

"I could eat this forever."

Biggs right hand was down on his groin, stroking, manipulating. He slid a couple of fingers inside her. Got enough juice on the fingers, and then rubbed all that juice over the knob. He was ready now for round two, more than ready, Cecil figured.


He rose to his feet, spread the woman's cheeks, and guided his member toward her cunt. Slid it in. Stroked several times, backed out, and then squeezed it inside and up the stripper's tight butt. He heard her wince, but it was not much of a sound.

Damn, it felt good in her like this. Snug fit. It was warm inside her asshole and he stroked it. Heard the woman emit a gasp or two. He thrived on that, of course. The louder the better.

"Oh, yeah. . . ."

He gripped handfuls of her ass and pressed the cheeks against his groin and held on to the buttocks this way. Bitch continued to make sounds. Even tried to shake him off at times, it seemed. Biggs stayed right in there.

"I think Trusty's in love, Pearleen baby. This must be love. . . ."

He eased up some. Only because he'd wanted to make it last longer, draw it out. Gave her a few more strokes. Cupped, then gripped her tits in both hands. Gripped some more, pinching her nipples, as he proceeded to climax deep inside her. Had his arms wrapped around her wet back and belly during this part of the phase and held on for dear life . . . until totally spent. Subsequently, he jammed it in her mouth and had her finish him off.

# CHAPTER 238

**Later that evening members of the "inner circle" were seated at the large dinner table in the kitchen on the first floor.** The menagerie consisted of Julian "Red Menace" Ionesco, "Big Tex" Leo Nix, Miss Betty Lou Rutterschmidt and her daughter Mildred, Patience McDaniel, Lawrence "Sassy" Sassounian, Norbert Fimple, Olin "Swine Vomit" Goodfellow. Marvin R. Muck was seated in a barber's chair off to the side getting his curls clipped by Biggs with a hair clipper. Greta Otto, the cook in the Cupid mask, served her specialty: that suspect jambalaya that Norbert Fimple seemed to favor so much and never could get enough of.

Biggs finished up with Marvin. Gave him the hair clipper, and sat at the head of the table to his strawberry-and-cream-filled *Twinkie*, chased with a cold soda. Picked up the *Wall Street Journal*.

"Who be next?" Marvin was itching to clip hair. Biggs pointed to Julian Ionesco.

"You're up, cabbie."

"*Ja ja, kurva*," said the Rumanian, the "cabbie" moniker having rubbed him the wrong way. He rose from the table and sat in the barber's chair. Kept on how upon first arriving in America with his "dear wife" he'd been forced, *forced* to operate a taxi for a living.

"I have better life in Rumania, much better."

Marvin didn't give a damn about any of that. Ran the clippers over the guy's skull. Not doing a great job of it, either, but he was getting it done. Biggs was saving money this way by not having to pay to have anyone's hair cut by a professional. That was all that mattered.

"I am tired of all you foreigners coming over here and running down this country, my country." Biggs snapped at the fat man. "What the hell you greasy bastards come here for then if you don't like it?"

"Free Ride" Muck was nodding his head and agreeing with his mentor. "That be right. Tell him, Brotha Trusty. America be good."

"I come to see Cowboy and Indian."

"Boo-shit."

Biggs looked at Ionesco good and hard. "You come here chasing the dollar. Commie bastard."

"My wife and me we have dream: Go to America. All people say America is best country."

"Yeah, I know about dreams. Don't tell me about dreams. I dream all the time: about *big, ugly, fat, green flies*—that's what I dream about."

"How much of this mofo' hair I should get, Cecil?"

"All of it. Get it all. Do all of them the same way. You know the routine."

There was hair behind Ionesco's ears that Marvin was overlooking, not that it mattered. He got most of it.

"My beloved Rumania; I was engineer . . ."

"Here we go again. You were a *peasant*. Learn to tell the truth around me, or keep your mouth shut."

"How you know what I do? Who tell you? Leo Nix tell you?"

"What's the difference?" Biggs wanted to concentrate on the *Journal*.

How was he doing? Was his portfolio up? Years of studying the stock market was paying off handsomely. Compensated for the loss in income at having his haunted house shut down. Not entirely, but it did help. Had no idea when he'd be able to re-open, either. It was on his mind. Couldn't stop dwelling on it. Loss of that kind of revenue was not unlike losing an extremity. Caused greater anguish. No doubt about it. Goddamned wetbacks. See: kindness backfires once again. And all this dumb Commie can think to whine about is this obsession he has with the Wild West that never existed. "All you Reds are the same. You were a cab driver over there and you drove a cab here. A lowly cabbie. Let that be the end of it. And, oh yes: you had that gig in Beverly Hills as 'gardener to the stars.' Good for you. Your wife Anastasia did janitorial work, cleaned toilets and wiped some forgotten silent movie star's wrinkled bunghole after he took his daily dump."

"*Bunghole?* I am sorry, I do not understand."

"Butt crack."

"Asshole, you say? No. Never. We do not do this. *We refuse.*"

"You were refusniks."

"Of course. Refusniks."

"Fine and dandy. I stand behind my claim: Janitors and dog walkers. Wiped little Timmy's dripping nose and changed old geezer Tom Mix's underwear, after you and your loving wife first gave him a careful and cautious sponge bath, making sure his sweaty balls and smelly rectum were properly swabbed."

"No janitorial. *Never. We do not do this.* We do not go near privates, or this *bunghole* you talk about. I do not know this Tom Mix, you speak of, sir. I never see one single bunghole in Beverly Hills or Bel Air, not one; it is also true we see many assholes. My wife was *nanny*, please. *Nanny.* I was *butler.*"

# CHAPTER 239

**Marvin was finished with the former Beverly Hills butler and nudged him to get his heavy ass out of the chair and let Big Tex park his skinny one in it.**

Ionesco reclaimed his seat at the table, dug into the stew.

"How you get *Rolls-Royce* and *Cadillac*, Bishop Cecil? My wife always want *Cadillac* for me. She love *Cadillac* for me. Very nice. Comfortable. Class automobile, no?"

"Eat the goddamn jambalaya and shut up about Rumania."

"You are boss, *Tovarich.*"

The Rumanian ate his stew. Norbert Fimple indicated with his hands and slobbering tongue that he was ready for seconds. Julian looked at Lawrence Sassounian who still wore Lana's scalp on his head. Long strands of matted hair dangled over his eyes and below. Sassounian adjusted the scalp so that the hair did not block his mouth. He wiped some more. Picked up the cutting board Greta Otto had left on the table and began to hammer himself over the head with it and stayed with it until blood materialized from underneath the scalp. Soon enough Sassy lost consciousness and his face fell forward, landing into the nearly empty bowl before him, and dozed. Some stared. Biggs wasn't bothered.

"At least he's not banging away at walls and bunks, as is the norm for him."

Marvin Muck was smiling and shaking his head. "That ain't for me. Ain't no way I could do that to myself. Man gotta be a *fuckin' 'tard.*"

"He do all the time."

"One of these day' that old fool gonna mess up all his brains, then what he gonna do when he don't even have enough sense to piss and shit in the crapper like Norbert was doin' all that time? Goodfellow, too. Guess who gonna be followin' after the mothafuckah wiff the *honey bucket* pickin' up after him? Me; I be the one."

"I talk to him. He tell me he do this to find *what make him tick.*"

Big T. looked at the foreigner. "How's that?"

"He hope for *revelation*. Vision will come if he hit brain long enough, special vision—"

"You *shit*, too. He don't talk to nobody about nothin'."

"Why he wanna put himself in pain?"

"Don't ask fool questions, boy," said the man from Texas. Added under his breath: "Dumb sumbitch."

"You think he feel guilty about something in his life that happen many years before?"

Marvin was done with Big T. He wasn't getting any better at it, but at least 95 percent of Big T.'s hair was off.

Leo Nix stood up. Walked to his chair at the table. Sat down.

"I don't rightly give a rank fart, my Pinko sumbitch. Gimme some of that down home cookin'. Lordy. . . . Porterhouse steak, mashed taters, gravy, corn-on-the-cob, Billy Bob's and Bob Wills, Hank Williams. Don't bother me, *Com-raide*. Can't relate to all that *hogwash* you're yappin' about, on account you're yappin' outta your hind end, boy—'cause your yap sure knows better."


Big Tex removed his weather-beaten, sweat-stained Stetson, reached inside for a worn, dog-eared color snapshot of his wife, two young girls, and family dog. Big Tex looked at the photo and it brought back memories, good memories, and the subsequent tragedy.

"Who be my next victim?"

Biggs looked at Norbert. "Your turn."

Norbert was not inclined. Didn't want a haircut.

"Would you rather undergo another session of Pit Therapy instead?"

That made him comply. Mr. Fimple walked to the barber chair and sat in it. Marvin began cutting the hair off of the big head.

"You feel bad, my American *comrade*," Julian said to the Texan. Biggs hadn't cared for the melancholy tone the conversation was headed in; it kept him from enjoying the good news about his stock jumping in value.

"Caught her with my best amigo in a No-Tell Motel," Big T. said to no one in particular. Perhaps only recounting the event for the hundredth time for no one's benefit but his own, perhaps in a dire hope that as he retold it, the ending, the tragic ending of it might somehow amend itself, magically transform into something not as burdensome and heartbreaking. Only it never did. Life didn't work that way. Big Tex always recalled the blood and finality of it. Death.

"I wiped the smile off her face with a *.50-.50*, then dropped that two-timin' whore's body down a mine shaft. I shot the family dog and my two baby girls. . . ." And tears filled his eyes, slow, quiet tears that kept forming in his pain-wracked eyes, one after another. "Lord, how come things don't ever turn out the way they ought to?"

"Best not to have dream, my friend. No dream, no disappointment. . . . But then: no dream, no life—no hope. Hard to do, no?"

Julian patted Big Tex on the shoulder. Patience walked over to him with her sweater in her hands. Draped it about the cowboy's back. The cowboy wept on the table top, face down this way.

"Don't worry, my friend, on the other side we will be happy. . . . There will be much love. . . . I promise you. . . . I know my wife, too, she wait for me on the other side. You needs to take it easy on you, my American buddy. . . ."


Patience was back in her chair, shivering. Wiped a tear or two from her eyes. Tex was sitting up now, staring off in the distance, staring at a cobweb up in a corner, above the pennies embedded in the wall, the fat spider in the cobweb, not seeing anything other than his past, images of something he'd once been a part of, a sanity and love that he'd once known, and then it had all gotten short-circuited somehow.

"High school sweethearts, we was. Down a mine shaft. . . . You could hear them hit bottom. . . . Couldn't see nothin' down there; it was pitch black . . . but I heard them hit bottom . . . one after the other. Dropped them right down that mine shaft. . . . Shot the sumbitch's privates right off. He lived. . . . Don't believe he spends a whole lot of time schemin' how to get into poontang what ain't his no more. . . ." Big T. cleared his throat. "If I had it to do over again, I wouldn'ta done it that way. No, sir.

My baby girls wasn't guilty a nothin'. . . . I'da just blowed my own dang head off instead." Big Tex looked at Julian Ionesco and the others. "Then again, who knows?"

Biggs lowered the *Wall Street Journal*.

"Yeah, well. You people have a way of cheering a fellow up." He had another *Twinkie*, sip of his soda. "You can't dwell on the past; it will only pull you down. Regret is for the birds. Dwell on things you didn't do right, the times you went wrong—for whatever reason, and all you're doing is pecking at wounds. Not good for you at all. We have a lot to be grateful for. You're well fed, and you got a roof over your head. Beats being homeless, doesn't it? Beats having to sleep in some public park somewhere, beats being on The Row, or sleeping on a cot, bus bench, in some doorway. You're a lot better off than all those homeless out there, and my stock is up."

"And you got them heathen fornicators what need to be shown the Way of the Lord."

"You certainly are right about that, Miss Betty Lou. I've been working hard on that. What I was doing earlier: reading from the *Bible* to that amoral hussy. Did my desperate best to set her straight. She'll eventually see the light by the time Bishop Cecil O. Biggs is done with her. Want to ensure your place in Heaven? Making the Lord a big part of your life here and now is the only way. There is no other."

Marvin was done cutting Norbert's hair. Both returned to their places at the table. Norbert did not waste time chowing down,while Marvin picked at his.

"Amen, Pastor."

Others readily agreed with Betty Lou Rutterschmidt.

# CHAPTER 240

**Early next morning Marty Roscoe squeezed through a flimsy section of the picket fence that separated his backyard from the one belonging to Cecil's church.** One thing was certain, the closer he got to Biggs's front door the stronger the odor became. It was unusual for Roscoe to be up this early in the day and the smell didn't make it any easier. When you had need, you had need.

He pounded on the door.

Eventually the four-by-ten-inch security slot slid open and Deacon Marvin's tired eyes were giving the redneck the twice over.

"Like to join up with this here Christian Church of Re-Newed Hope."

"Got to be jivin' me, man."

"No jive. I got religion. Something come over me said it was time for religion; time to reconnect with the Lord."

"Membership be by special invite only."

"The kind of *House of Worship* is this anyway, buck? I want to come in and thank the Maker for my good fortune over the years: marriage, health—all that good shit."

"What keep' you from doin' it from your own cribby?"

"My 'cribby' ain't a church, is it?"

"You gonna have to talk to Bishop Bigg'."

"Get him out here, then. We're wasting time. You tell *'Bishop Bigg'* you got a sinner here wants to join his church. That should make him feel damned good. I know how important membership is to a half-ass parish like this. What are you waitin' for? Move your behind."

Marvin stood there looking at Marty Roscoe and not knowing how to react to this off-the-wall request. He stood and thought about it. *Ofay mofo gotta be out of his mind. Last thing Bishop gonna want is this dumbass redneck runnin' 'round in his house.*

Roscoe was clearing his throat. "I like the looks of this church and I want to be part of it. It's convenient for me and my lady. We been talking about joining up. We don't belong to no church right now and we sure could use some spiritual guidance, you might say—if you know what I mean?"

Marvin remained unconvinced. *Don't nobody know what the cracker mean. Prob'ly don't even know it hisself.* Marvin's lack of reaction was enough to piss Roscoe off.

*"Are you deaf, buck? Tell the bishop."*

"You don't be gettin' it. Be by *invite* only."

"Huh? What kind of shit are you talking now?"

"Membership be by invite. You got to be brung by a member, and since you don't know nobody who be a member—"

"I know Peaches LaBelle. She's a member, ain't she?"

"No, she ain't."

"I seen her and her friends comin' in here—"

"That don't mean she a member. You just wastin' yo' time, brother—and mine."

"You saying I'm not good enough? Are you calling me a redneck? I get enough of that shit from my old lady."

"I ain't said nothin'—"

*"You said I ain't good enough to join your church. I don't like being called a redneck, punk. You tell that to your 'Bishop'. You understand?"*

# CHAPTER 241

**The church door opened and Biggs appeared.** The odor of decay, heavy Lysol and lemon-scented ammonia mixed-in hit Marty Roscoe full on. He coughed, did his best not to be too obvious about it. Only there it was: that odor. It had been wafting in periodic waves out through the open slot all during his conversation with the flunky, but now that the door was wide open the stench was difficult to take.

Still, Marty Roscoe could not stop thinking about Peaches LaBelle. She was beyond reach for him, and yet, she could stoop low enough to waste her time on nothing losers like Cecil Biggs and Marvin Muck.

"What kind of parish you running here anyway, Biggs? Buck here claims I ain't welcome."

Biggs handed him a church flyer. The legend across the very top in heavy black letters read: UNITED CHRISTIAN CHURCH OF RENEWED HOPE. There was writing in much smaller print underneath that, and the bottom was signed: Bishop Cecil Omar Biggs.

Roscoe glanced at the flyer.

"The hell is this?"

"Fact is, we've got all the members we can handle. Read the flyer."

"I don't have time to read this shit. Fine print hurts my eyes." Roscoe balled the flyer up and tossed it over his shoulder. "Look, I just felt like coming inside to say a couple of prayers. What's the big deal in that?"

"Where were you when the church first opened years ago, Roscoe? I delivered pamphlets door-to-door. Everyone in the neighborhood was invited to come in and worship: the lame and the insane, rich and poor— all were invited back then. Times have changed since all that. We have rules to abide by as implemented by the board of directors—for security reasons. I may be the bishop, I still have rules and guidelines I am expected to abide by."

"'Security Reasons'? What for?"

"I've been threatened. We receive our share of death threats. No point being reckless."

"Hogwash, Biggs. You don't think we know about the pole crawlers and the rock-n-roll?"

"He's desperate to go inside because he saw those ghetto ballerinas with tits out-to-here go in the other night!" Petunia Roscoe shouted from the sidewalk. Gave her husband a real start. He'd never heard her walk up. Roscoe had been so preoccupied in dealing with Biggs and his crackhead secretary, or whatever Muck was to him, that he'd had no idea that his wife had tracked him to Biggs's smelly abode. But there she was—and she wasn't through.

"Isn't that right, Marty honey?"

"What ghetto ballerinas?"

*"Whores."*

"Whores? Can't you see that's an insult to the reverend and all he stands for? He's a *Man of God.* This ain't no *whorehouse.*" Roscoe pointed at the plaque on Biggs's door. "This is a church. See that? *United Christian Church of Re-Newed Hope. It don't say Church of Made-Over Hoes*, does it? Besides, *hoes* got just as much right to worship as anyone else."

Biggs stepped past the redneck in order to unlock the front gate as an invitation for Roscoe to take a walk and get lost, and stay lost.

A disappointed Marty Roscoe took the hint: left the premises, grumbling. "I ain't givin' up, Biggs. I need the Word. You ain't seen the last of me."

He rejoined his wife on the sidewalk and the verbal sparring continued as they made it back to their prefab shanty.

# CHAPTER 242

**Biggs noticed the mail carrier drop a bunch of advertisements in his mailbox, glance nervously at him, and quickly drive off in the postal Jeep.** Everybody was nervous these days. He didn't care for it. It wasn't good for his condition. He unlocked his mailbox to retrieve the bundle inside and could easily hear the Roscoes going at it on their front porch.

"Don't lie to me, Marty. I hate it when you lie to me. You know how much I hate that, Marty."

"What's the big deal? What the hell did I do now?"

"You know exactly what this is about. You can smell those sluts a block off—especially if they've got tits out to here."

"What's wrong with tits? You got tits. That's how I got interested in you, ain't it? You never complained about that."

Even though they were inside by now and their front door closed, the back-and-forth shouting was easily audible.

Biggs locked his gate back up, went through the mail as he walked to his front door. He shook his head, cursing under his breath.

"I don't believe it."

"What do it be, Brotha Lusty?"

"Roscoe put my name on a smut list. I'm being sent smut now. Some of this is *fag porn*. How can they do this? How can they send smut to a reputable church?"

Marvin's reaction was a double take. Do the mofo be serious? Can't be. After all he be doin' to the bitches, he complainin' 'bout weak shit like this?

He followed Cecil inside. The front door was locked. They were in the living room. The Roscoes could still be heard: the battle raged on in their domicile.

# CHAPTER 243

**Biggs had tossed the queer porn in the trash, and was rubbing himself while going over the straight porn catalogue and flyers.** He stood at the shuttered window facing the Roscoe house as he did this.

He dropped the smut on the futon. Only then did he notice, among the porn, the white envelope that had been sent by the PI he kept on retainer to track Tillie down.

Marvin was all over the smut at this point. Agog.

Cecil yanked the envelope from the stack. There it was. The name. In the left-hand corner: **Philbert Coyne, Private Investigations**. He suspected what was inside. Hated to open it. Did so just the same. Another bill, or rather the same one. PI insisting he be paid for work rendered during the past few months or so.

Bill was too high, thought Biggs. Exorbitant. Otherwise he would have paid it by now, not to mention the private detective hadn't given him anything he could use against her, such as photos that caught her mistreating the kid in some way or that showed her for being the rotten, lying gold digger that she was who would spread her legs or blow cock at the drop of a peso.

Not only had he not given him anything to use as leverage to counter her demands for increased child support and alimony, but this was the same grifter who hadn't been able to provide him with any evidence to nail her with while the divorce was going through, that she had lied about being a virgin and that she'd been running around on him while they lived as husband and wife.

The other thing that nagged at him: Why were women never penalized for being lame lays and/or for refusing to take it in the ass or for not knowing how to give satisfactory head? Why was the blame always left at the man's doorstep? And when the marriage unraveled, which was bound to happen, the husband was punished once more with demands of money and property—when all he had been interested in in the first place was spicing up the lackluster union?

It's the Betty Friedans of the world. Bull dyke bitches built like longshoremen and truck drivers who had started it; the two Glorias: Steinem and Allred. Then you had the Commie-loving, capitalist-hating filthy rich celebrity bag of excreta called Jane Fonda.

There was a time when cunts knew their place. Not these days. Not anymore. *Until he got his hands on them and showed them what was what.*

Stapled to the back of the bill was a brief note regarding the two Mex turds, former employees, who were doing their best to shake him down for a substantial wad of cash over the incident with Greta. They'd found a liberal ambulance chaser to take their case on. Charges were serious enough: Assault and Battery, and should have been against *them*. For assault with intent to invade a lady's poop chute without proper consent.

Everything was upside down these days. He and his attorneys should've been suing the other party instead. Wouldn't happen. Mexicans haven't got a pot to piss in. No. So instead you sue the hard-working small businessman like himself and do your damned best to liberate him from the few dollars he has managed somehow to set aside over the years for his retirement. On of the things he found annoying about the system. He was all for liberty, capitalism and free enterprise. Problem was, it also fostered underhanded practices such as this. Nation was lawsuit happy. And it had gone way overboard with no end in sight.

When you thought about it, though, looked at it logically and with a calm mind, Greta had been at fault. Yes. Entirely. For not taking them both out. Bitch had fucked up by not crushing the vermin out of existence. Right there in the women's john. Flushed them away. And no one would have faulted her for it. She claimed she'd tried, and that they'd been too quick for her, and that Violeta, a girlfriend of one of the Mexicans, had used pepper spray on her. You couldn't make this shit up. Sprayed with *pepper spray* by a *pepper belly*. Too much. Worth a chuckle. Even from him. Almost. But not quite. Only because there was nothing funny about any of it. What it was, instead, was stress-inducing; what it did was to make certain that his sleep disorder would never abate. Slugs. Were humans slugs? Humans were slugs. Everywhere you turned. And then you had that certain segment of society acting like they're appalled and thoroughly repulsed when his type responded in kind. Trusty, Mr. Turnbull, took it. With all due respect, sir; this is what did you in. They crushed you because you were a saint. You were good and you took it. Cretins like J.J. make it a point to seek out and disassemble your kind. Your demise and destruction is their life's goal and sole intent.


Cecil folded the notice. A thought occurred to him as he stuffed it in his shirt pocket: What if he dealt with this latest request for remuneration from this bogus shamus by simply enlarging the already dug hole in his garage floor—to accommodate not only Agenda Marie and this *cum stain* Honesto, whom she claimed was his, but PI Philbert Coyne as well? And adding the two Hispanic shakedown artists and their shady lawyer as icing on the cake.

Something to ponder over. It was about timing, usually. It came down to timing. Timing was everything—and having a plausible alibi, as well as a more accommodating dumping site—preferably away from his property. He had enough stiffs on the grounds to start his own graveyard as it was.

You had to ask yourself, too, would the risk even be worth the trouble? A PI is not going to be dumb enough to leave himself unprotected. And the illegals had been his employees for close to a year now. How would he go about eliminating the ungrateful motherfuckers? And then there was their lawyer. Actually, that one was simple: if wetbacks, Arturo and Bartolo, as well as their accomplice and so-called witness Violeta, should suddenly vanish off the face of the earth, so would their claim against him.

# CHAPTER 244

**He unlocked the inside shutters.** Peered through the vertical crack that the outer shutters allowed. The belligerent Roscoes were taking it to the next level. Biggs pulled up on the lower half of the window to open it an inch or so. Had his hands on the shotgun mic and headset. Slid the latter over his ears, the former was aimed in the direction of the white trash couple he loathed with a seething passion.

"I have more respect for the common fag than I do a spineless punk like that. How do you let a chunky, homely twat emasculate you that way? How do you do it? How does he live with himself? Where is his self-respect?"

"*Pussy-whip.* That be it. Redneck Romeo ain't nothin' but *pussy-whip.*"

"You said it."

Biggs reached for his binoculars. Petunia was on the verge of tears. She was still screaming, but her eyes were about to well up.

"I can't live like this, Marty. There's nothing wrong with tits, only I can't look like those eighteen- and twenty-year-old bimbos. I can't keep up with that. *I am forty-two years old. Overweight and miserable. . . .*"

"Nobody's asking you to keep up with nobody, babe."

"There's times I'm convinced I'd be better off without you, Marty."

Roscoe wrapped his muscular arms around her waist. Slid a hand up inside her blouse. Grabbed a handful of breast, waited and felt a nipple harden. "You don't mean that, babe. I'd be lost without you."

Biggs could see that Petunia was mellowing, responding to the redneck's touch.

"Just long enough until you found yourself another meal ticket."

Roscoe nibbled on her ear. Kissed her neck down and then the back of it.

"That's cold-blooded."

"I can't help it. You make me feel that way sometimes."

"I'd lose my mind without you, babe. I'd go nuts if we ever split up. Probably jump off a bridge. . . ."

"Not you. That's isn't you, Marty. . . ."

"You don't know me, babe. You don't know how much you mean to me. I couldn't make it without you. . . ."

Marty Roscoe walked her to the sofa. Sat her down. He pulled her blouse off, undid the bra, and Petunia's forty-four triple Es spilled out. Her nipples stayed firm, and she was starting to give in to the overture.

"I wish you were like this all the time, honey. I can't stand it when you notice other women. I hate it so much. I want to be the best for you, Marty. . . ."

Roscoe played with her nipples. He flicked them with his tongue. Kneaded the heavy flesh. There was plenty there for both hands. More than enough.

"You are, babe. You're the best. Even if you are nutty sometimes. . . ."

"Promise me you'll stay away from that creep and his 'church' and his tramps in there."

"You got it, Pet. They just don't make them like you no more. None of those sluts could touch you."

"You mean that, Marty?" She wanted to meet his eyes. Marty Roscoe looked right at her.

"I do mean it, babe."

He buried his face between the huge mounds of pale flesh in his hands.

# CHAPTER 245

**The SUNSHINE SHOESHINE sign sat atop the roof of the cinder block hovel at the corner of Chandler and Lankershim.**

It was ninety-two degrees in the shade, and if not for the awning Harold Crust had fashioned by securing either corner of his tarp to the roof itself, while having secured the opposite corners to a couple of extended push broom handles that he had positioned at an angle (with the heads) against either wall at the base and braced this way with sandbags, so that the makeshift canopy provided enough protection from the blazing Valley sun, the heat would have been far more difficult to bear up under.

Mr. Crust's place of business was just about large enough for a mini fridge, tools of the trade, portable fan, radio, and two customer's chairs, in one of which he whiled away the time by gazing at the latest *Sports Illustrated, Special Summer Bikini Edition.*

Lightnin' Hopkins' *"You better watch yourself"* played softly in the background. One of his favorites. Blues made life's ups and downs easier to take usually. Another thing that mattered just as much, if not more so, were the regulars, one of whom drove past in his shiny *Mercedes.* Honked his horn. A Universal executive on his way to the studio. Harold glanced up. Waved back with a ready smile. What the *Sunshine Shoeshine* stand was about: being positive, no matter what. The only way to be. What kept folks coming back. Only thing was you had to stay cheerful somehow through the dry spells. Everybody had them. Even movie studios. Speak of studios, someone else connected to them in a much lesser way than the studio man, was Marty Roscoe.

Dude rolled up on his weighted down bicycle with the fat tires and wire baskets in back and the one large in the front, all of them crammed with old style, out-of-date black phones with rotary dialers, used record albums, figurines of *Bugs Bunny* and *Minnie Mouse*, and other doodads and knick-knacks he'd picked up that day at various garage and yard sales throughout North Hollywood. That wasn't all: his neighbor had a box of *Fruit Loops* stuck in there among the junk in the front.

Seems Roscoe never went anywhere without them *Fruit Loops*. Harold didn't get it/couldn't understand it. How can a grown man eat so much of that crap? Didn't he know this kind of cereal with its strong sugar content was bad news? All that sugar could fuck his heart up. Ain't nobody hipped him to it?

Then you had them clothes he had on: bright enough to blind a blind man—even on a hot mother of a day like today was: canary yellow sweat suit that matched his yellow eyes. What usually made Harold uncomfortable about Roscoe: them yellow cat peepers that did nothing but remind him of Delonzo, his wife Fay's disagreeable cat and how much he despised the tom.

To go with the bright yellow sweatpants and sweatshirt, or maybe not to go with them, depended how you looked at it, was a red kerchief with white polka dots tied round his neck and a red ball cap that sat half-cocked up there on his head the way that tee-vee character Johnny Yuma liked to wear. There it was: crud-covered and sweat-stained and had embroidered letters across the front that spelled out something only someone like Marty Roscoe could find remotely amusing:

### WHO FARTED?

Harold almost laughed at the stupidity of it. A grown man with something like that on his head. The shoeshine man watched as Petunia's husband lifted that sorry excuse for a hat and wiped his face and neck with that red kerchief with the white polka dots; wiped at the sweat that rolled down.

There was something else that Harold never failed to notice: Roscoe's collar-length hair was brown, except where it had blond streaks in it. Hilights, they called them. Roscoe had told him how he did it once, a while back: dipped his thumb and index finger into a bottle of peroxide and ran them down his hair, at intervals. Let the sun do the rest. Gave him that Malibu surfer look. Never mind that the Arkansas native never cared for sand and feared the ocean. Said Latinas liked the streaks. "Negro" chicks, too. Said it was a horndog's duty to resort to any and all tricks at his disposal to reel in poon.

Couldn't get enough "strange." What Roscoe liked to call pussy he got on the side: *Strange.* So long as Petunia didn't get wind of it. It wasn't that Harold was judging, far from it, it's just that he wondered if Roscoe would ever mature in time before his marriage fell apart.

Harold knew better than to say anything about it. Kept his notions to himself. Watched Roscoe wipe the sweatband inside his cap and wipe additional sweat and smog crud from his brow.

He wound the kerchief round his neck, tied the ends, and went about brushing his hair back from the sides of his face with the free hand—in a manly manner, always, making certain it was fluffed in back, as opposed to flat against his neck, and had the cap back on his full head of hair, half-cocked as before.

Harold knew the score. Used to have that same attitude himself once. Thought he was the cock of the hen house. Petunia's husband, no doubt, felt certain the women of the world found this not only attractive, but irresistible. Wanted no one but him, and those who didn't only *thought* they didn't.

# CHAPTER 246

**Harold lowered his reading material, and was not entirely aware that he was rubbing the tips of his fingers up along the vertical scar at about the center of his chest, then running his fingers down the scar left there by the surgery.**

His fingers wandered to the left of his heart, feeling the mound 'neath the skin, a mound about the size of a man's watch, his pacemaker. The tips of his fingers lingered there, as they often did, while Harold wondered if and when the battery would run out of juice. Batteries in these things lasted anywhere from five to eight years, supposedly. He wasn't certain. What he had been told. He had also been told to have the generator checked every three months, at least. His next visit to the cardiologist was due in one month.

Just as he became aware that he was doing the thing with the fingertips, he stopped doing it. Didn't like thinking about the pacemaker, thinking and worrying and wondering if and when the damn battery would run down on him without warning—and he'd have to either recharge it or replace it.

The experts said not to worry; the experts. Easy for them to say. He'd be fine. Like the year before when he'd had the heart surgery. He'd be like new, they'd said. Sure. But then "complications set in." "Should have a pacemaker put in, to be on the safe side. Got an irregular heartbeat."

What happens when booze and toot come into play. Living the good life. You paid. He was paying now. The thing with the fingers was part of it—and he didn't know how to stop himself from doing it, either, after four months of it. And now Marty Roscoe had to stop by and probably bug him about Cecil O. Biggs and his lap dog Marvin Muck. The white dude couldn't quit about Biggs. Roscoe and them fake blond streaks in his hair like some California beach bum. Never mind he couldn't tell a surf from a Smurf; couldn't tell a surfboard from the kind you ironed your clothes on. World was a funny place.

Harold reached in his mini fridge for a couple of cans of diet soda.

Handed one to Roscoe. Roscoe cracked the top and had a long pull. Made a face.

"This is some *foul-tasting toe juice*, Harold."

"You're welcome."

"Don't mean to be rude, and I thank you kindly, but this crap causes cancer in lab mice."

"My doc recommends it."

"No disrespect meant, but doctors don't know *zilch* now days. Half of them are quacks. Get their medical trainin' in some *third world burrito nation*. I don't ever eat anything that says *fat-free*, don't drink nothin' that says *"diet"* on it. That's just me. Or *lite beer*. Gotta be the worst. A waste."

"They don't want me drinking regular sodas. Seems I'm at their mercy."

Roscoe nodded. Had a longer pull this time that finished off the can. Handed the empty back to Harold. Belched loud and long. Sounded like a fog horn to the shoeshine man. It takes all kinds, thought Harold.

"See what I mean? What diet pop does."

Roscoe dug the box of *Fruit Loops* out. Offered to let Harold have a few. Crust declined with a wave. Couldn't be interested.

Roscoe shook out a mound of the breakfast cereal into his right palm and shoved the lot in his mouth.

"How's the *ticker*? How's the shoeshine business?"

"Ticker's tickin'. So far. Business could be better. Good to be above ground, though. I'm grateful for that. Fay's always reminding me of it, too. And she's right. Slow time of the month; that's all it is. You get used to it—and roll with the flow. If you're looking for work I can let you use this other chair for a reasonable fee—"

"No, nothing like that." Roscoe stuck the box of *Fruit Loops* back in the basket. "I wouldn't be caught dead shining shoes, Harold. No offense. Got my hands full with garage sales, swap meets. I do okay."

"Up to you. Jesus Ortiz been asking about it, showed interest. Just might let him rent it. Gotta have a job to keep his parole officer off his ass."

"Jesus Ortiz? You mean *Ace? Junkie who shits his pants?* All you're gonna draw is *flies* with him."

"Maybe so. I hope not, anyway."

Harold looked at all the useless knick-knacks the guy had in the large wire basket attached to the handlebar, and then at the baskets hanging from either side of the rear wheel.

"You actually make money buying that kind of crap at garage sales and then selling it again to people at swap meets? Hard to believe."

"Not to 'people'. Not stuff like the rotary phones. To the studios. Art directors need props all the time. Pay a pretty penny, too."

"For old phones like that?"

"Hell, yes—if they're doing a period picture. You better believe it. Old phones, soda machines, blenders, radios, clocks, hair dryers, watches; whatever you can get. All you gotta do is wait; there will be a call for it eventually. Only problem is storage. Garage is packed to the roof. Had to rent storage space recently to keep it all. Got stuff in the house, too. Petunia's not happy about it. Except when the studios call and pay for what they need, if I got it—and I make them pay. You betcha."

Harold still couldn't quite understand that what the man did to make a buck was hardly worth the trouble.

"Been doing it for years. Beats punching a clock, bein' on the road. Thing is, you gotta be patient when it's slow; gotta know how to weather the slow times, when tee-vee programs is on hiatus, when none of the studios are doing any period shows." Marty Roscoe was anxious to change the subject. "Listen, Harold: the hell's going on with Biggs?"

"You don't want to talk about him again? Dude's gotta be bad news, Marty."

"My wife could be right, Harold, about something funny going on in there. It's that goddamn smell lately—like hair or something burning. I don't know—"

"You smelt it, too? My old lady brought it up the other night. Foul, ain't it?"

"Petunia says it smells like *burnin' flesh.*"

"*Flesh?* Now you starting to sound like Lloyd Dicker and that grandson of his. What's his name? Wilford? Wilmer?"

"Wacky Wilburn Flinger. "

"That's the one: Wilburn Flinger. Got purple lips from suckin' on them Popsicles all the time; Popsicles and pomegranates, or he's suckin' them raw eggs he lugs in that old mail bag. Kid is always sayin' shit, makin' up shit about people that don't add up. He ain't right in the head, Marty, is what I'm gettin' at."

"I don't know. Smells like flesh. It's the most godawful odor. . . . I knocked on Biggs's door the other day, had to get the old lady off my back; knocked on his door to talk to him about all the noise—"

"Bet he didn't come to answer it. See the sign on his fence? *No visitors, agents, peddlers, or salespeople—admittance by appointment only.* What kind of welcome sign is that for a church to have on its front gate?"

"The way I see it the only way we'll find out anything is to go inside and take a look."

"*You* can go *'inside.'* If you can get past that locked gate and odor. Me? I'm too old for that shit. I don't have to tell you." Harold indicated the lump in his chest, more out of habit than anything else. "I don't need no kind of excitement in my life these days. My pump couldn't take it."

Roscoe nodded.

"Petunia's been calling the cops. Called them a few times myself. Hell, you know all this. Asshole plays that music *24/7.* And he don't never play nothin' I like, neither. I ain't got nothin' against Jackie Wilson and them. Prefer Charley Pride, though. He don't never play no Pride; don't never play no George Jones or Tammy Wynette; don't never play no Flatt and Scruggs. Good bluegrass would sure pick up my spirits some. Take my mind off my finances. I ain't exactly religious. Don't mind gospel now and then. But, sweet Jesus, *not all day and all night.* When he plays it. Or he plays *Barry White.* Deep fuckin' baritone rattles my doors and windows."

"Ain't no different on our side. Makes Delonzo nervous enough so that he goes right on the carpet. Goes to the bathroom right on the living room carpet."

"You know what I'm saying. We call to complain and guess what happens? Nothing gets done about it." Roscoe paused to wipe his brow with the damp kerchief. Sweat poured on down. Valley heat spared no one. Once Roscoe was through with what he had to do to battle the sweat attack, he looked at the shoeshine man.

"Something peculiar is going on in that *'church,'* Harold. I'd bet my last *Mickey Mouse* watch on it."

"You wouldn't want to do that. Some art director might want one to put in a movie." When Harold saw that the half-hearted joke laid an egg, he apologized.

"It's like this, Marty: I mind my own business these days. Live the quiet life. The way I like it." He turned his head briefly to wave to a passing motorcycle cop, then redirected his attention to Marty Roscoe. "I remember when Biggs married that young Filipino woman, the one run off on him finally? They was fighting like cats and dogs, out in public, too. Me and my missus kept our nose out of it. That's the best way. Don't need the excitement, like I said. And then when he had the church really goin' strong, lettin' all that riffraff come in off the street: car thieves, hopheads, runaways, porn hoes hooked on crack. All them crazy people looked like the Manson Family reunion. Well, they made noise, carried on. Me and my wife Fay stayed out of it. Best way. Oh, Fay *dropped a dime* on him from time to time only 'cause it got too loud for her to be able to hear the tee-vee preachers. For the most part, we kept our nose out of it. Ain't got no use for trouble in my condition."

"Yeah. Only your wife don't stay on your ass like Petunia. If it ain't the noise she's bitching about, it's the stench; if it ain't that it's the sluts in their 'short skirts'; and if it ain't *that*, it's something else about Biggs himself and that strange buck he runs with."

"Sounds domestic from where I'm sittin'."

"What do we do about Biggs?"

"Me—I keep away from him. Mind my own business."

"Sure seen some big titters go in that 'church' lately. Gotta be some mighty interesting preaching going on in that house these days."

"You talking about Peaches LaBelle—"

"Her and some others. She takes her clothes off for a living, the hell would she be doing in his church?"

"Prayin', what else? What a church is for, ain't it? Where you go to be at one with the Lord."

"She's prayin' all right: On her knees. Peckerwood's got the bank account."

"Peckerwood? Take my advice, Marty: that's one *'Peckerwood'* you don't want to be messin' with. Man got that look to him like there ain't nothin' living inside of him, like even if there was at one time it died a long time ago—like maybe he's dead inside. I know he's breathing, walking and shit; talking. His eyes blink, seem to. He looks and appears human. There's something cold-blooded about that dude. . . . Manson's like that. . . ."

Marty Roscoe nodded. "I get chills every time I look at the creep. It ain't that I'm afraid of him, because I ain't. I can take care of myself. I ain't exactly a wimp—but you're right about them psycho eyes."

"Stay away from Cecil O. Tell your woman to do the same. If he got the *cash* to pay for all that *gash* and all them young hoes to do their number for him that's his business. If I was twenty years younger and single and had his bank account, shit, I'd probably be doing the same thing. Come to think of it, did have me a taste of life in the fast lane. What caused the ticker trouble. What the hell. You go around one time."

"I suppose you're right." Roscoe re-joined as an afterthought: "Petunia was wondering if Fay might go inside and take a look."

"Inside where?"

"Preacher's place."

"After what I just said? Come on, Marty. Gimme a break."

"She's been after me to talk to you. I don't want a divorce on my hands. I know she's emotionally unstable. I also know that she's got good qualities that a lot of people don't see, maybe don't want to see. She just got promoted to assistant manager at the supermarket where she works. This would get her off my back; if Fay could go in there and talk to the man, look around."

Harold Crust was shaking his head. "There's a saying I like a lot, Marty. Goes something like this: Leave well enough alone."

"What about the stench and the screaming at all hours of the night?"

"Don't know. Could be *sounds* like screams—could be music—"

"Your wife's religious, ain't she? Man's a pastor. Got a lot in common right there."

"Ever seen James Brown scream?"

"Sure. He screams."

"Could be what you heard; what all of us been hearin'."

"It ain't me—it's the old lady. I went over there. Tried to get in, tried to join. I don't get along with the man. He knows I got no respect for him. Claims our dogs chewed up his cat. When I tried to join up he tells me they're full up, ain't taking no new members. What a crock. A Lhasa apso and a Boston terrier ain't tough enough to kill no alley cat. It's just an excuse he uses to keep me out."

"I wouldn't know. Ain't seen a sign of the Ripper since my operation— or of that dog he had. Could be your answer to the odor problem. Got 'em layin' around somewhere. Never bothered to bury 'em. Heard of stranger things."

"No disrespect meant, Harold, I think what it comes down to I ain't got the right *paint job* to set foot inside."

"You sayin' you got to be black?"

"Muck's colored, ain't he? So's Peaches LaBelle. Probably Biggs got some negro blood, else why would he be runnin' with all them colored and showin' off that *Cadillac* all the time?"

"Maan, I don't get you."

"Ain't nothing *to get*, really. Me and my wife, we ain't prejudiced. Just figured it would be easier for you and Fay to talk to Biggs and them."

Harold Crust looked at the other man. Ran a handkerchief across his forehead and neck. He blew his nose. Wiped back and forth a couple of times, and jammed the handkerchief into his hip pocket.

"I suppose somebody should find out what's going on over there in that man's place. Somebody's got to put an end to all that racket; put a stop to

Marvin playin' with firecrackers. Them firecrackers can burn a place down, easy. Don't even want to think about it."

"Firecrackers?"

"Sounds like it."

"Either that, or they're shooting off guns."

"Might be. Can't say. Whatever it is, it can't go on."

"Thanks, Harold. I'm beholden."

"Before you take off, let me ask you somethin' about somethin' else."

"What else?"

"Now, I know you like your beer—but how in hell you get them big arms eatin' *Fruit Loops* all the time?"

"Why do you ask?"

"Don't mean to pry. If you'd rather not say, that's fine. Your business. Only reason I ask is because I used to have me some powerful legs, strong legs; shoulders, too. Was strong up in here. Was tellin' Fay the other day. Then, all of a sudden, seems it happened overnight: my weight an' all that muscle seemed to shift down to my belly. All my damned weight settled in my midsection. I thought you might have a suggestion or two as to how I might build up my shoulders some. Could be hopeless. Since my surgery an' my age. All that fast livin'."

"I take little blue pills."

"Little blue pills?"

"Little blue pills. *D-Balls*. It ain't the *Fruit Loops*; it's the pills. If you want, I can get you some. Know stuntmen who use them to build themselves up. Take some hard falls. The only way they can keep from ending up in a wheelchair, crippled."

"No, thanks, Marty. My doctor would kill me if he found out."

"If you change your mind, let me know."

Marty was back in the saddle.

As Petunia Roscoe's husband wobbled off on his heavily weighted down bicycle, the shoeshine man noticed a paperback entitled *The Coming Race War In America* sticking out of his back pocket.

If he ain't racist, and I ain't sayin' he necessarily is, thought Harold, what's he doing carrying that kind of reading material around? Why would any decent man be interested in that kind of *vile shit?*

# CHAPTER 247

**That same day, in a basement several miles south of the shoeshine stand, Cecil Omar Biggs was pursuing his favorite pastime.** He was somewhat amazed that Stella Martel had lasted as long and as well as she had with such a badly wounded leg and hole in her back from the meat hook.

Biggs had his gear on: Parfrey pig mask, with goggles over the eyes. Yellow slicker. Heavily stained and soiled bib apron over that. Leather work gloves on his hands, knee-high rubber boots on his feet. Durable. Warehouse type for manual labor. Certainly suitable for the task ahead.

He was in the Fun Room with Marvin, while the readily-willing and available Pinko Punisher was assigned to stand outside the door and wait to be alerted to employ the hose that they had connected to the spout out there by the pit as needed. The shower head that was part of the old style tub functioned well enough, to be sure, Biggs supposed. However, as a precautionary measure, it was decided that it would not be used in this case. There was that risk that it might get in Trusty's way and hamper his concentration and detract from the way he liked to conduct a demanding scenario such as this one was—especially when a *Black & Decker* was involved.

Stella had been secured to the specialized copper bathtub: arms hanging over either rim and fastened at the wrist to the tub's claw feet with nylon rope restraints; her legs, at the other end, bent at the knee, hung over either side and were tied at the ankle with the same type of rope to the tub's other feet, so that her body hung over the bathtub in a particular way: not entirely taut, but taut enough: swaying, but nowhere near the bottom.

Pearleen Bell was also in the room. Cecil wouldn't have wanted her to miss out on any of it. He'd had her secured to the torture board that hung from the wall to the left of the metal cabinet: wrists at either end at the top, ankles at either corner at the bottom. He hadn't bothered to gag her this time. *Let's see how she takes it.*

# CHAPTER 248

**Biggs gave each *Stanley* glove a tug in turn, and held out for the *Black & Decker*.** Marvin handed the chainsaw to him. Noticed Bishop's eyes was already fillin' up wiff blood, turnin' a *deep red*. They gonna be *glowin'* pretty soon, too, like two *round chunk'* of *hot coal'* right in his skull. It was times like this the mothafuckah give him chills. *No shit.* Up and down his spine.

Bishop yanked on the starter handle with his left hand, while the index finger of his right hand applied pressure to the accelerator control. Gray exhaust billowed. He watched the blade spin, the noise music to his ears. He only wished Stella hadn't been so out of it. She might not be able to feel enough pain at this stage, might not twist and jerk around and put on a good enough show if she were as weak as she appeared. This was a concern.

"Get some water on her face."

Bishop adjusted the snout and goggles. Slightly off initially; both were. Marvin opened the door to let the Commie scumbag in and ordered him to spray the ho on the face. The in denial, slobbering *Pinko a-hole* was way too eager to oblige, as far as Marvin was concerned. Waited for him a minute or so, saw that the ho got her enough water to nearly drown, then told the Russian, or wherever the fuck he was from, to get back out there— and not to come back until he was called.

"Of course, Tovarich," said Ionesco.

"You call me that again, *mothafuckah,* and I'll kick you so hard in yo nutsack your cracked balls gonna pop right outta yo America-hatin' mouth."

Muck readily slammed the door shut in the red creepo's face as he exited the room. The naked victim's eyes were open now and they were looking up at her masked executioner with the wide tongue dangling from between crud-encrusted fangs and crimson eyes that glowed from inside the scuffed lenses of his goggles.

"Don't . . ."

"What was that?"

Her head moved. She was trying to say she did not want to go bye-bye. Hell, they all went through it. Pretty much said the same thing.

"How about a little more life? Put a little zip into it. Come on, Stella. You can do it."

"Please help me. . . . Daddy. . . ." Her eyes closed. She seemed to go out. Giving up. Resigned to it.

*"WAKE UP, BITCH.* Come on. Wake up. More water. *MORE WATER, I SAID.* My erection's going down again. The cunt refuses to stay awake long enough."

"Yeah? Yo eyes be red; that means yo dick should be up, don't it?"

Biggs did a double-take: *You're talking shit at a time like this?*

Ionesco was permitted to rush back in with the hose and spray her considerably. Then Muck told him to get his fat ass back out there again.

"Give her a whiff of the smelling salts."

Marvin waved his hands. Didn't have it on him. Biggs took his right hand off the handle, pulled his glove off and reached inside the apron pouch. He uncapped the tube. Passed it under the victim's nose. She showed some life. That's it, Biggs thought. Got his glove back on. Gripped the chainsaw handle.

"I didn't want to have to kill you this soon. What choice did I have? What was I supposed to do? I can't let a quack come in here." Biggs looked at Marvin, who was fiddling with the *Polaroid* camera. "You taking pictures of this? I better at least get one great one worth framing. I want some good shots for the collection. This is what we base the exhibits at the Bordello on, the real McCoy."

"Why you tellin' me? I know, man."

"Because your composition is always off, that's why. You don't have a good eye; never did. You like to act like you're fucking *Fellini*, but you haven't got a clue. That's why."

"Hey, man, how about if you mention just once somethin' Marvin Muck be good at, Hoss? Like to talk about *me* bein' negative."

Biggs ignored him. "I'd like to be able to relive this later on. Should be able to get some good ones."

"See me tryin'," said Marvin. "Can't do mo' better than that." And did as instructed. Clicked off *Polaroids* of the action from various angles. He didn't much care for what was going on at this point, but did what he had to do. It was a waste of good trim, that's all. Ho be put on ice so *Parfrey* could get his dick up. Dude always be havin' trouble wiff his dick that way. Gotta see blood; gotta cut 'em up. Me, I ain't never had me that kinda problem. Wiff me it be the other way 'round. Can't keep my mofo dick down, no matter what. That be the thang I be good at right there. Only a dude like that ain't never gonna say it. Jealous, is what. Sho nuff. Fuck him; fuck 'em all. Everybody.

# CHAPTER 249

**Stella Martel was in and out of it, even after having been exposed to the smelling salts.** It was a bitch. The bitch was being—what else? A bitch.

Cecil eyed Pearleen from time to time, wanting to determine how she was handling it. If she freaked, and started sobbing, like the time Lana's ass got chewed up by the rat, then perhaps there was no hope for her—

and there never would be.

If they couldn't take what he was about, couldn't relate—or refused to understand . . . they weren't worth keeping around any longer than the rest of those worthless cunts.

Well, she looked on. Wasn't turning away, like she did before. There was moisture around the eyes. Couldn't tell what it meant exactly. Peering out through the eyeholes in the mask itself, and then the goggle lenses made it difficult to determine if it was perspiration . . . or something like tears.

She went out from time to time. Faded in and out, not unlike Stella. Although, for the most part, Pearly Girlie Pearleen seemed to show promise. She was handling it so far. Bearing up. Showed promise. Wait until we get into the thick of things here, thought Biggs. Wait until the plasma begins to spray.

On the other hand, the McVictim was not doing as well. Can't let the *hen-pecker* short-change me this way.

He lowered the blade against Stella's right thigh, above the knee. Pushed it in. Blood appeared. More pressure was added. Stella showed life. Not much. There were signs. The will to live making a comeback, Biggs noted. *Yeah. Good.*

See what happens when they're at your mercy? See how they behave? Spineless cunt. All the same. *Dog shit.* Look at her.

Had nerve to go prowling around in his cribby, his sanctuary. Bad-mouthed him behind his back every chance she got. Schemer. No different from Agenda Marie. Users. Abusers.

"Come on, ballbuster. I hate your guts. Hate every one of you fucking pole crawlers. Die, cunt."

The blade cut through flesh and bone. The leg dropped off, landing in the puddle of fresh as well as not-so-fresh blood. Stella shook her head. Screaming now.

"Go ahead. Scream your head off. Scream the way I screamed when I was being beaten by the bitch and her hick for wetting the bed. Day after day, week after week. *Scream the way they made me scream.*"

He stood, waited, watched. Take it for all it's worth. They put out, all of them—as long as the price was right, just like Charlotte Yvonne. Little nothing whores. Scum-sucking bimbos.

The screams subsided to whimpers. . . . Biggs ran the blade up and down her belly vertically. Watched all that precious bright red gush out. He placed the blade against the other thigh, same way, above the knee. He sliced through bone. Witnessed more flailing, frothy blood gushing from her mouth, then she went out with a final roar. Too bad.

Ordinarily the blood would have been more abundant. You had to take into account what she lost in the tunnel, and then the cooler, hanging on the hook.

He glanced at the high yellow. Pearleen had fainted. Couldn't take it after all. Weak. Ballbuster was weak. Hanging there on the board like a limp human sack of flesh. *What the fuck?*

# CHAPTER 250

**Biggs stopped the chainsaw.** Yanked the goggles off, then the Parfrey pig mask, Stanley gloves, and reached for his chalice. He dipped the chalice into the blood. Drank it down. Ionesco, who had been pacing impatiently outside the door with his jaw hanging and mouth salivating, had been allowed to enter by the bishop, as well as granted permission to stick around as compensation for helping out.

"Get your own." It was directed at the Commie, as well as Cecil's primary water carrier. The Rumanian did not need to be reminded a second time. Grabbed a Styrofoam cup. In fact, dipped it *twice*. Liked it. Smacked his lips.

"America good?"

*"Ja ja, sir. America very good."*

The deacon passed. Was busy spreading *Polaroids* on a small, flimsy metal folding table.

"I'm watching you, Base. I got my bloodshot eyes on you, Sam the Sham."

"Got me a bellyache all of the sudden. Some other time."

"You're either in, or you're out, 'Free Base.' Get me? No in-between."

"Man, all I ever be wantin' was *vagina*. I ain't no *vampire*. Bloodsuckin' be for vampire'."

Biggs looked at him. There was absolute silence in the room.

"You step on your dick now, my black American friend."

The Rumanian was shaking his head. Biggs's eyes were on the Rumanian, and his gaze shifted back on Marvin.

"Are you calling me *Dracula*, punk?"

"Didn't mean it like that, Omar. I mean Cecil. Keep forgettin' you don't like for nobody to call you Omar. I remember that. Said your old daddy give ya that fuckin' name on purpose. He be the one hatin' yo gut' before you was ever born. What you said, Cecil. Kicked yo mamma in her belly so the ho could miscarry. What you said. Remember?"

"You called me a *vampire*."

"Tol' me so yo'self yo' daddy expected he wasn't even yo' real daddy— an' that be why he was kickin' yo mamma in her belly, and then give ya one of them *A-rab* name' when you was born."

"You have no idea how nasty kids can be when you have a name like Omar." The intimidating black eyes stared at Muck, but his head was somewhere else. Images of his childhood flashed in his mind, images of being mocked by the other kids for being different and "weird," mocked for the dented forehead and for having a strange and fucked-up family: street whore for a mother, a dogcatcher stepfather who beat dogs he caught, and for having a sissy name like "Cecil Omar."

"He couldn't have picked a worse name to give me. *Goddamned Cecil Omar. . . .*"

"He don't be right, to give somebody that name."

"On the other hand, it could have been worse: It could have been

*Marvin Ritalin Muck.* How do you name someone after a drug used to treat depression and hypersensitivity?"

"Have to *aks my mama.* Only—"

Biggs finished it for him: "Ho be dead." As an afterthought, or something like it, added: "That's all right. Cecil suits me just fine these days. Cecil O. Biggs. It's mine."

Indicated to Marvin to get himself a cup. Muck did not have to be told "*twiced*" this time. Scooped up half a cup of blood. Shut his eyes tight, and drank it down. He felt an immediate urge to throw up. Fortunately it didn't happen.

"That's better."

# CHAPTER 251

**Biggs got his gear back on: mask and goggles, the gloves.**

*"More water!"* The stripper was brought back to life. She was breathing. Biggs wished this were Marty's wife Petunia before him. What a treat that would have been.

Crimson continued to pour out of the blond. Trusty the Clown, wearing the heavily-stained and flesh-pocked Parfrey hog mask, proceeded to cut her head off at just above the collar bone.

"Turn the music up!"

Marvin threw up instead. Biggs grabbed him by the scruff and dunked his head in the tub, all the way down in there in the blood and muck, and held it like that until Marvin started kicking out with his legs, then shot up, gasping for breath.

The Rumanian was laughing. Biggs would have if he could have. Marvin suspected *he thought* it was funny. Whirled away, raging.

*"Hey, fuck you, Cecil! Get me? FUCK YOU, MAN! WE AIN'T PARTNER' NO MORE! NOT LIKE THIS! GOIN' BACK TO THE*

*HOOD! I DON'T NEED THIS SHIT! I WAS COOL ON MY OWN! I AIN'T NO GODDAMN VAMPIRE, CECIL! I'M A PIMP, ME! MY NAME DON'T BE DRACULA! YOU WANTS TO DRINK BLOOD? NO PROBLEM! ONLY LEAVE ME THE FUCK OUT!"*

"Ungrateful. Don't you think, Bishop Biggs?"

"Nah. Just a little pissed. Eh, Deacon? Craves it as much as I do. Only I'm honest about it."

"Marvin should be honest with Marvin."

*"Keep yo mouth shut, Commie Dawg. You ain't even prob'ly got yo green card and you be tryin' to tell everybody what to do. We don't need that in America, greasy-ass punk."*

"How you know I don't have green card? Maybe I got green card and you don't know, *'Dawg.'* My business, don't you think? Truth be, you got weak stomach. Bishop should make *me* deacon. I help pick up big Eastern European woman all the time. I take you to Mediterranean restaurant in San Fernando Valley, Bishop Biggs."

*"SHUT YO MOUF, NAZI MOTHAFUCKAH!"*

"Maybe even down to Fairfax Avenue. Down there plenty of European place' to eat, West Los Angeles; we go all over. This black boy not very intelligent."

Marvin had hosed the blood off his face. Turned the hose on the Rumanian. Moved in. Whipped the hose against his face and kept whipping him until gouts of blood appeared in his mouth and Ionesco reeled against the wall, slipped, and went down.

Biggs scooped up limbs and other body parts and viscera and dropped them into a galvanized bucket. Got out of his gear and clothes, reached for the chalice and stepped into the tub. Lowered his body until he was sitting in it. He enjoyed watching Free Ride kick the living daylights out of the foreigner.

"Let me drown in it."

Biggs dipped the chalice in. Raised it over his head and let the red pour down, and followed this procedure with two more helpings, pouring blood all over his face as he tilted his head back, allowing plenty of it to wind its way inside his open mouth, the red matching the red of his eyes.

Marvin kicked Ionesco in the groin. Watched the man twist around in the blood and water on the cement floor and liked it.

*"WHO YOU BE MAKIN' FUN OF NOW, NAZI ASS-HOLE?"*

"I am not *Nazi.* You are not correct, boy. I no *Nazi.* I am Rumanian. My dear wife and I come to America to see Cowboy and Indian."

Marvin stood back. Shook his head incredulously.

"Fulla shit, too. *Punk.* You don't never call me '*boy*' neither. We don't got no boy' in America. What we got is *mens* in America. *Mens.* I be a *man,* me."

The Rumanian was too preoccupied spitting blood to answer. Muck kicked him in the belly, then picked up the hose again and began to whip the man on the floor some more with it—and mistakenly whacked his right knee. Cursing, Marvin dropped the hose and reached down for the pain.

"That's enough, Brother Marvin."

Biggs was calm. Well immersed in his own ritual and wanting to enjoy it to the fullest. His erect penis, not unlike *Nessie*—the Loch Ness monster—rose up through the blood in degrees . . . and he gripped it in his right hand.

# CHAPTER 252

**Marvin was on the floor rubbing his knee.** Ionesco took the opportunity to send a fist into the light-skinned black's crotch and watched his head drop back down against the cement. The Rumanian scooted over, so that he was within spitting distance, and spit in the deacon's face, then sent a hard fist into his jaw. He followed that up with another to Muck's nose and fell back, his fist aching.

Muck sat up. Managed it. Wiped at the mucous and blood with the back of his sleeve. Both men were too exhausted to do anything else just then.

"Leave." Biggs meant it. Had his eyes closed. "I want to be *alone*. . . ."

The Rumanian crawled away in the direction of the door, with Marvin doing the same.

"*I could leave, me.* Keep right on goin'. Leave this plantation for good. Don't be no future here for this nigga."

"You'll leave all right. Feet first. . . ."

"Feet first?"

Marvin paused. Turned his head.

"You know too much."

"I know too much? You the one be all the time sayin' I know shit about nothin'."

"You'd never make it out there, Free Ride. Don't act like this is news to you."

"Could find me a rich ol' ho. All it take'. Down in Beverly Hill'. One of them old bitches don't nobody want' 'cause she had too many face lift'; got her face all messed up. Me? I don't mind. Give her the black mamba, the big black dick—'cause that be all they want. They be wantin' it and can't get it. Yo. Them Hollywood faggot' don't like fuckin' them over-the-hill ho. Them big shot studio mothafuckahs be busy payin' outcall hoe' to do the golden shower on 'em. Some of them rich dude' be akskin' the hoe to shit on 'em, too—for big bread. I know that scene; ain't nothin' new there. Why there be so many unhappy over-the-hill old bitches in Bel Air and Beverly Hill' and Malibu."

"And you're going to solve everyone's problems with a big dick? Is that it?"

"What I said."

"Close the door on your way out."

Marvin crawled out of the room and kicked the door shut behind him.

Sure thing, he thought. "And fuck you, too, *Omar*. Fuckin' Omar gotta have his way. Like I ain't suppose' to want nothin', like I ain't got my own need', too. Makin' me drink blood like Dracula. Always be talkin' 'bout: *Don't cross me. It be about trust. Trust be everything.* Meantime, *Trusty* be the one you *can't trust.* I don't drink blood. Don't need it, me. Base don't be needin' it. Ain't my style. Iceberg never dranked blood; never got into that shit. Neither did Dolemite; Mr. Moore. Man want' to drink blood like a vampire that be his business. I don't be doin' it 'cause I don't like it. Fuck them vampire'."

His belly went tight on him. Grumbled some more. Marvin found himself throwing up again near the pit and could not stop. *Feet first.* Two words. Could not shake the threat anymore than he could stop vomiting. Mothafuckah be always makin' threat'.

"Lord, that hurt'. *Damn, my gut' be fucked up real bad. . . .*"

When the deacon lifted his head he could see that the Rumanian was in the john and had left the door wide open as he urinated standing up. Missed the bowl more often than he should have, spraying the tank and floor.

Marvin was dry heaving at this point. All he wanted was for the pain to go away.

## END OF BOOK ONE

# Interview with Kirk Alex

**How do you write something as graphic and twisted as *LUSTMORD: Anatomy of a Serial Butcher* and live with yourself? How do you sleep at night?**

I'm not making excuses, but this is who they are, how they behave. Take a pit bull pup, mistreat it, beat it—abuse it—and you end up with a killing machine. Why should a human be any different? Granted, the occasional bad seed happens. Have been reading true crime for decades. You pick up knowledge, learn how serial killers operate. I know how the cowardly fuckers think, and what they're about. Bundy, Gacy, Manson—pussies and punks. Prey on victims who can't fight back. Having said that, yes, there were two scenes, well, more than two actually, but two specifically that literally caused me to lose sleep. One in particular, that I won't mention, that during the initial two-and-a-half years it took to write the first draft, I kept taking out and putting back in, taking out and putting back in. It was no easy task, mind you, since the four-hundred thousand-plus word novel was written (primarily) on a typewriter. Taking out the scene made me feel that I was being less-than-honest with what I was dealing with, the material that I was tackling; leaving it in turned my stomach because the scene, in its graphic depiction, and it is graphic, is absolutely abhorrent.

Finally, I said: *Fuck this shit.* Leave it in. I'm leaving the goddamned scene in. Not only that one, but the others as well, because that's the way these assholes (serial killers) are. Very few give a damn about the victim, very few feel any remorse afterwards. It's all about them, getting their rocks off, having their fun—or else it's about filling that void, the hollowness within—that never gets filled; the "wound" never heals; the psychological wounds caused by a brutal childhood are never mended, not by hurting the innocent who never did them any harm, anyway. But they have themselves convinced that killing is the answer, that taking life, crushing, destroying, maiming, torturing, will somehow make them whole. . . It gets convoluted, because you're dealing with psychosis; it ties in: getting their jollies, while at the same time needing to "fill the void." In BTK's case, for instance, I doubt he was needing to fill any void; he was strictly out for kicks, thrills—and in doing so left devastation in his wake. Ruined lives. Every now and then you get one of these guys (even their female counterparts, who do exist, by the way) who feel a degree of remorse and turn themselves in, or commit suicide—but it's rare. It happens, but not very often. In BTK's case, he was heartless, so was Bundy, so was Gacy; Richard Ramirez, the Night Stalker, is another one. Just cold-blooded sociopaths. Selfish and remorseless. I know it's a long answer, but it's also a tough question. Also, you want to keep in mind that the book was begun way back around 1987, and wasn't finished until about 2013. That's how many years? Twenty-five, twenty-six years? Give or take. Long fucking time. On and off. Still a long time to spend on a single book. Because the subject matter is so brutal and psychologically taxing. Somewhere in there was a five year period when I wouldn't go near it. In the mid-90s, I believe. I'd done several drafts by then . . . still felt it needed more work, polish, revision. The characters wouldn't let me be. They had additional things they wanted to do and say. The way it is when the people in your tale are three dimensional: they tell YOU what they want, and not the other way around. I go with the flow when it gets like this. The book leads, and I go along where it wants to take me. In addition to the above, there was a period after that five year hiatus when I could only bear to work on the book four, five, maybe six months out of the year (for about three years)— and that was it. I'd be off working on other things that had nothing to do with killing and mayhem. That shit can pull you down, give you nightmares. Like I said: That's the subject matter, that's the tale. I wanted to do it justice. I refused to whitewash any of it.

## All right. Fine. But why horror?

Why not? I have as much respect for horror as I do any other genre. Horror is just as valid, if not more so. I feel the same way when it comes to horror flicks. To me, the great ones, and they are few and far between, but the best ones like Polanski's *Repulsion*, or *The Tenant*; George Romero's and John Russo's *Night of the Living Dead* (Yes, I'm aware they "borrowed" heavily from Matheson's *Last Man On Earth*, starring the late, great Vincent Price); Fred Walton's (original) *When A Stranger Calls*; Friedkin's *The Exorcist*; the 1974 original *Texas Chain Saw Massacre*; John McNaughton's *Henry: Portrait of a Serial Killer*; William Lustig's (original) *Maniac*, starring the late, amazing Joe Spinnel; I'll even toss Bergman's *Virgin Spring* in there (and I'm no Ingmar Bergman fan, by the way)—are as worthy of praise as any of the great films in the other genres, be they drama, western, comedy, etc. That's part of the reason, the other reason is I'd rather not keep painting the same painting over and over, working in one genre, writing the same type of book each time out. I can remember when I was down, as a young man, broke, living in tiny furnished rooms in LA, on my own, no prospects, no woman in my life—no one to love, or be loved by—and there you are, feeling worthless, no money in the bank, no car, between cab gigs, or some kind of low-wage day gig—but I'd always been able to scrape together enough change to go see a horror flick, because nothing takes you away from your troubles the way a good scare flick can. Nothing. Not for me, anyway. Sure, running helped, but you can't do that night and day; guzzling brew helped—but you can't do that 24/7. It's no good to sit there in the dark playing Billie Holiday records or Janis Joplin or Roy Orbison and sucking down brewskies, because that's a sure way to push yourself over the edge. So, I'd find a movie, preferably a horror flick—to take my mind off my troubles. Mind you, we're talking when I was in my 20s, 30s. But finding a great horror film is not easy—because most of them suck. Hell, most films, most of anything sucks: books, music. Just the way it is.

# ZIGGY POPPER AT LARGE

14 Tales of General Degeneracy, of Mayhem & Debauchery – for
the Morally Conflicted & Borderline Criminal

**Raw** and **loony, filthy** and **funny gutbucket belches** from **Kirk Alex**,
author of the acclaimed and controversial *LUSTMORD: Anatomy of a
Serial Butcher.*

This collection includes tales such as the sexually graphic and outlandishly
violent, *"Ziggy Popper at Large,"* featuring a fresh out of the joint ex-con
sitting in a dive bar in seedy East Hollywood nursing a beer and minding his
own business, when a scrawny a-hole walks in and parks his butt on the stool
next to his and offers him money to shag his wife. Hardboiled and packing a
punch of LA attitude in its gritty realism and black humor, "Ziggy Popper"
shows what can happen when a man's past catches up to him.

The compilation also includes the cab stories *"Don't chu want it?"*
*"Cruising for Action,"* and *"You should have done what I did,"* as well as
the seriously raunchy and absurd noir parodies, starring low-rent, private
eye **"Choo-Choo" Buschitski** in a series of adventures entitled: *"Bone,"*
*"My Kind of Client,"* *"Angel–the Crazy Woman,"* and *"The Case of the
Vengeful Vixen,"* et al.

Praise for *Ziggy Popper at Large* (crime noir single) "★★★★1/2 out of five." –**GoodReads.com**

Praise for *Fifty Shades of Tinsel: Portrait of a Heartthrob:* "This story is a bit dark and to say there is a lot of sex is an understatement. Jimmy's journey is an interesting one. ★★★★ out of five." –**NetGalley.com**

Praise for *nonentity:* "You can digest this book in two hours – it will stay with you forever." –Steven Rosen, **Curled Up With A Good Book**

# ZOOK

## By KIRK ALEX

## Blurb & Novel Excerpt

**Some very strange things are taking place at the New Pueblo Funeral Home . . .**

War vet, Ray Zook, a PTSD afflicted former grunt, is about to regret that he ever set foot in Tucson, Arizona.

All he wants is to gain the courage to face his inner-demons and somehow explain to the widow of his best friend what *really* happened to him during their stint in the military. But when Zook is mugged and takes a temporary job working the night-shift at a crematory run by a couple of unsavory employees, those plans get derailed.

After witnessing a series of disturbing incidents—like the shady "after hours" business taking place—that hurl him into an immoral world of grave robbing, coffin swapping, and even disappearing bodies, Zook finds himself caught in the middle of a twisted power-struggle to control ownership of the funeral home.

If Zook hopes to escape this utter mess with his sanity intact, he must rise above his fears and confront the dark deeds before he ends up back in the looney bin . . . for good this time.

# CHAPTER 1

**I had just gotten off the bus and the two of them followed me: the dim-witted young chick with the dishwater hair and the beastly two-hundred-pound butch dyke with her: all tats and rings and studs and chains.** Lots of black leather. Blue/black crew cut. Demanding money.

"For what?"

"BJ."

The other one was quiet. Just wasn't there mentally. Didn't seem like it mattered to her, either. It was the bitch built like a dozer who was after my cash. I dared her to take it, which hadn't been a wise move at all. She cold-cocked me. By the time she was done I was on the ground, nearly out. She'd flipped me over on my belly and sat on my back. I could hardly breathe, let alone do much of anything else at this point. She'd taken my wallet, extracted the bills, tossed it back at me. Spit in my direction, and they walked off. With close to eighty dollars of my jack. My roll. A good chunk of it. If it hadn't been for the paper money I'd kept stashed inside my sock I'd have been up the creek. I was, but at least with what remained I'd be able to rent a room, buy something to eat, a newspaper, and look for work.

I had been sound asleep, as comfortable as one can possibly be on a Greyhound bus. Been pulling on a bottle of hooch all the way from Phoenix. The idea was to stay on in Tucson long enough to beef up the roll and continue on to Ft. Worth. The ex had family there and I hoped that's where she'd ended up. I didn't have a need to connect with her. It came down to my kid. In her early teens by now. Hadn't seen her in years. I'd been to LaFayette, Indiana; Bowling Green, Kentucky; Lawrence, Kansas, and dozens of other towns, large and small. I stayed on the move; perpetual motion seemed to keep the demons at bay—at least I had myself convinced of it. I had war- related nightmares I couldn't shake, and some other things I was trying to live down. Staying on the move seemed to be the answer. Only how in hell do you get away from yourself? I'd been given the boot by more apartment managers and motel desk clerks for kicking the floor and walls in my sleep than I cared to remember.

It was usually some indiscriminate setting, me unarmed, being chased by the enemy in some far-off land. Commies? Mid-East zealots? Your run-of-the-mill America haters? Who knew? Or maybe I was in denial. Unwilling to face my demons. It took a lot to deal with that shit.

That was where they got on, though: Phoenix. The young one: couldn't tell how old, didn't look half bad in tight jeans, pink blouse, although the heavy one with the butch cut made me want to retch. This was one unappealing broad. And wouldn't you know it, she was the one who dropped her sweaty and mean ass in the seat next to mine. She wanted a hit off my hooch. I told her to piss off. Took the occasional nip from the bottle, pulled the blanket up to about my neck. I had no idea how long I'd be staying in Tucson. Didn't know a soul in town, not really. It was just a place to drive through, or maybe spend a week in, look around. Been in the 'Old Pueblo' before. Worked as a busser at some sports bar some years back, did a bit of panhandling.

What nudged me awake was the two of them switching seats. Now the young one was sitting next to me. Before the fat one gave up her seat, she whispered in my ear: "My cousin gives great head."

"How much?"

"Forty bucks."

I told her to get lost.

They switched seats, and before I knew it, 'cousin' had her hand under my blanket. Inched it slowly toward my crotch and was rubbing it, just running her fingers gently over it, and I'll be damned if my groin didn't begin to stir. All that vino, and there I was: getting wood. She proceeded to unzip my fly. I let her; pretended I was asleep, and let her do what she wanted. I figured if I acted like I was dozing, they wouldn't be able to claim I owed them money later, her and the beast she was with.

She had it out, stroking, slowly, taking her time. Then she ducked her head under the blanket. I let her. Of course, I let her. It had been a while. No love, no sex. Traveling the country on buses, when the money was there, hitching when it wasn't.

She had her tongue on it, licking; then she had the shaft inside, all of it. I didn't have a tremendous whole lot, but it was all right; there were some poor bastards who envied what I did have. You lived with the hand the Dealer laid on you—and this time the Dealer had shown me some kindness, I thought. That head of hers bobbed up and down, not fast, gently, gradually, taking her time. And the fact it was night provided adequate cover. Passengers were zoned out, with the exception of some punk in his teens, across the aisle, watching out of the corner of his eye. Let him. Probably wished he was me, the big shot, getting his nuts off on a Greyhound bus to nowhere.

The licking went on. She played with the head, flicking it thoroughly. This chick had been around, knew her business when it came to licking balls and sucking cock. It had been such a long time, too. Probably did this to get by: sucked off strangers for whatever they could pick up. Who knew? Did it matter? Only I'd had too much wine. Couldn't make it. It was no good. Wine and sex didn't mix, not for me.

She lifted her head. I pulled out my wallet. Extracted a tenner for her effort. She did what she could. Not her fault. Before the young hooker had had a chance to even take a good look at it, the beast, her freakish 'relation,' stuck her hand in and snapped up the sawbuck. She sniffed it. Looked it over. She was not pleased. Tough, I thought. That was a ten dollar try.

"My name is not Bill Gates and I don't own *Microsoft*. Besides, I never got off."

"You're lying." She yanked her 'cousin' out of the seat, and lowered that wide posterior next to me.

"We agreed on forty."

"Like hell we did."

"That was a forty dollar BJ. You never had anything that good in your life."

"How would you know? Maybe I had better." For a fact. Only my ex-wives wanted nothing to do with me, especially the last one. I had no idea where she was. Ft. Worth was nothing more than a guess, a vague one, like all the other towns I'd been to. She'd taken the kid and disappeared off the face of the earth. Could explain the roaming. If I admitted it to myself. I didn't need the exes back, only ached to see the kid. A girl. Must have been six years ago I saw her last. I didn't blame the wife for leaving me. Couldn't take the screaming in the middle of the night, the kicking at the floor with my feet, the times I was stationed out of the country, or stuck in some bug bin here in the states. I drank to fight the demons. Only made everything worse. They had me on *Prozak*, then *Paxil*, at the VA. While I was in the whack ward the wife dropped the bomb: wanted out. I couldn't stop her, didn't try. She never mentioned custody, only because she figured she was entitled. She'd given birth to the child and that was that. Frankly, I was in no shape to take care of a kid, couldn't even take care of myself. I let it go; let them both go. The ex had a man, in fact, had been shagging a neighbor while I was stationed overseas. The way it usually went. I'd had it done to me once before. Kid could be his, biologically. Probably. Don't matter. I treated her like she was my own. You get emotionally attached. Kids are all right. Always wanted a family. Always did. Things kept going wrong somehow. Something would always happen to turn things upside down. This was divorce number three. You know what they say: three strikes and you're out. Three marriages, three divorces. I was defective, a loser. Something was seriously the matter with me. It was the war; it was other things.


"I doubt it." She looked at me. "Not with that nose and those teeth." My nose was bent, both ways, in bar brawls that I usually started and lost, so were my teeth—born with them that way—the ones still there: black, yellow. Of the uppers in front, I had but one left. In the middle.

I pulled the blanket up, and pretended to go to sleep. Only she wouldn't let me.

"Thirty bucks. You can't deny that was worth thirty bucks."

"You got what it was worth. And that's the end of it. I never got rocks. You bitches came on to me. Before I knew what was going on, your nympho girlfriend was molesting my privates."

"You owe us money."

"Fuck off, or I go to the driver."

"He's our friend. That wouldn't get you anywhere."

"What does *he* pay for it?"

"That's a different case. He gets a discount—and has nothing to do with you."

"I feel drained for some strange reason and crave rest." And this time I shut my eyes and kept them shut. I could feel them switch seats again. As she got up, I turned my head, and caught her cousin going down on some geezer way in the back. I guessed the freak was on her feet in order to collect payment, and before I knew it, the young bitch was back sitting beside me. It wasn't long before she had her hand under my blanket again. This time I slapped it away, and she left me alone.

We got off the bus. I had my old backpack; walking down in search of a cheap motel along Drachman. Then I turned down an alley. Big mistake. They'd had friends waiting for them. Indians. Looked like. I was jumped, knocked down. She stood on one side, while one of those drunk Indian friends of hers stood on the other, and they took turns delivering a couple of very effective, if unsteady, kicks to my kidneys. The beast had emptied my wallet, rummaged through the backpack, spat in disgust and left me lying there in the puke and blood.

Welcome to Tucson, Arizona. To be fair, this was no slam against the Old Pueblo, and besides, the bitches had hopped on in Phoenix.

I was up, wiped vomit from my chin. Dug my hand inside my left sock. At least I still had that. Jammed the spare socks and underwear, photo album, toiletries, back in the pack. Checked into a motel, washed my face, showered, then plopped down on the floor and slept the rest of the night and most of the next day when I had to go out and find a bar, or *Circle K*, to buy a can of *Spam* and a 6- Pack of *Red Dog*, a newspaper. At this rate, my money wouldn't last long and I'd be stuck here indefinitely. Taking a look at the job ads was in order.

* * *

# About the Author

Kirk Alex's novel *Lustmord: Anatomy of a Serial Butcher* was a finalist in the Kindle Book Review's Best Book Awards of 2014. He is also the author of *Zook, Fifty Shades of Tinsel,* the story collection: *Ziggy Popper at Large,* the *Love, Lust & Murder* series: *Throwback & Backlash,* the Eddie "Doc" Holiday Private Eye Series, and a few other novels & shorts.

http://www.kirkalex.com